Rage of A Demon King

Other books by Raymond E. Feist

Magician
Silverthorn
A Darkness at Sethanon
Faerie Tale
Prince of the Blood
The King's Buccaneer
Shadow of a Dark Queen
Rise of a Merchant Prince

With Janny Wurts:

Daughter of the Empire
Servant of the Empire
Mistress of the Empire

Rage of a Demon King

Volume III of the Serpentwar Saga

Raymond E. Feist

AVON BOOKS NEW YORK

This is a work of fiction. Names, characters, places, and incidents either are the product of the author's imagination or are used fictitiously. Any resemblance to actual events, locales, organizations, or persons, living or dead, is entirely coincidental and beyond the intent of either the author or the publisher.

AVON BOOKS
A division of
The Hearst Corporation
1350 Avenue of the Americas
New York, New York 10019

Interior design by Kellan Peck
Visit our website at **http://AvonBooks.com**
ISBN: 0-380-97473-8

Library of Congress Cataloging in Publication Data:

Feist, Raymond E.
Rage of a demon king / Raymond E. Feist.
p. cm. — (The Serpentwar saga ; v. 3)
I. Title. II. Series: Feist, Raymond E. Serpentwar saga ; v. 3.
PS3556.E446R34 1997 96-30715
813'.54—dc20 CIP

First Avon Books Printing: April 1997

Printed in the U.S.A.

FIRST EDITION

QPM 10 9 8 7 6 5 4 3 2 1

For Stephen A. Abrams,
who knows more about Midkemia than I do

Acknowledgments

For reasons far too complex to detail, I am indebted to the following people:

To William Wright, Lou Aronica, and Mike Greenstein, for bringing order out of chaos and getting the program pointed in the right direction.

To Adrian Zackheim, for getting me to Hearst Books; Robert Mecoy, for keeping the inertia heading in the right direction and being the world's most indefatigable cheerleader; Liz Perle McKenna, for taking time from a very busy schedule to keep a perplexed author informed; and John Douglas, for some timely hand-holding. All were my editors for a while during that chaos.

To Jennifer Brehl, my editor, for hitting the ground running and not missing a step.

To everyone else at Hearst Books/Avon Books, for getting behind the series.

To Jonathan Matson, for all the usual reasons.

To my children, Jessica and James, for showing me magic every day.

And to my wife, Kathlyn Starbuck, for more reasons than I could ever list here.

—Raymond E. Feist
Rancho Santa Fe, California
June 1996

Cast of Characters

ACAILA—leader of the eldar, in the Elf Queen's court
ALFRED—corporal from Darkmoor
AGLARANNA—Elf Queen in Elvandar, wife of Tomas, mother of Calin and Calis
AKEE—Hidati hillman
ANDREW—priest of Ban-Ath in Krondor
ANTHONY—magician at Crydee
AVERY, ABIGAIL—daughter of Roo and Karli
AVERY, DUNCAN—cousin to Roo
AVERY, HELMUT—son to Roo and Karli
AVERY, KARLI—wife of Roo, mother of Abigail and Helmut
AVERY, RUPERT "ROO"—young merchant of Krondor, son of Tom Avery

BORRIC—King of the Isles, twin brother to Prince Erland, father of Prince Patrick
BROOK—First Officer, *Royal Dragon*

CALIN—elf heir to the throne of Elvandar, half brother to Calis, son of Aglaranna and King Aidan
CALIS—"The Eagle of Krondor," special agent of the Prince of Krondor, Duke of the Court, son of Aglaranna and Tomas, half brother to Calin
CHALMES—ruling magician at Stardock

D' LYES, ROBERT—magician from Stardock
DE BESWICK—captain in King's army
DE SAVON, LUIS—former soldier, assistant to Roo
DOLGAN—king of the dwarves of the west
DOMINIC—Abbot of Ishapian Abbey at Sarth
DUBOIS, HENRI—poisoner from Bas-Tyra
DUGA—mercenary captain from Novindus
DUKO—general in the Emerald Queen's army
DUNSTAN, BRIAN—the Sagacious Man, leader of the Mockers, used to be known as Lysle Rigger

ERLAND—brother to the king and Prince Nicholas, uncle to Prince Patrick
ESTERBROOK, JACOB—wealthy merchant of Krondor, father of Sylvia
ESTERBROOK, SYLVIA—Jacob's daughter

FADAWAH—general commanding the Emerald Queen's army
FREIDA—Erik's mother, wife of Nathan

GALAIN—elf in Elvandar
GAMINA—adopted daughter of Pug and sister of William, wife of James, mother of Arutha
GARRET—corporal in Erik's Company
GRAVES, KATHERINE "KITTY"—girl thief in Krondor
GREYLOCK, OWEN—captain in Prince's service, later General
GUNTHER—Nathan's apprentice

HAMMON—lieutenant in King's army
HANAM—Lorekeeper of the Saaur
HARPER—sergeant in Erik's company

JACOBY, HELEN—widow of Randolph Jacoby, mother of Natally and Willem.
JAMES—Duke of Krondor, father to Arutha, grandfather to James and Dash
JAMESON, ARUTHA—Lord Vencar, Baron of the Prince's Court and son of Duke James
JAMESON, JAMES "JIMMY"—elder son of Arutha, grandson of James
JAMESON, DASHEL "DASH"—younger son of Arutha, grandson of James

KALIED—ruling magician at Stardock

LIVIA—daughter of Lord Vasarius

MARCUS—Duke of Crydee, cousin to Prince Patrick, son of Martin
MARTIN—former Duke of Crydee, great uncle to Prince Patrick, father of Marcus
MILO—owner of the Inn of the Pintail in Ravensburg, father of Rosalyn
MIRANDA—magician and ally of Calis and Pug

NATHAN—blacksmith at the Inn of the Pintail in Ravensburg, former master of Erik, married to Freida
NAKOR THE ISALANI—gambler, magic user, friend of Calis and Pug
NICHOLAS—Admiral of the Western Fleet, Prince of the Royal Family, uncle to Prince Patrick

PATRICK—Prince of Krondor, son of Prince Erland, nephew to the King and Prince Nicholas
PUG—magician, Duke of Stardock, cousin to the King, father to Gamina and William

REEVES—captain of *Royal Dragon*
ROSALYN—Milo's daughter, wife of Rudolph, mother of Gerd
RUDOLPH—baker in Ravensburg, husband of Rosalyn, stepfather to Gerd

SHATI, JADOW—sergeant in Erik's company
SHO PI—former companion of Erik and Roo's, student of Nakor's
SUBAI—captain of the Royal Krondorian Pathfinders

TITHULTA—Pantathian High Priest
TOMAS—Warleader of Elvandar, husband of Aglaranna, father of Calis, inheritor of the powers of Ashen-Shugar

VASARIUS—Quengan noble and merchant
VON DARKMOOR, ERIK—soldier in Calis's Crimson Eagles
VON DARKMOOR, GERD—son of Rosalyn and Stefan von Darkmoor, nephew to Erik
VON DARKMOOR, MANFRED—Baron of Darkmoor, half brother to Erik
VON DARKMOOR, MATHILDA—Baroness of Darkmoor, mother to Manfred
VYKOR, KAROLE—admiral of the King's Eastern Fleet

WILLIAM—Knight-Marshal of Krondor, Pug's son and Gamina's adopted brother, uncle to Jimmy and Dash

BOOK III

The Mad God's Tale

We are the music makers,
We are the dreamers of dreams,
Wandering by lone sea-breakers,
And sitting by desolate streams—
World-losers and world-forsakers,
On whom the pale moon gleams:
We are the movers and shakers
Of the world for ever, it seems.

—Arthur William Edgar O'Shaughnessy
ODE, ST. 1

Prologue

Breakthrough

THE WALL SHIMMERED.

In what had once been the throne room of Jarwa, last Sha-shahan of the Seven Nations of the Saaur, the thirty-foot-high wall of stones opposite the empty seat of power seemed to waver, then vanish as a black void appeared. Nightmare creatures gathered, things of terrible fangs and poisonous claws. Some wore the faces of dead animals, while others were humanlike in aspect. Some bore proud wings, antlers, or bull's horns. All were beings of massive muscle and evil intent, dark magic and murderous nature. Yet all in the hall remained motionless, terrified of that which was appearing on the other side of the newly created gateway. Demons who stood as tall as trees crouched low trying not to be seen.

Immense energy was required to open a gate, and for years the demons had been thwarted by the accursed priests of the distant city of Ahsart. Only when the mad High Priest had unsealed the portal, admitting the first demon to deny his city to the conquering host of the Saaur, was the barrier breached.

Now the world of Shila lay in tatters, the remaining life reduced to lowly creatures at the sea bottom, lichen clinging to rocks upon distant mountain peaks, and tiny creatures that scuttled under rocks to avoid detection. Anything larger than the smallest insect had been devoured. Hunger now gripped the demon host, and again they returned to their ancient habit of feeding upon one another. But internecine conflict was put aside among the elite of the host as a new gate from the Fifth Circle to Shila was completed, opening the way for the supreme ruler of the demon realm to communicate.

The demon without a name stood at the edge of those summoned to this once-grand hall. He peeked out from behind a stone column, lest he call attention to himself. He had captured a unique soul and had been harboring it, using it, becoming cunning and dangerous. For unlike most of his brethren, he had discovered guile worked better than confrontation in gaining valuable life force and intelligence. He still showed the proper mix of fear and danger to those directly above him, enough fear so they judged him under their sway, yet dangerous enough for them to avoid attempting to consume him. It was a perilous pose, and had he made one misstep, calling attention to his uniqueness, those captains nearby would have destroyed him utterly, for his mind was turning alien and was now self-aware enough to be a threat to all of them.

This demon knew he could easily defeat at least four of the demons who presumed superiority and stood before him, but to rise too quickly among the host was to call unwanted attention to oneself. He had, during his short life, seen no fewer than a half-dozen others rise too quickly, only to be destroyed by one of the great captains, either against that day they might themselves be challenged, or to protect a favored servant.

Mightiest of these captains was Tugor, First Servant of Great Maarg, who was now making his will known. Tugor fell to his knees, placing his forehead to the floor, and others followed his lead.

The demon without a name heard a faint voice and knew it came from the soul he had captured, and he tried to ignore it, but it always said something he knew to be important. "Observe," he heard in his mind, as if it were a faint whisper in his ear, or a thought of his own.

A great rush of energies bathed the room as the shimmering wall seemed to ripple outward, then vanish as a gate to the home realm opened. A wind filled the chamber, from air sucked through the gap between worlds, as if everything in this hall was being urged to return to its home realm. By their nature, demons instinctively felt an awareness of those far mightier than themselves, and being close to Tugor caused the nameless demon to nearly faint in terror. But the presence that emanated through the rent in the fabric of space nearly reduced him to babbling incoherence.

All those present stayed on their knees, keeping foreheads to the stones, save the nameless demon, still hidden behind the column. He watched as Tugor stood to face the void. From within the gap in the wall came a voice that was filled with the echoes of rage and dread. "Have you found the way?"

Tugor said, "We have, most mighty! We have sent two of our captains through the rift to Midkemia."

"What do they report?" demanded the voice from beyond, and in it the nameless demon detected a note of something besides anger and power, a hint of desperation, perhaps.

"Dogku and Jakan do not report," responded Tugor. "We know nothing. We believe they are unable to hold the portal."

"Then send another!" ordered Maarg, Ruler of the Fifth Circle. "I will not cross until that way is clear; you've left nothing upon this world that I may consume. Next time I open the way, I will cross, and if there is naught for me to devour, I will eat your heart, Tugor!" The sound of air being sucked from the room ceased as the rift between the worlds closed. Maarg's voice hung in the air as the shimmering vanished and the wall was as it had been before.

Tugor rose up and shouted in rage, venting his frustration. The others stood slowly, for now would not be a good time to draw the attention of the second most powerful among their race. Tugor had been known to snap the heads from the shoulders of those who appeared to be growing too powerful, so that no rival would appear who might contest his position. It was even rumored that Tugor harbored his strength against the day when he might challenge Maarg for supremacy among the race.

Tugor turned and said, "Who goes next?"

Without quite knowing why, the nameless demon came forward. "I will go, lord."

Tugor's visage, a horse skull with great horns, was nearly expressionless, but what expression it was capable of reflected puzzlement. "Who are you, little fool?"

"I have no name yet, Master," said the nameless one.

Tugor took two large strides, pushing aside several of his captains, to stand towering over the small demon. "I have sent captains, who have failed to return. Why should you succeed where they did not?"

"Because I am meek and will hide and observe, Master," the nameless one said quietly. "I will gather intelligence, and I will stay hidden, harboring my strength, until I can reopen the portal from the other side."

Tugor paused a moment, as if considering, then drew back his hand and struck the smaller demon, driving him across the room into the wall. The demon had small wings, not yet sufficient to fly with, and they felt as if they had been broken by the impact of the stone wall.

"That is for being presumptuous," said Tugor, his rage just below the killing level.

"I shall send you," he said to his next most powerful captain. Then he spun and grabbed another, ripping out the hapless demon's throat as he screamed, "And this is for the rest of you for not showing as much courage!"

Some of the demons at the edge of the group turned and fled the hall, while others fell to the stones, throwing themselves on the mercy of Tugor's whim. He was satisfied with killing one of his brethren, and drank blood and life energy for a moment, before tossing aside the now-empty husk of flesh.

"Go," said Tugor to the captain. "The rift is in the distant hills, to the east. Those who guard it will tell you what you must know to return . . . if you are able. Return, and I will reward you."

The captain hurried from the hall. The small demon hesitated, then followed, ignoring the fiery pain in his back. With food and rest, the wings would heal. As he left the palace he was challenged twice by other demons driven by hunger. He quickly killed them. Drinking their life energies caused the pain in his wings to fade, and as before, new thoughts and ideas manifested themselves. He suddenly knew why he was following the captain sent to reopen the rift.

The voice that had once come from the vial he wore around his neck, but that was now inside his head, said, "We shall endure, then thrive, then we shall do what must be done."

The little demon hurried to the rift site, the location of the fissure between worlds where the last of the Saaur horde had fled. The little demon had learned things and knew that somehow an ally had betrayed the demons, that this gate was to have remained open, but instead had been closed. Twice it had been forced open, but closed again quickly, for those on the other side used counterspells to keep the portal sealed. At least a dozen powerful demons had died at Tugor's hands because of the host's inability to cross.

The captain reached the portal site as a dozen other demons surrounded him. They were there to aid the captain in the crossing. Unnoticed, the little demon followed the larger as if accompanying him.

The rift site was unremarkable, a large patch of muddy earth, the grass crushed by the passing of thousands of Saaur horses and riders, their wives and children accompanying them. Most of the grass surrounding the rift was withered and blackened by the tread of demons, but tiny patches of green could be seen here and there. Should the rift remain closed much longer, even those tiny sources of life energy would be sought out and devoured. Squinting his eyes, the tiny demon saw the strange twist in the energy that hung in the air, difficult to notice unless one specifically looked for it.

What the Saaur and other mortal races called magic was but a shifting of life energies to the demons, and some of these might die in opening the rift. Until the wards on the other side were removed, it would be impossible to keep the rift open for more than a few seconds at a time, and many demons would die to achieve even two or three such passages. No demon gave his life willingly—it was not in their nature—but all feared Tugor and Maarg, and harbored the hope it would be the others in their company who paid the ultimate price, while they survived to gain reward.

The captain commanded, "Open the way!"

The demons given the task glanced at one another, knowing that some would die in the attempt, but at last they opened their minds and let the energies flow. The little demon studied the air and saw the shimmering as the opening appeared, and the captain crouched, timing his jump to the brief opening.

As he launched himself, while demons around the site screamed and fell, the little demon leaped upon his back. Taken totally by surprise, the captain bellowed his shock and outrage as they fell into the rift. The urgency of the little demon's purpose helped him ignore the disorientation, while it only added to the captain's surprise.

As they emerged into a dark and vast hall, the little demon bit as hard as he could into the base of the captain's skull, where it met the neck, the weakest point on his body. Instantly, an electric pulse flowed into the little demon as the captain's outrage turned to terror and pain. He flailed about in the darkness, desperately seeking to dislodge the assassin. The little demon clung viciously to his victim's back. Then the captain flung himself back, attempting to crush the smaller demon against the rock face of the cavern, but his own powerful wings conspired to prevent that.

Then the captain collapsed to his knees, and at that moment the smaller demon knew he was victorious. Energy flowed into him until he felt as if he might literally explode from it; he had feasted to insensibility before on those he had taken, but never in one feast had he consumed so much energy. He was now more powerful than the one he fed upon. His legs, longer and more muscular than they had been only a moment before, stood upon hard stone as he lifted his diminishing victim, who now could only mew weakly as his life force was drained.

Soon it was over and the newly victorious demon stood in the hall, almost drunk from the infusion of power. No food of flesh or fruit, no drink of ale or wine could bring one of his kind to this state. He wished for a Saaur looking glass, for he knew he was now at least a head taller than a moment before. And upon his back he felt the wings that would one day carry him through the sky begin to grow again.

But something distracted him, and he again felt alien thoughts entering his mind. "Observe and beware!"

He turned and altered his perceptions to pierce the darkness.

The vast hall was littered with the bodies of mortal creatures. He saw both Saaur and those called Pantathians, and a third type of creature, one unknown to him, smaller than the Saaur and larger than the Pantathians. There was nothing left of their life energies, so he quickly dismissed them.

The wards were still in place, the barriers that caused the death of those demons who attempted to pass through unaided. He inspected them and saw that they should have been easily removed by those demons sent before him.

Again regarding the carnage in the room, he realized that great magic had been brought to bear to prevent the demons who came before from destroying the wards. Then he wondered what had happened to his brethren, for if they had been destroyed in this battle, there would have been a lingering energy, but there was none.

Fatigued from his battle yet intoxicated with his new life force, the demon reached to remove the first ward, but the alien voice said, "Wait!"

The demon hesitated, then reached down to the vial he wore about his neck. Without considering the consequences, the newly empowered demon opened the vial and the soul trapped within was loosed. But rather than fly to join that great soul of his ancestors, the soul in the vial passed into the demon.

The demon shuddered, closing his eyes as a new mind took control. Had the demon not been caught up in the change after the victory, he would not have succumbed so easily to the demand to free the soul in the vial, and had he not been so disoriented, that other intelligence would not have been able to achieve dominance. The mind now in charge of the demon reserved some essence in the vial and replaced the stopper. Some of his essence must remain apart from the demon, an anchor of sorts against the demands of demon lust and appetite. Even with that anchor, withstanding the demon's nature would be a continuous struggle.

Seeing through nonhuman eyes, the newly formed creature inspected the wards again, and, rather than destroy them, he chanted an ancient Saaur summoning of magic and strengthened them. The creature could only imagine the rage of Tugor when the next messenger exploded into flaming agony upon attempting to pass into this realm. The setback would not keep the demons from entering this realm forever, but it did gain this new creature valuable time.

Flexing talons, and then arms that seemed suddenly too long, the creature wondered about the third race who lay dead upon the floor. Was it ally or foe to the Pantathians and their dupes, the Saaur?

The creature put aside such considerations. As the new mind, made up of the little demon and the captured soul, melded into one, knowledge unfolded. It sensed at least one mindless demon wandering these halls and galleries of stone. It knew that the wards had protected the little demon as he rode the back of the captain through the rift, and that the captain had been stunned, robbed of wit and rendered animal-like, no matter how powerful. But this new creature that had once been a demon knew that eventually, as the other demons already here fed and grew in power, cunning, then intelligence would return. And with memory would come the need to return to this cavern and destroy the wards, opening the way.

First the creature must hunt down those demons, ensuring that did not happen. Then would come another search. "Jatuk." The creature spoke the name softly aloud. The son of the last ruler of the Saaur on the world of Shila would rule here, over the remnants of the last Saaur host, and this creature had much to tell him. As the melding continued, the demon's nature was controlled and contained, then fused with that other intelligence. The father of Shadu—who now served Jatuk—took control of this false body and moved toward a tunnel. The mind of Hanam, last of the great Loremasters of the Saaur, had found a way to cheat death and betrayal and would now find the last of his people to warn them of the great deception that would doom another world to destruction if not halted.

One

Krondor

ERIK SIGNALED.

The soldiers knelt just below his position in the gully, watching as he silently motioned where he wanted each of them. Alfred, now his first corporal, gestured from the far end of the line and Erik nodded. Each man knew what to do.

The enemy had camped in a relatively defensible position on the trail north of Krondor. About three miles up the road was the small town of Eggly, the objective of the invaders. The enemy had stopped their march before sundown, and Erik was certain they would launch an attack just before dawn.

Erik had watched them from his hidden vantage, his men camped a short distance away while he decided his best course of action. He had observed the enemy erect their camp, and saw they had been as disorganized as he had suspected they would be; their pickets were placed poorly, and were undisciplined, spending as much time looking into the camp to chat with comrades as actually watching for an enemy approach. The constant glances in the direction of the campfires were certainly diminishing their night vision. After gauging the strength and position of the invaders, Erik knew his choices. He had decided to strike first. While outnumbered by at least five to one, his men would have the advantage of surprise and superior training; at least, he hoped the latter was true.

Erik took a moment for one last inspection of the enemy's position. If anything, the pickets were even more inattentive than they had been when Erik had sent for his company. It was clear the invaders thought their mission one of minor importance, taking a small town off the beaten track, while major conflicts would be raging to the south near the capital city of Krondor. Erik was determined to teach them that there were no minor conflicts in any war.

When his men were in place, Erik slipped down a small defile, until he was almost within touching distance of a bored guard. He tossed a small stone behind the man, who looked without thought. As Erik knew would be the case, the man glanced back into the camp, at the nearest campfire, which blinded him for a moment. A soldier sitting near the fire said, "What is it, Henry?"

The guard said, "Nothing."

He turned to find Erik standing directly before him, and faster than he could shout alarm, Erik hit him with his balled fist, catching him as he fell.

"Henry?" said the man at the campfire, starting to rise, vainly trying to see into the gloom beyond the campfire light.

Erik attempted to imitate the guard's voice. "I said, 'Nothing.' "

The attempt failed, for the soldier started to shout alarm and pulled on his sword. But before he could clear the blade from his scabbard, Erik was upon him like a cat on a mouse. Grabbing the man by the back of his tunic, Erik pulled him over backward, slamming him hard into the ground. Putting a dagger at the man's throat, he said, "You're dead. No noise."

The man gave him a sour look, but nodded. Softly he said, "Well, at least I get to finish my supper." He sat up and returned to his dinner plate, while two other men blinked in incomprehension as Erik circled the campfire and "cut" each of their throats before they realized an attack was under way.

Shouts from around the camp announced that the rest of Erik's company was now in force among the enemy, cutting throats, knocking down tents, and generally creating havoc. The only prohibition Erik had put on them was no fires. Although tempted, he thought the Baron of Tyr-Sog would not appreciate the damage to his baggage.

Erik hurried through the struggle, dispatching sleeping soldiers as they emerged from tents. He cut a few ropes, trapping soldiers inside as the canvas fell upon them, and heard shouts of outrage from within. Throughout the camp, men cursed as they were "killed," and Erik could hardly contain his amusement. The strike was fast and he was at the center of the camp within two minutes of the start of the assault. He reached the command tent as the Baron came out, obviously half-asleep as he buckled his sword belt around his nightshirt, and clearly displeased by the disruption. "What have we here?" he demanded of Erik.

"Your company is destroyed, my lord," said Erik with a light tap of his sword upon the Baron's chest. "And you are now dead."

The Baron studied the man who was sheathing his sword: he was tall, unusually broad across the shoulders without being fat, like a young blacksmith, with unremarkable features. His smile was engaging, however, friendly and open. In the firelight his pale blond hair danced with ruby highlights.

"Nonsense," said the stout Baron. His neatly trimmed beard and fine silk nightshirt said volumes about his campaign experience. "We were to attack Eggly tomorrow. No one said anything about this"—he waved his hand around the campsite—"business of a night attack. Had we known, we would have taken precautions."

Erik said, "My lord, we are attempting to prove a point."

A voice came out of the darkness. "And you proved it well."

Owen Greylock, Knight-Captain of the Prince of Krondor's Royal Garrison, came into the light. His gaunt features gave him a sinister appearance in the dancing shadows of the firelight. "I judge you've killed or incapacitated three-quarters of the soldiers, Erik. How many men did you bring?"

Erik said, "Sixty."

"But I have three hundred!" said the Baron, clearly disturbed. "With an auxiliary of Hadati warriors."

Erik glanced about and said, "I don't see any Hadati."

From out of the dark came an accented voice. "As it should be."

A group of men dressed in kilts and plaids entered the camp. They wore their hair tied atop their heads in a knot, with a long fall of it spilling down their backs. "We heard your men approaching," said the leader, looking at Erik, who wore an unmarked black tunic, and guessing at his rank, "Captain?"

"Sergeant," corrected Erik.

"Sergeant," amended the spokesman, a tall warrior who wore only a simple sleeveless tunic above his kilt. His plaid would provide warmth in the mountains if unrolled and worn around his shoulders. Below night-black hair, his features were even, nothing out of the ordinary, save for dark eyes that reminded Erik of a bird of prey's. In the campfire light, his sun-darkened skin was almost red. Erik didn't need to see the man draw the long blade he wore on his back to know him for a seasoned fighter.

"You heard us?" asked Erik.

"Yes. Your men are good, Sergeant, but we Hadati live in the mountains—often sleeping on the ground near our herds—and we know when we're hearing a group of men approach."

"What's your name?" asked Erik.

"Akee, son of Bandur."

Erik nodded. "We need to talk."

The Baron said, "I protest, Captain!"

Greylock said, "What, my lord?"

"I protest this unannounced action. We were told to play the role of invaders and expect resistance by local militia and special units from Krondor at the town of Eggly. Nothing was said of a night attack. Had we known, we would have prepared for such!" he repeated.

Erik glanced at Owen, who signaled that Erik should form up his company and depart while the Prince's Knight-Captain soothed the ruffled feelings of the Baron of Tyr-Sog. Erik motioned Akee to his side and said,

"Have your men gather their kits and find my corporal. He's an ugly thug named Alfred. Tell him you'll be coming with us to Krondor in the morning."

"Will the Baron approve?" asked Akee.

"Probably not," answered Erik, turning away. "But he doesn't have much to say about it. I'm the Prince of Krondor's man."

The Hadati hillman shrugged and motioned to his companions. "Let those men free."

"Free?" asked Erik.

Akee smiled. "We captured a few of those you sent to the south, Sergeant. I believe your ugly thug may be among them."

Erik let fatigue and the pressure of the night's exercise get the better of his usually calm nature. Swearing softly, he said, "If he is, he'll regret it."

Akee shrugged, turning to his companions and saying, "Let's go see."

Erik addressed another of his company, a soldier named Shane. "Get the men formed up at the south end of the camp."

Shane nodded and started shouting orders.

Erik followed the Hadati to a point outside the perimeter of the Baron's camp and found a pair of Hadati sitting next to Corporal Alfred and a half dozen of Erik's best men.

"What happened?" Erik asked.

Alfred sighed as he stood. "They're good, Sergeant." He pointed to a ridge above them. "They must have moved the second they heard us coming, 'cause we were up there on that ridge, and I would have wagered everything I own it wasn't possible they could have come up out of that camp, crossed the ridge, lay low, then come up behind us as we headed down." He shook his head. "We were being tapped on the shoulder before we heard them."

Erik turned to Akee. "You'll have to tell me how you did that."

Akee shrugged, saying nothing.

To Alfred, Erik said, "These hillmen are coming with us. Take them down to the camp and let's get back to Krondor."

Alfred smiled, forgetting the tongue-lashing he was likely to receive from Erik when they were back at the garrison. "A hot meal," he said.

Erik was forced to agree it would be welcome. They had been out on maneuvers for a week, eating cold rations in the dark, and his men were tired and hungry. "Get moving" was all he said.

Standing in the dark, Erik considered what was at stake in the impending war, and wondered if a hundred such exercises would prepare the men of the Kingdom for what was to come.

Tossing aside such concern, he conceded that probably nothing would prepare them fully, but what other choice did he have? He considered that Calis, Prince Patrick, Knight-Marshal William, and other commanders were operating throughout these mountains, conducting such exercises this week;

at the end of the week a council would be held to tally what needed to be done.

Erik said to himself, "Everything, everything needs to be done," and he realized his black mood was due more to fatigue and hunger than to Alfred's failing to avoid the Hadati ambush. Then he smiled. If the hillmen from northern Yabon had gotten up over that ridge that fast, it was a good thing they were going to be on the Kingdom's side, and even better, thought Erik, under his command.

He turned toward the camp and decided he'd better join Greylock in mollifying the distressed Baron of Tyr-Sog.

The soldiers stood to attention as the courtyard resounded with the echo of their boot heels striking cobbles as one, motionless while the Prince of Krondor made his appearance on the dais.

Roo looked at his friend Erik and said, "Nicely done."

Erik shook his head, indicating that Roo should keep silent. Roo grinned but stayed quiet while Prince Patrick, ruler of Krondor, accepted a salute from the assembled garrison of the palace. Next to Erik stood Calis, Captain of the Prince's special guards known as the Crimson Eagles.

Erik shifted his weight slightly, uncomfortable with the attention being drawn to him and the others. The survivors of the most recent expedition to the distant land of Novindus were being presented with awards for bravery, and Erik wasn't sure what that entailed, but he knew he would prefer being back about his usual duties.

He had returned from the exercises in the mountains expecting a quick council, but Calis had informed Erik and the others that with Prince Erland's return from a visit to his brother King Borric, a ceremony was scheduled and awards would be conferred, but beyond that, Erik knew little. He glanced sideways and saw his Captain, Calis, also looking impatient to see the fuss over with. Renaldo, one of the other survivors, turned to look at Micha. Both soldiers had accompanied Calis on their flight from the halls of the Pantathian serpent priests. Renaldo had his chest puffed out as the Prince of Krondor presented him with an award, the White Cord of Courage, which would be sewn to his tunic sleeve, marking him a man who displayed conspicuous bravery for King and Country.

Roo had sailed one of his largest ships to Novindus to bring the Kingdom's soldiers home. Erik and his companions had rested and healed on the return journey. Their captain, the enigmatic man reputed to be half-elf, was almost completely recovered from injuries that would have killed any other man. Two old companions of his, Praji and Vaja, had died in the magical blast that had caught Calis, and half his body had been burned as if set on fire. Yet he hardly showed the slightest scar, his face and neck only marked by flesh just a little lighter in color than the rest of his sun-browned skin. Erik wondered if he would ever know the full truth about the man he served.

And thinking of enigmas, Erik regarded another of his companions over the last few years, the odd gambler, Nakor. He stood apart from those being honored, a half-mocking grin on his face as he watched the awards ceremony. At his side stood Sho Pi, the former monk who now regarded himself as Nakor's acolyte. They had been residing in the palace as the guests of the Duke of Krondor for the last month, Nakor showing little motivation to return to his usual occupation, fleecing the unsuspecting in card rooms across the Kingdom.

Erik let his mind wander as the Prince cited each man, and he wondered who would honor those who were left behind, particularly Bobby de Loungville, the iron-tough, unforgiving sergeant who, more than any other, had forged Erik into the soldier he had become. Erik felt a tear gather in his eye as he recalled holding Bobby in the ice cave in the mountains as his lungs filled with blood from a sword wound. Silently Erik said to himself, See, I got him out alive.

Blinking away the tear, Erik once again glanced at Calis and found the Captain watching him. With a barely perceptible nod, Calis seemed to say he knew what Erik was thinking, and was also remembering lost friends.

The ceremony dragged on; then suddenly it was over, the assembled garrison of the palace in Krondor dismissed. Knight-Marshal William, Military Commander of the Principality, motioned for Erik and the others to attend him. To Calis he said, "The Prince asks you all to join him in his private council room."

Erik glanced at Roo, who shrugged. On the return voyage, the two boyhood friends had caught up with each other's news. Erik had been half-amused, half-astonished to discover that his best friend had, in less than two years, contrived to become one of Krondor's preeminent merchants and one of the Kingdom's richest men. But as he saw the ship's master and crew snap to every order Roo gave, he realized that Rupert Avery, barely more than a common thief as a child, and hardly more than a boy now, truly owned that ship.

Erik had told Roo of what he and the others had discovered, and he needed no embellishment to convey the horror and disgust he felt at fighting through the Pantathian birthing halls. Of those who had not traveled to Novindus with Calis on his most recent journey, Roo, Nakor, and Sho Pi had been there previously, and knew what the others faced. Slowly, over the voyage, Erik had provided enough grisly details about the slaughter of Pantathian females and infants, as well as about the mysterious "third player" who had accomplished more carnage than Calis's raiders ever could have done. Unless there were birthing crèches located elsewhere—and it seemed unlikely—the only living Pantathians were those close to the Emerald Queen. If they were finally defeated in the coming battle, the Pantathian serpent priests would cease to exist, a fate most fervently hoped for by the two boyhood friends from Darkmoor.

Roo and Erik had parted almost as soon as the ship had berthed, as Roo had businesses to oversee. Two days later, Erik had left on maneuvers, evaluating the training Jadow Shati had inflicted upon the men while Calis had been gone. Erik was pleased that the new men under his command for the last week were as disciplined and reliable as those he had trained with when he had been a common soldier.

Entering the palace, Erik was again uncomfortable at finding himself in the halls of power and in the presence of the great of the Kingdom. He had served for a year in Krondor before leaving with Calis on the last voyage, but had confined himself to the training grounds most of the time. He came to the palace proper only when summoned or to borrow a book on tactics or some other aspect of warcraft from Knight-Marshal William. He was never comfortable with the supreme commander of the King's Armies of the West, but he finally grew used to spending hours over ale or wine discussing what he had read and how it would bear on the armies he was helping fashion. But, given a choice, Erik would rather be in the drilling yard, working with the armorers around the forge, or tending to the horses, or most of all, out in the field, where life was too demanding to think much about the larger consequences of the coming war.

In the Prince's private chamber, actually, Erik thought, a small hall, other men waited, including Lord James, Duke of Krondor, and Jadow Shati, the other sergeant in Calis's company. Erik expected Jadow would be promoted to sergeant major to replace Bobby. Upon the table a lavish board of cheeses, meats, fruit, bread, and vegetables had been laid out. Ale, wine, and frosted pitchers of fruit juices were also waiting.

"Set to," said the Prince of Krondor, removing his ceremonial crown and mantle and handing them to waiting pages. Calis picked up an apple and bit into it while others moved around the table.

Erik motioned to Roo, who came over to him.

"How did you find things at home?" Erik asked.

Roo said, "The children are . . . amazing. They've grown so much in the months I was gone I scarcely recognize them." His faced creased in a thoughtful expression. "My business endured my absence well enough, though not as well as I expected. Jacob Esterbrook had the better of me three times while I was gone. One transaction cost me a small fortune."

"I thought you and he were friends," said Erik, taking a bite of bread and cheese.

"In a manner of speaking," said Roo. He had thought better of mentioning his relationship to Sylvia Esterbrook, Jacob's daughter, given that Erik tended to have a narrow view of family and vows of faithfulness. " 'Friendly competitors' would be a more accurate description. He has a stranglehold on trade to Kesh and seems reluctant to relinquish even a small part of it."

Calis came up to them and said, "Roo, will you excuse us a moment?"

Rupert nodded, said, "Of course, Captain," and walked over to the table to take advantage of the fare.

Calis waited until they were out of earshot before he asked, "Erik, has Marshal William had a chance to talk to you today?"

Erik shook his head. "No, Captain. I was busy getting back into the rhythm of things with Jadow . . . now that Bobby's no longer here. . . ." He shrugged.

"I understand." Calis turned and motioned for the Knight-Marshal, who joined them. Calis looked at Erik. "You've got a choice."

William, a short, slender man whom Erik knew to be one of the best riders and swordsmen in the Kingdom despite his advancing age, said, "Calis and I have talked about you, youngster. With things . . . as they are, we have more opportunities than we have men with talent."

Erik knew what William had meant by "things as they are," for he knew that a terrible army was massing across the sea and would be invading in less than two years' time. "Choice?"

"I'd like to offer you a staff position," said William. "You'd hold the rank of Knight-Lieutenant in the Prince's army, and I'd put you in charge of the Krondorian Heavy Lance. Your skill with horses—well, I can't think of a better man for the job."

Erik glanced at Calis. "Sir?"

"I'd like you to stay with the Crimson Eagles," said Calis in a flat tone.

"Then I'll stay," said Erik without hesitation. "I made a promise."

William smiled ruefully. "I thought as much, but I had to ask."

"Thank you for asking, m'lord," said Erik. "I'm flattered."

William grinned at Calis. "You must use magic. He's halfway to being the best tactician I've ever met—and if he keeps studying he will be the best—and you want to waste him as a bully sergeant."

Calis smiled slightly, an expression of wry amusement Erik had come to know well. The half-elven Captain said, "We have more need of bully sergeants to train soldiers right now than we do tacticians, Willy. Besides, my bully sergeants are not the same as yours."

William shrugged. "You're right, of course, but when they come, each of us is going to want the best we can find at our side."

"I can't argue that."

William left and Calis said, "Erik, thank you."

Erik repeated, "I made a promise."

"To Bobby?" asked Calis.

Erik nodded.

Calis's expression darkened. "Well, knowing Bobby, I'd best tell you now, I need a sergeant major, not a nursemaid. You kept me alive once,

Erik von Darkmoor, so consider your promise to Bobby de Loungville discharged in full. If it comes to a choice between my life and the survival of the Kingdom, I want you to make the right choice."

It took Erik a moment to comprehend what had just been said. "Sergeant Major?"

"You're taking Bobby's place," said Calis.

"Jadow has been with you longer—" Erik began.

"But you have the knack," interrupted Calis. "Jadow doesn't. He'll do fine as a sergeant—you saw how the new men are shaping up—but promoting him any higher would put him in a situation where he would be a liability instead of an asset." He studied Erik's face a moment. "William wasn't overstating the case about your abilities as a tactician. We'll need to work on your comprehension of strategy as well. You know what's coming and you know that once the struggle begins, you may find yourself out there with hundreds of men looking to you to keep them alive. An ancient Isalani general called it the 'fog of battle,' and men who can keep other men alive while chaos erupts around them are rare."

Erik could only nod. He and the others around him who had traveled with Calis had seen the army of the Emerald Queen, had been a part of it for a time, and he knew that when that host of hired killers arrived on the shores of the Kingdom, chaos would ensue. In the midst of that chaos, only well-trained, disciplined, hard men might survive. And it would be upon those men that the fate of the Kingdom—and the rest of the world of Midkemia—would rest, not on the Kingdom's traditional armies.

"Very well, Captain. I accept," said Erik.

Calis smiled and put his hand upon Erik's shoulder. "You didn't have a choice, Sergeant Major. Now you need to promote some men; we need one more sergeant for the balance of this year, and a half-dozen corporals besides."

"Alfred of Darkmoor," said Erik. "He was a corporal and a bully until I got through with him. He's ready to take on the responsibility, and at heart he's still a brawler and we'll need that when the time comes."

"You have that right," said Calis. "Every man a brawler, for that matter."

Erik said, "I suppose we have enough potential corporals around. I'll make up a list this evening."

Calis nodded. "I must talk to Patrick before this turns into a full-blown reception. Excuse me."

Roo returned when he saw Calis leave, and asked, "Well, did you get promoted or did Jadow?"

"I did," answered Erik.

"My condolences," said Roo. Then he grinned and struck his friend on the arm. "Sergeant Major."

"What about you?" asked Erik. "You were telling me how things are at home."

Roo smiled weakly and shrugged. "Karli is still upset I took off to go after you on such short notice, and she was right: the children don't recognize me, though Abigail does call me Daddy, and little Helmut just gives shy grins and gurgles." He sighed. "I got a warmer welcome from Helen Jacoby, truth to tell."

"Well, from what you told me, she is in your debt. You could have turned her and her children out on the streets."

Roo chewed on a piece of fruit a moment. "Not really. Her husband had no part in the plot to kill my father-in-law." He shrugged. "I've got a few loose ends to tie up; Jason, Duncan, and Luis have been careful in seeing to my company while I was gone, and my partners in the Bitter Sea Company haven't robbed me too outrageously." He grinned. "At least, I haven't found any proof yet." His expression turned serious again. "And I also know that this army you're about to become a significant part of will need provisions, weapons, and armor. Those don't come cheaply."

Erik nodded. "I have some small idea of how we're going to meet the Emerald Queen, and while we'll never put as large a force in the field as she will send against us, we'll have to mount the most ambitious campaign since the Riftwar, and one never matched before."

"How many men under arms do you think?"

"I'm speculating," said Erik. "But at least fifty, sixty thousand more than the current armies of the East and West."

"That's close to a hundred thousand men!" said Roo. "Do we have that many?"

"No." Erik shook his head. "We have twenty thousand in all the Armies of the West, including the ten thousand directly under the Prince's command. The Armies of the East number more, but many of them are honor garrisons. With our long-term peace with Roldem, the other eastern kingdoms are calm, not willing to try anything without Roldem distracting us." Erik shrugged. "Too much time spent with Lord William, I guess, talking strategy . . . We now must start building for the battle here." With a shake of his head he said softly, "We lost too many of our key men on our last trips to Novindus."

Roo nodded. "There is a large debt to be repaid to that green bitch." Then he sighed audibly. "And a huge billing to finance it."

Erik smiled. "Our Duke is getting into your pocket?"

Roo returned the smile, though his was far more wry. "Not yet. He's made it clear that taxes will remain reasonable because he expects me to underwrite a large portion of the coming fight and to convince others, like Jacob Esterbrook, to provide funds as well."

Mentioning Esterbrook, Roo again thought of his daughter, Sylvia, Roo's mistress for the better part of a year before his sailing to rescue Erik, Calis, and the others. He had seen her only once since returning two weeks ago, and he was planning on seeing her tonight; he ached for her. "I think I should call upon Jacob soon," he said as if the thought had just come to him. "If he and I together agree to participate in financing the war, no one else of importance in the Kingdom would refuse the Prince's request." Dryly he added, "After all, if we fail in this, repayment of loans will be the last of our worries." Then he whispered in a somber tone, "Assuming we can worry about anything."

Erik nodded noncommittally. He had to admit that Roo had proven beyond any doubt he understood matters of finance far better than Erik and, should his phenomenal success be any indication, better than most of the businessmen in the Kingdom.

Roo said, "I should make my excuses to the Prince and get about my own business. I suspect those of us here who are not part of your military inner circle will be asked to find other things to go do soon, anyway."

Erik took his hand. "I think you're right." Other nobles, not part of the military, were presenting themselves to the Prince. Roo left his boyhood friend and joined the line of those begging the Prince's leave to depart, and soon only the Prince, his senior advisers, and members of the military remained.

When Owen Greylock entered, Patrick said, "We're now all here."

Knight-Marshal William motioned for them to gather around a circular table at the far end of the room. Duke James sat to his Prince's right, and William to the left.

It was the Duke who began. "Well, now that the pomp is over, we can get back to the bloody work ahead of us."

Erik sat back and listened to the plans for the final defense of the Kingdom begin to take shape.

Roo reached the gate where his horse was waiting for him. He had left his carriage at home for his wife's use, for he had moved his family to an estate outside the gates of the city. While he preferred the convenience of his town house, across the street from Barret's Coffee House—where most of his business day was spent—the country house offered a tranquillity he couldn't have imagined before the move. He had grounds for hunting if he chose, and a stream with fish, and all the other advantages granted to the nobility and rich commoners. He knew he would have to find time soon to enjoy those pastimes.

Not yet twenty-three years of age, Roo Avery was the father of two, one of the richest merchants in the Kingdom, and privy to secrets shared by few. The country house was also a hedge, as the gamblers called it, a place from which his family could escape the oncoming invasion to safer refuge to the east before the mob fled the city, trampling everything in its path. Roo had endured the destruction of Maharta, the distant city crushed three years before by the armies of the Emerald Queen. He had been forced to fight his way through the mass of panic-stricken citizens, had seen innocents die because they were in the wrong place. He vowed he would spare his children that horror, no matter what else might come.

He knew what he had been told, years before, along with the rest of Calis's company, on the shore of that distant land called Novindus, that should the Kingdom of the Isles not prevail, all life as they knew it would cease on Midkemia. He still couldn't accept that deep within, but he acted as if it was true. He had seen too many things on his trip south to know that even if the Captain's claims were overblown, life under the yoke of the Emerald Queen's advancing army would bring only a choice between death and slavery.

He also knew that if that event should come to pass which the Captain warned of, the invading army reaching some unnamed goal, then whatever preparations he made would be meaningless. But short of that, he was determined to take whatever steps necessary to keep his wife and children alive and away from harm. He had purchased a town house in Salador, presently used by an agent he had hired to run his affairs in the Eastern Realm, and he would probably buy another in the city of Ran, on the Kingdom's eastern frontier. He was next going to inquire of foreign agents in the East about the availability of property in distant Roldem, the island kingdom most closely allied with the Kingdom of the Isles.

Gathering his thoughts, he realized he was halfway to his office. He had told Karli he would spend the night at the town house, claiming that the affairs at the palace would force him to work late into the night. The truth was he was going to send a message to Sylvia Esterbrook, asking to see her tonight. Since returning from rescuing Erik and the others, he had thought of little else. Images of her body haunted his dreams, and memories of her scent and the soft feel of her skin made him unable to think of more important things. The one night he had spent with her after his return only reinforced his hunger to be with her.

He reached his office and rode through the gate, past workmen hurriedly attempting to finish the improvements to the property he had ordered when first back from his sea voyage. A second story was being added to the old warehouse, a loft, actually, where he could conduct business without being on the busy warehouse floor. His staff was growing and he needed more room. He had already made an offer for a piece of property adjoining his from the rear, and would have to completely tear down an old block of apartments rented to workmen and their families, and then build new facilities. He paid too much, he knew, but he was desperate for the space.

He dismounted and motioned for one of the workers to take his horse. "Give him some hay; no grain," he instructed as he made his way past wagons being loaded and unloaded. "Then saddle another horse and have it ready for me." Workers repairing broken wheels and replacing shoes on draft animals set up a raucous hammering, and men shouted instructions to one another across the floor.

Overseeing the chaos were two men, Luis de Savona, Roo's companion from the early days of Calis's "company of desperate men," and Jason, a former waiter at Barret's who had been the first there to befriend Roo, and who was also a genius with figures.

Roo smiled. "Where's Duncan?"

Luis shrugged. "Abed with some whore, probably."

It was midday, and Roo shook his head. His cousin was reliable in certain ways, but in others he had no sense of loyalty. Still, there were only a handful of men in the world Roo would trust at his back in a knife fight, and Duncan was one of them.

"What news?" asked Roo.

Jason held out a large document. "Our attempt to establish a regular route to Great Kesh is 'under consideration,' according to this very wordy document that just arrived from the Keshian Trade Legate's office. We are, however, welcome to bid on odd jobs as they come to our attention."

"He said that?"

"Not in so many words," said Luis.

"Since we took over the operation of Jacoby and Sons, I halfway expected we'd keep their regular clients."

"We have," said Jason, "except for the Keshian merchants." He shook his head, his young features a mask of solemnity. "Once it became known you'd taken over on Helen Jacoby's behalf, every Keshian trading concern began canceling contracts as fast as possible."

Roo frowned. Tapping his chin with his finger, he asked, "Who's getting those contracts?"

Luis said, "Esterbrook." Roo turned and stared at his friend, who continued. "At least, either companies he holds a minor interest in, or ones owned by men he has major influence over. You know he was doing a lot of business with the Jacobys before you finished with them."

Roo glanced at Jason. "What did you find when you went over the Jacoby accounts?"

Jason had thoroughly investigated all those accounts while Roo had sailed across the sea to rescue Erik. Roo had killed Randolph and Timothy Jacoby when they had tried to ruin him, and rather than put Randolph Jacoby's wife, Helen, and their children out on the streets, he had agreed to run Jacoby and Sons on her behalf.

Jason said, "Whatever business Jacoby and Esterbrook had, there was little record keeping involved. There were some minor contracts, but nothing out of the ordinary, just a few odd personal notes I can't make sense of. But one thing doesn't fit."

"What?" asked Roo.

"The Jacobys were too rich. There was gold accounted to them in several countinghouses that . . . well, I don't know where it came from. I have accounts going back ten years"—he waved at a pile of ledgers on the floor nearby—"and there's just no source for it."

Roo nodded. "Smuggling." He remembered his first confrontation with Tim Jacoby, over some smuggled silk Roo had managed to get his hands on. "How much gold?"

Jason said, "More than thirty thousand sovereigns, and I haven't found every account yet."

Roo considered silently for a minute. "Don't say anything about this to anyone. If you have any reason to speak to Helen Jacoby, just tell her things are going better than we had thought. Keep it vague, just enough solid information to reassure her that she and her children are protected for life, no matter what happens to me. And ask her if she needs anything."

"Aren't you going to see her?" asked Luis.

"Soon." He glanced around. "We need to build more resources, and fast, so start keeping your ears open for businesses we can buy into or take over outright. But keep it quiet; any mention of the name Avery and Son or the Bitter Sea Company and prices will rise faster than a spring flood." The others acknowledged his instructions, and Roo said, "I'm going next to Barret's, to see my partners, and if I'm needed, that's where you'll find me for the balance of the day."

Roo left his associates and mounted his fresh horse. As he considered what he had been told, he reached Barret's Coffee House before he knew it.

Roo dismounted, tossing the reins to one of the waiters. He pulled a silver coin from his vest and handed it to the boy. "Stable him behind my house, Richard."

The youngster led the mount away, smiling. Roo made it a point to remember the names of all the waitstaff at Barret's and to tip lavishly. He had been employed there only three years before and knew how difficult the work could be. Besides, if he needed something from a waiter, a message carried across town or a special dish prepared for a business associate, he got quick service in exchange for his largesse.

Roo moved past the first rail as another waiter quickly opened the gate for him, then made his way to the stairs up to the balcony overlooking the central part of the floor. His partners, Jerome Masterson and Stanley Hume, were waiting for him. He took his seat and said, "Gentlemen?"

Jerome said, "Rupert. A pleasant morning to you." Hume echoed the greeting, and they began to conduct the morning business of the Bitter Sea Company, the largest trading concern in the Kingdom of the Isles.

Two

Warning

ERIK FUMED.

He had spent the day working on a plan to employ the Hadati hillmen he had taken from the Baron of Tyr-Sog, only to be told they had left the Prince's castle, and no one seemed sure where they had gone or at whose orders. He had finally ended up outside the office of the Knight-Marshal of Krondor, who was ensconced within his private chamber in a meeting with Captain Calis.

Finally a clerk indicated Erik could enter, and both William and Calis greeted him. "Sergeant Major," said William, indicating an empty chair. "What can I do for you?"

"It's about the Hadati, m'lord," said Erik, not taking the seat.

"What about them?" asked Calis.

"They're gone."

"I know," said Calis with a faint smile.

Erik said, "What I mean is, I had plans—"

Knight-Marshal William held up his hand. "Sergeant Major, whatever plans you had are certainly similar to our own. However, your particular talents aren't needed in that area."

Erik's eyes narrowed. "In what area?"

"Teaching hillmen how to fight in the hills," said Calis.

He motioned for Erik to sit, and Erik did as he was instructed.

William pointed to a map on the wall across the room. "We've got a thousand miles of hills and mountains running from just north of the Great Star Lake up to Yabon, Sergeant. We're going to need men who can live up there without supplies from Krondor."

Erik said, "I know, m'lord—"

William interrupted him again. "Those men already meet our needs."

Erik was silent a moment, then said, "Very well, m'lord. But, for my curiosity's sake, where are they?"

"On their way to a camp north of Tannerus. To meet with Captain Subai."

"Captain Subai?" asked Erik. The man named was head of the Royal Krondorian Pathfinders, an elite scouting unit that traced its lineage back to the Kingdom's first foray into the West. They had long since changed their mission of being trailbreakers and explorers; they now served as long-range military scouts and intelligence officers. "You're turning them over to the Pathfinders?"

"In a manner of speaking," said Calis. He sounded tired, and Erik studied his leader's features. There were dark smudges under his eyes, as if he hadn't slept much in recent days, and his face was a little more pinched than usual. Those signs might go unnoticed by someone who hadn't spent every waking moment for months in Calis's company, but to Erik they communicated much: Calis was worried and was working late into the night. Erik suppressed a rueful smile. He had started to think like the very nursemaid Calis had warned him not to become, and besides, he was just as guilty of overwork as his leader.

Calis spoke. "We need couriers and exploring officers."

This was a term new to Erik. "Exploring officers?" he asked.

"It's a madman's job," offered Calis. "You pack your horse with a few rations and a canteen of water; then you ride like hell through the enemy's pickets, move behind their lines, stay alive, meet with agents and spies, occasionally assassinate someone or burn down a stronghold, and otherwise wreak havoc wherever you can."

"You forgot the important part," offered William. "Staying alive. Getting back with what you know is more important than all the rest."

"Information," said Calis. "Without it, we're blind."

Erik realized with a sudden clarity that what he had lived through on two journeys to Novindus—the hardships, the loss of good men—was all to return with vital information. As with many things that Erik had learned in the military, he thought he understood something only to discover later he possessed merely a surface apprehension of the way things were, as a deeper appreciation of the topic seem to unfold in his mind. Tactics and strategy were like that. William kept telling him he had a knack, yet often Erik felt stupid, as if he were missing the obvious.

Almost blushing, Erik said, "I understand."

"I'm sure you do," said Calis in a friendly tone.

William said, "We're delighted to put the Hadati to such use, though they will likely be used as scouts and couriers; few of them are competent enough horsemen to serve as explorers."

"I can train them," said Erik, suddenly interested.

"Perhaps. But we've got some Inonian mountain rangers coming in from the East. They are experienced riders."

Erik had seen the occasional Inonian in Darkmoor. Swarthy, tough little men from the Inonia region along the coast of the Kingdom Sea nearest the southeastern borders with Kesh, they were reputed to be as fierce in their ability to defend their mountain highlands as the Hadati or dwarves. Erik knew them firsthand only for the excellent wines they traded in exchange for Darkmoor's best; their wines were distinctive, using different varieties of grapes from those found in Darkmoor, often spiced or treated with resins or honey, but treasured for that very difference. The Inonians also produced the finest olive oil known, and that was the primary source of their prosperity.

"From what I understand," offered Erik, "Inonian horsemen are able enough."

"In the mountains," said William, standing up as if to throw off the weight of fatigue. "Hit-and-run tactics are the rule. They also don't marshal many men at a time, doing most of their damage with a dozen or fewer raiders." He waved to a bookshelf on the opposite side of his office. "We have at least one account of the Kingdom's conquest of their region in there. They have some nasty tricks that may help us when the invaders get here." He stretched. "They ride small, tough ponies, and getting them to accept our faster horses may take some doing; you may have to give them some instruction, too."

Calis grinned, and Erik knew without asking that the eastern hill fighters were unlikely to take being trained gracefully. "But for the moment," the Captain said, "you're to head back into the hills with another batch of soldiers."

"Again?" Erik barely suppressed a groan.

"Again," said Calis. "Greylock and Jadow have got sixty survivors of their boot camp they swear will take to your training like a baby to the teat. You and Alfred and another six of your men will take them out tomorrow morning."

William said, "Teach them everything you can, Sergeant Major."

"And keep your eye out for potential corporals," Calis added. "We need more sergeants, too."

"Yes, sir." Erik rose, saluted, and turned to leave.

Calis said, "Erik?"

"Yes?" asked Erik as he paused at the door.

"Why don't you go out tonight and have some fun? You look like hell. Consider that an order."

Erik shrugged, shook his head, and said, "You're no daisy."

Calis smiled. "I know. I'm taking a long hot bath; then I'm turning in early tonight."

William said, "Go find a girl and a drink and relax."

Erik left the Knight-Marshal's office and moved to his own quarters. He had been working in the marshalling yard all day, and if he was going anywhere he wanted to bathe and change.

After his bath and in a fresh tunic, he felt hunger and considered heading to the mess. He weighed his choices and decided a meal in town might be just the thing.

Erik decided to walk to the Broken Shield, the inn operated by Lord James for the men, giving them a place to drink and meet the whores handselected by the Duke to ensure no one said anything to a potential agent of the enemy.

Evening was falling and the city was ablaze in torch and lantern light as Erik reached the inn. James had picked a location far enough from the palace to look a likely hangout for soldiers wishing to be away from the scrutiny of their officers, yet close enough that a message could reach anyone in minutes. Only Erik, the officers, and a few others realized that every person within the inn was an agent or employee of the Duke.

Kitty waved as Erik entered the room and he found himself smiling at her. He had been the one who had told the girl of Bobby de Loungville's death, and since then he had looked in on her from time to time. She had shown no reaction to the news, excusing herself for a few minutes, and when she had returned, only slightly red eyes had betrayed her feelings. Erik suspected the former thief had been in love with the man who had held the position of sergeant major before him. Bobby had been a difficult, even cruel, man at times, but he had treated the young girl with nothing but respect since she had come to the inn.

Erik had asked James if the girl did more than tend bar, but the Duke had simply replied he was pleased with the girl's services since she had become one of his agents. Erik knew her primary job was to keep alert for any Mocker, a member of the Guild of Thieves of Krondor, attempting to enter the Broken Shield.

"What's new?" asked Erik as he reached the bar.

"Not much," said Kitty, retrieving a large jack from under the counter, then filling it at the ale tap. "Just those two in from somewhere." With a motion of her chin she indicated two men sitting at a corner table.

"Who are they?" asked Erik, then took a long pull on the ale. Say what you will, he thought, about being told to frequent only this one inn: at least the Duke kept it serving only the finest ale and food.

Kitty shrugged. "Didn't say. They sound like Easterners to me. Certainly not from around here." She picked up a bar rag and began wiping imaginary spills. "One of them is quiet, the dark fellow in the corner, but the other talks enough for both of them."

Erik shrugged. While the inn was known to locals as being the hangout of garrison soldiers off duty, a few strangers wandered in from time to time, and although the staff was always on the lookout for spies and informers, most of those strangers had legitimate business in the area. Those few who didn't were either followed out by Duke James' agents or conducted to a basement room for interrogation, depending on the Duke's instructions.

Erik glanced around and noticed that none of the girls who serviced the soldiers were in view. He glanced at Kitty and found he preferred talking to her for the moment. "The girls keeping out of sight?"

"Meggan and Heather are working tonight," said Kitty. "They ducked out when the strangers arrived."

Erik nodded. "The special girls?"

"One's on the way," said Kitty. The special girls were agents of the Duke, and when a stranger stayed too long at the inn, one quickly appeared, ready to accompany the stranger and ferret out whatever information might prove useful.

Erik found himself wondering who had taken up the role of "Spymaster," as Erik was certain that had been one of Bobby de Loungville's many masks. Certainly it wasn't Captain Calis, and Erik knew it wasn't himself.

"What are you thinking?" asked Kitty.

"Just wondering about our"—glancing at the two strangers, he changed what he was about to say—"landlord's employees."

Kitty raised her eyebrows in question. "What do you mean?"

Erik shrugged. "It's probably none of my business, anyway. A man can get too curious."

Kitty leaned forward, elbows on the bar, and said, "Curiosity is what got me the death mark."

Erik raised his eyebrow. "The Mockers?"

"Rumor reached me a few weeks ago. An old friend thought to warn me. The Upright Man has returned, or at least someone claiming to be the Upright Man, and I'm being blamed for some troubles beyond the death of Sam Tannerson."

Tannerson had been a bully and thief who had killed Kitty's sister as a warning to Roo not to do business in the Poor Quarter without paying bribes. It had been a bloody business and had resulted in both Roo and Kitty finding themselves in need of the Duke's protection.

"What sort of troubles?"

"Something to do with the previous leader of the Mockers, the Sagacious Man, having to flee Krondor." She sighed. "Anyway, if I venture out of this inn after dark, or into the Poor Quarter at any time, I'm dead."

Erik said, "That's a heavy burden."

Kitty shrugged as if it wasn't important. "Life is like that."

Erik sipped his ale. He studied the girl. When she had first been captured, she had stripped before Bobby and the men who had captured her, partially in defiance, partially in resignation. She was pretty—a lithe body, long neck, and big blue eyes that any man would notice—but hard. There was an element of toughness in her which took nothing away from her features but which underlined them, as if life had forged her in a hotter fire than most. Erik found it attractive in a way he couldn't articulate. She wasn't remotely provocative, like the girls he slept with at the Sign of the White Wing, or playful and mildly taunting, like the whores who worked this inn. She was guarded, thoughtful, and, Erik had decided, very smart.

"What are you staring at?" she asked.

Erik lowered his eyes. He hadn't realized he had been staring at her. "You, I guess."

"There are plenty of girls around here to scratch your itch, Erik. Or there's the White Wing if you want something special."

Erik blushed. Suddenly Kitty laughed. "You're a child, I swear."

Erik said, "I'm not in the mood . . . for that. Just thought I'd have a drink or two and . . . talk."

Kitty raised an inquiring eyebrow, but said nothing for a moment. Finally she said, "Talk?"

Erik sighed. "I'm spending so much time shouting at men, watching them fall all over themselves trying to anticipate my next order, or in meetings with the Captain and the other court officers, I just wanted to talk about anything that doesn't have something to do with"—he almost found himself saying "the invasion" but caught himself—"being a soldier."

If Kitty noticed his slight hesitation, she said nothing. "So, what do you want to talk about?" she asked, putting away her bar rag.

"How are you doing?"

"Me?" she asked. "Well, I'm eating better than I ever have. I've gotten used to not having to hold a dagger in my hand when I sleep—I just keep it under my pillow. That's another thing I'm getting used to: sleeping in a real bed.

"And not having lice and fleas is good."

Suddenly Erik laughed. Kitty joined in. Erik said, "I know what you mean. The pests on the march can be as maddening as anything."

One of the two strangers approached. "From your garb I take you for a soldier," he said.

Erik nodded. "I am."

With a friendly manner the fellow spoke. "It's kind of quiet here tonight. I've been in a lot of inns, and this isn't exactly what I'd call lively."

Erik shrugged. "Sometimes it is. Depends on what's going on at the palace."

The man said, "Really?"

Erik glanced at Kitty, who nodded slightly, said, "Got to check some inventory," and left through the rear door.

"We've got a big parade coming up soon," said Erik. "Some embassy or another from Kesh is coming for one of those state visits. The Master of Ceremonies has the Captain of the Prince's Household Guards half-crazy with all the nonsense the garrison's going to go through to get ready for this.

I'm in for a quick ale and a chat with my friend; then I've got to head back."

The man glanced at his empty ale mug. "I need another." He turned and shouted, "Girl!"

When Kitty didn't answer, he turned back to Erik. "Think she'd mind if I fill my own?"

Erik shook his head. "If you leave your coins on the bar, she won't."

"Buy you one?" asked the man as he moved behind the bar.

"What about your friend?" asked Erik, indicating the other man at the table, the darker stranger Kitty had referred to as the quieter of the pair.

"He'll keep. He's a business associate of mine." The man lowered his voice and in a conspiratorial tone said, "Truth to tell, he's a terrible bore. All he talks about is trade and his children."

Erik nodded, as if agreeing with the man.

"I'm unmarried myself," said the stranger, coming around the bar, handing a foaming mug to Erik. "Name's Pierre Rubideaux. From Bas-Tyra."

"Erik." He took the mug.

"Your health," said Pierre, hoisting his own mug.

Erik took a drink. "What brings you to Krondor?" he asked.

"Business. In particular, we're looking to set up some trading with the Far Coast through the port."

Erik smiled. "You'll be wanting to talk to a friend of mine, I think."

"Who's that?" asked Rubideaux.

"Rupert Avery. Owns the Bitter Sea Company. You trade in Krondor, you do business with either Roo or Jacob Esterbrook. If you're talking about Kesh, that's Esterbrook. If you're talking the Far Coast, that's Roo." Erik took another long drink from his mug. Something slightly bitter lingered after the ale, and he frowned. He didn't remember his first mug being off.

"As a fact, I am looking for Rupert Avery," said the man.

The other man stood, nodding to Pierre. "It's time," he said. "We must leave."

"Well, Erik von Darkmoor, it's been more of a pleasure than you know."

Erik started to say good-bye, then frowned. "I never told you my full name—" he began. Suddenly a pain ripped through his stomach, as if someone had plunged a fiery knife in his gut. He reached out and grabbed the stranger by his tunic front.

As if removing the grip of a baby, the man pulled Erik's hands away. "You've got only a few more minutes, Erik, but they'll be long ones; trust me."

Erik felt the strength drain from his legs as he attempted to step forward. The blood pounded in his temples and darkness began to close around his field of vision. He was dully aware of Kitty reentering the inn. Her voice sounded distant and he couldn't understand most of what she was saying, but he heard a man shout, "Take them!"

Then he was looking upward through a tunnel of light as darkness moved in from all sides. His body was afire with pain as if each joint was swelling inside him. Hot spikes of agony traveled up and down his arms and legs, and his heart pounded faster and faster as if trying to erupt from his chest. Perspiration ran from his face and drenched his body as Erik felt his muscles tighten, disobeying his command to let him stand. As Kitty's face appeared at the end of the tunnel of his vision, he attempted to speak her name, but his tongue wouldn't work and the pain made it almost impossible to breathe.

The last thing he heard as darkness overtook him was a single word: "Poison."

"He'll live," said the voice as Erik found himself regaining consciousness.

Pain exploded behind his eyes as he opened them, causing him to groan. The sound of his own voice caused the pain to redouble, and he bit back a second groan. His body ached and his joints were burning.

"Erik?" came a woman's voice, and Erik attempted to find the source. Strange blurry shapes hovered at the edge of his vision, and he couldn't make his eyes obey his will, so he shut them.

Another voice, Roo's, said, "Can you hear me?"

"Yes," Erik managed to croak.

Someone put a damp cloth on his lips and Erik licked them. The moisture seemed to help, so he sucked on the cloth. Then someone held a cup of water to his lips, while someone else held his head so he could drink.

"Just a sip," said the woman's voice.

Erik sipped, and while his throat hurt worse than he ever remembered, he forced himself to swallow. In a few seconds the returning moisture to his mouth and throat eased the discomfort.

Erik blinked as he realized he was in a bed. Hovering over him were Kitty, Duke James, Roo, and Calis. Another figure was barely visible at the periphery of his vision.

"What happened?" asked Erik, his voice still hoarse.

"You were poisoned," said Roo.

"Poisoned?" he asked.

Nodding, Duke James said, "Henri Dubois. He's a poisoner from Bas-Tyra. I've run afoul of his handiwork before in Rillanon. I didn't expect to see him this far west."

Glancing around, Erik assumed he was in a back room at the inn, a priest of an order he didn't recognize standing behind the others.

"Why?" asked Erik. Assuming no one in the room was ignorant of the coming invasion, he still didn't want to betray anything Lord James wanted kept secret.

"Nothing to do with the coming troubles," said Calis. He glanced pointedly at the priest, which Erik took to mean the man was not fully trusted.

"A personal matter," suggested Lord James.

Erik wasn't sure what he meant, for a moment, then realization struck.

"Mathilda," he whispered. He sank back into the bed. His father's widow, mother to his murdered half brother, who had vowed revenge on Erik and Roo, had sent someone to see the matter disposed of.

"They were coming after Roo next," said Erik.

"That's logical," said James.

"Who was the other man, the quiet one?" asked Erik as James helped him to sit upright. Nausea struck him, his head rang, and his eyes watered, but he stayed conscious.

"We don't know," answered Calis. "He got out of the inn while we were subduing Dubois."

"You captured him?" asked Erik.

"Yes," answered James. "Last night." He indicated Kitty. "When she left the inn to fetch some of my agents, then returned to find you on the floor, she surmised at once what was going on. She hurried down to the nearest temple and brought a priest to heal you."

"Half dragged, you mean," said the nameless priest.

James smiled. "My men took Dubois to the palace and we questioned him all night. We're certain the late Baron of Darkmoor's widow sent him after you." James raised one eyebrow and motioned with his head toward the cleric.

Erik said nothing. He knew the Lady Gamina, James's wife, could read minds, which was why they were certain who had sent the assassin. No confession was needed.

The priest said, "I think you should rest. The magic that cleansed your body of the poison didn't reverse the damage already done you. You will need at least a week of bed rest and a bland diet."

"Thank you, Father . . . ?" began Erik.

"Father Andrew," answered the priest. He nodded once to the Duke and left without further comment.

Erik said, "That's an odd priest. I don't recognize his regalia."

"I would find it strange if you did, Erik," answered the Duke as he moved toward the door. "Andrew is a priest of the order of Ban-ath. Their shrine is the closest to this inn."

The god of thieves was not one commonly worshipped by most citizens. There were two holidays when small votive offerings were made to protect the home, as an appeasement, but mostly those who frequented the temple were on the dodgy path, as it was called. It was rumored the Mockers' Guild sent a tithe to the temple each year.

James said, "I'm going to leave you now. You stay here a couple of days, then you've got to get that happy little band of cutthroats we've recruited for you up into the mountains and teach them what they need to know."

Erik glanced around. "Where is here?"

"My room," said Kitty.

"No," said Erik, trying to rise. He almost fainted from the effort. "Give me a little while to catch my breath and I'll get back to the palace."

Calis turned to leave. "Stay here."

"I've slept with worse company," said Kitty. "I won't mind a pallet on the floor."

Erik tried to protest, but fatigue was making it hard to keep his eyes open.

He heard Calis say something to Kitty, but couldn't remember what it was. During the night, chills racked his body for a few minutes, until a warm body slipped into bed with him and he felt reassuring arms encircle his waist. But when he awoke in the morning he was alone.

Erik rode in silence. His strength was slowly returning after a few days in bed, and a week in the saddle. Since leaving Krondor he had left it to Alfred to bully the men, doing little more than give instructions to Alfred and another corporal named Nolan. He had inspected fortifications only once or twice. Jadow and the other sergeants had done their work in Krondor. The men were adept at using the ancient Keshian Legion techniques for making camp each night. Within a hour of the order being given, a tiny fortress was in place, with breastworks, defensive stakes, and removable planks used to get in and out.

Erik was getting to know these men, though he still couldn't remember every name. He knew many of them would die in the coming war. But Calis and William were doing a nearly perfect job of picking the right men for these special companies. The men before him were tough and self-reliant and, Erik suspected, would be able to live by their own wits for months up in these mountains if the situation required, once they had learned the particulars of mountain living.

Erik considered all the things he knew from living in Ravensburg: the tricks the wind played with sound, the threat of a sudden storm being felt before it was seen, and the dangers of being exposed to such a storm. He had seen more than one traveler dead from spending the night in the cold, only miles from the inn where Erik had grown up.

The wind from the north was cold, for winter was coming quickly. Erik realized that was why he was thinking of the trader they had found when he was ten; the man had tried to shelter under a tree, with his cloak wrapped around him, but in the night the wind had sucked the warmth from his body and killed him as if he had been encased in ice.

They were making their way along a small mountain trail, used for the most part by hunters and a few shepherds, one which ran roughly the same course as the King's Highway from Krondor to Ylith, but which veered to the northeast about fifty miles from the Prince's city. Several little hamlets dotted the way up to another fork, where the road turned west again, eventually leading to Hawk's Hollow and Questor's View, while a smaller trail led to the northeast, toward the Teeth of the World and the Dimwood. In the foothills of those great mountains and in the various meadows, valleys, and stretches of the forests existed some of the most dangerous and unknown territory within the boundaries of the Kingdom.

Fate had conspired to keep Kingdom citizens out of those areas, for there were no natural trade routes, little desirable farmland, and few mineral riches to lure men there. Erik had decided, without asking anyone, to take his trainees farther on this march than ever before. He had an instinct that the more the Kingdom knew of the north, the less likely they would be to have unwelcome surprises when the Emerald Queen's army came.

As if reading his mind, Alfred rode up next to him and said, "Bit far to go for drilling, isn't it, Erik?"

Erik nodded. He pointed to a pass off in the distance. "Send a squad to scout out that rise so we don't find a band of Dark Brothers marching over it unexpectedly, and look for tonight's camp." He glanced around, then said softly, "Hunting parties tomorrow. Let's see who knows how to find his own dinner."

Alfred shivered. "This is a cold place to camp."

"The farther north we go, the colder it gets."

Alfred sighed. "Yes, Sergeant Major."

"Besides," said Erik, "we're almost where I want to be."

"And would you be in the mood to share that tidbit, Sergeant Major?" asked Alfred.

"No," said Erik.

Corporal Alfred rode off, and Erik suppressed a smile. The old Corporal had served in the garrison at Darkmoor, for Erik's father, for fifteen years before they met. He was a full twenty years older than Erik's twenty-two. He had also been an early convert of Erik's, having been one of the first picked to accompany the levy of men Erik's half brother sent to the Prince, and he was one of the few survivors of that journey. Erik had been forced by circumstance to physically beat Alfred three times, the first when Alfred had sighted Erik in an inn in the town of Wilhelmsburg and Alfred had attempted to arrest Erik. The second time had been during his first week of training under Erik and Jadow Shati; and the third, when he had gotten too sure of himself and thought he could finally best the young sergeant. Then they had voyaged to the far continent, Novindus, and from there they had returned, two of the five men who survived that expedition. Now Erik trusted the man with his life and knew Alfred felt the same way about him.

Erik considered that odd forged bond of soldiers, men who otherwise might have no use for one another but who after serving together, facing death together, felt like brothers. Then, thinking of brothers, he wondered if James would be able to convince Erik's half brother's mother to cease her attempts to kill him. Erik considered that if anyone could do so, it would be Lord James.

The men marched and Erik considered the coming war. He was not privy to all the plans of Lord James, Knight-Marshal William, and Prince Patrick, but he was beginning to suspect what they would be. And he didn't like what he was beginning to suspect.

He knew more than most men what was coming, but he had reservations about what would be the price of victory, and as he rode down the small path, he heard one of the men pass the word, "Scouts coming!"

A man sent ahead with three others jogged at a good pace past the column of men marching ahead of Erik and stopped before the Sergeant Major. His name was Matthew, and he struggled for breath as he said, "Smoke, Sergeant!" He turned and pointed. "Far ridge. About a dozen fires I think."

As Erik searched the distant ridge, he started to notice the low-hanging smoke, easily mistaken for ground fog at this distance. "Where are the other scouts?"

The soldier, catching his breath, said, "Mark has moved out, while Wil and Jenks are staying where we first saw the smoke." He blew out his cheeks a moment, then said, "And Jenks will follow about now, I guess."

Erik nodded. It was the standard procedure for any encounter with potentially hostile soldiers. The scouts always left camp an hour before the main column, moving along the road in pairs, two on each side, scouting for potential ambush. If any potential enemy was spied, orders were for one man to return, the other to scout ahead. If the advance scout didn't quickly return, a second would follow, to determine if the first was dead, captured, or observing the enemy. If the latter, the advance scout would return as soon as he was relieved, carrying the most up-to-the-moment intelligence while leaving another pair of eyes to watch.

Erik nodded and wished they were training these men as mounted cavalry. That would start next month, but right now he wished for the speed.

Erik signaled and said, "Hand signals only!"

The men at the rear turned to look, then started tapping the men in front on their shoulders, relaying the silent order. Alfred motioned and Erik nodded. He signed that he would ride with the advance scout to the van, while Alfred was to bring up the column. He indicated he wanted two squads on the wings, one to the right and one to the left, and ready for anything.

Erik motioned for the scout to take the lead and rode after. The man jogged at a good pace, and Erik trotted along after him.

After moving up the road for nearly a half hour, they found the first of Erik's scouts, watching ahead. He held up his hand and Erik dismounted. Keeping his voice low, he said, "No sign of Jenks or Mark, Sergeant."

Erik nodded, handing his reins to Matthew. He motioned for Wil to come with him and moved along the trail. Glancing across a small valley, he could clearly see smoke from fires along a distant ridge.

He moved another quarter mile along the trail, then paused. Something ahead wasn't right. He listened, then realized that while sound was echoing from all around this narrow pass, it was silent ahead. He motioned for Wil to move to the other side of the trail, then he continued down into the thick brush on his side.

The going was slow as Erik carefully picked his way through the dense undergrowth. The trees in this rocky hillside stood in clumps, with relatively bare spots between. At the edge of one such clearing, Erik saw Wil on the other side of the road. With hand gestures, he indicated Wil should loop around and approach the next group of trees from a position farther off the trail.

Erik watched and waited. When Wil didn't appear again, Erik was certain he knew where whoever was taking his scouts was secreted. Erik surveyed his own surroundings and decided to move farther down slope.

He backed away from the edge of the trees he had hid within, and after a few scrambling half-slides, he was down at the base of a dry creek. During the next rain this defile would be flooded, he knew, but at present there was only a bit of damp soil underfoot to remind him of the last rain in these mountains.

The scent of smoke was now evident, and Erik knew there had been other campfires closer than the ones that now burned; he suspected that another company of men had broken camp here the night before. A familiar odor greeted Erik and he glanced up the slope. A good job of hiding horse dung had been accomplished, but to someone who had grown up with the animals the scent was unmistakable. The animals had been staked out a short distance from the clearing where his scouts had vanished. The lingering pungency of horse urine would be gone in another day.

Erik moved to the point on the opposite side of the road where his scout had disappeared, and paused, listening. Again there was a dead spot of sound nearby, as if the animals had left and would not return until the present occupants departed.

Erik skirted the edge of the brush, reached the next grove of trees from the downslope side, and started working his way back to the trail. Suddenly he knew: someone was watching him.

While short on years, he was long on experience in warfare, and he knew that he was about to be attacked. He rolled over as a body landed upon the spot he had just vacated.

The man landed lightly on his feet, despite his intended victim's not being where he had expected, and as he turned, Erik did the unexpected. He rolled back into the man, yanking him down on top of him.

Few men Erik had met were as strong as he, so he felt more confident with both of them in close than having his opponent upright while he tried to rise. Erik rolled the man over and got on top of him.

His opponent was strong, and quick, but Erik soon had his wrists confined. Seeing no weapon in the man's hand, Erik released his wrist, drawing back his own fist to strike, but hesitated, as he recognized the man.

"Jackson?"

The soldier said, "Yes, Sergeant Major."

Erik pushed himself off the man and rose to his feet. The soldier was one of Prince Patrick's Household Guards. But rather than the ceremonial uniforms of the palace, or even the daily drilling regalia, he was dressed in a dark green tunic and trousers, with a leather breastplate, short dagger, and metal bowl helm.

Erik extended his hand and helped the guardsman to his feet. "Want to tell me what this is all about?"

Another voice said, "No, he doesn't."

Erik looked to the source of that voice and saw a face familiar to him: Captain Subai of the Royal Krondorian Pathfinders.

"Captain?"

"Sergeant Major," said the officer. "You're a bit off your course, aren't you?"

Erik studied the man. He was tall, but rangy, close to gaunt, in appearance. His face was sunburned and looked like dark leather. His eyebrows and hair were grey, though Erik suspected he was not that old a man. He was rumored to be originally from Kesh, and was counted a fierce swordsman and an exceptional bowman. But like most of the Pathfinders he tended to stay among his own, not mixing with the garrison or Calis's Eagles.

"I was told by Prince Patrick to drill my new company and thought I'd wander them a bit through some rougher terrain than just outside Krondor." With his chin he indicated the distant smoke. "Your fires, Captain?"

The man nodded, then said, "Well, take your men north if you want, but don't come this way, Sergeant Major."

"Why not, Captain?"

The man paused and said, "That wasn't a request, Sergeant Major. That was an order."

Erik wasn't incline to argue the chain of command. This wasn't some noble's hired mercenary but a Knight-Captain of the Prince's army, a man with rank equal to Calis's. Erik thought Bobby de Loungville might have a clever rejoinder in this situation, but all Erik could think to say was "Yes, sir."

Subai said, "Your scouts are over there. They need some work."

Erik crossed the road and found another pair of soldiers standing guard over Wil, Mark, and Jenks. His men were tied up, but not uncomfortable. Erik glanced at the two guards and saw that one was a Pathfinder and the second another of Prince Patrick's Household Guards.

"Cut them loose," said Erik, and the two guards complied. The three rose slowly, obviously stiff from their confinement, and flexed a bit as the two guards handed them back their weapons.

Wil began to speak, and Erik held up his hand. A faint noise came to him and he recognized it, then another, and a third. "Come along," he ordered his men.

After they were well away from the Pathfinders, Erik asked, "They jumped you from the trees?"

Mark said, "Yes, Sergeant Major."

Erik sighed. He had almost been taken that way as well. "Well, look up more often."

The men waited for an outburst, or some other form of recrimination for allowing themselves to be captured, but Erik's mind was elsewhere.

He mused on the presence of Prince Patrick's select guard along that distant ridge, working hand in glove with the Pathfinders and their odd Captain. More odd yet was the presence of many soldiers on a distant ridge where every map said there were no trails, and oddest of all was the faint sounds that had carried to Erik. The second had taken him longer to recognize, but he knew it had been the sound of axes felling trees. That and the sound of picks on rock had not come to him as quickly as the first sound, one he knew well from his childhood: the sound of hammers striking iron on an anvil.

As they cleared the ridge to where the remaining scout waited, Jenks made bold to ask, "What are those blokes doing over there, Sergeant Major?"

Without thought, Erik said, "They're building a road."

"Over there?" asked Wil. "Why?"

Erik said, "I don't know, but I intend to find out."

The problem was, Erik had a good idea why they were building a road along that distant ridge, and he didn't like the answer.

Three

Queg

ROO SCOWLED.

Karli stood aside, obvious awe on her features, as the Duke of Krondor entered their home. She had met Lord James once before, at a gala Roo had thrown to mark the advent of his success with the founding of the Bitter Sea Company. Outside the door a carriage waited. Four mounted guards, one carrying a spear from which hung the ducal banner, stood holding their horses' bridles.

"Good evening, Mrs. Avery," said the Duke. "I'm sorry for the unexpected intrusion, but I need to borrow your husband for a bit."

Karli was nearly speechless, but she managed to say, "Borrow?"

Duke James smiled and took her hand, squeezing it slightly. "I'll return him to you undamaged. I promise."

Roo said, "Shall we talk?" He indicated his study.

The Duke said, "I think so."

He removed his cape and handed it to the astonished serving girl who had come to see who was at the door, and swept past her and Karli.

In his study, Roo closed the door. "To what do I owe the pleasure?" he asked.

James sat in a chair opposite Roo's desk. "From the expression on your face when I appeared at the door, pleasure isn't what I think you feel."

Roo said, "Well, it's not often we have the Duke of Krondor show up unannounced a few minutes before bedtime."

"I can do without the fuss of letting you know I'm coming and throwing your household into an uproar. I don't need another large meal with all the neighbors invited," said James. "Truth to tell, I know most of those with estates near here, and you're among the few with whom I can have an interesting discussion."

Roo looked dubious. "Would you care to stay the night, m'lord?"

"My thanks for the offer, but I must continue my journey. I'm heading to your homeland, to have word with the Dowager Baroness and her son. She sent assassins to kill Erik."

"I was warned," said Roo. "I was also told you took the assassin into custody."

"Yes," said the Duke. His features were drawn and he looked as if he had done without sleep for too many days recently, but his eyes were still alert and they studied Roo's face for a moment. "He's been . . . seen to. The other man, though, he's still out and about, and if he's merely Baroness Mathilda's errand boy, he'll be back to Darkmoor by now and she may be hatching another plot. I have plans for you and Erik, so I'm personally going to see she stops trying to kill you," he said lightly. Then, with complete seriousness, he added, "Neither of you is to die until I say so."

Roo sat back. There was really nothing more for him to say until the Duke told him what was on his mind. Roo knew he owed James several serious favors for his intervention in Roo's almost unheard-of rise to power and wealth, and he was certain James was here to collect one of those favors. He wouldn't stop by just to let Roo know he was personally seeing to Erik's and his safety.

After a moment of silence, James said, "I could do with a drink."

Roo had the good grace to blush. "Sorry," he said, rising from his chair. He retrieved two crystal goblets and some expensive brandy in a matching decanter from a cabinet built into the wall next to a window overlooking one of Karli's many gardens. He poured two generous measures, then handed one to the Duke.

James sipped and nodded his approval.

When Roo had returned to his chair, the Duke spoke. "I have a favor to ask."

Roo was surprised. "You sound as if you really mean that."

"I do. We both know you owe me in a very large measure, but I can't demand you go."

"Go where?"

"Queg."

"Queg?" Roo's astonishment was genuine. "Why Queg?"

James paused a moment, as if weighing how much to tell Roo. He lowered his voice. "Confidentially, we're going to have our hands full with the Emerald Queen's fleet when it clears the Straits of Darkness. Nicky's got some notion of hitting it halfway through, but to do that he's got to have the bulk of our fleet on the Far Coast. That means we have no way of protecting our shipments from the Free Cities and Ylith when the enemy is in the Bitter Sea."

"You want to make a deal with Queg not to raid our shipping?"

"No," said James. "I want you to negotiate a deal to hire Quegan warships as escorts for our ships."

Roo looked like an owl greeted by a bright light. Then he laughed. "You want to bribe them."

"In a word, yes." James sipped at his brandy, then lowered his voice, "And we want fire oil. Lots of it."

"Will they sell it?"

James sipped his drink. "Once, no. But they know we have the knowledge of making it, and have had it since the fall of Armengar. What we don't have is the production facilities. Our agents tell us they have an abundant supply. I need at least five thousand barrels. Ten thousand would be better."

"That's a lot of destruction," whispered Roo.

"You know what's coming, Roo," the Duke answered, his voice equally low.

Roo nodded. There was only one merchant in Krondor who had traveled to that distant land and seen firsthand the destruction visited upon innocents by the Emerald Queen. But there were other merchants with far better connections to be made with Queg. "Why me?"

"You are a well-regarded curiosity, Roo Avery. Word of your rise has spread from Roldem to the Sunset Islands, and I'm counting on that curiosity to tip the balance."

"What balance?" asked Roo.

James set his goblet on Roo's desk. "Queg has many quaint and original laws, and not the least of these is the simple fact that a non-citizen of that mad little Empire has no legal rights. If you set foot on Quegan soil without a Quegan sponsor, you're property for the first Quegan with a strong enough arm to toss a rope around you and make it stick. If you resist, even to save your life, that's assault on a citizen." He made a rowing motion. "How do you feel about long ocean voyages?"

"How long?"

"Twenty years is the shortest sentence we've heard of."

Roo sighed. "How do I get a sponsor?"

"That's the tricky part," said James. "We've had strained relations with Queg lately. Too much smuggling and raiding from our point of view, too little paying of duties for sailing on *their* ocean from their point of view. Our delegation was expelled from their court four years ago, and it's going to take a while to get another installed."

"Sounds difficult," said Roo.

"It is. But the thing you need to know about the Quegans is that their government serves two purposes: to keep order—by keeping the peasants beaten down—and to defend the island. The real power rests with their rich merchants. The oldest families have hereditary rights to a place on their ruling body, the Imperial Senate. Those with enough money can buy a seat."

Roo grinned. "Sounds like my kind of place."

"I doubt you'd like it. Remember, aliens have no rights. If you irritate your sponsor, he can withdraw his protection at whim. That means you have to be *very* polite. Take lots of gifts."

"I can see what you mean." Roo reflected on what he had been told for a moment, then asked, "How am I supposed to get ashore to make this sort of sponsorship contact if you can't provide an introduction?"

"You're an enterprising lad," said James, finishing his brandy. He stood. "You'll find a way. Start sounding out your business associates. Once you get some names to contact, I can arrange to have one message smuggled into Queg without too much difficulty, but that's about the limit of what I can do."

Roo rose. "I suppose I'll find a way." Already his mind was turning to the problem.

"My carriage is waiting and I have some distance to travel," said the Duke as he reached the doorway.

James followed him and motioned for the serving girl, who was rooted to the same spot he had left her in, still holding the Duke's cloak. She quickly helped the Duke on with it, and James stood aside while Roo opened the door.

James's carriage was waiting just beyond the portal, and Roo's gateman made ready to escort the carriage back to the entrance to Roo's estate.

As the carriage door was closed by a guard, James leaned out the window and said, "Don't be too long. I'd like you to leave next month at the latest."

Roo nodded, and closed the door. Karli hurried from the upstairs to ask, "What did the Duke want?"

"I'm going to Queg," answered Roo.

"Queg?" responded his wife. "Isn't that dangerous?"

Roo shrugged. "Yes. But for the moment, getting there is the problem." He yawned. Slipping his arm around her waist, he gave her a playful squeeze. "Right now I need some sleep. Let's go to bed."

She returned his merry tone with a rare smile. "I would like that."

Roo led his wife upstairs.

Roo lay in darkness listening to Karli's even breathing. Their lovemaking had been uninspired. Karli did nothing to arouse his desire the way Sylvia Esterbrook did. He thought of Sylvia during his love play with his wife and felt vaguely guilty for it.

He had visited Sylvia almost weekly, often twice in a week, since the award ceremony at the palace, and he was still as excited by her as he had been the first time he had come to her bed. He quietly stood up and moved to the window.

Through the flawless glass, imported at great expense from Kesh, he could see the rolling hills of his estate. He had a brook that provided, he had been told, excellent fishing, and he had a small stand of woodlands to the north teeming with game. He had said he would fish and hunt like a noble, but he never seemed to find time. The only thing that he could remotely consider recreation was his time spent with Erik at the Sign of the Broken Shield, making love to Sylvia, or practicing his swordplay with his cousin Duncan.

He reviewed his life in a rare moment of reflection and had to consider himself both lucky and cursed. He was lucky that he had survived the murder of Stefan von Darkmoor, the journey to Novindus with Captain Calis, and his confrontation with the Jacoby brothers. More, he was now one of the wealthiest merchants in Krondor. He felt blessed to be a family man, though his wife was not someone he cared to consider; he had long since admitted to himself he had married Karli out of pity and guilt: he felt responsible for the death of her father.

His children confused him. They were alien little creatures, demanding things he could only vaguely recognize as needs. And they tended to smell at the most inconvenient times. Abigail was a shy child who often burst into tears and ran from him if he raised his voice even in the slightest, and Helmut was teething, which led to his constantly spitting up the contents of his stomach, usually on a fresh tunic that Roo had just put on. He knew that had he not married Karli, he would now be wed to Sylvia. He didn't understand love, as others talked about it, but Sylvia consumed his thoughts. She took him to heights of passion he had only dreamt of before he met her. He even imagined that had Sylvia been his wife, his children would be perfect, blond little creatures who smiled all the time and never spoke unless it was required by their father. He sighed. Even if Sylvia had been their mother, Abigail and Helmut would be odd, alien creatures, he was sure.

He saw a cloud moving across the sky, blocking the big moon, the only one showing this time of night. As the vista beyond the window darkened, so did his mood. Sylvia, he wondered silently to himself. He was beginning to doubt she was in love with him; maybe it was some doubt about himself, he thought, but he just couldn't truly believe someone such as himself could capture her interest, let alone her heart. Still, she seemed relieved when he could arrange to visit her and her father, especially if he could spend the night. Her lovemaking was always inventive and enthusiastic, but as the months wore by, he suspected everything wasn't as it seemed to be. He also suspected she might be giving information to her father that cost Roo in his business. He decided he would have to be more careful what he said to Sylvia. He didn't think she was getting information out of him to give to her father, but a chance remark repeated over dinner might give the crafty old Jacob enough of an edge to better his younger rival.

Stretching, he watched as the cloud glided past. Sylvia was a strange and unexpected presence in his life, a miracle. Yet doubts continued to stir. He wondered what Helen Jacoby would make of this. Thinking of Helen made him smile. While she was the widow of a man he had gotten killed, they had become friends and, truth to tell, he enjoyed talking to her more than either Karli or Sylvia.

Roo sighed. Three women, and he didn't know what to make of any of them. He softly left the bedchamber and crossed to the room he used as his office. Opening a chest, he extracted a wooden box and lifted the lid. In the moonlight rested a brilliant set of matched rubies, five large stones as large as his thumb and a dozen smaller ones, all cut in identical fashion.

He had tried to sell the set in the East, but too many gem merchants recognized it for what it was, stolen goods. The case was inscribed with the name of the owner, a Lord Vasarius.

Roo laughed softly. He had cursed his luck at being unable to sell the gems, but now he counted himself fortunate. He knew that in the morning he would tell his apprentice Dash to inform his grandfather, Duke James, that when he was ready to send his message to Queg, he knew what it would say:

"My Lord Vasarius. My name is Rupert Avery, merchant of Krondor. I have recently come into possession of an item of great value I am certain belongs to you. May I have the pleasure of returning it to you in person?"

The ship rocked gently inside the huge harbor that was the entrance to the city of Queg, capital of the island nation of the same name. Roo watched with fascination as they edged close to the quay.

Huge war galleys crowded the harbor, along with dozens of smaller ships and boats, from large trading vessels down to tiny fishing smacks. For an island the size of Queg, it seemed an improbably busy port.

Roo had studied as much as he could on the hostile island nation, asking his trading partners, old soldiers and sailors, and anyone else who could give him an "edge," as the gamblers liked to say. When the Empire of Great Kesh had withdrawn from the Far Coast and what were now the Free Cities, pulling out her legions to send south to fight rebellious nations in the Keshian Confederacy, the Governor of Queg had revolted.

A child of the then Emperor of Kesh, from his fourth or fifth wife, he claimed one gods-inspired divine reason or another that led to the founding of the Empire of Queg. This tiny nation of former Keshians, mixed with local islanders through intermarriage, would have been something of a joke save for two factors. The first was that the island was volcanic and had some of the richest farmland north of the Vale of Dreams, surrounded by unusual local currents so that it was the most clement climate in the Bitter Sea—meaning it was self-sufficient when it came to feeding its populace—and the second was its navy.

Queg had the largest navy in the Bitter Sea, a fact of life constantly driven home by its regular harassment and occasional seizure of Kingdom, Keshian, and Free Cities ships. Besides Queg's claim that it had territorial rights throughout the Bitter Sea—a legacy of that long-ago claim on this sea by Kesh—there was the additional irritation of its pirates. Often galleys without flags would raid along the Kingdom coast or the Free Cities, down even along the far western coast of the Empire in a bold year, and at every turn the Emperor and Senate of Queg denied knowledge.

More than once Roo had heard from a minor palace official, "And all they'll ever say is 'We are a poor nation, surrounded on all sides by enemies.' "

Odd shadows skimming across the water caused Roo to lift his eyes aloft, and they opened wide in amazement. "Look!"

Jimmy, grandson of Lord James, and his brother, Dash, both looked up and observed a formation of giant birds flying out to sea. Jimmy was along at his grandfather's insistence, which caused Roo no small amount of discomfort. Dash worked for him, at least nominally, and was a reliable apprentice trader. Jimmy worked for his grandfather, though Roo wasn't certain in what capacity. He was certain it wasn't accounting. For a brief instant Roo wondered if the Quegans would hang the entire party if the boys were accused of being spies, or just him.

The brothers didn't resemble each other much, Jimmy looking mostly like his grandmother, fine-boned and with pale hair; Dash, like his father, Lord Arutha, with a mass of curly brown hair and a broad open face. But they shared more than most brothers in attitude and cunning. And he knew where they got that attitude: from their grandfather.

"Eagles," said Jimmy. "Or something like them."

"I thought they were only a legend," said Dash.

"What are they?" asked Jimmy.

"Giant birds of prey, harnessed and ridden like ponies."

"Someone's riding on them?" asked Roo in disbelief as the ship was hauled into the quay by dock workers catching ropes tossed to them by deckhands.

"Little people," said Jimmy. "Men who have been chosen for generations for their tiny size."

Dash said, "Legend has it that a Dragon Lord flew them as birds of prey, as you or I might fly a falcon, ages ago. These are the descendants of those birds."

Roo said, "You could do a lot with a flock of those in battle."

"Not really," suggested Jimmy. "They can't carry much and they tire easily."

"You suddenly know a great deal about them," suggested Roo.

"Rumors, nothing more," said Jimmy with a grin.

"Or reports on your grandfather's desk?" suggested Roo.

Dash said, "Look at the reception committee."

Jimmy said, "Whatever you wrote, Mr. Avery, it seems to have done the trick."

Roo said, "I merely informed Lord Vasarius I had something of value that belonged to him, and wished to give it back."

The gangway was rolled out, and as Roo made to leave, the ship's Captain put a restraining hand on his chest. "Better to do this by custom, Mr. Avery, sir."

The Captain called ashore. "Mr. Avery and party from Krondor. Have they leave to come ashore?"

A large delegation of Quegans stood waiting, surrounding a man in a litter, carried by a dozen muscular slaves. Each wore a robe with a fancy drape that hung over one shoulder, what Roo had been told was called a toga. In the cold months, the locals wore wool tunic and trousers, but in the hot months of spring, summer, and early fall, this light cotton garb was the preferred dress of the wealthy. One of the men said in the King's Tongue, "Please come ashore as our guest, Mr. Avery and party."

The Captain said, "Who speaks?"

"Alfonso Velari."

The Captain removed his hand from Roo's chest. "You are now invited to set foot on Quegan soil, Mr. Avery. You're a free man until that Velari fellow withdraws his protection. By custom he's supposed to let you know a day in advance. We'll be waiting here, ready to up anchor and set sail at a moment's notice."

Roo regarded the man, one of his many ship's masters, named Bridges, and said, "Thank you, Captain."

"We're at your disposal, sir."

As he stepped on the gangway, Roo overheard Dash mumble to Jimmy, "Of course he's at Roo's disposal. Roo owns the ship!"

Jimmy laughed softly, and the brothers fell silent.

Roo walked down the gangway and stopped before Velari. He was a short man of middle years, with hair cut close to his head and oiled. Roo was reminded of Tim Jacoby, for he also had sported a Quegan style of hair. "Mr. Avery?" asked the Quegan.

"At your service, sir."

"Not mine, gentle Mr. Avery. I am but one of many servants to Lord Vasarius."

"Is that Lord Vasarius in the litter?" asked Roo.

The Quegan returned an indulgent smile. "The litter is to transport you to Lord Vasarius's home, Mr. Avery." He made a gesture that indicated Roo should enter the litter. "Porters will secure your baggage and bring it to my master's home."

Roo glanced at Dash and Jimmy, who nodded briefly. Roo said, "I was planning on staying at one of your city's better inns. . . ."

Velari made a sweeping gesture with his hand, as if to brush aside the remark. "There are none, sir. Only common travelers and seamen stay at our public houses. Men of rank always guest with other men of rank."

As if that settled the matter, he held aside the litter's curtain and Roo awkwardly entered. Instantly he was inside, the litter was picked up by the eight slaves, and the procession set off.

Roo could see the city of Queg as he was carried through. He glanced behind and saw that Jimmy and Dash were having no trouble keeping up, and he settled in to view the splendor of the Quegan capital.

One of Queg's greatest exports lay in quarries at the center of the island. Marble of unsurpassed quality was cut there and exported at great expense to nobles in the Kingdom, Kesh, and the Free Cities who wanted impressive façades on their homes, or stunning fireplaces. But here it was used everywhere. The common buildings seemed to be fashioned from stone and plaster, but the larger buildings on the tops of the surrounding hills all glistened white in the morning sun.

Already the day was warm, and Roo wished he had cooler clothing. The tales about the climate here were understated if anything. While the weather in Krondor was still brisk in the morning and mild in the afternoon, here it was almost like summer. Rumor had it that much of the warm currents that surrounded the island came from undersea volcanoes, venting nearby. It had been said on more than one occasion by those to whom Roo spoke that occasionally prayers were said to Prandur, Burner of Cities, that the entire island should blow up.

Despite the Quegans' reputation as a people hostile to outsiders and generally unpleasant to deal with, the common folk of the city seemed much like those of Krondor to Roo. The only marked difference was dress, as the laborers wore only breechclouts and headbands as they loaded and unloaded cargo at the docks, and the common workers wore short tunics of what looked to be a light spun wool, and cross-gartered sandals.

Occasionally Roo spied a noble in a toga, but mostly the men affected the short tunic. Roo saw women wearing long skirts, but with their arms bare and their heads uncovered.

The sounds of the city were much like those of Krondor, though horses seemed rare. Roo judged a population of this size must require a very high percentage of the land be put under cultivation, which wouldn't leave much room for grazing non-food animals. Horses on Queg would be a luxury.

The party wended its way up a series of hills until at last it reached a large building behind a high stone wall. The gate opened and they were admitted by two guards wearing the traditional Quegan military uniform: breastplate, greaves, shortsword, and helm. Roo realized they looked similar in attire to the legendary Legionaries of the Keshian Inner Legions. He had practiced Legionary tactics when he had served with Calis's Crimson Eagles, and he knew much about them. But this was as close as he had come to ever seeing one.

As the litter was gently deposited on the stones before the entrance to the building, Roo considered it likely it was as close as he was ever likely to get to a genuine member of the Keshian Inner Legions. Rumor had it that they were still the finest body of soldiers in the world, despite their never having ventured outside the immediate vicinity of the Overn Deep, the inland sea upon which the city of Kesh had been built ages before. Absently Roo wondered if their reputation was earned, or the legacy of ancient conquest.

The language of Queg was a variant of the ancient Keshian spoken at the time of the Empire's withdrawal from the Bitter Sea, so it was related to the languages of Yabon and the Free Cities. It was also similar enough to the language spoken in the land of Novindus that Roo could understand most of what was being said around him.

He thought it best to feign ignorance.

As he exited the litter, a young woman slowly walked down the three stone steps that led to the wide entrance to the building. She wasn't beautiful, but she was regal: slender, self-assured, and possessed of an attitude that spoke volumes of her contempt for this alien merchant who stood before her, all the while masking that contempt behind a welcoming smile.

"Mr. Avery," she said in accented King's Tongue.

"I am," said Roo with a noncommittal half-bow.

"I am Livia, daughter to Vasarius. My father has asked me to show you to your quarters. Your servants will be seen to." As she turned away, Jimmy stepped forward and cleared his throat.

The young woman turned. "Yes?"

"I am Mr. Avery's personal secretary," said Jimmy before Roo could comment.

The girl raised one eyebrow, but simply turned, and Roo took that as acquiescence to his coming with Roo. Softly Roo said, "You're my what?"

Jimmy whispered back, "I won the coin toss. Dash gets to be your servant."

Roo nodded. One inside with Roo, one outside to see what there was to see. Roo was certain that Lord James had other tasks for these two beyond seeing that Roo didn't end up dead or chained to a galley oar.

Roo and Jimmy were led into a large entrance area, open to the sky, then through a series of hallways. Roo quickly decided the building was a hollow square, and his suspicions were verified when he glimpsed a garden through a doorway off to one side.

The girl led them to a large apartment, with a pair of beds, surrounded by white netting, and a large bathing pool that was built into the floor. The room overlooked the wall to the city, and Queg could be seen below in the distance, while the nearby houses were blocked from view. Privacy and panorama, thought Roo. Livia said, "These will be your quarters. Bathe and change. Servants will show you to our table for dinner. Rest until then."

She walked off without further comment, ignoring Roo's thanks. Jimmy smiled as a young man took his bag from his hand and started to unpack. He winked at Roo and inclined his head slightly.

A young girl was unpacking Roo's belongings, including the wooden case containing the rubies. She set them aside on a table as if they were but another possession, took his clothing, and went to what appeared to be a blank wall of marble. She pressed it lightly and a door popped open, revealing a wardrobe.

Roo said, "That's amazing," and moved to inspect the handiwork. "Jimmy, look at this."

Jimmy came to see what Roo was pointing to, and saw that a slab of marble, cut thin but still more than a man's weight, was cleverly hinged and counterweighted, so the door moved almost effortlessly.

Roo pointed to the hinges. "Very well engineered."

"Expensive," said Jimmy.

The girl barely suppressed a giggle, and Roo said, "Our host is among the wealthiest men in Queg."

The boy who had unpacked Jimmy's baggage and put his belongings in a chest near the foot of one of the beds came to stand next to the girl and waited.

Roo was uncertain exactly what came next, but Jimmy said, "We can bathe ourselves, thank you. It is our custom. If we may have some privacy."

Without any expression the two young people waited. Jimmy pantomimed bathing and pointed to himself and Roo, and then to the servants and the door. The servants bowed and retired from the room. Roo said, "Bath servants?"

"Very common here and in Kesh. Remember, they are slaves, so living in the luxury of a house like this is dependent on pleasing the master and his guests. Even the slightest fault might earn one of them a quick trip to a brothel along the docks, or the quarry, or anywhere else strong young slaves are needed."

Roo looked appalled. "I never thought much about it."

"Most people in the Kingdom don't." Jimmy began undressing. "If you don't want to share the bath, I can go first or wait."

Roo shook his head. "I've shared cold rivers with other men, and that pool is big enough for six of us."

They stripped and entered the water. Roo looked around and said, "Where's the soap?"

"This is Queg," said Jimmy, indicating a line of wooden sticks arrayed along the edge of the bath. "Scrape the dirt off with these."

Roo longed for a cake of hand-milled Krondorian soap, and looked dubiously at the sticks as he picked one up and followed Jimmy's lead. After a sea voyage of two weeks, he wasn't as dirty as he had been many times in his life, but he was far from being fresh. But as Jimmy showed him how to use the sticks, called a *stigle* in the local language, he found that the dirt came off quickly in the hot water.

His hair was another matter. Repeated ducking under the water didn't seem to rid him of that not-quite-clean feeling, but then Jimmy pointed out that most Quegan men oiled their hair.

"What about the women?" asked Roo.

"I hadn't thought of that," said Jimmy as he rose from the pool and wrapped himself in a large bath sheet.

After they had dressed, they found nowhere to sit, so they lay down, waiting for the call to dinner. Roo dozed a bit in the warm afternoon, until he was awoken by Jimmy.

"Time to eat."

Roo came to his feet and found Livia waiting for them at the door of their suite. He picked up the wooden case with the rubies inside, and moved to the door. As he started to greet her, the girl said, "Were the servants unsatisfactory?"

Roo had no idea what she was saying. Jimmy, however, said, "No, milady. We were weary and wished to rest."

"If you see one among the servers at the table whom you find desirable, mark that one by name and we shall send him or her to your room tonight."

Roo said, "Ah . . . milady, I'm a married man."

The girl looked over her shoulder as she led them down the hall. "This is a problem?"

"In my nation it is," said Roo, blushing. While cheating on his wife with Sylvia seemed as natural to him as breathing, the thought of one of those young girls—or boys—being sent to his bed, much like an extra blanket, positively scandalized him.

Jimmy worked hard at not laughing.

The girl seemed indifferent as she led them into the dining room. The table was a long slab of marble, resting upon a matched set of ornately carved supports. Roo assumed that the table had been hauled into the room by a derrick and the roof added after this massive piece of stone had been installed inside. Along each side sat a half-dozen chairs, open-backed, little more than half-circles of matching stone with thick pillows upon them, small benches, really, thought Roo. One didn't move the heavy chairs to sit and dine, one stepped over them. Livia pointed to a chair to the left of the man sitting at the head of the table, indicating Roo should sit there. Then she moved to the chair on her father's right. Jimmy sat at the remaining place, to Roo's left.

Lord Vasarius was an impressive man, thought Roo. His toga was worn off one shoulder, and Roo could see despite his age he was still a powerfully built man. He had the shoulders of a wrestler and the arms of a blacksmith. He had sandy hair that had turned mostly grey, and he wore it oiled and close to his head. He did not rise or offer his hand in greeting, but merely inclined his chin. "Mr. Avery," he said.

"My lord," Roo returned, bowing as he would before the Prince.

"Your message was cryptic, but the only thing of worth you might possibly have of mine in the Kingdom was a set of rubies stolen over a year ago. May I have them, please?" He held out his hand.

Roo started to hand the case across the table, but a servant intercepted it and carried it the short distance to his master. He flipped open the case, briefly regarded the gems, then closed the case.

"Thank you for returning my property. May I inquire how you came by it?"

Roo said, "As you may have heard, m'lord, I have purchased several different companies lately, and this item was discovered among the inventory of one of them. As there was no lawful bill of sale attached and as your name was prominently noted on the case, I assumed them to be stolen goods. I thought it best to return them personally, given their unique beauty and their value."

Vasarius handed the case back to a servant without looking. "Their value is only they were to have been a gift for my daughter on her most recent birthday. Both the servant who removed them from this house, and the captain of the ship that took him from our island, have been found and dealt with. I have only to discover to whom they were sold and all those hands who have soiled them until you returned them to me. All will die painfully."

Thinking of his friend John Vinci, who had bought them from that Quegan captain, Roo said, "My lord, they were in an inventory box with other items of dubious origin. I doubt it possible to trace who dealt them along from the captain to myself. Why trouble yourself further, now they have been returned?" Roo hoped Lord Vasarius listened. Obviously the now-dead captain hadn't implicated John, else he and Roo would already be dead men.

Vasarius said, "My name was upon the box, Mr. Avery. Any man who saw it knew it to be my property. Any man who did not return it as you have done is a man without honor, a thief, and one who should be thrown to the animals in the arena, or tortured slowly."

Roo considered that he had been among those attempting to sell the stones and the only reason he had been distracted from that undertaking was the murder of his father-in-law. He maintained an indifferent manner. "Well, m'lord, perhaps that is as it should be, but now that you have those gems back, at least that portion of the affront has been somewhat lessened."

"Somewhat," agreed Roo's host as the servants began bringing out the evening meal. "As I haven't been able to find those others besides the captain who insulted my honor, it may be a moot point."

Roo sat motionless, hoping against hope that was the case, as he was served by young men and women, all attractive by any measure. Whatever other vices Lord Vasarius might have, it was clear he enjoyed the beauty of youth on every hand.

For all the splendor of the setting, Roo found the fare at Lord Vasarius's table rather plain. Fruits and wine were served, and some flat bread with butter and honey, but the cheese was bland, the wine unspectacular, and the lamb overcooked. Still, Roo dined as if it were the finest meal he had ever tasted; the gods knew he had eaten far worse with gusto in his soldiering days.

There was almost no conversation over dinner, and Roo caught a few meaningful glances pass between Livia and her father. Jimmy seemed bored, but Roo knew he was noting every detail he could. When at last the meal came to an end, Vasarius leaned forward and summoned a servant bearing a tray with a goblet and metal cups.

Roo found the notion of drinking brandy from a metal cup odd, as a metallic taste was imparted to the drink, but he ignored it, being nothing of the wine purist most people born in Ravensburg were. Besides, not offending his host was far more critical.

Vasarius raised his goblet, said, "To your health," and drank.

Roo did as well and said, "You're most kind."

Vasarius said, "Now, to the matter of what you expect in repayment for returning my property to me, Mr. Avery."

Roo said, "I expect no repayment, m'lord. I merely wished for an opportunity to visit Queg and explore the possibility of trade."

Vasarius regarded Roo a moment. "When I received your letter," he said, "I was inclined to believe it another plot by Lord James to infiltrate our state. His predecessor was a clever man and again, by half, but James is a demon incarnate." Roo glanced at Jimmy to see if he was reacting to his grandfather's being described that way, but Jimmy maintained a façade of indifference that suited his pose as Roo's personal secretary. "I am willing to put that by, as your reputation precedes you. To return those rubies is of little consequence to a man of your wealth, Mr. Avery, but gaining a trading liaison in Queg, now that is something worth the price of such baubles."

Vasarius sipped his brandy, then asked, "Do you know much of my people, Mr. Avery?"

"Little, I'm afraid," admitted Roo. In fact, he had attempted to study as much about the Quegans as possible, but he felt feigning ignorance was far better for his own purposes.

Livia spoke in the Quegan dialect. "If you're going to give a history lesson, Father, may I be excused. These barbarians sicken me."

In Quegan, Lord Vasarius replied, "Barbarians or not, they are guests. If you're bored, take the young secretary and show him the garden. He's pretty enough to be diverting. There's a chance he might know a trick that's new even to you." His tone hid nothing of his disapproval; it would have been evident even if Roo and James didn't speak the language used.

Vasarius turned to Roo. "Forgive my daughter's lapse of manners, but speaking the King's Tongue is not something we do often here. It was only her teacher who insisted she learn the languages of our neighbors."

"He was a Kingdom-born slave," supplied the girl. "I think the son of some nobleman or another. So he claimed." To Jimmy she said, "Business bores me. Would you care to see the garden?"

Jimmy nodded, excused himself, and left Roo and Vasarius alone.

The lord of the house continued, "Most of those outside our borders know little of us. We are all that is left of a once proud and great tradition, the true inheritors of all that was once Great Kesh."

Roo nodded as if hearing this for the first time.

"We were founded as an outpost of the Empire, Mr. Avery. This is important. We were not a colony, as was Bosania, what you know as the Free Cities and the Far Coast, or a conquered people, as were those of the Jal-Pur or the Vale of Dreams. Those primitives who lived on this island were quickly absorbed by the garrison placed here to protect Keshian interests in the Bitter Sea."

Raped by the soldiers and getting half-breed children, thought Roo. He had no doubt that the men living here when the Keshians showed up were either killed or enslaved.

"The garrison was pure Keshian, men from the Inner Legions. The reason I point this out to you is that you of the Kingdom have often treated with Kesh's Dog Soldiers. Their leader was Lord Vax, fourth son of the Emperor of Great Kesh.

"When the legion was called home to crush the rebellion in the Keshian Confederacy, he refused to abandon his people. This was Kesh, and Queg has endured as the sole repository of that great culture since the fall of Bosania to the Kingdom. Those who sit upon the Throne of the Overn Deep are a fallen people, Mr. Avery. They call themselves 'Trueblood,' but they are a base and degenerate people."

He stared at Roo, awaiting a reaction. Roo nodded and sipped his brandy.

Vasarius continued. "This is why we have few dealings with outsiders. We are mighty in culture, but otherwise we are a poor nation, surrounded on all sides by enemies."

In other circumstances, Roo would have burst out laughing, as that phrase had been repeated to him so often it was something of a joke. But in the midst of this splendor, Roo understood. While there were many things of beauty, one couldn't eat marble or gold. You had to trade. Yet this was a nation of people who distrusted, even feared outsiders.

Roo considered his words. "One must be careful with whom one is trading." He waited, then said, "Else one must consider the risk of contamination."

Vasarius nodded. "You are very perceptive for . . . an outsider."

Roo shrugged. "I am a businessman, first and foremost, and while I have been lucky, I have also had to live by my wits. I would not be here if I didn't sense an opportunity for mutual gain."

"We do not permit many to trade in Queg, Mr. Avery. In the history of our people there have been fewer than a dozen such concessions granted, and all have been to merchants in the Free Cities or from Durbin. Never has a Kingdom merchant been permitted such a privilege."

Roo weighed his options. If this had been a Kingdom merchant or noble with whom he was speaking, he would have judged it time for a "gift," as bribery was part of doing business. But there was something about this man that warned him away from making such an offer. After a moment he said, "I would be content to remain in Krondor and let my Quegan partner conduct the business at this end. I am a shipper, and a . . . cooperation with a Quegan of rank and influence would be beneficial. Also, there are cargoes that are difficult to secure anywhere else than Queg."

Vasarius leaned forward, his voice dropping. "You surprise me. I assumed you wanted to establish a presence here in Queg, Mr. Avery."

Roo shook his head. "I would be quickly disadvantaged by your local businessmen, I am certain. No, I need the sure hand and practiced intelligence of a man known in Queg for his perspicacity and wisdom. Such a man would benefit from such an arrangement, as would I."

Roo fell silent. Vasarius knew what he had to offer. He could bring in foodstuffs to make this the most lavish table in Queg. Wines unmatched in all the world. Silks from Kesh for his daughter and mistresses. Luxury items that these people obviously craved.

Roo glanced around the room. He knew why these buildings were marble: there was abundant marble on Queg. Wood was scarce. Most of the arable land had been cleared centuries ago for crops. Sheep were the livestock of choice, as you got more meat for less grass than with cattle. Everything about this meal tonight spoke of a people who had prospered, but at a price. No, Queg smelled ripe for imported luxury items from the Kingdom.

Vasarius said, "What do you offer?"

Roo said, "Almost anything you can imagine, m'lord." He paused, then he said, "Luxuries, rarities, and novelties." Vasarius didn't blink. Roo spoke again. "Lumber, coal, and beef." A spark ignited in Vasarius's eyes, and Roo knew he was now an equal player in this game. He felt a warm tingle of success begin to spread inside him; Roo was in his element. It was time to haggle.

Vasarius said, "What cargo would you wish to secure?"

"Well, as a matter of fact I have a commission, which, should I fulfill it, would be a great beginning to any such trading association."

"What do you seek to buy?"

"Fire oil."

Vasarius blinked. It was the most overt reaction Roo had witnessed so far, and he knew that this was a man he didn't want to face in a card game. But he knew he had surprised him.

"Fire oil?"

"Yes, I'm sure your intelligence has told you the Kingdom is preparing for war." He slipped into the speech James had had him memorize. "Kesh moves along the Vale again, and we fear it seeks to invade. With a new Prince in Krondor and no practiced General leading the Armies of the West, it would be prudent to equip as well as possible. We are training additional men for the Prince's army and seek to bolster our defenses with fire oil. We know how to produce it, as I am sure you're aware; it's no longer a secret. But we lack facilities to produce it in sufficient volume to provide any viable amount."

"How much do you desire?"

"Ten thousand barrels."

Roo watched and again there were flickers in the man's eyes: shock, followed almost at once by greed. Roo reconsidered, and wondered if he could get this man into a game of cards.

Four

Relationships

DASH LAUGHED.

Jimmy said, "And then I asked, 'Are the red bulbs more difficult to cultivate than the yellow?' "

Owen Greylock, Knight-Captain of the Prince's Army of the West, said, "You came close to a personal insult, James."

Jimmy smiled. "In that strange land, what I said was far more important than what I meant." He took another drink from his ale. "I might have found the girl attractive in different circumstances, but her contempt for me simply because I came from another land . . . it made any notion of romance impossible."

Roo said, "Well, you didn't seem to have any problems with that young serving girl later that night."

Jimmy smiled. "I thought you were asleep."

Roo shook his head. "I was, but you woke me up. I decided it was less awkward to feign sleep. Besides, I've had friends coupling a few feet away before, in camp." He glanced at Erik.

Kitty, who had been standing behind Roo, filling ale tankards, said, "Oh?" in a meaningful tone, then turned and walked away.

Roo laughed, and so did the others as Erik began to blush. "What's this, then?" asked Duncan Avery. "Something going on between you two?"

Erik said, "Not that I'm aware of." He glanced at Kitty's retreating back. "I don't think so, anyway."

"Think so?" said Jadow Shati. "Man, there either is or there isn't. That's simple enough even for someone as dim as you, and that's the truth."

Erik stood up. "I guess. Excuse me."

Jadow laughed as Erik followed Kitty. The Sergeant from the Vale of Dreams said, "Man, if that boy was any dumber when it comes to women, we'd have to kill him to put him out of his misery."

Jimmy glanced at his brother, and Dash said, "I don't know. Kitty's a strange girl. I think she just . . . likes having someone solid around."

Roo said, "Erik's that."

Erik reached the bar and said, "Kitty?"

"Yes, Sergeant Major?" she asked coolly.

"Ah . . ." He blushed again. She fixed him with an unwavering glance. "I . . . uh."

"Spit it out before you choke."

"What did you mean, at the table?"

"Mean?" she asked, a skeptical expression on her face. "By what?"

"By that 'Oh.' "

"Nothing. Just 'Oh,' as in 'Oh.' "

Erik suddenly realized he was being made a fool of, and he felt his color rising. "You're making sport of me."

She reached across the bar and patted his cheek. "It's so easy to do."

"What is this?" he asked, losing any sense of humor in the situation. "Are you mad at me?"

She sighed. "I'm just mad at men in general."

Erik said, "Well, take it out on someone else."

Her eyes narrowed. "You've suddenly got a tender side for a man who's killed dozens and bedded whores next to his friends."

Erik felt flustered. This girl's attitude was getting under his skin. "What would you have of me?" he asked in exasperation.

Kitty studied his face a long, silent moment, then said in a low voice, "I don't know."

Erik stared at her. The torchlight reflected off a faint sheen of moisture on her upper lip. She was perspiring lightly despite the cool of the evening.

After a moment, she asked, "What do you want?"

Erik shook his head. "I don't know either, but I . . . I didn't like the way things felt when you . . ."

"Said 'Oh'?" she finished for him.

Said that way, it sounded so silly Erik had to laugh. "Yes, I guess that's what I mean."

"Come with me," she said. She gestured to one of the other girls that she was leaving, and led Erik through the kitchen, past the cook and his helpers, through a rear door into the courtyard behind the inn.

For a moment Erik experienced an odd sensation of familiarity; he had grown up in such a yard, with the stable and forge, well and hayloft, behind an inn. There was a wooden bench around the well, used by those too short to pull up the bucket easily, and Kitty went and sat on it, motioning for Erik to sit next to her.

Erik said, "It's quiet back here."

Kitty shrugged. "I never noticed. I'm usually too busy."

Erik sat and Kitty leaned over and kissed him. He held still an instant, then returned her kiss. After a long moment, she sat back, looking at him. Finally she said, "I've never done that before."

"Kissed a man?" Erik said, his voice showing his surprise.

"I'm a thief, not a whore," she said. "I've been raped and had men stick their tongues in my mouth, but I've never kissed anyone before."

Erik's mouth hung open, and then he shut it. "What about Bobby?" he asked finally.

She shrugged. "What about him?"

"Well, I thought . . ." He hesitated. "Well, we just assumed you and he . . ."

"I would have, if he'd asked. He was good to me. Better than I deserved, I think. I mean, he treated me roughly that night you caught me, and he threatened to hang me and the like, but mostly he made me laugh. And he kept others from hurting me." She pointed to the back of the inn. "I've got to watch for Mockers, or anyone else nosing around, but what I am now is just a barmaid. That's not bad, 'cause I won't whore."

She looked down. "I would have lain down for Bobby, 'cause he was good to me, but he didn't love me and I didn't love him. Not that way." She looked at Erik. "I don't think there was anyone he loved, maybe 'cept for Captain Calis."

"Bobby was devoted to him."

"I thought for a while he might be one of those men who love other men." She made a motion with her hand, as if flipping something over. "Not that I care; I'm no follower of Sung the Pure, but you do wonder. Then I heard he was a regular down at the White Wing, so I figure he's just got it in his head to get his itch scratched by someone who's . . ." She searched for a concept.

"Not special to him?" Erik supplied.

"Ya," she agreed. "That's it. Like if he did it with me or someone else who wasn't a whore, it might make things . . . you know, different."

Erik nodded that he understood.

She sighed. "Bobby joked and made me laugh. At first I was scared of him, because he said he would kill me if I betrayed the Prince or the Duke, and I saw in his eyes he meant it. But after a while, when folks here treated me right, well, I stopped being afraid.

"I've got no place to go, so, like it or not, this is my home." She was silent awhile, looking at the inn. "It's not a bad life. I know something big's coming. You can't work here and not figure out a few things. Soldiers who aren't bragging on what they're doing, they're keeping secrets. So something big's coming. I don't know what, and I think I don't want to know." She paused, and stared up at the pale moon.

Suddenly, she turned her head to face Erik. "But with Bobby gone, you're the man who's been nicest to me. The men sometimes say things to the other girls, about me, but I don't mind. It's just, well, you've never been anything but nice to me."

Erik shrugged. "I know what it's like to have some tough luck, I guess."

"You can't know what life is like on the street."

He said nothing, simply watching her in the flickering torchlight. She went on, "Girl children aren't thought much of, except for whores. There's good money for little girls in some places." She hugged herself. "My mum was a whore, that's the truth. No one knows who my father was. My mum threw me out when I was six. I think maybe she was keeping me from the crib. Her whoremaster kept looking at me funny.

"I got found by this man, named Daniels, and he took me to this place in the sewers. They gave me food and told me they'd take care of me, but I had to do what they said. There were other children there, too. They didn't seem too bad off. They were dirty, mostly, but they were fed.

"I begged, and I learned the best dodges. I could cry like I was lost and if some mark stopped to see what the problem was, someone else cut his purse. I started being the holder after a while."

"Holder?" asked Erik.

"Cutpurse, he gets spotted, he gets stopped by the City Watch, he'd better have nothing on him that don't belong. So most Mockers work in teams. The cutpurse hands off the score as soon as he can, and the holder moves to the bagman, who takes it to Mother's."

"Mother's?"

"That's what the Mockers call the place we all live . . . lived."

"Oh."

She said, "Anyway, I saw me mum and we talked after I'd been gone a few years. She told me I had a sister, who was a whore. That was Betsy."

"You found her, then?"

"Yes, and we got along good. She didn't like me being a thief and I didn't care much for her whoring, but we got along. I liked her. She was the only one I knew who wasn't always after me for something.

"When I got these"—she pointed to her breasts—"some of the men got rough with me. If I could stay close to the other cutpurses or hang out at Mother's, I was all right. But sometimes you just can't stay in a crowd, you know what I mean?"

Erik didn't, but he nodded as if he did.

"I got poked a lot until I started dressing like I was when you found me, like a boy, staying dirty, not smelling good."

Erik didn't know what to say, so he remained silent.

"What I'm saying is I've never done nothing with a man that was 'cause I wanted."

Erik waited, and when she didn't speak, he softly asked, "Are you telling me you want to now?"

Tears welled up in her eyes as she almost imperceptibly nodded. He sighed as he gathered her into his arms. Erik had never felt so unsure of himself before. He had been with whores since he had joined the army, and he remembered what the first one told him, to go easy, but every woman he had lain with knew more than he did. Now he was being asked to lie with a girl who knew only violence at the hands of men.

He kissed her on the cheek and then the chin, then the lips. At first she was very still, then after a few more kisses she began responding. Soon she stood and took him by the hand and led him into the barn, toward the loft.

"Erik!" came the familiar voice. "You up there?"

A sleepy "Wuzat?" came from Kitty as she nestled in his arms. Their lovemaking had been tentative, slow, and awkward at first, then building until Erik felt he was in the midst of battle, as Kitty exploded in a riot of emotions in his arms. Laughter mixed with tears was unleashed by his touch, and at the end she lay exhausted, as did he.

A while later they made love a second time, and Kitty was much more sure of what it was she wanted. Erik had never experienced anything like this with another woman.

He wondered if he was in love.

He raised up on one arm as the caller again shouted his name. "Nakor, I'm going to kill you," Erik muttered as he sat up and began to dress.

Kitty came awake. "Is that the funny gambler?" she asked.

Erik said, "He's not being very funny at the moment."

As he pulled on his boots, she slipped her arms around his waist and said, "Thank you."

He stopped. "For what?"

"For showing me what the other girls always talked about."

Erik sat motionless for a moment. "You're welcome, I think."

She leaned her head on his shoulder. "You think?"

"It wasn't a favor," he said in a curt tone.

"Oh, you enjoyed it, too?" she asked innocently.

Erik realized she was again teasing him. He was pleased it was too dark for her to see him blush. "I ought to spank you for that," he muttered.

She kissed his shoulder. "Some of the girls at the White Wing charge extra for that, I've been told."

A wave of uncertainty gripped Erik, as real as a sword thrust in his chest. He turned and gripped her by the arms, harder than he intended, and when he saw the look of panic in her eyes, he instantly released his hold. "I'm sorry," he whispered. "But I can't stand it when you mock me."

She looked at his face as tears formed in his eyes and suddenly she was crying. She laid her chin on his shoulder, cheek to cheek with him, as she whispered, "I'm sorry, too. I don't know how to be any other way."

"I will never hurt you," he whispered.

"I know," she whispered back. "I'm all jumbled inside." Then she pulled back and he saw she was smiling. "And it's your fault, Erik von Darkmoor."

He kissed her.

Soon a cough sounded and Erik turned to see Nakor's head poking up from below as he stood on the ladder to the loft. "There you are!"

Without a word, Erik extended his leg, pushing the ladder away from the loft, and watched it vanish, with a satisfying squawk from Nakor, into the gloom. A loud thud and an "Oof" of breath exploding from Nakor's lungs followed.

Kitty laughed and Erik finished dressing. After a moment, as Nakor lay groaning dramatically from atop a pile of hay, Erik said, "When you're done with your act, put the ladder back up."

The groaning was instantly replaced by a chuckle. "You know me too well," said Nakor.

The ladder reappeared at the edge of the loft and Erik glanced at Kitty, who was dressed. He went down the ladder first, and she followed.

Nakor said, "Sorry to have bothered you and your lady friend, but I needed to see you."

"Why?" asked Erik.

"To say good-bye for a while."

Erik saw that Sho Pi, his onetime comrade-in-arms and now Nakor's student, was standing silently by the doorway of the barn. "Where are you going?" asked Erik.

"Down to Stardock again. The King has asked me to return there while Lord Arutha returns to work for his father." Then his expression turned serious. "Something's going on. Prince Erland sailed into port tonight aboard a Keshian cutter."

Erik said, "Nothing we can talk about."

Nakor nodded. "I think I know what you mean."

Erik said, "Well, have a safe journey and let me know when you return to the city."

Nakor nodded. "We'll be back." He motioned for Sho Pi to follow as he left the barn, and Erik watched them vanish into the night.

"That is the strangest little man," said Kitty.

"You are far from the first to observe that," said Erik. "Still, he's a good man and worth six when you're out on the trail. The things he knows are astonishing. He claims there's no magic, but if there's anyone who's a better magician out there, I've not met him."

Kitty came and leaned in to Erik and he slipped his arm around her waist. "What did he mean, 'Something's going on'?"

Erik turned and kissed her. "You catch spies, and you want me to talk about secrets?"

She nodded, resting her cheek against his chest. "I sometimes think I know what is going on, Erik, as I piece together bits of things heard here and there. Other times I'm not sure even what I'm doing here. Since Bobby died I often think I'm in one of those places the priests talk about, one of the lesser hells. I can't leave the inn unless I've a pair of guards with me. The Mockers have put the death mark on me, but they're the only family I've known."

Erik couldn't think of anything to say. He hugged her. "If I get some time off soon, I'll take you somewhere, someplace different, away from the city."

She clung to him a minute, then said, "I have to get back."

He walked toward the rear door of the inn and removed his arm from around her waist when they got there. Saying nothing, he followed her inside. She silently moved through the kitchen and took her usual station behind the bar.

Jadow Shati and Owen Greylock still sat at the table, but Roo had departed.

"Where's Roo?" Erik asked as he sat.

"When you didn't come back, he, Jimmy, and Dash left. Something about an important appointment," answered Greylock.

"Did Nakor find you?" asked Jadow innocently.

"Yes," answered Erik as he sat.

"Not at too awkward a moment, I hope," said Jadow, his face splitting into a wide grin.

Erik blushed and said, "No."

"That's good," said Jadow. Then he exploded into a laugh so infectious Greylock and Erik were forced to join in.

Kitty approached with a fresh pitcher of ale. "What's so funny?" she asked.

Her tone was one of potential injury, and her expression spoke volumes: if she was the butt of some joke told by Erik, some brag of conquest, no repair would ever be possible to the damage done.

Adroitly Greylock said, "Nakor," and started to laugh again.

"Oh," said Kitty, as if that explained everything. She smiled at Erik and he returned the smile.

After she left, Jadow said, "So there is something going on with you two?"

Erik nodded. "And it scares the hell out of me."

Greylock held up his fresh ale, as if in a toast. "That's serious."

Jadow nodded sagely. "Very serious, man. It can only be one thing."

"What?" said Erik, a tone of worry in his voice.

"Oh, man, he does have it bad," said Jadow.

"That's the truth," answered Greylock.

"What?" demanded Erik.

Greylock said, "Never been in love before?"

Jadow retorted, "He's too stupid to know if he has."

Erik sat back and said, "I guess not." His brow furrowed and he stared into his ale as if he'd find an answer in it. Then suddenly he grinned and looked at the faces of his two friends. "I guess not."

He turned to gaze at Kitty, who was busy cleaning behind the bar, talking quietly with another of the working girls, then turned back to his friends. "I'm in love," he said as if it were a revelation.

Suddenly Greylock and Jadow couldn't contain themselves and started laughing again. After the mirth died, Jadow said, "Come on, boy. You need another drink."

Greylock shook his head and sighed. "Ah, to be young again."

Erik just sat silently, wondering at all the odd feelings of delight and uncertainty within. He stole a glance at Kitty and saw her watching him. He smiled at her and she returned it, and he felt joyous inside.

Then, while Jadow and Greylock exchanged witty remarks, a dark cloud descended over Erik, as he considered the coming battle. How could he afford the time for anything other than that, he wondered to himself.

Sylvia bit Roo playfully on the neck.

"Ow," he said, half in jest, half in real pain. "That was too hard."

She pouted. "I need to punish you. You've been gone too long."

She snuggled down into the crook of his arm as he said, "I know. The closer we get—" He caught himself. He was about to say "to the invasion."

"Closer to what?" she asked, very attentively.

He studied her face in the candlelight. He had come to her house late and they had gone straight to bed. Her father was away on business, she said, so he planned on spending the entire night, rather than returning to his town house before dawn, as was his habit when Jacob Esterbrook was at home. Thinking about what he had found about her father's advantage over Roo's companies in trade with Great Kesh, he again wondered if he was saying anything that she was repeating to her father. He pushed aside the concern. "I mean, as I get closer to this goal I have, controlling all shipping on the Bitter Sea, I seem to have less time for anything else."

She bit him on the shoulder again, this time hard enough to make him genuinely cry out. "Explain that to your wife," she said, indicating the teeth marks she'd left. She got out of bed, and Roo marveled at the sight of her naked body. She was the most beautiful woman he had ever encountered, and in the light of the single candle she seemed sculpted from living marble, without flaw. He thought about his own wife's pudgy body, without a hint of strength in the muscle, the marks on her left by childbirth, and he found himself astonished by his ability to make love to Karli.

As Sylvia put on her robe, he said, "What's gotten into you?"

"You have time to spend with Helen Jacoby, but you spend days away from me."

Roo said, "You can't possibly be jealous of Helen?"

"Why not?" She turned, an accusatory expression on her face as he sat up in her bed. "You spend time with her. She's not unattractive in a raw-boned peasant-girl fashion. You've mentioned you respect her wit, far too many times for my liking."

Roo got out of bed, and said, "I killed her husband, Sylvia. I owe her some comfort. But I have never touched her."

"You'd like touching her, I wager," said Sylvia.

Roo tried to put his arms around her, but she brushed him aside and moved away. "Sylvia, you're being unfair."

"I'm being unfair?" she said, turning and allowing her robe to fall open.

Roo found himself beginning to become aroused at the sight of her.

"You're the man with the wife, children, and reputation. I was one of the most eligible daughters in the Kingdom until I met you." Pouting, she moved toward him, letting her breasts rub against his bare chest as she said, "I'm the mistress. I'm the woman of no status. You can leave whenever you want." Her hand began tracing small circles on his stomach.

Roo's breath came hard as he said, "I would never leave you, Sylvia."

Reaching down, she stroked him and said, "I know."

He pulled off her robe and carried her so quickly to the bed he almost tossed her onto the covers. Quickly taking her, he pleaded his undying love while Sylvia looked at the canopy overhead, fighting off a yawn. A self-satisfied smile then formed on her lips that had nothing to do with physical pleasure, and everything to do with power. Roo was on his way to being the most important merchant in the history of the Kingdom, and he was clearly under her power. She listened to Roo breathe more rapidly as his passion mounted, and she detached herself from the experience. The novelty of his lovemaking had long since worn off, and she preferred the talents of his cousin Duncan, who was far more attractive, and whose appetite for inventive love play matched her own.

She knew Roo would be appalled to discover that she and Duncan often shared this bed, and occasionally invited one of the servants to participate as well. She knew that Duncan would be malleable as long as he had access to fine clothing, good food, rare wine, pretty women, and the trappings of prosperity. He would make a fine lover after she wed Roo, and a completely socially acceptable replacement for him one day. As Roo neared the pinnacle of his ardor, Sylvia absently wondered how long she need wait to wed the repellent little man after she arranged the murder of his fat wife. At the thought of taking control of both her father's financial empire and Roo's, Sylvia found her own passion mounting at last, and as Roo could control himself no longer, Sylvia joined him in a paroxysm of release, imagining herself as the most powerful woman in Kingdom history.

Erik knocked on the door and William looked up. "Yes, Sergeant Major?"

"If you have a minute, sir?" he asked.

William waved him to a chair and Erik sat. "What is it?"

"Nothing to do with training," said Erik. "That's going well. It's a personal matter."

William sat back. His expression was neutral. While serving together, each man had occasionally let the other glimpse some facet of his personal life, but neither had intentionally opened a conversation on a personal subject. "I'm listening," said the Knight-Marshal of Krondor.

"I know this girl, and, well, if you don't mind, I just need to talk about being a soldier and getting married."

William said nothing for a moment, then he nodded. "It's a difficult choice. Some handle family matters well. Others don't." He paused. "The man who held this office before me, Gardan, was once a sergeant like yourself. He served Lord Borric, Duke of Crydee, when my father was a child there. He came to Krondor with Prince Arutha and rose to this office. All the while he was married."

"How did he do with it?"

"Well, all things considered," said William. "He had some children, one of whom became a soldier like him. He died in the sacking of the Far Coast."

Remembering what his stepfather, Nathan, had told him of those days, Erik knew that many had died during those raids. "Gardan was already dead by then. Some of the other children survived, I believe."

William rose and closed the door behind Erik, and came to sit on the edge of his desk. Erik noticed that apart from the formal tabard of his office, the Knight-Marshal elected to wear a common soldier's uniform, without markings of rank. "Look, with what's coming . . ." William began. He fought for words, then said, "Is any sort of relationship wise?"

"Wise or not, I have it," said Erik. "I've never felt this way before about a girl."

William smiled, and for a moment Erik saw years drop from the man. "I remember."

"If you don't mind my asking, have you ever been married, sir?"

"No," said William, and there was a hint of regret in his voice. "My life never seemed to have room for a family."

He moved to his own chair and sat. "Truth to tell, my family hasn't had much room for me."

"Your father?" asked Erik.

William nodded. "Time was we didn't speak to each other from anger. We've since gotten over that. But it's hard. If you'd ever met my father, you'd think he was my son. He looks but ten years older than you." William sighed. "The ironic thing, it turns out, was that becoming a soldier, as I did, had been his own boyhood dream. He insisted I study magic."

William smiled. "Can you imagine growing up somewhere where everyone practices magic, or is married to someone who does, or is the son or daughter of someone who does?"

Erik shook his head. "It must run in your family, though. I met your sister."

William smiled ruefully. "Another irony. Gamina's adopted into our family. And she's far more adept at things magical than I.

"I have one pitiful talent. I can speak with animals. They tend toward short, uninteresting conversations. Except Fantus, of course."

At mention of the firedrake, Erik said, "I haven't seen him around the palace lately."

"He comes and goes as it pleases him. And if I ask him where he's been, he pointedly ignores me."

Erik said, "I still don't feel any closer to a decision than I did before."

William said, "I know that feeling, too. There was a young magician from Stardock, a girl from the desert stock of the Jal-Pur, who came to study with my father when I was a boy. She was two years older than I.

"She was the most beautiful thing I'd ever seen, dark skin and eyes the color of coffee. She moved like a dancer and her laughter was musical.

"I was smitten the first time I saw her. She knew me as the Master's son, Pug's boy, and she knew I was infatuated with her. I followed her around, making a pest of myself. She put up with me with good grace, but after a while I think I wore her nerves thin."

William gazed out the window that overlooked the courtyard and said, "I think her indifference to my plight was one of the big reasons I chose to leave Stardock and come to Krondor." He smiled in remembrance. "She came two years later."

Erik raised an eyebrow in question.

"Prince Arutha's father had a magical adviser, a wonderful old character named Kulgan. Far from the most powerful magician around, he may have been among the most intelligent. He was like a grandfather to me in many ways. His death hit my father very hard. Anyway, Prince Arutha decided he wanted a magical adviser in his court, so he asked Pug to send his best to Krondor. Father surprised everyone by sending her instead of one of the masters; I thought at first he was sending her to check up on me." He smiled ruefully in memory.

William was almost laughing as he went on, "You can imagine the consternation among the nobles when she showed up and turned out not only to be Keshian, but to be distantly related to one of the most powerful noble lords among the desertmen of the Jal-Pur. It took Prince Arutha's iron will to force the court into accepting her."

William sighed. "Things got very difficult here the day she showed up, some things I can't talk about, but suffice it to say by the time we were done she and I had learned we were very different people than we had been at Stardock. We also discovered that my feelings hadn't changed, and I was astonished to discover that the two years apart had changed the way she looked at me. We became lovers."

Erik said nothing for a moment as William became lost in a moment of remembering.

"We were together for six years."

"What happened?"

"She died."

Erik said, "If you don't want to talk about it—"

"I don't," interrupted William.

Erik looked uncomfortable. "Well, I'll go, sir. I didn't mean to open old wounds."

William waved away the apology before it came. "You didn't. Those wounds are with me every day and they are always open. It's one of the reasons I've never wed."

As he reached the door, Erik said, "If you don't mind my asking, sir, what was her name?"

Without looking at Erik, still staring out the window, William said, "Jezharra."

Erik closed the door behind him. As he walked along the corridor leading to the marshalling yard, he considered the conversation. No closer to knowing what he should do, he decided to put his mind to the matters before him and let his feelings for Kitty come as they might.

Five

Elvandar

TOMAS SAT MOTIONLESS.

King Redtree, *Aron Earanorn* in the elves' language, spoke. "In the years since we abandoned the Northlands to *return*, we have attempted to understand our cousins." The leader of the glamredhel, the "mad" elves, those left to fend for themselves in the Northlands above the Kingdom ages ago, fixed Queen Aglaranna with a steady stare. "We bow to you as ruler, *here*, lady"—he made an all-encompassing gesture with his right hand—"in Elvandar. But we do not accept any suggestion that you rule us, absolutely."

Tomas glanced at his wife. The ruler of the Elves of Elvandar turned her softest smile on the warrior who had ruled over his followers for almost as many years as she had reigned in the elven glades. "Earanorn, no one here is suggesting anything," she countered. "Those who chose to come to Elvandar, by the call of ancient blood or as guests, are free to leave at any time. Only those who choose to remain here of their own accord are subject to our rule."

The former King tapped his chin. "That's the rub, isn't it?" He looked at the assembled elves in the Queen's Council: Tathar, her senior adviser; Tomas, the half-human Warleader and prince consort; Acaila, leader of the eldar who had remained on the world of Kelewan until the human magician Pug had found them; and others, including Pug and his current companion, Miranda. After a long silence, the old King asked, "Where would we go? Back to the Northlands and our less generous cousins?"

Tomas glanced at Pug, his boyhood companion, foster brother, and ally in the Riftwar, and his eyes revealed that he, too, knew the answer: there was nowhere else for these "wild" elves to go.

Tomas turned his attention to Acaila, whose knowledge and power never failed to astonish Pug, and raised a finger so slightly the human magician barely noticed it. Acaila inclined his head but a fraction of an inch, yet the Queen returned the barely perceptible nod.

"Why leave at all?" asked the leader of the Eldar, those ancient elves who were closest to the Dragon Lords, and who kept their lore and knowledge. "You have found your lost kindred after centuries of isolation and no one seeks to return you to slavery, yet you seem ill at ease. May one ask why?"

Redtree let out a long sigh. "I'm an old man." At this, Tathar, Acaila, and some others laughed, without malice but with genuine amusement. "Very well, so I'm merely three hundred seventy years of age, while some here are twice that, but the truth is the Edder Forest of the Northlands is a harsh place, rife with enemies and scant of food. You have little sense of that here, in the midst of Elvandar's bounty." He hugged himself slightly as if memory of the Edder was chilling. "We numbered no Spellweavers, and the healing magic of Elvandar did not exist. Here a mild wound heals with rest and food; there festering can take a warrior as surely as an enemy's arrow." He held out his hand in a balled fist, anger coloring his words. "I have buried my wife and my sons. By my people's experience, I am a *very* old man."

To Pug, Miranda whispered, "And a long-winded one, too." She stifled a yawn. Pug tried not to smile on the heels of the old King's emotional words, but he, like Miranda and the others, had heard the tale of Redtree's battles and losses many times in the months they had lived with the elves.

Calin, Aglaranna's older son and heir to her throne, spoke. "I think over the last thirty years we have demonstrated our goodwill, King Redtree. We mourn your losses"—others of the council nodded agreement—"yet here rests your people's best chance to thrive, returned to the heart of our race.

"During the Riftwar and the Great Uprising, we lost many who now rest in the Blessed Isles, yet we have gained, by your having found your way here. In the end, all of elvenkind are profited."

Redtree nodded. "I have considered my people's choices." He seemed to let go of something, a hint of pride. "I have no sons." Looking at Calin, he said, "I need an heir."

A young warrior of the glamradhel stepped to his King's side, handing over a bundle wrapped in leather and tied in thongs. "This is the mark of my rank," said Redtree, untying the bundle. As much as elves could display surprise, the assembled council was surprised. Inside the skins was a belt of marvelous beauty: silken threads that Pug judged were something more alien than silk held gems of stunning brilliance in a pattern both lovely and compelling. *"Asle-thnath!"* proclaimed Redtree.

Pug studied the belt, shifting his perceptions. To Miranda he whispered, "This is a thing of power."

"Really?" she asked dryly.

Pug glanced at her and saw her smile, as she tried to keep from laughing at him outright, and again he was visited by the certainty that her power and knowledge were more than she revealed.

Acaila stepped down from the circling benches and came to stand before Redtree. "May I?" he asked.

Redtree handed him the belt.

He examined it and then turned to Tathar. "This is a great and wonderful magic. Did you not know it was here?"

Tathar, senior among the Queen's Spellweavers, shook his head. With a hint of irritation, he said, "Did you?"

Acaila laughed, as he had often laughed when teaching Pug for the year the magician had lived with the eldar, in Elvardein, Elvandar's twin forest, magically hidden under the ice cap on the world of Kelewan. There was no mockery in that laugh, ever, but with a hint of irony, Acaila said, "There is that." He turned back toward Redtree, and the ruler of the glamredhel nodded slightly. Acaila turned as Tathar stepped down from his place in the Queen's circle. Even though Acaila was the undoubted leader in age and experience among the Queen's advisers, he was a newcomer, and Tathar was Aglaranna's seniormost adviser.

As Tathar took the belt and turned to present it to Calin, Redtree spoke. "The belt is worn in high council and is passed from the King to his son. As he who was my father gave the belt to me to mark my position as heir, so I give this to you, Prince Calin."

The Elven Prince bowed his head as Acaila handed him the belt. He took it and touched his forehead to it, and said, "Your nobility is unquestioned. I accept your generosity with humility."

Then Aglaranna rose and said, "Again our people are one." To Redtree she said, "You are truly Aron Earanorn." She bowed her head to him. An elf appeared behind him with a new robe, and at the Queen's bidding, he placed it over the armor and furs Redtree wore in the fashion of his people. "You would honor our council by accepting a place in it."

The old King said, "The honor is mine."

Acaila put out his hand and led Redtree to a place between Tathar and himself.

Pug smiled and winked at Miranda. By placing the glamredhel above himself in council, yet behind Tathar, the wise leader of the eldar avoided years of possible resentment by the glamredhel. Redtree would stand second only to Tathar in council.

Miranda motioned with her head for Pug to move away from the council and when they were safely away from the discussion, she said, "How long is this going to continue?"

Pug shrugged. "Redtree's people first came here about thirty years ago, twenty years or so after Galain and Arutha ran into him after the fall of Armengar."

"They've been arguing who's in charge for thirty years?" asked Miranda, her face showing disbelief.

"Discussing," said Tomas, appearing behind them. "Come with me."

Tomas led Pug and Miranda to a private area, screened from the Queen's court by cleverly arrayed branches. On the other side, he could look out over the tree city of Elvandar.

Pug asked, "Do you ever get used to it?" He studied his friend, again finding the echoes of his foster brother in the alien-etched features of the tall warrior.

Even in his ceremonial robes, Tomas radiated strength and power. His pale blue eyes, nearly colorless, gazed across the vista of Elvandar as he said, "Yes, but its beauty never fails to move me."

Miranda said, "No one who's alive could not feel something."

It was evening and Elvandar was ablaze with a hundred cooking fires, some on the ground below, others on platforms erected in the branches of the trees. Throughout the community, glowing lanterns had been ignited, but rather than the harsh yellow flame of a city lamp, these glowed with a softer, blue-white light: elven globes, part natural, part magic, and unique to this place. But the trees themselves also were alight, branches illuminated with a soft glow, a faint bluish or greenish haze, as if the leaves were phosphorescent.

Tomas turned, the golden-trimmed red robe flaring slightly, and said, "Is it time for me to don my armor, old friend?"

"Soon, I fear," said Pug.

Almost wistfully Tomas said, "When we were victorious at Sethanon, I hoped we were done with this business."

Pug nodded. "Hoped. But we knew sooner or later the Pantathians would come again for the Lifestone." Pug's forehead furrowed, as if he was about to say something additional, but he halted himself. "So long as your sword rests within the stone, and so long as the Valheru are not finally vanquished, we did but buy time."

Tomas did not reply, but continued to stare out over the railing at the splendor of Elvandar. "I know," he said at last. "There will come a time when I must retrieve that sword and finish what we started that day." He had listened with keen interest when Miranda had recounted what she and his son had discovered on their last voyage to the southern continent. Tathar, Acaila, and the other Spellweavers had questioned her repeatedly over the months since she had come, ferreting out details she had forgotten. While Miranda's patience had been worn thin on many occasions, the long-lived elves took the interminable investigation as a matter of course.

The sounds of voices announced that Aglaranna and her advisers were coming to join her husband in their private quarters. The Queen, followed by Tathar, Acaila, Redtree, and Calin, entered.

Miranda and Pug bowed their heads, but the Queen said, "Court is over, my friends. We are here to discuss important issues in an informal fashion."

Miranda said, "Thank the gods."

Redtree scowled. "My familiarity with your race is limited"—he glanced at Acaila, who mouthed a word—"milady." He pronounced the word as something alien. "But this rushing to action I've observed in humans . . . it's incomprehensible!"

"Rushing!" said Miranda, allowing her astonishment to show openly.

Pug said, "We have been dealing with the Pantathians for fifty years, Redtree."

The old elf took an offered goblet of wine and said, "Well, you should have come up with some sense of the enemy, then."

Suddenly Pug realized that the old elf had his own sense of humor. It was different from Acaila's: while just as dry, it had a mocking edge. Pug grinned. "You remind me of Martin Longbow."

Redtree smiled and years dropped from his face. "Now, there's a human I like."

"Where is Martin?" asked Tomas.

"Here," came a voice as the old former Duke of Crydee climbed into view, mounting a flight of steps from below. "I don't move quite as spryly as I once did."

"You're still a fair hand with a bow, Martin," said Redtree. Then he added, "For a human."

Martin was the oldest living human Redtree might call a friend. Nearly ninety years of age, Martin looked a man in his late sixties or early seventies. His powerful shoulders and chest were still broad, though his arms and legs were thinner than Pug remembered. His skin looked like old leather, sun-dried and wrinkled, and his hair was now completely white. But his eyes were still alert, and Pug realized that Martin, over the months he had stayed in Elvandar, continued to have his wits around him. There was no hint of the doddering in this old man. While not quite rejuvenating him, the magic of Elvandar kept him vigorous.

Nodding at Miranda, Martin smiled. "I've known the edhel," he said, using the elves' own term for their people, "since I was a baby, and their humor is often lost on humans."

Miranda said, "As is their sense of haste." She looked at Pug. "For months now, close to a year or more, you've been saying that we must be about this or that—mostly, 'We must find Macros the Black'—yet I find us spending a great deal of time sitting around doing little."

Pug's eyes narrowed briefly. He knew Miranda was far older than she looked, perhaps even older than his own seventy-odd years, but often she displayed what he could only call an impatience that surprised him. He seemed about to say one thing, then another. At last he said, "Macros's legacy to me included many things—his library, his commentaries, and, to some extent, his powers—but nothing could replace his experience. If anyone can help us unlock the mystery of what is behind all we face, it is he." Pug stood before Miranda and looked into her eyes. "I cannot help but feel that behind all we have seen lurks another mystery, one far more profound and dangerous than what we yet know." Then his tone lightened slightly as in a mock-chiding voice he added, "And I would expect you, as much as anyone, to realize that often when one is motionless, the most thought is being applied to the problems at hand."

Miranda said, "I know, but I feel like a horse too long held under rein; I feel the need to be *doing* something!"

Pug turned to Tomas. "There we have the problem, don't we?"

Tomas nodded, glancing at the oldest, wisest minds in the Council of Elvandar. "What is to be done?" he asked.

Pug said, "Once you found Macros by leading me into the Halls of the Dead. Would it be useful to return there?"

Tomas shook his head. "I don't think so; do you?"

Pug shrugged. "Not really. I'm not even sure what I would say should we again face Lims-Kragma. I know more now than I did then, but of the nature of the gods and those other agents who serve them I still feel ignorant. In any event, I'm grasping at straws." He was silent a moment, frustration clearly evident on his features. Then he said, "No, the realm of the dead would be a waste of time."

Acaila said, "Those beings are not meant for easy apprehension by those who live mortal spans. But indulge me one question, Pug: why would it be a waste of time to seek this person in the Halls of the Dead?"

Pug said, "I really don't know. A feeling, nothing more. I'm certain Macros is alive." He then described how when they had last sought the Black Sorcerer, Gathis—then Macros's and now Pug's majordomo at Sorcerer's Island—had indicated that there was a bond between them, and should Macros be dead, Gathis would somehow know it. Pug finished by saying, "Several times over the last few years I've had this sense that Macros was not only still alive but . . ."

Miranda now looked thoroughly irritated. "What?"

Pug shrugged. "That he was somehow close by."

Under her breath she let out a sound of aggravation. "That wouldn't surprise me."

Martin smiled with wry amusement and asked, "Why?"

Miranda glanced out over the lights of Elvandar and said, "Because my experience is that most of these 'legendary' individuals turn out to be no more than a well-constructed sham, designed to convince us all of their importance, rather than any real indication of their true significance."

Aglaranna sipped her wine and sat next to Tomas on a long bench by the railing. "You sound more than irritated in a general way, Miranda."

Miranda dropped her gaze a moment; when she raised it again to the Elf Queen, she was composed. "Forgive my petulance, lady. We of Kesh often struggle with issues of appearance, rank, and court standing that have nothing to do with worth or value in any real sense. Many rise high by dint of birth while others far more worthy never achieve any significance, their lives spent in trivial work. Yet those 'great' nobles have no sense they achieved high rank by a simple accident of birth." She made a sour expression. "They think the fact their mothers were who they were ample proof of the gods' favor. Given my . . . history, I have had to deal with more than my share of such men. I have . . . little patience, I fear, for such as they."

"Well," said Tomas, "Macros did construct his own legend to protect his privacy, I'll grant, but as one who stood beside him more than once I can attest his legend is nothing but a shadow of his real power. He faced a dozen Tsurani Great Ones in this very forest, and while the magic of our Spellweavers aided our struggle, against the alien magicians he alone strove, and he destroyed their works and sent them fleeing to their own world. He is alone among men I would dread opposing. His power is nothing short of astonishing."

Pug nodded. "Which is why we need to find him."

"Where do we start?" asked Miranda calmly. "The Hall?"

Pug said, "I don't think so. There are too many people willing to sell information who live in the Hall of Worlds." Dryly he added, "And not all of it is accurate." He sat across from the Elf Queen and said, "I thought we might journey to the City Forever and question the Dreadmaster we imprisoned there."

Tomas shrugged. "I doubt he would know much more than we already discovered. He was but a tool."

Acaila said, "Have you considered this sorcerer might be here on Midkemia?"

Martin said, "Why?"

The eldar said, "Pug's 'feeling.' It is something I would not dismiss or set aside lightly. Often such feelings are our own minds informing us of something we haven't apprehended consciously."

"True," said Redtree, taking a bite from a large red apple. "In the wilds one's instincts must serve, else a hunter doesn't return with food for his family, or a warrior is left behind on the field of battle." Looking at Pug, he said, "Where did you feel this Macros's presence the most?"

"Oddly enough," said Pug, "at Stardock."

"You didn't say anything," offered Miranda, her voice almost accusing.

Pug smiled. "I was often distracted."

Miranda had the grace to blush. "You could have said something at one time or another."

Pug shrugged. "I dismissed it as stemming from the fact that most of his powerful tomes and scrolls are housed in my tower. I often feel as if he's looking over my shoulder when I read them."

Tathar said, "There is also this matter of that artifact retrieved from the southern continent."

Aglaranna spoke. "The Spellweavers feel there is something alien about it."

"Absolutely," said Tomas. "And it is more than the Pantathian presence. There is something about this that is alien even to the Valheru."

Martin said, "There is something I don't understand."

"What, old friend?" asked Calin.

"In all of this, since the first Tsurani ship was wrecked on Crydee shores to the fall of Sethanon, no one has asked one important question."

"Which is?" asked Acaila.

"Why have all these plots, all these plans, involved such chaos and destruction?"

Tomas said, "It is the nature of the Valheru."

Martin said, "But we haven't faced the Dragon Lords; we've faced only their agents, the Pantathians, as well as those who've served or were duped by them."

Pug tried to dismiss Martin's observation. "I think we've seen ample proof of the nature of the Pantathians."

Martin said, "You mistake my meaning. What I'm saying is that in all of this, much is without apparent motive. We've assumed things, over the years, about why and how the Pantathians were acting in the fashion they have, but we don't *know* why they're behaving the way they are."

Pug said, "I must be guilty of some oversight. I still don't see your meaning."

Miranda said, "Because you're not paying attention." She stepped past Pug to stand before Martin. "You've got an idea." It wasn't a question.

The old bowman nodded. Turning to Tathar, Acaila, and Redtree, he said, "Feel free to correct anything I say that isn't as it should be." To Pug and Tomas he said, "You have powers I cannot begin to imagine, but I have spent most of my life here, in the West, and I know the lore of the edhel as well as most men, I wager."

"Better than any human living," offered Tathar.

"In the lore of the eledhel," said Martin, "some things are said about the Ancient Ones." He faced the Queen. "Most Gracious Lady, why is that usage preferred?"

The Queen considered the question a moment, then said, "Tradition. It was once believed that to use the name of the Valheru would be to call their attention."

Miranda said, "A superstition?"

Martin looked to Tomas. "A superstition?" he repeated.

Tomas said, "Much of the memories given to me of the ancient times is clouded, and even those that are well remembered are the memories of another being. We share much, but much is also unknown to me. The power was once given to the eldar to call us by speaking our names aloud. That may be where this belief originated."

Martin better than anyone, except Pug, fully understood the strange duality of Tomas. He had known this half-alien man when Tomas and Pug had been boys at Castle Crydee, and had watched as the mystic armor of the long-dead Dragon Lord Ashen-Shugar had transformed Tomas into the strange being he was today, neither fully man nor Dragon Lord but something of both.

Tomas looked at the eldar and said, "Acaila?"

The old elf nodded. "The legends say such. We who were first among the slaves of the Valheru were able to contact them. This may have given rise to the practice of never speaking their names aloud."

Miranda said, "What, then, is your point?"

Martin shrugged. "I'm not even sure I have one, but it seems to me that we're making many assumptions here, and if any one of them is incorrect, we risk all by building our plans upon such mistaken beliefs." He stared into Miranda's eyes. "You returned from the land on the other side of the world with artifacts, apparently made by the Ancient Ones, yet Pug and Calis both say they are 'tainted,' not what they seem to be."

Acaila again nodded. "They are not pure. We know enough of our former masters to recognize that another hand has touched these items."

"Yet they sing to you?" offered Pug.

"Yes, they are much of the Valheru," offered Aglaranna.

Martin said, "So, then, whose is that other hand?"

"The third player," said Pug. Looking at Miranda, he said, "The demon, I assume that's who he meant."

Martin nodded. "I think so, as well. What if the Pantathians are not tools of the Ancient Ones but rather are tools of these demons?"

Tomas said, "That would explain a few things."

"Such as?" asked Redtree, taking a sip of wine.

Pug said, "The Dread, for one."

Acaila asked, "What of them?"

Tomas said, "They are an unlikely ally for my brethren." He used the term *brethren* for the Valheru when he was caught up in thinking as one.

"And an even less likely tool," supplied Acaila. "What lore has passed down through the generations of the eldar always shows the Dread to be rivals to the Valheru on the occasions when they crossed paths."

"Yet," said Pug, "we didn't consider the oddity at the time."

With a faint smile, Tomas said, "We were a bit preoccupied."

Pug's brow furrowed and his expression was a question.

"The Riftwar?" Tomas added, with a laugh.

Pug returned the laugh. "I know what you mean, but what I mean is, why didn't you think of this before?"

It was Tomas's turn to look perplexed. "I don't know. I just assumed the presence of the Dreadmaster in the City Forever and the Dreadlord at Sethanon were part of the Valheru attempt to distract us. I assumed somehow the Pantathians made contact with those creatures—"

Acaila interrupted. "You have memories and some knowledge, and great power, Tomas, but you lack experience. You are less than a century of age, yet you wear powers not gained in five times that span." He looked around the gathering. "We are as children when we speak of beings like the Valheru and Dreadlords. We are presuming when we attempt to understand them, or apprehend their purpose."

Pug said, "I grant that, but we must try, for there are things that cannot be allowed to simply come to us; we must discover the purpose behind those who seek to take the Lifestone and end us all."

Miranda said, "All of which brings us back to this: we know little and we need to find Macros the Black, and you still haven't suggested where we start to look."

Pug looked defeated. "I don't know."

Acaila said, "Perhaps you should cease looking for a place and begin looking for a person."

"What do you mean?" asked Pug.

The ancient elf said, "You spoke of a sense of Macros being close by. Perhaps it is time to turn your focus on that sense, look for the presence, and let it lead you to the man."

Pug said, "I don't imagine how that is possible."

"You studied with me for a brief time, Pug. There are many things we have to teach you still. Let me instruct you and Miranda now."

Pug looked at his companion, who nodded.

"Do I need to come along?" asked Tomas.

Acaila looked at the Warleader of Elvandar and shook his head. "You'll know when it is time to leave, Tomas."

To those of the Queen's court he said, "We will need to retire to the contemplation glade. Tathar, I would appreciate your help in this matter."

The old elven adviser bowed to his Queen and said, "By your leave, lady?"

She nodded and the four of them left the Queen and Tomas's private quarters. Down through the bowers that formed the elven city in the trees they moved, until they came to the ground, where large cookfires were brightly burning.

They moved silently away from the heart of Elvandar until at last they came to a tranquil glade. Here Tomas and Aglaranna had pledged their vows; here only those ceremonies most important to the elves were conducted.

Pug said, "We are honored."

"It is necessary," said Acaila. "Here our magic is most potent, and I suspect we need to use it to ensure your survival."

"What do you propose?"

"Tomas spoke to me of your previous travels to the Halls of the Dead, through the entrance at the Necropolis of the Gods. While we have a different vision of the universe and its order, we elves understand your human vision enough to know that only Tomas's raw strength allowed you to survive that journey."

"I awoke with my lungs burning and feeling as if I had been frozen to my bones," said Pug.

Acaila said, "You do not enter the realm of death while you are alive—not unless you make extensive preparations."

Pug said, "Are we to return to Lims-Kragma's halls?"

"Perhaps," said Acaila. "That is why we must do what we are to do here. Time passes differently in other realms, that much we remember from our Master's travels across the dimensions. You may be gone but hours, yet experience years. You may be gone months, yet experience minutes. We have no means to know which will be true. However long it takes, you are to leave your bodies for a while. Tathar and I will ensure your bodies are ready to receive you when you return. We shall keep you alive."

Miranda said, "We appreciate the effort."

Pug turned and saw her dubious expression. "You don't have to come," he said.

"I must," she said. "You'll understand."

"When?"

"Soon, I think," she answered.

"What must we do?" Pug asked Acaila.

"Lie down," he answered.

They did as he bade and he said, "First, you must remember what I said about the passage of time. This is important, for you must hurry while you are in spirit form. If you linger but for an hour, months may pass here on Midkemia, and we know how quickly the enemy approaches. Second, your bodies will follow your spirits. When you return, you may not find yourselves here. If all goes as we hope, you will arrive where you need to be, and Tathar and I will know you were successful because you will awaken here or your bodies will vanish from our sight. Last, we cannot help you return. This is something you must accomplish by your own arts. We shall know if you fail only when your bodies die despite our efforts. Our arts can do only so much.

"Now close your eyes and attempt to sleep. You will see visions. When they first come to you, they will be as dreams. But they will become more real to you as the moments pass. When I call to you, stand up."

Pug and Miranda closed their eyes. Pug heard Acaila's voice as the ancient eldar Spellweaver began chanting. There was something tantalizingly familiar about the words, but he could not quite recognize them. It was as if he heard the words of a song forgotten the moment he heard the words.

Soon he dreamed of Elvandar. He could see the faint glow of the magic-imbued trees above him, as if his eyes were open. But they appeared to him as brilliant shimmering colors, blues and greens, golds and whites, reds and oranges, and the sky was as black as the darkest tunnel under the mountains.

Pug "looked" deep into that void and soon found specks of color appearing against the blackness. Time passed unnoticed as he saw the spirits of stars dance across the heavens. A strange, distant keening sound intruded on his awareness, also familiar yet unrecognized.

Time continued to slip by, and Pug was lost in an awareness unlike anything he had ever experienced. The texture of the universe lay open to him, not the outer shapes, or even the illusions of matter and time, but the very fabric of reality. He wondered if this was the "stuff" Nakor spoke of, the fundamental matter of all that was.

His mind started to soar, to voyage through the distances, and he discovered he could move at will from place to place. Yet he sensed he still lay in the grove. Something about his body had changed, and he felt alien powers and odd sensations course through him.

Not since his time on the Tower of Testing, high above the Assembly on the distant world of Kelewan, had he felt so connected to the world around him. Thinking of that time in his life, he turned and looked "down" at Midkemia.

Suddenly he floated miles above the highest peaks of the Kingdom, with seas and coastlines looking like maps to his perception. But rather than flat lifeless things, the very land and seas were living things, pulsing with power and beauty.

He shifted his perceptions and saw every fish swimming in the sea. How very much like being a god! he thought.

"Pug." A distant call and one that almost caused him to lose his perception.

"Find Macros," came the instruction. "And 'ware the time!"

He glanced one way and another, and every being on the world had a signature of energy, a line of force that started at Sethanon, at the Lifestone, which bound all living things in Midkemia together. As time passed, lines vanished as beings died, and new lines sprouted from it as births occurred. It looked like nothing so much as an emerald fountain of pulsing energy, life incarnate, and it took Pug's breath away.

Among the myriad strands he sought one, one with a familiar quality to it. He lost track of time, and did not know if hours or years passed, yet eventually he saw something familiar.

The Sorcerer! he thought, seeing a particular pulsing line of force. How strong and distinct it was, he thought as he focused. But it was odd. It existed in two places at the same time.

"Arise!" came the spoken command, and Pug stood up.

He saw Acaila and Tathar, but they looked alien to him, beings of coarse matter and finite energy, while he was a creature of enhanced perception and unlimited power. He glanced at Miranda and saw a being of stunning beauty.

She wore no clothing and revealed no hint of sex. Where he should have seen breasts and hips, as familiar to him as his own body, he saw only smoothness, featureless and without distinguishing marks. Her face was an oval, with a pair of burning lights where eyes should have been. She had no nose. A single slit where her mouth should have been moved, but rather than his hearing her voice, her mind touched his.

"Pug?" Miranda asked.

"Yes," he answered.

"Do I look as odd to you as you do to me?" she said.

"You look stunning," he replied.

Suddenly he was seeing himself through her eyes. He was as featureless as she. They were of like height and they both existed with a shimmer of energy illuminating them from within. Neither had hair or sexual organs, teeth or fingernails.

From a great distance they heard Acaila's voice. "What you see are your true selves. Look down."

They did, and saw their own bodies lying on the grass, as if asleep.

"Hurry, now," said Acaila. "Follow the thread that leads you to Macros, for the longer you are out of your bodies, the harder it will be for you to return. We will keep you alive, and when it comes time to return, you only have to think of it. Your bodies will appear wherever you need them to be," he repeated. "May your gods protect you."

Pug sent, *"We understand."* He said to Miranda, *"Are you ready?"*

"Yes," she replied. *"Where do we go?"*

With a thought he made the thread appear to her, and he said, *"We follow that!"*

"Where does it lead?" she asked as he reached out with his mind and "took her hand," leading her along the thread's path.

"Don't you sense it?" he asked. *"It is going to the one place I should have expected it to lead us. It's taking us to the Celestial City. We travel to the home of the gods!"*

Six

Infiltration

CALIS POINTED.

Erik nodded, then signaled for his squad to move out behind him. The men duck-walked in the gully, keeping their heads below the rim of the wash through which they were approaching their opposition.

Erik was both sick to death of this drilling and frantic that it might not be enough. In the six months since he had taken the first band of soldiers into the mountains, he had judged he had a solid twelve hundred soldiers under his command, reliable men who would survive on their own for as long as possible.

There were another six hundred men who were close, needing a bit more training.

The band he led now was those he feared would never become the soldiers needed to win this coming war.

Alfred tapped him on the shoulder and Erik turned. The Sergeant pointed to a man on the other side of the gully, who was not walking as instructed, letting the discomfort in his knees drive him to recklessness.

Erik nodded, and Alfred nearly dove to get to the man and pull him to the floor of the gully. Sharp rocks cut both men, but Alfred's hand clamped hard over the soldier's mouth, preventing his cry from being heard by the nearby sentries. Erik could hear his corporal's whisper: "Now, Davy, your sore knees just got you and your comrades killed."

A distant voice told Erik the exercise was a failure, and as if reading Erik's mind, Calis stood and said, "This is done."

Erik and the others rose and Alfred jerked the soldier named Davy to his feet with one powerful tug. Now his voice was unleashed in all its volume and fury. "You rock-headed layabout! You sorry excuse for a water boy! You'll regret the day your father looked at your mother when I'm done with you."

Calis heard a challenge, turned, and called out the password. He motioned to Erik, and the Sergeant Major and his Captain walked away from the men. Calis said, "Sergeant, start them back to camp."

Alfred shouted, "You heard the Captain! Back to camp! Quick march!"

The soldiers set out at a ragged run, and the Sergeant harried them every step of the way.

Calis watched in silence until the men were out of sight; then he said, "We have a problem."

Erik nodded. The sun was setting in the west and he said, "Each day about this time, I feel as if we've lost another step. We're never going to get six thousand men trained in time."

"I know," said Calis.

Erik looked at his Captain and sought any hint of his mood. In the years he had spent with Calis he had come no closer to being able to read him than he had the first day they had met. He was an enigma to Erik, as unreadable as one of those foreign texts William kept in his library. Calis smiled. "That's not the problem. Don't worry. We'll have our six thousand men in the field when the time comes. They won't be as well trained as either of us would like, but the core will be solid, and that backbone of really fine soldiers will help keep the others alive." He studied his young Sergeant Major's face for a while, then said, "You forget that the one thing you can't teach is the seasoning you get in combat. Some of the men you judge fit will get themselves killed in the first few minutes, while some you would wager everything you have will perish will survive, even flourish in the midst of the carnage."

His smile vanished. "No, the problem I speak of is we've been infiltrated."

Erik said, "Infiltrated? A spy?"

"Several, I suspect. It's a hunch, nothing more. Those we face are occasionally heavy-handed, but they're never stupid."

Erik thought it time to broach his own unease. "Is that why the Prince's guards are ensuring no one sees the Royal Engineers building supply roads along the rear of Nightmare Ridge?"

"Nightmare Ridge?" asked Calis. His expression was clear to Erik. He wasn't being disingenuous; he didn't recognize the name.

"That's what we call it in Ravensburg," answered Erik. "It's probably called something else up north." He glanced around. "I ran a company up into the north and took them farther than usual. We ran into a company of Pathfinders and a bunch of Prince Patrick's Household Guards. I could hear the sound of tools coming from the other side of the valley we entered, echoing from behind the ridge: trees being felled, anvils striking steel, and spikes being driven into rock. The Prince's corps of engineers is building a road. That ridge runs all the way from the Teeth of the World down through Darkmoor, and halfway to Kesh. It's almost impossible to cross anywhere there isn't a road, and more than one traveler's been found dead up there. That's why we call it Nightmare Ridge. You get lost anywhere up there in cold weather, you're a dead man."

Calis nodded. "That's the place. You weren't supposed to be there, Erik. Captain Şubai was not pleased, nor was Prince Patrick. But yes, that's why no one is permitted to go there, in case the enemy does have agents snooping around outside Krondor."

Erik blurted, "You're going to abandon the city."

Calis sighed. "I wish it were that simple." He was silent as he watched the sunset. Brilliant orange and pink faced by black clouds far away, over the sea, gave an unreal quality to the approaching evening, as if nothing that beautiful should exist in the same world as the coming evil.

Calis looked at Erik. "We have several plans in place. You need worry only about the disposition of soldiers under your command. You'll be told where to take them and what your options are. Once you are in the mountains with your soldiers, you'll have to make the decisions, Erik. You'll have to judge what is best for both your men and the overall campaign. A great deal will ride on your judgment.

"But until the Prince and Knight-Marshal are ready to brief you on the overall operation, I will not give you details you might blurt out to the wrong person."

"The infiltrators?"

"That, or if you're abducted and some agent of the Pantathians doses you with some potion to make you speak, or if they have mind readers like the Lady Gamina in their employ. We have no idea what might happen. That's why whatever you hear you share with no man, and you're only to be told what you need to know."

Erik nodded. "I'm worried . . ."

"About the girl?"

Erik was surprised. "You know about that?"

Calis motioned they should start walking after the departing soldiers, and said, "What sort of captain would I be if I didn't know about my Sergeant Major's life outside the barracks?"

Erik had no answer for that. He said, "Of course I'm worried about Kitty. I'm worried about Roo and his family, too. I'm worried about everybody."

"Now you're starting to sound like Bobby, though he would never have voiced it that way." Calis smiled. "He'd have said, 'We've got too damn much work to do and half the time needed, and a bunch of incompetent fools doing it.' "

Erik laughed. "That sounds like him."

"I miss him, Erik. I know you do, as well, but Bobby was one of the first I picked. The first of my 'desperate men.' "

Erik said, "I thought you fetched him from the Border Barons to work for you."

Calis laughed. "Bobby would have put it that way. He failed to mention he was going to be hanged for having killed another soldier in a brawl. I had to beat him a half-dozen times to get him to control his temper."

"Beat him?" asked Erik, negotiating his way over a large rock as they followed the gully downward.

"I told him each time he lost his temper I'd strip to the waist and we'd have at it. If he was standing and I was not, he was a free man. It took that fool six beatings before he finally realized I am a great deal stronger than I look."

Erik knew that was the truth. The Captain's father was a man called Tomas, some sort of lord or another up in the north. By all rumors, his mother was the Elf Queen. But whatever the truth of his parentage, Calis's strength was unmatched by that of any man Erik had run across. The former smith from Ravensburg had been the strongest man in his village, and of all those soldiers who had served with him on his first voyage to Novindus, only the huge man named Biggo was his equal. But Calis had done things that Erik could only judge impossible. He had once seen the Captain easily pick up a wagon so Erik could replace the wheel, when Erik knew from experience he would have needed the help of at least two other men to duplicate the feat.

Considering Bobby de Loungville's nature, Erik said, "I'm surprised you didn't have to kill him."

Calis laughed. "I came close, twice. Bobby wasn't a man to take defeat easily. When I came back from that first trip to Novindus, and we came limping into Krondor harbor like whipped hounds, Prince Arutha called me the 'Eagle' because of the banner on our ship." Erik nodded. He knew as well as any man that in that distant land Calis played the part of a mercenary captain, and his company was called the Crimson Eagles. "Bobby elected to call himself the Dog of Krondor. Prince Arutha seemed less than pleased, but said nothing."

Calis stopped and restrained Erik. "Don't say anything to anyone about what you suspect, Erik. I don't want to lose another sergeant major. Bobby may have fancied himself a dog, but he was a loyal and tough one. You're just as loyal and just as tough, though you don't know it yet."

Erik nodded at the compliment. "Thank you, sir."

"I'm not through. I don't want to lose another Sergeant Major because Duke James hanged him to keep him silent." He looked Erik in the eyes. "Do I make myself clear?"

"Very."

"Come along, then, we've got to march this lot back to Krondor and hand them over to William to turn into garrison rats. If they somehow find themselves in the mountains, they may survive a little longer than the average soldier, so we've done them a favor, but none of these men will be of service to us."

Erik said, "That's the truth."

"Go find me some more men, Erik. Desperate men if you must, but get me some men we can train."

"Where should I seek them?" asked Erik.

Calis said, "Go see the King before he leaves Krondor. If you ask him nicely, he may give you a warrant so you can steal the Border Barons' best men from them. The Barons will not be happy when you do this, but if we lose this war, invasion from the Northlands is the last thing we'll need worry about."

Erik, remembering the map of the Kingdom in William's office, said, "That means a journey to Northwarden, Ironpass, and Highcastle."

"Start with Ironpass," instructed Calis. "You'll have to move fast, and while you're bringing the men south, march them through the Dimwood and avoid Sethanon. Get them here as soon as you can." Then with what Erik had come to think of as Calis's evil grin, he said, "You have two months."

Erik suppressed a groan. "I need three!"

"Kill some mounts getting there if you must, but you have two. I need another six hundred good men, two hundred from each of those garrisons here in Krondor in two months."

"That will leave them with less than half their standard garrison! All of the Barons will object."

"Of course they'll object," said Calis with a laugh. "That's why you need the King's Warrant."

Erik hesitated, then set off in a jog, leaving a startled Calis behind. "Where are you running to?"

"Krondor," said Erik. "I need all the time I can squeeze, and there's someone I must say good-bye to."

Calis's laughter faded into the background as Erik continued to run. He was still running when he passed a startled Alfred and the men marching back to camp.

Erik had spent a difficult day with the King and then with Kitty. While the King wasn't too adverse to stripping his northern garrisons of soldiers needed there to defend his realm from the marauding goblins and dark elves, he was less than enthused with Calis entrusting the task of selecting those men to a sergeant. He reminded Erik that he carried court rank now, and he shouldn't let any of the Barons question his right to carry out those orders, but silently Erik wondered how he would force a nobleman with nearly four hundred armed men trained to obey to do what Erik wanted should the King's Warrant prove insufficient.

He told Jadow that Calis would be returning later with the men who were to be reassigned to the Prince's garrison, and then left to find Kitty.

She took the news of his two-month absence with a calm exterior, but Erik had come to know her well enough to see she was upset. He wished he could spend one more day with her, but knew that Calis's time limit was nearly impossible.

They slipped out of the inn and spent an emotional hour together, and at the end Erik had come as close as he dared to breaking his word to Calis about not repeating what he suspected. He just warned Kitty that should he not be around when that "something big" she suspected finally happened, she should slip out of Krondor and head to Ravensburg. He knew that when word of the invaders finally reached the city, there would be a little time to flee before the Prince ordered the city sealed. Kitty was smart enough to know what he meant, and she would head to the Inn of the Pintail in Ravensburg to be with Freida, his mother, and Nathan, his stepfather. He promised he would find her there.

Erik left two hours before sundown. He knew he would have to put up at an inn along the way, but every hour he could steal would be worth the extra expense. Besides, he was spending the King's gold, not his own.

Sundown found him still an hour from the nearest inn. The little moon was up, so it wasn't completely dark, and the King's Highway was a clearly marked way, but Erik walked his horse rather than risk an injury by having the animal stumble.

His horse was a tough little roan gelding he had selected himself. It wasn't as strong or as large as most of the horses in the Prince's stable, but it was likely to possess more endurance than most of the animals Erik might choose. He would switch mounts often on this journey, and he would be in the saddle from before dawn to after dusk for nearly two weeks to reach Ironpass, and even then he would have to push the horses to the end of their endurance, but it could be done.

Silently Erik cursed his Captain and rode into the night.

Nakor pointed. "There, again!"

Sho Pi nodded. "As it was last time, Master."

Nakor resisted the impulse to tell the young man to cease calling him master. It was as pointless as telling a dog not to scratch fleas.

"Keshian patrols along the south coast of the Sea of Dreams," observed Nakor. "Last time Calis informed the garrison commander, yet here again we see Keshian lancers riding with their colors unfurled." After a moment, he laughed.

"What is funny, Master?"

Nakor struck the young man lightly with the back of his hand on Sho Pi's shoulder. "It's obvious, boy. Lord Arutha has made a deal."

"A deal?" asked Sho Pi as the boat's Captain turned his craft toward the shore.

"You'll see," said the little man.

He and his disciple had taken ship from Krondor and sailed through the inlet into the waterway between the Bitter Sea and the Sea of Dreams. They were now on a river boat heading to Port Shamata, where they would buy horses and ride to Stardock. Nakor carried documents for Lord Arutha and orders from Prince Patrick and Duke James. Nakor had a nagging suspicion he knew what was in those documents, for several of them bore the King's own crest, not that of the Prince.

The balance of the journey passed uneventfully, and eventually Nakor and Sho Pi found themselves on the raft that served to carry passengers and goods across the Great Star Lake to the island of Stardock, and the community of magicians that resided there.

Arutha, Lord Vencar, Earl of the King's court and son of Duke James, met them at the landing. "Nakor, Sho Pi! It's good to see you two again." He laughed. "Our last meeting was far too brief."

Nakor also laughed. He had spent less than two minutes in the newly arrived Earl's company before departing with Sho Pi and Pug to travel to Elvandar.

As they jumped the narrowing gap between barge and dock, Nakor said, "I have messages from your father."

Arutha said, "Come with me, then."

"How did you know we were on the barge?" asked Nakor.

As they walked to the huge building that was Stardock, the man the King had sent to administer the island of magicians said, "Something mundane. Our lookout saw you from up there." He pointed to one of the windows in a high tower. "He sent word to me."

"Must be one of my students," said Nakor, nodding.

Inside the building, they traversed a long hall and moved toward what Nakor knew would be Arutha's office. It was the same one he had taken when he had been placed in charge of the island by Calis. "Are Chalmes, Kalied, and the others giving you any trouble?" asked Nakor.

At mention of the Keshian-born traditionalist who resisted the idea of this island's being subject to the King's law, Arutha shook his head and said, "None worth mentioning. They grouse a bit now and again, but as long as they're free to teach and do their research, they don't complain too much about my administration."

Nakor said, "I suspect they're plotting."

"No doubt," agreed Arutha as they reached his office, "but I think it won't amount to much without outside help. They're too spineless to attempt to secede from the Kingdom without a strong ally."

Once inside the office, Arutha closed the door. "And we're prepared for that," said the Earl as he took the packet of documents his father had sent. "Excuse me a moment," he said, and broke the seal on the first of those, a personal message from the Duke.

As he read, Nakor studied the Earl. He was as tall as his father, but looked more like his mother, with fine features and an almost delicate mouth. His eyes, though, thought Nakor, were his father's; they were dangerous. His hair was like his father's, too, as it had been when James was a young man: tight dark brown curls.

After a moment, Arutha said, "Do you know what's in here?"

"No," said Nakor, "but I can guess. Erland has just returned from Kesh. Did he pass this way?"

Arutha laughed. "Not much gets by you, does it?"

"When you've lived by your wits as long as I have," said Nakor, "you learn to pay attention to everything."

"Yes, Erland stopped for one night on his way home."

"Then you've made a deal with Kesh."

Arutha said, "Let's say we've come to an understanding."

If Sho Pi was lost in the conversation, he gave no sign, seemingly content to let his master and the Earl speak uninterrupted.

Nakor laughed. "Your father is the most evil, dangerous man I've ever met. It's a good thing he's on our side."

Arutha looked rueful. "You'll get no argument from me in that regard. My life has never been my own."

Nakor took the message as Arutha handed it across the desk. "You don't seem particularly bothered by this," observed the gambler.

Arutha shrugged. "I had the usual rebellious nature most young men possess, but truth to tell, most of what my father had me do was interesting; challenging even. My sons, as you may have gathered, were a completely different case. My wife is quite a bit more forgiving of 'adventuresome' natures than my mother was." He stood up as Nakor read the Duke's message. "I have often thought what Father's life must have been like, to be literally raised a thief in the sewers of Krondor." He glanced out a small window that overlooked the shoreline. "I've heard enough 'Jimmy the Hand' stories to last a lifetime."

"I didn't think your father was much on bragging," observed Sho Pi as Nakor continued to read.

"Not from Father, but from others," said Arutha. "Father has changed the history of the Kingdom." He fell into a thoughtful silence. "It can be a difficult thing to be the son of a great man."

Nakor said, "People expect much of a great man's son." He put the document on the desk. "You want me to stay?"

"For a while," said Arutha. "I need someone trustworthy here when this all breaks out. I need some reassurance that Chalmes and the others don't react badly."

"Oh, they'll react badly enough when they see what your father and Prince Erland have cooked up," said Nakor with a small laugh, "but I'll make sure no one gets hurt."

"Good. I'll leave next week, after I've seen to a few more necessary details."

"You need to return to Krondor?" asked Nakor.

Arutha nodded. "I know my father."

Nakor sighed. "I understand."

Arutha said, "You have the same rooms as before, so rest and I'll see you at dinner."

Sensing they were being dismissed, Sho Pi rose and opened the door for Nakor.

After they had left the Earl's office, Sho Pi said, "Master, what did you mean by asking Lord Arutha if he needed to return?"

"His father ordered him to Rillanon, on a thin pretext of carrying messages to the King," said Nakor as they turned a corner leading to the suite of rooms set aside for them. Climbing a flight of stairs, Nakor continued, "Arutha knows his father is unlikely to leave Krondor when the fighting starts. He wants to see that his sons don't stay with their grandfather."

"I know war is risky," said the former soldier, "but why should the Duke's grandsons be at any greater risk than anyone else?"

"Because it is unlikely that anyone who is in Krondor when the Queen's fleet arrives will survive," Nakor answered flatly.

Sho Pi remained silent as they reached their quarters.

Erik signaled and the riders stopped. One of his scouts was riding back toward him. He had spent the better part of two months raiding the Border Barons for their best men, and now almost six hundred men rode in three columns spread out over twenty miles behind him. It had been an exhausting ride, and Erik was cursing Calis with almost every mile of it, but he had his men.

Each Border Baron he had visited had read the King's Warrant with a mix of disbelief and outrage. Each Baron was unique in that he was a vassal of the Crown, answerable to no Earl or Duke. To have a mere sergeant major of the Prince's garrison walk in with orders to let him handpick men to be taken away, while promises of replacements were vague at best, was more than they could withstand.

Baron Northwarden had even considered attempting to hold Erik for confirmation of the order, but by then Erik had an armed company of nearly two hundred men with him and the Baron thought better of it.

At Highcastle, the Baron merely looked as if another weight had been added to his already abundant burden, and complied with a minimum of complaint. Erik suspected the company of four hundred men from Northwarden and Ironpass also convinced him.

They had ridden through the vast grasslands of the High Wold, home to nomadic tribesmen, herding their sheep and trading with the Barons and those small villages that survived this close to the Northlands. Several times they had found camps recently abandoned, as if the approach of so many armed men had caused bandits to flee into the hills.

After the third such camp had been encountered, Erik had ordered two of the men from Ironpass to ride advance scout. Erik found it slightly discomforting to think of any problems this far within the border of the Kingdom, but of all the lands between the Far Coast and the Kingdom Sea, those lands between the Teeth of the World—the great northern mountain range—and the boundary of the Dimwood were among the most hostile. Raiding parties of goblins and dark elves were known to have traveled as far south as Sethanon in the years before the Riftwar, and no matter the frequency of Kingdom patrols through these areas, they still remained wild and inhospitable.

They were presently riding through light woodlands, leading toward the far denser Dimwood, and now Erik had lost count of the ideal places for ambush he had ridden past.

The first scout reined in and said, "An armed camp, Sergeant Major. At least a hundred men."

"What?" said Erik. "Did anyone see you?"

"No, they post no scouts and seem unconcerned about it; I believe they think themselves alone here."

"Could you mark them?"

"No banner flew and they wore neither uniform nor tabard. They look like brigands."

Erik dismissed the scout and turned to the man he had named acting corporal, a sergeant from Ironpass named Garret. "I want a skirmish line behind us by fifty yards—half the men. At the first sound of trouble, I want them to sweep in from either side. The rest should ready themselves to hit hard up the middle if needed, by column of two. Get four of your best and ride with me."

At least a decade Erik's senior, the man showed no hesitation in taking orders from the younger man. Erik liked his attitude and his discipline and planned on making him a sergeant as soon as possible, because in Garret he sensed someone who'd keep his men alive.

That was the one thing about Calis's plan Erik grudgingly approved of: the men he had been sent to fetch had been hardened by years of fighting goblins, dark elves, and bandits. Most of them were mountain fighters by experience, and it would take little to meld them into the force Erik already had under his command.

Like the trained soldiers they were, the first twenty men spread out behind Erik. He told Garret, "Get ready for trouble."

Orders were passed, and Erik, Garret, and the four men he had chosen rode forward.

They slowly picked their way through the trees and came within sight of campfires. Close to eighty men lay about or stood talking in a clearing in the woods. A few dozen tents of various size were erected in haphazard fashion, and some men tended cooking fires and saw to provisions near the middle of the clearing. Erik saw baggage wagons and horses staked out near the far edge. To Garret he said, "This is no band of outlaws."

The older soldier nodded silent agreement. "We better hit them hard." There was no question in his mind; they were heading for a fight. Erik wondered. While it was not quite midday, many of the men were sleeping. Erik held up his hand and spoke softly. "They're waiting for someone."

"How do you know, Sergeant Major?" asked Garret.

"They're bored and they've been here for at least a week." He pointed to a slit trench over to their right.

Garret said, "I can smell it. You're right. They've been here for a while."

"And unless I'm mistaken, there's nothing here worth waiting for, so they're waiting for someone else to show up."

"Who?"

"That's what I intend to find out."

He motioned the men forward and they walked their horses to within sight of the camp.

A bored soldier sat polishing his sword and he glanced up as Erik and the others hove into view. His eyes widened and he shouted.

As soon as Erik heard the man's voice, the hair on the back of his neck stood up and he shouted to the rear, "Attack!"

Swords were in hands without thought, and the sound of the riders coming hard filled the afternoon air. In the camp, men ran to bedrolls and pulled on armor as they could, or grabbed shields and swords, bows and arrows, and the fight began.

As Erik had planned, the column of twos rode into the center of the camp behind him just as the sweeping skirmish line encircled the camp. Men screamed as arrows filled the air and steel rang upon steel as the riders swept into the clearing. Many of the men who rode with Erik were mounted bowmen and quickly picked off targets as men struggled to don armor.

Erik rode down two men as he headed for the center of the camp. Whoever led these men was certain to be there, and he intended to find the leader before some overly eager Kingdom archer skewered him with a bowshaft.

Erik saw the leader.

The man was an oasis of calm as those around him ran in every direction. He shouted orders and attempted to bend his men by force of will into an effective fighting force. Erik put heels to his horse and charged him.

The leader sensed more than saw Erik approach, so intent was he on directing his men. He turned to see the horse and rider almost on top of him and dove to one side, avoiding Erik's charge.

Erik turned his mount and found the man now armed with sword and shield, quickly retrieved from the ground. Erik knew he faced a tough opponent, for the man had dived in the direction of his weapons. He would not rattle.

Erik knew better than to charge him again, for to do so was to risk having the man duck under his attack and hamstring his horse. He was probably calm and confident enough to attempt that dangerous move.

His men were taking a terrible toll on those in camp, and Erik circled his opposite number, waiting. The man eyed him warily, ready for the charge that didn't come, and Erik shouted, "Keep as many of them alive as possible."

When it became clear that the men in the camp were hopelessly outclassed by those on horseback, soldiers began throwing down their weapons and crying for quarter.

Quickly the matter resolved itself in Erik's favor, and when at last there was no doubt, the leader threw down his weapon. Erik knew that in Novindus, it was the accepted sign of surrender by mercenaries.

Erik glanced around and saw a banner lying on the ground, its emblem familiar to him. Erik rode his horse toward the man. Garret and the other soldiers looked perplexed as the Prince's Sergeant Major spoke in a strange tongue.

To the man, Erik said, "Duga and his War Dogs, if I'm not mistaken."

The man nodded. "Who are you?"

"I rode with Calis's Crimson Eagles."

Captain Duga, mercenary leader of one hundred swords, sighed. "You were to be killed on sight, and that was on the other side of the world."

"You've come a long way," observed Erik.

"That's the truth." He glanced around and saw his men being disarmed by Erik's. "What now?"

"That depends. If you cooperate, you'll get a chance to stay alive. If you don't . . ."

"I won't break oath," Duga said.

Erik studied the man. He had been almost a classic mercenary captain in Novindus. Clever, if not intelligent, but smart enough to keep his men alive, a requirement of any captain. He'd be tough enough to keep a surly band of cutthroats in line, and he'd be honest enough to keep contracts, else no one would hire him.

"No oath need be broken. You're our prisoner, but we can hardly give you parole to return home."

Bitterly the man said, "I don't even know where home is."

Erik pointed to the southwest. "That way—on the other side of the world, as you said."

"Care to loan us a boat?" Duga asked with bitter irony.

"Perhaps. If you share some information with us, you might find yourselves with some opportunity to return home." Erik didn't comment on how slim the chance of that occurring might be.

"Talk," said Duga.

"Start with, how did you get here?"

"Through one of those magic gates the snake men make." He shrugged. "They offered a bonus for any captain who led his men through." He glanced around. "Though where I'll spend it, the gods only know."

Erik said, "How long have you been here?"

"Three weeks."

"Who are you waiting for?"

"I don't know," said the Captain of mercenaries from Novindus. "All I know is the orders from General Fadawah were simple. Go through this rift thing and find a place to camp nearby. Then wait."

"For what?"

"I don't know. I just know we were told to wait."

Erik felt a stab of uncertainty. Until the next element of his column arrived, he had almost as many prisoners as he had men to guard them, and at any moment new enemies might appear. Thinking quickly, he said, "Limited parole. You'll not be harmed, but we won't let you ride away. We'll negotiate better terms when we get to our camp."

The mercenary considered it for a moment, then said, "Done." With obvious relief, he shouted to his men, "No more fighting. Now, let's eat!"

Erik once more was amazed at the attitude of mercenaries from Novindus, who treated conflict and fighting as jobs, who faced men across the line one day who might have been allies the year before, and might be again someday, and who carried little or no ill will as a result.

Erik motioned to Garret and said, "After things settle down, make camp and let the men eat."

The sergeant from Ironpass saluted, and started giving orders.

Erik stretched in the saddle and felt as if every bone were jangled out of its joint. His backside was sore and he couldn't remember ever having been this tired. With a silent groan he dismounted and, smelling the food on the fires, realized he was hungry.

Before beginning the questioning of the prisoners, he paused once more to curse his Captain. He started to tend his horse and again paused a moment to curse Calis.

Seven

Schemes

ROO NODDED.

The trade delegate had been speaking for nearly an hour, and Roo had sensed the entire course of negotiations within the first five minutes, but protocol dictated he endure the entire presentation before declining the opportunity. Roo wished the man would come to an end, as he knew this meeting was entirely pointless.

Since seizing control of the grain market in the Western Realm of the Kingdom, Roo had seen the control of his various companies, especially the Bitter Sea Company, grow by the month, until he had only one rival in the Western Realm in commerce: Jacob Esterbrook.

The one area where Jacob completely dominated was in trade with Kesh. The profitable luxury trade with the Empire was like a locked room to Roo, and no attempt of his to gain a foothold in that lucrative market had resulted in anything more than a minor contract or a marginally profitable trade.

He had again sought to gain a concession into Kesh, but now he was being told at great length by this minor Keshian functionary that his latest attempt would come to naught.

At long last the man finished, and Roo smiled at him. "So, to put it another way, the answer is no."

The trade delegate blinked as if seeing something for the first time and said, "Oh, I think it too harsh to simply say no, Mr. Avery." He put the tips of his fingers together. "It is far closer to the truth to say that such an arrangement is not feasible at this time. However, that is not to say that at some future date such an accommodation might not be possible."

Roo glanced out the window of the upper floor of Barret's Coffee House. Night was approaching. "The afternoon is late, sir, and I still have much to do before enjoying my evening meal. May I say that when next we speak, I plan on starting a great deal earlier in the day."

The Keshian rose, his expression showing Roo's humor was completely lost on him, and bowed slightly, then departed.

Duncan Avery, Roo's cousin, sat almost asleep in the corner, and stretched as he rose. "Finally," he said.

Luis de Savona, Roo's general manager, said, "I agree. Finally."

Roo said, "Well, we had to try." He sat back in his chair, glanced at the coffee and rolls that had sat upon the table for hours and were now cold and stale, and said, "Someday I'm going to figure out how Jacob has such a stranglehold on Keshian trade. It's almost as if . . ." He left the thought unfinished.

"As if what?" asked Duncan.

Luis glanced at Roo's cousin. The two men barely got along, though they remained civil with one another. Luis, a former comrade-in-arms with Roo, was hardworking, conscientious, and meticulous in every detail of whatever task lay before him. Duncan was lazy, paid no attention to detail, and was in Roo's employ only because he was his cousin. He was also charming, funny, and an excellent swordsman, and Roo enjoyed his company.

Luis said, "When did you become interested in trade?"

Duncan shrugged. "Roo started to say something. I just wondered what. That's all."

Roo said, "Never mind. I have some things I need to investigate."

Duncan said, "Anything you want me to do?"

Roo shook his head. "No, but I need to speak to Duke James." He stood, walked to the rail, and shouted down, "Dash?"

"Yes, Mr. Avery," came the response from below. Dash looked up from a Bitter Sea Company desk where he was going over shipping invoices with two of Roo's scribes. "What can I do for you, sir?" While informal when alone with his employer, Dash always observed the formalities at Barret's and other public places.

"I need to see your grandfather at his earliest convenience."

"Now?" said Dash, half rising.

Roo waved him back into his chair. "Tomorrow is soon enough."

From the doorway a voice said, "Now would be better."

Dash looked up as Roo craned his neck to see who spoke, and Dash said, "Grandfather!"

The Duke of Krondor entered, flanked by two palace guardsmen. A general stir sounded in the lower floor and several of the members rose and bowed slightly as word of the visitor spread. James came to the railing that prevented non-members from entering the trading floor, and one of the guards opened the gate. James passed through and mounted the stairs to the upper floor of Barret's. It was a tremendous breach of protocol for a non-member to do so unless he was there on business, but Roo decided it wasn't the time to inform the most powerful noble in the Kingdom of that detail.

James spoke to Luis and Duncan. "Leave us." He leaned over the railing and said, "Dash, ensure we're undisturbed."

Dash moved to the foot of the stairs and tried not to grin as he saw his grandfather's guards also take up position at the foot of the stairway.

Keeping his voice low so as not to be overheard below, James said, "It's time for us to do some business."

Roo didn't like the sound of that, but he shrugged. "Sooner or later."

"I need two million golden sovereigns."

Roo blinked. His net worth was several times that, but he wasn't that liquid. To put his hands on that much gold would require some restructuring of his business. "How soon do you need it?"

"Yesterday, but tomorrow will suffice."

"And the interest?"

James smiled. "Whatever you like, within reason. You understand that we may not be in a position to repay this loan."

Roo nodded. "If you can't repay this loan, I doubt I'll be in a position to complain."

James said, "How soon can I see the gold?"

"I can have a half-million golden sovereigns at the palace by the end of business tomorrow. The other million and a half will take a few days to arrange. I'm going to overtax most of the moneylenders in the city. I'm going to have to do some business in the East, as well." Leaning back, he said, "Would you do me the courtesy of a bit more advance notice next time, Your Grace?"

"No," said James. "Things come up."

"Speaking of which," said Roo, "I just got another trade concession rejected by the Keshian trade legate. Is there anything you can do to help me overcome this problem?"

"Possibly," said James. "Right now we're doing a lot of business with Kesh."

"The gold?" asked Roo, raising an eyebrow in question.

"A very fat bribe for several well-placed Keshian nobles."

"Very fat," agreed Roo. "Are you attempting to overthrow the Emperor?"

James stood. "It would take a great deal more gold than that to even dream of such a move. There may not be enough gold in existence to overthrow Great Kesh." James hesitated, then said, "So you know. We have a southern border to worry about."

Roo nodded. "I figured out that much by myself." He stretched and stood up. "I am interested in how you propose to deal with Kesh during the coming invasion."

"I'm working on several different contingencies," said James. "But one of them is to ensure that enough Keshian soldiers are in the right place to encourage the Emerald Queen's army to stay where we want them."

Roo nodded. "No sweeps south of Krondor, up into the mountains from the Vale of Dreams."

"Something like that. That sort of move would require that the Emerald Queen overrun the dwarves at Dorgin, which has never been done." James smiled ruefully. "But even old King Halfdan's army would be put to rout by this host, I'm afraid."

Roo shrugged. He had heard stories of the dwarves' fierceness in warfare, but had never met one of them.

As James turned to leave, Roo came around the desk. "No need to see me to the door," said the Duke. "I can find my own way."

As he reached the top of the stairs, he said, "Oh, by the way, stop trying to squirrel away your wealth in the East and the Free Cities. I'm going to need most of it for the war."

Roo didn't even attempt to look shocked or deny the truth; he had been taking small amounts of capital and moving it quietly out of Krondor. "Very well," he said with honest resignation in his voice. "Trying to outfox you is a waste of energy."

James nodded. "Don't forget it."

He left and Roo stood alone, wondering again at his failed attempt to get a trade concession into Kesh. He had a theory, and he needed to put it to the test, but right now he had a more immediate concern: how to raise a huge amount of gold quickly without causing every moneylender in the city to double his interest rates.

He sighed as he thought about his planned visit to Sylvia. He would have to give Duncan a note to take to her, since he would be here until well past midnight. He sat down and started to write.

Once done, he called down to Dash. When Dashel was standing before him, Roo said, "Give this to Duncan to take to the Esterbrook house. He'll know what to do." Roo stretched again. "Then please send word to my wife that your grandfather is keeping me too busy to come home for the next few days." Actually, Roo had already told his wife he was staying in the city to work, but had planned on seeing Sylvia that night. Now he felt obliged to see Sylvia the next night, or the one after that, before returning home.

Roo glanced out the window at the sunset, and he heard the city noises outside as the day wound down and shops began to close. "I need to take a break before I start doing your grandfather's bidding," said Roo, standing up. "I think I'll pay a visit to Helen Jacoby and her children."

Dash nodded. "After that?"

"I'm going to Avery and Son for an hour or so this evening," and with a sour face he added, "Then it's back here. I'll most likely be here all night."

Dash nodded. "Anything else?"

"No, that's all. Come back here first thing in the morning. I expect I'll have a great deal for you to do. Have Jason come along, as well."

As Dash hurried toward the door, Roo walked down the stairway. He reached the entrance to Barret's and considered crossing the street to his town house, to saddle up a horse and ride over to Helen's. Then he decided he'd rather walk.

He wended his way through the busy streets. Roo never tired of the crowds and clamor of the city. A small-town boy, he saw Krondor as a never-ending source of stimulation. Just by walking he could refresh himself and conceive of anything being possible. But today as he walked, the distant specter of the Emerald Queen and her approaching host intruded on his appreciation of the robust city.

On one level, he knew that eventually Krondor would be attacked, probably overrun. He had seen what happened when her conquering General Fadawah crushed a city: he had barely escaped the destruction of distant Maharta. He knew it was coming. He had a faint hope the Kingdom army, far better trained and more dedicated than anything encountered by the invaders, might keep them out of Krondor, but he recognized it was probably a vain hope.

On another level, the coming seemed an impossibility. He was rich beyond even his boyish dreams of avarice; he possessed the most beautiful woman in the world; and he had a son. Nothing remotely evil could be allowed to touch that perfection.

Roo stopped; he had been so intent on his imagining, he had neglected to turn on the street that led to Helen Jacoby's home. He turned and thought he saw a figure duck out of sight. He quickened his steps and turned the corner, and glanced both ways.

Shopkeepers were closing for the day, and workers were hurrying along, either on their final errands for their masters, or to home or a friendly inn. But the figure he had glimpsed was nowhere to be seen.

Roo shook his head. It must be fatigue, he thought. But he couldn't shake off the feeling he had been followed. He glanced around, then set off toward the Jacoby house.

He thought it had to be the realization that the Emerald Queen's fleet was getting ready to sail. He didn't have any direct intelligence, but he knew enough to understand it was a certainty.

He'd watched as her army had swept over the continent of Novindus, and had sat in council while plans were made to defend the Kingdom against her attack. He could read the signs. He provided as much transport as any firm in the Kingdom; he knew where the supplies were being stored; he knew where the shipments of arms and reserve horses were being readied. He knew the attack was coming soon.

It was early fall in Krondor, which meant it was spring on the other side of the world; soon the massive fleet would be loading, and would start its months-long voyage. Time and again Roo had heard Admiral Nicholas talk about the dangers of sailing through the Straits of Darkness. Difficult in the mildest of weather, it was nearly impossible in the winter. To bring so large a fleet through safely, the ideal time would be almost exactly upon Banapis, Midsummer's Day. Tides and winds would make the narrow passage between the Endless Sea and the Bitter Sea clement enough for those inexperienced ship masters who must be in command of the bulk of the fleet. Given the wholesale carnage visited on Novindus by the Queen that Roo knew about, he couldn't imagine there were six hundred competent captains left alive down there. Besides the wholesale devastation her conquest had visited upon the populace, Novindus boasted no deep-water sailors; they were all coast huggers, captains who didn't suspect there was a land across the sea until Nicholas and his crew had visited there twenty years before.

Roo also suspected Nicholas had a surprise or two in store for the visitors when they attempted to clear the Straits, which was why Roo had made the journey to Queg. The only reason Duke James might require Quegan ships to act as escort for Kingdom merchants would be if the entire Royal Navy was busy elsewhere. No, Nicholas would have something waiting for the invaders as they pushed through the Straits.

He reached the Jacoby house and put the troubling thoughts of invaders behind him for a while.

Helen Jacoby answered his knock, and Roo said, "I hope you don't mind an unannounced visit?"

She laughed and Roo was struck by how nice that sounded. "Rupert, of course not. You are always welcome here."

From behind came the sound of her children calling his name, and Roo found himself struck by a refreshed feeling he seldom experienced elsewhere. "Uncle Rupert!" said Willem, the five-year-old. "Did you bring me something?"

"Willem!" said his mother. "That's no way to treat a guest."

"He's no guest," said Willem indignantly. "He's Uncle Rupert!" Seven-year-old Nataly rushed forward and threw her arms around his waist in a welcoming hug.

Rupert smiled at the boy's brashness and the girl's affection as Helen moved to close the door behind him. As it latched, he realized something: if his calculations were accurate, the invaders would be in sight of Kingdom soil in seven months.

Acting Corporal Garret had looked dubious, but he accepted Erik's orders without comment. After questioning Duga and his men all the previous day, Erik had decided on a course of action. He ordered Garret to lead half the men requisitioned from the Border Barons on a slow march to Krondor, while Erik kept the remaining half with himself. They had turned in their tabards when they left their previous commands, but they still looked like soldiers.

Erik then had them swapping clothing with the captured mercenaries, and after a while judged the results sufficiently chaotic to give the illusion of this being a very large company of mercenaries.

Duga gave his approval: "They look like my boys."

Erik had spent the previous evening talking with Duga. He had come to like the man, a simple no-nonsense captain with a company of eighty men who had come to realize they were in over their heads. It had taken all night, but Erik had at last convinced him that it was in his own best interest to give more than his parole; rather, he should switch sides. Several of his men seemed dubious, and Erik had marked those and sent them off with Garret's squad, while the rest stayed with Erik and Duga.

Later that same day, the second contingent of Kingdom soldiers had ridden past, and Erik instructed them to follow Garret's company. When Duga saw the third company of two hundred come past early the next morning, he commented that he and his men had been led to believe they were invading a country of weak, ill-prepared cities.

Erik had gone on at great length, patiently explaining how things were different here in the Kingdom, and while he downplayed the relative sizes of the two armies, he emphasized the training and equipment of the Kingdom soldiers. Fortunately for his case, he had been aided by the sight of six hundred of the toughest veterans in the King's army riding by.

Duga gladly accepted the rations carried by Erik's men, which they shared for breakfast. "You know," he commented as he ate, "there's not a lot keeping the Queen's army together but fear."

Erik nodded. "I saw that at Maharta."

"It's gotten worse." He glanced around. "Some of the captains tried to desert after that, when we got word we were turning east toward the City of the Serpent River."

"I heard what happened," said Erik. Prince Patrick's spies had reported about the captains being impaled along with some randomly selected soldiers.

"It's as if we're all guarding each other. No one wants to be there, but everyone's afraid to say anything." He shook his head. "No, if you say the wrong thing to the wrong man, you've got a stake pounded up your arse."

Erik considered his next question. "Has anyone asked why you're sent halfway around the world?"

"There's nothing left at home," he said. "Not much plunder when a city's burned to the ground." He lowered his voice. "I don't believe this, but those snakes that stay close to the Queen have been telling everyone who'd listen that this is the richest place in the world, that there's this city called Sethanon"—he pronounced it "Seeth-e-non"—"where the streets are marble, the door handles and latches are all gold, and they use silk for curtains." He sighed. "After what I've seen for the last ten years, I can understand why men want to believe, but you've got to elect to be stupid to believe that nonsense." He lowered his voice even more. "Some of the captains . . . we've talked about trying to do something, but . . ."

"But what?"

"But she's just got too much control."

"Tell me about this," urged Erik.

He motioned with his chin that they should take a walk. When they were out of earshot of the men, Duga said, "I've probably got an agent or two of hers in my company now. You never know. This General Fadawah, he's a bloody genius with his tactics and knowing when to send the men and the like, but he's also a murderous dog. You heard what happened to General Gapi?"

Erik nodded. "Staked out naked over an anthill because he failed."

"And most of the generals and captains had to watch." He hit himself in the chest with his thumb. "I was one of them. It wasn't pretty, I can tell you that."

Duga looked frustrated as he tried to explain. "It's the way they've got us all," he said, closing his hand slowly to demonstrate. "At first it was just another fight. You'd sign up at the rendezvous and go fight, loot, then spend your money. Then we started sacking cities. I remember Calis's Crimson Eagles were on the other side at . . . where was it?"

"Hamsa," supplied Erik. "That was before I signed on, but I heard the story of the siege."

"That's when it started to get ugly. For two hundred sixty–odd days the Queen starved those pitiful bastards; then she unleashed those Saaur raiders on those that fled."

Erik had heard the story of how the survivors of Calis's company had made it to safe haven with the Jeshandi, the nomadic riders of Novindus.

"Things started to look funny to us. We had a captains' meeting, decided some of us had had enough, and went to see General Gapi. He took three of our captains to meet with the Queen, and they never came back.

"That's when we knew. We were in this war as long as it was going to be fought, and any man tried to leave, he was the enemy.

"For a while it wasn't too bad, though. There was plenty of plunder. Women, too, both willing and unwilling. But after a while you get tired, you know?"

Erik nodded. "I know."

"Some of my boys—" He stopped. "None of us are boys anymore. Not a man in my company under thirty years of age, Erik."

Erik said, "I don't know what I can promise you. This is different than anything you've ever seen. This is a nation at war, but I think if you'll either switch sides or stay out of the way, if we get through this we'll find some way to get you home."

"Home?" asked Duga, as if he didn't understand the word. "You have any idea what it's like back home?"

Erik shook his head.

"Farms burned, cattle slaughtered, fruit left to rot on the branches because there's no one to work the orchards. Fields lying choked with weeds because the farmers are either dead or in the army.

"We ate everything."

Erik said, "I don't understand."

"We fought this war for over ten years, from the Westlands through the Riverlands into the Eastlands, and we left nothing behind us.

"Whoever's living down there now is scraping by. There may be some people still living in the burned-out cities. I hear there's a city full of dwarves somewhere up in the Ratn'gari Mountains the Queen was smart enough to leave alone, but if it had humans in it, it was burned to the ground."

Erik could hardly credit what he heard. "Nothing left?"

"Some people hid, and others just lived too far away to bother with, so there's someone living down there. But most of those we left behind were dead, Erik. There are no cities left, and only a few towns with a building standing. If a farmer lived enough distance away, he might have a crop, unless those fleeing the cities ate it. And the sickness . . ." He sighed. "With that many dead, it had to come. Some of our own men got the runs so bad they died from them; couldn't even hold down a drink of water in their stomachs. Others got the black pox. Or some got fevers with no herbs or temple priests around to heal them. It's pure misery back home, that's what it is."

Erik studied the man's face and saw something in his eyes he had never seen in a soldier before. There was a deep horror that had been held in check so long it was not even being acknowledged, and when it at last came to the surface, who knew what might be the result.

Erik put his hand on Duga's shoulder. "There are plenty of living people here." Raising his voice a little, he said, "And I intend to see they stay that way." Smiling, he added, "Even if they're a bunch of scruffy mercenaries too damn far from home for their own good."

Duga's eyes widened slightly as he searched Erik's face, then he nodded once, and turned away quickly, to keep Erik from seeing the moisture gathering in them. To his own men, he shouted, "Look lively, then, we've got to show these Kingdom lads how to be properly scruffy mercenaries."

That got a laugh from some of his men, though most of the Kingdom soldiers didn't understand the dialect he spoke.

Now the camp looked much as it had when Erik had encountered it, save that more than half the men were Kingdom soldiers, and a squad of thirty bowmen was lurking in the trees just out of sight to lend support.

On the third day after the surrender, a sentry reported riders approaching from the south.

"Get ready," Erik instructed his men.

Duga's mercenaries moved with the slow confidence of bored soldiers, while Erik's men kept swords and shields very close to hand. In the trees the archers made ready.

A few minutes later three riders entered the clearing, each dressed in a traveling robe. The leader threw back his hood and revealed a man of middle years, with grey-shot black hair. "Who leads?"

"I do," said Erik.

"What company?" asked a second man.

"Duga's Black Swords," answered Erik.

"You're not Duga!" said the first man.

"No, Kimo, I am." Duga stepped forward.

The man named Kimo said, "He claims to lead."

Duga shrugged. "We got bored waiting for you. He challenged me, and won." He made a show of rubbing his jaw. "Look at the size of him. Damn near broke my head. So, he's in charge."

"What's your name, 'Captain'?" asked Kimo.

Not knowing why, Erik answered, "Bobby."

"Well, Bobby," said Kimo, "your orders are to take your men west from here. Three days' march, you'll come to a small valley with a village in it. Leave that village alone. Don't let them even know you're here. Move past it at night, and head up into the mountains. Find a river that feeds that village, then follow it upward until you come to a branch. Follow the northern branch. You'll find a nice little valley with game. We've also laid in supplies there. Wait until someone comes for you. When that happens, you must return down the river and take that village."

Attempting to look confused, Erik said, "Why wait? Why not just take the village now?"

The man who had been silent spoke, and the hair on Erik's arms and neck stood up, for the voice wasn't human. "You are not paid to ask questions, boy." To Kimo the creature said, "Should we kill this one and turn command back to that one?" He pointed at Duga, and Erik saw a scaled hand, green, with black talons. He had seen Pantathians before, even killed a few, but he felt relaxed only around the dead ones.

"No, we have no time for this. There are other companies to find." The second man took out a map and started to read it.

Erik didn't hesitate. "Kill them!"

The air filled with arrows, and before Kimo and his companions could act, they were literally lifted from their saddles as arrows struck them. Duga's eyes widened and he said, "Why did you do that?"

Erik crossed first to the Pantathian and kicked it to make sure it was dead. Then he went to the second man, and as he knelt next to him, he said, "Because I need this map."

He studied it a moment; then his eyes widened. "Nelson!" he shouted, and one of his men ran over.

"Yes, Sergeant Major!"

"Take two extra horses and go find our men. I want them back as fast as you can bring them. Meet us . . ." He studied the map a moment. "Meet us at the northern bank of the river Tamyth, where it falls. Three days to the east of the road to Hawk's Hollow."

"Yes, Sergeant Major!" Nelson said with a salute and turned.

"And, Nelson," Erik said, halting the man.

"Yes, Sergeant Major?"

"Get your uniform back on. Garret may shoot you down for a bandit before he recognizes you."

Nelson nodded and ran off.

"What's this all about, then?" asked Duga.

Erik held up the map. "There are twenty companies like yours scattered through these hills. And if I read this right, they're all going to seize key points in the hills, opening up the way for the Queen's army to breach those mountains."

Duga said, "I don't follow."

"No," said Erik, "but I do. Jack!"

Another soldier hurried over. "I'm going to draft a message for Knight-Marshal William. You take six men and ride like hell for Krondor."

The soldier hurried off to get ready. Duga followed Erik as he moved toward his own horse. Erik pulled parchment, pen, and ink from his saddle bag. Duga said, "What is this about key points in the hills?"

Erik turned and said, "If you'd moved about much outside this clearing, you'd have seen a range of mountains west of here." With his chin, he indicated a vaguely southeast direction. "Sethanon, that city you spoke of is down that way. There's nothing of marble, gold, and silk about her, but she's important. I'm not quite sure why, but I have it on good authority that if we let your former comrades get there, we're all dead, even those in the Queen's army."

"That doesn't surprise me," said Duga. "She kills men every night."

"Tell me about it later," said Erik. Duga fell silent as Erik wrote. When he was finished, he handed the parchment to the soldier named Jack and said, "With your life!"

The soldier saluted. "Understood, Sergeant Major." Then he ran to where the other six riders waited.

Erik turned to Duga. "Looks like you're about to enlist in the King's army. You're going to fight for gold after all—just on the other side."

Duga shrugged. "I've done it before."

"As I was saying, Sethanon's down there, and the mountains are over there. And the Queen's army is coming over those mountains to get there."

"Ah," said Duga. "Now I see why they went to the trouble of getting us here." He shook his head. "Some of those Pantathians collapsed when they sent the lads in front of us. It took some powerful magic by the look of things. Some of them died."

"That doesn't break my heart," said Erik as he started shouting orders to strike camp.

"What I mean," said Duga, "is they can't send any more soldiers with that magic. Because if they could, they would, don't you see?"

Erik stopped. "You must be right. Else why hide you all down here?"

He scratched his beard. "Some very odd goings-on, if you ask me. Why didn't they just put us in this city of Sethanon?"

"Because you'd all be dead before you got your bearings," answered Erik. He thought it best not to elaborate. The truth was, he didn't know why that was so, but all Duke James and Knight-Marshal William would say was that it wouldn't be possible for the Pantathians to send men directly into Sethanon. Erik suspected it had to do with one or another of the magicians that James was talking about, Pug or that woman Miranda.

Erik didn't dwell further on the question. He had too many things to do. "Duga?"

"Yes?"

"These other companies, do you know them?"

"A couple. Taligar's Lions were the first through. They'll not throw down swords easily—Taligar's got a bitch of a temper and he just doesn't like to lose. Nanfree's Brothers of Iron might listen to reason if I can talk to them before people start bleeding." He grinned. "Nanfree's a smart old fox who likes to work as little for as much gold as he can."

Erik said, "Good. We'll go in and talk to them first, if we can, but if we need to fight, I expect you to know which side you're on."

Duga shrugged. "I forgot which side I was on years ago." He glanced around the woods. "This seems like a nice place. I've had my fill of killing and burning. Might as well pick this land to call home and die for. Don't see much back where we started worth that."

Erik nodded. "That's as good an answer as I could expect."

Duga turned and shouted to his men, "Up we go, lads. It's time to earn some pay." He glanced at Erik, then with a grin he shouted, "You're all soldiers of the King now, so behave yourselves!"

"Wait!" Erik instructed softly.

The defenders had holed up behind some rocks, and Erik had sent bowmen along a ridge above to provide cover fire. For a month he had swept through the Dimwood, using the map to locate and encircle the various companies of the Emerald Queen who were hidden there.

Of the first dozen companies Erik and his men had routed, eight had surrendered and four had fought. Erik had been forced to delegate some of his men to escort the captured soldiers who refused to turn coat to a safe holding place.

His company now numbered eleven hundred men, spread out in five squads. Coordinating efforts was difficult, and he regretted the many horses that were lamed as messengers raced between squads, but all reports indicated the sweep of the Dimwood was going well.

More than once he had wondered how much of this Calis had anticipated, for it seemed too providential that he should just happen to be riding through here with six hundred crack soldiers when the Emerald Queen's advance forces popped into view. Sometime he'd have to remember to ask just where Calis got so much good intelligence.

A scout came running toward Erik, and one of the enemy soldiers behind a rock loosed an arrow that barely missed the man. Erik grabbed him by the tunic and demanded, "What's wrong?"

The soldier was one of Duga's mercenaries. Short of breath, he could blurt out only one word: "Saaur!"

"Where?" demanded Erik.

"That way," said the soldier, turning to look back over his shoulder into the wood.

"How many?" Erik asked as he heard the thunderous pounding of their gigantic mounts echoing through the trees.

"Fifty!"

Erik stood, risking an arrow, and shouted, "Fall back!"

The bowmen who were climbing a distant ridge turned to see what the shout was, and saw Erik waving them back down toward the tree line. They waved acknowledgment and started down.

Erik ducked as two arrows flew at him from the defenders' position and shouted, "Archers! Kill anything coming through those trees."

Erik had fought the Saaur once before, and he had no illusions of this being a simple fight. He might have two hundred men with him, but fifty Saaur were easily their match. And he had a hundred-plus mercenaries who could sally forth at any time, putting Erik squarely between two armed foes.

Erik ran back to where the horses were picketed, and climbed into the saddle. He shouted to one of the nearby soldiers, "Ride to the north. James of Highcastle is up there with his men. Tell him to come as fast as possible."

Even if the soldier found the Corporal from Highcastle and his men and they rode straight back, it might be too late.

The sound of the advancing Saaur was now like a storm about to break over them. Erik glanced around frantically, looking for any advantage. The Saaur averaged nine feet in height, with horses twenty-five hands at the withers. "Into the woods!" shouted Erik.

Then the Saaur came crashing into view. Armored with helms, breastplates, greaves, and bracers, the riders looked like a soldier's worst nightmare. Reptilian faces showed more emotion than Erik ever would have imagined before meeting them, and the expression on their faces was anger. A Saaur wearing the flowing horsetail plume of an officer led the charge. "Die, traitors!" he cried as he saw Erik's men pulling back.

The fight became a blur. Erik dodged around trees, attempting to strike at the hocks of the larger animals, avoiding the powerful blows of the Saaur. Erik had once charged a Saaur rider, and he knew just how much more powerful they could be. From the screams around him, punctuated with curses, it was clear other men were discovering this fact the hard way.

Erik lost track of time and let the battle flow. He knew that by giving his men a chance to survive in the trees he had lost any hope of organizing the fight. More distant shouts led him to believe the company they had been readying to attack had joined the fray.

A Saaur bore down on him from behind, and Erik felt the approach more than heard it, moving his horse around a tree just in time to avoid being overrun. As the alien rider swept past, Erik put heels to his horse's flanks and took out after another Saaur, moving in a different direction. It was clear to Erik that attacking these giant creatures from behind was the best course of action.

The air hissed with arrows and Erik prayed they came from his archers taking Saaur riders out of saddles, and not the other side killing his men. He came up behind the Saaur he followed as the rider reined in to catch his bearings. The creature was half-turned in the saddle when Erik caught him with his sword point, thrusting as deeply into the creature's ribs as he could. The shocked Saaur looked down at the smaller human, astonishment being the only possible word to describe the expression on that alien face, and then he fell backward out of the saddle, almost ripping the sword from Erik's hands.

Throughout the afternoon they rode through the trees, a crazy weaving dance of death with both sides dying more from blunders than from the other side's tactics. Then a horn sounded and Erik turned to see more riders entering the woods. He expected to see his men from the north, but these riders were coming from the south, as best he could judge.

"What now?" he muttered to himself, his voice barely more than an exhausted croak.

Suddenly Calis rode into view, and horse archers started picking off Saaur who were locked in combat with Erik's men. Erik saw his Captain point behind Erik and shout something, but he couldn't hear what he said over the din of fighting.

Then the world exploded in pain and Erik saw the ground rising up to strike him. The breath was knocked from him. His shrieking horse fell on his leg, and he barely kept his wits about him. More by instinct than thought, he disentangled himself from his thrashing animal, blood spraying from a wound to the horse's flank.

A Saaur rider turned his animal as Calis charged, and Erik struggled to his feet. He put his hand to his head and found his helmet gone. Blood covered his hand when he brought it away, but he couldn't tell if it was his or the horse's.

The rider ignored Erik and charged Calis. Erik braced his hand on the trunk of a tree to support himself, then knelt to pick up his sword. Nausea knotted his stomach and his head swam from the effort, but he stayed conscious. He quickly killed his dying horse and looked to see Calis engaged with the Saaur.

If the Saaur that Erik had killed had looked surprised, it was nothing compared to the expression on this one's face at the first blow Calis delivered to the creature's shield. Erik was certain nothing could have prepared that rider for the impact of someone as strong as Calis. The blow knocked the creature from his saddle.

Then it was quiet. Erik opened his eyes and realized he was sitting on the ground, his back against the tree. Someone had put a tunic over his legs and a rolled-up shirt behind his head.

A familiar voice said, "You took a nasty one to the head."

Erik turned to see Calis standing nearby. Erik said, "I think I've been hit worse."

"I'm sure. Blade glanced off the back of your helmet and that rock head of yours and struck your horse behind the saddle. Broke its spine. You're a lucky man, von Darkmoor. A couple of inches farther forward and he would have split you in two."

Erik's head rang and throbbed. "I don't feel lucky," he said. Taking a drink of water from a skin held before him, he asked, "What brings you to this dark and lonely place?"

Calis said, "I got your message, but mostly it was because I gave you orders to be back in Krondor in two months."

Erik smiled and it made his head hurt worse. "I told you I needed three."

"Orders are orders."

"Does it help that I brought you two thousand men instead of six hundred and have captured or killed another thousand of the Queen's army?"

Calis considered this a moment. "A little. But not much." Then he smiled.

Eight

Evolution

MIRANDA SPOKE.

"Where are we?"

Pug heard the words, though he knew they were projections of her mind. He wondered at that peculiar aspect of the human mind which sought always to force something to fit its perceptions, irrespective of what the true nature of the thing might be.

"On our way to heaven," he answered.

"How long have we been traveling?" she asked. "It seems like years."

"Funny," answered Pug. "It seems but moments to me. Time is warped."

"Acaila was right," she observed.

"He usually is," said Pug.

The region they traveled through was a multicolored distortion of space, or at least that was how Pug viewed it. Stars swam through vortices of violent colors, rather than the void of night he expected. And the stars were as often as not colorless.

"I've never seen anything like this," said Miranda, and to Pug's mind she seemed to whisper in awe. "How do you know where to go?"

"I follow the line," he answered, indicating with a thought the fragile line of force they were following from Midkemia.

"It goes on forever," she said.

"I doubt it, but I think Macros the Black went on a very long journey when he last left Midkemia."

"We're following his journey?"

"Apparently," said Pug.

They voyaged through the cosmos, and at last they descended to a world, a green and blue orb that circled a star. Around it circled three moons.

"We're back where we started," said Miranda.

Pug turned his attention to the world below, and it was indeed Midkemia. "No," he said. "I think we've come to a time much earlier than when we left."

"Time travel?"

"I've done it before," he answered.

"You must tell me of this someday."

Pug projected amusement. "I've never been fully in charge of those events. And I've always felt the risks far outweighed the benefits."

"You don't think traveling in time to kill this Emerald Queen in her crib would be a good idea?" she asked, and Pug detected the familiar dry humor in the question.

"We can't, or else we would have."

"There is that paradox, isn't there?"

"More, there are laws that we can't begin to contemplate." He fell silent, and Miranda couldn't judge if it was a moment or a year before he spoke again. "All of reality as we know it is but an illusion, a dream of some agency we can barely comprehend."

"It sounds so trivial, put that way."

"It's not. It may be the most profound thing humankind is able to comprehend."

They moved down toward a scene familiar to Pug. Standing near the wreckage of the city of Sethanon was an army, led by King Lyam. Pug felt odd emotions as he viewed himself, fifty years earlier, listening to Macros's good-bye, again.

"What's he saying?" asked Miranda.

"Listen," said Pug.

A younger Pug said, "Yes, but it is still a hard thing."

A tall, thin man, wearing a brown robe with a whipcord belt and sandals, said, "All things come to an end, Pug. Now is the end of my time upon this world. With the ending of the Valheru presence, my powers have returned fully. I will move on to something new. Gathis will join me, and the others at my island are cared for, so I have no more duties here."

Miranda said, "Gathis didn't leave!"

Pug said, "I know."

She focused her attention on her lover and felt something that was familiar. "You find this funny?"

"Ironic, perhaps," came the answer.

Macros the Black, legendary sorcerer supreme, was bidding good-bye to a younger Tomas, who stood resplendent in his gold-and-white armor.

Miranda said, "He's doing it again, isn't he?"

"What?" asked Pug.

"Lying to you."

"No, not this time," answered Pug. "He honestly believes what he's saying about the Pantathians and Murmandamus."

Macros said, ". . . the powers granted to the one who posed as Murmandamus were no mean set of conjurer's illusions. He was a force. To have created such a one and to have captured and manipulated the hearts of even a race as dark as the moredhel required much. Perhaps without the Valheru influence across the barriers of space and time, the serpent people may become much as others, just another intelligent race among many." He stared into the distance a moment. "Then again, perhaps not. Be wary of them."

"He was right on that count," said Miranda. "The Pantathians could never be redeemed. The Valheru heritage has warped them beyond redemption."

"No," said Pug. "It's something else. Something much larger."

Pug and Miranda watched as Macros finished his good-byes, and Pug felt stirrings of old emotions. "It was a difficult time," he said to Miranda.

He sensed more than heard her understanding.

Macros, more than any other man in Pug's life, was the central figure in Pug's development. Pug still had dreams of his days in the Assembly of Magicians on the world of Kelewan, dreams in which Macros was among his teachers. Pug knew there were things still locked away in his head, things that only Macros or time could unlock.

Pug and Miranda saw Macros turn and walk away from the assembled army, from Pug and Tomas. As he moved, he began to fade from sight.

"Cheap theatrics," said Miranda.

"No, more," said Pug. "Watch."

He shifted his perceptions and saw that Macros was not vanishing from sight but was changing. His body continued to walk, but it became intangible, a thing of mists and smoke. Power flowed upward as Macros spoke to some unseen agency.

"What is this?" asked Miranda.

"I'm not sure," answered Pug. "But I have suspicions."

"Master," said Macros to the unseen agent. "What is your bidding?"

"Come, it is time," said the voice.

Miranda and Pug sensed joy in the sorcerer as he rose up on mystic energies, flying into the void much as Miranda and Pug had in Elvandar.

"Look!" said Miranda, and below they could see his body lying upon the ground. "Has he died?"

"Not really," said Pug, "but his soul is moving elsewhere. That is what we must follow."

Through years and across vast distances, they flew in close pursuit, chasing the very essence of Macros the Black. Again time had no meaning as they moved across the vast gulf between stars, only to return to Midkemia at last, to be confronted again with a new vista, as they descended from the skies to a point high above the vast peaks of the Ratn'gari Mountains.

"We've been here before!" said Miranda.

"No," said Pug. "I mean, yes, we've been here, but not yet."

"Look, there's the Celestial City you created."

"No," answered Pug. "This is the real thing."

Across the peaks of mountains capped with snow sprawled a city of incredible beauty. Crystal pillars held aloft roofs like giant diamonds, brilliant facets sparking with an inner fire. Pug said, "Below, thousands of feet below the clouds, rests the Necropolis. This is where I led you, and this resembles the illusion I created for you, but mine was a shadow to this."

Miranda agreed. "This is solidity where your illusion was smoke and shadow, but it also feels less real."

"What I built was created to fool your physical senses. This is a thing of the mind. We are experiencing it through direct contact, without any instrument of perception intervening."

"I understand," she said, "yet I am disoriented."

Pug suddenly shifted before her eyes, and he was as she knew him, a man of solid form, a body as familiar to her as her own. "Is this better?" he asked, and the words seemed to issue from his mouth.

"Yes," she answered.

"You can do the same. You have only to will it so."

She concentrated and suddenly felt herself become solid, and, holding up her hand before her eyes, she saw it as she expected it to be, solid flesh.

"It is but another illusion," said Pug, "but one that will give you a firmer foundation upon which to stand."

The hall in which they stood was similar to the one of illusion Pug had created to deceive Miranda when they had first met. When she had first come searching for Pug, he had led her a merry chase, finally ending up in the Ratn'gari Mountains, only a short distance from here. He had created an illusionary version of this place in which to hide from her.

Miranda said, "This is similar, but so much more!" The ceilings above were vaults of heaven themselves; lights shone down that were stars. Miranda saw that where in Pug's illusion small areas had been set aside for the worship of each of the gods, here the areas were the size of cities.

In the distance, the line of energy they had followed from the time of Macros's departure to the present descended in a gentle arc, coming down from the ceiling, and disappearing beyond their perception.

As they moved toward it, they passed an intersection of two paths, and stood where the areas of four gods touched. Odd stirrings in the air caused Miranda to say, "Can you feel that?"

"Again, shift your perception," Pug told her.

Miranda experimented, and suddenly the hall was filled with shadowy figures. Like the energy beings they had become in the groves of Elvandar, these beings lacked features and identifying marks. But where Pug and Miranda had been brilliant beings of light, these were shadowy figures, barely perceptible with a faint illumination.

"What are they?"

"Prayers," answered Pug. "Each person who prays to the gods is heard. We perceive that prayer as an icon of the person praying."

Miranda moved down the path and looked upward. A huge statue, many times the size of a human, rested upon a throne of azure. The figure was of a man, still and white, with a faint blue tinge. His eyes were closed. Few of the shadow figures moved near this statue.

"Who is this?" she asked.

"Eortis, dead God of the Sea. Killian tends his domain until he returns."

"He's dead, but he's returning?"

"You'll understand more, soon, but for now suffice it to say that if my suspicions are right, there is far more concerned with this war than merely defeating mad creatures bent on mindless destruction." He led her to another intersection. Pointing at a distant wall, he said, "Turn your mind's eye toward that distant vista, and tell me what you see."

She did as she was bid and at last a giant symbol appeared on the wall. It was incomprehensible to her for what seemed a very long time, then it resolved itself into a pattern. "I see a Seven-Pointed Star of Ishap, above a field of twelve points in a circle."

"Look deeper," he instructed.

She did so and after a minute another pattern resolved itself. "I see another pattern, with four bright lights overlapping the top four points of the star. And there are many dim points between the twelve bright ones."

"Of the three points of the star below those that are brightly lit, tell me what you see."

Miranda concentrated on them, and after a moment she saw what Pug meant. "One of them is dimly alight! The one in the center. The one to the right of it . . ." She faltered.

"What?" he asked.

"It's not dim! It's . . . blocked. Something is preventing it from being seen!"

Pug said, "That is what I perceive, too. What of the remaining light?"

"It is dead."

"Then I think I may be close to knowing the truth." The tone he projected into her mind led her to think he wasn't pleased to learn this particular truth.

They continued along. They reached the farthest corner of the Hall of the Gods and found themselves between two statues. One was totally lifeless, and Pug said, "Wodar-Hospur, the dead God of Knowledge. So much we might know if he were to return."

"Does no one worship knowledge anymore?"

"A few," said Pug, "but might and riches seem to occupy humankind's time more than anything else. Of all the men I've met, only Nakor seems truly driven to know."

"Know what?"

"Everything," he answered with amusement.

They turned and regarded the other statue. The faint line that had been the spirit of Macros descended into the head of the statue. Miranda looked at the features and gasped. "Macros!"

"No," answered Pug. "Look at the name across the foot of his statue."

"Sarig," she said. "Who is he?"

"The not-quite-so-dead God of Magic."

"That's Macros the Black!" she blurted, and for the first time since he had known her, Pug saw in Miranda's visage true confusion and even a little fear. "Macros is a god?" asked Miranda, and for the first time since he had met her, Pug sensed a genuine flash of concern in her voice. The mocking, dry humor was gone.

"Yes," he answered, "and no."

"Which is it?"

"We'll know better when we talk to him," answered Pug. "I think I know the answer, but I want to hear it from him." Pug willed himself into the air, until he stood before the giant, immobile statue's face. Loudly he called, "Macros!"

He was greeted by silence.

Miranda "moved" to stand next to Pug, and said, "What now?"

"He sleeps. He dreams."

"What is all this?" she asked. "I still don't understand."

"Macros the Black is attempting to rise to godhood," answered Pug. "He seeks to fill the void left by the departure of Sarig. Or Sarig created Macros the Black so that someday he would rise to replace him. Something like that." He pointed to the line of force. "That line still functions, and at the other end we'll find the mortal body that we know as Macros, but the mind, the essence, the soul—that is here, within this being that is forming. They are one and yet different, connected yet apart."

"How long will it take, this rising to godhood?" asked Miranda, not attempting to hide the awe in her voice.

"Ages," answered Pug softly.

"What do we do?"

"We wake him up."

The illusion that was Pug closed his eyes and focused his attentions within. Miranda felt energy building within the sorcerer and a mighty magic being forged. She waited, but when she expected some sort of release of energy, it continued to build. Soon she was in awe, for while she had thought she understood the magic arts and the limits of Pug's talents, she saw she was wrong on both counts. After moments more, she became truly astonished, for while her own knowledge of magic was not inconsequential, this was a feat beyond her capacity.

Suddenly an explosion in the air rent the image before them. The sound of a thousand cymbals clashing rang, deafening the senses. Light exploded outward, and Miranda saw something, for only an instant: the eyes of Macros opened, regarding them.

Into darkness they plunged, and the last thing she heard was a faint, plaintive "No!"

Pug's mind reached out to touch her own. "This is difficult. I will attempt to follow him to where he flees. Our bodies will appear wherever we wish them to be, so follow me as I follow Macros."

"I know how," she answered, and sensed him leave.

Suddenly the blackness was everywhere, and for an instant Miranda felt fear, for she had no point of reference.

Then she opened her eyes.

She was cold. The stone floor of the room seemed to drain the warmth from her body, and she sat up, shivering. She was in Pug's study at Stardock! She knew what the elven Spellweavers had told them, that their bodies would appear wherever they were needed when they returned from their spiritual journey, but she had expected to be still in Elvandar. Now she was hundreds of miles distant. Pug lay unconscious next to her, barely breathing. She had no idea how long they had been gone from Acaila and Tathar's care, but it was clear to her that Pug was only minutes from death if he did not revive. Miranda tried to focus a spell of location to cast upon him; he might vanish at any second, and if she didn't have the spell ready, finding him might be more difficult.

Forcing herself to clarity, she was about to chant the spell when Pug sat up. He took a gasping, painful breath, and then another.

Aborting the spell, she said, "What?"

Pug blinked and took more deep breaths. "I don't know. The line that bound Macros to Sarig was severed, and that which recoiled flew back toward Midkemia. I followed Macros's mind and suddenly I was here."

Miranda stood up, and Pug did likewise. Both of them were cold and stiff, and movement was difficult at first. Pug paced a little to restore circulation. "That's the second time I've done this, and it was no more pleasant than the first."

"Where is Macros?" asked Miranda.

"He must be close by. That's the only answer."

He moved to the door of the study and opened it, hurrying down the stairs of the tower. He pushed open the lower door and almost knocked over a young student, whose eyes widened. "Master Pug!" he exclaimed.

Pug and Miranda ignored the startled student and moved toward the main entrance to the Academy. As they passed, students and teachers both turned to stare, and by the time they reached the main entrance to Stardock, the calling of his name had almost become a chant: "Pug! Pug!"

Pug was breathless from excitement. "I can feel him! He's close by."

Miranda said, "I can, too."

They went outside and looked around. Pug pointed. "There!"

At the edge of the lake a knot of excited students had gathered, and Pug could hear Nakor's voice shouting, "Stand back!"

A man hung in the air, and Pug could sense the energies that danced around him. He was a beggar by his look, filthy, wearing only a dirty loincloth, his hair and beard a dirty mat, but he exuded power. The air sparkled as he seemed to be drawn up in the air, along the thread of energy that Pug had followed from the Celestial City.

Pug and Miranda hurried to where the students were assembled, and Pug ordered, "Stand aside."

One looked over his shoulder. "Master Pug!" At the sound of his name, others backed away.

Sitting at the edge of the water were Nakor and Sho Pi, watching in rapt attention as the man hovered in the air.

"Do you see?" said Nakor as Pug came up to him. "He attempts to rise, but that other force, that thing in the air, it's falling back here, toward the water."

If Nakor felt any surprise at Pug's appearance at Stardock, he did not show it. "Something marvelous has happened," said Nakor, "and soon we shall know a truth." He glanced at Pug. "Or maybe you know it already."

The beggar floated down into the water, where he sat, waist deep. Pug watched as the thread of energy coiled down from the sky and at last seemed to vanish into the water around the man. He was weeping.

Pug moved into the water and knelt next to the man. "Macros?"

After a moment, the slender man turned to regard Pug. In a hoarse whisper he said, "Do you know what you've done? I was on the verge of godhood." He closed his eyes for a moment and a sob shook his shoulders. Then he took a deep breath. "The knowledge, the understanding—it's leaving, like water spilling from a vessel too shallow to hold it." He pointed to his own head and closed his eyes, as if trying to hold on to some image. At last he went on, "It's as if I saw the universe in its entirety, but was looking through a hole in a fence, and as you pull me back from the fence I see less and less by the second. . . . Moments ago I could have told you the secrets of the universe! Now, even as I try to remember, concepts fall away from me, and all I'm left with is the knowledge of what I've lost! Years of work undone."

"We had need," said Pug softly.

"My time here was done!" insisted Macros, standing and looking at his successor. His knees were wobbly. "It was not your place to call me back. My next mission was beyond your understanding."

"Obviously not," said Miranda.

Macros looked to the woman without recognition. Then his eyes narrowed. "Miranda?"

"Hello, Daddy," said the woman. "It's been a while."

Pug turned, his face showing surprise.

Nakor laughed as he echoed, " 'Daddy'?"

Macros the Black, sorcerer of legend, glanced from Pug to Miranda and said, "We need to talk." He took a deep breath and said, "I think I've regained my composure."

"Good," said Miranda, "because we're about to hand you another shock."

Macros paused and seemed to brace himself. "All right, what is it?"

"It's Mother," answered Miranda. "She's trying to destroy the world."

Even Nakor could barely contain his astonishment at that remark. Finally Macros said, "I need a drink."

Miranda wrinkled her nose. "First you need a bath."

While Macros bathed, Miranda, Pug, and Nakor sat in Pug's study. Sho Pi was attending the needs of the sorcerer, and Pug was opening a bottle of particularly good wine from Darkmoor.

"You need to share something with me," said Miranda.

Pug looked at his lover and said, "Seems we both need to do some sharing. 'Daddy'?"

Nakor grinned. "I think that would make me your stepfather, except I was Jorna's first husband, and Macros her second."

"She called herself Jania when I was born," said Miranda. She seemed oblivious to the little man's delight in all this, and instead revealed what looked to be barely controlled fury. To Pug she said, "That stunt of yours in the Celestial City, when you removed Macros from the consciousness of Sarig—"

"What!" said Nakor, his eyes wide. "I must hear of this."

"What about it?" said Pug.

"I could feel what you were doing."

"And?"

"The power, the sheer scope of the energies you used . . . you could have destroyed the Emerald Queen and her pitiful band of Pantathians as I could step on an anthill! Why has this war gone on so long, Pug? Why haven't you acted to stop it?"

Pug sighed. "Because, like ants, those that survived would only scurry off into the dark and begin again. And there's more."

"What?" asked Miranda.

From the door, Macros said, "Nothing we can speak of here, not yet. Pug, it's too dangerous."

Pug indicated an empty chair and the freshly bathed sorcerer sat and took the cup that was waiting for him. Macros wore a borrowed robe, black instead of his usual brown. After a long sip he said, "Excellent. There are advantages, after all, to being alive."

Nakor said, "I'm Nakor."

Macros's eyes narrowed. He studied Nakor's face a moment before the recognition dawned. "The Isalani! I know you. You cheated me at cards once."

"I'm the one." With enough emotion to almost bring tears to his eyes, Nakor admitted, "You were my greatest challenge." He turned to Pug. "I was wrong when I said Macros wouldn't remember me."

Macros pointed at Nakor. "That scoundrel did the only thing he could: he made me think he was using magic so when I erected my defenses he could manipulate the cards with simple sleight of hand."

"Sleight of hand?" said Pug.

"He stacked the deck!" Macros said with a laugh.

"Not really," said Nakor modestly. "I switched the cards and slipped in a cold deck."

"Will you stop it!" exclaimed Miranda, slamming her hand on the table. "This is not some reunion of dear friends. This is . . ."

"What?" asked Pug.

"I don't know. We're trying to save the world, and you're reminiscing about card games."

Pug saw Sho Pi in the doorway, and he motioned for the young man to close the door, leaving the four of them in privacy. Sho Pi nodded, shut the door, and left.

Pug said, "First, I'd like to ask about this relationship. Seems you all have ties I knew nothing about."

Macros said, "To all of you."

Pug suddenly looked alarmed. "Don't tell me I'm your unacknowledged son." He glanced at Miranda and saw his concern mirrored on her face.

"You can relax," said Macros. "You're not her brother." He sighed. "But when I said you were as much a son to me as any I have fathered, I meant it." He sipped his wine and remembered. "When you were born, I sensed greatness in you, lad. You were the son of a maid in Crydee, and a wandering soldier. But as the Tsurani sense power in children and train them to the Assembly, I saw you had greatness, perhaps more than any living magician on this world."

"And you did what?" asked Nakor.

"I unlocked that magic. Else how could Pug have come to the Greater Magic?"

"Sarig?" asked Pug.

Macros nodded. "I am his creature."

"Sarig?" said Nakor. "I thought he was a legend."

"He is," said Miranda, "and a dead god, to boot. But he's obviously not as dead as some think."

Pug said, "Why don't you start at the beginning."

"And this time, the truth," added Miranda.

Macros shrugged. "The story I told you and Tomas, to wile away the time we spent in the Garden of the City Forever, was a far more entertaining one than the truth, Pug.

"I was nothing as a child. A city boy from a distant land—"

"Stop it!" said Miranda. "You're doing it again, Father!"

Macros sighed. "Very well, I was born in the city of Kesh. My father was a tailor and my mother a wonderful person, a woman who managed my father's accounts, kept an orderly house, and raised a willful and disobedient son. My father had many rich merchants among his clientele and we lived well enough. Satisfied?" he asked his daughter.

She nodded.

"But I developed a taste for adventure, or at least for rough company. When I was little more than a lad, I went on a trip with some of my friends, without the knowledge or blessings of my parents. We bought a map, one reputed to show the location of a lost treasure."

Nakor nodded. "Slavers."

Macros said, "Yes. It was a trap to lure foolish boys who would end up on the Durbin slave block."

"How long ago was this?" asked Pug.

"Nearly five hundred years ago," said Macros. "At the height of the Empire's power.

"I escaped the slavers and hid in the mountains, but I got lost. Almost dead from starvation, I found an ancient, abandoned temple. Half delirious, I collapsed on the altar and prayed to whatever god ruled that shrine to save me, in exchange for which I'd serve him."

Macros blinked, as if trying to remember. "I don't remember exactly what occurred next. But I think I spoke to Sarig, and either I died and he took me before I went to the Hall of Lims-Kragma, or he got me just before my death; but from that moment on, I was Sarig's creature.

"It may be my prayer was the first to him since the Chaos Wars, though someone had to have built that shrine. Maybe someday I'll know. But whatever else, that dying prayer opened an avenue, a conduit if you will, and from that ruined temple I emerged no longer a boy but a man of magic. I knew things as if I possessed memories of them, yet I know they weren't my memories. Sarig was within me, and part of me was within Sarig."

"No wonder you had such power," said Pug.

Macros looked from face to face. "To understand what I'm about to tell you, you need put aside all prejudices and preconceptions.

"The gods are both real and illusion. They are real in that they exist and exert force over this world and our lives. They are illusions in that they are nothing like what we perceive them to be."

Nakor laughed his cackling laugh. "This is wonderful!"

Pug nodded.

Macros said, "Forces exist in nature, and we interact with them. As we think of them, some of them become what we think."

"Wait a minute," said Miranda. "You've lost me."

"Think of ancient humans, huddled in a cave and contemplating the wonder of fire. On a cold, wet night, it's their friend and a source of life. They give to that fire a personality, and after a while they worship it. Then that evolves into the worship of the spirit of fire, which in turn becomes the god of fire."

"Prandur," said Pug.

"Exactly," said Macros. "And when enough people worship, the energy that we call Prandur begins to manifest certain aspects, certain attributes that match the expectations of the worshippers."

Nakor was almost beside himself with glee. "Man creates the gods!" he exclaimed.

"In a manner of speaking," said Macros. His eyes reflected a deep pain. "For most of my life I've been a part of Sarig, his agent on Midkemia and elsewhere, his eyes and ears, and I thought my ultimate fate was to merge with him, to assume his mantle and return magic in all its glory to Midkemia." Glancing at Pug, he said, "You were one of my better experiments. You returned the Greater Magic to Midkemia."

"This is all very interesting," said Miranda, "but what about Mother?"

Nakor lost his grin. "I think Jorna is dead."

Miranda said, "What? How do you know?"

"When I last saw her, I sensed that another inhabited her body, and that which we knew as your mother was absent. I can only assume she is dead, or hidden away someplace."

Pug asked, "How do all of you fit in this?"

Nakor said, "When I was young, I met a girl named Jorna, who was beautiful and smart and who seemed interested in me." He grinned. "I am not what you would call a handsome man, nor was I when I was young. But as all young men, I wished to be loved by a beautiful woman.

"She didn't love me, however. She loved power, and she hungered after what you call magic. She wanted to stay young and beautiful forever. She feared death, and growing old even more.

"So I showed her tricks. I showed her how to manipulate what I call 'stuff,' and when she had learned all I could teach her, she left me."

"And found me," said Macros. He glanced at Miranda. "I met your mother in Kesh, and she was as Nakor described, a beautiful young woman who pursued me with ardor. I ignored her hunger for power. I was blinded by youthful romance. Despite my age and ability, I acted young and foolish. I discovered her deceit later, after you were born, Miranda, but before she could learn all I could teach—she was centuries removed from that possibility, though she didn't know it—and I refused to show her more."

Miranda said, "So you took me from her and left me with strangers. I was ten years old!"

"No," said Macros. "I accepted you when she left us both, and found you good people to raise you. I know I only visited you briefly, from time to time, but . . . it was difficult."

Pug said, "And was this when you became the 'Black Sorcerer'?"

"Yes," said Macros. "Dealing with humanity at that level was too painful, and I didn't know it at the time, but Sarig had uses for me. The gods move in ways we cannot understand, so much of what drove me was compulsion or desire, and clear goals were seldom mine. I found that island, abandoned by those who lived there, the people who had built that lovely villa. I assume they were a family of Keshians, probably nobles from Queg, who fled there when the secession occurred. And I built the black castle, to scare away travelers, and life became much as it was when you first came to the isle, Pug. What was that, fifty, sixty years ago?"

Pug nodded. "Sometimes it seems like yesterday when Kulgan and I stood on the beach reading your message." Pug studied the sorcerer's face. "But so much of what you've done, so much of what you've told me, it's all been lies and deceit."

"Yes, but much of it was truth, as well. I could sense my future, even see it clearly at times. That was never a lie. My life was shown to me in idle thoughts, random dreams, and visions that would come unexpectedly. Were he still living in full, Sarig could have given me more, but were he still alive as we think of such things, he wouldn't need me."

"So when you told me that I was to take your place," said Pug, "you really thought you were done here?"

"Yes," said Macros. "That bit of story telling I gave you, about kings to advise and wars to stop, was just that, something to divert your interest from me, to let me find my own way without your coming to find me when you needed some advice!"

Pug saw Macros's anger growing again. "If you were to have become one with Sarig, I would not have been allowed to draw you back, Macros. He wouldn't have permitted it."

The anger lessened but didn't entirely vanish. Pug could see it smoldering below the surface, like a banked fire.

"There is that," Macros admitted. "The problem is that I know how much I've forgotten." Tears gathered in his eyes. "I . . . can't explain."

Nakor's gaze narrowed. "But was it you?"

"What do you mean?" asked Macros.

"Were you the one who knew, or was it this God of Magic?"

Macros said softly, "I don't know."

Pug said, "What do you mean?"

"Correct me if I'm wrong," Nakor said to Macros, "but as you became more godlike, didn't your sense of 'self' lessen? Didn't you feel more detached from who you were?"

Macros nodded. "That is true. My life became a dream, a dim memory."

"I suspect that had you achieved godhood, you'd not have known it, for you, the mind we call Macros, would have ceased to exist," observed Nakor.

Macros considered this. "I will have to ponder that."

Miranda said, "What about the Queen? Why isn't she my mother?"

Nakor shrugged. "I don't know. Maybe she made the wrong deal with the Pantathians. When she was Lady Clovis, she was hungering after eternal youth, and she was practicing some very nasty necromancy. Bad things to do, and she really was in over her head. That was twenty years ago, so who knows what has happened since then. She may have been punished for her failing in the plot with the Overlord of the City of the Serpent River and his magician, or it may be simply expedient for whatever has taken her over to use her this way. I don't know. But I do know that the woman who was once wed to both of us is probably dead."

Pug turned to Miranda. "If it's time for making a clean breast of things, why don't you tell us your part in this?"

Miranda said, "When I began to manifest powers, I hid that fact from my foster parents. They tried to get me interested in marrying one of the local merchants, so I ran away." She glared at Macros. "That was two hundred fifty years ago, if you'd bothered to come investigate!"

Macros could only say, "I'm sorry."

"I found a magician, an old woman named Gert." She smiled as she said, "When I need to, I can look like her, and given some men's response to a pretty face and a round bosom, it's a good thing to know."

"That's a very good trick," agreed Nakor.

"She was hideous to look at, but she had the soul of a Saint of Sung, and she took me in. She quickly recognized my abilities and taught me what she knew. After she died, I began seeking out others who could teach.

"About fifty years ago, I was arrested by the Keshian Secret Police. A fox of a man named Raouf Manif Hazara-Khan saw in me a great weapon, so he recruited me."

"Hazara-Khan is a well-known name in Krondor," said Pug. "Wasn't he the brother of Kesh's ambassador to Krondor?"

"The same. His brother had reported some very strange things about the battle of Sethanon, not the least of which was the appearance of dragon riders in the sky, a gigantic explosion of green fire, and the utter destruction of one of the Kingdom's more modest cities.

"So they set me to the task of discovering exactly what was going on."

"And?" said Pug.

"And I deserted."

Nakor positively cackled with glee. "That's wonderful!"

"When I began discovering the truth, I realized we were involved with much more important things than serving one nation or another."

"That's certain," said Pug. "We've got some interesting problems to confront, and some choices to make."

"Most important," said Nakor, "we have to discover who is behind all these things that are going on."

"The third player," said Miranda.

Macros said, "I know who it is."

"The Demon King," said Miranda.

"No," said Pug. Looking at Macros, he said, "If it's as I think it is, the situation is such that we may not even discuss it safely."

"Certainly not here," agreed Macros. "And we could use an expert on certain lore from the Order of Ishap."

"Which means we need to go to Sarth," said Pug.

Macros yawned. "Very well, but I could use a nap first."

Nakor got up. "I'll take you to my apartment. It has extra bedrooms in it."

Pug stood as well. "Don't let him keep you up all night," he said to Macros, and he and Nakor left.

Pug turned to Miranda. "Well, it seems we're finally getting to the heart of things."

Miranda said, "Maybe. My father is a self-confessed liar, remember?"

"And you?"

"I've never lied to you," she said defensively.

"But you've hidden things from me."

"What about you?" she said, her tone accusatory. "You still haven't told me why you don't just fly across the water and sink the Queen's fleet. I saw what you did. I couldn't believe the power you control."

Pug said, "I can explain that, but not until we're someplace safe."

"Safe from what?"

"I can't explain that until then, either."

Miranda shook her head. "You irritate me at times, Pug."

Pug laughed. "I expect I do. You're not exactly without edges yourself."

She stood up and crossed to stand before him. Putting her arms around him, she said, "One truth: I love you."

He said, "I love you, too. . . . And I never thought I'd hear myself say that to another woman after Katala died."

"Well, it's about time," she said.

Pug hesitated. "What about Calis?"

"I love him, as well." When she felt Pug tense, she said, "But in a different way. He's a friend and very special to me. And he needs a great deal and asks for so very little. If we live through this, I think I can help him find happiness."

Pug said, "Does that mean you're choosing him?"

Miranda drew back slightly so she could look Pug in the eyes. "No, stupid. It means I think I know a few things about him and what he truly needs."

"Like what?"

"Let's all live through this, first, then I'll tell you."

He smiled and kissed her. They lingered in their embrace, then she hugged him tight and whispered in his ear, "Maybe."

He slapped her on the bottom and she laughed. Then he kissed her again.

Nine

Plots

ERIK SHIFTED HIS WEIGHT.

His dress uniform was uncomfortable, and his head still hurt from the blow he had taken the previous week. Now it was merely a dull throb when he turned too quickly or when he was exerting himself, which was every day.

The Novindus mercenaries who had agreed to come over to the King's service were proving an interesting training problem for Jadow Shati and the other sergeants. With Alfred promoted to sergeant, Erik was depending on a new bully in his company, a Corporal Harper.

As Erik rubbed absently at the back of his head, Calis said, "Still hurts?"

Erik said, "Less each day, but you were right about that Saaur's blow. Two inches more and I'd have been cut in half."

Calis nodded as the Prince and his retinue entered the room. Patrick said, "Let's get this meeting under way."

Nicholas, uncle to the Prince of Krondor and Admiral in command of the Western Fleet of the Kingdom, said, "Our latest intelligence tells us they will absolutely be coming this way: a quick strike through Krondor and over the mountains to Sethanon."

Patrick nodded. "I agree, though my father is still concerned about the possibility we're being intentionally fed false reports and the fleet will end up sailing around the world to Salador, in an attempt to reach Sethanon from the east."

"That was a possibility, but always very unlikely," said Calis. "Now we know it's not remotely probable."

Erik studied the others at the conference, feeling far out of his depth. Sitting next to the Prince was James, Duke of Krondor, and on the Prince's other side William, Knight-Marshal of Krondor. Owen Greylock, former Swordmaster at Darkmoor and now a Knight-Captain of the King's army, sat next to William. Nicholas sat next to James, and Calis between Erik and Nicholas. On Owen's other side sat a man unknown to Erik, a scribe who wrote down whatever was said in an odd script unlike anything Erik had seen before.

Calis said, "Our enemy is many things, but subtle is not one of them. They tried subtle once, when they abducted your cousin Margaret and the others from Crydee."

Patrick snorted. "Sacking the Far Coast wasn't exactly my idea of subtle."

"That's the point," said Calis. "Had they abducted a few commoners here and there, and let their infected duplicates wander through Krondor . . ."

"Why even bother with the abductions?" asked James.

"My point exactly," said Calis. "They do not think as we do. I doubt we will ever understand them." He pointed to the map on the opposite wall, showing the Kingdom from Land's End to the eastern border outside the city of Ran. "Salador and Krondor both present problems, and the route from Salador to Sethanon is easier, but getting to Salador presents many additional problems.

"It's a longer journey, which means an additional risk of unexpected damage to stores or to ships by storm. And it's a route far more likely to bring the Empire's attention to bear upon the fleet."

He stood and walked over to the map. He motioned and a servant removed it, replacing it with one in smaller scale, showing the entire world as they knew it. Waving at the bottom half of the map, where Novindus was shown, Calis said, "Currents here force anyone coming this way to move in a straight line from the eastern shore of Novindus to a point just southeast of the tip of the Triagia, then they have to move almost due north to strike the southern coast of Kesh. That right-angle route adds a month of travel time. We found that out when we used that Brijaner longship to get to Novindus last time. But crossing the Endless Sea to reach the Bitter Sea from the City of the Serpent River is a direct line by comparison." He pointed to the long, curving coast of Kesh on the eastern side of the continent and said, "South of the Kingdom Sea, the Brijaners and other Keshian raiders trade regularly. Additionally, here"—he pointed to the area of the ocean just northeast of the range of mountains called the Girdle of Kesh—"is the heaviest concentration of the Empire's Eastern Fleet. They are not going to sit idly by and watch six hundred hostile ships float past, even if they know the Kingdom is their ultimate target." He shook his head. "Plus the invasion fleet would have to sail past Roldem and the other Eastern kingdoms who might harry them in their passing.

"No, they will come this way. The mercenaries we've captured all tell of similar assignments: to capture and hold vital points along the mountains, so they can allow additional forces to pass over the ridge unopposed."

William turned to Admiral Nicholas. "Nicky, we've talked about the risk of the Straits of Darkness passage. . . ."

Nicholas said, "It's not that risky if you know what you're doing, even in late fall. Amos Trask and my father once sailed it in the dead of winter." He considered. "But for this fleet to clear the straits and reach Krondor, they would be best to come through no earlier than late spring or early summer. Midsummer is perfect. The weather's the best, the tides the most forgiving. . . ." He paused and looked into space.

"What?" said Prince Patrick after a minute.

"I still urge you to let me sail against them before they enter the Bitter Sea."

Patrick sighed and looked at James. The Duke of Krondor said, "Nicky, we've been over this territory before."

"I know," said Nicholas. "And I know it's risky, but think of the benefits!" He rose, came to stand next to Calis, and motioned to the servant. "Give me the larger map."

At once the scribe stood, removed the map of the world from the wall and rapidly hung another of the same size, but of much larger scale, showing the Western Kingdom and major portions of Kesh and the north, from the Far Coast to Malac's Cross. Pointing to the Straits of Darkness, Nicholas said, "They're bringing six hundred or more ships. They can't have six hundred captains and crews worth spit." He slapped his hand against the wall for emphasis. "If we bring the fleet down out of the Sunset Islands or closer in, say, Tulan"—his finger stabbed at the southernmost city on the Far Coast—"we can catch them as they begin to come through the straits. I can put thirty warships of size at their rear and another two or three dozen fast cutters. We sail in, slash them from behind, and sink as many of the wallowing barges they're carrying their troops in as possible; then when their escort ships turn to fight, we sail off. I don't care how good their escort ships or captains are, we know the winds and current better than they. We can get away!" He was the most animated Erik had ever seen him as he said, "If we're fortunate we'll catch them with their escorts coming through the straits before the troop ships, unable to turn and come back because of their own ships! We could sink a third, perhaps a half of their fleet!"

"Or if they split their escorts and put half of them at the rear, you could lose every ship we have in the West without doing any real damage," said Patrick. He shook his head. "Nicky, if we had the Western Imperial Fleet with us, or if Quegan war galleys would sail from the eastern side of the straits, maybe I could see risking this." The Prince sighed. "We are the smallest sea power in the West."

"But we have the best ships and men!" said Nicholas.

"I know," conceded Patrick, "but we don't have enough of them."

"Nor time to build them," said William. "Pursuing this discussion further is pointless."

"Maybe," said James.

"What?" asked Patrick.

The old Duke smiled. "Something you just said. About Queg raiding from the east. I might be able to arrange that."

"How?" asked the Prince.

James said, "Let me worry about that."

Patrick said, "Very well. Let me know what you're dreaming up, though, before you get us into another war with Queg."

James smiled. "I'm waiting for some reports from Queg, and when I have them"—he turned to Nicky—"you can sail your fleet to Tulan. And tell Duke Harry to cut his fleet loose from the Sunset Islands and put it under your flag. That squadron of cutthroats will swell your flotilla to what, fifty ships?"

Nicholas was enthusiastic. "Sixty-five!"

James put up a hand in a restraining gesture. "Don't get too carried away. This plot of mine may not work. I'll let you know one way or another in a month or so."

Turning to the others at the table, the Prince asked, "Anything else?"

"Why Krondor?" asked Greylock.

Patrick said, "Captain?"

"I mean, I agree it's likely they'll come into the Bitter Sea, but why attack Krondor?"

"Do you see an alternative?" asked the Prince.

"Several," answered Greylock. "None of them obviously superior, but the two that would appeal to me most if I were the Emerald Queen's commander would be either to land north of Krondor, keep the defenders bottled up inside the city with a small force, moving the army around the city, then into the East, over the King's Highway, or to put ashore between Land's End and Krondor, moving to the south of the city along the Keshian border, then north to the pass to the east. I would lose some portion of my army holding Kingdom forces inside the city, but less than in a full assault."

Patrick said, "William?"

"We've considered it, but there's nothing in our reports that would indicate this General Fadawah, who commands for the Queen, is inclined to leave anything alive behind his lines."

"Food?" suggested Erik.

"Pardon?" asked the Prince of Krondor.

"I'm sorry, Highness, but it seems to me that with all the numbers of ships and men we've tossed about over the last few years, if they're bringing even as few as six hundred ships . . . I could show you my calculations, but I think they're going to be out of food when they get here."

Nicholas said, "Yes, that's it!" He pointed to the island nation of Queg. "They can't raid Queg for food, nor down here along the Jal-Pur Desert.

No, they need to sack Krondor to provision their army before they move east."

Patrick said, "I agree. Which is why, if James's plan doesn't work, I want the fleet deployed to the north near Sarth. When they attempt to come ashore, that's when you harry them."

Nicholas swore. "Damn it, Patrick, that's the worst time! You know they'll bring their fastest ships into skirmish along their perimeter. They'll need only one or two large warships to break through whatever we have at the harbor mouth if we take all our big ships up the coast. Then they sail their troop ships into the harbor and seize the city! You can't have it both ways, Patrick. If you want me to defend the city, my fleet needs to be equally divided between ships inside the harbor and those defending outside the seawall."

Erik said, "Excuse me."

"Yes?" said Patrick.

"If it's not too late, you could change the way ships enter the harbor."

James grinned. "We're already working on that, Sergeant Major. We're going to make them come to a complete right-angle turn through a new set of breakwaters—"

"No, m'lord," interrupted Erik. "I mean build another wall along the northern jetty to the harbor, put a sea gate in between the new wall and the old one, make them sail against the wind, not with the currents at the old breakwater, so they're as slow as can be when they have to turn into the harbor proper. Maybe even have it so they have to be towed around."

"Why the new wall?" asked Calis.

"Catapults and ballista platforms," answered Greylock. "Burning anything coming around that corner that doesn't fly Kingdom colors."

"If you sink the first two or three ships as they come in . . ." said Nicholas.

"They'll have to turn away from the harbor and land on the beaches to the north of the city!" finished Patrick.

"Or attempt to land on the wall itself!" said William. "Sergeant Major, I'm impressed."

Patrick looked at Duke James. "Can we do it?"

"We can, but it will be expensive to do it in time. And the merchants will set up a howl about the inconvenience."

Patrick said, "Let them."

A door opened and a squire in the livery of the palace entered, carrying a document to Duke James. He opened it and read. "They've sailed!"

Patrick said, "We're certain?"

Duke James nodded to Calis, who said, "We left a few agents behind after the fall of the City of the Serpent River. It's been more difficult to get intelligence out of that region, but we left behind one fast ship, and our best crew, in a safe location. It took a messenger two days by fast horse to reach our ship, then the ship left at once. We know it's faster than anything the Queen has, and they're moving at the speed of the slowest ship in the flotilla." He calculated, then looked around the table. "They will be at the Straits just before Midsummer's Day."

James said, "That leaves us three months to prepare."

Patrick said, "Do what you must, and let me know the details of this Quegan plot of yours as soon as possible." He stood and the others in the room rose. "This meeting is adjourned."

Duke James motioned Erik over to his side. "Sir?" said Erik.

"Send a note to that friend of yours and tell him to get here as soon as possible. I think I need Mr. Avery to run an errand for me."

Erik nodded. "Yes, sir."

After Erik had left, James beckoned to William. "It's time to tell young von Darkmoor the truth, I think."

Owen Greylock, who had followed William to the Duke's side, said, "He won't like it."

"But he'll follow orders," said William. "He's the best."

James smiled. "He is that, isn't he? We're lucky to have him." James's smile faded after a moment. "I wish others could be as lucky as that."

William said, "If there were any other way . . ."

James held up his hand. "I believe we shall see more pain and destruction in the next half year than the Kingdom has known in its history. But when the smoke settles, there will still be a Kingdom. And a world. And those who survive will be the luckiest of all."

"I hope we may be among them," said Greylock.

With a bitter note, James said, "Don't count on it, my friend. Don't count on it." Without further words, the Duke departed.

"Again?" said Roo. "Why?"

"Because I need you to buy more Quegan fire oil."

"But, Your Grace," said Roo, as he sat uncomfortably before the Duke of Krondor. "I can send a message to Lord Vasarius—"

"No, I think you need to go in person."

Roo's eyes narrowed. "You're not going to tell me what this is about, are you?"

"What you don't know can't be tortured out of you, can it?"

Roo didn't care for that answer. "When do you wish me to leave?"

"Next week. I have a few things I must do before then, and then off you'll go. It'll be a short trip, don't worry."

Roo stood. "If you say so."

"I do. Now good day."

"Good day, my lord," said Roo, and his tone showed he was less than pleased to have to endure another visit with his erstwhile partner. It wasn't that Lord Vasarius was not a hospitable man, but his idea of hospitality was to bore his guest with interminable stories over bad food and wine. And that daughter of his! Roo thought she was enough to make him give up women. Then he thought of Sylvia, and he amended that to almost enough to make him give up women.

As he left the Duke's private chambers, another door opened and a squire said, "Lord Vencar, Your Grace."

"Send him in, please."

A moment later, Arutha entered the room, still covered with road dust. "Father," he said in greeting.

James kissed his son on the cheek. "Is it done?"

Arutha grinned and for a moment James saw a hint of himself in his son. "It's done."

James struck his fist into the palm of his left hand. "Finally! Something is going our way. Is Nakor willing?"

"More than willing," said Arutha. "That madman would have done it simply for the pleasure of seeing the faces of those other magicians when it happens, I'm certain, but he also understands we have to protect our southern flank."

James regarded the map in his office. "That's one problem."

"There's another," said Arutha.

"What?"

"I want Jimmy and Dash out of the city."

James waved away the request. "I need them here."

"I mean it, Father. They have your impossible sense of immortality, and if you leave it up to them, they'll cut things too close and be trapped in the city when it falls. You know that's true."

James studied his son's face, and sighed. He sat behind the desk and said, "All right. When the Queen's fleet is sighted off Land's End, send them away. Where do you want them to go?"

"Their mother is visiting family in Roldem."

"That's convenient," said James dryly.

"Very," said Arutha. "Look, you and I stand scant chance of surviving this. You can lie to me, even yourself, but you can't lie to Mother."

James nodded.

"She's had a look on her face I've not seen before, ever, and I've seen her go through most everything I can imagine." He met his father's gaze with an unwavering one in return and said, "Being a member of your family provides ample opportunity to test one's temperament."

James grinned, and for a moment he looked like the young father who had told stories of Jimmy the Hand when Arutha was a child. "But it's never been dull, has it?"

Arutha shook his head. "Never that." Then he studied his father. "You're staying to the end, aren't you?"

James said, "This is my home. I was born here." If there was any regret in his statement, he hid it well.

"You plan on dying here?"

James said, "I don't *plan* on dying, but if I must, I wouldn't be anywhere else." He slapped the desk with the palm of his hand. "Look, there are a lot of things we can't plan on, and staying alive until tomorrow is one of them. Life has shown me all too often it's a fragile gift. Remember, no one gets out of life alive." He stood up. "Go get refreshed and come have dinner with me. Your mother will be pleased to see you again. If I can get word to your sons we'll have a family dinner."

"That would be nice," said Arutha.

He left, and after the door was closed, James crossed the room to another door, slipping through. He moved down a corridor to a small door where he had to duck his head to pass through. Down a flight of twisting stairs and through another long corridor. He reached a door and tested the handle, finding it locked. He knocked twice, then when a single knock came from the other side, he knocked again. The latch clicked and the door swung open.

Behind the door he found Dash and Jimmy, and a pair of men wearing unmarked uniforms and black hoods with eye slits. Inside the room, instruments of torture were waiting, and along the wall empty shackles hung. A man sat tied to a heavy wooden chair, his head slumped forward on his chest.

"Anything?" asked James.

"Nothing," said Dash.

"Get back to your employer. I've just told him you're going to Queg again. He's not very happy and will be even less so when he discovers you're not at the office doing whatever it is he pays you to do."

Dash said, "Queg? Again?"

James nodded. "I'll explain latter."

As Dash reached the door, James said, "Oh, by the way, your father's back, so join us for dinner tonight."

Dash nodded and the door closed. His grandfather said to Jimmy, "Revive him."

Jimmy threw a cup of water into the man's face and he roused. James grabbed the man by the hair and looked him in the eyes. "Your masters would have been kinder had they not put those blocks around your mind. My wife lies abed with a nasty headache and that puts me in a foul temper. So we must do this the old-fashioned way."

He nodded to the two torturers. They knew their craft and quickly and efficiently set about applying the tools of their trade. The prisoner, an agent of the Emerald Queen picked up the day before, began to scream.

* * *

Roo attempted to look alert as Vasarius told a remarkably boring story of a deal negotiated with a trading combine from the Free Cities. The story itself didn't hold Roo's attention. He was more curious about matters of business than anyone he knew, and the particulars of the trade were unusual, but Vasarius managed to tell the story in the most convoluted, tedious way, denuding it of anything remotely like personality, color, or humor. What held Roo's interest was the very ineptitude of his storytelling. Roo at this point no longer had any idea who the principals were, why they were enmeshed in this contract, or even what the transaction was about, or why this story was supposed to be funny, but he was certain that with a little urging on his part, Vasarius could make it even more pointless and rambling before he finished.

"And then?" Roo supplied, causing Vasarius to launch into another parenthetical exposition on some topic that was, to him and him alone in the world, somehow relevant. Roo let his gaze wander to Livia, who seemed to be involved in some sort of silent communication with Jimmy. Roo wasn't sure, but the girl seemed somehow put out with Roo's personal secretary, and Roo wondered what had passed between them on their last visit. To hear Jimmy tell it, he had been the complete gentleman, even to the point of ignoring hints that *might* have led to a sexual encounter.

Aware suddenly that Vasarius had become silent, Roo said, "My, my. How fascinating," without missing a beat.

"Very," said the Quegan noble. "You don't play fast and loose with Lord Venchenzo's cargo and then go brag on it."

Roo thought he better discreetly ask around who Lord Venchenzo might be, so if the topic ever came up again he might have at least a hint to what this story had been about.

The meal was at last over, and Vasarius sent Jimmy off with his daughter and offered Roo a rather decent brandy. "It's one of the ones you were kind enough to send me," explained the Quegan noble.

Roo thought he'd have to send him something a little better, against the possibility he was going to be ordered back here one more time. After they had sipped the brandy, Vasarius asked, "What's the real reason for your visit?"

Roo said, "Well, I do need additional oil."

"You could have sent me a purchase order, Rupert. You didn't need to come here personally."

Roo looked into his cup. As if weighing his words, he hesitated; the truth was James had rehearsed him relentlessly until he was perfect in what he was to say next: "Actually, I need a favor."

"What is it?"

"I'm sure your Empire has agents, or at least 'friends' who pass along certain types of intelligence."

"I would be insulting you if I claimed otherwise. No nation on Midkemia is without such resources."

"Then you may have wondered about the buildup of military forces in the Kingdom."

"It has come to our attention that a great many military projects are under way."

Roo sighed. "The truth is there are reports from Kingdom agents in Kesh that the Emperor is thinking of reclaiming the Vale of Dreams."

Vasarius shrugged. "So what else is new? The Kingdom and Kesh fight over the Vale like two sisters over a favorite gown."

"There's a bit more. It looks like Kesh may launch a full assault toward Krondor, with an eye to cutting off all roads between Krondor and Land's End."

Vasarius said, "If true, that would isolate Land's End."

"Not to mention cutting off Shamata and Landreth, and giving the Empire control of Stardock."

"Ah," said Vasarius. "The magicians."

Roo nodded. "The Kingdom considers them something of an unknown factor."

"As well you should," said Vasarius. "We have our own magicians, here within the Empire, but all are willing servants of the Imperial court."

Roo mentally added the "or else they're dead" part.

Vasarius continued. "That many magicians, unsupervised, could prove troublesome."

"Well, be that as it may, the point is we're going to be putting men and matériel into Krondor in abundance. We're going to be shipping troops from Ylith and other parts of Yabon, as well as in from the Far Coast."

"You still haven't given me any inkling of what this has to do with me."

"I'm coming to that." Roo cleared his throat dramatically. "We need to protect certain critical shipments and, well, it would benefit us if they were carried on Quegan ships, as the Empire of Great Kesh is less likely to expect such cargo to be carried on Quegan galleys."

"Ah," said Vasarius, and fell silent.

"I need a dozen heavily armed war galleys in Carse by the third week after Banapis."

"A dozen!" Vasarius's eyes widened. "What are you carrying?"

"Weapons and other items."

Roo could see the eyes of the man spinning with greed. Roo knew that Vasarius was assuming it was a huge shipment of gold, coming down from the Grey Towers, mined by the dwarves and exchanged for Kingdom goods, to be shipped to Krondor to pay soldiers. Which was exactly what Duke James wanted him to think. Roo knew Vasarius would assume twelve war galleys were far too much security for a weapons shipment.

Vasarius said, "Which means they'd have to leave here three weeks before the Festival of Midsummer." He calculated. "That would put them in the Straits of Darkness about Midsummer's Day. It would mean you need the gold in Krondor two months after Midsummer."

"More or less," said Roo, pretending to ignore Vasarius's reference to the gold.

"A dozen Imperial Galleys will prove costly."

"How costly?" asked Roo.

Vasarius gave him a figure, and Roo haggled halfheartedly in an attempt to look as if he was trying to beat down the price. Roo knew that the gold would never be paid to Queg, because Vasarius intended to steal the shipment, and there wasn't any gold in any event. There would be six hundred hostile ships showing up about then, however. And Roo knew that Vasarius wouldn't send twelve galleys, he'd send every one he controlled, which could amount to two dozen or better, if he could recall them to Queg in time to pass along orders.

They talked into the night, and Roo wished the brandy was better. Absently he wondered how Jimmy was getting on with Livia.

Jimmy licked the blood on his lip and said, "What?"

Livia slapped him again and then bit him hard on the neck as she said, "Oh, I wish you barbarians spoke a civilized tongue!"

The girl sat astride Jimmy, with her toga pulled down around her waist. Jimmy was drunk on drugged wine and trying to keep his wits, but the combination of narcotics, alcohol, and a young, healthy, half-naked woman attempting to have sex with him was making it difficult for him to keep his focus. It was all he could do to pretend he didn't understand her language.

At some point Jimmy got the impression that Livia was furious with him for not having tried to make love to her on their last visit. He was certain that was more for the lost opportunity of rejecting him than for any lust for him, but given how temperamental this Quegan lady was, Jimmy couldn't be sure. At the present it was clear that she was trying to prove a different point to him, one which seemed to involve a lot of slapping, some biting, and a lot of promises that he would never be able to make love to another woman after having Livia. In a semicomatose state, Jimmy fervently hoped the last was not true. Though the way she was jumping up and down on him made him think there might be enough permanent damage to prevent him from being interested in testing the claim for some time to come.

He said, "Enough!" and tried to sit up, which got him another ringing slap across the face. As tears came to his eyes, Livia started tearing his clothing off.

Somewhere along the way he remembered getting serious scratches on his back and buttocks, and at another point someone—a servant he thought—threw a bucket of very hot water on them, followed by one that was very cold. Then Livia was doing interesting things with a feather and a jelly made from gooseberries.

Finally, as they lay exhausted in each other's arms, she mumbled something about never having known anyone like him. Jimmy never considered himself a lady's man, for although he loved women and their company, having a grandmother who read minds taught a young man things about women few men even imagined. For years every time he glanced at a comely wench with a lustful intent, his grandmother would drag him off for a lecture on his attitude toward women. It took a while, but he finally came to look upon women as friends and enemies, just like men, except when he was sleeping with them, when they were decidedly unlike men, for which he was eternally grateful.

This one was something outside his experience, however, and he wasn't sure he welcomed any repeat of the experience. Knowing he'd been drugged, he had practiced some of the mental techniques taught him by his grandmother, and when the girl had started her questioning, he had started telling lies.

By now Jimmy was certain that when she and her father compared notes, the plan conceived by Jimmy's grandfather would swing into motion. He tried not to laugh, for every part of him hurt too much to move. As he let sleep overtake him, he wondered how Dash was doing.

"Ah, you're a lying sack of dung, and a Kingdom dog to boot, and that's a fact." The sailor looked at Dash with a challenge.

Dash stood up, dramatically swaying far more than was due to anything he had drunk. He had years before mastered the art of appearing to drink more than he had, and he could pass himself off as a drunk as well as any actor. The trick was to get a tiny bit of pepper or ale on your finger, rub your eyes, and get them red. His grandfather had taught him that trick. "No one calls me a liar!" He glared at the Quegan sailor. "I told you I saw it! With me own eyes!" He lowered his voice to a conspiratorial whisper. "And I can tell you when and where, too."

"When and where what?" asked another of the card players.

Dash had returned to the dockside tavern he had visited on their last voyage to Queg—where he had established his identity as a Kingdom sailor with a night off—and had entered a friendly game of Pashawa. After winning a little and losing a little, he had started to win, just enough to keep people paying attention to him.

Finally a couple of local card sharks had shown up and asked to join the game. As he expected, Dash was offered round after round of drink, in the hope his card sense would be dulled.

He accommodated them, and lost enough money to keep them around, then won back enough to keep them interested. While he played, he talked.

"Like I told you: my father sailed with Prince Nicholas and Amos Trask himself! He was the first to reach the land across the Endless Sea."

"There is no such place," scoffed a Quegan sailor.

"How would you know?" retorted Dash. "You're a bunch of coast huggers. Not a deep-water sailor in this entire nation."

That got him the undivided attention of every man in the inn. Several were ready to teach him manners should he start insulting their homeland. Dash started talking to his captive audience. "It's true! For almost twenty years the Prince of Krondor has had men down there tradin' with the natives! They're a simple people, who worship the sun, and even their children wear gold trinkets and play with toys fashioned from gold. The Prince has them mining gold for glass beads. I've seen the gold. With me own eyes! It's the largest cargo in the world, enough gold to fill this room. More! As tall as two men, one upon the other's shoulders, it was. And at the base, it filled a room twice the size of this inn."

"There isn't that much gold in the world," said the man who had named himself Gracus. He was a skilled gambler, and Dash suspected a confidence man, a thief, and a potential murderer. But for Dash's purpose he possessed the signal ingredient of nature: he was greedy to a fare-thee-well.

"Look, I tell you this: when Mr. Avery's ship leaves here, and after we take him back to Krondor, we're going out with every ship of the fleet, beyond the Straits of Darkness. Why?"

The men muttered as several asked why.

"Because the biggest fleet of treasure ships in the history of the world is headin' this way, even as we sit here gabbin', and it's going to come through the Straits on Banapis."

"Midsummer's Day?" asked Gracus.

"Think on it!" said Dash. "Where will your galleys be? Where will all those Keshian pirates from Durbin be?"

One of the sailors said, "He's got a point, Gracus. Our ships will be in port so the crews can celebrate. Even the galley slaves get a drink of wine that day."

"And it's true in Durbin," said another. "I've sailed into that port on Midsummer's Day, and if there's a crewman sober by sundown, he's not trying."

Gracus said, "That may be all well and good, but it's still a little difficult to believe."

Dash glanced around the room, as if looking to see he wasn't being watched, which was difficult to do with a straight face when every man in the room was watching him closely. He reached into his shirt and pulled out a small purse. He opened it up and let the contents fall on the table.

A tiny whistle and a small top fell with a clatter, and Gracus picked up the whistle. "Gold," he whispered.

"I traded a copper piece to a little boy for that whistle," said Dash. "And he was glad to have it. He'd never seen copper before, but gold was everywhere."

The top and whistle had been fashioned from some of the King's currency, melted and reforged, and James had sent back the items twice because the goldsmith couldn't get it through his head that the Duke wanted them to look crudely fashioned. Dash took the whistle away from Gracus. "This boy gave me a voyage's pay in gold for a copper piece.

"I've seen other men come back from there with enough gold in their kit to retire for life to a gentleman's farm in the country, that's the truth." He glanced around the room. "If any of you lads have visited the Anchor and Dolphin in Krondor, Dawson who runs it, why he got the gold to open that inn by trading his clothes to the natives. Came back smelling like a skunk, 'cause he didn't have a change of clothing for three months, but he came back rich."

Dash could see he had them, and he knew that whatever doubt might linger in the minds of some of these men would be far outweighed by the desire to believe in others. By the time Banapis arrived, every Quegan pirate crew able to sail would be waiting at the Straits of Darkness.

Putting away his trinkets, Dash decided he'd better lose enough to have to give those trinkets away to the winner of the pot, for the story would be more convincing with physical evidence. Additionally, he thought, as he glanced around the room at a gallery of naked greed, if he was broke he stood a far better chance of getting back to his ship alive.

Pug said, "Are you ready?"

Macros and Miranda nodded, and held hands.

Nakor said good-bye to Sho Pi, gripped Macros and Pug's hands, one in each of his own. Pug and Miranda joined hands and the circle was closed.

Pug incanted and suddenly they were standing in a courtyard, high up in the mountains somewhere. A startled monk dropped a bucket of water he was carrying and stood open-mouthed and wide-eyed. Pug looked at him and said, "We need to see the Abbot."

The monk could not bring himself to speak, only nodding and running off. They waited while several monks poked their heads through windows to get a look at the intruders.

Macros said, "I suspect you know what you're doing?"

"Cooperation between magicians and clerics is rare, but it has happened in the past," said Pug.

They stood in the courtyard of the Abbey of Ishap at Sarth, in the mountains north of Krondor. Pug had visited there occasionally, after having made the acquaintance of the present Abbot, who had been a simple priest then.

A moment later a grey-haired man about Pug's height, and looking to be in his late seventies, moved briskly toward them. At his side a younger cleric, carrying a war hammer and bearing a shield upon his arm, approached. When the man got close enough to recognize Pug he called him by name.

"Hello, Dominic. It's been a very long time."

The Abbot of Sarth nodded. "Nearly thirty years, I believe." Glancing at Pug's three companions, he said, "I expect this isn't a social visit." He turned to his companion. "Put away your weapons, Brother Michael. There is no threat."

As the warrior priest walked away, Dominic said, "You've really injured his pride, Pug. You went through his protective wards as if they weren't there."

Pug smiled. "They weren't. Tell him to put some *below* the libraries in the mountain. We came through the floor."

Dominic smiled. "I'll tell him. Would you care to join me for some refreshments and tell me what this is all about?"

Macros said, "We need your knowledge, Abbot. And we may not speak safely here."

The Abbot said, "And you are . . . ?"

Pug said, "Dominic, this is Macros the Black."

If Dominic was impressed by the name, he did not show it. "Your reputation precedes you."

"I am Nakor, and this is Miranda."

Dominic bowed to the two of them. "This abbey may be the safest place on Midkemia—if we get those wards established under the library," he said with slight smile.

Pug said, "For what we need to discuss, there is no safe place on Midkemia."

"Do you propose to take me to another world, as you did so many years ago?"

"Exactly," said Pug. "Only this time you won't be tortured."

"That's a relief." He studied Pug. "You haven't changed, but I have. I'm an old man, and I need a persuasive reason to leave this world at my age."

Pug considered his reply. "We need to talk about your most precious secret."

Instantly Dominic's eyes narrowed. "If you're fishing for something, I will not break my oath, so tell me what you know."

Macros said, "We know the truth of the Seven-Pointed Star, and the Cross within it. We know the fifth star is dead, as is the sixth." Lowering his voice, he said, "And the seventh star is not dead."

Dominic remained motionless for an instant, then turned to a nearby monk. "I will be going with these people. Tell Brother Gregory he is in charge as long as I'm absent. Tell him also to send the sealed chest in my study to the High Father at our temple in Rillanon." The monk bowed his head and hurried off to carry out the Abbot's wishes.

"Let us leave," said Dominic, and they formed a circle.

Pug said, "Macros, I have the power, but not the knowledge."

Macros said, "I have both. Follow me."

Suddenly they were gone, and around them a void could be sensed, rather than felt or seen.

Miranda's thoughts came to Pug. "When I first entered the Hall of Worlds I asked Boldar Blood what happens when you step into the void."

Pug's thoughts returned out of the featureless grey. "This is the void between realities. Here nothing exists."

"There is something," came the thoughts of Macros. "There is no place in the universe without something residing within. It may not be apparent to those who pass through, but there are creatures that live within the void."

"Fascinating," came Nakor's thoughts, and the word was tinged with excitement.

Suddenly they were in a star-filled night of pure black, encapsuled in a bubble of air, warmth, and gravity. Below them, swimming through the void, was a place Pug had never thought to visit again. "The City Forever," he said.

"What alien beauty," said Nakor. Pug glanced at the Isalani and saw his eyes wide with wonder.

"It is that," said Pug.

The city spread out below in a twisted symmetry, one that sought to capture the eye, but somehow eluded it. Towers and minarets that looked too slender to support their own weight rose up against the vault of the City's self-contained sky. Arches that could have soared miles above Krondor's highest rooftop spanned the vast distance between buildings of alien design.

Downward they sped, yet they felt no sense of movement save what they saw with their eyes. "Who built this place?" asked Miranda.

"No one," said Macros. "At least, no one within this reality."

"What do you mean, Father?"

Macros shrugged. "This place was here when our universe came into being. Pug, Tomas, and I witnessed the birth of what we know as our reality. This place was already here."

"An artifact of an earlier reality?" suggested Nakor.

"Perhaps," said Macros. "Or something that simply is because it needs to be."

Dominic had remained silent but now asked, "Why this strange and incomprehensible place, Pug?"

Pug said, "Because it is perhaps the only place we may speak freely and not fall prey to the agency behind all the woe and destruction unleashed upon our world."

They moved over a vast square, many times the size of the city of Krondor, where city-size tiles changed color in a hypnotic pattern. As they approached the surface of the street, they saw the pattern echoed in streets that left the enormous square.

Miranda said, "It's a city. It has buildings, what look to be houses, and yet it is devoid of life."

"Don't make that assumption, daughter." Macros pointed. "That fountain may be a decorative creation, or it may be a life form so alien to our understanding that we will never communicate with it."

"What if the city is the life form?" asked Nakor.

"Possible."

Dominic said, "Why would the gods create such a place?"

"Depends on which gods we're talking about," said Macros.

The orb settled across a gulf of the void, onto a lush green lawn surrounded by trees and plants, all beautifully tended. Then the orb vanished.

"This may be the most remote corner of reality," said Macros. "The Garden."

Pug said, "Now we may speak, but first there is something I must do."

"What?" said Miranda.

But Pug had already closed his eyes and was mumbling an incantation. Everyone present felt a fey energy gather around Pug, then suddenly it was gone and he opened his eyes.

Miranda's eyes narrowed. "This is a powerful spell of blocking. Why do we need protection from eavesdropping in this remote corner of reality?"

"All will be made clear," Pug answered. He looked at the Abbot. "It is time," Pug said to Dominic.

"What would you know?" asked the Abbot of Sarth.

"The truth," said Pug. "Ishap is dead."

Dominic nodded. "Since the time of the Chaos Wars."

Miranda said, "Ishap, the One Above All? The Greatest of All the Gods is dead?"

Pug said, "I'll explain. Nearly forty years ago, an agency of some unknown origin sought to destroy an artifact of the Ishapians, a magical gem known as the Tear of the Gods."

Dominic nodded. "This is not widely known. Only Prince Arutha, a few of his trusted advisers, and Pug knew of the theft.

"To understand the importance of that attempt, you must know something of the nature of the gods and their role in Midkemian life."

Macros said, "Dominic, explain to Miranda and Nakor."

Dominic spied a bench nearby and said, "I'll sit, if you don't mind."

They followed him there. The old Abbot sat, Nakor and Miranda sat at his feet, and Pug and Macros remained standing. Dominic said, "At the time of the Chaos Wars, a new order came into existence on Midkemia. Before the Chaos Wars, a primal force of creation and one of destruction ruled hand in glove; these forces were worshipped by the Valheru as Rathar and

Mythar, She Who Is Order, and He Who Is Chaos, the Two Blind Gods of the Beginning.

"But with their raiding across the heavens, the Valheru were an unintentional agent of change. For each realm they visited, each realm they connected with the one of their birth, they created ripples in the time stream and changes in how the universe was ordered.

"The Chaos Wars were an upheaval on a cosmic scale, as the universes sought to reorder themselves in a fashion more finely drawn, more clearly delineated than before, and as a result, the gods arose."

Dominic looked from face to face. "Each world in the cosmos, each planet and star in the multitude of universes shares a common property, energies existing on a multitude of levels. Many of these worlds gave form to those energies as consciousness, while others formed what we call magic. Some have no life as we think of it, while others are teeming. In the end, each world sought out its own level."

Nakor seemed riveted by this. "But they are all connected, right?"

Dominic said, "Ultimately, they are, and therein lies the heart of this matter.

"When the gods came into existence they ordered themselves in ways we can only guess at; but as time passed they took on properties that clearly revealed their natures. For the most part, they were organic things, if energy or mind can be called organic, that is to say, without consciousness as we think of it."

Macros nodded. "I know that for certain."

Dominic continued. "Seven beings existed, who had ultimate responsibility for the ordering of Midkemia. They were given names by mankind, though what they think of themselves is beyond our ability to know. They were Abrem-Sev, the Forger of Actions; Ev-Dem, the Worker from Within; Graff, the Weaver of Wishes; and Helbinor, the Abstainer.

"These are the four remaining Greater Gods," said Dominic, "those who survived the Chaos Wars when the Lesser Gods rose and the Valheru last flew Midkemia's sky."

"What caused the Chaos Wars?" asked Nakor. "Why did the Lesser Gods rebel against the Greater Gods?"

"No one knows," said Dominic. "Mankind was young on this world, having fled to Midkemia from other worlds as the Valheru raged across the multiverse."

"The Mad God," said Macros.

Nakor said, "Who is he?"

"The Unnamed," supplied Pug. "And the reason we're here."

Miranda said, "You said seven greater beings existed, yet you named only four."

Dominic nodded. "Originally, there were seven. Besides the four we call the Builders, there were three others. Arch-Indar, the Selfless, the Goddess of Good, was she who drove every creative and positive impulse on our world. We think she sacrificed herself to ultimately banish the Unnamed from Midkemia."

Miranda said, "So who is Ishap?"

"He was the most powerful of all the Greater Gods," said Dominic. "He was the Balancer, the Matrix, the one whose ultimate task was to keep the other gods in their places."

"Who is this seventh god," asked Miranda, "this Unnamed?"

Pug said, "Nalar."

There was a momentary silence and Pug said, "That's a relief."

"What's a relief?" asked Miranda.

Dominic said, "Nalar is unnamed, for even to say his name is to risk becoming his tool. He has been cast out by the other four Greater Gods, to keep something of a balance, while we labor to return Ishap to life."

Miranda said, "So you're praying every day, trying to return the Greatest of All the Gods to life?"

"Yes."

Miranda said, "Have you anticipated how much longer you need to do this?"

"Centuries," said Macros. "Millennia, even. Our lives are but passing moments in the age of the universe."

Dominic said, "This is so. This is why we who worship Ishap are the self-appointed keepers of Knowledge. Wodar-Hospur, the God of Knowledge, also died in the Chaos Wars, and knowledge serves us in attempting to return the order of the universe to what it needs be."

Miranda said, "This is incredible."

Pug said, "I know. It means that what I've been living through—the Riftwar, the Great Uprising, this constant attacking by the Pantathians, all of which is apparently some plot by the trapped Valheru to gain their freedom—all of it is simply a ruse."

"By Nalar?" said Miranda.

"What would he gain by the destruction of the world?" said Nakor.

Dominic said, "You do not understand the nature of the gods. No man does. It is his nature to do that which man calls 'evil.' He is an agent of destruction much as Arch-Indar was an agent of creation. To destroy, tear down, and render all life to a basic form is as much a part of his nature as it was of Mythar, the ancient God of Chaos. But it is more, for while Mythar was mindless, Nalar has a mind, a consciousness. More to the point, a self-consciousness.

"While the other Controller Gods were alive, all was in balance. And his tendencies to destroy and cause evil were kept in check by a mind aware of its own purpose, and by the forces of Ishap and Arch-Indar, supported by the other four, the Builders.

"But during the Chaos Wars, Nalar went mad."

Pug said, "Another name for the Chaos Wars is the Time of the Mad God's Rage."

"Or perhaps," said Nakor, "it was his madness that caused the Chaos Wars."

"We'll never know," said Dominic. Glancing around the circle of faces, he said, "Even so powerful a company as this is trivial compared to the might we're discussing."

"We are candles to their stars," said Macros.

"But a lifeless world is no problem for a god who exists for eons," said Dominic. "Life is persistent, and eventually it would return to Midkemia, either arising in the lifeless soil and water of its own accord, or brought there from other worlds, and as it waited, the dead world of Midkemia would provide Nalar with an opportunity to escape his prison, for the other gods would be weakened. The Lesser Gods would probably die with the planet—they are agents who work between living beings and the Greater Gods—and the Greater Gods would be greatly reduced in strength."

"Why didn't the other gods simply destroy Nalar?" asked Miranda.

"They couldn't," said Dominic. "He was too powerful."

Miranda sat back on her heels. "Too powerful?"

"Yes," answered Dominic. "The entropic nature of destruction, the forces used by Nalar, are the most powerful in the universe. Without Arch-Indar and Ishap, the Builders could not destroy him. They could shut him away. He is entombed under a mountain as large as the world of Midkemia, upon a planet the size of our sun, in a universe as distant from our own as can be imagined, yet he is still powerful enough to reach out and influence the minds of his servants."

Pug spoke. "Those who serve him often have no idea on whose behalf they labor. They have need to do things, but no reason."

Dominic said, "The other gods gave to my order the Tear of the Gods. It is why we have any power at all. All clerical magic is prayers answered, but with Ishap dead, we have no one to answer our prayers."

"So every one hundred years, this mystic gem is born, in a cave high in the mountains," said Pug, "and it is transported to Rillanon, where it is placed in the inner sanctum of the Temple of Ishap."

Dominic said, "It is there so we may speak to the other gods, and so we may work magic and do good works, and cause men to come to the worship of Ishap so that someday he will return to us and restore the balance."

"But until then," said Macros, "we have a problem."

Miranda said, "That's one way of putting it. Let me try another: the Valheru, the demons, the wars and destruction, all are tiny diversionary tactics by a Mad God who is so powerful that the other Greater Gods and Lesser Gods combined can't destroy him, so it's up to us to face him?"

Macros said, "Something like that."

Miranda could only sit in stunned silence.

Ten

Dedication

MIRANDA YAWNED.

After the initial shock of the enormity of the task before them wore off, boredom set in. Macros, Pug, and Dominic had resolved not to leave the Garden of the City Forever until a plan of some sort had been worked out.

They had spoken for hours, or at least Miranda had gotten hungry a couple of times, and had napped once. The only person who had seemed completely enthralled by the experience was Nakor.

The little man was sitting on a bench and seemed lost in thought when Miranda approached him with an armful of pears. "Want one?" she asked.

He grinned as he nodded and took one. "My orange trick still works, if you want one of those."

"Thanks, maybe later." Then she said, "But how does it still work?"

"I don't know," he said with a perplexed smile. "Maybe the stuff I'm moving around doesn't care where I am."

"But we're nowhere."

"No," Nakor disagreed. "We're somewhere, we just don't have any idea of where."

"Or a frame of reference," she added.

"Yes, you do understand."

"You seem impossibly cheerful for someone who has just been told he's got to go fight a god."

Nakor shook his head as pear juice ran down his chin. "No, not yet. And I don't think ever, maybe. We need to find a way to defeat his plans, not him. If four Greater Gods can't destroy this one, then who are we? Besides, the plan is already in place, we just have to realize what it is."

"I'm not sure I understand."

He stood up and said, "Come along, I'll explain."

He led her to where Pug, Macros, and Dominic sat, under a large tree of alien foliage, and said, "How are you doing?"

Pug said, "We've restated the problem many times, but we seem without a hint of what to do next."

"That's easy," said Nakor.

Macros's eyebrows raised. "Oh, really? Care to share this insight with us?"

Nakor nodded and in a single motion sat cross-legged on the ground. "We have to fix what's broken."

Dominic said, "That is what the Order of Ishap has been doing."

"I know," said Nakor. "I mean all of it. Look, you've got to take some time to bring back the dead god. That's not an easy thing to do."

The old Abbot's eyes narrowed. "Thank you for understanding," he said dryly.

"But there's a lot of mischief that's gone on since this all began that we need to do something about *now*!" said Nakor.

"Such as?" asked Pug.

"Well, one thing," answered Nakor, "we have those demons. We can't have them running around. They cause much too much trouble. Even the little ones can be very dangerous."

"I remember when Murmandamus's magicians gated in some flying demons years ago, before the Great Uprising was crushed. That should have alerted me that something was amiss. I mistook it for a common spell of summoning," admitted Pug.

"We can spend a lifetime in regrets," said Macros, "if we let ourselves." He looked at his daughter, who returned his scrutiny with a neutral expression.

"Yes," said Nakor. "Regrets are foolish. Now, your other question. As for putting things right, that's simple. We defeat the Emerald Queen, get this invading army turned around and headed home, kill all the Pantathians who are left alive—because we can't change their nature—and make sure no one gets to the Lifestone. Oh, and chase all the demons back to their own realm."

"Is that all?" Miranda said sarcastically, with mock wide-eyed wonder.

Dominic said, "Nakor, you pose very interesting questions, intriguing solutions, but little advice on how to go about reaching those solutions."

"That's easy," said Nakor. "We have to go plug up the hole."

"What hole?" asked Macros.

"The one the demons are coming through. That could be very nasty in a short while."

Pug sighed. "He's right. The Emerald Queen's army is a catastrophe, but a major invasion of demons would make it look like a bunch of street roughs trying to roll a drunk."

"But I think that might wait until we defeat the Emerald Queen," said

Nakor. "What we've seen of the demons indicates they haven't fully reached into this realm yet, and while they're influencing the Emerald Queen, she is the one who is here. For all we know, once she has the Lifestone, she may use it to bring the demons into our world."

"What are we missing?" said Miranda.

"What do you mean?" asked Pug.

"I don't know," she said, concern clearly written on her face. "Somewhere in all of this is a missing piece, something to do with why we're not swooping down on the invasion fleet as it reaches the deepest part of the ocean and sinking it."

"There are a lot of Pantathian priests on those ships," said Nakor. "They may not have Pug's power, or Macros's, or yours, but together—"

"Pug could destroy them in seconds," Miranda interrupted. "I saw what he did in the Celestial City; I'm not a beginner. I've been studying magic for two centuries, and what he did is so far beyond my abilities it's staggering."

Macros nodded. "He forced himself into my mind . . . Sarig's mind, and ripped me away like pulling a cork from a bottle. This was no trivial thing."

Pug said, "It's not that simple."

"It *is* that simple," said Miranda. "If we don't act, a lot of people are going to die."

"What if we're wrong?" asked Pug. "What if we die in the attempt?"

"Life is risks," answered Macros's daughter, and for a brief second Pug saw the resemblance between father and daughter.

"If we perish," said Pug, "then there is nothing to stop the Emerald Queen from taking the Lifestone."

"There's Tomas," reminded Miranda.

Pug thought it over for a long time, then said, "First we must make sure that Tomas knows what we are going to do."

"Agreed," said Macros.

"Send Nakor and Dominic to Tomas," said Macros.

"No!" said Nakor. "I want to see what you're going to do."

"Your curiosity is endless," said Pug, "but we're going to be facing something awesome by any standards." As Nakor started to object, Pug raised his hand and cut him off. "You claim there is no magic, but you know more about the workings of magic than just about anyone else in Midkemia, save Macros, Miranda, and me."

Nakor's eyes narrowed. "I always wanted to ask you about that," he said. "You told James to tell me 'There is no magic' a long time ago, to get me to go to Stardock, and I always wanted to know about that."

Pug smiled. "I'll tell you when this is all over."

Nakor's grin returned. "Very well, but we have a few problems to address before we return."

"Yes," said Dominic. "No one may return to Midkemia with the knowledge of Nalar or even a desire to discover that knowledge intact. While the God of Evil is locked away, Midkemia is his home, and he will attune his influence to anyone who is receptive, much as Sarig took Macros to his service all those years ago."

"Have you the means to remove the memory of Nalar, Dominic?" asked Pug. "We can put blocks on our own minds, not letting the knowledge surface, but it will still be there."

Dominic nodded. "Among our order it is common to deal with just this sort of problem, as we cannot let anyone know the secret of Ishap and the other Controller Gods. If you do as I instruct, we will leave here ignorant of Nalar." He turned to face Macros. "You trod perilously close to becoming Nalar's tool, had you not been protected by the lingering magic of Sarig. Even though the God of Magic gave you that protection, it will not last."

"I know," said Macros, "but we had to understand what we faced."

"Agreed," said Dominic, "though the Father Prelate in Rillanon will find it difficult to accept my word."

"Is that what you did, sending that sealed chest?" asked Miranda.

Dominic nodded. "Each Abbot at Sarth prepares against the time of great trial, when we shall see the abbey destroyed. Against that day we are preparing another place, one that will be called That Which Was Sarth. The repository exists and awaits, and we only waited for the foretold sign."

"And we were that sign?"

Dominic nodded. "In our dealings with the Greater Gods, we have come to understand their limits as well as their power; they communicate to us in a fashion that can be only called disjointed. One thing above all else, though, was the event of our first contact, ages ago, when we were warned that one would come, with companions, who knew the secret, and at that time the world would change. Yes, your arrival is the signal that we need to begin moving the great library at Sarth to That Which Was Sarth."

Miranda said, "Where are you moving the library to?"

"To a location, high in the mountains of Yabon, where it will be safe."

"Well, if the Emerald Queen gets her hands on the Lifestone, nothing will be safe," Pug observed.

Miranda said, "Then let us set about forgetting the reason behind this horror."

Dominic indicated they should sit in a circle and join hands. The old cleric said, "Close your eyes, and open your minds to me. When we have finished you will know nothing of Nalar. You will only know that you have forgotten something, but rather than be curious, you will be relieved. You will know that it is vital that you not remember this thing, for to do so would bring danger beyond any you imagine. You will remember enough of what we have talked about to be aware of your chosen course of action, but of Nalar, the only thing you will recall is that out there, somewhere, a grave danger lurks, one against which you must remain vigilant, but one which you must never seek to know."

Dominic began his incantation and all of them felt a strange presence enter their minds, which began to order knowledge. For a brief instant each felt a mild discomfort, and a flash of fear, which was instantly replaced by a calm reassurance, and then, suddenly, it was done.

Pug blinked and said, "It's over?"

Dominic said, "Yes. You remember what you need to remember, and the rest is safely locked away. It must be so."

They took what he said at face value. "We must go now," Dominic said.

"First I will take you and Nakor to Elvandar," said Pug. He glanced at Miranda and her father. "Then we go to face the Emerald Queen."

Tomas awaited in the glade where Tathar and Acaila had overseen their protection. He stood resplendent in his armor of white and gold. Behind him waited the warriors of Elvandar, Calin and Redtree at their head.

"It is time?" asked Tomas as soon as they materialized.

"Not yet," said Pug, "but soon. Get word to Stone Mountain and the Grey Towers. Call the dwarves to war. You know where to lead them when they gather."

Tomas nodded, and started issuing instructions to elven runners nearby. Pug had alerted him of their coming, using a mental call agreed upon by the two boyhood friends years before. Nakor and Dominic moved away from the three magicians, and Pug came up to Tomas. "We go to challenge the Emerald Queen before she reaches our shore. Should we fail, the war will come to you eventually. You know the stakes. You must convince Dolgan and Halfdan down in Dorgin to come to the Kingdom's aid."

Tomas nodded. "Dolgan will come. He and I have too much between us for him to ignore my call. Halfdan will come because Dolgan comes." He smiled, and for a moment Pug saw his boyhood friend again, behind the mask of the alien warrior. "The dwarves of Dorgin never forgave Dolgan for not inviting them to the last war."

Pug looked around the glade, as if drinking in the calm beauty, imprinting it on his memory. It was early evening here in Elvandar, so it would be morning where the invading fleet would be found.

Pug gripped Tomas's hand and said, "Good-bye, my friend."

Tomas squeezed lightly. "Be well. I will see you when we celebrate this victory."

Pug only nodded.

He turned and came to where Macros and Miranda waited, reached out and took their hands. Suddenly they were gone.

Nakor said, "We have much to do, and less time to do it in than we might wish for."

Tomas nodded. "I fear you are correct."

Dominic said, "I need to reach our abbey in the Grey Towers. From there our brothers can transport me to anyplace in the Kingdom where we have an abbey or temple."

Tomas motioned to an elf. "Galain, see to horses for the morning." To Nakor and Dominic he said, "You will dine and rest, and leave in the morning."

Nakor said, "No, Sho Pi and I will stay here. I think we will be needed here, soon."

Nakor was without his ever-present grin, and Dominic said, "You're fearful?"

"Yes," said the little man. "I know why Pug does this thing, and it is unwise, I think. He does it as much to prove his love for Miranda as to defeat the enemy, and while I believe she is right in assessing his power, I think she underestimates the power of the Emerald Queen and the Pantathians." Then he added in a low voice, "And vastly underestimates the third player."

Dominic's eyes widened and he pulled Nakor aside as the elves walked on. "What do you remember?"

"All of it," said Nakor. Something strange burned in the little man's eyes. "I have my own ways of protecting my mind, Abbot, just as you do. Those three magicians like to think they know a lot about the many paths of magic, but they still think too much along one path. You and I know there are many paths, many ways to proceed. Or no paths, if you look at it another way. You have no need to worry about my falling under the Nameless One's influence."

"Who are you?" asked Dominic.

A grin spread across Nakor's face. "Just a gambler who knows some tricks."

Dominic said, "If you weren't clearly working for our cause, I would fear you, I think."

Nakor shrugged. "Those who aren't my friends do well to fear me, for as I said, I know a few tricks."

With that enigmatic pronouncement, Nakor walked after the elves, leaving a very shaken old Abbot with much to ponder.

"What next?" said Miranda.

Macros pointed downward. "There!"

The three magicians hovered high above the clouds as hundreds of miles of shimmering water spread out below. Pug turned his eyes to the point Macros indicated and saw the fleet of the Emerald Queen.

"It's huge," said Miranda.

"More than six hundred ships," said Macros. "Close to seven hundred."

"They must have been building somewhere we didn't know about," offered Pug. He, like Miranda, had stayed abreast of the intelligence coming from Calis's agents in Novindus.

"We need a plan," said Miranda.

Pug said, "Here's the plan: I will swoop down to confront the Emerald Queen and her Pantathian servants. When they spring whatever trap they have waiting for me, you two come in and catch them by surprise."

Macros said, "No, I'll come in. Alone."

As Miranda started to object, Macros said, "Your job is to get us out of there if this doesn't work."

She considered a moment, and while the wind sent her hair streaming out behind her, Pug thought he had never seen her looking more beautiful. "Very well," she said.

Pug quickly kissed her and said, "Place a spell of recall upon us all."

Miranda said, "Where do we travel if we have to leave in a hurry?"

Pug had already considered the question. "Elvandar," he said. "The elves have the best healers in the world, and we may need them. They also have the best magic wards if something tries to follow us."

She nodded. "Telling you to be careful would be the height of foolishness." She kissed her father's cheek. "Be careful."

Then she kissed Pug passionately. "Stay alive."

Pug and Macros lowered toward the fleet and Macros said, "Am I going to be a father-in-law?"

Pug said, "If we somehow live through this."

Macros said, "Then I'll see you do."

"I'm counting on it," said Pug, and Macros laughed. "What do you propose to do?" he asked.

"I think a direct approach is best." Pug considered a moment. "I'm certain they expect me to come at them sometime between now and when they reach the Straits."

"They might expect you at the Straits."

"That is too late. If I fail, there is no time to regroup, but if I come now . . ."

"What should I do?"

"Be ready to provide me with a distraction. They have no knowledge you're back." Then he muttered, "At least, I hope they don't." He spoke up: "If I get into trouble, do something to give me a chance to escape, but don't put yourself at risk; rely on Miranda to get us both out."

"I'll do what I must," said Macros.

"Then let us begin," said Pug.

He faded from Macros's sight, and the sorcerer knew he was attempting to get as close as possible to the ship upon which the Emerald Queen rode before revealing himself. Macros let his own enhanced senses reach out and locate Pug, following him as he approached the fleet.

Pug swooped down over the vanguard of the flotilla. A full score of warships formed a V at the head of the fleet. On either flank another twenty ships guarded the bulk of the armada. At the rear came a squadron of faster warships, tacking back and forth, ready to race forward and give support on either side if the need arose.

Pug saw the Emerald Queen's ship, dead center of a huge cluster of transport ships. Pug used his magic vision, attempting to locate his quarry.

As if watching through a crystal, he saw her with the lens of his magic perception: she rested upon a throne, set amidships, upon a wallowing galley rowed by three banks of oars. Surrounding her were an honor guard of some of the most evil-looking creatures Pug had ever spied. Each exuded a miasma of foulness like a cloud of smoke, trailing along behind him.

Two men stood on either side of the Queen. To her right was a human whom Pug took to be General Fadawah. There was nothing soft in his features or demeanor. He looked as if carved from unyielding stone. His head was shaved, save for a single topknot of hair gathered together and allowed to fall down his back. His face was scarred, and Pug recognized the marks; they had been described to him by those who had faced the moredhel outlaw chieftain Murad, when Prince Arutha had quested after the Silverthorn plant that he needed to save his betrothed's life.

At the Queen's other hand a robed figure stood, a Pantathian to outward appearance. Pug could detect no features beneath the creature's hood. Pug gently sent energies down to the ship, attempting to detect any countermeasures. There was a flow of communication between the ship and other agents, near and far away. And there were detection spells, which he easily avoided.

That made him suspicious and he sought to investigate behind those spells. As he suspected, there was a second array of wards, cleverly masked by the clumsy detection spells, and he had been close to activating them.

He studied his enemy's defenses and made ready his attack.

Pug gathered his energies, determined to blast this ship from existence. He would deal with the other ships and the serpent priests who rode them after disposing of the Queen. As energy gathered around him, Pug sensed probing energies of an alien nature, from an unknown source.

Suddenly those on the ship below were running and pointing. A handful of robed figures appeared upon the decks and began incanting wards of protection.

But they were too late, as Pug unleashed a tremendous blast of mystic energy, enough to ignite the entire ship in a funeral pyre. A crimson ball of fire exploded from his fingertips, hurling like a comet of death at the Emerald Queen's ship. The explosion was deafening and blinding, and as it ignited, Pug suddenly sensed his mistake.

"Flee!" he sent to Macros and Miranda. "It's a trap!"

The bolt of energy encountered a counterspell, one woven into the very fabric of the ship itself. Weeks of execution had been involved in this, the most subtle thing the Pantathians had undertaken since Pug's first encounter with them years before. The cloth in the sails, the tar in the deck, the nails in the hull, and the wood of the spars—all had been imbued with this counter-magic. And the wards of detection and the incanting of the Pantathian priests had been nothing more than masks to hide the telltale traces of this subtle magic.

Pug's defenses were hardly in place when his own magic was turned back upon him. The fireball ran back up its previous course, seeking its source. Furious energies exploded around him, blinding and deafening him, rendering him near-senseless. Reflexes took over, and he attempted to put distance between himself and the ship. Red flames consumed Pug, and only his own incredible power and instinct kept him from being incinerated in an instant.

Then those upon the ship unleashed their own attacks, and Pug suffered.

A presence manifested itself to Pug as he struggled to avoid the next wave of pain. "Puny mage! Do you think we were unaware of your pitiful scheming? You are but a pawn in a game so much more vast than any you can imagine. Now die!"

At that instant, Pug saw the face of his true enemy. Where the Emerald Queen had sat, the illusion was pierced. A demon crouched upon the golden throne under the canopy athwart the galley. Mystic chains went from his taloned hand to magic collars around the necks of the Pantathian and General Fadawah. They were clearly under the demon's control and both looked upward helplessly.

"I am Jakan, and I shall rule here!"

Agony raced through every fiber of Pug's being as his protective wards were stripped away from him. The robes on his body burst into flames and his hair and skin began to burn. A scream erupted from lungs scorched and blistered and his eyes shriveled in his head. He struggled to escape, but the pain was overwhelming, and he lost all control. His mind fled from the pain, and as he felt darkness closing around him, he also felt himself tumbling through the air.

Then a pair of arms grabbed him, and a groan of agony came from Pug as he was carried aloft, every movement an agony for him. Macros sent word to Miranda: "Get us out of here now!"

Even the chilled air burned his flaming skin as Pug lapsed into darkness.

"Will he live?" asked Miranda, fear etched into her features.

"I don't know," answered Tathar.

Dominic and Nathan looked on in horror at the thing that had been Pug. His body was smoking and charred, and in several places white bone showed through. Acaila said, "It's a miracle he lives still."

Nakor pushed through and said, "Life is strong in this man. It holds strongly here. We must help it."

Nakor put his hands above his head a moment, then incanted. He placed his hands upon Pug's chest, over his heart, and said, "I need whatever strength you can spare."

Instantly the Spellweavers of Elvandar began to spin their magic. Dominic lent his skills, using a spell of healing, the most powerful he knew.

Nakor felt the energy course through him, down his arms and into Pug's chest. Faintly, under the palm of Nakor's right hand, he could feel the fluttering beat of Pug's heart. Slowly it strengthened, as if drinking the energy from Nakor and the others like a dry sponge in water.

Nakor felt himself tingle with the flow, but he focused, and attempted to see the energy sites in Pug's body. "One of you, put hands over his head," he said.

Acaila did as he was bid and Nakor closed his eyes a moment.

In the elven glade more and more came to witness the healing. Tomas strode into the ring of watchers, who stepped aside to let him approach his friend. Nakor opened his eyes and said, "Good. Put your hands over his throat. He burned his lungs, and I need help."

Nakor closed his eyes and directed the energies flowing into Pug.

Time passed and night gave way to day, and still they labored, kneeling for hours letting the healing energies of their own bodies as well as the ancient magic of Elvandar flow into the injured magician.

Near noon, Nakor faltered and found familiar hands gripping his arm. "Master?" came Sho Pi's inquiry.

"I'll be fine," said Nakor. "I just need rest."

"I'll take over," said Nakor's student, and he stepped into the position his master had occupied, placing his hands upon Pug's chest.

Miranda came over, and from her drawn expression and red eyes Nakor could see she had been weeping. "Will he live?"

Nakor said, "I don't know. A lesser man would have died instantly. Most greater men would be dead now, but there's something in him that hangs on." He looked at the man lying on the floor of the glade, upon the grass, and said, "He looks very small and vulnerable now, doesn't he?"

"Yes," said Miranda, her voice heavy with emotion.

Nakor sighed. It was obvious he was exhausted from his efforts. "The longer he hangs on, the better his chances that he will survive. We are all channeling healing energies to him, and as long as he has a will to live, he continues to live. I told Nicholas once that in some men life is weak and in others it is strong. For one such as myself, your father, or yourself, it must be strong for us to abide all the years we continue to exist, but for Pug it's something more." Trying to be reassuring, he added, "I think he will live."

Miranda looked into Nakor's eyes. "You don't think that, do you?"

Nakor tried to force a grin, but it failed. "No, I don't. We will do all we can, but he is injured far beyond what I've seen any man endure." His eyes revealed a hint of deep regret, then he forced back that doubt and assumed his usual cheerful mantle. "But what do I know? I'm just a gambler who has some tricks, and Tathar and the other Spellweavers are working vigorously." He patted her hand in a fatherly fashion. "He will be all right, I'm sure."

She looked into Nakor's face and saw the words were empty, but she appreciated the gesture and nodded, walking over to stand beside her father.

Nakor watched her move away, then looked at Pug's face, the oozing, cracked skin, the blackened arms and legs. "But if he does, it will be a very long time before he fights again."

Days passed, and Pug's condition remained unchanged. The Spellweavers, Nakor, and Sho Pi worked in shifts, pouring as much healing magic as possible into the unconscious magician. Only exhaustion forced them from his side.

Nakor returned from another half day spent healing Pug, and sat down heavily next to Macros and Miranda, who were eating their supper next to a fire.

"How is he?" asked Miranda.

"The same," said Nakor, shaking his head slightly. "I fear he grows weaker."

Miranda's grief was openly revealed as tears gathered in her eyes. "He's not going to live, is he?"

Nakor shrugged. "I do not know. It may be a long time before we do know."

Macros placed his hands upon his daughter's shoulders. "And we don't have a long time, do we?"

Nakor shook his head. "No. And again we find another mystery."

Macros said, "Yes."

Nakor said, "I'm going to sleep awhile; then I think we need hold council with the Queen and Tomas."

"I agree," said Macros.

The three of them rose to find places to sleep and parted company. Nakor couldn't help returning to the clearing a moment and looking at Pug. The magician remained motionless, the only sign of his still being alive the slight rise and fall of his chest as Sho Pi continued to keep his hands upon Pug's charred chest. Perhaps it was wishful thinking, but Nakor thought Pug's breathing might be slightly deeper and more regular than before. Again he wondered at the small magician's strength and will to live.

Aglaranna looked around the circle and said, "Tathar says Pug will live. It will be a long time before he regains consciousness and longer still before he heals, but with our arts we can restore his damaged skin and hair, heal the broken bones and burned tissue."

The relief was almost tangible in the council, especially on the faces of Tomas and Miranda.

Macros said, "Pug was right and we were not."

Miranda's expression showed she felt terrible guilt over her part in Pug's precipitate attack. "It is my fault."

Nakor said, "It is no one's fault or everyone's fault. No one forced Pug, your father, and you to attack the Emerald Queen. We thought it risky and it was."

"They were better prepared than we anticipated," said Miranda.

"More than that," said Macros. To Miranda he said, "You were too far removed from the battle to see what Pug and I saw, and you have no way of knowing."

"What?"

"The woman who was your mother is but a shell, an illusion. I suspect she is long dead. The creature at the head of this army is a demon. He identified himself to Pug as Jakan."

"Jakan?" said Nakor.

"You've heard of him?" asked Miranda.

"In a roundabout way," said the little man. "He's a demon captain, not a big one, like Tugor, First Servant to Maarg, Ruler of the Fifth Circle, but one with some reputation."

Tathar said, "We have had contact with such once or twice in the history of our race. How do you know of them, human?"

Nakor shrugged. "You hear things, here and there."

Miranda said, "You're an infuriating little man."

Nakor grinned. "Your mother said the same to me when we were married." He sighed. "I wish I had had a daughter like you."

Macros said, "No you don't."

Suddenly laughter filled the council and everyone knew the relief was at Pug's apparent recovery as much as from the banter. Then Nakor's expression turned serious. "About a century or so ago I found my way into the Hall of Worlds and spent some time at Honest John's. It's a good place to gamble." He made a sour face. "Hard place to cheat. Anyway, in the course of my time there I heard about some troubles with the demons."

"Such as?" prompted Macros.

"That someone was stirring them up and they were attempting to breach the barriers out of the Fifth Circle into the higher realms."

"Someone provided them a way," suggested Macros.

"That's what worries me," said Tomas. "In the memories of the Valheru, we struggled with the demons, and among our foes, only the Dread were more powerful. But the Dread and the demons were confined to realms far from our own, and for them to be here, both at the time of the Riftwar and now, means an agency of great power is behind all of this."

Macros and Miranda exchanged looks. "I sense we know something . . ." said Miranda.

"Knew something," said Macros. To the Queen and Tomas he said, "There are larger forces at play here, but I also have some sense that we have limits to what we may do. I suggest we consider what may be our next best course of action."

Tomas said, "It's obvious the fleet is well protected and that another attack of the sort Pug mounted would prove unwise."

"Agreed," said Macros. "They may not know my and Miranda's abilities, but they must know Pug has allies of significant power and have defenses in place. This demon who has taken the Emerald Queen's place may not be a great demon lord, but he has firm control of those around us, from what little I glimpsed as I saved Pug.

"We must consider the risk that the demons are in a position to slip more of their captains and lords through into Midkemia. We must attend to that danger, while I think we'd best leave the more mundane concerns of invasion to those who are best equipped to meet it: Prince Patrick, Duke James, and Knight-Marshal William."

Tomas said, "We will, though we will aid them when the time comes."

"I understand," said Macros. He stood and moved to the middle of the circle. "With Pug injured, I must again put myself in the center of this struggle."

Aglaranna said, "Years ago you came to us and were instrumental in saving our home, Macros. Your wisdom is always welcome here."

Macros rubbed his beard. "My wisdom is somewhat lacking at the moment, lady. Before, I had Sarig's gift of future sight, and the ability to travel at will back and forth through time. Since the severing of our ties, I fear I have but a bare sense of where to start looking next for our course of action."

Miranda said, "Well, we need to find the Rift and close it forever."

"Perhaps you need to look at the place Calis and Miranda found those tainted artifacts." It was Tathar who spoke. "I've studied the artifacts our Calis sent to us as much as anyone, and while I can put no name to the alien presence that has touched it, I can say it is powerful, and what is there is well hidden. It must be the demons, and that must be where they are entering our world."

Acaila held up his hand and nodded in agreement. "Absolutely. Tathar and all the Spellweavers have indicated this is magic of great power and subtlety, well hidden, masked to disguise its origin, and clever in its construction."

Macros said, "That sounds likely."

Tomas said, "I will go with you two."

Miranda said, "I thought you never left Elvandar."

Tomas said, "I vowed never to leave save at great need." He turned to his wife. "It is time."

The Elf Queen's face was an expressionless mask, yet her eyes betrayed a flicker of emotion. Then she calmly said, "I know."

Tomas asked Macros, "Should I call a dragon?"

Macros said, "No. Miranda knows where the entrance to the caves is. If you guide me," he said to her, "I can take the three of us there."

Miranda said, "No need. I can do so."

Tomas said to his wife, "Abide, and keep hope in your heart. I will come back."

No one spoke until a few minutes later Tomas reappeared, and even though he had seen him dressed so before, Macros felt awe.

Tomas stood dressed in armor fashioned of gold, a helm and coif, chain shirt and leggings. His white tabard, bearing a golden dragon design, was cinched by his black belt, and his boots were black leather as well. His scabbard was white, looking as if carved from ivory, but it was empty.

Calin came and withdrew his own sword, handing it to his mother's husband. "A loan," he said.

Tomas took it, nodded once, and slipped it into the scabbard. "I will return it soon," he said. To Macros and Miranda he said, "Come. It is time."

He motioned and Miranda rose, took his hand and Macros's, closed her eyes, and they were gone.

Redtree watched the empty space and said, "Until I saw him in that armor, I had doubts. But he is Valheru."

Acaila said, "Not truly. A fact for which we should all be eternally grateful."

No more was said.

Bitter winds swept the mountains as they appeared. Miranda blinked at the bright sunlight after the cool evening light of Elvandar. The rising sun was shining directly in her eyes. "Over there." She pointed to a cave mouth.

They moved quickly toward the dark opening and entered. Once they were inside, the noise of the wind was cut and Tomas said, "I see in the dark, but what of you?"

Macros raised a hand and a nimbus of light surrounded him, illuminating the cave mouth. He looked around.

Miranda said, "This tunnel was one I found by accident. Boldar Blood was killing some serpent warriors who were trying to block our path and I noticed a faint light from above."

At the mention of the mercenary from the Hall of Worlds, Macros said, "I wouldn't mind his sword with us, now."

Miranda said, "Not to mention all those other exotic weapons he bears."

Macros spoke under his breath, "But not at the prices he charges, I wager."

Tomas laughed. "You keep your sense of humor, old friend."

"Well," said Miranda, "you'll find little to laugh about ahead. This way."

She led them into the tunnel, one low enough that Tomas had to duck to enter. They half scrambled, half walked down a narrow, steep incline, entering another tunnel by having to slide almost sideways into a stone alcove, about six feet above a larger tunnel.

As they jumped to the floor of the second tunnel, Macros said, "It's a miracle you even noticed that entrance."

Miranda said, "I was motivated. Boldar is a fearsome fighter, but he survived to reach Elvandar with me only because we were fighting a rearguard action up that narrow crawlway. Else we would have been overwhelmed."

Macros looked around. A few bones littered the passage, and what looked to be a broken sword hilt. "Something has disposed of most of the mess."

Tomas said, "Scavengers?"

"Perhaps," said Macros. He asked Miranda, "Which way?"

She pointed and started walking without saying anything.

Twice they had paused to rest, though it was not so much that anyone was fatigued as to stop a moment and get their bearings. Once they opened a small bag that Macros carried, which held some small slivers of a food for travel prepared by the elves. Another time they drank from a waterskin Miranda carried.

Then they reached the first major gallery of the Pantathians. "There's something close by," Tomas said in a low voice.

"I feel it, too," said Macros.

"Then we have a consensus," offered Miranda. "It's that way."

She pointed across the hall, now blanketed by dust, but full of dead and dying Pantathians when she had last passed that way. "Up there," she said, "we came into this hall. We saw the demon fighting the Pantathians down on the floor." She indicated the ridge that ran around the gallery, above their heads. "We crossed along there, and lowered ourselves down a rope to there." The location she indicated was marked by a low door, now hanging open.

"Some Saaur and Pantathians objected, and we fought our way down that corridor." Glancing around, she commented, "I didn't realize how close we came to doubling back when we fled down that hallway."

Tomas said, "Sometime I'll tell you of the time a wraith chased me through the ancient Mac Mordain Cadal. I survived only because I could double back and lose it in those confusing tunnels."

Macros said, "I'm astonished you can find your way through here at all. It's been over a year, and you've only been through here once."

Dryly Miranda said, "When your life is in the balance, you'd be amazed what you remember."

She led them to the open door. "It was down this way we found the artifacts."

Tomas said, "We can go that way later. I'm inclined to discover who or what we feel up that way." He pointed to the tunnel opening Miranda had indicated she and Calis's party had used to enter this area the previous year.

"That way lies a passage to a central corridor, a large vertical shaft that runs from the bowels of this mountain to the peak."

"I know," said Tomas. "That was a common feature of the Valheru mountain holdings. Otherwise a dragon had no means to enter the central hall."

Miranda led and they followed, and soon they were walking through another dark passage.

Time passed without measure and they went on without pause. On two occasions Macros asked Miranda if she needed to rest, a question she dismissed with a sarcastic remark. After the second rebuff, Macros decided to stop asking.

Miranda wished they could use their magic to transport ahead, but it was decided there was too much chance they might miss something. Also, without exact knowledge of the location to which they were moving, there was always the risk of materializing inside solid rock.

They descended the large shaft Miranda had described. As if the center of the mountain had been hollowed out, a large ramp spiraled up and down, cut into the stone of the mountain. The central shaft was unguarded by rail or barrier, and the wind gusts were strong enough to give one the feeling of being sucked over the edge. Large areas had been carved out of the stone at various locations, for what purpose only Tomas might know. Macros thought he might ask him sometime, but at the moment the magician was disinclined to speak without need. This wasn't the time or place for idle chatter.

They came to another large tunnel that intersected the shaft and a faint, unpleasant odor reached them.

"It's near," whispered Tomas, as they moved into the large hallway.

Macros sniffed and identified the stench as something rotting. "A lair?" he whispered in return.

Tomas only drew his sword and moved forward. Macros let Miranda follow and took up his position at the rear of the file. The white-and-gold-clad warrior was first to enter another large gallery, near the bottom of the circular shaft.

Macros saw Miranda abruptly step to the side, making way for him, as Tomas shouted a war cry and leaped over the edge. Macros took a quick step and met a sight that made him hesitate an instant.

A creature sat upon its scaled haunches gnawing on a bone. It was scaled in black glinting with a faint green shine. Large batlike wings were folded upon its back, and its head was something alien, looking roughly like that of a crocodile fashioned from grey stone, with a stag's antlers rising from the skull. If skin protected that skull, it was taut enough not to be evident at first glance, and was pulled back so that an impressive array of teeth was always on display.

Powerful shoulders melded into long arms, ending with hands tipped with talons the size of daggers.

Miranda said, "A demon."

Macros was beginning an incantation, one designed to stun the creature, as Tomas landed on the stone floor before it. The demon rose, standing a full head taller than the half-human warrior, and for an instant Macros was concerned for Tomas's safety.

But, rather than attack, the creature pressed itself against the wall, and spoke.

A single word, in a language unknown to Miranda, but the effect on Macros and Tomas was instantaneous. Macros ceased his incantation and Tomas halted an attack in mid-strike, turning his blade so that, instead of cleaving flesh, Calin's blade struck the stone next to the creature. Sparks erupted on the wall as he cut a furrow in the stone next to the demon.

Macros leaped to his companion's side as the brute attempted to avoid Tomas's strike. Again the alien word was repeated and Tomas stepped back.

"What is it?" shouted Miranda from above.

Macros stood at Tomas's side, not taking his eyes from the demon. The fearsome-looking being remained motionless, as if waiting, and Tomas said, "He yields!"

Miranda asked, "How do you know?"

Tomas turned to his friend. "That's what he shouted. He yields."

Miranda also jumped down, landing heavily next to Macros. "I speak a dozen tongues. I've never heard that one before. What is it?"

Tomas regarded her with confusion clearly marking his half-alien features. "It is the language of the Valheru. It's the ritual phrase of submission. Our servant races spoke it as a greeting."

Miranda looked from Tomas to the cowering demon and let out a long, slow breath, while wishing her heart would cease pounding its way out of her chest. "Isn't that something?"

Eleven

Alarm

ERIK RAN.

Drums rolled as he dashed through the halls of the old castle at Tannerus. He reached the open doorway at the top of the stairs leading down into the courtyard. In one quick glimpse he saw it all: the assembled soldiers bearing witness to the execution, the four men standing upon wooden supports, the ropes already around their necks. Erik shouted, "No!" as he leaped over the railing to the second landing below, but the sounds of the drums drowned him out. Erik half flew down the remaining stairs into the courtyard as the drums halted and the supports were kicked out from under the condemned. He ran the twenty yards to where his soldiers stood at attention, and saw that three of the men had died instantly of broken necks, and the fourth had ceased his brief twitching.

Erik stopped. "Damn!" he swore.

The order to dismiss the formation was given, and the troops of the Tannerus garrison broke ranks and hurried back to their duties. No man wanted to linger while another soldier twisted in the wind.

Erik stood nearly breathless as he watched his men swinging below the makeshift gallows. The Captain had wasted little time in putting the condemned to death. Had he ordered a half-decent gallows be erected, Erik would have gotten here in time. Erik searched the faces of the dead. He knew them by sight, but not yet by name. Still, they were his men.

Captain Simon de Beswick turned his horse and saw Erik standing there. "Is something amiss, Sergeant Major?"

Erik studied the foppish officer, just rotated in from the East. Erik and another company of the Prince's soldiers had been ordered into the field, and he discovered that de Beswick would ride with them to Tannerus. De Beswick was seconded to the Prince's court, and assigned garrison duty in the north. The two men had taken an instant dislike to each other.

The only person to whom de Beswick was civil was Owen Greylock, because of his rank, senior to de Beswick's. He refused any conversation with any enlisted man save in the line of duty, and was uniformly rude and abusive to the men. It had been with relief that Erik had taken half the men into the field for a week's field training, while the other half had remained to be trained in garrison defense. Erik had just returned to be informed at the gate that four of his men were being hanged. Erik balled his right hand into a fist, and said, "Why were those men executed?"

"They pilfered stores," said de Beswick, raising his eyebrows as if asking a question.

"Those were *my* men," Erik said with menace in his voice, almost a growl.

"Then tend to them better, Sergeant Major, and address me as 'sir' in future."

The Captain made to ride past, and Erik seized the reins of his horse. "You had no right to hang my men. We're not even in your command!"

De Beswick said, "I had every right, as commander of the garrison here at Tannerus, and I certainly do not need to explain my actions to you, *Sergeant Major.*" Slowly drawing his sword, he said, "Now, please be good enough to release my horse, or I shall be forced to kill you for assaulting an officer."

Owen Greylock caught up with Erik, and said, "Put up that sword, de Beswick!"

"Knight-Captain?" said the garrison commander.

"That's an order," said Greylock calmly.

Reluctantly de Beswick put the sword away. Owen put his hand on Erik's shoulder and said, "Sergeant Major, see to your men. I'll take care of this."

Owen waited until Erik had left, then turned and grabbed de Beswick by the boot, lifting suddenly. As Owen expected, de Beswick came flying out of his saddle, and as his horse galloped away, the Captain from Bas-Tyra landed hard upon the dirt of the courtyard.

Owen grabbed the young man by the collar and hauled him to his feet. Looking into his eyes with an expression that could only be called murderous, he said, "We have a war coming and you're killing *our* soldiers?"

"They were thieves!" said the now-fearful de Beswick.

"Half the men in this army are thieves, you idiot."

Owen let him go with a slight shove, and de Beswick landed hard upon his backside again. Leaning over, Greylock pointed to where Erik had gone. "That man may be the best soldier I've ever known, and I've been training them for thirty years. When this war comes, you incompetent lily, he is your best hope for staying alive. If you have the brains the gods give a flea, you will try to learn everything he has to teach you about surviving in these mountains. If you cross him one more time, I will give him permission to call you out, and if you face him with sword in hand, he will kill you. Do you understand?"

"Yes," said the younger Captain, and it was obvious he didn't like what he was hearing.

"Now get yourself back to your command, de Beswick, while I decide what I'm going to say to Knight-Marshal William in my next missive."

As the Captain started to leave, Greylock said, "One more thing, de Beswick."

"Sir?" asked the Captain.

"If Captain Calis had been here, he would have killed you, and that's a certainty."

After the young commander of the garrison had departed, Owen went looking for Erik. He found him in the soldiers' commons, asking the men of his command what had happened.

"It was nothing," said a man named Gunther. "It was a lark, pure and simple, Sergeant Major. We were tired after a long day of parading—"

"Parading?" asked Erik.

"Yes, standing formations, marching up and down, turnin' right, then left, that sort of business."

Another man, an old soldier named Johnson, said, "It's that Eastern Army sort of business, Sergeant Major. Not fighting, but marchin' in lines and the like."

"Anyway, those four lads just wanted to nick a little ale from the ale shed, nothing criminal."

Erik could see the men were in a foul mood, and he didn't blame them. If caught, the men should have stood extra punishment watches, or at worst a flogging, but to hang them was beyond excuse. He was about to say something when Greylock spoke. "Erik, a word with you."

Erik came over to the former Swordmaster from Darkmoor and said, "I know, I shouldn't have interfered."

Seeing they were out of hearing range of the soldiers, Owen said, "Probably you should have killed him, but that's not the issue. Give him a wide berth; he may be looking to goad you."

"Why?"

"He's from a well-connected family in Bas-Tyra. His father is a cousin to the Duke of Ran."

Comprehension dawned on Erik. "Which means his family is probably close to the von Darkmoors."

"Maybe. I know they know each other, but close? I don't really know. He could be one of Mathilda's agents," said Owen. The slender man rubbed his chin in thought. "Or some idiot who thinks to curry favor from the Baron's mother by ridding her of a bothersome threat to her son's title."

Erik sighed. "How many times do I have to tell the world I have no interest in my father's title?"

Owen said, "No matter how many times you do say it, Mathilda won't be satisfied until you're dead."

"What should I do?"

"I'll send a note to Duke James and let him intercede with William to transfer this idiot to someplace where he may die gloriously for the King. I'm going to recommend he command the catapults on the seawall they're building in Krondor."

Erik winced. "I thought it was going to be manned by volunteers."

"It is. We'll just see that young de Beswick volunteers." Owen smiled. "Take your other company out at first light. Don't linger here. I have to move on to Eggly and see to the defenses there. We're going to have to put up a convincing fight throughout these hills to force the Emerald Queen's army where we want it."

Erik sighed. So much to do and so little time to prepare. He knew the fleet had departed from Novindus; all those who had served with Calis across the sea knew that. "What of Krondor?"

Owen shrugged. "Rumors. Some timid folks are starting to leave the city. Nothing that's stirring up real alarm. There's a lot of movement along the Keshian frontier, so many folks are thinking we may have war in the south again."

"It's going to be difficult to keep the city under control once the fleet clears the Straits," said Erik.

"I know. I expect James and William have come up with a solution."

Erik said nothing more. The Queen's fleet would clear the Straits in less than a month's time, at the Midsummer Festival. He had fears that the city would be the ultimate sacrifice for the good of the Kingdom, but the problem for him was that the girl he loved was in the city. As Erik left Owen, and gave orders that the company in the garrison would be rotated out in the morning, he wondered if he could prevail upon Roo to help get Kitty out of Krondor.

Roo looked at the books and said, "I don't understand."

Jason took that to mean he was vague on the methods of accounting, and began explaining it again.

"No," interrupted Roo. "I know the sums and the calculations. What I mean is I don't understand why we're losing money."

Jason, the former waiter at Barret's who had become the chief accountant for Roo's financial empire, said, "It's a problem with too many debts not being paid to us and too many bills we're paying in timely fashion. We're borrowing money for things we should have paid for out of our cash reserves."

"Which are nonexistent," said Roo. He had lent every available golden sovereign to Duke James. "Well, I have about as much chance of a loan repayment from the Crown anytime soon as I do of learning how to fly."

He sighed, stood up from the table in his office and said, "What do you recommend?"

Jason, still looking much like the youth who had first befriended Roo three years earlier, said, "You could sell off some of our less profitable concerns."

"True, but I hate to get rid of capital assets." He yawned. "I'm tired." Glancing out the window, he saw that night had fallen. "What of the clock?"

Jason turned and looked down the hall to where the fancy Keshian timepiece had been erected. "It's almost seven of the clock."

"Karli will be furious," he said. "I promised to be home at six."

"The family's in the city?"

"Yes," said Roo, grabbing his cloak and hurrying down the hall.

Fortunately, by the time Roo reached his house, he found Karli lost in conversation with Helen Jacoby. The two women had struck up a guarded friendship after the death of Randolph Jacoby, awkward because Randolph's brother had been responsible for the death of Karli's father. But in the main they seemed to enjoy each other's company, and the four children played well together. And Roo found that he always enjoyed those evenings when both families gathered.

"There you are," said Karli. "Supper will be served in a few moments."

Cries of "Daddy!" and "Uncle Rupert!" filled the hall as the children swarmed over him. Laughing, Roo fought his way through the tangle of legs and grasping hands, and made his way to the stairs.

As Abigail started to follow him up the stairs, he said, "I'll be down shortly, darling."

"No!" she announced imperiously. "Go away!"

With a regal turn, she walked to the end of the hall and stood with her arms crossed. From his position on the stairs, Roo glanced at the two women in the parlor, and Helen was laughing, while Karli looked astonished.

Helen said, "They all go through that."

Roo nodded and hurried up to his and Karli's room, where he washed up and changed his shirt. He returned to the dining room, where the children carried on at one end of the long table while Roo and Karli sat with Helen Jacoby at the other end.

Roo noticed Helen had taken to wearing her hair up in the new style, curls set around the forehead, and ringlets falling from an odd-looking comb. Roo wondered if it would be rude to ask what the comb was made of, then realized he had almost no idea what the latest fashions in the Prince's City were.

He thought Sylvia would know, and then realized he rarely saw Sylvia dressed anymore, and besides somehow it seemed improper to be thinking of her while his wife and Helen were sitting next to him.

"Why, Roo," said Helen, "you're blushing!"

Roo feigned a cough, then said, "Something in my throat." He made a display of furiously coughing, then dabbing at nonexistent tears in his eyes with his napkin.

Helen laughed again, and Roo was astonished to discover how lovely she was. He had always thought of her as a fine-looking woman—nothing like the beauty Sylvia was, but in her evening finery with her hair done up, she was quite attractive.

Karli said, "Helen tells me you are doing well by her in running her company."

Roo shrugged. "It pretty much runs itself. Tim Jacoby"—he was about to say the man was a swine who knew his business, but given his sister-in-law was sitting there, he changed it to—"was very organized."

"Yes, he was," agreed Helen.

Conversation turned to discussing small items of importance to the children and the landmarks of their growth. The boys were starting to act like boys and the girls were becoming girls, and the mysteries of children still seemed to Roo uncharted territory.

He looked at his own children and realized he knew next to nothing about them. He barely paid them any attention, and suddenly he felt very odd about that. Perhaps when they were older, they'd have something interesting to say to him.

His gaze wandered again to Helen Jacoby, and after a moment she looked his way. Realizing he was staring, he said, "Would you care for brandy?"

Karli looked surprised. In their house, he had never offered brandy to anyone but his business associates.

"No, thank you," she said. "By the time we get home it will be the children's bedtime."

The Jacoby family departed, riding in one of Roo's carriages, and Karli put the children to bed. Roo sat alone in his study for a while, drinking a brandy that he could hardly taste. His mind was lost in worry; he knew that the war was coming and that it was time to get his family to the East, or at least out to his estate, ready to flee from there.

Conversations with Erik and Jadow Shati and others who trusted him had revealed the presence of invaders already within the borders of the Kingdom. Most of those had been neutralized, but when the fighting erupted, who knew how dangerous travel to the East would become.

Karli came down the stairs and asked, "Are you coming to bed?"

"Yes," said Roo, "in a few minutes." As his wife started to turn away, he observed, "You seem to like Helen and her children."

Karli said, "Yes, I do. Her people and mine came from the same village, and we have a lot in common. And her children are sweet."

An idea came to Roo. "When the Midsummer Festival has passed, what do you say to having the Jacobys out to the estate for a few weeks? The children can swim in the stream, and ride horses."

"Roo, they're too little to ride."

"Well then, we'll get them some pony carts." He stood up. "The weather will be beastly hot and it will be much nicer out there."

Karli said in a guarded tone, "You're not trying to get me out of the way, are you Rupert?"

Alarmed that she might suspect his affair with Sylvia, Roo took her in his arms. "Not that. I just think I'd like some quiet time with my family, that's all."

"Having four children in the house instead of just two is hardly my idea of quiet," said Karli.

"You know what I mean," he said, playfully swatting her bottom. He kissed her, and she responded, "Let's go to bed."

While somewhat distracted by worry, he was still able to please Karli, and after their lovemaking she lay asleep in his arms. He found himself visited by an odd confusion, for as was often the case he was thinking of someone else while making love to his wife, but this time he found himself thinking not of Sylvia Esterbrook but rather of Helen Jacoby.

Remembering Gwen, the serving girl back in Ravensburg whom he had lost his virginity to, he silently said to himself, "Gwen's right; we are all pigs."

Fatigue drove away this moment of lucidity, and Roo fell into a deep sleep.

Erik read the orders and said, "We're recalled to Krondor."

Corporals Harper and Reed both saluted and moved out briskly, calling out commands to the soldiers spread out in the hills.

Erik wiped his brow and calculated. He knew that most of the men in the hills were among the last to be trained, the last to be considered for the critical task of limiting the ability of the invaders to expand their front anywhere except where Prince Patrick and his advisers permitted. Most of these men would be assigned to the defense of the city, and if Erik judged things rightly, those garrison units slated to defend in the hills would soon be moving along in small groups, patrols ostensibly, so the Emerald Queen's agents would have little to report.

Erik admired Knight-Marshal William's plans, for it now looked as if all units scattered throughout the West were being recalled for the defense of the city.

Erik squinted at the sun. Midsummer was less than two weeks away, and he knew the Emerald Queen's fleet must be nearing the Straits of Darkness. It was hotter than usual for this time of the year, and he knew that meant it was likely to be a miserable summer.

As the men gathered, he considered that even if the weather were perfect, it would be a miserable summer. Still, by the time the invaders reached these mountains, it would be late fall, and if they could hold them until the winter snows, the Kingdom would survive.

Harper returned, saying, "Word's been passed, Sergeant Major, and we'll be ready to march within the hour."

"Very good," said Erik. "Have you spotted Captain Greylock in the last few hours?"

"About an hour ago, that way." The Corporal pointed down the road.

"When they're ready, don't wait for me, start them for Krondor." He glanced around the hills. "We have four hours of sunlight left, and I want a good ten miles behind us before we think about making camp."

"Yes, Sergeant Major."

Erik mounted his horse and headed down the road to find Greylock by the side of the road, reading a map.

"Owen," said Erik as he rode up.

"Erik," said Owen. "Are you ready to march?"

"In the process," said Erik, as he dismounted. "The corporals are getting them ordered and they should be under way in the next few minutes." Erik sat heavily on the side of the road and said, "I guess we're done up here."

"Done with training," said Greylock. He let his horse crop grass at the roadside as he sat with Erik. "Next time we're up here, we'll be doing it for real."

Erik said, "I've wished a thousand times for a few more days, a week, anything, to get these men into better shape."

"You've done wonders," said Greylock. "Honestly, I can't imagine anyone could have gotten more from the men than you did, Erik. Not Calis, not Bobby de Loungville."

"Thanks for that, Owen." Erik sighed. "I still worry that it's not enough."

"That hardly makes you unique, my young friend."

"Has Lord William told you what we're going to do?"

"Yes," said Greylock. He nodded back up the road. "At least our part of it. I can guess the rest."

"We're going to lose Krondor, aren't we?"

"Probably," said Greylock. "You've seen what happens to cities that resist the Queen, but we've got to hold her at Krondor long enough so she gets into the mountains late."

Erik looked up at the high, pale blue sky streaked with faint clouds far above. "If this weather holds, it could be a long summer."

Greylock sighed. "I know. Prince Patrick has had some magicians with weather sight trying to gauge that, and they all say a long summer is likely."

Erik said, "I keep wondering about those magicians. The Queen uses them. Why don't we?"

Owen smiled. "I expect we'll have a few magical surprises in store for them. But do you remember Nakor's explanation of why you don't use magicians in warfare? He repeated it often enough."

Erik laughed. "Yes, I remember. 'First magician throws spell in battle, then second magician throws counterspell, then third magician try to help first magician, and fourth magician try to aid second, then army shows up and chops them all while they're throwing magic around,' " he mimicked.

Greylock laughed. "You do a terrible impression of Nakor."

Erik shrugged. "But the point is, if we don't do something to counter her magicians we let them have a terrible advantage."

Greylock stood. "Ah, my bones are getting too old for all this riding over the countryside." As he pulled his horse away from the grass at the roadside, he made a display of being old. Erik laughed. Greylock put the reins over the horse's head, then set foot into stirrup and mounted. Once in the saddle he said, "Erik, the more you talk, the more you sound like a Knight-General instead of a Sergeant Major. So don't be asking those sorts of questions around the Prince, or he might promote you."

Erik laughed. "In other words, keep my mouth shut."

"As I said," continued Greylock. "The Prince has some surprises up his sleeve, I'm sure."

Erik mounted. "I'll see you when I get the men back to the city."

"Good," said Greylock. "Oh, and one other thing."

"What?"

"The local commanders are being called in for a last-minute council. The cover story is they're coming in to celebrate Banapis with the Prince, but we know why. So that means de Beswick will be in Krondor."

"I'll keep my eyes open."

"Good. The festival in Krondor is nothing like what you're used to."

Erik nodded. Since coming to the Prince's service, he had managed to be out of the city every Banapis. He had never seen the city celebrate the Midsummer Festival. "I'll try not to get too distracted."

Erik rode back toward where his men should be mustering. He hadn't encountered de Beswick since leading this second company into the mountains. But the suspicion that he could be one of Mathilda von Darkmoor's agents was not lost on Erik. Besides, Erik had four reasons to keep an eye on the man even if he wasn't.

Erik stood stiffly at the rear of the room, the only non-titled non-officer in the room. Captains Calis and Greylock, the only men he knew well, were across the room with Knight-Marshal William, the Duke of Krondor, and the Prince, the only other men he was familiar with.

He recognized some of the others, members of the Prince's court, officers of the palace, local nobles, though he had spoken to only a few of them, on rare occasion. He knew within an hour or so he'd be dismissed and he could squeeze out some personal time before having to get back to the orders that were sure to be waiting for him.

Patrick stood. "My lords, and gentlemen. I'm pleased to see you all in attendance. You will be given a full briefing in select groups. It's no secret a hostile army is heading our way, and we've spent the last several months in preparation for this coming invasion.

"Some of you know a great deal more than others, and for reasons of state security, I command you not to speculate among yourselves or share information. Assume that the man next to you is as knowledgeable as you, no more or less, and cannot give you any more information than you already have, so don't ask questions."

Some of the nobles seemed a bit taken aback by the order, but no one made a comment. A few glanced around the room, attempting to measure the reactions of others.

"Now, to the general situation. This is what you must all know before hostilities begin." The Prince motioned to two squires, who removed a large cloth hanging from the wall. Behind the hanging was an immense map of the Western Realm, from the Far Coast to Malac's Cross. The Prince picked up a long pointer and moved at once to the far left edge of the map. "Here," said Patrick, pointing to the Straits of Darkness, "we expect the enemy's fleet within the next week."

A few nobles muttered to one another, but the room quickly fell silent. "Between then and when they reach here"—he pointed north of the city of Land's End—"we need to be fully mobilized. Therefore, you will spend the next week before Banapis in meetings, getting orders, and making ready. We shall all celebrate the Midsummer Festival as if nothing were amiss—we can't alarm the populace, and already rumors are starting to circulate. Lord James?"

The Duke of Krondor said, "I have agents in the city right now, adding to those rumors. We're not trying to deny the possibility that war is coming to Krondor, but we are giving the impression the trouble springs from Great Kesh. As Krondor hasn't seen a Keshian army in over two hundred years, the population is currently more concerned about rising taxes and the possibility of travel to Shamata and Landreth being curtailed than about any immediate danger."

James's expression darkened. "That will quickly change. When ships due in from the Free Cities and Far Coast fail to appear because of the invaders' fleet, word will quickly circulate from the docks to the outlying farms that something is coming from the west. When that happens, we'll have to lock down Krondor."

"Martial law?" asked one of the local nobles.

"Yes," said Prince Patrick.

Duke James said, "Our enemy is dangerous, far more so than many of you can imagine. By the time we're finished with all our meetings this week, you'll have a better appreciation of that danger, but until then accept what I say: Krondor has never faced a trial such as the one coming.

"We will impose curfew and, if possible, permit an orderly evacuation of the city before it is encircled. But once the enemy has landed, we will close the gates and Krondor will have to hold."

"Hold?" said another noble. "What about help from the East?"

Patrick put up his hand. "Silence. As I said before, we will tell you only what you need to know. You will obey." His tone indicated there was to be no debate on this matter. If any of the nobles present felt slighted, they hid the fact.

The Prince said, "So we are clear on the chain of command. First of all, Knight-Marshal William is now commander of the Armies of the West." He held up a document. "By order of the King." A few nobles looked interested, but no one seemed shocked. By tradition, the Knight-Marshal of Krondor held rank equal to that of a Duke, and occasionally in the past, the Duke of Krondor had held both offices. Patrick then pointed to Calis. "Captain Calis has the acting rank of Knight-General of the Kingdom." Patrick held up another document. For a moment, the significance of what he had just said did not penetrate; then the jaws of several of the nobles dropped in astonishment, reflecting Erik's own shock. Knight-General of the West would have placed him second in command of Principality troops. But Knight-General of the Kingdom put him second in command to Knight-Marshal William, and the superior of any Duke in the Kingdom.

Calis said, "I prefer to be referred to as 'Captain,' in any event." Pointing out Erik, he said, "My second in command is Sergeant Major Erik von Darkmoor. Despite his modest rank, assume he speaks with my voice when he comes to you with orders."

This set up a resentful muttering in the room. Patrick wasted no time in ending it: he struck the table with the pointer, letting the loud crack silence the nobles. "This special unit will operate independently of the traditional order of the Armies of the West, but if at any time you find yourself in a situation where you must decide if you are required to follow the orders of an officer of that special unit, let me make it clear: you will obey orders from any officer of any rank from that special unit as if they originated with the Crown. Is that abundantly clear?"

That left no room for misunderstanding. "Yes, Your Highness," said several of the nobles.

"The units of the Special Command, under Lord Calis, the Royal Krondorian Pathfinders, and other special auxiliaries are all included in those orders. You will be provided with a complete list of those units before you depart for your own commands."

Erik glanced around the room. Several of the Dukes in attendance were close to enraged at the orders, and hid the fact poorly. Patrick showed the training of his office by slamming the pointer on the table hard enough to break it. "My lords!" he said in a loud but controlled voice.

Then he lowered his voice. "When this is over, you will understand why the creation of special units and the operation outside the traditional organization of the Armies of the West are imperative. I needn't remind any of you what history taught us during the Riftwar: that a unified command is essential. As I have only one Knight-Marshal, I must leave it to him to decide how the troops under his command will be disposed."

William, as if an actor moving on a cue, said, "We'll organize the defense of the area around Krondor, utilizing most of the soldiers under your command, my lords. Those of you in command of nearby garrisons will return to those the day after Banapis. Those of you who have been called in from distant garrisons can expect to have your troops seconded to the Prince's Garrison, under my direct command. A few of you will be asked to volunteer for particularly dangerous duty. Now, again I caution you about speaking to anyone outside this room about anything that you are privy to in the next week. Our foe is cunning and has agents everywhere, perhaps in your own commands. Trust no one outside this room. Until we meet with each of you in private, you are given leave to depart."

Erik watched as the lords of the Western Realm of Krondor departed, many still barely in control of their fury. When the room was empty of all but Patrick, James, William, Calis, Erik, and a handful of court officials, Patrick said, "Well, that went better than I expected."

Erik's expression was open amazement. Calis said to him, "He means we didn't have open rebellion."

William laughed. "We held off telling them they'd been relegated to a secondary role until the last possible minute, but we could hold off no longer."

Erik said, "I don't think I fully understand."

Calis said, "That's as it should be." He asked his Prince, "Have I your leave to depart?"

"Yes, you'd better hurry," said Patrick.

Erik glanced at William, who said, "A special mission."

Erik had gotten used to Calis's special missions since becoming his Sergeant Major. He put aside his curiosity and said, "Yes, sir."

"I've got a lot for you to do, Sergeant Major," said William. "But no need to start until I get through with those nobles who just left in such a foul mood. Take some time off this evening and relax. Starting at noon tomorrow, until Banapis, you're going to be working from dawn to dusk."

"Yes, sir," said Erik. "Is there anything else?"

"Nothing right now, but start thinking about which of those last batch of trainees might serve in the mountains. Have a list of the fifty best on my desk by noon tomorrow."

"Yes, sir."

William said, "I've already ordered three hundred of your best out at dawn tomorrow, under Colwin and Jadow Shati. Most of your command is moving out in small groups this week. I'll bring you up to date at noon tomorrow. Until then, your time's your own."

Erik saluted, bade the Prince, the Duke, and the others good day, and departed. He hurried to his own quarters and sat down, going over a list of men with whom he had just returned from the mountains.

For a moment he felt defeat. The names meant nothing to him; how would he pick fifty to give some slightly better chance of survival to? Then a name caught his eye, a man named Reardon. He remembered him because of a particularly funny off-color remark he had made at a difficult moment, when lesser men would have been losing their tempers. The men around him had laughed, the tension had lessened, and the men had managed the task Erik had given them.

He saw the man's face, and then began remembering the men who had been with that group, Reardon and his five teammates, and the other group. Within moments, Erik recalled a dozen names.

At the end of an hour, Erik had a list of fifty men he judged fit for the extraordinary duty required in the mountains. Feeling better for having that task out of the way, he visited the enlisted baths, finding several off-duty soldiers cleaning up. He overheard the barracks gossip and, by the time he was refreshed, was certain that the entire garrison was abuzz with some sense of impending conflict.

Erik changed into fresh clothing and, as fast as he could, found his way to the Inn of the Broken Shield. The inn was fairly crowded, but that didn't stop Kitty from nearly jumping over the bar as she flew into his arms. Erik laughed, and as the slender girl kissed him, he said, "Slow down, woman. Do you want people to think you've no morals?"

Kitty said, "Who cares what people think?"

Several of the nearby patrons laughed at the remark. One of the whores employed by Duke James said, "I certainly don't, dearie!"

Erik said, "How have you been?"

She pinched his cheek playfully and said, "Lonely. How long before you have to go back to the palace?"

Erik smiled. "I don't have to be there until noon tomorrow."

Kitty almost squealed in delight. "I opened today, so I get off in two hours. Have something to eat and don't drink too much with your low-life barracks mates, because I have plans for you."

Erik blushed, and several of those within hearing range laughed at Kitty's remarks.

Erik crossed to the corner of the inn, where Sergeant Alfred sat with other men from Erik's unit. Erik pulled up a chair, and one of the other serving girls came over with a pitcher of ale and a fresh mug for him. She topped off the other mugs and left the men to themselves.

"Why so somber?" asked Erik.

"Orders," said Alfred.

Another soldier, a Rodezian corporal named Miguel, said, "We leave at sundown tomorrow."

Erik took a long pull of his ale. "So."

Alfred said, "It's beginning."

The other soldiers nodded.

Erik, the only man in the room who had served with Calis on his voyages to Novindus, said, "No, it began a long time ago." He looked off into the distance, then at his companions, and said, "But now it's here."

Kitty snuggled into the crook of Erik's shoulder. "I hate that you have to leave tomorrow."

"I know," said Erik.

"What's wrong?"

"What makes you think anything is wrong?"

They lay in the relative solitude of her room. Erik could afford to take a room had he wished, but having spent his childhood in a similar loft, he found the odor of hay and animals, leather and iron familiar and reassuring.

Kitty said, "I know you, Erik. You're worried."

Erik weighed his words. Finally he said, "Do you know a way out of the city?"

"You mean where the gate is?" she said in a joking fashion.

"No, I mean if the city was sealed, do you think you could find a way out?"

Kitty raised herself up and leaned on an elbow, looking down at her lover. "Why?"

"Just answer: could you?"

"Without running into the Mockers, probably not."

Erik considered his next words, for what he was going to say bordered on treason, and at the very least was a direct circumvention of orders. "I have a favor to ask."

"Anything."

"When the festival winds down next week, just before sundown . . ."

"Yes?" she prompted.

"Find your way out of the city; leave with some farmers heading back to the nearby villages."

"What?" she asked, her expression one of open surprise.

"I can't tell you exactly why, but I don't want you in Krondor after Banapis."

"You mean you won't tell me. What is this all about?"

"Duke James has agents at every gate of the city, without question, and besides looking for enemy agents, my guess is they also have orders to stop you, or anyone else he's forced to serve, from fleeing. Banapis is the best chance you have of getting out of the city without being stopped."

"Why do I need to leave Krondor?" said Kitty.

"Because if you stay, I don't know if you'll survive. I can't say more."

"You're frightening me," she said. Erik had never heard Kitty admit to being afraid of anything, so the words carried weight.

"Good. You have to fear what I can't talk about more than Duke James's long reach. Get out of the city and make your way to Roo's estate and hide there. I'll make arrangements for him to get you out of the West. And say nothing to anyone."

"Where are you going to be while I'm hiding in the East?"

"Fighting a war."

Erik felt her melt into his arms, and her hot tears fell on his chest. "We're not going to see each other again, are we?"

Holding her close, he stroked her hair and kissed her cheek. "I don't know, but it won't be for the lack of trying, my love."

She kissed him back. "I want to forget what you said."

"You can forget until Banapis," said Erik.

"Until Banapis."

Twelve

Midsummer

ROO POINTED.

"Nothing like that in Ravensburg, is there?"

Erik said, "You've got the right of it."

Below the palace, the courtyard was filled with visiting nobles, waiting for the traditional noon start of the Festival of Banapis, Midsummer's Day. Erik glanced around and felt conflicting emotions; Banapis was traditionally the happiest day of the year, the day when everyone in the Kingdom was counted one year older, a day dedicated to drinking, gambling, making love, dancing, and anything else people could traditionally think of as pleasure. Servants were free to roam after noon and, once the tables were laid out for the nobles, were free to mingle with them or to head into the city to partake of the merriment there.

Back in Ravensburg, things were considerably less formal. The servants worked through the night and morning to prepare the meals, then the town burghers, the members of the local guild, the Growers' and Vintners', would leave their hall to signal the beginning of festivities. Everything in Ravensburg was free that day, with those of great and lesser means sharing. Whatever could be was brought to the community table, and at noon the feasting began.

Here there were servants whose part in the festivities wouldn't commence until the Prince and his family had retired for the night. Some of them would be permitted to leave early, then forced to return to take the place of others, for no matter what the tradition in other parts of the Kingdom, the royal family could never be without servants.

Erik knew from having been involved in the passing of orders that soldiers were warned to limit their imbibing and that any man returning to quarters obviously drunk would be called out for punishment duty the next day. Normally that would have been insufficient to deter some of the younger soldiers, but word had been passed that punishment would consist of a full day beside the convict labor building the new jetty in the harbor.

And that was the reason for the dark shadow that hung over Erik's otherwise jovial mood. In the back of his mind he couldn't forget the coming battle, and he fretted over Kitty's planned escape from the city.

He wrestled with his conscience. He should have gone directly to Lord James and asked him to send Kitty away, but fear of the Duke saying no had led Erik to this implicit defiance of orders. He could claim that because James had not overtly forbidden Kitty to leave Krondor, no one was being treasonable, but Erik knew it to be a petty legalism, and that he was violating the spirit of Kitty's conditions of service to Lord James, if not the word.

Yet a part of him didn't care. Her safety was paramount to him, matched only by his fear for his mother and Nathan, her husband. Kitty would carry a letter drafted by Erik to Ravensburg, after Roo gave her shelter. The letter would tell Nathan to take Freida to the East.

Erik understood that should the Kingdom fall, nowhere on Midkemia would prove safe, but he knew that the fighting would eventually reach Darkmoor, and even should the Kingdom prevail, Ravensburg was on the wrong side of the mountains. It would surely be overrun by the invaders.

Roo asked, "What's the matter?"

Lowering his voice, Erik said, "Come with me a moment."

Roo signaled to Karli that he would be with Erik, and she nodded. The children were freshly scrubbed and on their best behavior, as Roo and a score of the most important merchants mingled with the assembled nobles as guests of the Prince, at a private reception of his prior to the general festivities.

Duncan Avery was deep in conversation with Sylvia Esterbrook, and Erik absently wondered if Roo had intentionally inflicted his boorish cousin on the girl to keep Karli free of suspicion.

Roo asked, "What is it?"

"Ah," Erik began, then he said, "I see you brought Helen Jacoby and her children."

"Yes," answered Roo. "They're quickly becoming a fixture in my life." He grinned. "Actually, Helen is a wonderful woman, and she and Karli hit it off. And the children get along like kittens in a litter.

"Now, tell me what's really on your mind. You didn't ask me over here to talk about Helen Jacoby, and you've got something stuck in your craw. I know you too well, Erik von Darkmoor; I'm your best friend, remember? You want a favor. You've *never* known how to ask for one, so just say it."

"I want you to hide Kitty," he said softly.

Roo's eyes widened. Of those not members of the Prince's court he knew more of what was going on in the Kingdom than any man. He had served with Calis's forces and had seen the ravages of the Emerald Queen. He knew about the preparations for the coming war, as his various companies were doing more business with the Crown than any other like concerns. He could judge to a fairly accurate degree just what sort of defense was being mounted and where, because it was his wagons that were carrying arms and provisions throughout the Principality.

He also knew Kitty's status and who she had been before being captured by Lord James, and he knew what it meant to run afoul of the Duke of Krondor. He hesitated an instant, then said, "Done."

Erik's relief was almost too much. Tears began to gather in his eyes. Getting his emotions under control, he whispered, "Thank you."

"When do you plan to sneak her out of the city?"

Glancing around to see they weren't being overheard, Erik said, "At sundown. I've gotten her some common clothing and a theatrical wig. She will mingle with farmers leaving to return to the nearby villages.

"I've left money and a horse for her at the Inn of the Silent Rooster near the village of Essford. The innkeeper thinks the daughter of a wealthy merchant is eloping with me, and he's been paid enough not to ask questions."

Roo grinned. He had borrowed money from Erik to start his enterprises nearly two years earlier, and that relatively little bit of gold Roo had taken had come back to Erik a thousandfold. "So you've finally found a use for the money I've made you?"

Erik managed a faint smile. "Yes, finally."

"Well, I hope you didn't overpay him. That's one of my inns, and you could have gotten the service for free."

Erik laughed. "Is there anything in Krondor you don't own?"

Roo glanced to where Sylvia was laughing at something Duncan had said, and replied, "Yes, I'm sorry to say there is."

Erik ignored the reference. "When are you leaving for your estates?" he asked.

"Tomorrow. Kitty need only spend tonight at the inn. Tomorrow she can come to my home. I'll put her to work in the kitchen and tell Karli and the rest of the staff I'm doing her a favor." He thought about it, then added, "I'll make up some story about her being from one of my other inns, I'll decide which later, and some business about a squabble." He lowered his voice. "Then I'll tell Karli the truth, and she'll gladly remain silent. She loves the notion of romance."

Erik shook his head. "Whatever, Roo. And thanks."

"Come on," said the little man. "We better get back to the pleasures of the day and mix around. I take it you're heading to the Sign of the Broken Shield?"

"As soon as it's politic for me to go." Erik smiled. "People would wonder if Kitty and I had a falling out if I didn't go spend Banapis with her."

Roo had an idea. He whispered into Erik's ear, "Take her to the temple and marry her. If James discovers what's afoot, he'll think less ill of you for trying to save your wife from the coming carnage."

Erik stood dumbstruck. "Marriage?" He looked at his friend. "I never thought of it."

Roo's gaze narrowed. "You've been a soldier too long, friend."

They both laughed, and then Erik turned to find Karli approaching. He said, "Mrs. Avery, I return your husband to you."

Karli smiled. "Thank you. The children are bored with all the adult talk and we're taking them down to the courtyard to see the jugglers and jesters."

Roo said, "'Ware the mountebanks. Don't buy anything! I'll be along in a moment."

Erik saw he was joking, and Karli pointedly ignored him. She and Helen took the children, bade good-bye to the Duke's wife, and departed.

Suddenly both Erik and Roo felt a stab of panic as the Lady Gamina turned her gaze upon them. Both men were all too familiar with her talents in reading men's minds, and both instantly knew she had sensed something in what they were doing.

She paused a moment, and a look of sadness mixed with resignation crossed her face; then she approached them. Both men bowed, and Erik said, "Duchess, it's a pleasure."

Lady Gamina said, "You'll never make a convincing liar, Erik, so don't try." Glancing at Roo, she said, "Don't attempt to teach him, either. Men as honest as Erik are few and far between." She studied Erik's face. "I never willingly intrude on another's thoughts, unless I'm bidden by my husband for the good of the state"—her eyes hinted at some regret at that—"but occasionally thoughts come to me unbidden, by those who don't realize they are 'shouting' their concerns. Usually, it's something to do with great emotion." She smiled slightly. "So why did you suddenly shout 'marriage,' Erik?"

Erik blushed furiously. "It's just . . . I'm going to marry Kitty."

Gamina looked at him a moment, then smiled. "You do love her, then, don't you?"

"I do."

The old woman reached out and gently patted Erik's hand. "Then get married, young man. I don't know how pointless it is to wish someone happiness in the days to come, but grab what you can." Glancing over her shoulder to where her husband stood surrounded by other nobles, she said, "Enjoy your youth, and if all ends well, treasure her. I know how hard it is to be one who serves the King. And I know even more what it is to be married to one who serves the King."

Saying nothing more, she moved away toward her husband.

Roo glanced at Erik and with a nod of his head indicated they should move out of the crowded reception chamber. In a hallway, relatively empty, Roo whispered, "Do you think she knows?"

Erik nodded. "She knows."

"But she isn't going to say anything?"

Erik shrugged. "I don't think she'll lie to her husband, not for you or me, but I think she's not going to volunteer anything either." He was thoughtful a moment. "There is something very sad about her."

Roo shrugged. "If you say so." He glanced into the reception room. "I'd better see what Duncan is up to."

"Right," said Erik with a heavy dose of sarcasm. He knew full well it was Sylvia to whom Roo wished to attend. "I've got a few things to do around here before I can see Kitty." He whispered in his friend's ear, "Thank you. I'll tell her to go to your estate tomorrow."

Roo whispered back, "I'll dress her up as a maid when we travel east, in a month's time."

"That's cutting it close."

"Any earlier and the Duke will find an excuse to arrest me, you can be certain." He squeezed Erik's arm and went back into the room.

Erik walked to his quarters, where he planned on changing out of his black tunic with the crimson eagle on it, preferring to wear common garb on Banapis. He reached his small quarters, and stripped off his tunic. As he folded it, he regarded the red bird sewn on the chest.

What was Calis doing this Banapis, he wondered.

Calis pointed. "There!"

Anthony closed his eyes and muttered a series of soft syllables under his breath, and the air before them shimmered. It seemed to bend and contract and suddenly a lens appeared before them, upon which they could clearly see the fleet of the Emerald Queen as it progressed through the Straits of Darkness.

The old magician gasped a bit for breath. "That is perhaps the most useful thing I have ever learned to do. It bends the air into a spherical lens to magnify light. Very passive, and we should not be detected at this distance unless the Pantathians are being supremely suspicious."

The two men stood high atop a peak overlooking the Straits, the southernmost spire of the Grey Towers. "Sit down," said Calis. "You're short of breath."

"It's the altitude," said Anthony. As he sat, he added, "And the age." He glanced at the morning sun. "And being forced out at such a foul hour to climb mountains. Transporting us here was more strain than I thought."

Anthony was a slender man in his late fifties, his hair faded from pale yellow to grey-white, though his skin was still relatively unwrinkled. He let out a long breath and drew a deeper one. "I used to be able to climb around up here without passing out."

Calis turned and smiled at his old friend. "Perhaps you exaggerate? The South Pass is a full three thousand feet lower than this spire. I doubt you've ever been close to any elevation greater than that."

"Well, all right, so I exaggerate." The brother-in-law of the Duke of Crydee lay back on the rocks, attempting to get as comfortable as conditions permitted. "I'm too tired to look. What do you see?"

"The vanguard is through the Straits and has fanned out in an attack formation. How do I turn this thing?"

Despite the season, the wind was chilled, for they sat atop a peak eight thousand feet in the air. Anthony said, "I have to turn it. Which way?"

"First to the right. I want to see what the bulk of her fleet's deployment is."

Anthony held up his hand until it was parallel to the air lens, then he slowly turned his hand in a half-arc. The lens moved in a similar arc.

The two men had been companions on Calis's first trip to Novindus. Anthony had been the court magician to Duke Martin, and had been in love with Martin's daughter, Margaret. He had voyaged with Nicholas, Calis, and others in an attempt to recover the kidnapped Margaret and other hostages, and they had sailed halfway around the world.

Anthony said, "Have I mentioned that whenever you show up, things seem to get very bad for me?"

"Coincidence," said Calis with a smile. "I'm almost certain." He glanced at the lens. "Hold it there a moment." He studied the deployment of the fleet and said, "Damn."

"What?" asked Anthony.

"They're being very cautious."

"How?"

"They've sent skirmishers farther up the coast than Nicky thought."

"That's bad."

"It means Nicky's going to have fight warships and will do little damage to the fleet even if he wins."

"That is bad." Anthony sniffed at the air. "Do you smell something?"

"No. Why?"

"Just asking," said Anthony as he sniffed again.

"Swing this back a little." Anthony did as Calis bade, and when Calis again said, "Hold it here," he stopped. Calis said, "The Queen's got a circle of warships around her craft, and . . ." He paused a moment. "That's odd."

"What?"

"Take a look."

Anthony got up with some theatrical groaning and moved to look over Calis's shoulder. "Gods and fishes!"

"What do you see?"

"I see a demon sitting on a throne."

Calis said, "Looks like Lady Clovis to me."

"Well, you're not a magician," said Anthony. He took out a bag of powder and said, "Sniff this."

Calis did as Anthony instructed, and suddenly sneezed. "What was that?"

"Sorry, one of the ingredients is pepper. Don't wipe your eyes."

Trying to blink away tears, Calis looked through the lens. For a moment he could see two figures upon the dais in the center of the ship, the illusion of the Emerald Queen and the demon. "That might explain what happened to Pug."

"I'd like someone to explain to me what happened to Pug," said Anthony. "I'm a simple magician. Truth to tell, I haven't worked very hard at it since I got my title."

"That's what comes of marrying into nobility," said Calis.

"There's little call for magic when you've got estates to manage."

"You've filled in for Pug admirably so far," said Calis dryly. "Think you could drop down there and dispose of that creature?"

Anthony closed his eyes and incanted a silent phrase, then he made a loud snorting noise as he smelled deeply. He made a face and said, "No, and I doubt Pug could either."

"Really, why?"

"Because I may not have as much power as Pug or be as clever as some of those fellows down at Stardock, but one thing I'm very good at is smelling magic."

"Smelling magic?"

"Don't ask. Secrets of the trade and all that."

"Anyway, you were saying?"

Anthony said, "I'm serious; I can smell the reek all the way up here, and we're miles away. Something big went off around that ship, and it could have been Pug. If what I smell lingering is what's left over, it was a magical exchange of tremendous powers. Given that creature is still there, and Pug's nowhere to be seen, we can only assume the worst."

Calis sighed. "That seems to be the way things have been working, hasn't it?"

"Can we leave? I'm getting cold."

"In a while. Move this thing back to the left; I want to look down across the southwestern horizon if you can manage that."

"It's like a glass; you can see only as far as you could with your own eyes from this perspective, if your own eyes could see that far. For what you're asking, you need a crystal, and I neglected to bring one. Besides, if I had a crystal, which I don't, the first person who turns it on that creature is likely to get his eyes blistered for trying."

"Well, as far that way"—Calis pointed—"as you can manage."

Anthony did as he was asked, and heard a satisfied "Ah" from Calis.

"What?" asked the magician.

"The Queen sends a skirmish line up the northern coast toward Tulan. But she only lightly guards her southern flank."

"Well, there're a lot of deserted islands and the Trollhome Mountains to the south of the Straits. I doubt she fears a troll navy, as they haven't evidenced one in recent memory."

"No, but Keshian Elarial is but a week's sailing down the far Keshian coast, and Li Meth is only two days' travel to the west of her vanguard. And those deserted islands are just the place for pirates to hide."

Anthony was silent a moment. Then he said, "James?"

"Most certainly. He's been spreading rumors for months of a treasure fleet from a fabled land coming this way."

"He is a sneaky bastard, isn't he?"

Calis said, "I think I see sails." He extended his hand to the southeast. "Please move the lens that way."

"I get a headache every time I do."

"Please," Calis repeated.

"Very well." Anthony did as he was asked, and Calis said, "It's a raiding fleet from Durbin and Li Meth! Must be a hundred warships!" He laughed. "It must be every Keshian pirate between Elarial and Durbin."

Anthony looked. "And a few of them appear to be irritated to discover they have neighbors visiting."

"The captains of Durbin are not exactly what you'd call welcome guests in Li Meth, as often as not. Move the lens over there, please."

Calis watched as the lens swung around to an orientation slightly north of west. "Ah, the Quegans!"

"How far?"

"Two days, maybe, if I judge the magnification."

Anthony waved his hand and the lens vanished. "Good. Now can we go home?"

"Yes. I need to see my father. If something has happened to Pug he's the most likely to know about it." Silently he thought that his father would also know if something had happened to Miranda. Nakor had indicated that Pug and Miranda were together, and something about the little man's silence after he said that set Calis's mind to worry.

Calis reached into his cloak and pulled out a old-looking metal sphere. He motioned for Anthony to stand next to him, and the magician put one hand upon his friend's arm and activated a lever in the side of the sphere with his thumb.

Instantly they passed through the void, and found themselves, feeling slightly disoriented, standing in the rear courtyard at Castle Crydee. Three figures stood waiting.

"What did you see?" asked Duke Marcus. He was a man nearly equal in height to Calis, and once he had been powerfully built, but while age showed little on the half-elf, on the fifty-year-old Duke it was starting to take a toll. Marcus was still a robust man, but some of his muscle had turned to fat and his hair was now completely grey.

Beside him stood two women, one obviously Marcus's sister by the family resemblance. She had a straight nose, like her brother's, and her eyes were even, unblinking, and despite the lines of age and sun, a striking brown. She was also strong-looking for her age. Lady Margaret, the Duke's sister and Anthony's wife, said, "Anthony?"

He smiled as he said, "It's cold up there, dear, even at this time of the year."

Marcus smiled. "So you got where you wanted to go?"

"Let's have a drink and we'll talk," suggested the magician.

The third person greeting them, the Duchess Abigail, said, "There's a meal waiting. We didn't know how long you'd be." Marcus's wife lacked his or his sister's outward signs of vitality, but her step was quick and her slight figure hinted at a dancer's lithe strength. She smiled quickly as she motioned for Calis and her brother-in-law to come through the rear entrance to the castle.

"Wasn't much to see, really," said Anthony. "The battle's not yet begun." Glancing toward the height of the sun, he added, "It will not begin until tomorrow. How far away did you say the Quegans were? Two days?" he asked Calis.

"Quegans?" asked Margaret.

"We'll explain everything inside," said Calis.

They mounted the steps to the central keep. For Calis, Crydee had been his second home. His grandparents had lived here, years before, and his father had spent his childhood working in the kitchen and playing in the courtyard of the castle.

The castle had been gutted in the sacking of the Far Coast, thirty years earlier, when Calis had taken his first trip to the distant continent. Then he had been a simple observer, on behalf of his mother and father, but he had returned since several times, much to his sorrow and regret.

They moved down the long hall to the dining hall. A table long enough to seat a score of dinner guests formed the top of three sides of a square, in the old court fashion. The Duke and his wife would dine at the center of the top table, while guests and court officials would be seated in descending order of rank from there to the farthest seat.

Calis glanced around the hall. Brightly colored banners hung where once ancient and faded ones had been displayed. Calis remembered them from his childhood. They had been the war trophies of the first three Dukes of Crydee.

"It's never the same, is it?" asked Marcus.

"No."

"How's Father?" asked Margaret.

"He's fine," said Calis. "At least, he was the last time I saw him, which was more than a year ago. But his life is easy and I expect he's unchanged. Had anything happened, Mother would have sent you word immediately."

"I know," Margaret said. "It's just we miss him."

Marcus said, "Yes, but it's better to have him there, happy and living, than here, in the burial vault."

Calis said, "Well, when this business is done, you could go visit. Mother and Tomas would certainly welcome you."

Marcus smiled and Calis said, "Do that more often; it makes you look like Martin."

A corner of the left and head tables had been set, at Marcus's instructions, so the five of them could gather close. Wine, ale, hot food and cold waited.

Anthony said, "Ah, a little wine will warm me up."

Abigail said, "It's still early, so not too much, else you'll be asleep before the festival is half-over."

Marcus indicated they should sit. "We need to hurry, for I need to be in the courtyard at high noon to see things started."

"There's not much to tell," said Calis as he broke off a hunk of bread. "Things are pretty much as we expected, with one change."

"What?" asked the Duke.

"Where the Emerald Queen was supposed to be sitting, in the middle of the biggest ship in the fleet, a very ugly demon squatted. Looked like he had some sort of mystic chain of control around the neck of all the 'advisers' who surrounded him . . . or it . . . whatever."

"A demon!" Marcus's face showed surprise.

"Well, we knew there were some involved, after that last business down in Novindus I told you about."

"But we thought they were destroying the Pantathians, not controlling them."

Anthony sipped his wine. "Maybe there are different demons."

"Maybe so," said Calis as he took a gulp of wine. "Humans certainly come with enough politics to keep the world at war eternally. Who says demons can't have politics?"

"Not I," said Marcus.

"Well, I'm off. I've got to talk to Mother," said Calis, rising. "And you have a festival to start. If my sense of timing is right, it's nearly noon and the populace will not be pleased if you're late." He stuck out his hand. "Thanks for the help, Marcus. Can I have the loan of a horse?"

"Aren't you going to use that Tsurani transport thing to get to Elvandar?" said Anthony.

Calis tossed it to him. "You keep it. You know how to use it better than I, magician. And use it you must. Rest tonight, then back to that peak we used first thing in the morning. Take Marcus, and observe the battle. If you need to get word to me in a hurry, send a runner to the banks of the river Crydee. I can be back here in a week.

"I'll ride, and if Pug or Miranda is at Elvandar, they can get me back to Krondor. If not, I'll return this way and use that thing."

Marcus said, "Good-bye, Calis. Your visits are far too rare."

Margaret and Abigail both kissed him on the cheek, and Anthony shook his hand.

Marcus signaled for a squire to escort Calis to the stable and give him whichever mount he chose. Then the Duke of Crydee and his family hurried to the main entrance of the castle to begin the Banapis festival for another year.

At sundown, farmers and citizens who lived outside the walls of the city began to trickle through the gate. The guards stood idly by, watching only with cursory attentiveness. Erik held Kitty in a close embrace, deep in the shadows of a nearby alley.

"I love you," Kitty whispered into his chest.

"I love you, too," Erik said.

"Will you come for me?"

"Always," said Erik. "No matter what, I'll find you."

As the lamps were lit and those shops still trying to conduct business opened their doors to reveal the light inside, the sound of traffic increased. While the celebration would last long into the night, there were more sober souls who knew that come dawn there would be work to be done, and that to be at their best the next day would require a good night's sleep.

Erik held Kitty away from him a moment. A dark wig peeked out from under the plain hood of a farmer's cloak of homespun. The dress she had selected was equally nondescript. To any who failed to inspect her closely, she looked like nothing more than another common farmer's daughter on her way home with her family. A small bag was clutched under the cloak, and in it Kitty carried a modest fortune in gold coins, as much of Erik's personal wealth as he could put his hands on in short order. She also carried a pair of daggers.

"If something goes wrong, get to my mother in Ravensburg." He grinned. "Just tell her you're my wife and stand back."

Kitty put her head on his chest again, and said, "Your wife."

Neither of them could believe it. They had simply walked into the temple of Sung the Pure and joined a line of other couples who had come to be wed. Impulsive marriages on Banapis were hardly uncommon, and after the priest had asked pointedly if they were intoxicated and how long they had known each other, he had consented to marry them. The ceremony had been brief, less than five minutes, and they had been hustled outside by an acolyte seeking to make room for the next pair.

Erik said, "You have to be ready."

"I know," said Kitty. She understood that at any instant a group of farmers was likely to come though whom Erik judged appropriate and she would have to act without hesitation. "I don't want to leave you."

"I don't want you to leave." Then fiercely he said, "But I don't want you to die, either."

"I don't want you to die," she answered, and he could feel her tears fall on his bare arm. "Damn. I hate crying."

"Then stop it!" he said lightly.

She started to say something, but he said, "Now!"

Without even a kiss good-bye, she turned and walked out of the side street, up to a young woman who was walking next to a hay wagon, upon which rode a half-dozen children. An old man drove the wagon, and behind it walked another three men and a woman.

Kitty said to the young woman, "Excuse me?"

As the wagon rolled up to the gate, Kitty was hidden from observation on one side, and had her back turned toward the guard on the other as she appeared lost in conversation with the young woman to whom she spoke.

Erik listened as she said, "You're not from Jenkstown, are you?"

"No," said the young stranger. "Our farm is only a few miles from here."

"Oh, I thought you might be someone I knew a while back in Jenkstown. You look a great deal like her, but prettier."

The girl laughed. "You're the first to call me that," she said lightly as the wagon rolled through the gate.

Erik strained to hear what was said next, but the voices were drowned out in the sounds of celebration. Soon he could tell that Kitty was safely through the gate and beyond the scrutiny of the guards. He waited another full minute, half expecting the sound of alarm to be raised. But all he heard was the city at play, and he forced himself to take a slow, deep breath, then turned back toward the palace. He decided his best course of action was to be seen around, and should anyone ask about Kitty, make up some plausible excuse, that she was in another room, or off visiting the jakes. There would be enough traffic through the palace that he might get through the entire evening without anyone asking after her.

As Erik vanished into the crowd, two figures who had been hiding in the shadows across the street emerged. Dash turned to his brother and said, "I'll follow the girl."

"Why bother? We know she's heading either for Avery's estates or to Ravensburg. Those are the only places he'd send her."

"Because Grandfather wants to know," said Dash to Jimmy.

Jimmy shrugged. "Very well, but you're going to miss the height of the celebration."

Dash said, "It's not the first time I've missed out on some fun because of Grandfather. If Father asks about me, make up some excuse. If the girl's bound for Ravensburg, I won't be back for a week."

Jimmy nodded and slipped into the crowd. His younger brother turned and made his way through the gate, keeping sight of the distant hay wagon.

* * *

The next day dawned on two fleets locked in combat, skirmishing in the predawn gloom. They had caught sight of each other as the darkness had lightened in the hours before the sun finally climbed into the sky. Now, as the sun lay still hidden behind the distant mountains, yet illumined the morning, the battle was almost decided.

Nicholas cursed and shouted, "Order Belfors and his three to sail to windward! They're attempting to hold us into the coast!"

A signalman high above shouted, "Aye, aye, Admiral!" and began waving signal flags. He soon shouted back, "Orders acknowledged, Admiral!"

The battle was going badly. If he lost any more ships, Nicholas was going to have to withdraw, and while he had no doubt he could outsail his opponent, the failure of his plan put a sour taste in his mouth.

Of all his father's sons, Nicholas was the most like him when it came to achieving a stated goal, and he had intended to maul the Emerald Queen's fleet. She knew the Far Coast well enough to understand that the risk to her fleet would come down the coast from Tulan. Nicholas's only belief for some benefit to his Kingdom came from the belief that James's plan was working and flotillas from Kesh and Queg were hitting the fleet as well.

It rankled him that he was only engaging warships, without even sighting the troop convoy, and the sole comfort that afforded him was the thought that should either the Quegans or Keshians intercept this fleet, there were that many fewer guardians to protect it.

Seeing no benefit in dying or taking his command with him, Nicholas shouted, "Word to the fleet! Withdraw!"

A red banner was run up while the lookout frantically signaled orders. Two ships were engaged in boarding actions and could not withdraw safely.

Nicholas weighed his options and ordered them left to fend for themselves. Each of his ships was rigged with a dozen barrels of fire oil down below, and if they were taken, the captains were ordered to put them to the torch, in the hope they'd take along an enemy ship grappled alongside as well as deny them a Kingdom prize.

The fleet off the Far Coast were the best deep-water sailors in the world, and their ships the most nimble. As soon as the order was relayed, like a finely practiced team the ships turned upwind and took a following reach, disengaging themselves from the slower ships of Novindus design. A few of the war galleys could stay with the Kingdom ships for a short burst, but as the slaves below became exhausted, they were no match for the Kingdom warships.

Nicholas saw his fleet moving away successfully, and said, "Captain Reeves, what's the count?"

His second in command, the son of the Baron of Carse and a lifelong sailor, was officially the Captain of the *Royal Dragon*, though he knew he would never give orders as long as the Admiral was aboard. He said, "Seven of the enemy sunk, three burning, five more severely damaged." Both men wore the duty uniform of the Kingdom fleet—blue jackets and white trousers, newly instituted by Patrick's order—but even the Prince of Krondor couldn't make Nicholas wear the new fore-and-aft hats the Eastern Fleet wore. He instead affected a broad-brimmed black hat with a very faded red plume, a legacy from his first voyage as a boy with the legendary Amos Trask. No man who sailed in the fleet made sport of that hat.

"And of our own?"

"We lost six, and five more are limping up the coast to Carse."

Nicholas swore. At least sixty-five ships had sailed north against his own sixty, and this had been little more than a sparring match.

Nicholas looked at the morning sun. "Orders, Captain Reeves."

"Yes, m'lord?"

"Signal the fleet to head west. Let them think we're running to the Sunsets." He gripped the railing on the quarterdeck. "At sundown, we turn south. Before dawn tomorrow, we'll turn east and hit them while they're outlined against the rising sun and we're still in darkness."

"Understood, sir!"

Nicholas watched the ponderous ships of the Emerald Queen fall away behind, finally turning southward as they gave up their attempt to overtake the Kingdom ships. Nicholas looked to the east, where he was leaving one of his ships crippled and sinking slowly, while his other boarded ship burned.

"This one is far from over," said Nicholas to no one in particular.

Thirteen

Improvisation

CALIS KNELT.

"How long has he been like this?" he asked, using the subtle speech of his mother's people.

"Weeks," Calin told his half brother.

Pug lay unconscious in the center of the contemplation glade, at the very spot where he had first been placed, while Spellweavers worked around him to keep him alive. "Tathar?" Calis asked.

"We think he regains his strength, slowly. The wounds are also healing, slowly."

Calis regarded the silent magician. His body was covered with huge scabs and scars, with flakes of dead skin peeling off, as if burned by the sun. Under the flakes, raw pink skin could be seen. Most of his hair, beard, and brows had been burned away, so he looked even younger than usual.

Acaila said, "We've tried mind probes, of the most cautious sort, and no one was able to reach him."

Calis stood. "We were counting on his holding back until the end."

Calin said, "I think he acted imprudently, but that is judging after the fact. At the time he took the risks, he thought the outcome worth it."

Calis nodded. "Sinking the Queen's fleet in the deepest part of the great ocean would have simplified many of our problems." He shook his head in regret. "But I would rather have him standing healthy at Sethanon."

Calin said, "Tomas will go to Sethanon."

"What of the dragons?"

Calin looked concerned. "They doubt Tomas. Not his word, but they doubt his apprehension of the risk. For all their wisdom, only a few grasp the concepts of magic we know to be at play."

Calis looked at his half brother for a long moment, then said, "May I speak to you alone?"

Calin moved his hand in agreement, indicating the younger man should follow him. When they were away from the others, Calis said, "Miranda?"

"No word from either Miranda or Macros since they brought Pug back. They went with Tomas to seek information on the demons under the mountains where you last found them."

Calis looked off at the trees of Elvandar. He was silent for a long time, and his half brother didn't say a word. In the fashion of the elves, Calin knew the other would say what was on his mind when he was ready.

After several minutes of silence, Calis said, "I miss her."

Calin put his hand upon his shoulder. "You love her?"

"In a fashion," said Calis. "Nothing like among the eledhel; it feels nothing like what I have been told of the recognition. But she found me, back when this all began, and she fills a dark and cold place within me as no one else has."

"If it is still dark and cold when she is not with you, it is not truly filled." Calin sat upon a large rock and said, "When your father first saw your mother I was there; I thought him but a boy smitten by the beauty of one without peer, a boy who had no conception of the feelings between a man and woman." He sighed. "I certainly had no idea of what the future would hold."

Calis had heard the story of his mother's first visit to Castle Crydee, when the Tsurani had first threatened the Far Coast, and of his father's first glimpse of the Elf Queen.

Calin said, "You are still very young, my brother. You have seen much, experienced much, but you've not begun to understand yourself. In many ways you are human, but in many others one of us. Patience is required in most things. Your father realized that quickly, when he first came to us, and for a human boy, those years he spent here taught him much."

"Father's unique. He possesses knowledge tens of thousands of years old."

"Does he?" said Calin.

Calis turned to look at his half brother. "Ashen-Shugar?"

Calin said, "Macros said something to me a few days before he left. He said Tomas had Ashen-Shugar's memories, but that all memories are suspect."

Calis sighed. "All of this is suspect."

Calin agreed. "I have stopped looking for reasons when it comes to the enemy." His eyes took on a distant look. "When your father first came here, after the Riftwar and in the years that followed, I presumed to think that the worst was behind us. The war with the Tsurani was over, and the risk from the moredhel and the open rift calling back the Valheru was at an end." He smiled a half-smile that Calis recognized as a mirror of his own. "I now realize that forces much more enigmatic and far more vast than I had imagined were involved."

"What do you mean?" asked Calis, as he sat cross-legged at his half brother's feet.

"Primal forces are moving, forces next to which the Valheru are minor annoyances. Other forces move to counter them, and I fear you and I, and those we love, may be crushed between them."

"Have these forces names?"

"Many," said Calin. "I speak of the gods."

"The gods war?" asked Calis.

"It is the only explanation that fits all of what we know and still makes some sort of sense." The still-youthful-looking elf said, "Tomas and I have talked many times about his memories. He counts me among his oldest friends, from that time of the first visit to Crydee. Much of what Tomas remembers is colored by how Ashen-Shugar saw the universe and his place in it. Some of that was tempered by the magic Macros used to place my mind in bond with his, ages ago, but Tomas still must rethink much of what he presumed to be true."

"The Chaos Wars?"

Calin nodded. "We can speak of this at length tonight, after we dine with Mother."

Calis got to his feet as his brother stood. Calis said, "I do owe her more of my time."

"It's been years since we've had you here," said Calin, without any indictment, but clearly with regret. "It is easy to think we have ages, given our people's heritage, but we both know how fragile life is."

"True," agreed Calis. "I promise that should we endure, I will return for a long visit."

"Why not to stay?"

Calis shrugged as they walked toward the Elf Queen's court. As they passed through a series of small clearings, many elves who had not yet greeted the Queen's younger son did so. Calis smiled and returned each greeting, but when the brothers were again alone, he said, "I do not know if my place is here. My life is neither human nor elf, nor Valheru."

"A legacy of magic," said Calin. "You must define yourself, for no one else has the wisdom to do it for you." He was thoughtful for a moment, then said, "Much as your father has had to do. As long as the mark of the Valheru exists, he will never be free of a certain suspicion."

"I understand," said Calis.

They moved into another clearing, this one loud with the voices of children at play. A half-dozen elven youngsters were chasing after a ball, kicking it back and forth.

"Football? In Elvandar?" asked Calis.

Calin laughed. "See those two over there?" He pointed to twin boys, children Calis had never seen before.

"Yes?"

"They taught the others. They are from across the sea. Miranda brought them and their mother here. Their father is now in the Blessed Isles."

"Have many of those across the ocean reached us?"

"Not enough," said Calin, as he resumed the walk. The ball shot toward them, and Calis deftly caught it on the instep of his left boot.

With a laugh, he kicked the ball high and stepped under it, bouncing it off his head a few times, then heading it back to one of the children, who caught it on a knee, bouncing it a few times as the other children "ooed" and "ahed." "I remember playing on Sixthday at Crydee with Marcus when I'd visit Grandmother and Grandfather," said Calis.

The twin who caught the ball on his knee kicked it to his brother, who passed it to a third child. The twins regarded Calis with suspicion. He said, "You two look very serious."

When they didn't reply, Calin said, "They struggle with their natural tongue."

Calis nodded. In the dialect spoken in the Riverlands of Novindus, he said, "You play well."

Instantly both boys' faces were illumined with smiles. "Will you teach us how to bounce the ball on our heads?" asked one.

Calis knelt and said, "I must leave first thing tomorrow, but someday I will come back and teach you."

The second twin said, "Promise?"

Calis said, "I do." The boys turned and ran off to resume their game, and Calis turned to his half brother. "They asked me if I was telling the truth."

"They grew up among humans. It has been very difficult for the ocedhel. They wrestle with what is natural to us. Learning our ways comes hard."

Dryly, Calis said, "That I can understand."

"You will resolve your struggle," said Calin as he motioned for his half brother to continue the walk to the Queen's court, "someday."

Calis nodded, and silently added, "If I live that long."

Ships burned at dawn. Nicholas's fleet had lost sight of the Emerald Queen's northern squadron after sundown the night before, and had turned south, piling on all the canvas the ships' yards could hold. Two hours later, the entire fleet had swung toward the east, and the Straits of Darkness.

They had been rewarded with the sight of fires before dawn as they encountered smoking hulls, burned to the waterline and sinking, both Queen's ships and Keshian. Lookouts reported fires farther to the west.

As the sun rose, Nicholas saw the vast navy that still waited to slip through the Straits. He couldn't judge how many had already made the difficult passage; perhaps as many as a third.

To the south, fighting was still under way as Keshian ships from Elarial were engaged with an equal number of the Queen's warships.

Captain Reeves said, "Where are the rest of her escorts?"

Nicholas shouted, "We have her!" To the lookout aloft he cried, "All ships: attack!"

As the orders were relayed, Nicholas turned to Reeves. "We've outrun those ships we were tangling with yesterday." He calculated. "We have perhaps an hour to do as much damage as possible before they come into sight. What she's got left here are engaged with the Keshians, and the rest of them are on the other side of the Straits!"

He went to the quarterdeck rail and shouted, "Ready ballistas!"

Ballista crews ran to the fore of the ship, where a pair of huge crossbow-like engines of war waited. Each could launch an iron-headed missile three times the size of a man, used to strike at the waterline, or to foul rigging. Instead of the usual missile, though, a special shaft had been designed, one filled with the deadly Quegan fire oil. To use them was dangerous, for any mistake could result in the *Royal Dragon* burning to the waterline.

Behind him the attacking fleet, forty-seven of the original sixty ships he had left Tulan with, fanned out in attack formation. Nicholas's ship lost wind, dropping her speed so the two flanks of the flotilla could sweep in from either side, doing the most damage to the huge body of ships milling in the water, almost at a dead stop, waiting for orders to enter the passage.

Nicholas shouted, "Master of Arms! Fire as you bear!"

The officer in the bow shouted back, "Aye, aye, Admiral!"

Two of the larger ships at the rear turned to engage, wallowing awkwardly, but potentially dangerous. The lookout shouted, "They bear catapults, Admiral!"

Nicholas said, "So I see," as a huge war engine on the aft castle of the closest ship unleashed its cargo, a huge net of rocks. "Port your helm, Captain Reeves."

"Aye, aye, sir," came the calm answer as the net unraveled at the top of its arc, releasing the shower of rocks, each the size of a man's head—or bigger.

The more nimble Kingdom ship swerved to the left and the rocks splashed harmlessly to the right of where Nicholas stood. "That would have made a fair mess of the rigging, sir," said Captain Reeves.

"Take us back to starboard," said Nicholas.

The helmsman did as ordered, and the bow of the warship swung back on line, bringing it to where it would cross to the port of the big ship. They were close enough now that Nicholas could see the catapult crew frantically attempting to reload. "Bad choice," said Nicholas. "Takes too long to reload and the men are exposed."

As if reading his mind, bowmen in the rigging began firing on the catapult crew on the enemy ship. The Kingdom's Royal Marines were ground soldiers, yet experienced at fighting aboard ship. They used short bows with good effect. Then the Master of Arms ordered the starboard ballista fired and it struck the middle of the enemy ship with a fiery explosion. Men screamed and Nicholas could see the mid-deck was packed with soldiers, many looking sick from the months at sea. At least a score fell over the side, partially or completely on fire. Others frantically and vainly attempted to beat out the fire, but discovered to their horror the secret of Quegan fire oil. Once it was ignited, only smothering in sand could put it out. Those throwing buckets of water on it were just spreading the flaming oil faster.

Nicholas tore his gaze from the grisly sight and looked at their course. "Hard to port," he said. "It's a mess in close, and I don't want to get stuck in there with no place to turn around. We'll keep nibbling at the edges."

Orders were passed, and other ships in the flotilla did the same, launching their fiery cargo, then turning hard lest they become entangled with the ships they were attacking.

The lookout above shouted, "There are two war galleys backing oars in the middle of those burning ships there, Admiral."

Nicholas said, "They want to come out and fight, but they have no room to maneuver. Let's find something else to burn before they do find a way out."

He ordered the flotilla to a southerly course, sailing toward where the Keshians had been battling the invaders. Smoke was beginning to obscure Nicholas's vision. "Lookout!"

"Sir?"

"Keep a watch out for that northern squadron of theirs. If you catch sight of them, I want to know it before you can think!"

"Aye, aye, sir!"

For an hour they hunted. Men screamed and died, and still the invaders' ships seemed without number. Nicholas had personally fired four ships, and was approaching the fifth when the lookout shouted, "Ships to the north, Admiral!"

"How many?"

"I count at least a score of sails. . . . I count thirty. . . . Forty!"

"It's their northern element, returning to find they've been outrun," said Captain Reeves.

Nicholas swore. "Look at all these fat wallowing barges! We could sink them all day long without danger."

Then the lookout shouted, "Admiral! Those two war galleys have turned and have gotten free of the sinking ships!"

"Well, that makes it interesting," said Reeves.

Nicholas nodded. "I could use some more time. Master of Arms!"

"Sir?" came the reply.

"How stands our arsenal?"

"We have another forty missiles, Admiral."

Nicholas shouted to the lookout. "How far do you judge those two ships?"

"Less than a mile, Admiral."

"Reeves, who's to our north?"

Reeves knew the Admiral knew the disposition of the fleet as well as he did, but wanted to hear it from another to help crystallize his thoughts. "Sharpe's squadron, Wells's squadron, what's left of Turner's group, and a full third of the fast cutters."

Nicholas said, "Orders! Sharpe and Wells are to move to the north and intercept. I want them to harry and delay, but not to engage!"

The lookout shouted, "Understood," and started signaling.

"Then I want the cutters to burn those galleys!"

Nicholas knew he was sending several of those fast little ships to the bottom. They had limited offensive capacity, but if two or three could get close enough, they could fire those war galleys, while the Kingdom-class warships could sink three dozen troop ships each under ideal conditions.

"Acknowledged, sir!" shouted the lookout as the first order was received.

The carnage continued throughout the morning, and at an hour before noon, word came the concentration of enemy warships was too heavy. The northern element of the Queen's fleet had ignored Wells's and Sharpe's squadrons when it became clear they wouldn't engage. Now they were bearing down on the heart of the fighting. Nicholas saw that the cutters had one of the huge war galleys burning and another surrounded. The concentration of bow fire from the galleys was incredible, a veritable rain of arrows, and these ships manned ballistas. With calm precision, their crews would reload and fire, and each time another of the small cutters was damaged or sunk.

Nicholas took one last look at the damage he had done, then said, "Captain Reeves, it's time to run for Freeport!"

Captain Reeves did not hesitate, for he could see another huge war galley that had followed the first two out of the mess of troop ships, now rowing furiously in their direction. Captain Reeves gave orders to the helmsman, and Nicholas shouted, "Master of Arms!"

"Sir," came the reply, hoarse from hours of breathing the stinking smoke of burning oil.

"As we bear, I would appreciate your putting a missile down the throat of that galley that's racing toward us."

"Aye, aye, sir."

As the ship heeled, the ballista was fired, and the fiery projectile hurled across the gap, striking the forecastle of the approaching galley. Flames exploded across the upper third of the ship's bow, but only those men on deck were killed. Below, the horator steadily beat his drum and the galley slaves pulled as the ship bore relentlessly down on the *Royal Dragon*.

Nicholas calculated and decided they were unlikely to get clear of the ship. "Lookout!"

"Aye, sir?"

"Does she bear a ram?"

"An iron-clad one, sir, at the waterline."

"Well, Reeves," said Nicholas, "unless we get a sudden burst of wind, I'm afraid I'm about to get your ship sunk."

"Always a risk, sir," came the impassive reply.

The men stood calmly watching as the huge warship bore down on them, its bow now completely engulfed in fire. Reeves looked up and shouted, "Trim the topgallants, Mr. Brooks."

His first officer shouted the order, and men quickly tied off ropes and moved yards.

The *Royal Dragon* heeled over, hard to port, as the galley bore down. Nicholas could feel the heat of the flames across the narrowing gap. His marines began firing down into the deck of the enemy ship.

"Master of Arms!" cried Nicholas.

"Sir!"

"See if your marines can distract their helmsman!"

"Aye, sir!"

Without waiting for the order to be relayed, those bowmen aloft started peppering the rear of the enemy ship with arrows. Nicholas didn't know if they could see the enemy helmsman, but he thought it likely an incoming fusillade might cause him to duck and lose hold of the helm. Even a deviation of course by a few yards might spare the *Royal Dragon*.

Nicholas watched in mute fascination as the enemy ship bore down relentlessly on his ship. He could hear the faint thud of the horator's drum from belowdecks as he shifted tempo, and he knew the call for ramming speed had been given. "I think you'd best grab on to something solid, Captain Reeves."

"Aye, sir."

Then the *Royal Dragon* moved, slightly, and heeled over even more, as the wind freshened. Whether it was the incoming arrows, or the blinding smoke from the flaming bow of his own ship, the steersman on the galley did not compensate for the speed of his target.

The grind of steel against metal accompanied the sight of the *Royal Dragon*'s helmsman being flung from his wheel as the other ship's ram struck hard into the tiller of the Kingdom ship. A low grinding continued, and the flames from the galley fired the *Dragon*'s spanker. "Fire stations, Captain Reeves," said Nicholas evenly.

"Sir," said the Captain. He started shouting orders, and the crew raced towards the buckets of sand. Men aloft started cutting away rigging to loose the flaming sail.

As if being pushed along, the *Royal Dragon* jumped forward, and another sailor hurried to grab the helm as the helmsman lay stunned. "Well, Reeves," said Nicholas, "it seems providence may be with us for a moment."

"Sir," said the Captain, relief on his face as the two ships separated. "I hope we don't come that close again any time soon."

"Agreed—" said Nicholas, then his eyes widened. He looked down to see the shaft of an arrow protruding from his stomach, and blood beginning to flow down his white trousers. "Oh, damn," he said. His knees gave way.

A flight of arrows struck the rigging above their heads as the marines from an enemy ship nearby launched a random attack on the *Dragon,* hoping to strike anyone. Captain Reeves shouted, "I want best speed!"

Men flew through the rigging and the Kingdom fleet disengaged itself from the struggle. "Get the Admiral below!" Reeves shouted.

A short time later Nicholas lay on his bunk with the ship's chirurgeon attending to the wound. Captain Reeves entered and said, "How is he?"

The chirurgeon said, "Bad, sir. I fear the worst. If we can keep him alive until we reach Freeport, a healing priest may be able to save him. But he's beyond my meager talents."

The Captain nodded and returned to the quarterdeck, where his first officer waited. "Mr. Brooks?"

"We lost the *Prince of Krondor*, the *Royal Swift*, and a score of the cutters. We estimate we sank thirty or more of their cargo ships, and a half dozen of their war galleys."

Reeves glanced to the stern, where the enemy fleet was now a low black mass on the horizon. "Is there no end to them?"

"Apparently not, sir." The first officer asked, "How is the Admiral?"

"Touch and go."

"Can we turn to Tulan?"

"No, we must make best speed for Freeport. Those are the orders."

"But the Admiral?"

Reeves said, "Those are *his* orders." He sighed. "We wait a week in Freeport, then we head to Krondor." Softly he said, "Those are the orders."

"What then?"

"I don't know. Until Lord Nicholas recovers, everything rests in Lord Vykor's hands in Krondor."

The first officer saw how troubled the Captain was, and felt the same. Prince Nicholas, youngest son of Prince Arutha, had been Admiral of the Prince's fleet, supreme commander of the Royal Navy in the West, as long as either could remember. He was the man who held the fleet together and, more, he was royalty, the King's youngest brother. For him to die on any captain's watch would be difficult enough, but for him to die when the Kingdom needed her fleet at its best was tragic.

Reeves, who was Nicholas's second in command, said, "Orders to the fleet. I'm taking command. Pass word of the Prince's injury. Then order best speed for Freeport."

"Aye, sir."

Nakor studied Pug. Calis asked, "Will he wake soon?"

"Maybe. Maybe not. Who can say?"

The Isalani watched as his student continued to administer the healing energies, aided by the Spellweavers of Elvandar. Nakor had dined with Calis, Calin, and their mother the night before, and they had discussed the best course of action.

Nakor had agreed to ride with Calin to Crydee, where they would use the Tsurani transport device to get to Krondor. Sho Pi would remain behind in Elvandar and continue to help heal Pug.

"I wish I knew what was going on in there," said Nakor.

"In where?" asked Calis.

"In Pug's mind. Something is happening, and only the gods know what it is."

Pug floated in a void, and again he knew he was detached from his body. Only this time he had none of the references he had possessed when he had been aided by the elven Spellweavers. He did not even know how he had come into the void. The last thing he remembered was preparing to attack the fleet of the Emerald Queen. Then there had been a blinding flash and he had found himself floating.

He also had some sense that time was passing, but he couldn't tell how long he had been here. In the void there was no way to orient himself, either in space or time.

Then a voice came: *Greetings.*

Pug spoke with his mind. *Who is there?*

Suddenly Pug was someplace else, a realm of shadows but still without any physical frame of reference. Mountainous figures, dwarfing him to insignificance, ringed his position. They were near enough that he could sense how large they were, but distant enough that he could apprehend their overall shape. They were roughly human in form, but that was a generous use of the term *human*. Each rested upon a gigantic throne. Pug sensed these figures were living, though they resembled nothing so much as figures carved from a dark rock of unknown nature.

Pug attempted to see detail, but it was as if his mind would not hold the image of what he saw. He turned from figure to figure, and as he thought he recognized a detail, it would flee.

"Who spoke?" he asked aloud, but no words echoed in the air. He heard his voice in his own mind, but the sound was absent.

A figure emerged from the surrounding gloom, a figure robed in black. Pug waited patiently as the figure approached, and at last she removed a veil that hid her features. Pug asked, "Do I know you?"

"We have met once before, magician," came the icy voice, and Pug felt physical pain as it ran through him like a frozen blade.

"Lims-Kragma!" he said.

The goddess nodded.

Pug looked around and said, "But this is not your realm."

"Everything is within my realm, eventually," said the Goddess of Death. "But it is not the place of our previous meeting, magician."

"Who are these mountainous figures?"

The goddess held out her hand. "These are the Seven Who Control."

Pug nodded. "Where are we?"

"We are in the realm of the gods," said the goddess. "This is what you thought you saw when you sought to tear Macros the Black from within the mind of Sarig." She waved her hand and a faint image of the Celestial City sprang up, surrounding the lower third of the mountainous seven Greater Gods. "But that, like this, is simply another level of perception. Despite your powers, nearly unmatched for a mortal, you have not the ability to truly apprehend our reality."

Pug nodded. "What am I doing here?"

"You are here to make a decision."

"What?"

"To live or to die."

Pug said, "Is that a decision to be made?"

"For you, magician." She placed her hand upon his shoulder and, rather than discomfort, he felt a strangely soothing touch. "You will never enter my realm unbidden, for to you has fallen a curse."

"A curse?"

"You will not realize it at first, but eventually you will know it for what it is."

"I don't understand."

The Goddess put slight pressure on Pug's shoulder and walked him forward slightly. Other figures came into view and Pug could see that most of them stood motionless, with eyes closed. One or two had their eyes open and regarded them as they passed.

"This is the closest a mortal may come to viewing the gods, Pug of Crydee." Pug glanced at the goddess and saw that she again looked as she had when he and Tomas had first visited her hall years before, but smaller. On that visit she had towered over them both.

"How is it this time we are of equal size?"

"It is a function of perception," she said, stepping away from him. Instantly she towered over him as she had before. "Now look at the Controllers."

Pug did, and all he could see were the foundations of the Greater Gods' thrones; they appeared a distant range of peaks, nothing more, their tops lost in the dim sky.

Then the Goddess returned Pug to the size he had been when they first met.

"What have you to say to me?" he asked.

"You are at a nexus. You have three choices. You may release your hold on life now, and enter my realm. You will be rewarded for the good that you have accomplished. Or you may choose eternal life."

"As did Macros?"

"Macros makes assumptions about his existence that are not valid. The sorcerer's fate is not what he thinks it to be."

"You said I have three choices?"

"The third is that you can escape the curse and return to living now, but you shall know the loss of those you love, the pain of thousands, and the sting of bitter failure at the end of your life. You will die in futility."

Pug said, "You paint three difficult alternatives."

"I will tell you this, Pug," said the Goddess. "Your position in our universe is unique. Macros unlocked your potential as a baby, before leaving you where you would be found. He ensured that your Tsurani training would be modified, so that you would return the Greater Magic to Midkemia, and he saw to it that you survived the Riftwar. Because of the sorcerer's interference over the centuries, you play a role far more critical than your birth would have predicted. You stand poised to shake pillars upon which gods rest. This cannot go unnoticed.

"But in doing this, he also created other situations, ones you know nothing of. And as a result you must eventually pay the price for his meddling. And at the end of your life, that price will be terrible."

Pug didn't hesitate. "You leave me no choice. A terrible foe stands on the brink of destroying everything I love. I must live."

"Then I will help you live. You will know things, and you must act." She placed her hand upon his face, covering his eyes.

Suddenly Pug felt the void around him tear, and a great pain shot through his body.

He sat up, a dry scream ripping from his throat.

Nakor held him. "Drink this."

A bitter brew of herbs touched his lips, and Pug drank deeply. He blinked and found his entire body throbbed with pain. Nakor said, "This will lessen your suffering."

Pug focused his mind and the pain subsided. "I can deal with pain," he said, and his voice was a stranger's. "Help me to my feet."

Sho Pi, Calis, Calin, and Aglaranna stood nearby as the magician got to legs shaky with weakness. A robe was brought, and Pug said, "I seem to be the worse for wear."

"You will heal," said Nakor. "A good healing priest can even rid you of the scars." He touched the magician's cheek. "Though it seems you're managing well enough on your own. Someday we must talk about your abilities."

Pug smiled and his face hurt. "Sometimes I think the same of you."

Nakor also smiled. "We came to take a last look at you before saying farewell."

"Good. Where were you going?"

Calis said, "Nakor and I are bound for Crydee. Anthony has one of the old Tsurani transport orbs, and we are going to use that to get to Krondor."

Pug said, "Let me rest this day and tomorrow we'll all three go straight to Krondor."

He glanced around. "How long since I was injured?"

"Two months," said Nakor.

"What's the date?"

"Two days past Banapis," said Calis.

"Then the Emerald Queen's fleet . . . ?"

"At the Straits of Darkness," answered the Elf Queen's younger son. "Anthony gave me a viewing lens made from air, and we watched."

Pug said, "Miranda? Macros?" He glanced at the group. "Tomas?"

"When you were injured they went to look for answers under the Ratn'gari Mountains," said Calis. "Will you join them?"

Pug said, "I don't think so. You and I need to go somewhere else."

"Krondor?"

"First; then we must go to Sethanon."

Calis said, "I have much to do before I set foot in Sethanon."

"No," said Pug. "You must go with me to Sethanon."

"How do you know?" asked Calis.

Pug said, "I have no answer. I just know this to be true." Looking at the Elf Queen, he bowed. "Lady, when your husband returns, please let him know that is where we will be."

Aglaranna nodded. "First you must eat and rest. You've been kept alive by magic arts and your body is not strong."

"A fact I am painfully aware of," said Pug, as his eyes rolled up and he collapsed into Nakor's arms.

Consciousness returned slowly, but at last Pug awoke, finding Sho Pi sitting watch with him. "How long?"

"Another day, a night, and most of this day."

Pug sat up. His skin itched and his muscles protested, but he found that while still weak, he no longer felt unable to function. He rose unsteadily and looked around. He ran his hand over his chin and felt the stubble of beard returning. He had been moved to a small room, carved from within the bole of a huge oak, and found, stepping beyond a heavy curtain, that it opened into the private garden of the Queen and Tomas. Aglaranna sat with her two sons, in calm discussion.

Calin said, "Welcome."

Pug sat down slowly, allowing Sho Pi to hold his elbow. "My thanks for all you've done," said Pug.

"We only aid those who are fighting to preserve this," said the Queen, motioning with her hand to indicate all of Elvandar.

"A bit more than that," said Nakor, entering the glade. "The entire world."

The Elf Queen said, "For the eledhel, Elvandar is the world."

Nakor sat down next to Pug and regarded him. "You'll live."

"Thank you. I needed the reassurance," said Pug dryly.

Nakor laughed. "When do we leave for Krondor?"

Pug glanced at the falling light. "It's evening there already. We should leave first thing tomorrow."

"Another night's rest will help you," said Sho Pi.

"Besides, Nakor," said Pug, "you and I need to discuss some things."

Calis said, "Such as?"

Pug said, "Some things, I am sorry to say, must remain between Nakor and me."

Calis shrugged. "That's as it should be. But I will be glad to return to Krondor. There is still a great deal left to do."

Pug said, "You must go to Sethanon."

Calis's gaze narrowed. "I have duties."

"Be that as it may, you must be in Sethanon."

"My father?" asked Calis.

"He may have something to do with this, but I think it is something only you are capable of seeing done."

"What is that?" asked the Queen.

Pug sighed. "I don't know."

Nakor laughed, a loud, long guffaw. "That sounds like something I would say."

Pug shrugged. "I can't say how I know, Calis, but you must be in Sethanon at the end. And you can't risk not getting there. Which means we cannot have you in the battle. You must go straight to Sethanon—*now*."

Calis looked torn. Pug and his father were nearly legendary figures, men whose wisdom and power were undoubted, but he had seen to the forging of the Prince's defenses as much as William, James, or the others. "But there are so many things for me to do."

"There are many men to do those things," said Nakor, "but if Pug is right, there is only one man who must be at Sethanon when the battle ends."

"Why?" asked Calis.

"We will know when the time comes," said Nakor with his nearly ever-present grin. "All will be made known."

Calis said, "What of the others—my father, Macros, and Miranda?"

Nakor shrugged. "They have their own concerns, I am sure."

Macros said, "Whenever I think I've seen everything there is to see, something new and perplexing shows up."

Miranda and Tomas were forced to agree as the demon shifted its weight uncomfortably upon the ground. They had been communicating with it constantly since it had spoken, and had revealed problems. The demon itself appeared to be nearly mindless, but some other intelligence was in control. The problem was that this intelligence was limited in how much of the demon's nature it could stem. Twice Macros and Miranda had been forced to restrain the creature and listen to it howl in rage for days.

But at the end of a month of give and take, all parties had arrived at a clear understanding.

The demon was controlled by a being named Hanam, a Saaur Lore-master from the Saaur home-world of Shila. Between the four of them—Macros, Hanam, Miranda, and Tomas—they had pieced together a picture of events.

A dark power, vaguely known to Macros and Miranda, but whose name was hidden from them, had influenced the priests of a city called Ahsart, manipulating them into opening an ancient barrier between the demon realm and this one. The demons had come into the world of Shila, destroying an ancient empire and everyone in it.

The Pantathians had shown up in providential fashion, offering the remaining Saaur refuge on Midkemia in exchange for a generation's service, thirty Midkemian years.

For half that time the Saaur had been growing in power on the continent of Novindus, then aiding the Emerald Queen in conquering the entire continent in anticipation of this attack on the Kingdom.

Miranda sighed. "We have, it seems to me, two options."

"Which are?" asked Tomas.

"Reveal the betrayal of the Saaur by the Pantathians, allowing them an honorable avenue to withdraw from the war, or find this entrance from the demon realm and close it."

Tomas said, "We must do both."

Macros said, "I do not like this choice, but Tomas is right."

"Can we do one, then the other?" asked Miranda.

The voice of the demon still sounded like grinding rock, but Hanam said, "The demons' King, Maarg, rages and has destroyed many of his own in frustration. He does not know the Pantathians have ceased to exist as a force." Pointing with a clawed talon toward a distant tunnel, he said, "The rift between Shila and this world is but a half day's walk from here. But on the other side of that rift wait Tugor and his minions." The demon stretched his arms, now reaching nine feet from talon to talon, and said, "I am half his size, and I lack his demon's cunning."

Tomas said, "A demon lord I can best."

"But it's the numbers," said Macros. "Save the Demon King himself, none of that realm is the match of any single one of us." He glanced at his daughter. "Including you, I think, if you keep your wits."

"Thank you for that," she said dryly.

"But a dozen or more of them at once . . ." Macros shook his head. "That's a different matter."

Tomas said, "We delay, yet every day we spend here makes this a more difficult set of tasks."

Macros said, "There are times when strength aids and times when stealth does." He held up one finger. "Tomas, you are vital to the defense of Sethanon. I suggest you and Hanam attempt to divert the Saaur."

Tomas said, "Can we get close enough to . . ." He glanced at Hanam for a name.

"Jatuk, son of Jarwa."

" . . . Jatuk to let him know of the betrayal?"

"And will he believe a demon and a Valheru?"

Macros shrugged.

Hanam said, "If I can get him to listen, I know things only the Loremaster of the Saaur would know. If I can speak to Shadu, my student who took my place, I know I can convince him it is his old master who resides in this body."

"What of you?" asked Tomas.

Macros said, "My daughter and I need to close the pathway between the demon realm and here. Eventually Maarg will deduce he has been betrayed by one of those he sent through, even if he doesn't know which captain it is."

"Once Maarg realizes he's been betrayed," said Hanam, "his rage will be without equal. He will launch a blind attack through the rift, ignoring however many of his servants die for the effort, but once he has reached this world, the outcome will be the same as it was on Shila. Eventually, you will all go to the feasting pits."

Tomas said, "Do they suspect what is waiting at Sethanon?"

One of the longest debates that had gone on between Tomas and Macros had been over how much to tell the Saaur Loremaster. Eventually it had been necessary to tell him everything.

"No," said Hanam. "Jakan knows only that he took over an army in the middle of a war of conquest and destruction. That is as much his nature as anything else. He eats one of his own every night to keep up his power, and his men think they still go to the arms of the Emerald Queen.

"I suspect his ambition is to devour this world and eventually return to challenge Maarg. But if he should find this Lifestone he may attempt to seize it, thinking it a great prize. Who knows what may happen then?"

Macros sighed. "We are decided. Tomas, you must take our taloned friend here and convince his former student to listen."

"There is one other thing," said the Loremaster in demon form.

"What?"

"You must destroy me as soon as Jatuk is convinced. For this body and mind are a struggle to control, and I do not know how much longer I can maintain my dominance of them. It was long in gaining, but it may be over quickly."

"Wonderful," said Miranda, as she stood.

Macros said, "We will first find the rift into Shila, then we will cross over into that world and find the entrance in the city of Ahsart. And close that."

"Unfortunately," said Hanam, "there is one thing you're overlooking."

"What is that?"

"Maarg may already be on the world of Shila; if so, to close the entrance to the demon realm, you will first have to kill the Demon King."

Macros looked at his daughter, and neither could think of anything to say.

Fourteen

Betrayal

ROO FROWNED.

Jason continued to run down their losses which had resulted from the huge burden of debt they assumed to lend gold to the Crown. "And now he wants more," said Roo.

Jason said, "I don't know how we can raise more gold to lend the Duke. We would have to sell off some of our more profitable concerns, and that would increase our problems with cash flow." He shook his head. "Can you find someone else to lend the gold to the Duke?"

Roo laughed. "Well, perhaps I can convince Jacob Esterbrook to join me." He knew it was futile. The few times he had dined with Jacob he had been carefully deflected from any discussion of Jacob's aiding the Kingdom in the coming battle. Still, there were others, and Roo set about to see what he could do. "I'm going to be out for the rest of the day," he told Jason. "Would you send a message to my wife saying I may be in the city a few more days."

Jason jotted down a note.

"Then see what Duncan is up to and have him meet me here at five of the clock. And I'd like Luis here, too."

"Where will you be until then?"

Roo smiled. "Getting the Duke some money. I'll be at Barret's by three of the clock, and afterward I'll return here. Until then I'm out and about."

Roo took a cloak, a light one for fashion, as the day was hot, and wore a broad-brimmed hat with a stylish yellow plume and a very rich pair of riding boots. He carried his old sword at his belt.

He stepped into the busy streets of Krondor and turned to admire Avery and Son. He often paused to regard the huge warehouse he had converted to his business headquarters. He had purchased the land around the warehouse and had built office buildings attached to the warehouse, and now his wagons filled the great yard.

He turned and headed out to make his first call, on a banker who, while not a friend, at least owed him a favor.

"I need the gold," said Duke James.

"I know, m'lord," answered Roo, "but there's no more gold to be had."

"There's always more," said Duke James. Roo noticed he looked fatigued, with heavy circles under his eyes, as if he hadn't been sleeping much lately. The tension in the city was mounting and rumors of war were circulating. The word of a great sea battle at Banapis off the Straits of Darkness had been carried into the city the day before, and now ships were overdue from the Free Cities and Far Coast.

Roo said, "If you raise taxes, perhaps you can squeeze a bit more from the tradesmen and farmers, but the business community is very nervous now. Much of the gold you're talking about has been bleeding to the East for the last few months."

"No small part of it yours!" said the Duke, slamming his hand on the table.

Roo's eyes widened. "I've done nothing any man in my situation wouldn't have done, m'lord!" Roo's words were hot and for an instant he almost forgot who he was talking to, but he held his anger in check, if barely. "I have given you every copper piece it is prudent for me to give. If I give you more, you'll kill the cow for the milk."

James looked at the small man. "Then we kill the cow. I need another month's worth of stores and arms, and I need them yesterday."

Roo sighed. "I'm going to dine with Jacob Esterbrook tonight, and I'll see what I can squeeze out of him."

James looked at Roo for a long, silent minute. "He'll better you at this point."

"How do you mean?"

"He'll know you need to raise gold quickly, and he'll want something you don't want to sell him."

Roo considered that for a moment. "If this army isn't defeated, nothing I have will be of importance. If I have to take a loss now, what does it matter?" He stood up. "If I have your leave, I need to be back at Barret's by three of the clock, and I still have two other stops to make. I must set a few things up."

As Roo bowed and turned to the door, James said, "Rupert?"

"What, m'lord?" asked the little man, turning to regard the Duke.

"Have you many holdings in Landreth and Shamata?"

"Both, Your Grace."

James measured his words. "You might do well to move whatever you have of worth to the north side of the Sea of Dreams."

"Why, my lord?"

"Just a thought," said the Duke, returning his attention to the papers he had been reviewing when Roo had arrived.

Roo let himself out. In the outer office of James's secretary hung a large wall map of the Western Realm. Roo glanced at it, at the area around the Sea of Dreams. The Vale of Dreams had been in Kingdom hands for almost a hundred years, but had long been an area of dispute between the Kingdom and Great Kesh. Roo touched the map, at Land's End. There was the westernmost Kingdom outpost on the shore of the Bitter Sea. To the northeast of it lay a small inlet, called Shandon Bay. A small town, Dacadia, was the only population of size between Land's End and the Sea of Dreams. He traced his finger along a line of hills that moved eastward from the coast, south of Land's End, to a point where it met the river that linked the Bitter Sea and the Sea of Dreams. Then Roo looked at the surrounding countryside, from the Great Star Lake and Stardock, back up the river to the Sea of Dreams. To the east of the Great Star Lake, the mountains called the Grey Range rose up. Suddenly Roo's eyes opened. "He wouldn't!"

James's personal secretary said, "What, sir?"

Roo laughed. "Never mind."

As he left the office of the Duke of Krondor, Roo said, "By damn, I bet he did!"

With what was close to a dance step, Roo hurried down the stairs leading from the palace to the courtyard where a lackey was holding his horse. He took the reins, and as he turned his mount to the gate of the palace, he glanced around at the very busy marshalling yard and wondered where Erik was. He hadn't seen him since Banapis, and he was starting to worry about his friend.

Then his mood darkened as he considered that it was only a few more weeks before this city was in the grip of war. Putting heels to his mount, Roo moved toward the gate and threw a lazy salute to the lieutenant who commanded there. The young soldier returned it, for Roo Avery was a common sight at the palace and was known to be a friend of the Duke. Which, along with his vast wealth, made him one of Krondor's most important men.

Jacob Esterbrook said, "Have you given any thought to my offer?"

Roo smiled. "Considerable." He decided the best tack to take with his business rival was to tell him what he already knew, as if being frank. "I have lent considerable gold to the crown, for this coming war, and as a result I find myself somewhat cash-poor."

Sylvia smiled at Roo, as if everything he said was of vital importance. He returned her smile. "I'm not in a position to negotiate on behalf of the Bitter Sea Company without consulting my partners, but I think whatever I might agree to here would be agreeable to them after I explain the way things are." He paused to finish his last bite of dinner and dabbed at the corner of his mouth. "But I can certainly divest myself of any assets of Avery and Son, and there are several that might serve you as well as those we've discussed."

Jacob smiled. "You have a counteroffer?"

"In a word, yes," Roo said. "Since you seem to have a stranglehold on trade to Kesh, I'm considering abandoning my wagon yards in Shamata and my boat facility in Port Shamata. Both are fine facilities, but neither has realized me a coin of profit since I took them over, as you probably know." He said the last with a rueful laugh.

"Well, I do keep abreast of business to the south. I have enjoyed a long and profitable relationship with several prominent Keshian business concerns." Jacob pushed his chair back from the table as a servant hurried over to help him up. "My knees are not doing well. This weather, I think. When the sky is clear and things are hot and dry, they're almost as painful as when there's rain coming."

Roo nodded as he stood. "Would you be interested in those facilities?" he asked.

"I'm always interested, Rupert, in increasing my holdings. It is merely a matter of price."

Roo smiled. "As it should be."

Jacob said, "Let us retire to the garden for brandy and then I'll leave you to my daughter after that; I can't keep the late hours I used to."

They moved outside, under a warm and star-filled night. The garden was fragrant with the blooms of summer, and the night birds and crickets sang.

Roo sniffed his brandy. He was beginning to develop a taste for the distilled wine, but he still couldn't tell one from Kesh from one that was produced in Darkmoor, through he could tell quality like this one from the poor swill Lord Vasarius served. This one was pungent, tasted as much of wood as any he had tried so far, and gave him a pleasantly warm feeling inside, and the subtle taste of grape and wood lingered in his mouth for long minutes after he swallowed.

Sylvia sat next to Roo, absently letting her hand rest upon his leg, while her father said, "Why don't you prepare a list of particulars and send it over tomorrow?"

"I will do that," said Roo. "And as far as the properties here in Krondor you've inquired after, there are a few that I might be willing to part with, for the same reason I'm looking to get rid of those in Shamata."

"What about Landreth?"

Roo shrugged. "Well, I do manage a little trading from the north shore of the Sea of Dreams to Krondor, so they show a better profit. That, too, would depend on price."

They talked for an hour about business, and then Jacob rose and said,

"I must to bed. If you'd like, stay and have another brandy. Sylvia will entertain you until you leave. Good night, Rupert."

The old man left the garden, and after they were alone, Sylvia ran her hand up Roo's leg. "Shall I entertain you?" she asked playfully.

Roo put down his brandy glass and kissed her. After a moment, he said, "Let's go upstairs."

"No," she said, "I want to stay here."

"In the garden?" he asked.

"Why not?" she said, unfastening her bodice. "It's warm and I don't want to wait."

They made love under the stars, and when they were done, Sylvia lay upon the grass beside Roo, her head on his chest. "You've not been coming around enough, Roo."

Roo was jolted out of his pleasant half-dream state and said, "Things are getting frantic."

"I hear there is war coming," said Sylvia.

"A lot of people are saying that."

"Is it true?"

Roo considered what he should say next. At last he said, "It's true, I think, though I don't know if it's any time soon. But you should consider going East if you hear of trouble in Krondor."

"Krondor?" she said, playfully nipping his shoulder. "I thought Kesh was moving again."

"It is," said Roo, trying to tell her the truth; he loved her and wanted her safe, but he didn't entirely trust her because of her loyalty to her father. "But this time I don't think they're going to move in the Vale." He considered what that would do to his negotiations with Jacob. He decided it wouldn't hurt, so he decided to embellish.

"You know Lord Vykor was called from Rillanon to Krondor."

"Who's he?" said Sylvia.

Roo wondered if she really didn't know or just wanted to make him feel important. He ran his hand down her naked hip and decided it didn't matter. "He's the King's Admiral of the Eastern Fleet. He's lurking down in the Bay of Salts, with a huge flotilla, so that when Kesh sails out of Durbin, he can ambush it. Prince Nicholas took a large squadron to the west, out beyond the Straits, and will sail in behind the Keshians."

Sylvia started playing with the hair on Roo's chest. "I heard he was going out to meet a treasure fleet."

Roo then realized she knew a great deal more than she had ever revealed. Finding his ardor dying, he said, "I must go home, I'm sorry to say."

"Oh." She pouted.

"Sorry, but there is the matter of gathering the documents your father wants."

He dressed while she lay nude upon the grass, looking beautiful in the light of the large moon. When he was finished, she stood and kissed him. "Well, if you must run off, you must. Will I see you tomorrow?"

Roo said, "Impossible, but perhaps the night after."

"Well, I'm going to bed and I'll think of you as I lie in my sheets," she said, running her hand down his stomach.

"You're making this difficult," he groaned.

She laughed. "Well, you make my life difficult. How can I think of another man when I have you in my life?" She kissed him and said, "My father wants to know why I don't marry. He wants grandchildren."

Roo said, "I know. It's impossible."

She said, "Perhaps the gods will be kind and someday we'll be together."

Roo said, "I must go."

He left and she gathered up her gown. Rather than dressing, she carried her clothing through the house, and when she reached her room, she dumped it on the floor.

A soft moan from her bed caused her to smile and she crossed over in the dark, to find two figures entwined on the covers. She slapped the maid hard across her bare buttocks and the girl yelped in surprise.

Duncan Avery looked up at Sylvia in the pale light coming through the window and smiled. "Hello, my darling," he said with a rakish smile. "We got bored waiting for you."

Sylvia pushed the maid to one side and told her, "Pick up my clothes and take them to the laundry."

The girl regarded her mistress with an expressionless mask and slid out of bed. She picked up her own clothes and her mistress's and hurried out of the room, closing the door behind her.

Sylvia reached down and stroked Duncan, saying, "Well, at least she got you ready."

"I'm always ready," he said, kissing her on the neck.

She pushed him back and straddled him, saying, "I need you to do me a service."

"Anything," he said as they gazed into each other's eyes.

"I know," she cooed as she leaned over and kissed him.

"You smell like grass," he observed.

"No doubt," she said. "I was entertaining your cousin on the lawn."

Duncan laughed. "It would kill him to know you've gone from his arms to mine. He takes this sort of business far too seriously."

Sylvia reached down and gripped his face, letting her fingernails dig into his cheeks a bit. "And you had better, as well, my aroused peacock! I'm going to make you wealthy beyond your dreams." She knew she needed a man to be the public head of her father's and Roo's companies, and Duncan was stupid enough for her to control for years. When she got bored with him, she could dispose of him with ease.

Ignoring the pain, Duncan said, "I like wealth."

"Now, about that service."

"What?"

"I need you to kill your sister-in-law."

Duncan was silent for a minute as his breathing became heavy. Finally he said, "When?"

"Within the week."

"Why?"

"So I can marry Roo, you fool!" she said as her own pleasure was mounting.

"How is your marrying my cousin going to make me rich?" asked Duncan.

Suddenly Sylvia arched her back and shuddered, then collapsed on top of Duncan as he matched her passion. After a long silent moment, he said, "How is marrying—"

"I heard you," she interrupted him. How like him, she thought. Not willing to wait even a moment to let her linger in her pleasure. Finally she rolled off him and said, "Because, after an appropriate period, we'll make me Rupert's widow. And then, after an appropriate period of mourning, you and I can wed."

Duncan laughed and grabbed her hair roughly, pulling her head around without a hint of gentleness. "You are a woman to admire," he said, biting her on the lip playfully. "No soft romantic notions for you, my darling." He rolled her over and looked her in the eyes. "I *like* the notion of a marriage based on greed. That's something I can understand."

"Good," said Sylvia, slapping him across the face, almost hard enough to hurt. "Just so we continue to understand each other."

Sylvia lay back as Duncan began to arouse her again, and she thought his usefulness as a public head of the house, as well as his talents in bed, were equally balanced by his boorish behavior. Starting with the maid before she got here was unforgivable. She would punish the girl in the morning for not pointing that out to Duncan. She might not have a shred of jealousy in her makeup, but she insisted on obedience and she had not given the two of them permission.

She sighed and shivered as he began exploring her body, and thought, a year or two; she could put up with Duncan for a year or two before getting him out of the way. Then she would have to look for a young noble, perhaps that irritating grandson of the Duke who had been so resistant to her advances. He might be a welcome challenge. But whoever it was, she would have a title before she was done. She might even consent to have a brat or two for a baron or earl; it might prove necessary. She considered the price of losing her firm body to motherhood and wondered if there were potions or other magics that would keep her looking as she did now. Women had wondered that for years. Then she thought, why just an earl? Why not a duke? That Dashel who worked for Rupert had a brother, didn't he? And eventually he would rise to rank, perhaps that of duke. Then she wondered if he would be easier than his brother had been to charm, or if he would prove a challenge.

As Duncan kissed her stomach she thought, that's what she needed. Another challenge. All the men presently in her life were so predictable. As she closed her eyes and arched her back, she thought, the Prince is still unwed!

Pug materialized near the shore, where a group of students was listening to Chalmes lecture on magic. The master magician stopped when he saw who the three men were, for Pug had brought along Nakor and Sho Pi. Pug's outer appearance seemed different; he was thinner, and his hair and beard were short, as if just growing in. There was also a tired quality about his movement.

"M'lord," said Chalmes to Pug, "this is as unexpected as your last appearance."

Pug said, "There are matters of grave importance we must discuss. Gather the other leaders in the conference chamber. I will be along in a moment."

If the magician who was now the leader of the community objected to being ordered this way, he hid it masterfully. He put his hand over his heart in a Keshian gesture and said, "It will be done, m'lord."

Nakor looked at the students who sat with astonished wonder and said, "Shoo!"

They quickly departed, leaving the three men standing alone. They had transported into Krondor with Calin, whom Pug had left behind for a while, to oversee the coming defense of the city until such time as Pug came for him. Pug's grandson Arutha had managed to indicate he desperately needed to speak to him, so Pug felt the need to return quickly to the Prince's city. "You know what to do?" asked Pug.

"Certainly," said Nakor. "I don't know if I like this, but I can see why it's necessary."

Pug shrugged. "If we survive these next few months, we'll worry about what's happening here. Unless you've got a better plan?"

Nakor rubbed his chin. "I don't know. I might have something, but either way we must do this other thing first."

"Well, then, be off with you!" said Pug with a laugh. "When this is over, get horses and head for Sethanon. I don't think there's anything you can do in Krondor. And if I'm not there, see what you can do to help Tomas."

Nakor and Sho Pi hurried toward the ferry, which would take them to Stardock town, while Pug turned toward the great citadel of Stardock.

He hurried into the building and reached the central chamber where the senior magicians of the island were gathering. They rose to their feet when he entered, and he waved them to chairs as he moved to the seat traditionally occupied by the leader of the council.

"Things move quickly," he said without preamble. "I have been content to let you play your games of independence from the Kingdom and Kesh while peace reigned, but things cannot be allowed to continue in this fashion."

Chalmes said, "There are rumors of war. Do you wish the Academy to take the side of the Kingdom?"

"Yes," said Pug.

"Many here are of Keshian birth and feel no love for the Kingdom," said another magician.

"You are Robert d' Lyes?"

"Yes," said the young magician, inclining his head at the honor of being remembered.

"You're a Kingdom-born man."

"True. I merely point out the division of loyalties, after the loyalty we all feel to Stardock."

Pug said, "Let me be direct: Stardock is mine. It was built with my money on land deeded to me by the King, and until I say otherwise, it will continue to be mine."

"That is as it should be," said d'Lyes, "but many will choose to depart, and I see that as being a defeat of the principles that brought us together."

Pug smiled. "I understand, and I appreciate your Academy-born desire to sit here and debate the obvious until you've arrived at some profound philosophic insight, but given that the largest army in the history of the world sails to Krondor even as we speak, we cannot afford that luxury."

At mention of the fleet, several of the magicians in the room frowned. "We thought the gathering of Keshian soldiers to the south was a prelude to a war, my lord," said Chalmes. "What is this business of a fleet?"

Pug said, "Let me be brief. A huge army from across the Endless Sea, serving a demon lord, is sailing toward Krondor. Once the city has been reduced to ashes, that army intends to sweep out and conquer everything between this island and Ylith, Krondor and Salador. There will be blood and fire like nothing you could imagine."

The magicians spoke among themselves, and Pug let them for a minute. Then he held up his hand and the room fell silent. "But what is more critical is that their ultimate goal, without their own knowledge, is a prize which, if seized by them, could destroy all life on Midkemia."

"Is this possible?" said d' Lyes.

"Not only possible, probable," said Pug, "unless I get some help."

The young magician said, "I will help."

Pug smiled. "Youth is often underappreciated," he observed as the other, older magicians in the council remained silent.

Finally, Kalied, one of the senior magicians of Keshian ancestry, said,

"So much of what we have labored for is at risk, if that is true; would it not be wiser for us to remain here to protect the library and the other facilities?"

Pug said, "I cannot order you to willingness. I can order you to leave, but what purpose would that serve?" He stood. "I will retire to my tower for two hours. Call all the magicians capable of battle magic or protection or healing, and tell them what I have said. Those who will help I will take with me. The rest may stay here and defend Stardock, if they are able."

Pug left while the other magicians started discussing what he had just said. He mounted the stairs to his study and entered by the mystic door that barred others from entering; before the door had shut fully, he transported himself to Sorcerer's Isle.

Gathis, the goblinlike creature who had served Macros and Pug as majordomo, was at his usual post in the central room of the house, the one he used as an office, overlooking the lovely garden Pug had created. "Master Pug," said Gathis, "am I correct in assuming that Master Macros is back?"

Pug smiled. Gathis had once told him there was a mystic bond between himself and Macros. "Yes, that's true, though where he and Miranda are is not known to me."

Gathis stood and said, "What service may I perform?"

"I need a change of clothes, and bring me a hot meal while I bathe."

One of the pure pleasures of the house on Sorcerer's Isle, the one called Villa Beata, was the Keshian-style baths. Pug had ordered them restored to their former function, and when Gathis arrived carrying a tray with hot beef, cheese, bread, greens, and a chilled pitcher of white wine, Pug was sitting in a hot pool, relaxing.

Looking at the scars on Pug's body and his very short hair and beard, Gathis said, "It appears you have been in some difficulty."

Pug laughed. "I've always loved your knack for understatement, my friend." He took the goblet of wine the green-faced being handed him, and after a sip he said, "Did you know Miranda was Macros's daughter?"

Gathis said, "I suspected as much, though I've really had very little opportunity to talk to the young woman on the brief occasions when she accompanied you here from Stardock. As there is something about her manner that puts me in mind of the Black One, the revelation is no surprise."

"It was to me. Did you know her mother was the Lady Clovis?"

"Now, that is a surprise," said Gathis. "I met the Black One when he rescued me from my home world, quite some time ago, but that was after he had left Miranda and her mother, as I piece things together."

Pug said, "After I eat, I must return to Stardock. But before I go, I mean to see the defenses are in place. A very hostile fleet of great size is going to be sailing past here in a few days, and while their destination is Krondor, a few of them may be tempted to stop and investigate."

Gathis said, "I will follow your instructions in this." Then he smiled his toothy smile. "However, if I am to judge such things correctly, several of your students here would be most able to discourage such a visit by marauding malefactors."

Pug laughed. "I couldn't have said it better myself."

"Will you be returning soon?"

Pug's expression turned somber. "I don't know. I would be less than truthful if I didn't tell you that the fate of this planet is in the balance, so leave it that if we survive, I will return."

"And the Black One?"

Pug shrugged. "You know your former master far better than I, so you tell me."

Gathis returned the shrug; there was nothing more to say. Pug finished his meal and his bath and dressed in clean robes. He then transported himself to his study, and walked down the stairs to where a large number of students were waiting. When Pug saw them, he said, "Everyone, outside!"

The students started to hurry toward the main door, but Pug grabbed one by the sleeve, turning him completely around, and said, "What's your name?"

"John, Master," said the youth, almost beside himself to have been singled out by the legendary Master of Stardock.

"Go into the council hall and tell everyone there to join us outside."

The student hurried off to the council chamber, and Pug pushed his way through the crowd, which quickly fell back when the students saw who was attempting to get through. Pug reached a point where a large rock rose, a short distance from where the road to the docks wound down the slope, and he mounted the rock.

After a few minutes had passed, Pug turned and looked across the lake. He adjusted his mystic sight to study the distant docks, and was pleased to see Nakor, Sho Pi, and two soldiers. They were boarding the barge that served as a ferry between the shore and the island.

Chalmes and the other members of the council pushed their way through the press of students, and Chalmes said, "Pug, what is this about?"

Pug sat upon the rock, affecting the best Nakor-like pose he could muster, and said, "We are waiting."

"Waiting for what?"

Pug smiled and felt a perverse sense of pleasure in their frustration as he replied, "I don't want to spoil the surprise."

That caused them to fall silent, and for a very uncomfortable half hour they waited as the barge was poled across the lake. At last Nakor and the others came walking up the road, and Pug said, "I'm glad to see you."

Nakor said, "This is Captain Sturgess of the Shamata Garrison." The students began to mutter at the sight of the second soldier, who wore the uniform of the Keshian border legion. "And this is General Rufi ibn Salamon."

The General nodded. "My lord."

Pug turned to the assembled magicians. To Chalmes he said, "I suppose in the two hours I gave you, you have managed to dither the time away and do nothing that I ordered."

"We were discussing the best way to disseminate the information you gave us—" began the old magician.

Pug put up his hand, cutting him off. "Is Robert d' Lyes here?"

From the rear of the crowd, the young magician raised his hand. Pug pointed to him and said, "I believe he is the juniormost member of the council, is that right?"

The magicians nodded.

"Good. That means you're not totally without hope," said Pug.

D' Lyes looked confused at that remark. "Not totally," he said.

Pug laughed and stood up so all could see him. To the assembled magic users he said, "Even here I suspect you've heard rumors of war."

Some magicians said yes, and others nodded.

"The war is real, but it is not with our neighbors to the south.

"A great fleet comes from across the sea and brings with it an army of terrible size, perhaps a quarter-million men under arms." At that, several of the magicians began talking among themselves. Pug held up his hands and the group fell silent. "The Kingdom makes ready to defend itself, and as you can imagine, we need a secure border with Kesh. Toward that end, some changes have been made."

A hush fell over the crowd as they waited to hear what Pug said next.

"Great Kesh and the Kingdom have contested for years over the rich farmlands surrounding the Sea of Dreams. To end this eternal dispute, the Kingdom has ceded certain lands to the Empire of Great Kesh.

"To the southwest of Land's End is a great rocky prominence, clearly visible from sea and land, called Morgan's Ruin. Sailors know it well. From the tip of that great rock, straight east to the river Shamata, a new border has been drawn. The Empire of Great Kesh has been ceded all lands south of that line, along the southern banks of the river Shamata, the Sea of Dreams, and the Great Star Lake."

The assembled group gasped and a few shouted in anger. One man, obviously from the Kingdom, shouted, "You betray us!"

Pug said, "No. Prince Erland has been negotiating with the Emperor of Great Kesh for a long time on this matter. In exchange for Kesh's protecting our southern flank from the enemy, and for observing our current treaty while we are engaged with a mighty foe, the Kingdom chooses to grant several claims for territory Kesh has held for almost a hundred years. Those of you who are uncomfortable with this change in governance may leave.

"As it stands now, Stardock is still Kingdom territory; still *my* duchy." Pug glanced from face to face. "Shamata is now being handed over to the Keshians. The Kingdom forces are withdrawing across the Great Star Lake to Landreth. Any of you who wish may travel with them."

Several more protests were heard, but Pug ignored them.

General Salamon spoke. "We will honor the Kingdom's claim to sovereignty for Stardock Island. Stardock town will be Keshian. Until you have arranged for a portage or dock on the north shore, Kingdom citizens will be granted the right of free passage through Stardock town."

Someone in the crowd shouted, "When are you taking over?"

The General said, "We have taken over. My men are now occupying the small fortress at Port Shamata and the garrison in the city, and we will leave a small force across the water to ensure the peace." Looking at Pug, he said, "If there is nothing more, I need to return to my men, my lord."

Pug nodded and said, "Thank you for coming."

The General and the Kingdom Captain left together, heading down the hill toward the dock. Pug said, "That is the end of it. Now on to another matter.

"This invader I spoke of is an enemy of the most dangerous sort, and I need those of you willing to serve. We need those of you able to heal, able to act as conduits for intelligence, and those of you who may in some way stem the invaders' magic." He paused and then added, "They are served by Pantathians."

At mention of the hated serpent priests, several of those who had been quiet shouted, "I'll help!"

Pug waited and said, "Those of you willing to travel to Krondor, see Robert d' Lyes. He is to be my aide in this matter."

D' Lyes looked around, confusion on his face. "Aide?" he said as young magicians started to talk to him.

Pug jumped down from the rock and Nakor said, "What do we do now?"

Pug said, "We? I'm going to Krondor with this band, to get them ready; then I travel to Sethanon. You wait here to make sure that this band of fools doesn't start a war with Kesh in the next two weeks; when you're certain they won't, I want you to get to Sethanon." He reached into his robe and pulled out a Tsurani transportation orb. "Don't break it or lose it: it's the last one I have. And it's a long walk to Sethanon."

Nakor didn't look pleased. "Things are coming to a head, and you want me to stay here and wet-nurse this bunch?"

Pug grinned. "Who better?"

So saying he moved through the milling magicians and went to talk to Robert d' Lyes.

Sho Pi said to Nakor, "Master?"

"What?"

"Have you given thought to what Pug said about thinking of a different plan for Stardock?"

Nakor was silent for a moment, then turned to his student with a wide grin. "Of course I have."

Fifteen

Onslaught

ERIK FROWNED.

He put the papers on Lord William's desk and said, "That is what I'm to do?"

William and Calis nodded. "We've had a change of plans since my father appeared," said William, looking very tired. "He went into council with the Prince, James, and myself, and all I can tell you is he convinced us that Calis is needed elsewhere."

Erik had been operating on the assumption that he would be up in the mountains to the north and east of the city, awaiting the fall of Krondor to launch raids against the invaders as they moved eastward. Now he was being told the roles were being shuffled, like so many cards in a deck.

William said, "I am in charge of the defense of the city. That hasn't changed. Vykor's flotilla is hidden down in Shandon Bay and will sally against the raiders as they pass by, to be joined, we hope, by what is left of Nicholas's fleet after it's refitted at the Sunsets.

"Greylock will act as my second with the units up in the mountains." He pointed at Erik. "That means you will have to fill in for Greylock, where we had planned to use him."

"The retreat," said Erik flatly.

"Yes," said Calis. "By the time we lose this city, we're going to have a frantic population attempting to flee and a routed army trying to go with them. We can't allow that."

"How are you going to prevent it?" asked Erik.

William sighed. "This is what comes of making assumptions. If we had included you in our command meetings you'd know this already." He handed a large sheaf of papers to Erik. "Read these; the plan is outlined in detail and I want you to have it down cold by tonight. You and I will have dinner and we can dispose of any questions of yours then."

Erik turned to Calis. "When do you leave?"

"As soon as my father returns from Stardock," answered William for Calis.

Erik assumed it was implicit no one knew when that was. "Very well, m'lord."

Erik turned to leave the room, and as he reached the door, William said, "Oh, Erik, there's one more thing."

Erik turned and said, "What is that, sir?"

"From this moment on, you're a Knight-Captain in the Prince's army. I don't have time to waste making you a lieutenant, so you'll just have to skip a rank."

Greylock smiled, trying hard not to laugh at Erik's astonished expression. "Me, sir?"

"What's the matter, von Darkmoor!" shouted Calis in a fair imitation of Bobby de Loungville. "Are you suddenly hard of hearing?"

Erik blushed. "Ah, that means I need a new sergeant major, doesn't it?"

"Yes. Any recommendations?"

Erik almost said Jadow, because he was the most senior sergeant in the command, but the fact was that Calis had been correct originally when he had given Erik the job. Jadow just didn't have the command skills for the position; it required far more organizational ability than most of the sergeants possessed. After a while he said, "There are two or three men who would serve, but to be honest, the best of the lot is Duga, the mercenary captain. He's smart, he's tough, and he understands exactly what is at stake without our telling him everything. He's been very useful in persuading those other mercenaries we've captured into switching sides."

"I don't like it," said William. "The man's a turncoat."

Erik said, "You have to understand how things are across the sea, m'lord. Men there have no strong attachment to a city and there are nothing like the nations here; Duga has been a mercenary all his life, but down there mercenaries live by a strict code of honor. If he swears loyalty—and I can make him understand this isn't a contract where he can throw down his sword and switch back—he'll serve."

William said, "Let me think on this. Perhaps we'll make him a sergeant of auxiliaries, but I need someone else, now."

"Then Alfred," said Erik. "He's not as sharp when it comes to strategy and tactics as I'd like, but he understands how to get things done in a hurry with a minimum of fuss."

"Then he'll do," said William, glancing at Calis.

Calis nodded. "I agree. He's solid, and he'll do for what we have coming."

"Go tell him," said William, and Erik left.

After he was gone, Greylock said, "You neglected to mention he carries the court rank of Baron."

Calis smiled. "Let's not get him too upset right now."

William let out a long, tired sigh. "I'm going to have to deal with his upset when he reads the plans and sees what his role is to be."

Calis nodded. "There's no doubt about that." Then he laughed, a rueful, bitter laugh.

"Darkmoor!" Erik said. "You can't be serious!" At William's expression, he quickly added, "M'lord."

William motioned for Erik to follow him down the hall. "We're dining with my family tonight. We'll talk over a quiet meal."

As soon as they reached the dining hall, Erik felt his anger drain away. The "quiet" meal the Knight-Marshal spoke of included Duke James, Lady Gamina, their son, Lord Arutha, and his two sons, Dashel and James.

Erik almost blushed at being included with the Duke's family, and quickly took a seat to William's right. As servants began to bring in the food, the magician Pug entered through a door across from Erik's seat. Erik saw only that his hair and beard had been cut close, until he came to sit between William and Lady Gamina, at which point Erik saw what appeared to be faint burn marks on his neck and face.

Jimmy and Dash stood, as did Arutha, James, and Gamina. William hesitated a moment, and rose, while Erik quickly did as well. "Great-grandfather," said Dash in greeting.

Pug kissed Gamina's cheek and shook hands with James and then with William. "I'm pleased we're all together," said Pug.

Erik saw, and with sudden clarity realized, why there was a somber mood in the room; this might very well be the last time Pug's family would gather. And many of those here might not be alive soon.

Erik whispered to William, "If you'd prefer, sir, we can talk about my mission tomorrow."

William shook his head. "At first light tomorrow, I want you up in the hills inspecting the first line of fortifications outside the city to the east. Then you need to be back here by the day after tomorrow." He glanced at his family. "We don't have time, I'm sorry to say."

Pug said, "Before anything else, I have one thing I must say to all of you."

William turned to look at his father, as did James and Gamina. Pug said, "I have been absent from your lives far too long, and for this I must beg your forgiveness." He then reached out and placed his hands over William's and Gamina's. "And I also need to tell you how very proud of you I am."

William looked as if he didn't know what to say. Gamina smiled and moisture gathered in her eyes as she leaned over and kissed her father's cheek. Erik had seen enough strange things in the last four years to find nothing odd in the image of a woman who looked old enough to be Pug's mother being his daughter.

Gamina said something to her father by mind speech, and he smiled. "I wish she were here, too."

William said, "Thank you, Father."

Pug removed his hand from Gamina's and put it over the one that still gripped William's. "No, I must thank you, for being who you are, and for holding to your own dream, no matter what I thought you should be doing. I learn slowly at times, I fear."

William smiled and Erik could see the resemblance between father and son. There was a sheen of moisture in the Knight-Marshal's eyes, and Erik found his own throat tightening with emotion. This was what this war was about, protecting those we love, he thought. Somewhere in the night his mother and the only man he thought of as a father were sitting over a table in the back of an inn, and somewhere out there the woman he loved was hiding, on her way to join his mother and Nathan.

Erik suddenly felt a presence in his mind, a gentle touch, nothing more, but he knew it was the Lady Gamina. He glanced over and she saw was smiling at him. Then words came into his mind. *Your young woman is safe, I am sure.*

Without knowing quite how to do it, he tried to say, *My wife.*

Gamina laughed and William said, "What?"

The Duchess said, "Our young friend has gotten married since the last time we met."

Pug, William, Arutha, and Gamina all offered congratulations, while the two younger men glanced at their grandfather. Pug said, "James?"

The former boy thief shrugged and grinned, and there was a hint of boyish playfulness in his manner. "I knew. So did Dash and Jimmy."

Arutha said, "You knew?"

Duke James laughed. "I had to get Erik's mind back on the days to come, so I let him think he was being terribly clever sneaking his young wife out of the city." He pointed an accusatory finger at Erik. "Don't ever disobey me again, Captain."

At the admonition and use of his new rank, Erik couldn't help but blush.

"Captain?" asked Dash, nodding in approval.

Gamina and Arutha both said, "Congratulations."

William said, "We'll see how much congratulations are in order after this coming battle."

At mention of the conflict, the mood in the room fell somber again. After a moment of quiet, Pug slapped his hand on the table. "Enough! Let us steal a moment of happiness while we can." He glanced at his grandson, Arutha. "My only regret is that your wife is not with us."

Arutha smiled, and Erik again saw the echo of both his father and mother in his features. "She visits her parents in Roldem."

Jimmy said, "Perhaps we should all go to Roldem for a visit."

Pug laughed, and the others joined in. The meal passed quickly and pleasantly, as those dining together found reassurance in one another's company.

Erik was pleased to have the opportunity of seeing this family together, for in this room sat three of the most important men in the Kingdom, Lord James and his father-in-law and brother-in-law. The food was beyond a doubt the best Erik had ever had, and the wine was beyond comparison, wine grown in his own Darkmoor region, but too costly for a commoner like himself to have ever tasted. He and William quietly discussed the plan for the defense of those leaving the city, in the corner, while the other family members chatted about matters of small importance and ignored the darkness coming their way.

After supper they ate sweets and drank Keshian coffee with small glasses of an exquisite fortified wine from Rodez. As Erik felt a warm glow fill him from head to toe, Calis hurried into the dining room. "Sorry to intrude," he said without greeting, "but a message has arrived."

James stood and held out his hand, and Calis gave him the message. William said, "From Land's End?"

"Yes, by fast riders. The invaders' fleet was sighted just after dawn yesterday."

William said, "With a favorable wind, that will put them off the point the day after tomorrow."

James nodded. "It begins."

Erik squinted, trying to will sight in the gloom. He stood on the outer breakwater, on the forward firing platform. As he had threatened, Greylock had seen that Captain de Beswick was given the dubious honor of being the first officer to face the enemy at Krondor's wall.

If the formerly hostile Captain felt any resentment over Erik's promotion, placing him above the career officer from Bas-Tyra, he hid it well, and was nothing if not polite when Erik gave him orders.

"Where are they?" asked Erik.

De Beswick said nothing, realizing the question was rhetorical. As the sun lit the sky to the east, the western horizon continued to be cloaked in fog and darkness, accommodating the enemy's advance. De Beswick said, "I know little about this sea, Captain, but if the weather is at all like Bas-Tyra's, the haze should burn off by midmorning."

Erik said, "By midmorning you may have warships sitting close enough to throw rocks at." He looked over the defenses for what seemed to be the hundredth time since he had returned from his inspection of the nearby defenses to the east of the city.

Long minutes dragged on, and Erik kept returning to examining those forward elements. The outer breakwater had been restructured, so that to reach Krondor harbor a ship now had to sail as far south as possible around a large jetty, atop which sat the platform Erik stood on; that was manned by a company of catapult crews, bowmen, and a shoreside detachment, all armed to the teeth. Any ship approaching this end of the jetty would be fired upon. The seawall ran almost due north, separated from the inner wall by a distance of less than a quarter mile. At the north end of the wall, another company waited, and any ship attempting to come up the channel between the inner and outer walls would be subject to a withering cross fire. Across the water on the inner wall, another company of soldiers manned their war engines. Erik considered that once the enemy saw the new defenses, their only choice would be to attempt to seize all three platforms. If they were foolish enough to send ships into the channel before they cleared away the defenders, they ran the risk of a ship's being sunk to block the channel. What Erik knew and they didn't was that a clever set of traps awaited the ships that came through that channel, even if the defenders were swept away from the walls.

Erik looked at the small boat tied off below, less than twenty feet down a rope ladder dropped over the edge of the platform. "I'm going to leave you the boat," said Erik. He knew that the men on this and the next three stations were likely to be obliterated before they could withdraw.

De Beswick looked at Erik, and raised an eyebrow in question.

"If you need to send a message in a hurry, it's faster than running along the top of the wall."

"Of course," said de Beswick. Then, after a moment, he said, "Rather decent of you, actually."

Erik put his hand on the man's shoulder and said, "Good-bye and good luck."

He ran along the top of the jetty, along the small path cut atop the mountains of rocks placed there by convict labor so that the ballista and catapult platforms could be installed. For more than three quarters of a mile he trotted to the second platform, where he accepted the salutes of the officers waiting there. He didn't stop to speak, but continued along, turning eastward at the top of the inverted U the two walls formed. For a quarter mile the Knight-Captain of the Prince's army hurried along, then turned south. The day was getting warmer, and Erik was perspiring when he reached the third platform. He quickly inspected stores and equipment, then turned back north. The last platform was the most isolated, for as at the first one on the outer wall, the men would have to flee along the exposed path and across the rock jetty to reach the old north jetty, which had traditionally shielded Krondor's harbor from the Bitter Sea's south-running tides.

By the time Erik got to the point where the old jetty reached the northmost dock, he found a company of Palace Guards waiting for him. Erik mounted a horse being held for him, and led the patrol through the mass of soldiers on the docks. Every possible barricade had been erected, and the first three blocks into the city were a killing zone. Every upper window of every building housed an archer, and Erik marveled at the defenses planned by William and James. The lower windows were barricaded and the doors locked, and a clever set of easily moved ramps had been constructed so the defenders in the upper stories could withdraw by crawling from building to building, while others covered their retreat. What had surprised Erik wasn't the number of citizens who had fled the city once the construction of the defenses began but, rather, those who had to be evicted, despite the evidence before their eyes of the coming battle. Many had been carried by main force out of their homes, or marched out at spearpoint.

At the third corner from the docks, Erik and his men reached the first barricade. They were waved through and headed toward the palace.

As they moved away from the dock area, Erik saw the fearful faces of the populace, some peeking out of doorways, and others hurrying off on one errand or another before war came to Krondor. Many carried large bags of their belongings on their backs and were heading toward the east, where they would attempt to leave the city before fighting began.

Erik knew that James would allow refugees to trickle out of the city, in a controlled fashion, until the enemy were ashore and the eastern gates needed to be closed. From reports he had read the night before, Erik knew the foulburg—the portion of the city built beyond the ancient walls—was all but deserted. Local patrols of constables had arrested and hanged a dozen looters over the last week.

A trader with a pushcart hurried past, shouting he had food to sell, and Erik was certain the man would dispose of the last of his wares before noon. As Erik neared the palace, the level of traffic heading to the gate increased, and he ordered his escort to head around back toward the docks and then to the palace, to avoid the press of citizens.

They moved back down toward the docks, and as they rode along, one of the men in a second-story window above shouted, "Gods! Look at them!"

Erik lacked the man's advantage of height, but he knew that the man could see the hostile fleet. "What do you see?"

The soldier looked down to see who asked, and, seeing the officer's mark on Erik's tunic, said, "Ships, sir! Must be a thousand of them."

Erik didn't wait. He kicked his horse into a canter and moved as fast as safety permitted toward the palace. He knew there weren't a thousand enemy ships outside Krondor's harbor, but he knew there were at least four hundred, by cautious estimation of how much of the fleet had survived.

Nicholas had hit them on one side of the Straits of Darkness while a flotilla from Elarial hit them from the south. At the same time squadrons of warships from Durbin and Queg raided the forward elements. James had reviewed the reports from lookouts who attempted to judge the size of the remaining fleet as it sailed past, then sent word by a series of relay riders, who would change horses every few miles. The raids had reduced the invader's fleet by a fourth. Others had celebrated the damage done to the enemy until James had pointed out that left a mere four hundred and fifty warships heading toward Krondor.

So instead of three hundred thousand soldiers coming ashore within the next few days, only two hundred and twenty-five thousand would invade the Kingdom. Erik fought off the desire to surrender to despair.

He entered the palace via the sea gate, and gave his horse's reins to a lackey. "I need a fresh horse," he said, and ran off to his last meeting with Lord James and Knight-Marshal William.

He reached the conference room where William and James were overseeing the final briefing for the area commanders before they were dispatched to their respective garrisons. The palace gate out of the city was being held clear so that dispatch riders and those officers leaving could get out of the city before the riots of panic-stricken citizens began.

James stood by while William issued orders. "We should have ships beaching to the north of the city within the hour." He pointed to two of the commanders who would see to coastal defenses just outside the city. "It's time for you to be there, gentlemen. Good luck."

Erik saw the Earl of Tilden and a squire whose name was not known to him salute and depart. Erik had studied the deployment of troops for days since William had given him a copy of the battle plan, and he knew that nobles and their detachments would be the first to feel the brunt of the attack. From Sarth down to Krondor, from Krondor to the small villages north of Shandon Bay, every armed soldier that Patrick could squeeze out of the Armies of the West stood ready to repulse the invaders. But sixty thousand troops, most of them untested levies, were going to be overrun by more than three times their numbers in battle-hardened warriors. The only advantage the Kingdom possessed would be in discipline and training, and that wouldn't come into play until after Krondor fell.

For it was clear to Erik that his first suspicion had been correct: Krondor would fall. He glanced around the room and saw that Greylock was already gone, as was Calis. Greylock was riding for the first detachment directly under his command, a mixed company of Calis's Crimson Eagles, Hadati warriors, and the Royal Krondorian Pathfinders. Throughout the mountains to the north and east every experienced mountain fighter they could recruit from as far east as the hills above Ran and Pointer's Head was waiting.

The general plan was to bleed the enemy, killing as many of the invaders as possible going through Krondor, then to shred them as they made their way through the hills and mountains, where each of Greylock's mountain fighters would be the worth of five of the invaders. Erik had fought with the Emerald Queen's army; most of them were satisfactory horse infantry, and a few decent cavalry, but none were mountain men. The only thing Erik worried about was the Saaur riders, for while they might not be mountain fighters, they were warriors unmatched by any force the human defenders of the Kingdom could put in the field. Erik knew they would have lost a number of their horses on the sea journey. The fodder would spoil from to the constant moisture, and horses would colic, and some would be useless after six months in the hold of a ship, but enough would be quickly fit to make the Saaur a dangerous foe. And who knew what sort of magic the enemy might employ to keep the horses fresh?

William turned to Erik. "Ready?"

"Ready or not, our forces are in place. As I left the docks, the enemy was sighted."

William dropped what he was doing and hurried to the large window that overlooked the harbor. "Gods!" he said softly.

Erik and the others followed, and each in his own way was just as stunned. No matter what reports had said, none of them was prepared for the sight that greeted them. From the outer seawall to the distant horizon, clearing by the minute as the morning haze burned off the Bitter Sea, white sails could be seen. Erik craned his neck and looked as far north as he could manage, and could make out sails in the distance.

"They must have fanned out since yesterday," said William, turning away and hurrying back to the table. "They're going to wash over us like a tide." To the nobles in the room he said, "Gentlemen, you know what to do. May the gods protect us all."

Erik glanced around the room. "The Prince?"

"He left the palace last night," said William. "With my sister and her son and grandsons." William glanced at Erik and smiled. "Can't lose the Prince, now, can we?"

Erik shook his head. "Lord James?"

"In his office. Seems he felt obliged to stay."

After the nobles had left in an orderly fashion, Erik said, "There's nothing left for me to do here, sir."

"One thing," said William, reaching into his tunic. He pulled out a small parchment, rolled and tied with a ribbon, and sealed, the crest of his office pressed into the red wax. "When this is over, give this to my father if you can."

Erik frowned. "Sir?"

William smiled. "I would never order a man to the wall if I wasn't willing to go there myself, Erik."

For a moment, Erik was unable to move. He realized with dread certainty that the Knight-Marshal of the Kingdom did not intend to leave the city. He swallowed hard. While he and William were not close, he had come to admire the man for his honesty, bravery, and clear, cool logic in planning a battle. And for one night, when he had shared supper with the man and his family, he had glimpsed a personal history. He could not help but feel loss.

"Sir," he said at last, "good-bye."

William held out his hand. "Good-bye, Captain. Much of what will come rests in your hands. Know one thing: you are capable of far more than you know."

Erik put the scroll in his tunic and saluted as smartly as he could manage. The he hurried from the room. He returned quickly to the courtyard, where a fresh horse waited, and mounted. Unlike the others, who left through the one gate kept free of citizens, he turned back to the gate that led to the docks. He signaled for a patrol of lancers to accompany him, and the gates were opened as he reached them. Outside the gate a squad of foot soldiers held a small crowd at bay. Panic was beginning to manifest itself in the city as word spread of the approaching fleet. Some of the poor souls living along the waterfront, near the palace, were seeking to gain entrance into the city. Erik paused to shout, "There is no refuge for you here! The eastern gate is still open. Either leave the city that way or return to your homes! Now, clear the way."

He moved his horse forward, and citizens dove out of the way as the squad of riders followed behind him.

Erik moved through the city as quickly as possible. He knew his assignment in theory, but the difference between theory and practice was quickly becoming apparent. His job was to oversee the orderly withdrawal of the city's defenders to Greylock's first defensive position to the east, about a half day's march beyond the first farms outside the city. But everywhere he looked, Erik saw chaos, and he doubted anything remotely like order could be pulled from the mess. Still, he was sworn to succeed or to die trying. He put heels to horse and moved into the crowd.

Jason grabbed up every book he could and put them into canvas sacks, which he handed to boys who were waiting to take them to nearby wagons. Roo had overestimated the time left before the invaders reached Krondor, and now he watched as his employees evacuated his businesses. Everything he could manage to hoard—gold, letters of credit, and other items of wealth—was safely hidden at his estates. He already had a pair of wagons there waiting to take his wife and children, as well as the Jacobys, to the East. He hoped that Sylvia had listened seriously to his warnings and would join them as they moved to escape the coming onslaught.

Jason said, "That's the last of it, sir!"

Roo, sitting atop a fresh horse, said, "Get the wagons out of here!"

Fifteen wagons, carrying everything he could move, started out of the large yard into the street. Shouting people hurried past, some carrying their belongings on their backs, while others just ran. Rumors were flying—that the Prince was dead, that the palace had been taken, that all the gates were closed and they were trapped—and Roo knew that eventually he would have to leave behind his wagons and remaining goods if he didn't get out of the city by sundown.

He had hired the best private guards he could find, and there weren't many left in Krondor. Just about any man capable of carrying a sword or pulling a bow was now in the King's service. The squad of ten men he had hired were old men and boys, but the old men were veterans and the boys were strong and enthusiastic.

Whips cracked as the horses moved the heavily burdened wagons, which groaned under the weight. Roo was attempting to salvage everything of worth, inventory, tools, and furnishings. He had faith that eventually the Emerald Queen's army would be defeated, and he was attempting to ensure that he had as much of a start as possible in rebuilding his wealth after the war was over.

Roo said to Jason, who was now sitting on the first wagon, "Where is Luis?"

Jason said, "He went looking for Duncan when he didn't show up. I think he may have gone out of the city."

"Why?"

"Because Duncan said something about going to your estates on an errand for you."

Roo frowned. He had not seen Duncan for two days, which had put his cousin in the worst possible grace with Roo so far. He had excused a lot of Duncan's lapses, but with the invaders so close Roo had needed every pair of hands possible, and Duncan's preoccupation with his own pleasure was inexcusable this time. "I'm going on ahead to my estates. Meet me there."

Roo was going to let his wagoners rest the night at his estates, then send them on to Ravensburg. There Roo had planned to gather his employees and servants together and, if the enemy appeared, move on to Salador. He knew what few others knew: that if the invaders made it past Darkmoor, they'd turn toward Sethanon, for the fabled prize Calis had long ago told his men about, whatever it might be. Roo had no doubt that the Kingdom would be equal to the task; he had served with the invaders for a while when Calis had infiltrated their army, and while they had numbers, they lacked the Kingdom's training.

Then he remembered the Saaur.

Roo said, "I'm going to change orders. Continue past my estates and keep going until sundown."

"Why?" asked Jason.

"Something I just thought of. Head to our inn in Chesterton and wait. If you don't hear anything from me within a day that says otherwise, start the men toward Darkmoor. Refit there, change horses, whatever you need to do, then continue on to Malac's Cross. Wait for me to send you word there."

Jason seemed disturbed by the change of plans, but said nothing. He nodded and told the driver to keep moving.

Roo rode ahead and quickly became enmeshed in the crowd streaming for the eastern gates. He was on the verge of turning back, fearing a riot, when he saw Kingdom troops riding toward him from a street to his left. He saw a familiar figure at their head and shouted, "Erik!"

Erik reined in. "I thought you out of the city yesterday."

"Too many last-minute things to see to," answered Roo. "I've got wagons coming this way, then we're for the East."

Erik nodded. "Wise choice. You can ride with us to the gate, but the wagons are on their own, I'm afraid."

Roo pulled in next to his boyhood friend and asked, "When are they closing the gates?"

"Sundown, or when the first enemy is seen to the east, whichever comes first."

"They're that close?" said Roo in surprise.

"They hit the outer seawall an hour ago," answered Erik as he slowed his horse because of the press of people. The way was now lined with Kingdom soldiers, keeping the crowd moving in an orderly fashion. Those who heard horses coming from behind tried to move aside, but there was scant room and Erik and his squad were forced to slow to a walk.

Roo asked, "Where are you bound for?"

"Just outside," said Erik. "When the gates close, I'm going to ride rear guard behind those who are through."

"Nasty job," said Roo.

"Not as nasty as staying behind," said Erik.

Roo said, "I hadn't thought of it that way." He paused, then said, "What of Jadow and the others?"

Erik knew he meant the handful of men whom Erik and Roo had served with, across the sea with Captain Calis. "They're already gone, up in the mountains."

Roo said, "What's going on?"

"I can't tell you," said Erik.

Roo thought on it a moment; he had dispatched building materials for the Prince to odd destinations throughout the mountains, as well as provisions for men. He considered the fact that the best soldiers the Prince had were up in the hills, then asked, "Nightmare Ridge?"

Erik nodded. "Don't say anything, but in about a month you want your family east of Darkmoor."

"Understood," said Roo as they came in sight of the gate. A wagon had lost a wheel just outside the gate and the driver was arguing with the guards there, who wanted to cut loose the horse and drag the wagon out of the way, while the driver was insisting on waiting to fix the broken wheel.

Erik rode up and said, "Sergeant!"

The man turned and, seeing an officer in the black of the Prince's Special Command, said, "Sir!"

"Quit arguing and get that wagon out of the way." People on foot could get out of the gate around it, but a string of wagons and carts was building up quickly behind the broken-down wagon.

The driver was frantic. "Sir! Everything I own is in there!"

"Sorry," said Erik, and waved for a squad of men to move the man away, then drag the wagon off to the side of the road. "If you can fix it over there, good luck to you. But you're keeping people here who don't wish to linger."

Erik rode past and said to Roo, "Get away, Roo, now."

Roo said, "Why?"

Erik pointed to the north and Roo could see dust. The hair on his neck rose up. "Only one thing can raise that much dust in a hurry."

Erik said, "Either the biggest cavalry detachment this side of Kesh, or it's the Saaur!"

Roo turned his horse down the eastern road and with a shout had the horse cantering away from the city.

Erik turned to one of the soldiers at his side and said, "Pass word back into the city we've got visitors coming from the north." He glanced at the dust rising in the hills. "They'll be here in an hour."

Erik turned to the command at the gate and said, "Be ready to close up with no more than one minute's notice."

"Yes, sir!" came the response.

Erik rode a quarter mile to the north, where a company of heavy lancers waited, with two squads of bowmen to provide support. "Lieutenant!"

"Sir," said the leader of the Royal Krondorian Lancers.

"In the next hour some damned big lizards on giant horses are going to be coming down that north road. Can your men handle them?"

The lieutenant smiled. "Big makes 'em easier to hit, don't it, sir?"

Erik smiled. The young officer was probably a few years older than he, but Erik felt like an old man looking at his enthusiasm. "That's the spirit," he said.

He then turned his small patrol around and rode to the south, where another detachment of lancers waited. He dispatched those to support the group on the north. Whatever was coming from the south would be far less a threat than a full-blown Saaur attack, and those inside the city could deal with any human threat.

Then the sky seemed to open and a howl went up that had Erik and every man nearby covering his ears in pain. It went on while riders attempted to calm frantic horses that screamed and bolted at the sound. Several of the lancers were thrown from their saddles.

After a minute the sound ceased, and Erik could hear a lingering ring in his ears. "What was that?" he heard a soldier nearby ask.

"I have no idea," said Erik.

William and James stood on the palace balcony, overlooking the harbor, as the last echoes of the strange howling sound ended. A huge column of dust and steam rose at the mouth of the harbor. A blinding flash had accompanied the noise, and even though they had been inside, both men found themselves blinking away tears. Men below on the walls were wandering blind, crying out for someone to lead them away.

Soldiers raced through the palace shouting orders, for a tremendous sound had accompanied the explosion, and even the most veteran of them were stunned by it. "What was that?" asked William.

"Look!" said James, pointing to the harbor mouth.

The churning waters of the outer harbor seemed to be calming, and a great wave of foam and debris rolled in toward the docks. Upon its crest rode great ships, and they all carried invaders.

"They're in the harbor!" shouted William. "Damn! I thought we could hold them outside for a week."

James said, "Whatever they used, the two seawalls are gone."

William swore. "I had a thousand men on those walls."

"So much for those clever traps you rigged in the channel."

William nodded. "They must have been swept away when the enemy destroyed the defenses. What was it?"

"I don't know," said James. "I saw Guy du Bas-Tyra fire Armengar during the Great Uprising, and when those twenty-five thousand barrels of naphtha went up, the explosion could be seen for miles. This was something different."

"A magic of some sort?" asked William.

Dryly, James said, "Given your upbringing, you'd be in a better position to answer than I."

Turning away, William said, "We didn't encourage students to blow things up at Stardock. It disturbs the tranquillity." He hurried to where runners waited to carry orders, and to the first he said, "General order five. They are in the city."

William returned to where James stood, watching alien invaders sail into his city. "I will not let this happen," said the Duke.

William put his hand on his brother-in-law's shoulder and said, "It's happened."

"Remind me, what's general order five?"

William said, "We're locking the eastern gate, and firing on anything coming from the west. House-to-house for the first three blocks away from the docks."

"What about those nasty things you set up down at the docks?"

"Those are still in place. If the Pantathian magic users don't blow up the palace the way they did the seawalls, they'll find a surprise or two when they land on the docks."

James looked at William. "Have you gotten everyone out?"

William knew who the "everyone" was that James spoke of: his sister, her son, and her grandchildren. James had counted on William to see them to safety. "They're out of the city. They left in a special coach last night."

James said, "Then this is good-bye."

William looked at his brother-in-law and weighed the man in his memory. They had a long history together, back to the days when William was a young lieutenant in the Prince's Household Guards and James had run roughshod over the wild twins, Borric and Erland, now King and Prince respectively.

James asked, "It's been what, thirty years?"

"Closer to forty." They embraced.

When they separated, James said, "I only regret you never found anyone, William."

William said, "I did, once."

James said nothing, for he remembered the Keshian magician William had loved as a young man, and her untimely death.

William said, "I do envy you Arutha and the boys."

James said, "I must go."

William said, "If we do somehow manage to get out of this, I promise I'll give some thought to finding a good woman and settling down."

James laughed. He again embraced his brother-in-law and said, "See you in Darkmoor or see you in hell."

"One is as good as the other," said William, giving James a gentle push toward the door.

The Duke turned and hurried as fast as his old legs would permit. Outside, a squad of special soldiers, dressed in black tunics, leggings, and black-painted iron coifs, waited. They wore no markings, and they said nothing as they followed James down to his office. There he stripped off the marks of his rank, the golden chain holding the Duke of Krondor's seal, used to identify official decrees of the Principality. He removed his ducal ring, and set it next to the seal. After a moment he turned to one of the soldiers and said, "In the Prince's audience hall there's a sword hanging over the fireplace. Fetch it for me."

The soldier ran off while James removed his clothing and donned garb like that worn by the soldiers. He was dressed when the soldier returned carrying the sword. An old rapier, it bore an odd device, a tiny war hammer, that had been fused into the sword's forte.

He added this to the bundle and wrapped up the sword, ring, chain and seal, and a letter he had written the night before, and handed it to a soldier wearing the garb of the Prince's Household Guards. "Take this to Lord Vencar, in Darkmoor."

"Yes, my lord," said the guard and hurried away.

To the soldiers who were remaining, the silent men in black, James said, "It's time."

They left his office and hurried down into the bowels of the palace, down winding stairs that led to the dungeon. Past the cells, they moved to a seemingly blank wall. James said, "Put your hands here, and here"—he pointed—"and push up." Two soldiers did as bidden, and the wall slid almost effortlessly upward into the ceiling, revealing a door hidden behind the false wall. James pointed. Two soldiers moved to open the door; it protested at being disturbed after years of peace. But move it did, to reveal an opening, and a flight of stairs leading down. Lanterns were lit, two soldiers entered, and James followed. As the last of the eight guards passed through the door, it was drawn shut behind them, causing the false wall to return to its position.

Down the stairs the men hurried, until at last they came to another closed wooden door. One of the men listened and said, "It's silent, my lord."

James nodded. "Open it."

The man did so, and the door opened to the sound of lapping water. At a landing beneath the old citadel, the central part of the palace of Krondor, an underground waterway wended from the city into the bay. The stench of the place told every man what he already knew: this was a section of the great sewers of the city, which emptied into the bay a mile or more away.

A new longboat waited, tethered to an iron ring in the stone dock, and the eight soldiers entered, leaving a place in the middle for the Duke. James stepped into the boat. "Let's go," he said.

The boat was pushed off from the dock, and the men began to row, but rather than head for the bay, they swung the boat around and headed against the flow of the water, into the sewers of the city.

As they came to the entrance of a large culvert, one twice the height of a man, James whispered to himself, "Jimmy the Hand goes home."

Sixteen

Battles

ERIK SIGNALED.

"Over there!" he shouted.

Men turned their horses and charged. The battle for the city had been raging outside the northernmost gate in the east wall since the day before. The invaders were disorganized as they came ashore.

Erik's detachments had been struck twice, once at sundown, and again in the morning by a large detachment of Saaur horsemen. Erik had been pleased to discover that, despite their size, the Saaur horses were just as subject to the travail of travel as were the smaller animals humans rode. Also, for the first time in their memory, the Saaur weren't facing human mercenaries but true soldiers, Kingdom heavy lancers, and the impact of a disciplined foe with twelve-foot-long, iron-shod lances and a willingness to conduct an orderly charge had routed the Saaur. Erik had no idea what good this would do for the overall campaign, but the lift it gave his men to best the huge lizardmen in their first confrontation was incalculable.

Now they were engaged with a company of mercenary humans who, while not as individually threatening as the Saaur, were proving more difficult for their sheer numbers, and because they were relatively fresh, while Erik's men had fought two engagements in the last twelve hours.

But as fresh Kingdom riders approached from the south, Erik found his units able to roll back the invaders, who fled at last into the woodlands to the north. Erik turned and looked for his second in command, a Lieutenant named Gifford. He signaled the man and said, "Ride after, but halt a bowshot from the tree line. I don't want you riding into traps. Then bring the men back and re-form. I'm heading to the gate to see if there are any more orders." The Lieutenant saluted and rode off to carry out his orders.

Erik hurried his tired horse down the road toward the gate, past boarded up houses as if the owners expected to return to find them intact, as if this were only a storm striking Krondor. Other homes were obviously abandoned, with doors left open. A steady stream of refugees hurried along the road, moving in the direction from which Erik came, and he had to shout several times to get people to let him pass.

Already the tone of the flight was edging toward panic, and Erik knew that this would be his last trip to get any new orders. It took him nearly a half hour to ride a distance he could normally travel in a third that time, and when he reached the gate he saw the activity was up to a frantic pace.

He saw two other wagons pushed off the road, one into the small river that ran along the road into the city, through the sewers, and into the bay. Erik absently wondered if it might be one of Roo's. He suspected most of Roo's wagons had gotten clear of the city before the fighting at sundown, and were now safely on their way to Darkmoor.

Getting within hailing distance of the gate, Erik shouted, "Sergeant Macky!"

The sergeant in command of the gate turned to see who called, and when he spied Erik, he shouted, "Sir?"

"Any orders?"

"No, sir. As before" was all he said before turning back to hurry along those trying to crowd through the gate, while maintaining order.

Erik shouted, "Good luck to you, then, Sergeant!"

The soldier, an old man who had shared a drink or two with Erik and the other members of the Crimson Eagles, turned and said, "And to you, sir. Good luck to us all." Then he went back to his tasks.

Erik wished for a fresh mount, but he couldn't risk heading into the city. He would ride back to his command position and see if there was time to secure a remount. He had ordered the fresh horses kept far enough from the most likely points of combat that they were safe—but not convenient.

He forced his way back through the mob fleeing the city. He knew what the plan was, yet this frantic sea of humanity made him wonder if he could be as cruel as the Prince and Duke, for many of those he passed would be hunted down and killed by the Emerald Queen's raiders as they fanned out along the highway. Erik couldn't protect them all.

Erik reached the edge of the foulburg and found a few of his men resting in the shade of a tree. "Report!" he ordered one of them, and the soldier stood up. "We just got hit by another patrol, Captain. They came out of the trees and looked surprised when we filled them with arrows." He pointed toward the distant trees. "Lieutenant Jeffrey is over there somewhere."

It took Erik a moment to put a face to the name Jeffrey, and he realized suddenly how big his command had become. He had met every man in his unit for the first half year, but in the last two months the army of the Prince had doubled in size as units of troops sent from the Far Coast and down from Yabon arrived, along with detachments from the East. Many of the men who were now looking to him to survive were strangers, while most of the men he had trained were already up in the mountains to the east.

He rode on and found the lieutenant a short time later. The soldier, who wore the tabard of LaMut, a wolf's head on a field of blue, turned and saluted. "Captain, we had a patrol blunder right into us. They didn't know we were here."

Erik looked at the bodies littering the open ground south of the trees. "They're sending companies out without any coordination," he said. "The Saaur and the other companies we fought today haven't spread the word we're waiting."

"Can we expect this to last long?"

Erik remembered his own experience with the Queen's army in Novindus and said, "To a point. They'll never have the internal communication and discipline we do, but they have numbers, and when they come at us, they'll all come at once."

Looking at the afternoon light, he said, "Send a messenger down to where our reserves are and bring back two companies to relieve the men here, and"—he pointed to where the standard of the heavy lancers could be seen flapping in the breeze—"tell the lancers to stand down for a few hours."

"You think we've beat them back?"

Erik smiled. The older Lieutenant from LaMut knew better than that. He just wanted to see what kind of young captain he was taking orders from. "Hardly," said Erik. "We're just catching a little calm before the storm. I mean to take advantage of it."

Before the Lieutenant left, he said, "What about those serpent priests?"

Erik said, "I don't know, Lieutenant. We will certainly know when they arrive."

Jeffrey saluted, and as he departed, Erik called after, "And bring me a fresh horse!"

Miranda said, "Something's ahead." She spoke at a bare whisper.

Her father stood behind her, sweat beading his brow as he labored to keep a spell of invisibility around them. They had found the rift entrance that led into the world of Shila, and Miranda was attempting to probe it, to see what they could expect on the other side. From what Hanam had told them, they were likely to walk into the arms of some very angry demons if they just walked through.

They moved within sight of the rift gate, which to the normal eye appeared a blank wall. To Macros and his daughter the area was alive with mystic energy, and Macros said, "Something has tried to seal it from this side."

Miranda probed the rift. There were presences on the other side, and Miranda backed into the dark. "You can let the spell down. There's no one around."

Macros did.

"What do we do now?" asked Miranda.

Sitting down heavily, her father said, "We try to get through that rift with stealth, we try to fight our way through, or we search for a third way to get to Shila."

"The first two don't sound likely, and I especially don't find the second choice attractive," said Miranda. "What do you think of the third?"

Macros said, "If there's a way to Shila via the Hall of Worlds, Mustafa the fortune-teller would know."

"Tabert's?" asked Miranda.

"That's as good a place as any," said Macros. "I'm tired. Can you get us there?"

Miranda's brow furrowed in concern. "You, tired?"

"I would never tell Pug," said Macros, "but I suspect when he pulled me asunder from Sarig, I became fully mortal again. Most of my power came from the dead God of Magic, and with that link sundered . . ." He shrugged.

"Now is a hell of a time to tell us!" said Miranda. "We're about to face a demon king and you're suddenly not at your best because of old age?"

Macros grimaced as he stood. "I'm not quite ready for gruel and a shawl, daughter. I could still tear down this mountain if I had to!"

Miranda smiled as she took his hand and willed them to an inn in LaMut. The inhabitants of Tabert's were a mixed lot, but to the last, they rose and stepped back when the sorcerer and his daughter winked into existence a few feet before the bar.

Tabert was standing behind the bar, and he merely raised an eyebrow as Miranda said, "We need to use your storage room."

The barman sighed, as if to say, "What sort of story am I going to have to concoct to explain away this mystery?" but he nodded. "Good luck," he said.

They hurried behind the bar and through the door into the back room. Miranda led Macros down a flight of stairs and along a narrow hall. At the end of the hall was an alcove, separated from the rest of the hall by a plain curtain hanging from a metal rod. It was the portal Miranda had used when she had first entered the Hall of Worlds. They pushed aside the curtain that set apart the alcove, and as they stepped across the threshold, they were in the Hall of Worlds.

"I know the long way to Honest John's," said Miranda, pointing to the left. "Do you know a faster way?"

Macros nodded. "Over there," he said, pointing in the opposite direction.

They hurried on.

* * *

William watched as the battle raged below his vantage point. The defenders at the docks had started firing upon the ships that were moving toward the docks. Cleverly concealed ballistas and catapults had sunk three ships that had approached too close, but the fleet still came on.

One of William's most prized possessions was a spyglass, given him as a gift years before by Duke James. It had the usual properties of any good telescope, magnifying things to about a dozen times their normal size, but it also possessed an unusual attribute: it could pierce illusions. James, seemingly reticent to discuss its origins, had never revealed how he had come by the item.

He studied the approaching command ship and saw the hideous demon crouching amidships. Despite his revulsion, he studied the creature. All those nearby were being controlled by mystical chains and collars.

The expression on the demon's face was difficult to read, for it possessed nothing remotely like human features. Pug had warned Prince Patrick, James, and William of what had occurred regarding the death of the Emerald Queen and her replacement by a demon, but that information was being kept from all but a handful of officers. William and James had decided that there was enough for the men to worry about without having them fear the might of a demon lord.

William turned the glass ninety degrees, and the demon vanished from view. The illusionary woman who sat there was regal and beautiful and in an odd way even more frightening in aspect than the demon, who wore his rage and hate naked on his face for the world to see.

William returned the glass to the position that let him see through illusion and the demon popped back into view. William put down the glass.

"Orders," he said calmly, and one of the palace pages stepped forward. The squires were serving with the defenders along the wall, as aides to the various officers, and the pages were serving as runners. For a brief second William looked at the eager face of the boy who was ready to carry his orders wherever he was bidden. The boy couldn't have been more than thirteen or fourteen years of age.

For a brief instant, William was tempted to tell the boy to run, to leave the city as fast as his young legs could carry him; then he said, "Tell the dock command to wait until they've gotten close, then I want everything fired at that large ship with the green hull; that's their command ship, and I want it sunk."

The boy ran off and William turned to look. It was probably a futile gesture; the demon's ship was almost certainly afforded the most protection of any in the fleet.

Reports came in quickly that the enemy fleet had landed all up and down the coast, and units of cavalry had harried the northmost eastern gate. William considered his options and called for another messenger. When the boy voiced he was ready, William said, "Run down to the courtyard and tell one of the riders there to carry orders to the eastern gate. Seal the city."

As the boy turned, William said, "Page."

"Sir?"

"Take a horse and go with the rider; leave the city and tell Captain von Darkmoor it's time to head east. You stay with him."

The boy looked confused at being told to leave, but he simply said, "Sir," and ran off.

A captain of the royal guards glanced at the Knight-Marshal, who shook his head. "I might spare one of them at least," said William.

The Captain nodded grimly. The enemy fleet was attempting to dock. Lines snaked out from the ships as those on the railings attempted to throw loops around the cleats on the dockside. Arrows rained down on any who did not shield themselves, and men of the invading army fell into the water, their bodies pierced by multiple shafts.

But the first ship, then the second one, got a rope ashore, and they were slowly hauled in close to the docks. The only place they were unable to close was where the earlier three ships had sunk. Ships beyond were tossed lines, and William saw their plan. Originally they had thought they'd see a slow siege, with an orderly docking once this portion of the city was secured. But now he saw there would be no attempt to move empty ships away from the docks.

Only a few ships would actually tie to the docks, but they would act as shields for those farther out. They would be tossed grapples, and soon the ships would be tied off. A raft of ships would extend out into the bay, a platform that would let thousands of invaders race from deck to deck, to land on the docks of Krondor, across the breadth of the waterfront. It was a dangerous ploy, for if the defenders were successful in starting fires on any of the ships, all were at risk.

When the Queen's ship was close enough, every war engine within range launched an attack. A hundred heavy boulders flew through the air, accompanied by a dozen flaming bales of fire-oil-soaked hay. As William had suspected, all met an invisible barrier and bounced or slid off. He was pleased to notice that one large bolder crashed back onto another ship, which wasn't protected, doing significant damage to the soldiers packed tightly on the decks.

William turned to order as much fire oil directed at the frontmost ships as possible. The flames exploded along the entire length of the balcony. William was thrown backward as if batted by a blinding hand of fire, and lay stunned on the floor of the palace balcony. Blinking away tears, he could barely see, and everything was tinged red.

After a moment he realized his eyes were burned and bloody. The only reason he wasn't completely blind was that he had glanced behind him when the attack occurred. He felt around and saw a dim shape next to him, which groaned when he touched it. A pair of hands lifted him and a voice said, "Marshal?"

He recognized the voice of one of the pages, who had been standing back in the room. "What happened?" William asked in a hoarse croak.

"Flames erupted along the wall, and everyone . . . is burned."

"Captain Reynard?"

"I think he's dead, sir."

Voices from the hall shouted and men came running in. "Who's there?" William could see only shadowy shapes.

"Lieutenant Franklin, my lord."

"Water, please," said William, and he felt the Lieutenant take his from the squire, holding him up as he made his way to a chair. In his nose he could smell only the stench of his own burned hair and flesh, and no matter how he blinked, he couldn't clear his eyes of the blinding red tears.

Once he was sitting, William said, "Lieutenant, tell me what is happening."

The Lieutenant ran to the balcony. "They're sending men ashore. It's a dreadful fire we're pouring on them, but they're coming, sir."

The squire brought a basin of water and a clean cloth and William applied it to his face. The pain was incredible, but he used a trick taught him as a child by one of his teachers at Stardock to ignore it. The water didn't help his vision much, and he considered that he might be blinded for what would be the remainder of his life, however short that might be.

The loud sound of wood shattering followed by shouts and the sounds of fighting below caused William to ask, "Lieutenant, would you please tell me what is happening in the courtyard?"

The Lieutenant said, "Sir, they've crashed the royal dock. Enemy soldiers are landing."

William said to the squire, "Son, would you please help me to my feet?"

The boy said, "Yes, my lord," attempting to sound calm, but failing to hide the fear in his voice.

William felt young arms around his waist as he stood. "Turn me toward the door," he said calmly. The sounds of fighting were now echoing from the halls outside the room, as well as coming from the courtyard below as enemy warriors mounted the flight of stairs leading to William's command center. "Lieutenant Franklin," said William.

"Sir?" came the calm reply.

"Stand on my left, sir."

The officer did as he was bidden, and William slowly pulled his sword from its scabbard. "Stand behind me boy," he said softly as the sound of fighting in the halls grew louder.

The boy did as he was asked, but he kept a firm grip around the Knight-Marshal's waist, helping the injured man stand upright.

William wished he had something to say that would make this better for the boy, but he knew it would end in terror and pain. He just prayed it was quick. As the sounds of fighting got closer, and those remaining soldiers in the room rushed to defend the door, William finally said, "Page?"

"Sir," came the soft, fearful voice from behind him.

"What is your name?"

"Terrance, sir."

"Where are you from?"

"My father is the Squire of Belmont, sir."

"You've done well. Now help me stand fast. It wouldn't do to have the Knight-Marshal of Krondor die on his knees."

"Sir . . ." From the boy's voice, William could tell he was crying.

Suddenly there was a shout, and William saw a shadowy form heading toward him. He heard more than felt the blade of Lieutenant Franklin slash out, and the attacker fell back.

Another shadow appeared to the left of the first, on William's right hand, and the nearly blind Knight-Marshal of Krondor lashed out with his sword.

Then William, child of Pug the magician and Katala of the Thuril Hill People, born on an alien world, felt pain, quickly followed by darkness.

James moved slowly through the knee-deep sludge. The echoes of fighting rang through the sewers and his men walked with swords drawn. They opened shuttered lanterns from time to time to get their bearings, but mostly they negotiated through the murk by the faint light that came from above as they passed below culverts and drains from the streets.

"We're here," said a voice.

"Give the signal," said James, and a shrill whistle was blown.

One of the men kicked open a door and James could hear other doors being opened nearby. He followed the first two men into the cellar, and up a flight of stairs. They burst into a room illuminated by candlelight because it was still below ground level.

As James expected, resistance was light, but he was almost split by a crossbow bolt fired from behind a table, overturned to provide shelter. "Stop shooting!" he shouted. "We're not here to fight."

A moment of silence was followed by a voice saying, "James?"

"Hello, Lysle."

A tall old man stood up from behind the table and said, "I'm surprised to see you here."

"Well, I thought as long as I was passing by, I'd give you a chance to get out of here."

"Things are that bad?"

"Worse," said the Duke, motioning for the man who went by Lysle Rigger, Brian, Henry, and a dozen other names, but who, by any name, was the Upright Man, the leader of Krondor's Guild of Thieves: the Mockers.

James looked around. "Things haven't changed much—except it used to be more crowded."

The man whom James would always think of as Lysle said, "Most of the brethren are out of the city, running for their lives."

"You stayed?"

Lysle shrugged. "I'm an optimist." Then he said, "Or a fool." He sighed. "It's a tiny Kingdom, the Mockers, but it's my Kingdom."

James said, "True. Come along. There's one place we may survive."

James and his soldiers took Lysle and a scruffy assortment of thieves in tow and moved back into the sewers. "Where are we going?" asked Lysle as they slogged their way through the muck.

"You know where the river enters the city beside the abandoned mill?"

"The one that's paved over?"

"That's the one," said Jimmy. "We used it when we were smuggling with Trevor Hull and his lot, too many years ago to remember. If you'd been in Krondor when the Mockers and Hull's smugglers were working together, you'd have known about it. There's a huge staging area we've been stocking for months."

"For months?" said Lysle. "How did you manage that without us noticing?"

Laughing, James said, "From above. We did it during the day, when you and your thieves were asleep below ground."

"Why did you come fetch me?"

James said, "Well, you are the only brother I know about, so I couldn't let you die alone in that basement."

"Brother? Are you sure?"

"Sure enough to wager on it."

"I've wondered about that," said Lysle. "Do you remember your mother?"

"A little," said James. "She was murdered when I was a toddler."

"At the Sign of the Boar's Head?"

"I don't know. It could be. I was taken off the streets and raised by the Mockers. You?"

"I was seven when my mother was killed. I had a little brother. I thought he was dead, too. I was packed off to Romney and raised there."

"Father didn't want both his sons close by, I guess. Maybe we were targets for whoever killed our mother."

As they reached a huge intersection of culverts, with water flowing down from above to spray the center of the passages, Lysle said, "I always thought it odd that my foster parents in Romney raised me to work for a thief in Krondor."

"Well," said James as they moved around the small waterfall, "we'll never know. Father is dead many years and we can't ask him."

"Did you ever find out who he was? I never did."

James grinned in the dark. "Yes, I did, as a matter of fact. I heard his voice once and heard it again many years later, and after doing some snooping, I sussed out who was the original Upright Man."

"Who was he?"

"Did you ever have the displeasure of meeting a particularly surly and evil chandler whose shop was down by the south point, near the palace?"

"Can't say as I remember one like that. What was his name?"

"Donald. If you'd met him, you'd have remembered him, as he was a right nasty piece of work."

"A bit of a criminal genius, though."

"Like father, like sons," said James.

Reaching a place in the long passage where they were walking up an incline, Lysle said, "Are we going to get out of this alive?"

"Probably not," answered James, "but then no one gets out of life alive, do they?"

"There is that. But you have a hedge?"

"You always hedge a bet," said James. "If there's a way to get out of here alive, this is it." He indicated a large doorway, big enough to accommodate a wagon and team.

"I see what you mean about being able to smuggle through here," said Lysle as two soldiers opened the huge wooden doors. They swung open silently, showing recent attention, and inside, a bright light illuminated a hundred soldiers, readying with bows, crossbows, and swords.

"Here we are."

Lysle let out a soft whistle of appreciation. "I see you plan a warm welcome for whoever comes this way."

"Far warmer than you imagine," said James.

He motioned for Lysle and his half-dozen Mockers to enter and said, "Welcome to the last bastion in Krondor."

After James and those with him were inside, the doors were shut with a loud crack that had the ring of finality to it.

Erik heard the trumpet and instantly began shouting orders. They had been constantly fighting with smaller elements of the invading forces, and had reports that similar fighting had begun near the sea gate, the northwestern gate. And at that point only a few men had been sighted near the southern gate of the city, which was fine with Erik, as he had ordered as many men to the northern gate as possible. Both gates fed refugees in a steady stream to the eastbound King's Highway. And a mile east of where Erik and his companies stood, the two streams of humanity would come together, forming a clogging, slow-moving body of tired, frightened, and desperate people.

Erik's mandate was to defend the rear of that column of Kingdom citizens as long as possible. Erik knew that meant halfway from here to Ravensburg, if he was to judge things. At some point the enemy would likely cease harrying them. They had a city to sack and stores to replenish, and while the invaders were winning many battles, they were still disadvantaged from the long sea voyage.

Of the Saaur, Erik had seen little, and he wondered why they were being withheld after the first contact. He couldn't spend much time trying to outwit his adversary, for there was too much to react to: the enemy was hurling small squads of raiders at his position. The battles were short and intense, and Erik had won them all, but the men were tiring and his casualties were mounting.

He had commandeered a wagon in which he had loaded his wounded, sending them east with the refugees. Now he heard the trumpet telling him the gates were to close, and as he started organizing a retreat, a young boy came riding up to him. "Captain?"

"Yes, son, what is it?" Erik saw the boy was dressed in the uniform of a palace page. Tears were streaming down his face.

"Lord William ordered me to tell you to withdraw."

Erik knew that, from the trumpet, so he had no idea why the boy was here. "What else?"

"I'm to go with you."

Then Erik understood. At least one of the palace boys was spared. "Ride east, and you'll find a wagon with wounded in it. Attach yourself to them, and help tend the injured."

"Yes, sir."

The boy rode off and Erik returned to the business of managing a retreat. Everything he had read in William's library had told him an orderly retreat was the most difficult thing to accomplish in a battle. The tendency to turn and run was nearly overwhelming, and fighting a rear-guard action was alien to men who had been taught to move forward when fighting.

But he had discussed this with William in theory over the last two years, and in particular since getting his new command earlier in the week, and Erik was determined that no force of his would be turned to rout.

Throughout the afternoon the sounds of battle carried to Erik from distant locations, even though his command was being left alone. He decided it was because the invaders were in the city and didn't see the need to press the attack from the south or east.

He also knew that would change once James and William sprang their surprises.

A distant thud and, a moment later, a huge plume of dark smoke, and Erik knew the first of their nasty surprises was unleashed. Barrels of Quegan fire oil had been lashed to the supports of the docks, as well as laid in the basements and lower floors of the buildings that faced them, back for three city blocks. At the moment they were fired, the entire waterfront of the city erupted in a conflagration few could imagine, and the enemy soldiers within a hundred feet of any building were dead. Those not burned to a cinder died from lack of air as the fire stole it from their lungs.

Erik cast a glance to the southwest, toward the palace, dreading the thought that the Emerald Queen's soldiers might be within the keep. Then a shattering blast sounded and Erik knew what had happened.

A lieutenant whom Erik didn't know well, named Ronald Bumaris, said, "What was that, Captain?"

Erik said, "That was the palace, Lieutenant."

The lieutenant said nothing, waiting for orders. After a half hour, the flood of humanity out of the northernmost gate in the city fell off to a trickle, and Erik ordered his men to form up for a rear guard.

He watched as the civilians moved eastward, toward the coming night, and then he turned to the west, as fires burned in the distance, and he waited.

Honest John's was doing its usual business, and Macros and Miranda moved through the crowd. They waved politely to their host, but declined his invitation to a drink. They moved purposely to the stairs and mounted them to the upper concourse, to the gallery of shops.

Reaching the shop of Mustafa, they entered. The old man looked up and said, "So it's you again?"

"Yes," said Miranda.

"Did you catch up to Pug?"

Miranda smiled. "You could say so."

"What can I do for you? A divination?"

Miranda sat in the chair opposite the old fortune-teller, and said, "Do you recognize my father?"

Mustafa squinted. "No, should I?"

"I am Macros."

"Oh," said the old fortune-teller. "I heard you were dead. Or missing. Something like that."

"I need information," said Miranda.

"I deal in such."

"I need a way into the world of Shila."

"You wouldn't like it," said Mustafa. "It's overrun by demons. Some idiot unsealed the barrier between the Fifth Circle and that world, and now it is just gone to hell."

Macros laughed a dry laugh. "That's one way of putting it."

"Why do you need to go there?"

"To close two rifts," said Miranda. "One between Shila and Midkemia, then one between Shila and the demon realm."

"That's difficult." The old man rubbed his chin. "I have information that would prove useful, I think. I can tell you a doorway to a location not far from the city of Ahsart, which is where I think you want to go."

"How do you know that?" asked Macros.

"I wouldn't be much of a dealer in information if I didn't know that, would I?"

"How much?" asked Miranda.

Mustafa set a price, the souls of a dozen children who had never been born, and Miranda stood up. "Perhaps Querl Dagat will prove less outrageous in his price."

At the mention of one of his chief rivals, Mustafa said, "Wait a minute! Make me a counteroffer."

"I have a Word of Power, one that will gain you a greater wish."

"What's the catch?"

"You have to cast it on Midkemia."

The old man signed. "Midkemia, by all reports, is presently a less than hospitable place."

"That's one of the reasons we need to close those portals. If we do, then once the mess is cleaned up, you can travel to Midkemia, cast your wish, and be back before you know it."

Sighing, the old man said, "I would like to lose a few years. I don't age here, as you know, but I discovered the Hall late in life, and most of the youth cures I've discovered involve less than appealing requirements, such as eating the still-beating heart of your lover, or murdering babies in their cradles. My ethics do not permit such."

"If I were you," suggested Miranda, "I'd wish for eternal good health. You can be young and still have problems."

"That's not a bad idea. I don't suppose you have two of those wishes, do you?"

Miranda shook her head.

"Very well, I'll take it."

"Done."

The old fortune-teller reached under the table and pulled out a map. "We're here," he said, pointing to a large black square surrounded on four sides by lines that curved away after touching. "When you leave, tell the door witch you want exit number six hundred fifty-nine." His finger stabbed the map. "That will put you here. Go right, move down sixteen doors *on the right*—remember, the doors are staggered and if you count on the left, you'll go through the wrong one. The sixteenth door will open into a cave on Shila, about one day's ride by horse to Ahsart. I assume travel once you're there won't be a problem."

"It won't."

"Just travel due south and you'll see the city off to your right. Now, to give you a little insight into what you face," he said, putting away the map, "let me tell you a bit about demons.

"There are seven circles of what men call hell. The upper level is just a very unpleasant place populated by creatures not too different from those you meet on Midkemia. The Seventh Circle is populated by those you know as the Dread. They are life-drainers and beings of alien energy; they can't exist in your world without killing anything they touch. They are so at odds with life as we know it they aren't welcome in Honest John's."

Miranda took that to mean something significant, but without a context she had no idea what it meant. But being impatient to get on with the task at hand, she ignored the comment.

"The demons of the Fifth Circle aren't quite as alien as that. A particularly civilized one may wander in here from time to time, and as long as he doesn't try to eat the other patrons, John will put up with his business."

"What has this to do with us?" asked Macros.

"For a sorcerer of wisdom and power you tend to the impatient, don't you?" asked Mustafa. He held up his hand as Macros began to protest. "Silence. All will be made clear.

"The demons live on life. Much as you do, by eating plants or animals, they eat flesh and life. What you call life, mind, or spirit is like drink to them. Flesh builds their bodies, much as it does yours or mine, but spirit builds their powers, and their cunning.

"An ancient demon has devoured many enemies and will keep captured souls against the need to consume them later."

"I don't understand," said Miranda.

"Demons are like . . . sharks. Do you have sharks on Midkemia?"

"Yes," said Miranda.

"They swim in bunches, but for reasons unknown they will turn on one of their own, tearing him apart. If they enter a feeding frenzy, one shark may be eaten by another while it is in turn eating a third. Demons can be like that.

"They eat one another when there is no other source of spirit and flesh. When they find their way into a world on a higher plane, they pillage it, glutting themselves on flesh and spirit. As they steal spirit, or mind, they grow more cunning, but if they lack that new source, they become stupid. So the more powerful demons need more minds to keep from getting stupid."

"I think I understand," said Macros.

"Yes," said Miranda. "The demon who hurt Pug was betraying his master so he could feed unopposed in our world!"

Mustafa said, "That is likely. They do not possess what we would call a strong sense of loyalty."

"Thank you," said Miranda, starting to leave.

"Wait, there's more."

"What?" asked Macros.

"If you trap the demons between their own realm, where they can endure without needing to feed, and Midkemia, they will eventually destroy all life on Shila. Then they will begin feeding on one another."

"Do we care?" asked Macros.

"Not for the demons. Eventually there will be one demon left alive, probably their King Maarg if he's come through, or Tugor, his Captain. And without a source of food, he'll weaken, and eventually die. But before he becomes a starving, stupid demon, he's going to be a very angry, very powerful demon."

"Which means . . . ?" asked Miranda.

"Which means, just make sure you lock the door behind you when you leave."

Miranda blinked, then started to laugh. Rising, she said, "We'll do that."

"Not only the one into Midkemia; bar the door into the Hall when you return. An enraged demon king loose in the Hall would be most unpleasant."

"I'll remember that."

"What about my payment?" Mustafa asked as he stood.

Miranda smiled and there was an evil cast to her lips as she said, "I'll tell you on the way back."

Mustafa sat down as they left his little office and said, "Why am I always such a fool for a good-looking woman?" He pounded the table. "Get the money first!"

Seventeen

Destruction

ERIK SWORE.

"Yes, sir," said Sergeant Harper. "That's how I would have put it."

The message was from Greylock, and Erik now understood why the attacks throughout the previous two days had been so intermittent. The attackers had filtered through the woods and were now attacking Greylock's defenses, a half day's ride to the east. Greylock's message was calm, and he indicated he was having little trouble with the attackers, but stated his concern for the refugees, who were probably being preyed upon along the route of their retreat.

Erik's men were roughly organized in a camp at the moment the message arrived. The flow of people fleeing the city was down to a trickle. Erik had paused to talk to a few, but none of them could offer anything remotely like intelligence; they were too frightened, had no idea what they had seen, and were too concerned with escaping a city on the verge of being sacked.

One man was still slightly wet from having swum out through an underground street that he had known since he was a boy, his pitiful belongings in a pack on his back. He only knew that a major portion of the city was afire.

Erik didn't need him to tell him that. He could see the column of smoke rising to the west. He had seen the smoke as the city of Khaipur had burned, from a distance of over a hundred miles, a column of black smoke that had risen thousands of feet into the air until it had flattened out like a grey umbrella. The wind had blown the scent of smoke to them for days, and a fine soot fell for hundreds of miles. Erik had no doubt that when Krondor fell she would meet the same fate.

Erik gave orders, and the men hurried to obey. He detailed half his company, the heavy lancers, to follow behind the civilians, supported by a squad of bowmen who had wandered into Erik's area after being cut off from their own command. The light cavalry and horse-bowmen Erik took to ride to Greylock's position.

As he had feared, Erik had gone no more than a mile when he encountered the first sign of raider activity. Two wagons burned, and the ground around them was littered with the dead. Several women were stripped and obviously had been raped before being killed, and not one pair of decent boots or trinket of any possible worth was left behind.

Erik inspected the wagons and noticed a grain trail leading away from one. "They're hungry," he said to Sergeant Harper.

"Shall we hunt them down, Captain?"

Erik said, "No. I'd love to, but we need to support Greylock. If they reach the foothills to the north they'll turn eastward, and we'll encounter the swine soon enough."

Harper said, "Yes, sir."

They rode as fast as they could, permitting the horses rest when absolutely necessary, as Erik was determined to reach Greylock by sundown if at all possible. He knew some of the horses would be lame by the end of the ride, but he also knew that if the plans for the defense of the Kingdom were to be realized, they couldn't allow the enemy to quickly overrun the first positions of resistance.

Krondor was going to fall, and it had only taken three days. Erik surmised that the Emerald Queen and her magicians were desperate to get ashore. That meant stores were scarce. The use of magic to blow up the defenses of the outer harbor stunned Erik. The only time the Emerald Queen's Pantathians had resorted to magic was the light bridge across the river Vedra, and Pug had destroyed that, causing thousands of injuries and death. Erik had heard the report from a messenger from William with disbelief, but the fires on the docks proved the enemy was in Krondor.

As they rode, Erik wondered how Roo was faring. Had he gotten safely to his estates?

Roo sat heavily on the chair, holding a mug of cold water freshly drawn from the well. He said, "Thank you, Helen."

Helen Jacoby and the children were waiting in the anteroom of the estate house. Roo had just ridden up, after a desperate night of avoiding raiders, fighting, and keeping his wagons together. He had come to his estates the day before and, finding things peaceful, had returned down the road to join Luis in seeing the wagons safely home. The frequency with which he sighted invading soldiers, a full day's ride east of the city, told him more than he wanted to know about the battle for Krondor. He had seen firsthand the sacking of a city by the Emerald Queen and had no desire to repeat that experience.

Three additional wagons had been sent ahead two days before, and now servants were busily filling them with household possessions for the journey eastward. Given the rapidity of the enemy's advance, Roo was going to order them gone at sunrise, ignoring whatever was left behind. He now decided the entire train of wagons was going straight to Darkmoor, rather than stop at Ravensburg. He'd halt long enough to offer Erik's mother and Nathan, and perhaps Milo, Rosalyn, and her family, the opportunity to come along. He owed Erik that much, at least. But he wouldn't stop. The enemy was moving much too fast, and Krondor hadn't held as he had hoped it would.

One more day, he thought as he drank deeply of the cool, fresh water. If the invaders had been delayed one more day, he'd be free of worry. He also knew he would have to ride out this evening to the Esterbrook estates and insist that Sylvia and her father leave at once. They would have no way to know the enemy was as close as it was. He could provide quarters for them in his inns in Darkmoor and Malac's Cross without Karli becoming too suspicious, he thought; after all, half the population of Krondor was on the road eastward.

Finishing his water, he set it down and asked, "Where's Karli?"

"She's upstairs with your cousin Duncan."

Roo smiled. "I've been wondering where he's been." He stood up. "I'd best go see what they're doing."

Helen looked concerned. "He said something about helping her move some things."

Roo looked at her. "We still have plenty of time to get out of here. Stop worrying."

She smiled and said, "I'll try."

Roo went upstairs and found them in Roo and Karli's bedroom. Duncan was lifting a wooden box filled with Karli's best clothing.

"I have been looking for you for two days!" said Roo to his cousin.

Duncan smiled. "Things got pretty confused in Krondor. I went looking for you at Barret's, but you weren't there. By the time I got to the office, Luis told me you were back at Barret's, and then when I got back to the coffee house, and again found you not there, I headed back to our office.

"Things were pretty nasty in the streets by then, and when I finally reached them, your wagon train had headed out. I saw the mess at the northern gate, so I doubled back to the southern gate and rode here. I figured you'd want a reliable sword here to protect your family." He grinned as he took the box and carried it past Roo, then down the stairs.

Karli said, "Do you believe him?"

"No," said Roo. "He was probably with some whore when the panic set in, and he came straight here. But at least he's right about my wanting you protected."

Karli came and put her arms around her husband. "I'm afraid, Roo."

He made reassuring noises and patted her shoulders. "Don't worry. We'll be fine."

"Krondor is the only home I've known."

"We'll come back when this is over. I've made one fortune, and I can make another. We'll rebuild. But first we must see the children to a safe place."

At mention of the children, her own fear was put aside. "When do we leave?"

"At first light. Luis is bringing up the last wagons, with as many mercenary guards as he could scrounge up, and we're going to caravan to Darkmoor. I've got horses and equipment to repair wagons there, and once we've rested, we'll head down to Malac's Cross."

"Why there?"

Roo considered telling her what he knew, then decided it would only confuse and frighten her more. "Because the enemy will be stopped at Darkmoor," he said. "Malac's Cross will be far enough away from the fighting for us all to be safe."

Karli took Roo at his word and hurried downstairs to oversee the packing. Helen watched the children, and Roo was impressed with the calm manner in which she reassured them, keeping them diverted and entertained. He spent a few minutes with the four of them, listening to their prattle—children's issues of importance, he assumed, little of which made sense to him.

Toward the end of the day, a cold meal was prepared, and everyone ate. The presence of Duncan seemed odd to Roo, as Duncan had almost no interest in Roo's family, despite his attempts to charm Karli over the years. If anything, to Roo he appeared distracted.

When the meal was over, Roo said, "Duncan, I want you to wait down by the stable and let me know when Luis comes in with the last wagon."

Duncan nodded amiably. "After he gets here, I'm going to take some of the men and sweep the grounds. You never know when some of those invaders might come wandering down from the hills, or if local bandits are going to try to take opportunity of the confusion."

Roo glanced at the two women and the four children, shooting Duncan a black look.

Duncan quickly recovered by saying, "It's almost certain they aren't around, but it never hurts to be cautious."

After he left, Helen said, "Rupert, is it dangerous?"

Her calm and frank manner kept the children from sensing distress, and Roo thanked the gods she was here. He said, "War is always dangerous, especially when the invader is hungry and far away from home. That's why we're taking everything with us that might serve him, and what we can't take with us, we'll destroy."

"Destroy?" said Karli, looking confused. "Not my furnishings and things, certainly?"

Roo decided it best not to mention that the invaders would most likely smash everything in the house in frustration and burn it to the ground. He said, "No, merely that we'll burn the food we can't carry and make sure there are no weapons or tools left behind. If we can't take a wagon with us, we'll smash the spokes and break the yoke. If a horse goes lame, we'll put it down, and poison the meat. We'll dig up the garden tonight and make sure there's nothing here to help the enemy."

Karli looked very distressed at the news of losing her garden, but she remained silent.

Abigail said, "Father, where are we going?"

Roo smiled and said, "You're going to ride on a wagon tomorrow, my darling. It's a long trip, and you'll have to be on your best behavior. But we're going to the town where your father was born, and we'll go on to see other interesting places. Won't that be fun?"

"No," said Abigail. "I don't want to."

Helen smiled and said, "She says that a lot these days."

Roo looked at Karli, who said, "She doesn't know what any of this is about."

Roo said, "Children, we're going on a journey, and it will be a grand adventure."

Helmut grinned and drooled, while Helen's boy, Willem, said, "Is this like the sagas?"

Roo grinned at him. "Yes, just like the sagas! We're off on a great adventure and you must be very brave and do exactly what your mother and Karli tell you. There will be men with swords all around, and you'll see new places and great sights."

"Will there be fighting?" asked the boy with wide eyes.

Roo sat back and said, "If the gods are kind, no. But if there is, we'll protect you." He glanced from face to face, from the tiny perfection of the children to his wife's nervous smile to Helen's resolute expression, and said, "We will certainly protect you all."

Erik reached Greylock's position at nightfall. He had engaged the Emerald Queen's forces a half-dozen times along the way, and had witnessed the carnage they had left behind. Bodies littered the roadside, and it was clear that their first concern had been food. A few items of value, coins, jewelry, and the like, were found scattered around, but not one edible item could be seen.

After exchanging the password, Erik and his company rode in. Owen greeted Erik. "How are things? Bad?" he asked.

"Worse," said Erik, dismounting. He allowed one of Greylock's men to take the horse to tend to it and followed the former Swordmaster of Darkmoor to a campfire some distance behind the barricades they had erected across the road.

Erik left his own officers and sergeants to see to the horses and get the men fed. Greylock pointed to a pot of steaming stew and said, "Help yourself."

Erik took a wooden bowl and spoon and suddenly realized he was starving. As he filled the bowl, Greylock fetched him a small loaf of bread and a wineskin. "Tell me what you know," he said after Erik had shoveled in a couple of heaping spoonfuls of the savory stew and taken a drink of wine.

"If Krondor's not fallen this day, it will by tomorrow, no doubt. The palace is gone."

Both men knew that meant it was almost certain Knight-Marshal William was dead. Duke James might or might not have escaped. The Prince and the rest of his court, those nobles not in the field, were now safely in Darkmoor if everything had gone according to plan. Greylock said, "We've been pretty quiet. A few of the enemy's scouts have come close, but we chase them away, and when they see our fortifications, they seem inclined to move on."

Erik nodded as he chewed another mouthful of stew. After he swallowed he said, "If things are going according to plan, they'll waste a lot of time wandering north and south before they realize they've got to come back this way. Maybe we can pick up some of the time we lost at Krondor."

Greylock ran his hand over his face, and Erik could see that the older man was as tired as he was. "I hope so. There's still a lot to be done."

Erik put down his empty bowl and drank again from the wineskin. "Well, there are no more refugees behind us, so at least we no longer have to worry about a rear guard."

Owen nodded. "Now we just defend, making the bastards pay for every inch of ground." Then he grinned at Erik. "No offense," he said, remembering Erik's own sinister birth.

"None taken," said Erik. "I'm a bastard by birth; these invaders work at it." He sighed. "I've been more tired, but I can't remember when."

Owen nodded. "It's the pressure. The always being on guard. Well, as you and your boys have to take over here while I pull back tomorrow, we'll take the watch this night. You should be able to rest for one night."

"Thanks, Owen."

Greylock smiled, his narrow face looking almost sinister in the firelight. "I guess you should know, Prince Patrick has named me a Knight-General."

"Congratulations, I think," said Erik, "sir."

"Commiserations are more like it. I've got Calis's charge, defending the entire range from the Dimwood to Dorgin, and I think I'm going to wish you had the job before I'm done."

Erik said, "I'm in over my head already. I can't begin to understand what it is I'm supposed to do from here."

"You're just tired. Get some sleep and in the morning you'll have a better grasp on things. If you forget everything else, just remember you've got to slow the bastards down. We've got to hold them in the mountains for the next three months."

Erik sighed. "Until winter."

"When the snows fall, and they're on the west side of the mountains, we'll know we've won. They'll starve and die while we wait for spring, when we can chase them back where they came from."

Erik nodded, but he found his eyes were getting heavy and he couldn't think. "I'm going to find where that soldier took my horse, get my blanket, and go to sleep."

"No need," said Owen, pointing to a bedroll that had been made ready a short distance away. "I had that made up for you. Your men are also being told to get some rest. You just forget your worries this night, Erik."

"I won't argue," said Erik, moving toward the bedroll. He removed his sword and got his boots off, but he didn't remember anything after that as he rolled himself in the blanket and fell into a deep, exhausted sleep.

Roo kissed Karli on the cheek.

"I don't like this, Rupert," she said, near tears as she spoke.

"I know, but I have to see that everything is ready. Don't wait up for me, and take care of Helen and the children. I'll be back before sunrise."

They stood at the door of their estate house, and Roo kissed his wife on the cheek, then stepped through the door and closed it behind him. He hurried down to the servants' building and barn, where a dozen of his wagons had been gathered when they had arrived after sundown.

Luis de Savona, one of his old companions from Calis's army and now one of his most trusted aides, was seeing to the refitting. Luis had spoken little of his past prior to the day Roo met him in prison, save that he had once served a function in the court of Rodez, the easternmost duchy but one in the Kingdom. Roo didn't press him. Like many of those who had redeemed their lives in service to the Crown, Luis preferred to forget what had gone before, and Roo respected that.

There was something dark in Luis's nature, an anger that threatened to erupt at the oddest times, but Roo trusted him, one of the few men he did trust. And Roo felt the need of someone dependable at that moment.

Three times the mercenary guards and Rupert's drivers had fought off raiders. Two drivers had been injured, and a couple of the mercenaries had deserted when the fighting looked as if it was going badly, but while possessing a crippled right hand, Luis was still a fearsome foe with a knife in his left hand. He had killed three raiders personally, forcing the others to rethink their assessment of taking his wagon.

Roo said, "Luis, are we going to be ready at sunrise?"

Luis nodded. "Yes. We should probably leave an hour before, though, to steal a march on anyone coming down the highway."

"It's not the highway I'm worried about," said Roo. "Erik and the King's army are holding the highway. It's the raiders coming through the hills we have to worry about."

Roo's estate, like many of those settled to the east of the city, was far enough off the highway that they couldn't know the condition of the highway once they had left it. "I've got to see Jacob Esterbrook," he said, motioning for a fresh horse. "I'll swing back by the highway and see if we still hold it, or if we need find another route."

"Find another route?"

Roo nodded. "Yes, I know another way."

"Why don't you tell me now, just in case?" asked Luis.

Roo didn't like the idea of what "just in case" implied, but he agreed. "There's a road Erik and I used to reach Krondor, years ago. It's a small trail, really, but it will take wagons. You'll have to drive them in single file." He outlined how to get to the trail, little more than a goat path in places, but one over which he had taken wagons more than once. "You'll find a branch in the trail as you reach the foothills; take the southeastern one and you'll see the farms and vineyards to the north of Ravensburg. Pick up the King's Highway there if you can."

Luis nodded. "When will you be back?"

"If I don't encounter trouble, I'll be back before sunrise. If I'm not here an hour before sunrise, start without me. Tell Karli I'll catch up with you."

Luis looked around. "Duncan?"

"He's supposed to be conducting a sweep around the estate, making sure we're not bothered for a while."

Luis nodded. He and Duncan had shared quarters for almost a year, and during that time had developed an abiding dislike for each other. Luis didn't trust Duncan and put up with him only for Roo's sake.

The horse was brought over to Roo, who mounted.

"I'll see you sometime tomorrow."

Luis waved good-bye as Roo rode out, knowing what was unsaid: that if Luis didn't see Roo tomorrow, it meant Roo was dead.

Miranda said, "I don't like this at all."

They had gathered in the cave of the Oracle of Aal, after Macros and Miranda had returned to Midkemia, summoning the others.

Pug answered, "Who does, but we've got to be in two places at the same time."

Hanam growled and said, "Time grows short. My ability to contain the rage of this creature and not eat is about at its limit." The Saaur magician in demon form turned to Pug. "You know what must be done, what must be said."

Calis had sat listening to the exchange, silently observing the other four in the room. He finally said, "There is a chance none of you will return." While he spoke of all of them, his eyes focused on Miranda.

She nodded. "We know the risk."

He sighed. "I should be at Darkmoor."

Pug said, "No. I can't tell you why." He glanced at Macros and Miranda. "Things are hidden from us, and we sense that it is necessary to have these things hidden, for our own protection and that of others, but I *know* down to the fiber of my being that you must remain here."

Miranda and her father had found the door in the Hall and had entered it to the cave on Shila. They had watched from the mouth of the cave as demon fliers sped across the sky, and as demons of all sizes could be seen coming from the direction of where they had been told the city of Ahsart lay. After seeing far more demons than they could defeat, they had retreated to the Hall, returned to Midkemia, and sought out Pug.

They had spent two days evolving a plan, and now it was determined that Macros and Miranda would return to the tunnels beneath the Ratn'gary Mountains, while Pug and Hanam would go to Shila. Hanam in demon form would not attract attention, while Pug could better keep himself invisible than Macros could himself and Miranda.

Miranda and her father would attempt to seal the rift into Midkemia permanently, as Macros had once done with the rift between Midkemia and Kelewan, while Pug and Hanam would attempt to close the entrance to the demon realm.

Miranda glanced at her father, then at Pug, and said, "I need to speak with Calis, alone."

She rose and moved to where the half-elf warrior sat, indicating he should walk with her. They moved past the gigantic form of the sleeping oracle, a dragon of immense proportions who lay deep in a sleep of regeneration. Surrounding her were men, both young and old, the attendants who were also passing along their knowledge; the Oracles of Aal and their attendants would die in their time, but their knowledge would live on as long as new bodies could be found to contain their minds.

When they had walked far enough away from the others for some privacy, Miranda said, "What worries you?"

Calis laughed. "Everything." Then he said, "I fear I will never see you again."

She sighed and touched his cheek. "If that is our fate, we must accept it. If not, we shall see each other again."

With elven understatement, he raised an eyebrow slightly and said, "Pug?"

She nodded. "There are things that must be." She came close and leaned her head upon his chest, saying, "In time you will know so much more than you do now, and you will remember what we had as a gift, precious and wonderful, but you'll also realize that it was a lesson, for us both, that we might better learn what it is that we truly needed."

He gathered her into his arms and held her tightly for a moment, then slowly released her. When his arms were again at his sides, he said, "I will not claim to understand, but I do accept what you say as true."

She touched his face again and, looking into his eyes, said, "Sweet Calis. Always willing to serve. Always willing to give. Yet you have never asked of anyone for yourself. Why is that?"

He smiled and shrugged. "It is who I am. I have much to learn. As you delight in reminding me, I am still young. I feel that by service I can learn, and through learning, I can discover who I am."

"You are someone wonderful and unique," she said softly, kissing his cheek.

He nodded. "While I wait in this cave, can you at least give me a hint of what it is I'm to do?"

Miranda said, "I know only what Pug has told me."

"Then let me ask him one more time." He stepped past her and walked to where Pug and Macros were waiting with Hanam.

Calis said, "If you do not know why I'm here, can you at least tell me what you suspect?"

Pug turned and pointed to a huge dais that sat on the stone floor, within a few feet of the slumbering dragon. "That is why," he said, and everyone in the room felt a shift, as if they were moving slightly, yet no one budged. But where the empty dais had been, now a giant glowing green gem rested, with a golden sword embedded in it. It pulsed with a life of its own, and Calis instantly felt drawn to it and went over to it. "The Lifestone," he said quietly.

Pug said, "One has to be shifted slightly in time to see it."

Calis looked at the sword. "My father's sword."

"That portion of the Valheru which sought to seize this, embodied in the form of Draken-Korin," said Pug, "threw itself across this stone, and your father drove that sword deep into it. I do not know why, but that ended the Riftwar. The Valheru were drawn deep within its facets, and your father refused to risk retrieving his sword."

Calis nodded, not taking his eyes from the gem. "I will study this thing."

Miranda turned to Pug and said, "We can wait no longer."

Pug, Macros, and Hanam gathered, and Pug went to stand next to the demon. In his mind's eye he pictured the device over the door into Shila, the distinctive glyph that indicated which doorway they needed in the Hall. Miranda had memorized it, then given that memory to Pug, so it was if he himself had stood before it. He nodded once and blinked out of existence with the demon.

Miranda cast one last look at Calis, then nodded to her father, took his hand, and willed herself and Macros to the tunnels under the mountains across the sea.

* * *

"Message from Captain Breyer, sir."

Erik rubbed his eyes and blinked. He had managed an hour of sleep after the fighting. Since the day before, when Greylock had departed for the East, they had been attacked three times, most recently at sundown. They had easily defeated the forces thrown at them, thanks in part to Greylock's having left a squad of fifty additional archers behind, footmen with longbows. Erik knew he'd have to send them on ahead at least a day's march before he withdrew, for they could never keep up with the cavalry, but he was very pleased with their presence.

His mission was to hold at the road until it was clear that pressure along the front was roughly equal, then to pull out, leaving an obvious weakness in the defensive line. Prince Patrick and Lord William's plan was for the enemy to gain ground between Krondor and Darkmoor, but only where the Kingdom wanted them to.

Erik read the message. "So far, so good," he commented.

He dismissed the soldier and regarded the messenger, a Hadati hillman. "Get something to eat and rest, then leave at first light."

The hillman nodded and left, and Erik turned over, pulled his blanket around him, and tried to return to sleep. He lay there for a while, thinking of Kitty and wondering if she was well. He was almost certain she had left early enough to avoid the dangers of the road now being faced by those out there in the darkness. Then his thoughts turned to Roo. He wondered if he and his family were safe.

Jacob Esterbrook sat behind his desk, his face an impassive mask as Roo urged him to order his household packed and moved. "I understand the dangers, young man," he said at last. He rose and moved around the desk, pointing to a map of the Kingdom he kept on the wall, nestled between two large bookcases. "I have been doing business with the Empire of Great Kesh since before you were born. I have done business with Queg. If the politics of the area are about to change, I suspect I can do business with whoever is in charge once things settle down."

Roo's eyes opened in naked astonishment. He had ridden into the night, reaching Esterbrook's house two hours after sunset, and had asked to speak to the trader. "Jacob, no disrespect to your business acumen, but the point I'm trying to make is that an army of murderous thugs is heading this way. I know that army. I served with them for a time."

At that Jacob raised an eyebrow in interest. "Really?"

"Yes, and I don't have time to tell you the details, but trust me when I say these people have no interest in making deals; they will come here and burn this house to the ground after they strip it of everything worth more than a copper piece."

Jacob smiled and Roo didn't like the smile. "You are a very talented boy, Rupert, and I suspect you would eventually have done well enough for yourself, even without Duke James's help. Nothing like you managed to do with his help, but that business with the grain shortage in the Free Cities, that was brilliant." He sat down behind the desk and opened a drawer. Removing a parchment from within it, he placed it upon the table. "Of course, had you not had his help, I probably would have ordered your death when you became a nuisance, but as things worked out the way they did, I have no complaints." He sighed. "To put matters in the open, this is a commission"—he pointed to the parchment—"to negotiate with the invaders and to establish discussions with an eye toward ending hostilities."

Roo said, "After they burned Krondor?"

Jacob's smile broadened. "What concern does Great Kesh have with the destruction of a Kingdom city?"

"Great Kesh?"

Jacob said, "Rupert, don't be thick. You must have deduced I had something besides my not inconsiderable business skills in my favor when it came to trading to the south. I have friends in high places in the Emperor's court, and they have made it easy for me to keep you off the Keshian trade routes. Now they wish to come to a quick accommodation with the invaders, this Emerald Queen, and formalize a new border."

Roo sat stunned. "New border?"

"Prince Erland negotiated a treaty for noninterference with Great Kesh, in exchange for land concessions in the Vale of Dreams." He pointed at Roo. "Which I think you knew, given that sale of property to me in Shamata. You didn't realize that the new governor of Shamata would be more than happy to recognize my claims to those businesses, I know.

"But the point of the treaty is that while we are pledged not to invade the Kingdom, we agreed to nothing that prevents us from coming to a quick understanding with the new rulers of the land to the north of the Empire. Toward that end, a rather large army is marching now, even as we speak, seeking to occupy all lands in the Vale, not just those granted to us by the treaty, and we shall continue to hold those lands after this unpleasantness is over."

"You're a Keshian," said Roo softly.

Jacob spread his hands and shrugged. "Not by birth, dear Rupert; by profession."

"You're a spy!"

"I prefer to think of it as being a facilitator, one who conducts all manner of trade between the Kingdom and Great Kesh, goods, services, and . . . information."

Roo stood. "Well, you can burn in hell for all I care, Jacob. But I won't let Sylvia die here with you."

"My daughter is free to leave should she wish," said Jacob. "I have long since ceased attempting to control her. If she wants to travel with you, she may."

Roo left the old man in his study without another word. He hurried up the stairs toward Sylvia's room. Without knocking, he opened the door.

Sylvia was sitting on the bed while Duncan stood over her, one foot up on the bed beside her as he leaned forward. He had one hand on her shoulder, in a familiar fashion, and he was smiling his most charming smile. Sylvia appeared angry at whatever Duncan was saying, and they were so lost in their debate they didn't notice Roo for a moment.

"No!" said Sylvia. "You've got to go back and do it tonight, you fool. After he leaves the estate, it's too late!"

"What's too late?" said Roo.

Sylvia jumped to her feet as Duncan stepped away.

"Why, cousin," said Duncan, "I was just trying to convince Miss Esterbrook that she should evacuate."

Roo studied the tableau a long moment and slowly drew his sword. "Now I see just how much of a fool I've been."

"Roo!" said Sylvia. "You can't think . . . not Duncan and I?"

Duncan put up his hands in a gesture of conciliation. "Cousin? What do you think you're doing?"

"Since this has begun, I have never understood why I could never gain an advantage over Jacob. Now I discover that he's an agent of Great Kesh and that my own cousin has been feeding my lover information."

Duncan looked as if he was going to say something, then suddenly his smile turned to a snarl and he yanked his sword out. "Damn it, I have had enough of this charade."

He lashed out. Roo parried, then riposted. Duncan easily avoided the blade.

Roo said, "That makes two of us."

Duncan grinned, and it was an evil, hate-filled expression. "You have no idea how much I've looked forward to this moment, cousin. Taking your table leavings, running your errands, while you favored that one-handed Rodezian dog. Well, this will end that insult and I will no longer have to share Sylvia with you."

"That's the way it is, then?"

"Of course, you idiot!" screamed Sylvia. She rolled off the bed as a flurry of sword blows came perilously close to striking her.

Duncan said, "My love, I don't need to kill the fat cow. I'll kill Rupert here, then I'll marry Karli. When time enough has passed, we'll get rid of her and then you can marry me."

Rupert struck out with a blow aimed at Duncan's head, and as Duncan's sword came up to parry, Roo snapped the blade around to a side attack. Duncan merely turned his wrist, bringing his blade down to catch Roo's blade. "Nicely done, cousin," said Duncan. "But you were never my equal with the blade, and you know it. Eventually, you'll make a mistake and I'll kill you."

Roo said nothing. Hate filled his eyes at the realization of just how badly he had been played for an idiot. He feinted left, then came around from the right with a snapping blow that almost connected with Duncan's left arm, but the taller swordsman danced nimbly back. "Karli would never marry you, you swine. She hates you."

Smiling, Duncan said, "She just doesn't know me. She doesn't appreciate my better qualities." He lashed out with a full extension and almost took Roo in the shoulder. Roo ducked slightly and beat aside his cousin's blade, then he also tried a thrust, backing Duncan away.

Sylvia stood behind the bed, in the corner, clutching the curtains. "Kill him, Duncan!" she screamed. "Don't play with him."

Duncan said, "With pleasure," and suddenly attacked with more speed than Roo would have thought possible.

Roo did his best to defend, and he found his speed matched his cousin's, but Duncan was the more experienced swordsman. One advantage Roo had was he had fought a duel to the death only a year before, while Duncan hadn't faced a serious foe in years. Duncan began to improvise his attacks, and Roo saw his advantage. If he could wear his more skilled cousin down, tire him, he could eventually survive this duel. Roo then set about not to lose, as Duncan closed to kill.

Back and forth they moved, slashing and thrusting, blocking and parrying. A pair of candles threw dancing shadows across the room as the fury of moment caused the flames to flicker and gutter. The sound of steel on steel brought servants to the door of Sylvia's room. A wide-eyed maid looked in, and Sylvia screamed, "Get Samuel!"

Roo knew Samuel, the coachman, was a bull-necked thug of a man, and, now that he knew Jacob worked on behalf of Great Kesh, suspected Samuel might be one of Jacob's agents. He knew that if Samuel got into the room, Roo would be distracted enough that Duncan would probably kill him.

Roo tried to look hesitant, and when Duncan took the bait, overextending his attack, Roo launched a furious counteroffensive, forcing his cousin back against the far wall. Then Roo turned and hurried to the door, slamming it shut and throwing the bolt before Duncan could recover. "You'll have no help for a while, Duncan," he said, panting from exertion.

"I don't need any," said Duncan and began to stalk Roo across the room. Roo crouched low and waited.

Sylvia stood motionless in the corner, her face a mask of naked hatred as she watched the two men circle slowly.

Blows were exchanged, but no injury was done. Each man had the measure of the other; they had spent too many hours practicing with each other. While Duncan might be the better swordsman, Roo had spent more time drilling with him than any other; they were evenly matched.

Perspiration poured down both men's faces and drenched their shirts.

In the close air of the room on this hot summer night, they were quickly out of breath.

Back and forth to no advantage, the men fought across the room. Roo watched Duncan closely for any sign he was changing his style or fatiguing. Duncan's frustration was mounting, for while he had regularly defeated Roo in practice, this time the little man was holding his own, and if anything seemed to be gaining an edge.

Pounding on the door signaled the arrival of Samuel, the coachman. "Miss!" he cried through the door.

"I'm being attacked!" she screamed. "Rupert Avery is trying to kill me. His cousin Duncan is defending me. Break down the door!"

A moment later a thud signaled the assault on the door. The coachman and probably another male servant were throwing their shoulders into the door. Roo knew that the door was heavy oak, locked with an iron throw bolt; he had locked it himself enough times. They would have to find something to use as a ram; their shoulders would give out before the heavy door did.

Then Roo saw a flicker of movement and realized Sylvia was trying to run across the bed, past him, so she could unlock the door. He leaped backward and snapped a wild blow in her general direction, causing her to shriek and fall back. "Not so fast, my love," he said. "You and I have accounts to settle."

Duncan let out a sound of pure frustration as he lunged and drove Roo back to the side of the bed opposite Sylvia. He glanced at the door as if gauging his chances of opening it. When his gaze flicked to the door, so did Roo's blade, and a crimson stain spread on Duncan's white silk shirt, as he took a nick in the right shoulder.

Roo smiled. He knew that while it was a tiny wound, the blow to Duncan's vanity was immense. Roo had scored first blood, and Duncan would become even more dangerous and reckless.

Duncan swore and started to attack Roo as fast as he could, ignoring the door. He pushed Roo back to the corner, then lunged at him with a move designed to skewer the shorter man. Roo had anticipated the move, knowing that Duncan would follow his usual style and come at him angling toward Roo's right. The practice over the years had revealed Roo's tendency to move toward his own right when dodging. Roo knew Duncan knew this, and as it was the only likely move he could make, Roo did the unexpected. He leaped atop the bed on his left, bouncing off it as if he were an acrobat. He heard rather than saw Duncan's blade strike the wall. He leaped off to stand next to Sylvia, and he turned to see Duncan pull back his own blade and leap atop the bed.

Sylvia shrieked as she pulled a dagger from behind her pillow and struck at Roo. Roo's attention was fixed upon Duncan, but he saw movement in the corner of his eye and dodged forward slightly. Pain exploded in his shoulder, as the blow, intended for his neck, missed and the dagger point slid down his right shoulder blade, skidding off bone.

Duncan drew back his blade again, to skewer Roo as he had intended to do the last time. Roo fell back without conscious intent, and he struck Sylvia, who stumbled into the path of Duncan's lunge.

Both men froze a moment as Duncan's sword point drove deep into Sylvia Esterbrook's side. The beautiful young woman, her face contorted with hate and rage, suddenly went stiff and her eyes grew round with astonishment.

She looked down as if unable to comprehend what had just happened, and then she went limp. Duncan's blade was pulled forward briefly, and as he attempted to wrench it from Sylvia's dying body, Roo lunged. His aim was off and his arm weak from his injury, but Duncan was overbalanced and exposed, and the point of Roo's sword took him straight in the throat.

Duncan's eyes suddenly widened, his astonishment a match for Sylvia's. He stumbled backward and fell upon the bed, his head resting on one of his lover's pillows as his hands went to his throat. Blood flowed from his neck, mouth, and nose and he gurgled as he sought to stem the flow with his hands.

Roo stood there, bleeding, in pain, and out of breath as he watched his cousin lying on Sylvia's bed, his blood staining the satin sheets and pillows. After a moment, Duncan's hands went limp, falling from his throat, and his head rolled around to the left, as if he was staring at Roo and Sylvia, and the life fled from his eyes.

Roo looked down at Sylvia, who lay at his feet, staring up with eyes as vacant as Duncan's. The pounding on the door took on a steady, hard sound, and Roo knew they were using a table base or some other heavy object as a ram.

He stumbled over to the door and shouted, "Stand back!"

He unlatched the heavy iron latch and found three male servants, Samuel, a stablehand whose name Roo couldn't recall, and the cook, all standing there with weapons. The cook held a kitchen cleaver, but the other two men carried swords.

Roo glared at the three and said, "Stand aside or die."

Looking at the blood-spattered carnage behind the little man with the sword in his hand, the three servants moved back. Roo stepped into the hall.

Behind the three men waited the other servants, maids, cooks, gardeners, and the rest. Roo said, "Sylvia is dead."

One of the maids gasped, while another smiled in obvious satisfaction.

Roo said, "There's an army heading this way. It will be here sometime tomorrow. Grab what you can and run east. If you don't, by this time tomorrow night you'll be raped and dead or slaves. Now stand aside!"

No one hesitated. All turned and fled down the stairway.

Roo staggered down the stairs, and when he reached the bottom, he saw servants were busy stripping the house of easily transportable items. He thought of returning to Jacob's study and killing the traitor, but he was too tired. It would take all his strength to return home. His wound wasn't critical, but it could be serious if it wasn't tended.

Staggering outside, he found his horse where he had left it tied. He put his sword in its sheath, and by force of will he climbed into the saddle. Pointing the horse toward the gate, he put heels to sides, and the animal cantered off, heading home.

Luis dressed Roo's shoulder while Karli fussed about, holding a basin of water. "It's not bad," said Luis. "The bone's laid bare, but it's all over the shoulder blade." He was sewing up the wound with a piece of silk thread and a needle from Karli's sewing kit. "Very messy, but nothing permanent." As Roo flinched, he said, "Must hurt like hell, though."

Roo, pale from blood loss and pain, said, "It does."

"Well, if an artery had been cut you'd be dead by now, so count yourself fortunate." He pulled tight the last stitch and motioned for a cloth, cleaning off the wound. "We'll change the dressing twice a day and keep the wound clean. If it festers, you'll be very sick."

Both men had been trained in dressing wounds, so Roo knew he was in good hands. Helen Jacoby said, "I'm sorry about Duncan."

Roo had told them Duncan and he had been jumped by bandits, fleeing before the invading army. He looked at Karli and decided he'd tell her the truth when everything was over, when his family was safe and he could ask her forgiveness. He might never love his wife, but now he knew that what he had with her was a great deal more solid than the illusion of love he had felt for Sylvia.

All the way home, his wound pulsing with every heartbeat, he had cursed himself for a fool. How could he think she loved him? He had never been loved in his life, save perhaps by Erik and the other men who had served with him across the sea, and that was the love of comrades. He had never known the love of women, just their embrace.

Twice he had found tears running down his face as he thought of the number of times he had dreamed of that murderous bitch being the mother of his children, and his anger at himself mounted.

And his trust of Duncan . . . How could he have been so blind? He had let the fact of blood ties and easy charm mislead him about the man's true nature: he was lazy, self-serving, and conniving. He was a true Avery, Roo decided.

Drinking the mug of water Helen gave him, Roo said, "Luis, if anything happens to me, I want you to run Avery and Son for Karli."

Karli's eyes grew round and tears began to form. "No!" She knelt before her husband and said, "Nothing's going to happen to you!" She seemed almost desperate at the thought of losing Roo.

Roo smiled. "Something almost did, tonight. I don't plan on leaving this world any time soon, but I've seen enough of war to know that a man's not consulted about his time of death." He set down his mug and gripped her hands. "I'm talking about 'in case,' nothing more."

"I understand."

Then he looked at Helen and said, "I would like it if you'd stay with us for a while. After this is over, I mean. We're all going to have to rebuild, and we're going to need as many friends around to help as we can find."

She smiled and said, "Of course. You've been most generous to me and the children. They look upon you as they would a father, and I can't thank you enough for the care you've taken in conducting my business."

Roo stood. "I'm afraid both our companies are going to be the worse for wear when this war is over."

Helen nodded, and said, "We'll survive. Then we'll rebuild."

Roo smiled and looked at his wife, who still looked afraid. "You two get some sleep. We leave in a few hours. Luis and I have a lot to discuss before then."

"Your wound," said Karli. "You need to rest."

"I'll rest in the coach, I promise. I won't ride for a day or two."

"Very well," she said, motioning for Helen to accompany her upstairs.

Both women had awakened when Roo returned, and were wearing their long night shifts. As they climbed the stairs, Luis's eyes followed Helen until they vanished from sight. "She's quite a woman," said Roo's old companion.

Roo had admired the way the thin fabric of her nightdress had hugged the curve of her hip as she mounted the stairs, and said, "I have always thought so."

Luis said, "So what really happened?"

Roo looked at Luis. "What do you mean?"

"I know a dagger wound when I see one. I've given enough of them, and you were struck from the side and rear. Had that been a bandit who knew what he was doing, you'd have been dead." He sat down on a chair opposite Roo's. "And bandits don't jump armed men with nothing worth stealing."

"I went to the Esterbrooks' estate."

Luis nodded. "You found Duncan with Sylvia."

"You knew?"

The older fighter nodded. "Of course I knew. I'd have to be a blind idiot not to."

"I guess that makes me a blind idiot."

"Most men are when they think with that," he said, pointing to Roo's crotch. "Duncan's been bedding the wench for more than a year."

"You said nothing! Why?"

Luis sighed. "The reason I left the court of Rodez in shame was over a woman. I was made a fool of by a noble's wife. I wounded him in a fight. By the time I reached Krondor and was captured, he had died and I was to be hanged for murder. That's when I met you in the cell." He nodded in memory. "I know what it is to think you're in love, to be blinded by beauty and made stupid by the soft touch and warm scent. I know the lady who ruined me was a calculating bitch who had no more use for me after I left her bed than she had for the servant who cleaned her shoes, but even now the thought of her in the warm candlelight can arouse my hunger." He closed his eyes in memory. "I can't say that if she appeared outside now, inviting me once again to share her bed, I could be wise enough to say no.

"Some men never learn, and some learn before it's too late. Which are you?"

Roo said, "I never want to be that big an idiot again."

"Yet you gaze upon Helen Jacoby and wonder what it would be like to rest in those lovely arms, to rest your head upon that ample bosom, to feel her legs wrap around you."

Roo looked at Luis and his gaze narrowed. "What are you saying?"

Luis shrugged. "Part of it is what any healthy man would wonder, for Helen is a beautiful women, who has a warm and generous nature—I have thoughts about all such women, though I keep such thoughts to myself; all men do—but another part of it is Rupert Avery looking for something he doesn't have."

"What is that?"

"I don't know, my friend," said Luis, standing. "But you won't find it in the arms of another woman, any more than you found it in the arms of your wife or Sylvia Esterbrook." He reached over and touched Roo on the head. "You'll find it here." Then he touched him on the chest. "And here."

Roo sighed. "Maybe you're right."

"I know I'm right," said Luis. "Besides, Helen is as dangerous in her own way as Sylvia was."

"Why?" asked Roo. "Sylvia betrayed me and was using Duncan to try to kill Karli and marry me, then kill me to get my fortune." He looked hard at Luis. "You can't think Helen is like that."

"No," said Luis, with a sigh. "She's dangerous in a different way. She really loves you." Turning toward the door, he said, "When this is over, you would do well to send her away. See to her care if you must, but let her go, Roo.

"Now I must go see to the wagons. You rest. You need it."

Roo sat alone in the chair and felt all strength drain from him. It was all he could do to rise and move to a divan a few feet away and lie upon it, facedown so as not to put pressure on his shoulder. Helen in love with him? It couldn't be possible. Like him, yes. Be grateful for his care of her and the children, yes. But love him? It couldn't be.

Then Roo felt all the anger, pain, and loneliness of his life rush to the surface. He had never felt so stupid, inept, and ill-used. Two people he thought loved him had plotted to kill him and were dead.

Now Luis was telling him that the woman he admired the most in the world was in love with him, and he must send her away. Tears came unbidden as he lay there, feeling sorry for himself, and anger at his own shortcomings. Sleep came quickly as exhaustion overtook self-pity, and it seemed only brief moments of rest were his before Luis was waking him, telling him it was time to leave his home.

Roo rose on shaky legs and let Luis give him a hand to where the wagons were lined up. Roo blinked and realized Karli, Helen, and the children were all in his coach, ready to go. "I let you sleep to the last minute," said Luis, indicating that Roo should enter the coach.

Roo glanced to the west and saw the sun rising. "We should have been gone an hour ago," he said.

Luis shrugged. "We had much to do and little time to do it. An extra hour will not see us safe." He pointed to the west.

In the grey light of dawn, Roo saw towers of smoke in the distance. Burning homes. To the northwest faint glimmers of fire could be seen. "They're close," he said.

"Yes," said Luis. "Let us go."

Roo entered the carriage and crowded in beside Karli. Helmut, his son, sat on his mother's other side, while Helen was flanked by her two children. Abigail sat on the floor of the carriage, between Karli's feet, playing with a doll and singing a little song. Roo let his head loll on his wife's shoulder, closing his eyes.

The ride was bumpy and probably would not let him sleep, but he would rest his eyes awhile. As sleep returned to Roo, he wondered how Jacob Esterbrook would do in his negotiations with the invaders.

Jacob Esterbrook sat quietly behind his desk. He knew the first moments of his confrontation with these new invaders would be critical. If he showed fear or panic, any hint of uncertainty or hostility, they would react badly. But if he was calm and merely asked to speak to someone in authority, someone who could relay his message from key figures in the Keshian court to this Emerald Queen, he was certain his position would be protected.

He had experienced some surprising distress on discovering his daughter was dead. He had never liked the girl much, but she had proved useful, as had her mother before her.

Jacob wondered why some men felt so much concern over matters of children, who remained a mystery to him.

The sound of horses outside announced the arrival of the raiders, and Jacob composed himself. He had thought of what he would say. Footfalls echoed in the hall outside, and the door was thrown open.

Two oddly dressed men entered, one with a sword and shield, the other with a bow. Both had their hair heavily greased, with long braids that hung in a semicircle below their heads, and both wore scars on their cheeks, ritual in nature, Jacob decided, rather than from combat.

Jacob held up both hands to show he was unarmed, the scroll of credentials held in his left hand. His intelligence about the far continent had told him the denizens of that far land spoke a variant of the Keshian tongue, one used years ago in the Bitter Sea, related to the dialects of Queg and Yabon.

"Greetings," said Jacob slowly. "I wish to speak to someone in authority. I have a message from the Emperor of Great Kesh."

The two warriors looked at one another. The bowman asked a question of the other, in a language unlike anything Jacob had ever heard before, and the one with the shield nodded to the bowman. The archer raised his weapon and snapped off a arrow, which pinned Jacob to the back of his chair.

As the light fled from Jacob's eyes, he saw the two men pull knives and approach him.

Later that morning a captain of one of the many mercenary companies serving the Emerald Queen rode up with a squad of twenty men. They fanned out, ten circling the estate, while eight dismounted and hurried inside, the remaining two holding the horses. Every man in the company was starving and anything besides food was going to be ignored for a while.

A few moments later one of the fighters came out of the house with a disgusted expression on his face. "What is it?" asked the Captain.

"Those damn Jikanji cannibals. They're in there eating someone."

The Captain shook his head. "Right now I'm half-tempted to join them." He glanced around. "Where's Kanhtuk? He speaks their gibberish. We need to tell them to get down the road and find some food besides long pig."

The men returned and one said, "There's some livestock in back: chickens, a dog, and some horses!" Another rider came up and said, "There's cattle in the field, Captain!"

With a laugh, the Captain dismounted. "Take the horses for remounts. And let's slaughter those chickens. Get a fire going."

Men ran to do as they were bidden. The Captain knew the beef would have to go to the Queen's quartermaster, but he and his men were going to have some chicken first. At the thought of hot chicken his stomach cramped. He had never been so hungry in his life.

As men started killing chickens, the Captain shouted, "And slaughter that dog!"

He felt relief they had found food. How a land that looked so lush could be so devoid of anything to eat was a mystery. They had found gold and gems, fine cloth and items of rare beauty, everything that was usually hidden, and no food. Throughout his life as a soldier, those who ran took their gold and jewelry, valuables of every stripe, with them, but they didn't carry off grain, flour, vegetables, and fowl. Even game animals were scarce, as if they had been driven away. It was as if the enemy were retreating and taking everything they could eat with them. It made no sense.

The mercenary Captain sat down as a man emerged from the house holding bottles of wine. He greedily drank down the wine and absently wondered how long he could have resisted joining the Jikanji at their feast.

Wiping his mouth with the back of his hand, he realized he was free not to worry about that pass for a few more days. In the distance he heard the barking dog fall silent with a single whimper, and the squawk of chickens as their necks were wrung.

Eighteen

Delay

A LOUD RUMBLE came through the floor.

Lysle said, "Are you planning to blow up the entire city, Jimmy?"

James looked at the others in the gloom of the warehouse and quietly said, "Probably." He looked at his brother in the dim light of a single lantern. For two days his soldiers had been making forays into the sewers, gathering information, marking the progress of the fighting above, and coordinating the defense of the city. One of the things James had known was that the demon's magic would probably result in a quick entrance into Krondor. Rather than have everything committed to the walls and nothing inside, therefore, he had sacrificed the lives of hundreds of soldiers so that the enemy would think the city heavily defended, only to discover once inside Krondor that the battle had only just begun.

Between coordinating the defense from his underground command post and eating and sleeping only briefly, he had gotten the opportunity to know his brother. He found a sadness in realizing that as he neared seventy years of age, he had only spent hours with his brother. He knew that Lysle was a murderer, career thief, smuggler, and panderer, and guilty of as many crimes as a dung heap had flies, but in Lysle he saw himself, had he not chanced to encounter Prince Arutha so many years before. He had told Lysle about that meeting, catching sight of the Prince in the street as he sought to avoid being caught by Jocko Radburn's secret police, and how later he had saved Arutha's life from an assassin on the rooftops. That act had led to Jimmy the Hand, boy thief, becoming Squire James, and here, nearly fifty years later, James, Duke of Krondor.

James sighed. "I could have used you many times over the years, had I known I could trust you."

Lysle laughed. "Jimmy, in the short time I've known you—what? three visits in forty years?—I've come to love you like the brother that you are, but trust? You're joking."

James laughed. "I suppose. Given the chance, you'd have had me hung for treason and you'd be Duke of Krondor."

"Probably not. I never dreamed of ambition like that."

The two men heard another dull thump, and one of the guardsmen said, "That must be the abandoned warehouse in the mill district, down by the river. We stocked two hundred barrels in there."

Since before the siege, James's men had been moving through the city, leaving barrels of Quegan fire oil in strategic locations. "You should have seen the defense of Armengar," James told the guard. "That city was a defender's delight and an attacker's nightmare." He made a wavy motion with his hand, like a snake moving through grass. "No street longer than a bowshot without a curve in it. Each building with no windows at street level, heavy oak doors that could be bolted only from inside, and every rooftop flat."

The soldiers smiled and nodded, as one said, "Archery platforms."

James said, "Absolutely, so the defenders could move from rooftop to rooftop via long planks they pulled along after them, while those below were exposed to arrow fire every step of the way. When Murmandamus and his troops were in the city, Guy du Bas-Tyra fired twenty-five thousand barrels of naphtha—"

"Twenty-five thousand!" said Lysle. "You're joking."

"No, and when she blew . . ." He sat back against the wall. "I can't describe it. Just imagine a tower of fire that reached the heavens, and you'll have some idea. The noise. I was nearly deaf from it. My ears rang for a week."

A knock sounded on the door and men drew weapons. It was repeated in the expected pattern, and the single lamp was shuttered while a patrol was admitted.

A half-dozen soldiers were quickly inside, followed by three civilians. "Found them wandering around down here," said the leader of the patrol.

Rigger looked them over and said, "They're mine."

"And who are you?" asked one of the three men.

James laughed. "Anonymity has its drawbacks." To the three thieves he said, "He's your boss. This is the Upright Man."

The three looked at one another and one of them said, "And you're the Duke of Krondor, no doubt."

Everyone in the room laughed, except the three men. A young woman, one of Lysle's thieves, came and explained how things were. When it was clear she wasn't joking, and when one of the heavily armed soldiers also said it was true, the three men fell quiet. The Duke and the leader of the Thieves' Guild might be sitting in a basement connected to the sewer, but they were still the two most powerful men in the city.

At regular intervals, scouting parties went out and returned, bringing news of the fighting in the streets above. The defenders were making the invaders pay for every street and house, but the outcome was a foregone conclusion.

After having been cooped up for days, Lysle said, "If the battle's lost, why not order your lads out of the city?"

"No way to get the orders to them, sorry to say," said James, and his expression was one of genuine regret. "And for our plan to work, the invaders must think we've spent our entire army here."

"Gad, you're a bloody one," said Lysle. "I don't know if I could order that many lads to their death."

"Of course you could," said James matter-of-factly. "If your job was to preserve the Kingdom, you'd trade a city, even the Prince's."

"What's the plan, then?"

James said, "I've got a few thousand barrels of Quegan fire oil down here, and they're rigged to pour into the sewers. Sooner or later those bastards above us are going to figure out some of the populace is hiding down in the sewers, and when they do, I've got a surprise for them."

"A few thousand?" Rigger whistled in appreciation. "That's nasty stuff. The fire will burn right on top of the water."

"More," said James. He pointed to a chain, relatively new from the look of it, that hung near one wall. A soldier had been stationed to guard it at all times.

"I'd been wondering about that."

"It's something I picked up from old Guy du Bas-Tyra when we fled Armengar. Pull that chain and you'll release a light spray of naphtha into the tunnels. There's a series of small, closed-off drains, pipes, and culverts—"

"I know those. The old city's first sewers. But they were closed off when the deeper sewers were built a hundred years ago."

"Well, they're reopened." He sat back against the wall. "There are advantages to having every plan ever made for every building and public improvement in the city. When those culverts are filled with naphtha gas, they'll bleed the fumes into the larger sewer tunnels. There they'll combine with the existing sewer gas, the Quegan oil floating on the surface of the muck, and whatever barrels of oil we can cut loose up here, and when the fires hit them, the entire city is going to blow."

"Blow?"

"Explode," said James. "There won't be two stones in Krondor resting one atop the other when the dust settles."

"Damn me," said Rigger.

James said, "This is the only home I've known, sewers or palace, thieves or nobles. Krondor is where I was born."

"Well, if you're planning on dying here, would you allow me the opportunity to get a little distance away before you pull that chain?"

James laughed. "Certainly. Once we pull that chain we've got about an hour, unless there's already a fire at this end of the sewers." He shrugged. "I don't know how much time we'll have then." He pointed to a door in the easternmost wall of the basement. "There's a tunnel there that leads out to a building in the foulburg. As I said, this was Trevor Hull's and the Mockers' best route for smuggling into and out of Krondor."

"So you'll send everyone ahead, and pull the chain, then run like hell?"

James grinned. "Something like that."

Rigger sat back next to his brother. "Well, I don't fancy climbing into the daylight surrounded by an invading army, but I'll take my chances that way rather than sit here and fry."

A noise from above caused them all to look up at the ceiling, the floor of the basement of the old mill. The subbasement entrance was hidden, but guards moved quietly to their side of the trap, weapons drawn and ready.

"Sounds like they've reached this end of the city," said James softly.

"Or someone is trying to find a place to hide," whispered Lysle. "Maybe some more of my people."

James signaled one of his guards, who nodded. The man quietly put down his sword and shield and climbed up the short flight of stairs leading to the trap in the floor above. He pushed opened the door slightly, allowing him to peek through the door, and stepped back, obviously surprised. "M'lady," he said.

James's head snapped around as he saw his wife descending the stairs to the subbasement. "What are you doing here!" he shouted.

Gamina held up her hand. "Don't use that tone on me, Jimmy."

James's rage was barely held in check. "You were supposed to be in Darkmoor by now, with Arutha and the boys. How in heaven's name did you get here?"

She was muddy, with dirt on her face. Her hair was disheveled and covered with soot. She said, "You forgot Pug gave you one of those Tsurani transport spheres. I didn't."

"How did you know where to find me?" he said, his tone still seething anger.

Touching her husband's cheek, she said, "You foolish old man, did you think I couldn't hear your thoughts a world away?"

His anger fled. "Why did you come? You know there's a chance we won't get out of here alive."

Her eyes grew moist with emotion and she said, "I know. But do you think that after all these years together I could live without you?"

James gathered her into his arms and held her close. "You must go back."

"No, I won't," she said firmly. "I can't. The device is out of power. The best I could manage was to get to the market near the wall, and then I tossed it somewhere back in the mud. I had to make my way here on foot."

She moved close to him and held him, whispering in his ear, "If you can't live without this damn city, you must know I can't live without you."

He held her in silence. After nearly fifty years of marriage he knew he could not win an argument with her. It had been his intent to be the last to leave the city, and if fate decided he would die with Krondor, he thought it might be for the best; since constructing the plan for the defeat of the enemy he had constantly wrestled with the terrible price paid by the citizens of the Prince's capital. There could be no early warning for them, no orderly evacuation, for if the enemy had thought the city without plunder and food, they would have bypassed it. More, the enemy must think the bulk of the Kingdom army destroyed in Krondor.

James could hardly bear the idea of leaving so many people, so much of what had been his life, to die while he lived on. Perhaps it was fear of the ghosts of those who had paid the ultimate price so that James could buy time for the Kingdom; he didn't know. All he knew was that at some point in the planning for the defense of the Kingdom, James had decided that when it came time for his city to die, for Prince Arutha's city to die, he would most likely die with it. But now he had to leave, for he knew Gamina would not leave without him.

Lysle said, "This is your wife?"

James nodded, holding Gamina's hand. "This is the only woman I've loved, Lysle." He smiled at her.

Her head came around and her eyes widened. "Your brother?" He nodded. She turned to Lysle and said, "I've heard of you, but had no image of you." Glancing back and forth, she said, "It's obvious."

Motioning for his wife to sit down, James said, "Let me tell you of the time I first met this fellow, when people kept trying to pick fights with me up in Tannerus because they thought I was him."

Lysle laughed and said, "It's a good story."

James began, starting by explaining the odd mission Prince Arutha had sent him on, with his old friend Locklear, a young son of a local noble who happened to be an apprentice magician from Stardock, and a renegade moredhel chieftain. Gamina knew the story as well as James did, having heard it a dozen times, but she sat back, next to her husband, leaning her head on his shoulder, and let him tell it. The soldiers and thieves hiding in the gloom would be diverted from the terrible future that bore down upon them, and for a while they'd hear of better days, when the heroes were victorious and the forces of evil vanquished. Besides, she thought, as Lysle had said, it *was* a good story.

Calis watched. There was something within the Lifestone. He had noticed it within minutes of Pug shifting the Lifestone in time so that all could see it. He could sense energy inside, and as he watched for hours on end, after a while he believed he could see it.

The Oracle's companions, when they were breaking from their mystical lessons, would approach and some would stand watch with him for a time. They shared their food with him, though he couldn't really recall much of what they ate. He was preoccupied with the gem.

Calis relaxed and let his mind wander, and from time to time, flashes of images came to him. He saw people, beings looking much like his father, and he saw things: occurrences in places impossible distances away, creatures and beings from some other time. And he saw hints of forces moving behind those images, and those were the most compelling.

Hours stretched into days, and Calis lost track of time as he went deeper and deeper into the mystery of the Lifestone.

Erik shouted orders and his men began their orderly withdrawal. The enemy was less than a half mile down the road, in strength, and word had come from Greylock that the next fallback position had been secured.

Erik had decided the best way to gain back some of the time lost in the fall of Krondor was to do it a day at a time, rather than try to hold at the first defense for the extra three weeks. The original battle plan had called for them to hold the first defensive position for seven days; Erik had held it for nine.

There were seven more defenses until they reached the mountains at the pass to Darkmoor, and if he could add three or four days at each defense, they would have gained back much of the time they had lost. But Erik wasn't optimistic about realizing that goal; the plan for the defense of the West had the northmost and southmost defensive positions being unyielding, while Erik's center was the "softest" defense, withdrawing to lure the enemy along. The northern and southern flanks would funnel the enemy into the center, putting the bulk of the Emerald Queen's army on the King's Highway and within five miles of either side. The problem with that plan was that as the days wore on, more and more enemy soldiers would be thrown at Erik's position.

More than once in the first week of fighting, Erik wished that Calis hadn't been called off to whatever crisis needed his presence, and that Greylock had been in charge of the center. Erik would rather have had his original mission, holding the northern flank. Fighting from behind a strong defensible position was far easier than this delaying action.

Now his forward observers had seen battle flags going up, as the enemy prepared for a major offensive against his position. He had planned on being at least another mile down the road when the enemy got here. Erik used hand signals to order his men out of the area, while instructing the archers to fall back. Originally they were to harry the enemy along the line of march, but reports indicated there were too many gathering to risk exposing the bowmen. He'd improvise and find another location along the way to set them up, so that they could slow the enemy's advance, yet have a fair chance of getting away.

The difficulty was that during the first phase of the withdrawal, if the enemy attacked, they'd have little time to prepare themselves. If they could steal a march on the enemy, get far enough ahead, then they could quickly dig in and defend if they were overtaken, but if they were hit while they were in the process of withdrawing, the superior numbers of the enemy would prove devastating for Erik's command.

He had to get his men moving, down the road, and into the next prepared defensive position, where Greylock and his command were waiting. The two units would defend that position until the enemy pulled back, at which point Greylock's men would move out, falling back to the next position after that. That would be the pattern for the next three months, or until they reached Darkmoor. As the enemy withdrew from the extreme north and south flanks, those units were scheduled to move down the line, adding fresh soldiers to the center, but that phase of the operation wasn't scheduled until next month, and if the enemy didn't withdraw from the flanks, the support wouldn't materialize.

When the men were under way, Erik lingered at the rear, with his last line of skirmishers, who would hang back until the enemy was in sight. He looked to the west, to the late afternoon sky, and saw the smoke rising. Krondor was burning, and Erik wondered how William, James, and the others there were doing. He said a silent prayer to Ruthia, the Lady of Luck, that if the chance presented itself, those people might somehow get out.

Then he turned his horse and galloped off to overtake the front of the command. He knew he had roughly three hours to get to the next position, and another hour to dig in before night fell. He had no idea if the enemy would march until nightfall, then attack, or wait until dawn, but either way Erik intended to be ready.

Even in the bowels of the subbasement, the sounds of battle filtered down. The guards had been running to the various outposts in the sewers, and James had a rough idea of the enemy's deployment in the city. The fires raged through the center third of Krondor, and fighting in the eastern segment was light and sporadic.

The bulk of the enemy waited behind the flaming wall as the fires burned out. The one scout who had braved a look said thousands of armed men waited amid the burned-out cinders that was the westernmost third of the city. The palace was a mound of charred stone, still smoking, and James knew that his brother-in-law was dead. Gamina had confirmed that she could not reach William with her mind speech. While it was limited in distance, normally, with her family the question of range was less restrictive. She had found her husband from miles away.

James held his wife as they sat upon the stone floor of the damp and dark room. Those inside had fallen into long silences, as the sense of approaching doom grew. The escape plan required a lot of luck, and everyone was feeling short of luck at the moment.

James gave instructions to the scout who had found a way to the west, and the man hurried off to do as he was bid. Gamina dozed against her husband's shoulder while he waited, and at about what he judged was sundown, the scout returned.

Something in his manner alerted everyone in the room, and all listened attentively as he said, "M'lord!"

"Report," instructed James.

"Ships are attacking the invaders."

Gamina closed her eyes and said, "Nicholas isn't there."

James said, "Then it's Lord Vykor's fleet from Shandon Bay."

He patted his wife's shoulder, and stood up slowly. "I'm too old to be sitting on these cold floors."

He helped Gamina to her feet and said, "It's time."

"What do we do?" asked Lysle.

"Try to stay alive," he said, looking at his wife. He said, "Lord Vykor had a fleet in hiding down in Shandon Bay, and he was to link up with whatever was left of Nicholas's fleet after it came through the Straits, and follow the invaders. Once the invader's fleet was at anchor, they were to hit them as hard as possible, firing as many enemy ships as they could, while we set the city to the torch.

"As you can see, things didn't work out quite the way we planned. But if the bulk of their army, the key corps, are in the western third of the city waiting for the fires to subside, we can let loose the naphtha in the old sewers. That will blow the entire city under them, and with their ships afire, they've got no choice but to burn."

"You say that with a certain amount of glee," said Lysle.

"It's *my* city," said James through clenched teeth.

"So, what first?"

"Watch my men and stay out of the way," said James as he signaled to his soldiers.

With silent efficiency, six of them moved to a large pair of wooden doors and opened them, while two opened the outer doors. As these outer doors to the sewer swung wide, the six men on the other side were rolling barrels out of a huge storage area. Another two were attempting to work an ancient, rusted iron lever.

"Make your lads useful and have them put some weight on that," said James, pointing to the stubborn lever.

Lysle waved a hand, and four of his thieves hurried over and added their muscle to the effort. The lever began to move and they could hear the sound of running water.

James said, "There's an ancient cistern behind that wall, and that lever will drain it, setting off a very quick flow out to the harbor."

Lysle watched in fascination as the six black-clad soldiers began rolling barrels of naphtha down the ramp leading into the water. The current of the stream was noticeably faster, as the barrels were floating away from them at a good pace.

One of the rolling barrels struck the side of the door and cracked. The smell of Quegan oil filled the air. "A little on the surface is a good thing," said James with a grim smile.

"If you say so," said Lysle. "Now tell me again about the getting-away part of this plan of yours."

"As soon as the barrels are all moving toward the docks," he said. "We have an hour or so. Let's just hope the fleet's taking care of their part of things."

Lord Karoyle Vykor, Admiral of the King's Fleet in the East, shouted, "Fire!"

Another dozen catapults from the nearest ships lofted their flaming cargo high into the air, to come crashing down on the ships in the harbor.

"Mr. Devorak," said the Admiral.

"Sir?"

"Wasn't it cooperative of the bastards to tie all their ships together in a gigantic mass for us?"

"Sir, it was that."

The old Admiral was from Roldem stock, born in Rillanon, and had never set foot in the West until he had sailed his fleet through the Straits of Darkness in late spring. He had lost two ships in the passage, an acceptable toll for the early run, and he had been fortunate to have encountered only one foreign warship on the way to Shandon Bay, a Keshian cutter that had been overtaken and sunk before it could carry word to anyone that the bulk of the King's Eastern Fleet was now in the Bitter Sea.

Word of Admiral Nicholas's death had been tragic news for Vykor, for while he had met the man only twice on social occasions in the capital, his reputation and deeds were well known. Vykor did feel fortunate that at least once in his life he was able to go at the enemy under sail, with engines of war blazing, his men ready to fight hand-to-hand if need be. For most of his career he had been chasing ragged pirates, showing the colors to fractious neighbors in the Eastern Kingdoms, or attending state functions at the King's palace. Now he was doing what he had trained for all his life, and if what he had been told when he left Rillanon months before was to be believed, the fate of the Kingdom depended on this battle.

"Orders to the fleet, Mr. Devorak."

"Sir?" asked the Captain.

"Press the attack, and no enemy ship is to be let free."

"Aye, aye, sir."

"By sundown I don't want an alien ship afloat from here to Ylith. This is Nicholas's ocean, by damn, and I won't have them sailing on it."

Elements of the Bitter Sea and Sunset Island fleets moved away, heading north, to find those ships beached between the city and Sarth, while other ships moved farther north. The ships that had been beached between Land's End and Krondor had all been fired upon while Vykor's fleet passed, and to the last each had been burned to the waterline or sunk.

The Admiral's delight mounted as he saw his plan was working. He had ordered all fire to be trained upon the first row of ships, turning them into an inferno in minutes, before they could cast off from the ships farther in. Now the flames were moving inward, toward the city, as ship after ship caught fire. The missiles raining down on the mass of ships were adding to the destruction.

Vykor said, "Keep a sharp eye out for anyone attempting to get free."

Captain Devorak said, "Aye, aye, sir."

Lord Vykor watched as the *Royal Dragon*, under Captain Reeves's command, led a flotilla to the north, to sink any ships they could find. "Signal to *Royal Dragon*," said the Admiral: "good hunting."

"Aye, sir," said the Captain, relaying the order to the signalman.

Vykor knew that Nicholas had been buried at sea, on the way to the Sunsets, where the squadron had picked up fresh stores, repaired damage, and sailed back in record time. But the Admiral felt what any old sailor would feel, that Nicholas still somehow walked the quarterdeck of that ship. He saluted the ship and the memory of one of the two finest sailors he had ever known, teacher and student, Amos Trask and Nicholas conDoin.

Returning his attention to the matter at hand, he saw a small ship cut itself loose near the docks and make way toward them. "That ship, Captain Devorak. Please sink it, sir."

"Aye, aye, Admiral."

As they bore down on the enemy ship, Admiral Karoyle Vykor watched the Prince's city, capital of the Western Realm, burn. A profound sadness passed over him as he saw greatness destroyed; then he put aside his feelings until later, for there was still a battle to be won.

James pulled the chain. A rumbling from above told him the mechanism was working. "The naphtha will filter down through the drains and culverts, and will sprinkle through the sewers. If we're lucky, we have about an hour to get out of here."

Lysle said, "Then let's go."

Soldiers moved quickly up the stairs to the upper basement. One moved to another short flight of stairs and hurried up that, peeking through the trap. The soldier signaled the way was clear and they hurried up into the evening.

The evening was darker than it should have been, for the air was heavy with black smoke. Men coughed, and the soldiers took out cloths, which they tied over noses and mouths. The thieves tore rags off their shirts and did likewise, one of them handing a rag to Gamina.

They heard fighting all around, but no combatants were in sight. James's scouts hurried ahead, peering around the corner.

He waved them back and everyone who could ducked out of sight; others fell facedown on the street, hugging the walls as closely as possible, in the hope they'd be lost in the smoky gloom of evening.

Riders sped by, tattered, bleeding, scared soldiers of the Kingdom, obviously in full rout. James whispered to those nearby, "We have to find another way. Whoever's chasing them will be here in a moment."

As they retreated down the entrance to their belowground hideout, James's words proved prophetic: a thundering squad of Saaur riders came pounding hard after. It was James's first sight of the lizardmen and he said, "Gods, Calis's reports didn't do them justice."

The entire company made it back into the refuge without being discovered, and when they were safely into the subbasement, Lysle said, "Now what?"

"What's the only other sewer exit likely to be unguarded?" asked James.

"North gate outfall, but that puts us north of the city, not east," Lysle replied.

"True," said James, moving toward the loading ramp that led down to the sewer, "but we have less than an hour, and that gate is a half hour's walk from here. I'd rather be outside the city when it blows up than inside worrying about who's out there. If we can get into the woods to the north of Krondor, we might be able to find a way eastward."

He looked at the thirty soldiers and dozen thieves and knew it was probably futile.

But you must try.

James looked at Gamina. "Yes, we must try."

He led them off through the sewer.

Lord Vykor's eyes widened in astonishment. The creature seemed to appear out of nowhere, striding across the burning decks of the enemy fleet. Along the way to Krondor they had caught fifty ships on the beach, and fast-running cutters with men throwing bottles of oil, or larger ships with ballista or catapult, had burned all of them. Nearly twenty had been boarded, captured, or sunk, so that with the destruction of the ships in the harbor, more than half the enemy's fleet was destroyed. By rough count he assumed another hundred and fifty to two hundred ships were strung out along the northern coast of the Bitter Sea or already engaged with Captain Reeves's flotilla.

Now suddenly out of the inferno that was Krondor's harbor a demon walked purposefully toward him, striding across the decks of burning ships.

Calmly the Admiral drew his sword and said, "I think the creature means to board us, Mr. Devorak."

"Fire!" shouted the Captain, and ballista and bowfire were unleashed on the creature.

Some damage was done, and the creature howled as the arrows struck his fifteen-foot-tall body, but he walked on through the fire and seemed more irritated than injured.

"Veer off, Mr. Devorak."

"Aye, aye, Admiral."

The fleet was withdrawing, but Vykor's flagship, the *Royal Glory*, was closest to the burning fleet. The creature reached the outer railing of the last ship burning in the harbor, and stood up on the railing. With a prodigious leap and scream of anger, the beast unfolded its huge wings and sailed across the gulf between the damaged fleet and Vykor's ship.

"Signal to fleet," said Vykor as his personal doom sailed down upon his ship. "Make best speed!"

He never knew if the message got off, for Jakan, self-elected Demon King of the armies of Novindus, glided down upon him, scooping him up and crushing his spine as he bit off half his head. The Admiral had the brief satisfaction of driving his sword deep into the creature's side as it neared, but never heard the howls of pain, for he was dead before Jakan felt the wound.

Captain Devorak struck out with his blade and for his troubles had his head snatched from his shoulders. The bowmen above fired down upon the creature, to little effect, while the less brave among the crew dove over the side.

The two leading commanders in the Royal Navy were now dead, and each captain would have to make a decision on his own, seeking instruction from the seniormost among them until a command structure could be reformed, but at least the bulk of the invaders' fleet was destroyed.

Jakan killed and ate every man he could find, until he realized the ship had drifted to the northwest of the city. He hated the touch of seawater—it sucked energy from him—though he could abide it for a while. He abandoned the ship and launched himself into the air, attempting to glide back toward the inferno that was his fleet and city. Fire caused no pain for him, though it was a terrible waste of life energy and meat.

And something called to him. Something unspoken said he could not just start destroying this army that he had seized, but he must use it, must move to the east, must find this thing that called to him.

And from some dark source, across a vast distance, came a word, a place, a destination: Sethanon.

James saw the leading guard hold up his hand. Everyone stopped. They had passed others along the way, refugees and invaders. No one seemed eager to press an attack in the dark sewers, yet. But James knew that if the invaders were flushing out those hiding belowground, the city was now theirs.

He calculated the time in his head and knew they had no more than ten minutes. They were a dozen paces from the northern gate, near the so-called sea gate, the gate used most by smugglers and thieves to get in and out of the city.

Lysle sent one of his thieves forward, a young woman who nimbly climbed up and reported back that the way was clear. James signaled and the evacuation began.

Lysle said, "Out you go."

James said, "No. I'll go last."

"Captains and sinking ships?" asked Jimmy the Hand's brother.

With a smile that showed only pain and fatigue, he said, "Something like that."

"I'll wait with you," Gamina said.

James said, "I'd rather you didn't."

In his mind, James hear her say, *You don't want to leave, do you?*

I don't want to die, but I've caused so much death and destruction. This is the only home I know, Gamina. I don't see how I can live with this.

Do you think I don't understand that? she asked. *I hear your thoughts and I feel your pain. There is nothing you can say that I won't understand.*

He looked into her eyes and smiled, and this time the smile was one of love and complete trust.

Then the world around them exploded. The six men on the other side of the gate were knocked to the ground and stunned. Three who were in the gate were shot from it like corks from a bottle and flew through the air, one breaking his neck on impact twenty yards away, the other two sustaining broken bones.

Inside the tunnel the very air turned into flames for an instant. In that brief moment, Gamina and James were linked in mind, their memories unfolding together, from the first instant they met as James swam in the lake near Stardock, first espying the love of his life as she bathed.

Almost drowning, he had been rescued by this woman who looked into his mind and saw everything he was, everything he had been, and loved him, who loved him despite everything he had done since then, despite the things he had asked her to do that had caused her pain.

Everything around them was forgotten as they clung to that profound love they had shared, the love that had brought them a son who was safely away, and two grandsons they adored. For a brief instant they relived their lives together, from the journey to Great Kesh to the return to Krondor. As flames burned away the flesh from their bodies, their minds were deep within their love for one another and they felt no pain.

* * *

Pug cried out. "Gamina!"

Hanam said, "What is it, magician?"

Looking desolate, Pug whispered, "My daughter is dead."

The creature didn't dare touch the magician to comfort him. The hunger was too fierce, and the touch of human flesh might drive him into a feeding frenzy. "I am sorry," the creature said.

Pug took a deep breath and let it out with an audible sigh. "My son and daughter are both dead." He had felt William's death two days earlier, and now with Gamina's passing a portion of his life was closing behind him. "I knew I would outlive both of them, Hanam, but to know something and experience it are two different things."

"It is always thus," said the Saaur Loremaster from within the demon's body. "Among our race is a benediction that is repeated when a boy becomes a man and is given his first weapon: 'Grandfather dies, father dies, son dies.' Every Saaur repeats it when they get ready to ride into battle, sons beside fathers, for there is no crueler fate than for a parent to outlive a child."

"Macros called long life a curse, and now I understand. When my wife died many years ago, that was one thing, but this . . ." Pug wept for a while. Then he composed himself and said, "I knew William was at risk, for he chose a soldier's life. But Gamina . . ." His voice faltered, and again he wept.

Time passed, and the demon creature said, "We must hurry, magician. I can feel my control slipping."

Pug nodded as he stood up, and they left the cave.

Macros and Miranda should be in place.

Pug incanted, and suddenly they were invisible. He understood Macros's difficulty, for to do two things at once was always a problem, but coupled with the stress of expecting attack at any minute and the worry associated with achieving the goal, it was proving to be more than one of the most difficult things Pug had done.

Pug levitated and discovered that once over the initial strain of rising into the air, it was actually easier to float along toward the city of Ahsart than it was to walk.

Out of the air the voice of the demon said, "Fliers!"

A half-dozen winged creatures sped across the sky to the south, and Pug knew that if he and the Saaur Loremaster hadn't been invisible, the creatures would have swooped down and attacked. As foretold, life on this world was rapidly being devoured. The once-lush grasslands were now withered and brown; this was an absence of life so obvious that no one would have confused it with the sleeping dormancy of winter, where the plants would reawaken with spring's rain.

Trees, blackened and gnarled, dotted the landscape, and the waters ran with a clarity so profound that Pug knew not even algae lived in the pools. No insect buzz filled the air, and no bird call could be heard. The only sound was the wind.

"It is worse here," said Hanam, as if reading Pug's thoughts. "Here is where the creatures first came into our world."

"But soon it will all be like this?"

"Soon."

"Now I see why they are anxious to find new worlds." Pug said, "How is it they could reach this world, yet not ours?"

With what Pug had come to understand as a laugh, a barking sound came, followed by Hanam's voice: "In their rush into this world to feed, the demons destroyed the priests of Ahsart, the only ones on this world able to control the portal. I believe that what you've said about the Pantathians on your world means the demons have no allies on your world willing to bring them over."

As they approached the city of Ahsart, Pug said, "Nothing we've seen of Jakan says he's anxious to open the way for his brothers."

"Then let me give you this warning, Pug of Midkemia. Knowledge comes with the capture and devouring of souls. This would-be Demon King may know of the Hall and the ability of some of your people to make controllable rifts. If so, when he's captured enough of your land to feel firmly in control, he may start invading other worlds."

Pug said, "I deduced as much."

"Then you know that even if we win here, you must return and defeat Jakan."

Pug said, "If I don't, Tomas will."

They entered the burned-out city and started looking for the great temple, the entrance through which the demons had originally entered. Inside they found Saaur bones, dead priests torn limb from limb by the invading demons years before.

"It's not here!" said Pug.

"What?"

"The portal. The rift into this world from the demon realm. It's not here."

Pug let them become visible. "Where is it?"

Hanam said, "There can be only one answer."

"What?"

"They have moved the portal by magic means, somehow, to be near the rift into your world. That means they're preparing the way to your world for Maarg! He must be close to coming through!"

"Where is that?"

"On the other side of the world."

"I cannot fly us around the world *and* keep us invisible!" said Pug. "I can't transport us to a place I've never seen."

The demon with the Loremaster's mind said, "Then we must fly, quickly, and fight whoever gets in our way." He leaped to the air with what sounded like a war cry, and Pug followed.

Nineteen

Catastrophe

ROO GRIMACED.

His shoulder hurt to the touch, but Luis assured him it was without infection. When the bandage was changed, Luis said, "That should do it for now. We'll clean it again tomorrow night when we reach Wilhelmsburg."

Roo said, "A bed!" He grinned at Karli, Helen, and the children. For the first few days on the road the children had treated the journey like an adventure, but since this morning Abigail had been asking when they were going home. Karli had tried to explain that it would be a long time, but a "long time" more than five minutes was lost on the three-year-old.

Camp was relatively calm, though the mercenaries Roo had hired looked more and more nervous as the days wore on. Roo and Luis had spent enough time around soldiers to know these were men used to sitting quietly, scaring off bandits, and rarely having to pull sword or bowstring.

Krondor had fallen. That had become apparent from the incredible tower of black smoke that appeared in the west, two days after they left, and from the increase in traffic on the road east. More and more Roo spied the hired guards engaged in quiet conversation, and he suspected they were ready to bolt at the first sign of serious trouble.

Roo had talked to Luis in private about his doubts as to the reliability of the mercenaries, and Luis agreed. Luis saw to it he spent enough time around them both to bolster their resolve and to make it clear he was ready to deal harshly with anyone who didn't earn his pay. Roo knew that he had a better chance of keeping his little caravan intact once they reached Wilhelmsburg. They would rest, leave after a night in one of the inns Roo owned, then make for Ravensburg. Roo had promised the men a partial payment of their wages, and a little gold in their pockets would keep them in line.

If Erik's family and Milo's were still at Ravensburg, Roo would take them to Darkmoor. He knew that eventually Erik would end up there. Roo had thought about where he had been shipping arms and supplies for the last year, and where his wagons had taken tools and equipment, and the one thing Erik had said to him, "Nightmare Ridge."

He knew Royal Engineers had bolstered old roads or cut new ones along the rear side of the ridge, hundreds of miles long, that ran along the entirety of the eastern half of the Calastius Mountains. The range looked like a squashed, inverted Y, with one long leg and a short one. The long leg ran from just east of Krondor to the Teeth of the World, the great range that ran across the north of the Kingdom. The short, eastern leg ran from Darkmoor to north of the town of Tannerus, where the legs met. Roo had figured that with Sethanon as the aliens' ultimate goal, crossing the mountains north of Tannerus took them too far from their goal. Anywhere to the south of that point, they'd have to best Nightmare Ridge, and Roo knew that if the bulk of the Kingdom Army was waiting along that granite wall, there was a chance they'd survive. If the enemy could be kept on this side of the ridge until the snows fell, the Kingdom would be victorious.

But it was only three weeks after Midsummer's Day and the snows of winter seemed ages away in the warm evening. Raised in Ravensburg, Roo knew that the snows could come early, but he also knew they could come late, and that only an oracle would know which would be the case this year. In any event, the earliest they could see snow would be in six weeks, and ten or twelve was more likely. Perhaps heavy rains, they were common, but snow was months away.

Roo went to the fires and chatted with Karli and Helen and tried to talk to the children. Children were still a mystery to him, though their mere presence didn't inspire the great discomfort it once had. He even found little Helmut's insistence on putting everything in his mouth amusing, though it seemed to wear Karli to a thin edge. Jason spent time with the children, keeping them diverted, a talent for which Roo was greatly thankful.

Helen's children were older, and he could talk to Nataly and Willem, though the things they found interesting were a mystery to him. Helen was a calm in a sea of chaos, her ready smile and soft voice soothing to those around her. In the firelight, Roo realized he was staring at her as the children prattled, and he looked away. He saw Karli was watching him, and smiled at her. She smiled back, in a tentative way, and he winked and mouthed, "Everything is fine."

He sat back, trying to keep from putting pressure on his wounded shoulder, and let his gaze wander back to Helen. He yawned and closed his eyes, the impression of her burned on his memory. She wasn't pretty, though she was far from "raw-boned" as that bitch Sylvia had called her. She was what some men might call handsome. But her two most appealing features were large brown eyes and a broad, ready smile. And she had a firm, still-slender body.

Roo then wondered if Luis could be anything but mad to think this woman, this wonderful caring mother, could love a gutter rat like himself. Sighing, Roo let his body give in to a comfortable doze, as the chatter of the camp faded away, and the soothing warmth of the evening and the sound of Helen's voice lulled him.

Suddenly Roo was awake, as shouts from the distance turned the camp into bedlam. Men ran, and for a moment Roo blinked in disorientation as he tried to assess the situation. The children were lying under blankets, so some time must have passed since he dozed off.

After a moment, Roo had his bearings and his battle training came to the fore. Calmly, so as not to alarm the children, he said, "Karli, Helen, get up!"

Helen came awake and said, "What?"

"Get the children into that wagon!" He pointed to one nearby. "The coach won't last on these roads if we must run."

Luis ran up and said, "Riders, heading this way, fast." He had his dagger in his hand. Since his right hand had been injured, Luis never wore a sword anymore, but with his left he was still a deadly knife fighter.

Roo and Luis quickly doused the low-burning fire, in the hope the riders hadn't caught sight of the weak flames in the distance. Had they come hours earlier, they would have spotted the camp without difficulty.

Some of the mercenaries were now running for their horses, and Roo shouted, "Get the wagons going!" It was still two hours or more before dawn, but the horses had benefited from resting most of the night. With luck, they could be away before whoever approached saw them, and continue on, arriving at Wilhelmsburg early than anticipated.

Drivers ran to get the horses into traces, and Roo tried to help as well as he could with the injured shoulder. Jason knew nothing about weapons or wagons, but he carried whatever he was told to fetch, and Luis was a rock. But the mercenaries were Roo's biggest concern. Now they were being asked to stand steadfast against hard, vicious men who had been fighting for years.

The wagons began to get under way, and Roo got into the saddle for the first time. He felt stiffness in his right shoulder as he moved his sword, but he knew that his own was one of the few swords he could count on.

Roo hovered at the rear of the caravan, watching the west anxiously, to see the approaching riders. As the wagons rumbled toward the highway, Roo glimpsed figures in the west, darker silhouettes against the murk. He could only pray they would be cautious, fearing they were approaching some of the Kingdom's army, rather than a desperate band of civilians fleeing before them.

For long, terror-filled minutes, they moved over the grass, until they were back on the compacted dirt of the highway. As soon as the metal-bound rims of the wheels began to turn over the dirt and gravel of the road,

Roo felt his tension lessen. The farther along they were, the closer to Wilhelmsburg, the better their chances of survival.

Then a half hour later a man ahead shouted, while another screamed. Shouts from the south side of the road told Roo the riders he had glimpsed had crossed the highway, ridden up on a parallel course until they were certain this was no army column they shadowed, then ridden ahead to spring an ambush.

Roo shouted, "Turn north!" and drew his sword. Ignoring the pain in his arm, he pushed his horse forward to engage the first enemy fighter he could find.

It didn't take him long to find a ragged-looking rider hacking at the guard on a wagon six ahead of Roo's own. The mercenary guard was defending himself well enough, but other riders were coming fast.

Roo didn't try anything fancy. He slammed his heels hard into his horse's sides, forcing the animal into doing something it didn't want to do: crash into the other horse. The rider from the Queen's army was thrown to the ground as his mount reared unexpectedly, and Roo shouted to his guard, "Kill him!"

Roo urged his horse forward, toward the riders, who were only a wagon's length ahead. Then Luis was at his side, reins tied around his right wrist, dagger in his left hand. Roo wanted to tell him to get back and defend the women, but he was too busy trying to stay alive.

Roo killed one man and drove another off, turning his horse to find Luis nursing a cut on his right arm while holding his bloody dagger. Roo said, "You madman. Next time, stay behind with the women, and if you've got to cut throats, do it from there."

Luis grinned and said, "I think I have to. I've never been that good a rider." He used his chin to indicate his wound. "I'd do better on foot."

Roo marveled at his calm. "Go get Karli to dress that. I'm going to see how badly we've done."

Roo rode to the head of the little caravan and found that two of his guards were dead and two others had run into the early morning gloom. The remaining six, with Luis, himself, and Jason, were barely enough to defend two wagons, let alone a dozen. Roo didn't hesitate. He said to the mercenaries, "Get back to the last wagon." As they rode back to the end of the line of wagons, Roo turned to those drivers still on their wagons and said, "Get moving now! Straight on to Wilhelmsburg and to the Inn of the Morning Mist. You get there in one piece, I'll give you a year's wages in bonus."

The teamsters didn't hesitate, but at once shouted and got their animals moving. Roo rode to the remaining six guards and said, "We're going to defend the last wagon. I'll personally kill the first man who tries to run away."

Luis said, "You think they're coming back?"

"Absolutely. I think we just surprised them when we put up a fight."

"How many?" asked Jason, trying not to look frightened. The former-waiter-turned-bookkeeper had never been exposed to violence beyond an alehouse brawl before, and was trying mightily to be a calming influence on behalf of the children.

"Too many," said Roo. He got out of the saddle and led his horse to the rear of the wagon, tying her reins to the tailgate. He then moved to the front and mounted, picking up the reins from the wagon driver, who sat shaking, and said, "Hang on."

He turned the wagon northward and shouted, "Follow me!"

The six guards, Luis, Jason, and the wagonload of his family and the Jacobys headed away from the road. Roo knew it was a desperate gamble, but if he could get far enough from the highway when the raiders returned, they might not miss the one wagon seeking to find the small, little-used road eastward, while they pillaged the wagons trying to race to the east.

"They'll never make it," said Luis.

"Probably not, but if any does, I will make good on my word and give the driver a year's wages in gold, on the spot."

Luis settled back into the wagon bed. It was crowded as he and Jason sat with the children and the two women, but at least for the moment they were safe.

Their luck didn't hold long. Roo had found a small game trail that led into sparse woodlands, but it forced them into a gully that eventually became too narrow for the wagon to navigate. They backtracked until they found another route north, and again tried to find a way to the small road leading east.

Near midday, riders could be heard over a small rise, and for several tense minutes, Roo, Luis, and the mercenaries waited silently with weapons drawn while Karli, Helen, and Jason kept the children quiet. When the last rider passed, less than twenty yards off but out of sight, Roo signaled to turn toward the east and see if they could find yet another route.

By sundown they were completely lost in the woods. Around a cold camp, they discussed options, and one of the mercenaries said, "I'm for just leaving this wagon and striking east, Mr. Avery."

Roo said, "How well do you know these hills?"

"Not very, but our boys are to the east, so you said, and any road worth calling such is going to have enemy cavalry riding along more likely than not, so if we keep to the woods we could slip past them."

Roo said, "Between here and Darkmoor Province there are a dozen little villages, give or take, and we might blunder into one of them, but if we don't have a local guide, what we'll find is a sudden rise that turns into a big enough hill it might as well be a mountain for how easy we can get around it." He glanced around the quickly darkening woods and said, "It's easy to get turned around in the woods if you don't know the way. You could be heading right into the enemy's arms if you don't know what you're doing."

The camp was so somber the children were silent, looking at Roo and the other adults with large eyes. Karli and Helen did what they could to reassure them, but in a quiet way so as to encourage their continued silence.

After a moment, Roo said, "But I think you may be right. Unload the wagon and get blankets and food. Leave the rest and we'll start walking tomorrow."

The mercenaries glanced at one another, but no one seemed willing to say more, so they did as ordered. Roo sat and quietly watched his children, the Jacobys, and the others in the failing light.

Helen had his son on her lap, singing to him softly as Karli held Abigail in her arms. Willem leaned against his mother's shoulder, fighting off sleep, determined to stay awake, while Nataly was already asleep, on a blanket between Helen and Karli. Jason made himself useful repacking the food so it could be carried, and Luis kept close to the mercenaries, keeping them calm and promising them bonuses when they got to Wilhelmsburg.

When the children were all asleep, Karli came to sit next to Roo. "How is your shoulder?" she asked.

Roo realized that he had not thought about it since the encounter with the raiders, and he flexed it. "A little stiff, but I'll be all right."

She leaned in to him, whispering, "I'm frightened."

He put his left arm around her. "I know. But if we're lucky we'll be safe tomorrow."

She said nothing, just sitting there, stealing comfort from his presence. Throughout the night they sat silently, dozing, but unable to sleep, as the night noises of the woods kept startling them.

As the sky lightened, a few hours before dawn, Roo quietly said, "Get the children up."

As Karli did so, Roo said to Luis, "We need to be moving before dawn."

"Which way?"

"East and north. If we run into an obstacle in one direction, we head the other. But we only turn around and go south or west if there is no other way. Eventually we'll reach that road I told you of, or we'll hit the farms outside Wilhelmsburg."

Luis nodded. "The mercenaries are not to be trusted."

"I know, but if we make it clear they stand a better chance with us, staying in a group, than they would on their own—"

The sound of horses alerted them and they both turned, to see the six mercenary guards riding out in the predawn gloom.

"Damn!" said Luis.

Roo said to Jason and Helen, who were now awake, "We don't have time to eat. Grab what you can and let's get away. If there are any raiders nearby, they'll hear that clatter and come looking."

The children complained, but their mothers quickly silenced them and handed them pieces of bread to chew on while they walked. Roo had studied their surroundings the evening before and had spied a small dry creek bed that ran to the northeast. He decided that would most certainly take them upward, into the foothills, so he would follow it until they found a clear route to the east or north.

The going was slow. The children couldn't move quickly and they tired easily, but they managed to keep going for a full hour. Then they had to rest.

There were no signs of pursuit. After resting for a quarter hour, Jason picked up Helmut, freeing Karli from carrying the youngest of the four children.

They continued along, finding the way difficult, with deadfalls and debris providing constant obstacles. When it was near midday, they heard distant sounds of fighting echoing through the trees. They couldn't tell from which directions the sounds came.

They moved on.

Erik said, "We've done well."

Greylock said, "Given the total collapse at Krondor, well enough." He consulted reports that had come his way from positions to the north and south of him and said, "We have one nasty surprise."

"What?"

"Great Kesh has moved to occupy everything in the Vale of Dreams."

Erik said, "I thought Prince Erland had arrived at some sort of treaty with them?"

"Apparently the Keshians didn't agree."

Erik shrugged. He was eating his midday meal with Greylock. Owen's command would be pulling out after they finished eating, once Erik's men had finished occupying the position Greylock's command had dug. Erik's men were pleased they didn't have to create the barricades and could rest until the enemy put in an appearance.

"As I judge things," said Greylock, "you must hold here for five days instead of four."

"I'll try for six," said Erik.

Greylock nodded. "News from the north is good. Captain Subai and the Pathfinders have been able to get their men through the mountains with little trouble."

Erik laughed. "Wait until the enemy is up there in strength."

"Well, part of the plan is to keep them from getting up there in strength." Owen sighed. "Reports are the fighting is the hardest in the north. There's a company of Hadati alongside some of our boys, and they've dug in near a tiny pass southeast of Questor's View." Erik called up from memory the maps he had studied, and nodded. That position would have to hold; to let the enemy through in numbers up there would give them a clear route down the eastern face of the mountains, bypassing Darkmoor, straight to Sethanon. "But the enemy isn't up there in sufficient numbers to dislodge them."

Erik said, "I'm too tired to think. Once we're dug in, I'm going to sleep."

Owen rose, laughing. "I doubt it. You'll check everything twice before you'll decide you're sufficiently dug in, so you won't sleep until nightfall."

Erik shrugged. "How much time have we gained?"

"Two days. We still need to pick up three weeks."

Erik said, "I don't know if we can."

"If we don't, we'll have massive fighting in Darkmoor and along the ridge."

"What of the Armies of the East?"

Owen said, "They're behind the ridge, waiting."

Erik said, "I wish they were right over there." He pointed to an area where his men were readying weapons and supplies.

Owen put his hand on Erik's shoulder. "I understand. It's difficult watching your men get ground up bit by bit. But it's necessary."

Erik said, "Prince Patrick made that clear to me, as did Knight-Marshal William. But no one said I had to like it."

"Understood," said Owen. Turning to a Sergeant of his command, he said, "Sergeant Curtis!"

"Yes, General?"

"Get the men ready to march."

"Sir!" The Sergeant turned and hurried away, shouting orders.

" 'General,' " said Erik with a grin. "Suppose Manfred regrets discharging his Swordmaster?"

Owen said, "Ask him when you get to Darkmoor." Owen mounted his horse. "Besides, he really didn't have anything to say about it. It was Mathilda who gave me the boot."

At mention of his father's widow, Erik said, "I suppose I'm going to have to deal with her soon."

"Only if you stay alive, my friend," said Owen, then he turned his horse and walked him away. Over his shoulder he said, "So stay alive."

"Fare well, Owen."

Erik left the campfire and started inspecting his men's positions. Owen had been right, and it was hours after sunset before Erik found time to sleep.

Roo, Jason, and Luis stood with weapons ready as the two women hurried the children up the bank to a cave. They had moved without difficulty for two days, finding rough trails that kept moving toward their goals. They had found a woodsman's cabin, abandoned but untouched, where they had spent one night, risking a small fire, though Roo worried the scent of smoke in the air might reveal their position.

They had left the relative comfort of that cabin and were now no more than one day's travel from the road Roo remembered, when they heard the sound of riders, growing louder by the minute. Roo didn't know if the riders had picked up their trail or were just heading their way by chance, but either way they were rapidly getting closer.

From the sound of it, it was a small group, maybe a half-dozen riders or less, but with Roo's shoulder injury, Luis having only one good hand and a dagger, and Jason having no experience with a weapon, even two skilled mercenaries would have been dangerous. If the riders had bows, Roo knew they were lost. Their best chance for the women and children was for them to get out of sight and stay in hiding. Roo and the two other men were determined to delay anyone coming their way long enough to facilitate their escape.

Roo glanced over his shoulder and saw Helen usher the children into the cave's mouth, and he thought she smiled back at him. At this distance he couldn't be sure.

Soon four riders came into view, at the far end of the little wash Roo's band had been hiking. Roo said, "Jason, if this turns ugly, don't try to be a hero. Try to hamstring one of the horses and don't get killed. Luis and I will try to take care of the fighters."

Seeing three men in their path, the riders slowed to a walk. Luis said, "If they stay in single file, they'll talk. If they fan out, they're going to fight."

The four riders continued in single file. When they were a dozen paces away, the leader held up his hand and studied the three men. After a moment, he said, "Who are you?"

Roo realized they were speaking the language of Novindus, somewhat accented, so he judged they were from a different part of the continent than those Roo had visited. Roo hazarded a bluff. "My name is Amra."

Hearing their own tongue, the four riders seemed to relax a little. The leader pointed to Luis. "And you?"

"Haji, from Maharta," he answered without hesitation.

"And you?" he said to Jason.

Before Jason could open his mouth, Roo said, "He's mute. His name is Jason."

Jason couldn't understand a word of this strange dialect, but upon hearing his name, he nodded.

"What company?" asked the leader as the second rider moved out of line and came to stand next to him. Both men still held weapons, ready to act if they didn't like the answer.

Roo thought furiously. He knew things had changed radically in the Queen's army since Calis's Crimson Eagles had served in it. He knew the names of some companies, but had no idea if they still existed, or where they might be stationed. But he also knew no answer would get them killed as quickly as a wrong answer.

Softly, Roo said, "We were put into Shinga's Black Blades after the battle of Maharta."

The second rider said, "Deserters?"

Roo said, "No, we ran into some of the Kingdom's lancers and they cut us up."

Luis lowered his dagger slightly, as if relaxing, and said, "We got loose and ran. Somewhere along the way we got completely lost. We've been wandering around these woods for a week. We found a little food, but we're pretty hungry. We're trying to get back to our own side."

Roo said, "Can you help us get back? We're really not deserters."

The other two riders moved their horses and took up the flanks. The leader of the four said, "Not deserters? That's too bad. We are."

Suddenly they charged, and Luis and Roo were diving out of the way. Roo hit the ground, rolled, and came up in a crouch, in time to see Jason standing rooted in terror as he was ridden down by the second rider, who unleashed a blow at the clerk. Jason ducked and lashed out with his blade, and Roo saw it wrenched from his hands as he was knocked to the ground and struck in the shoulder by a horse's hoof. A horse's scream indicated he had done some damage with his sword, but he lay on the ground, in blinding pain, unable to move.

The horse he had wounded stumbled, its right foreleg bloody from the deep wound Jason's thrust had caused, throwing his rider over his shoulder. Roo had rolled and come up, ready for the second charge. Luis threw his dagger and took one of the men in the neck, killing him before he hit the ground.

The thrown rider was groaning as he lay on the ground, and Luis and Roo faced an equal number of opponents. Luis pulled a second dagger from his boot and crouched. The two men spoke softly to each other, obviously aware that Luis's ability to throw his weapon made him a more dangerous opponent.

They shouted as they urged their horses into a charge, and they appeared to be charging both men, but at the last instant, the one heading for Roo turned and circled around to attack Luis from behind. Luis threw his dagger at the rider heading straight for him, who dropped over the neck of his horse, presenting almost no target.

Luis had anticipated such a move, and had thrown low, aiming at the man's exposed thigh. The blade struck the man full in the right thigh, and he howled in pain as he sat up, trying to move away from Luis as his companion charged him.

Luis had a third dagger, carried in his shirt, out, and was throwing the moment the man sat up. He took the blade in the throat and fell over the rear of his horse.

Roo charged the man who rode past him, as soon as his back was turned. While he bore down on Luis, who was turning and attempting to get another dagger out of his sash, Roo held his sword above his head.

The rider slashed down at Luis, who attempted to dodge, but the rider compensated and caught Luis on his right shoulder, the blade biting deep. Roo's blow caught the rider from behind, slicing deep into his leg. Bone was exposed as the rider screamed in pain and attempted to turn, only to lose consciousness in the saddle as he went into shock.

Roo quickly killed him. He rushed to Luis and saw the man was barely conscious. He was about to speak to him when he heard a scream from behind.

Roo spun to see the rider who had been thrown standing over Jason. The young clerk was on one elbow, blood running down his face from a scalp wound, while the soldier drew back his blade for a killing blow.

"No!" Roo shouted as he started to run. His legs were leaden, each step impossibly slow and heavy. He tried to hurry, but the soldier's blow descended like a flash, and Jason screamed in pain. He had turned, and the thrust that should have silenced him left him contorted in pain, screaming.

Roo drew back his own blade, and swung with all his strength. He missed the soldier's body, but sliced through the man's wrist, and the sword tumbled through the air, the hand still holding the hilt.

The man looked at his bleeding stump in disbelief, not even seeing the next blow, which sliced the back of his exposed neck, causing his death as he slumped to the ground.

Roo knelt next to Jason, whose eyes were wide with pain and terror. "Mr. Avery," he said, clutching at Roo's shirt.

"I'm here," said Roo, cradling Jason's head.

Jason's eyes were unfocused, as if he couldn't see, and Roo saw the wound was a killing one. The head wound had come from the horse's flying hoof, but the gut wound pumped blood in a quick rhythm, and Roo knew an artery deep in the body had been severed. Jason's life was running onto the ground by the moment.

Jason said, "I'm sorry, Mr. Avery."

Roo said, "You did well."

"I'm sorry I betrayed you."

Roo said, "What do you mean?"

"I was the one who gave Sylvia Esterbrook information to pass along to her father," he said, then began coughing blood.

"I don't understand," said Roo. "How did you know her?"

"When you first came to Barret's, I told you of her, and told you she was wonderful."

Roo's head swam. The fight, his wound, and now this. "Jason, how did you and Sylvia do this?"

"I would pass her servant notes," said Jason. "She would write back to me. She promised that someday, when I was rich, she'd tell her father about me."

Roo was stunned. Sylvia had played himself, Duncan, and now Jason for fools. After a moment, Jason said, "Mr. Avery. Please, sir, forgive me."

Looking about the woods, with Luis lying unconscious or perhaps dead across the clearing, with the women and children hiding up in a cave, Roo could only say, "It doesn't matter, Jason. None of it matters."

Softly Jason said, "She kissed me once, Mr. Avery. When no one was looking, as she got into her carriage, she leaned over and kissed my cheek." Then his eyes rolled up into his head and he died.

Roo sat motionless, not knowing whether to cry or laugh. The boy had died thinking the murdering bitch was his perfect angel. Roo had not mentioned to anyone in the camp besides Luis that Sylvia was dead. Roo silently saluted her, for she had known what to do to get what she wanted from the men she had used. For Duncan, it had been the promise of power and money; for Jason, some child's story of the princess and commoner finding true love—a kiss on the cheek and love notes; and for Roo? Roo laughed a bitter laugh as he let Jason's head fall to the damp ground. He rose, thinking, For Roo she had promised a perfect love that doesn't exist.

Before meeting Sylvia, Roo never had any idea that love was anything other than a myth believed by people less intelligent than he, or a useful lie to get a town girl to spread her legs, but never had he felt the lie of love to be so monstrous as he did at this minute. Even from the grave Sylvia haunted his thoughts. He reached Luis's side thinking it unfathomable how three men could look at the same woman and see three different women, or how each could believe her lies so readily. And he couldn't understand how he could still feel such longing for her while detesting her so deeply.

Luis's breathing was shallow, and his complexion was waxy. He groaned when Roo tried to move him, and tried to help as Roo picked him up, slipping his uninjured shoulder under Luis's good arm. Half staggering, half dragging his friend, Roo tried to get him to the cave.

When he was a short distance from it, Helen Jacoby looked out, and when she saw Roo struggling to bring Luis to the mouth of the cave, she hurried down and helped the exhausted Roo.

They got Luis inside, and Roo discovered that the cave was large, though shallow. It was illuminated enough from outside that he could see everything clearly. Karli gasped as they entered the cave, and tears welled up in her eyes as she asked, "Jason?"

Roo shook his head.

Helen began tending to Luis while Karli tried to keep her own distress from further upsetting the children. "Who were they?" Karli asked.

"Deserters, from the Queen's army."

"Will there be more?" asked Helen.

"Undoubtedly," answered Roo, resting on the cave floor a minute. "I don't know if they're going to be heading this way, but it means we have to be wary of any riders or men on foot we spy until we know for a fact they're Kingdom soldiers."

He sighed and stood up. "I need to find those horses and see if they have anything useful on them." He also needed to bury Jason and the four dead men, but he thought it best not to speak of it.

Staggering down the hill, Roo saw that the wounded horse was only a few yards away, but the other three had wandered up the hillside and were trying to eat the small patches of grass that grew around a small clearing. Roo wasn't the expert that Erik was when it came to horses, but one look at the deep wound in the horse's flank told him he wouldn't recover without a healer's aide; there was bone exposed and the horse limped as if hobbled.

He walked as calmly as he could to where the three horses grazed, and made clicking sounds and talked softly. Two of the horses started to move away, but one remained close enough for him to get his hands on its bridle. Roo checked the bedroll and found a few items of worth inside, a silver candlestick and some coins.

Roo tied the first horse's reins to a branch on a deadfall and got the second. It also had a few items of worth on it, but nothing else of use.

The third horse was more interested in playing keep-away than in eating, so after Roo had chased it for about fifty yards, he started throwing rocks at it, attempting to drive it away so that should anyone else come across the wandering mount, it wouldn't lead them back to Roo's location.

Roo found one of Luis's daggers still stuck in one of the dead men, and he pulled it out. He quickly put down the lame horse, whose screams caused the two remaining horses to shy. But he had tied them well enough that they remained where he had left them. Then he turned to the grisly task of searching the corpses.

Like all former soldiers, he found the idea of rifling the dead repugnant, yet he knew that anything of real worth would be on these men. He discovered three pouches of gold and one of gems. Roo put the valuables on one of the two remaining horses and stockpiled the weapons. He had five daggers, a long knife, and six swords.

He carried these to the cave and deposited them inside. He asked Helen, "How's Luis?"

"Not good," she said softly. She looked at Roo and shook her head slightly.

Roo had seen enough wounds to know that Luis might not live through the night. He turned and went down the hill. He decided he'd move the horses after he disposed of the dead.

He had no shovel, so digging a grave was out of the question, unless he wanted to try to do it with one of the swords. He found a small fissure in the middle of the dry creek and rolled the dead into it. He hated the idea of burying Jason with the four deserters, but the safety of his family was more important than anything else.

He used the poorest of the six swords to dislodge dirt and cover the dead, then started carrying rocks to cover them. After an hour of this heavy labor, he was nearly exhausted and was on his knees piling up the rocks as best he could. He attempted to keep them below the lip of the fissure, so that when he sprinkled branches and leaves over it, anyone coming by might not notice the grave.

He was placing the last rock on the grave when something pushed him from behind.

Roo turned and was scrambling for the sword when he saw a curious horse looking him in the eye. The animal he had chased off had grown bored and returned, and had come down to see what he was doing. Finding the work uninteresting, the horse demanded Roo's attention.

Roo reached out quickly and grabbed its reins. The horse shied and pulled back, yanking Roo to his feet. He yanked once, cried, "Whoa!" and let pressure off so the horse didn't fly into a panic.

The animal responded and held its position. Roo led it to the others and tied it to the tree. He searched the blanket roll behind the horse's saddle and found some more gold and a gem.

Roo looked around and tried to spot a better location to hide the horses, but couldn't see one. If they were going to use them, he'd have to risk their being discovered.

Fatigue gripped him as he trudged up the hill. He thought it would be ironic in the extreme if he had gone to all the trouble of burying the five bodies only to have the three horses standing there give him away.

He looked at the dead horse and realized he'd have to attempt to cover it up before leaving, but decided he'd wait until the next day. Hiding the dead animal was pointless until he was ready to lead the living ones away.

He reached the cave mouth and found that Karli had distributed some more bread and pieces of cheese to the children. He took a hunk of each as it was handed to him and sat down. He couldn't remember ever having been this tired.

Helen said, "His breathing is better, I think."

Roo glanced over and couldn't see any difference. "I think you're right," he lied.

Roo chewed on the bread, finding it was drying out as the days wore on. Still, it was food, as was the hard cheese, and he welcomed the taste.

"We have a skin of wine," said Karli, and she handed it across to Roo.

He thanked her and took a mouthful. The wine tasted particularly piquant in combination with the yellow cheese, but Roo was glad for it.

Helen said, "What do we do?"

"There are three horses. If we can get Luis on one, and two of the children on each of the others, we can lead them out tomorrow."

Helen looked at Luis and her expression was dubious, but she said nothing. Karli tried a brave smile and failed.

Roo chewed and swallowed, and let his body rest as best it could against the rocks. After finishing his food, he stumbled out of the cave and down the hill, and returned with the four blanket rolls used by the deserters. He didn't care how filthy they were, these woods could get chilly at night and they couldn't risk a fire.

After the blankets had been spread and everyone bedded down for the night, he sat staring into the night. Time passed and for all his fatigue he couldn't risk sleeping.

Sometime in the middle of the night, Helen Jacoby appeared at his side, sitting down next to him. Softly, so as not to wake the others, she said, "I think he's going to be all right."

Roo whispered, "You've not seen a wounded man after he's been strapped to a horse for a day or two. We may kill him if we move him."

"Can't we stay another day?"

Roo said, "No. And Luis would be the first to tell me to try to get you to safety. Each day brings more soldiers, from both sides, as well as more deserters into this area."

Helen slipped her arm through his, putting her head on his shoulder as if it were the most natural act. She hugged his arm, and he was acutely aware of her full breast pressed against him and the scent of her hair. At last she said, "Thank you, Roo."

Roo said, "For what?"

"For being a kind and caring man. You've done everything for my babies a father would. You've protected us when other men would have left us in ruin and without resources."

They were quiet a long time, and then Roo felt warmth on his shoulder as her tears soaked into the fabric of his shirt. He patted her hand and could think of nothing to say.

After a silent time, she reached up and turned his head toward hers. She kissed him lightly on the lips, then softly she said, "You're a good man, Roo. The children love you." After a pause, she said, "And I love you."

Roo was silent; then he said, "You're the best woman I know, Helen. I admire you." He dropped his head, as if unable to look into her eyes, though how much she could see in this darkness was problematic. "And I'd be a liar if I said I haven't thought about you, as a man thinks of women, but to tell you the truth, I find that I can't bring myself to believe in love."

She said nothing for a long time, then rose silently and returned to the children. Roo sat alone through the rest of the night.

Twenty

Decisions

MIRANDA PACED.

Macros said, "Will you stop that, please?"

She sat. For days they had been studying the site of the rift between Midkemia and Shila, and had discovered that it had unusual properties.

Macros had spent a great deal of time investigating the structure of the magic involved and had arrived at the conclusion that the rift had been sealed from this side. He had voiced his suspicions to Miranda, who had said she had no idea what he was talking about.

Miranda said, "How long are you going to stare at that thing?"

"Until I know what it is I'm dealing with."

She sighed. "What else do you need to know?"

"Well, there is a great deal I would like to know. I would like to know how the Pantathians have succeeded in creating a rift that Pug couldn't detect. I'd like to know how they managed to create one that's different in several significant properties from any I've ever seen. This is very much like those rifts created by the accidental combination of too much magic, yet it also behaves in some very stable ways, much like the artificial rifts the Tsurani created. But what has me most concerned is that it has qualities of magic I've never thought of, let alone encountered. This one is almost 'organic,' if I had to find a word to use, something almost alive."

"Alive?"

"Most rifts are like tunnels or doorways. This one is like a . . . wound."

"You're not serious?"

"Observe," he said, and he waved his hand. Mystic energies came into being, a shimmering gate of blue-white light, woven closed with strands of what appeared to be blue-green energy, a threading of lines so tight nothing could squeeze through.

"The whiter light is the energy pulse of the rift. Notice how it seems to move slightly, like a thing breathing."

"Energy pulse?"

"Each occurrence of magic leaves a signature, a pattern of forces that can tell you a great deal about what has taken place. Rifts are both unique and common. They are unique in that each acts in a particular way, in where it comes from and where it goes to, but common in that they share many properties. This one is more unique than common. In fact, it's completely unique." He rubbed his chin. "I would love to have the opportunity to study the rift to the demon realm. It might give me a clue to who built this one." He sat back with a sigh. "I'm certain it wasn't the Pantathians. Someone else gave them the tools to do this."

"Who?"

"I don't know." He pointed at the rift. "This one was opened from the other side. If you get a chance to study enough of these fissures in space and time, you'll be able to tell the difference between the sending side and the receiving side, or if it's a two-way gate—this is a two-way gate." He shook his head in obvious wonder. "Now, this other energy," he said, pointing to the weaving, "this is even stranger."

"What is it?"

"A barrier, obviously, but one that puzzles me." He motioned for her to come closer. "What do you see here?" he asked, pointing to several of the strands.

"Dark green strands."

"Hmmm. To me they're more of a lime color. Anyway, look closer."

She leaned forward and studied the strands. "There's something irregular about this."

"Yes!" he said with delight. "I think they have been sundered and reconnected."

"By whom?"

Macros sat. "If what Hanam has told us is entirely accurate, he was the uninvited guest when the third demon was sent through. I suspect the first two encountered Pantathians. The first one fought and killed many, while the second, this Jakan, slipped away to safety. The first demon may have been the one you witnessed when you came here with Calis: the huge killer, driven mad or mindless by the Pantathians' magic."

"So Jakan slipped away, started sneaking around the halls, killing as he went and building up his strength," Miranda said.

"Yes. Eventually the Pantathians rallied, and sealed this rift again."

"That must have been when we found their deepest enclave and killed those high priests."

Macros nodded. "I wondered what happened to the first demon."

Miranda looked around. "Dead? I hope."

Macros laughed. "If he's still around, I think the two of us can deal with him. He won't have had much to eat, and from what you told me, he didn't appear to have much of a mind left."

Miranda said, "It's hard to appraise the intellect of a demon when it's embroiled in a battle with a dozen Pathathian serpent priests."

"True," he agreed. "There are three different ways we could approach this. We could wait to see if something else tries to break through from the other side. Or we could attempt to unwrap these barrier forces, letting whatever is on the other side come through unaided. Or we could destroy the barrier and go through to the other side."

"I like the fourth choice."

"Which is?"

"We do our best to reinforce the barrier."

Macros shook his head. "No, that won't do."

"Why not?"

Macros looked at his daughter. "I take it you haven't studied rifts much?"

"Not at all. I know next to nothing about them."

Macros shrugged. "Well, there's a large volume of my work on the subject in Pug's library. But given we can't risk the time to return there and wait while you study, let me sum up: no matter what barriers we add to those already in existence, as long as the rift exists it can be opened. We not only have to destroy it, we have to ensure that the demons don't create another."

"I was under the impression the demons followed the Pantathian rift," Miranda said. "Or is there something else here you're not telling me?"

"Not really. Just that it's foolish to make assumptions. We both know we have things locked away up here." He tapped his head with his forefinger. "We both feel comfortable that the knowledge is locked away for a good reason, but we are foolish not to draw a few likely conclusions from the fact of that hidden knowledge."

"Such as?"

"Such as there may be yet another player who had a hand in the creation of these rifts. From what we know, the demons seized the advantage when the mad priests of Ahsart opened the seal between their realm and Shila, but no one has asked who built that portal in the first place. Why were the priests of Ahsart driven to open the rift to the demon realm? What compulsion or obsession involved them in that particular idiocy?

"We also know that the Pantathians came here easily with the Saaur, yet the demons must struggle to come here, and given the conflict between them, they are not allies."

"Or at least allies who had a falling out."

"That's possible," admitted her father.

Miranda said, "Well, we can chat about this until the world ends. What do you suggest?"

"We wait. I have a feeling that when Pug and Hanam finish on their side of the rift, things might get lively here."

Miranda sighed. "Do we have the time?"

Macros shrugged. "Enough for a few more days."

She stood. "Then I'm going to transport to Sorcerer's Isle and get a bath. I'll bring back some food."

Macros shook his head. "Don't bother. Tell Gathis I'll be along shortly. I'll visit with him while I eat there. It will be good to see him again. Then I intend to take a bath as well."

She smiled. "Good. I wasn't going to say anything . . ."

He returned her smile. "I know I haven't been a father to you, but I must say I'm pleased with the woman I see here."

"Thank you," she said stiffly.

"Before you go, I would like to know one thing."

"What?"

"Pug?"

"What about him?"

"Are you going to wed?"

"If he asks me," she said. "I love him and think we could have a good life together."

Macros said, "I have demonstrated without question no expertise when it comes to falling in love." He sighed in memory. "Your mother was a woman of remarkable beauty and uncommon guile. I can't claim I was young, but I was inexperienced, and at first our time together was pleasant." He frowned as he said, "Your birth was something neither one of us dealt with well, and for that I apologize."

Miranda said, "What's done is done."

"True, but at least I can say I regret some of it."

"Only some of it?"

"Well, I do like how you turned out, and if I could I don't know what I would change, for to change anything in your past would risk turning you into less than you are now."

"Or more?"

He smiled. "I don't see how that's possible."

She smiled at her father. "Thank you for that."

"I mean it." He sat back and stared at the rift. "Pug is fortunate, and if he doesn't ask you, you do the asking. I think you need each other."

"I thought you said you had no expertise."

"It's a father's prerogative to give unwelcome advice. Now run along and take your bath."

She vanished, and he sighed. He let regrets about past failings fade into the background as he returned his attention to the rift and wondered what was happening on the other side.

* * *

Pug stood panting, his robe torn and his face bathed in perspiration. He and Hanam had fought a battle with six man-size fliers, and the conflict had come close to ending their quest.

One of the creatures alone would not be any match for either of them, but three on Pug and three on the Saaur Loremaster had proved a close thing. Hanam feasted on the three remaining dead demons. Pug had vaporized the other three.

He watched in fascination as Hanam ate flesh and drank energies. As he shifted his perceptions, he could see how the Saaur Loremaster had used his intelligence to subvert the creature. When he was finished eating, Hanam said, "This feast will make it easier for me to concentrate."

"How far have we to go?"

"The demons are not that clever, but they are being driven to wider patrols looking for anything to eat." Pointing to the bits of flesh thrown around the rocks on which they stood, he said, "These would have been required to bring back anything they found to Cibul, to feed those captains attempting to open the rift to your world." He glanced around, as if apprehensive about further detection. "By traveling along this course, we avoid many of the demons."

"We have been flying over ice and mountains for a day and more," said Pug.

"True." The demon form pointed to the south. "There we will find Cibul. We may be able to come close before we have to hide ourselves from demon sense. And be warned, the spells you use to confound the simple demons may not suffice for the captains and lords."

"I will do what needs to be done."

"Then we must plan," Hanam said. "I have no wish to continue this life. My soul begs to be joined with my brothers in the Sky Horde, here on Shila. So here is what I propose. Let me attack whichever great lord we may discover, drawing off any guards and servants nearby. That will give you time to examine and close the rift to the demon realm."

Pug said, "A brave plan, but I don't know if it will gain me enough time. There are things here that worry me. I have the vanity to think I know as much about the nature of rift magic as anyone, including Macros, and until I saw the empty altar at Ahsart, I would have told you that an open rift could not be moved in the fashion you describe. That means there are forces at play beyond my knowledge. It may also mean that closing the rift may be beyond my ability."

"What will you do if that is the case?"

Pug said, "I will do the only thing I can think of: destroy the rift to Midkemia and hope that is enough."

"With Macros attempting the same feat from the other side, will you be able to?"

"Undoubtedly one of us will succeed."

"Then let us go among them and do what we can."

The demon figure launched himself outward, with a snap of gigantic wings, gliding down the mountain slope rather than flying. He let his downward speed build up, and then, with a flex of his wings, he was soaring high in the air. Pug used his magic to fly after him.

They dove and flew close to the ground, in the hope of avoiding detection. Pug glanced to the west and saw the sun set. The lack of light would help a little, though demons saw at night almost as well as cats.

Above a world devastated by forces alien to anything Pug had witnessed in his life they flew; from trees to grass, from humans to the smallest insect, the lands around the once-great city of Cibul were devoid of life. Pug could sense it was more than the destruction of war or forest fire, where the land was burned, for there a sign of life would be seen here or there, even if only a blade of grass.

Here there was nothing.

They were within a mile of the city when Hanam said, "Cloak our passage, magician."

Pug forced his mind into the difficult task of rendering the two of them invisible while flying. He felt terrible pain from the unusual exertion but accomplished the requirements for both without faltering. For a few minutes the pain lingered, then it began to lessen as Pug mastered this combination of magics.

As they flew over the city, several demons below turned to look up, as if sensing something, but none gave alarm. Pug hoped they would reach their destination soon.

Hanam landed in what had once been a lush garden, and now was a burned-out mass of dead plants on rock. No moss or lichen, algae or mold clung to the tiniest corner of this formerly flourishing place.

Once they were safely inside a vast hall, Pug dropped the spell of invisibility. "Are you all right?" asked the Saaur Loremaster.

"It will take a minute for me to regain my strength. I need to catch my breath." Pug managed a smile. "It's getting easier to do this, but I'd rather not have to practice in the future under these conditions."

"Understood. Abide here awhile. I will be back."

So saying, the Saaur Loremaster in demon body left the room. Pug sat on the wreckage of a once-grand bed, on a piece large enough to provide him a comfortable resting place. The faint evening light could not hide the opulence of the residence. A Saaur noble of rank had slept here, perhaps the leader or his primary consort.

Pug heard a faint scuffle outside and was on his feet as Hanam entered, carrying a struggling demon by the head. As Pug watched, the Saaur cracked the skull and drank the creature's life energies.

"Is that wise?" asked Pug.

"Necessary. If I am to face Tugor or Maarg, and hold them at bay even for a few minutes, I must gather as much strength as possible. If I prayed for a chance of victory, I would lie in wait for months, killing as many demons as possible, until they became aware of my hunt and sought me out. After I battled the hunters and survived, I would then come and announce myself to the one whom I challenged. At that point I would be granted single combat.

"But I have no desire to win. I wish release from this prison." He tapped the crystal vial hanging from a chain around his neck. "This is a favor I must ask of you, magician." He removed the vial and handed it to Pug. "When the battle is high, release my soul by smashing the vial."

"What will happen?"

"I will be free, and the demon whose body I control will be destroyed. But if that vial isn't broken, any demon who found it would be able to continue my captivity."

Pug nodded and took the vial, placing it inside his robe.

"Time is short," said the Loremaster. "Come."

They hurried through several halls to a large chamber, where several other demons gathered. Two rifts hung in the air, only a few meters apart, while strange cloaked figures, hunched over and shambling, moved between them. The demons didn't notice them.

"What are they?" asked Hanam.

"I recognize them," said Pug. "They are Shangri, also called *Panath-Tiandn*, creatures I have faced once before. They live on a world called Timiri, where magic is a solid matter, manipulated by machine and will. They may be related to the Pantathians. I still don't know their part in all this."

"What are they doing?"

"They've moved both rifts!" Pug exclaimed. "They mean to create a direct path from the demon realm to Midkemia!"

"Then Maarg is soon to come through."

A demon turned and saw them, and screeched an alarm. Hanam didn't hesitate, but launched himself at the creature. Rather than engage the first creature, who crouched, claws extended in anticipate of the attack, he leaped past, slashing its throat with a talon.

One demon, larger than Pug could have imagined possible, turned and shouted, "Hold!"

Hanam screamed, "Tugor! I challenge! Meet me and die!"

The other demons fell back. Pug didn't know if they ignored him because of the challenge, but he rendered himself invisible.

Hanam and Maarg's captain squared off. Pug saw at once that Hanam had been right, for in a fair fight, Tugor would quickly destroy the lesser demon. But what the captain didn't understand was that the Loremaster of the Saaur faced him, not another lesser demon, and that being was prepared to die.

Pug hurried to the two rifts and attempted to make some sense of them. The two shambling creatures ignored the demons, working like automatons on the two rifts. When Pug had first encountered these creatures, years before, he had found them nearly mindless servants of an unknown dark power, technicians of magic, clever in their ability to work the solid form of what was an invisible force on Midkemia, but without a strong intellect. They had been servants of others then, and here again they were servants.

Once more Pug confronted the knowledge locked away in his own mind, and he intuited that these creatures were serving whatever the greater power behind this madness might be. He knew that to dwell further on their part in this would be to risk distraction.

He quietly stunned both creatures, letting them fall to the floor.

He quickly studied the rift to the demon realm, and realized it was readily opened at any time. He decided Maarg, their great ruler, was waiting safely in his own realm until his captain opened the rift to Midkemia. Then he could easily cross into the lush, life-filled world without long pause in Shila.

Pug turned to study the other rift with the thought that should Maarg reach Midkemia, he might be in for a rude surprise should Jakan reach the Lifestone.

Screams of pain and rage filled the hall as Tugor fought Hanam. The demon lord was injured, because rather than keep his distance, the smaller demon closed and accepted wounds in exchange for giving them.

Pug tried to ignore the combat, knowing seconds counted. He looked at the Midkemian rift and saw the Shangri were on the verge of punching through whatever barriers had been erected on the other side. His intervention had forestalled that.

Then a chilling presence behind Pug caused him to cease moving. A voice that ground his bones together said, "What have we here?"

Pug turned and looked into the face of horror.

A face the size of dragon's leered at him though the rift.

For a brief instant Pug was astonished to witness a rift that was as transparent as a window, that looked like a hole in the wall between two worlds, but that fascination lasted less than a second, for it was what confronted him through that transparent rift that demanded his undivided attention.

While the other demons looked muscular and powerful, Maarg looked gross. Jowls hung down from a face eight feet from brow to chin. Fire burned in the pits of its eyes, and evil emanated from it like a visible miasma of black smoke. The creature's face seemed fashioned from the skins of living beings, which still moved and twitched in agony. A face contorted in torment was stretched across Maarg's right cheek, mouthing silent screams while a clawed hand moved feebly along his right jawline. Details of the various bodies devoured and incorporated into the Demon King became evident as the creature moved closer to the other side of the rift to inspect Pug.

The figure behind the face was immense. Maarg must have stood thirty-five feet tall when upright. His body was likewise covered with other beings, twitching and undulating in the faint red light of the demon home world. Wings to hide the sun spread out behind him, and a long tail with the head of a serpent at the tip writhed behind him, hissing and spitting at Pug from over Maarg's shoulder.

Pug didn't hesitate. He knew instantly he was overmatched. He turned and with all the power he could muster, he blasted open the rift to Midkemia.

"Tugor!" came the cry from the other side of the demon rift as the room rang with the explosion of powers Pug unleashed. The rift to Midkemia seemed to contract, then expand, then rush forward with a tremendous ripping sound.

Then Pug was staring at Macros and Miranda.

Macros returned from his bath and a meal. "That was delightful. I can't tell you how much I've missed Sorcerer's Isle."

Miranda said, "Has it changed much?"

"A great deal. Pug has it crawling with students, some rather interesting ones, I must say. Gathis is the same as always. It's as if I had left yesterday." Macros sighed. "I'm afraid he's become something of a fixture there. It would be a shame to ask him to leave with all the good work he's doing for Pug. Why—"

Suddenly he looked wide-eyed and distracted.

"What?" asked Miranda.

"I don't know. Something—"

Before he could finish, the silence in the cave was shattered by a tremendous keening sound. Abruptly, the rift before them ripped open and Pug stood on the other side of a window between worlds, looking at them. Behind him a vision of horror reared up into view.

Miranda raised a mystic shield to protect herself, reflexively, but her father reacted by leaping forward, landing on the other side of the rift beside Pug. He unleashed a furious blast of mystic energy, which tore through the opened rift into the demons' realm, striking the Demon King in the face. The horror that was Maarg reared back, shrieking in pain.

Miranda followed her father and shouted, "What is going on?"

Pug said, "They've moved the rift. We arrived just as Maarg was preparing to come across!"

Macros said, "You must close both rifts, now!"

Pug looked at Miranda's father and said, "What are you going to do?"

"Distract that thing," he said, and he leaped through the rift into the demon realm.

"Father!" shouted Miranda. "No!"

Pug spared a glance to the other struggle, and saw that Hanam had managed to sink his fangs into Tugor's neck. Pug was no judge of such things, but it appeared to him the Loremaster might take his foe with him into death. The other demons in the room shrank back, for to them there would emerge a victor, Tugor whom they feared, or another who had destroyed Tugor, making him one to fear even more.

At the other side of the demon rift, Maarg fell back as Macros's flames seared his face. Then he raised an arm, to shield his face, and screamed in pain. Macros kept the blast of blue flame directed at the Demon King's head.

Pug quickly examined the rift. He said, "This one is much like that created by the Tsurani Great Ones, to reach Midkemia. It is vulnerable, from within."

"From within?" said Miranda in astonishment. "How do we get inside a rift?"

Pug looked around it one last time, and said, "By attacking it from the void."

They risked a glance at Macros as he continued to press his attack against the Demon King, who backed away. Perhaps it was that a relatively small creature dared to confront him, or that he had not been forced to face a challenger in years, but Maarg was on the defensive. He now used his great wings as a cloak, keeping Macros's flames from his eyes.

Macros's spell ended, and the flames vanished. Maarg regarded the intruder and reached forward, as if to seize Macros in his huge hand. Macros raised both arms above his head and brought them down in a quick gesture, and yellow flames seemed to explode from within his body. The Demon King seized him around the waist, and screamed in pain and fury as the sorcerer withstood his direct attack.

Miranda said, "Can we help him?"

Pug said, "No. We must close this rift."

"We can't. Father will be stranded in the demon realm."

Pug calmly said, "He knew that."

Miranda stared at her lover a long moment, then nodded once.

Pug said, "We also may not survive this closure."

Miranda said, "Tell me what to do."

"First, keep them off our backs." He pointed to two demons who had left the spectacle to investigate what was occurring between the two rifts.

Miranda said, "Gladly," and sent out a bolt of mystic energy, a blue light that engulfed the two demons and left them writhing in agony, while Pug finished his examination of the rift.

Pug turned his attention from the rift to the struggle beyond it, as the Demon King attempted to crush Macros with his bare hands. The sorcerer was held in the demon's grip, but he had his hands free, and he cast another spell while the mystic yellow flames kept him from being crushed. Sparkling white lights appeared around the Demon King and started spinning. Each looked like a diamond, reflecting light off myriad facets, and as they spun, they took on a sinister aspect. As they moved, they swooped in and out in a weaving pattern, and when they touched Maarg, he shrieked in agony.

"Kelton's knives," said Pug.

Miranda said, "That's a particularly nasty spell."

The mystic blades continued to pick up speed, buzzing around the Demon King, but while he was being cut over most of his body, he still held fast to Macros. "Human!" he shrieked. "You shall reside in a soul jar for eternity, to be tormented every instant for this!"

Macros managed to shout, "First you have to kill me."

Pug said, "It's time. Come with me."

He took Miranda's hand and they jumped into the rift, but rather than continue through, he halted their flight in the void.

Miranda waited to be told what to do. Pug had cautioned her that some rifts could be closed only from inside, and that was what her father and he had had to do during the Riftwar. The difference then was that Pug had been able to return to Midkemia from the void because of a staff Macros had given him, one that was linked with another that Pug's old teacher, Kulgan, had kept tightly bound to Midkemian soil.

Pug prayed that his advanced skills over the last fifty years would allow him to get home by force of will.

Miranda's thoughts came to him in the void. *I love you.*

Pug replied, *And I you. Let us begin.*

Cold unlike anything Miranda had experienced gripped both of them. Their lungs cried for air. But their magic gave them minutes where lesser beings would have perished in seconds.

Pug wove powerful magic. Miranda aided him where she could, taking instructions from him, and in this place without time it seemed to take forever for the great spell to form. When it seemed the task would never finish, it was done.

Pug said, *Now!*

Miranda gave him all her power and felt her body drain of strength.

Pug shattered the rift.

In a moment they saw the grey fabric of the void splinter into shards, and behind those shards they glimpsed another reality. Pug recognized it from his fever dream, when injured, and knew behind the void lay the realm of the gods.

Then they saw, as through a window, the struggle in the demon realm. Maarg gripped Macros and burned in flames that were running up his arms from the sorcerer, causing the demon's flesh to ripple and crisp, but Maarg continued to crush Macros's defenses, and the sorcerer screamed in pain as his will weakened. The Demon King dropped to his knees, as the sorcerer's attacks took their toll, but he refused to relinquish his grip on the Black One.

"Die!" he roared, and he attempted to bite Macros's head from his shoulders. But the legendary sorcerer's defenses held, and the foot-long fangs couldn't close on Macros.

Then the demon's tail appeared over his shoulder and the serpent head hissed, revealing long, poison-dripping fangs. The thing struck, but with an unbelievable display of will and strength, Macros seized the thing and turned it so that its fangs plunged into Maarg's wrist.

The Demon King cried out and released Macros, letting the sorcerer fall to the hot stone floor of his den.

Then the window seemed to close, to grow smaller or more distant, they couldn't tell which. Miranda shouted, *Father!*

Macros seemed aware of them, stealing a glance in their direction. He sent one thought, *They are creatures of fire*, then he redoubled his attack on the demon, one that was met by more fury.

As the window through which they looked closed, a chilling presence appeared. Pug felt fear beyond any he had known so far in his life, a fear that threatened to break his concentration as he attempted to return them to Cibul. The presence was outside the window through which they peered, and beyond it, next to them, and a vast distance away. It was everywhere. It was profoundly evil, and it was aware. Yet it seemed to be speaking from within the rift, from the demon realm. The presence said, *You are mine, at last!*

Macros shouted, "Never!" and before Pug and Miranda lost sight of him, he raised his hands high over his head, and for the briefest instant, instead of the plainly dressed sorcerer, clad in his familiar brown homespun robe with his whipcord belt, his cross-gartered sandals, and his plain oak staff, a being of profound wisdom and strength rose up, a godlike being of unknowable mystery. He lashed out with a white ivory staff that appeared out of the air, and, touching the Demon King, he created a blinding flash of white light that filled the closing window. With the dying scream of the Demon King, absent its rage and power, now the wailing cry of a creature reduced to terror and pain, a triumphal sense of victory washed over Pug and Miranda.

Pug did not know how he knew, but in that instant he felt the presence of Sarig, as Macros reached across space and time and reconnected with his god.

Then the rift was closed, and Pug said, *Now!*

Using what was left of his strength, he forced his way through the very fabric of the void, dragging himself and Miranda back to the hall of the Saaur in Cibul.

For one brief moment, they witnessed the finality of Hanam's battle with Tugor, as the two lay on the floor, each too weak to best the other, neither able to escape. When it was obvious that neither would survive, the remaining demons leaped atop the two, rending them limb from limb.

Remembering his promise, Pug withdrew the soul vial he had been given, and smashed it upon the stones.

A brief thought came to Pug, *Thank you!* and then it was gone.

Miranda was half-stunned from the experience, and Pug had to almost push her through the rift to Midkemia.

On the other side, back in the Pantathian mines under the Ratn'gari Mountains, Miranda sank down to sit on the floor, her back against the cool rocks.

Pug sat next to her, his head in his hands, and he said, "We only have a moment. We must close this rift."

She said, "How?"

"This is different from the first. This must be closed the way one would sew a wound."

He sat a long moment, then took a deep breath. He waved his hands, and faint energies left his fingers, snaking out toward the rift. Around the edges they flew, and as Miranda found her strength starting to return along with warmth, she saw Pug's energies forming a lattice work around the edges of the rift.

Then Pug changed the spell, and the binding energies he had cast around the edges of the rift began to contract. Miranda watched for a minute, then said, "I see."

She gathered together her strength, watching in fascination as the rift closed slowly. While she rested she considered what she had just witnessed. She had known her father briefly, having spent most of her life tracing him through his legend. He had not visited her since she had turned sixteen or seventeen, she couldn't remember which, and she had spent most of her life holding the man in contempt.

But as she had discovered her mother's part in the destruction of hundreds of thousands of lives, she reassessed her father's role in things. She was discovering that even at her advanced age, she still felt like a child in some ways.

She thought she would have grown to like her father, perhaps even love him someday, but now that day would never come. For that she felt regret.

But for the loss of his life compared to the deaths of thousands she had already seen, she couldn't find a means to compare; perhaps someday she'd mourn him, or at least mourn the loss of an opportunity, later, when she had time. If she had time.

Suddenly a face appeared on the other side of the rift, looking like a cow's skull stretched over with black hide, topped by a stag's rack of antlers. Coals for eyes burned in it, and they regarded the two humans.

With a howl of glee the demon, obviously the final victor in the carnage that had just finished in the great chamber in Cibul, flushed with a feeding of tremendous scope, started to leap through the rift.

"Stop it!" shouted Pug, and Miranda lashed out with all her remaining strength. It was enough to knock the demon back into the other world, and stun it.

Miranda almost fainted from the effort. In a hoarse voice she said, "Hurry. I have nothing left."

Pug concentrated his entire focus on continuing to close the rift. Miranda could see that as the rift became smaller the rate of closing was accelerating.

Then the demon was back, cautious in its approach. It feinted toward the rift, then ducked back, pausing a moment.

When no further attack came from Miranda, it tried to climb through, much as a human climbs through a window.

First the creature's head poked through, then one arm. It reached for Pug, but found him still too far away. The creature turned sideways, and started to put one leg through, but found its large wings a hindrance. It shifted position, and tried another angle, not noticing that the aperture was closing by the second.

Unable to pass, the creature became enraged with frustration, and tried to force his way through the rift. A headlong dive managed to get it wedged within the rift.

Then pressure began to exert as Pug continued closing the rift.

Rage turned to panic, then to pain and terror as the rift closed on the creature. Howling as it was being cut in two, the demon thrashed like a fish on the deck of a boat.

Miranda took a breath, tried to add her energy to Pug's, and felt the rift closing even more quickly. The demon's cries echoed through the Pantathian halls, resounding off the rocks and shaking the very mountains.

Dust rained down on Miranda and Pug as the creature's thrashing increased, then suddenly it went limp. A moment later, the rift closed, and the upper half of the demon fell into the cave.

Miranda looked at it and said, "We did it?" Then she passed out.

Pug said, "Yes," and he, too, collapsed on the floor, unconscious as the last reserve of his strength was paid out.

Twenty-one

Escalation

ERIK WATCHED.

In the fields below the foothills, a huge mobilization was beginning. He had just enjoyed a week of relative calm, but now that was obviously coming to an end.

For a month they had been relatively successful in forcing the invaders along the route they had designed for them. There had been reports of hard fighting to the north and south, but the Kingdom lines had held on both flanks as the middle had slowly retreated, drawing the invaders after.

Twice they had come close to disaster, narrowly escaping along the retreat route, and at each new position along the way fresh reserves were waiting. Erik was still far from optimistic about the success of the plan, but he was inching closer.

Since the fall of Krondor they had regained a week of the lost time; they had held here for ten days instead of seven. Now they had to fight a delaying action as they withdrew, slowing the enemy down by making them think there was going to be strong resistance in Wilhelmsburg. If they could keep the enemy cautious, they might be where they wished to be when the fighting reached Darkmoor. Every time Erik thought of the plan to hold the enemy on this side of the mountains, he wondered if they were going to be cursed with a late winter.

One advantage had been the arrival of a man named Robert d' Lyes, a magician who had several useful spells. He could send messages up the line quickly to another magician who was staying with Greylock, and he could tell what the weather was going to be like the next day. He also could see things better than a man with a spyglass, though he could do so only for a limited duration; and he lacked Erik's knowledge of what to look for, but he seemed to be catching on.

Other magicians were now scattered throughout the defenders' army, helping in whatever fashion they could. For this Erik was grateful. He didn't understand why the Pantathians were so conspicuous by their absence. Eventually they would take a hand, and when they did, Erik hoped the Kingdom magicians could counteract some of their advantage.

D' Lyes came to Erik's side and said, "General Greylock wants to know if you expect an attack today."

Erik said, "Almost certainly."

Erik glanced around. To the north the hills faded quickly into the late afternoon haze. They were entering the hilly vineyards and groves he had known as a boy. To the uninitiated, the terrain looked less severe than the low hills to the west, but it wasn't. Unexpected ridges and gullies could trap an enemy, slowing an advance. In the fervent hope this was going to be the case, Erik had positioned his most seasoned soldiers in key locations to the limit of his area. He would have to rely on Captain Subai and his Pathfinders and Hadati—what Greylock called the Krondorian Mixed Command—to hold beyond that point.

To the south, Erik threw his larger contingency, fresh replacements who were as yet untried. They would have an easier time of it because of the terrain, but they were also less ready to fight. Many of those carrying arms were town boys who had drilled less than two months and had never smelled blood.

Erik said, "Ask Greylock to be ready to support me to the south. I think my north flank is secure."

The magician closed his eyes, and his brow knitted in concentration; he said, "The message is understood." Then he sat down, obviously dizzy.

"Are you all right?" asked Erik.

The magician nodded. "It's just that I don't usually do this sort of thing more than once or twice a month. Once or twice a day is a bit much."

"Well, I'll try to keep message traffic to a minimum." He smiled. "I just wish I had more like you in a dozen locations."

The magician nodded. "As long as we're useful."

"More than useful," said Erik. "You may prove vital."

"Thank you," said the magician. "I am willing to help in whatever way I can."

Erik waited, and as the enemy staged below he found himself wondering aloud, "What is this, then?"

"Captain?" asked the magician.

"Just curious. They are staging for an assault, but it looks badly coordinated."

"How can you tell?"

Erik said, "This army we face is made up mostly of mercenaries: good fighters individually, but possessing almost no skills for large-scale fighting; they're used to winning by overwhelming whomever they face." He pointed to a small patch of uniformed men with green banners flying overhead. "That's what's left of the regular army of Maharta, which surrendered pretty much intact after the city fell. It's the only trained heavy infantry they possess. The other soldiers on foot are men whose horses were left behind or whose animals died along the way. They're useless for anything except swarming over a breach." Erik scratched his chin and felt four days' growth.

"I think I understand, but I may not. Are you saying they should have placed their men in a different arrangement?" asked the magician.

"Yes," said Erik. "The cavalry has to charge over hilly terrain, while the heavy infantry is being directed at the most heavily defended area of the line. The rest of the army looks poised to charge right across open territory where our catapults and archers will carve them up."

"I see."

Erik grinned. "You're being polite. Let's say that if I were on the other side, I'd use my cavalry in the middle, to screen and deliver cover fire, while I brought up my heavy infantry to attack just north of here." He pointed to a problem point in his defensive line, a modest gully where he hadn't had enough time or matériel to build a proper defensive position. "If I could punch through there, then that motley army down there could pour through and wreak havoc."

"Let's hope they don't think of it."

"They should," Erik said softly. "What I can't fathom is why they don't." Suddenly he said, "Send a message to Greylock, if you can. Tell him I think this massing here is possibly a feint to get us to concentrate our efforts, then spring an attack somewhere else along the line."

The magician smiled, though he looked fatigued. "I'll try."

Erik didn't wait to see if the magician was successful, but sent runners to the north, south, and east. After a few minutes, the magician shook his head and said, "I'm sorry, but I just can't focus my will anymore."

"You've done enough. We're pulling out tomorrow. I think it would be wise if you started toward the next defensive position to the east. If you leave now, you should reach a safe camp by sundown. Tell the quartermaster I authorized you be given a horse."

"I can't ride, Captain."

Erik looked over his shoulder. "Some sort of magic means to move quickly?"

"No, I'm sorry to say."

As trumpets blew down at the bottom of the hill, Erik said, "Then I suggest you start walking and get as far as you can on foot. If you're not near a friendly campfire, find someplace sheltered to hunker down. Sometime in the morning the wagon carrying the wounded will come past you; flag it down and get a ride. I'll pass word to pick you up."

"Can't I stay?"

Another trumpet blew and Erik drew his sword. "I wouldn't advise it." As he turned away he said, "Now, if you'll excuse me."

An arrow sped by overhead, a wild shot from someone below who was overanxious. Erik glanced over his shoulder and saw the magician running to the east with surprisingly renewed strength. Erik took the moment to indulge himself in a chuckle at the sight, then turned his attention to the bloody work ahead.

"All right," he shouted. "Archers, pick your targets and wait until I give the order."

A familiar voice came from behind as Sergeant Harper said, "Captain von Darkmoor, you're forgetting yourself. If you don't mind, sir?" He turned and said, "First one of you mother-lovers who lets fly an arrow before I give the word's going to have to run down there and fetch it back to me! Understood?"

Erik smiled again. He had never gotten the knack of being a proper bully sergeant and was pleased to have men like Harper, Alfred, and the others under his command.

Then the enemy came.

Erik welcomed the darkness. The enemy was retreating down the hillside, but had left his men in tatters. He had been wrong about the feint. The only reason he still held his position had been the enemy's ineptitude. They had charged straight up the hill, into first the withering missile fire of the Kingdom's archers, then a rain of the short, soft iron spears Erik's commands had been training with since he had first come to serve Calis. Hundreds of the enemy had died for each yard traveled, and they had still reached the first trench.

The defense had been a series of trenches and breastworks cut along the contours of the hillsides, and whatever natural slope of the landscape concentrated the attackers, there they found overlapping fields of missile fire waiting for them. When the survivors of the first wave reached the first breastwork, they found a highly banked, hard-packed earthen barrier, studded with sharp wooden spikes. The spikes caused little damage but forced the attackers to move slowly, making them easy targets for the defenders.

But they had come and kept coming. After the first hour, Erik felt as if he would never be able to raise his arms again, but still he had to fight on. During the fighting, someone—a squire or town boy, he didn't know which—had come by with a bucket of water and handed him a tin ladle during a tiny lull. He had drunk it quickly, handing the ladle back to the boy, and resumed fighting a moment later.

For what seemed an eternity, Erik fought, striking down any head that appeared on the other side of the redoubt. Then the enemy was fleeing, unwilling to continue pressing the attack as the sun began to sink beyond the western horizon.

Torches were lit, as much for reassurance as for the need—the twilight this time of year was lengthy—and those designated as hopitalers—local boys, old men and women, and court squires and pages—all started carrying water and food to the living, then carrying away the wounded and dead.

Erik turned and sat where he had been fighting, ignoring the dead soldier from Novindus who lay in the dirt next to him. When a boy with water came by, Erik took a single drink, passing along the rest of the water to the men nearby.

Soon a runner arrived with a note. He opened and read it, then, feeling so fatigued he didn't know if he could will himself to move, he shouted, "Fall back!"

As if by magic, Sergeant Harper appeared. "We're pulling out, sir?"

"That's it."

"Then we're making for the next defensive position?"

"We are."

The wily old Sergeant said, "Then we'll not be seeing much sleep tonight, will we?"

Erik said, "I expect not. What is your point, Sergeant?"

"Oh, none, Captain. I just wanted to make sure I understood everything."

Erik fixed the Sergeant with a baleful eye. "I think you understand just fine, Sergeant."

"Well, then, just so as it's clear I'm not the one making lads who've spent a half day fighting pick up and move without a drop to drink or a bite to eat."

Erik realized the men were ready to drop. "I think we can hold off, then, until we've eaten."

"That's lovely, sir. It'll give us a bit of time to haul away the dead and get the wounded out in the wagons. A wise choice, sir."

Erik sat down again. As Harper moved along, Erik said to himself, "And I had the presumption to call myself a sergeant."

The withdrawal was more difficult than Erik would have liked. Despite the food and rest for two hours, the men were still bone-tired when they were turned to march to the east.

Erik inventoried his assets and realized he was beginning to see elements of those men he had trained over the last two years, two companies of men who knew how to handle themselves, who had arrived from a position to the north.

Word came down that the enemy had broken through up north, but the gap had been closed. The bad news was that a contingent, numbering at least three hundred, possibly more, was loose on the wrong side of this current line of march. Erik sent his best scouts to the north, and hoped that if the invaders were coming this way, they would blunder into one of the heavier elements. Three hundred raiders could do quite a bit of damage to one of the smaller companies on the march before reinforcements could be summoned.

Just before sunrise, Erik found a solitary figure marching next to him, the magician Robert d' Lyes. "Hello, magician."

"Hello, Captain. I found a small rock under which to hide," he said with dry humor, "but instead of a wagon I find an army marching my way."

"I told you we were leaving," Erik said dryly. "I just didn't think we'd be leaving so quickly."

"So I see. How goes the war?"

Erik said, "I wish I knew. So far we've done well, but that last attack showed me we're still seriously outmanned."

"Can you hold them?"

"We will," said Erik. "We have no choice."

Ahead they saw lights as the village of Wilhelmsburg came into view. Entering the town they saw that it was completely taken over as a military site. The townspeople had been evacuated days earlier, and Erik knew that once his men had rested for a day, eaten and tended wounds, they would abandon this town, after putting every building in it to the torch.

A small figure ran toward Erik, shouting, "Captain von Darkmoor!"

Erik recognized him, despite the filth that clung to the tabard of a page of the royal court in Krondor. "Yes . . . what is your name?"

"Samuel, sir. A lady asked me to give this to you."

Erik took the note and sent the boy on his way. Erik opened the note. Inside, in simple handwriting, it said: "Gone to Ravensburg to find your mother. I love you. Kitty."

Erik felt relief that Kitty had reached here safely and was probably now staying at the Inn of the Pintail, where Erik had grown up. He turned to where the exhausted magician stood and said, "Let's get something to eat."

"An excellent idea," said the fatigued conjurer.

They reached the Sign of the Plowshare, the inn where he had first met Corporal Alfred and Roo's cousin Duncan. That caused Erik to wonder where his boyhood friend might be.

Inside the inn, they found the common room crowded. Half the floor was littered with blankets, where a makeshift infirmary had been set up, while the other half was jammed with starving soldiers, eating whatever was being passed across the counter.

A corporal whose name escaped Erik said, "We've got some rooms upstairs for the officers, Captain. We'll send up food."

"Thank you," said Erik.

He led Robert up the stairs, and when they got to the first room, he pushed open the door and found an officer in the tabard of Ylith, sound asleep on a bare floor. Two other men sat eating. They glanced over, and

Erik waved at them in apology and closed the door. He moved down to the next door and opened it, finding the room empty.

Inside were two simple mattresses, woolen blankets sewn together and hay-stuffed; to Erik they looked inviting. He struggled to get out of his boots, and by the time he did, the corporal had arrived with two wooden bowls of hot stew and two large mugs of ale. Suddenly fatigue was forgotten as Erik's mouth began to water.

As the corporal made to leave, Erik said, "Make sure someone wakes me an hour before dawn."

"Yes, Captain."

Robert said, "I don't envy you an early morning after a day such as you've just had."

"No need for you to envy anyone, magician. You're up at first light, too."

"I suppose it's necessary?"

"Yes, we need to be out of this town before the enemy gets here. It's the difficult part of this mission, keeping one jump ahead of the foe. When they reach Wilhelmsburg, they are to find only fire and ruin."

Robert said, "Such a waste."

"It's more of a waste to give the enemy anything to aid them on their march."

"I guess so." The magician ate a couple of spoonfuls of food, then said, "Pug said things were dire, and while he wouldn't be specific, he led us to believe that there's even more at risk than the sovereignty of the Kingdom. Or is that an exaggeration?"

"I can't say," replied Erik between bites of food. After he had swallowed a healthy drink of ale, he said, "But let me put it that none of us can afford a loss in this war. None of us."

Robert sat back, resting against the wall, with his feet stretched out. "I'm not used to all this walking."

"I offered you a horse."

"Truth to tell, they scare me."

Erik looked at the man, then laughed. "I have spent my entire life around them, so you'll forgive me, but I find that funny."

Robert shrugged. "Well, there are many who are frightened of magicians, so I guess I can understand that."

Erik nodded. "There was a time when I was a boy in Ravensburg when I would have been worried about you, if not frightened, but I've seen enough over the last few years that I choose to worry about things that I can face with a sword in my hand, and let the gods, priests, and magicians worry about the rest."

"Wise man," said Robert with a sleepy smile. "If you don't think it overly rude," he said, putting down his bowl and mug, "I think I'll get some sleep." His head barely touched the mattress before he was snoring.

Erik finished his ale and lay down, and it seemed only a minute after he closed his eyes when he found the young corporal shaking his shoulder, saying, "Captain, it's time to get up."

Roo motioned for everyone to stop. Luis was semiconscious, his feet tied to the stirrups of one horse—with the rope passed under the animal—so he wouldn't fall, as he hugged the animal's neck. His wound was still seeping blood, and Roo knew he would not survive another night without rest and better care than they could provide on the trail. Willem rode with his arms around little Helmut, while Nataly rode with Abigail before her. Roo, Karli, and Helen led the horses.

They had left the cave the morning before, trying to find a safe route to the northern road. Twice they had found themselves at impassable points in the woods, and Roo had followed his plan of going east when he couldn't go north, then turning north when he could no longer go east.

Only once had they found themselves blocked on the north and east, and he had cast back to the west and found another northern route.

Roo had halted them because of the sound of riders, some distance off, but close enough he started looking for a place to hide. "Wait here," he said softly, handing the reins of the horse he was leading, upon which Luis sat, to Helen. He drew his sword and hurried off, looking for some elevation to give him a better view.

He found a rise to the east and climbed it, which led to another, and that brought him to a relatively clear ridge. Sound was echoing, but when he stood still for a moment, he could hear that the riders were to his north.

"Damn," he said softly and hurried back to the others.

The children had fallen into silence, as they reacted to the obvious fear their parents tried to hide. Roo said, "A large band of riders to the north."

"That road you spoke of?" asked Helen.

"Yes, I think so."

"What do we do?" said Karli.

"We go quietly, and slowly, and we hope those are Kingdom cavalry."

Karli was handling her terror far better than Roo would have guessed. He admired her willingness to put aside her own fear to protect her children. Roo glanced at Luis, who had lapsed into a half-doze, barely able to sit upright. Perspiration ran from his face, although the morning was cool, and Roo knew he had fever from his wound.

"We've got to get Luis to a healer," Roo said, and Helen and Karli both nodded.

They set off slowly through the woods. A half hour later, Roo stopped. He glanced around a clearing and said, "I know this place."

"Where are we?"

Roo said, "Karli, this is where your father, Erik, and I camped, the second night we traveled together. We met him a half day's ride to the east." He calculated. "Damn. We got turned around someplace, and were moving northwest instead of north. We're not as far east as I hoped."

"Where are we?" asked Helen.

"Still most of a day's ride to a road that will fork down to Wilhelmsburg."

Karli lowered her voice. "Luis can't ride another day."

"I know," said Roo, "but we have no choice."

He led them through the clearing, and just a short distance to the north lay the road they had been seeking. Hoof prints showed that the patrol Roo had heard had ridden this way. He motioned to them to follow him down the road.

The day passed without incident. Near sundown, they left the woodlands and found an abandoned farm, a squat stone-and-log affair with a sod roof. "We can stay here tonight," said Roo. "The road that leads down to Wilhelmsburg is about another hour to the east of here."

They got Luis off the horse and into the house, laying him gently on a straw pallet. Roo took the horses into the unoccupied barn, untacked them, and found some hay there, which he let them eat. He knew from his training with Erik and the others while in the army that if the hay was bad the horses would colic and die, but from what he could tell, it still looked edible. He closed the door and went to the little house.

Helen was looking at Luis's shoulder. "We need to clean this," she said.

Roo looked around and found nothing. "Let me see if there's a well."

He went out back and found the well, and there was still a bucket in it. He pulled up fresh water, untied the bucket, and brought the water into the house.

Karli said, "I found this." She held out a small sack. "Salt." Roo took it while Karli said, "It must have fallen to the floor when whoever lived here fled."

Roo said, "It might help."

"Can we have a fire?" asked Willem.

Roo said, "No. Even if we hide the flames from sight, the smell of smoke could bring raiders."

Helen lowered her voice. "If I can boil some water, I can clean his wounds."

Roo said, "I know." He held out the salt. "Drink from the bucket, then when it's half full, pour the salt into the water. Bathe his wounds in that." He glanced at his unconscious friend. "It will hurt like hell, but I don't think he'll notice. I'm going to try to find something for a poultice."

Roo left the hut and stayed close to the buildings, in case someone might be coming along the road. He didn't want to take the chance of being spotted. He hurried past the barn and the now-empty fields, into the woods. He had seen several mosses on the rocks the way they had come. Nakor had shown them all how to make a poultice, and Roo wished he had paid closer attention. But he thought he knew what to look for.

After nearly an hour's search, as night was falling, Roo found the spiderweb-like moss, hugging tree trunks and rocks near a tiny stream. He gathered as much as he could carry in two hands, then hurried back to the farmhouse.

Karli and Helen had gotten Luis's shirt off and had bathed the wound with the salt water. Helen said, "He didn't move."

Roo said, "That's probably for the best." He studied his friend's face and saw it was covered with perspiration. He also saw that the wound to his shoulder had been caked over with dried blood, but now lay open. "That needs to be sewn closed."

Karli said, "I have needles."

"What?" asked Roo.

She reached under her dress and said, "Needles are expensive, and when we left everything, I made sure my needles were safe." She tore a seam in the hem of her dress and took out a tiny rolled piece of leather, which had been lying alongside the seam. She unrolled it and presented Roo with six finely tempered steel needles.

Roo blinked. "I'm pleased sewing meant so much to you," he said. "You wouldn't have any thread, by chance, would you?"

Helen said, "Threads are easy." She stood and lifted the hem of her dress. She reached under and pulled down one of her own underskirts, stepping out of it. With her teeth she worried a seam, and when she was satisfied with the damage done, she began unraveling threads. "Now, how long do you think?"

"A foot and a half," said Roo.

She took one of the needles and worked the tangle of threads, pushing the one she wanted clear, then she took it between thumb and forefinger and pulled. Roo expect it to break, but to his surprise, it unraveled and she pulled out three feet of thread. She bit at the hem, and yanked, and handed the linen thread to Roo.

Roo said, "I wish I knew what I was doing." He allowed Helen to thread the needle, then said, "One of you at his head, and one at his feet in case he tries to move."

The two women obeyed, Helen gripping Luis's legs while Karli put her hands on his shoulders, being careful not to touch the wound. Roo began to sew.

Throughout the night, Luis lay in a fever. He awoke enough to take a drink of water. Once they had to restrain him from attempting to scratch off the poultice that Roo had put on his wound.

Karli and Helen sat in the corner, with the children gathered around them, sleeping the best they could. Roo slept across the doorsill, sword in hand.

In the morning, Luis looked better. "I think his fever's broken," said Roo.

"Should we move him?" asked Helen.

Roo gritted his teeth. "I don't think we should, but we can't stay here. If those soldiers that rode by yesterday were Kingdom cavalry, the enemy will be here sometime today. If they were enemy soldiers, we're already behind the lines."

Luis's eyes opened, and he whispered, "I can ride."

"I wish we had something to eat," said Karli. "He needs it to regain his strength."

Roo said, "With luck we'll be in Wilhelmsburg by midday. We'll eat until we pop." He grinned at the children, who tried to smile.

They got the horses saddled and, with a great deal of difficulty, managed to help Luis into the saddle. Roo said, "Do you want me to tie you to the irons again?"

"No," said Luis, blinking against the morning sunlight. "I can manage." He looked at his heavily bandaged shoulder and said, "What did you do to my shoulder?"

"Salt water and a poultice," said Roo. "How is it?"

"It itches like nothing I've ever felt."

Roo said, "I think itching's good."

"Only if it's happening to someone else," said Luis.

Roo took the reins of his horse, and Luis gripped the horse's mane at the withers. The children rode as they had before, and Roo led them all down the road, eastward.

Erik rode quickly through the town and shouted, "Burn it!"

Men at the western edge of Wilhelmsburg ran through the town throwing torches. The larger stone buildings would be gutted, for most had bales of hay placed inside, and the buildings with thatched roofs caught quickly.

By the time Erik reached the eastern edge of the town, the western half was fully engulfed in flames. Erik waited until all his men were out of the town, then said, "Let's move."

Since before sunrise, soldiers billeted at Wilhelmsburg had been moving eastward, heading for a ridge line that they would defend for another week if possible. Erik knew that as they moved closer to Darkmoor they were going to encounter more towns like this one, Wolfsburg, Ravensburg, Halle, and Gotsbus. All would provide close support, but all would have to be torched before the defenders withdrew.

Robert d' Lyes rode over, obviously very uncomfortable on the horse Erik had secured for him. "How are you doing?" asked Erik.

"Only the thought of another day walking in the heat convinces me this is a good idea, Captain."

Erik smiled. "She's a gentle animal. Don't saw on her mouth and pay attention, and she'll take care of you. Remember to keep your heels down."

Erik turned and rode off, and the magician tried his best to keep up.

* * *

Roo lay back against the wall of the gully, his sword held close to his chest. The despair had almost been overwhelming when they had reached a point down the southern trail where they could see the smoke from Wilhelmsburg. Roo didn't have to see the town to realize it had been put to the torch.

They had halted on the road, trying to decide what to do: risk skirting the flaming town, trying to overtake the fleeing Kingdom army, or turn back north and take the less-used road into Ravensburg. While they debated, a shout from across a large clearing told them that they had been spotted by horsemen.

Roo took them into the woods at once, hurrying the frightened group as best he could. He found a gully that quickly deepened, turned to the north, then turned east again. He had shooed them all along, and had doubled back, sword in hand. Luis had followed, his dagger in his left hand. He was weak and disoriented, but he was willing to fight.

While Karli, Helen, and the children huddled deep at the end of the gully, against a steep wall of rocks, trying to keep the horses quiet, Roo and Luis waited just beyond the first turn in the gully.

Voices came from a short distance away, and Roo recognized the speech as being from Novindus. Luis nodded, and his thumb flexed along the hilt of his dagger.

The sound of horses approaching caused Roo to crouch, hugging the bank. The voices grew louder. "Some tracks in the mud. Look fresh."

"Keep it down. You want to send them to ground?"

The first rider came around the bend, looking backward over his shoulder, saying, "When you pay me, you give me orders, you—"

Roo sprang upward, striking straight into the exposed area under the man's right arm. The sudden thrust stunned the man, and Roo yanked him from his horse.

The horse shied, moving up the gully, past Luis.

"What did you say?" said the other rider.

Roo saw a dagger at the fallen's man's belt and pulled it, tossing it toward Luis. For all his fatigue and illness, Luis still managed to place his own dagger between his teeth and caught the one tossed him without missing a beat.

Luis flipped the blade in the air, caught it by the point, and pulled it back behind his ear and let fly with it just as the second rider came around the bend. "Hey! I asked—" the man said just as the blade caught him in the throat.

He gurgled as Roo dragged him from the saddle. Roo dumped the body next to the first one and with a swat sent the horse after the one heading toward Karli, Helen, and the children.

Roo signaled and he and Luis headed back to where the others waited. "They'll be here any second," said Roo.

"What do we do?" asked Karli.

Roo pointed to the rocks, a twelve-foot bank. "We climb up there. They can't follow."

He didn't wait, but started scrambling up to the top of the rocks. When he got up there, he would see glimpses of the other riders through the trees, calling questions back and forth, inquiring about the two missing men. Roo motioned for Willem to climb up, and he held down his hands, so Helen, who was taller than Karli, could hand up Helmut to him. The littlest child stuck out his lip as if about to cry, and Roo said, "Please, baby, not now."

As Roo took his son into his arms, Helmut cut loose with a pitiful wail, as if all the fear, hunger, and fatigue he had endured for the last three days were coming out at once. Luis turned and drew his dagger, for only a moment later, Helmut's cry was answered by the shouts of the horsemen.

Abigail and Nataly scrambled up the rocks, pushed by their mothers. Willem climbed without aid. Luis looked up, perspiration running off his brow, and said, "I can't make it."

Roo said, "Climb! It's just a short way."

Luis had one good hand, and that shoulder was the damaged one. He reached up, gritted his teeth, and pulled. He found toeholds, and took a deep breath. He let go and tried to push himself upward, grabbing frantically with his good hand, his withered right hand scraping uselessly off the rocks. Roo leaned over and grabbed his wrist. "I've got you!"

Roo felt his arms stretching as the larger man hung like dead weight. Nearly out of breath, Luis said, "Let me go. I can't do this."

"You'll do it, damn you!" said Roo, yanking hard, though he knew he couldn't pull the man up by main force.

Luis tried to climb, making little progress, as two riders turned into view. "There they are!" shouted one.

"Let me go!" said Luis. "Get away!"

"No!" shouted Roo. To Helen and Karli he said, "Get the children back into the trees!"

Roo pulled and Luis struggled, as a rider came into close proximity, with a sword drawn. "You the bastards killed Mikwa and Tugon? We'll settle—"

An arrow lifted the rider from his saddle and a second took the rider behind him out of his seat as well.

Strong arms reached past Roo and took Luis's wrist, lifting him easily to the edge of the rocks. Roo turned and looked up into a strange, alien, but handsome face. The elf smiled and said, "You seemed troubled, stranger."

"You could say that," said Roo, leaning back on his elbows, panting. Another elf appeared, shouldering his longbow. Roo flexed his left arm and said, "I don't know how much longer I could have held on."

A man in a black tunic came to stand next to the elf and a familiar grin split a dark face as he said, "If you aren't the sorriest-looking jokers I've had the misfortune to see, man, I don't know nothing."

Luis grinned and said, "Jadow. Glad to see you." Then he fainted.

"What's wrong with him?" asked Jadow Shati as he kelt next to his old companion from the campaign down to Novindus.

Roo said, "Shoulder. He's got a wound and it's inflamed. Loss of blood, the usual complaints."

"We can care for that," said the elf. "But we had best get you and your children away from here."

Roo stood up and said, "Rupert Avery."

The elf said, "I'm Galain. I'm on my way to bring messages to your General Greylock."

"General?" said Roo. "Things have changed."

"More than you know," said Jadow. "Let's get some distance between us and those other riders, and we can talk."

"How many of you are there?" asked Roo as he walked behind Jadow and Galain.

"Six elves from the Elf Queen's court, and a light company."

Roo knew a light company was ten squads of six men each. "Where are they?"

"A half mile that way," said Jadow. "Our friends here have remarkable hearing and told us there were horses over here, so I thought we'd check things out." He put his hand on Roo's shoulder. "We're on our way to Ravensburg. Care to come along?"

Roo laughed. "Thanks. We could do with some company. Now, what do you have to eat?"

Twenty-two

Ravensburg

ERIK SMILED.

Kitty seemed to fly into his arms, barely giving him time to dismount. "I was so scared I'd never see you again," she said.

He kissed her and hugged her tight. "Me too."

Soldiers milled about the stable yard of the Inn of the Pintail, and Nathan and Freida approached. Freida hugged her son, then Nathan shook his hand. "Congratulations!" said Nathan with a grin. "Made a Knight-Captain and married."

Freida said, "Why didn't you send word? When this girl first came to me I thought her mad, married to my boy." She fixed Kitty with a dubious look. "But after a while she told me enough to convince me she knew you quite well." Then she smiled.

Erik blushed. "Well, things were pretty confused and we had to act quickly."

"So she tells me," said Freida.

Nathan said, "You look all in. Come inside and have a bath and some food."

Erik said, "I will, but first I have to start getting people out of town. You're all going to have to be on the march by the day after tomorrow."

"Leave?" asked Nathan.

Erik nodded. "The enemy is no more than five days behind, perhaps as close as three, and some of his cavalry units may be closer. We'll defend the town for as long as we can after you leave."

"Then?" asked Nathan.

Erik looked down, almost ashamed to answer. "We'll have to burn it to the ground."

Nathan went pale. "Do you know what you're doing?"

Erik said, "I know. I've already put Wilhelmsburg, Wolfsburg, and a half-dozen villages to the torch."

Nathan ran a hand over his leathery old face. "I never thought I'd see it again."

Erik remembered he had lived through the sacking of the Far Coast, years before. "I can only tell you it's absolutely necessary."

A very tired-looking figure in a grey robe rode awkwardly into the courtyard and pulled up next to Erik's horse. Robert d' Lyes got off his horse, his trembling left knee barely able to support his weight as he dismounted. He looked almost bowlegged as he turned to Erik. "Do you ever get used to this?"

Erik smiled. "Mother, Nathan, this is Robert, and he's just learning how to ride."

Nathan winced in sympathy. "Come inside. I'll pour you some wine to ease your discomfort." Nathan signaled to Gunther, his apprentice, to take the magician's horse. The boy ran over, smiled at Erik, and looked questioningly at the former smith's mount.

Erik said, "I'll be needing her for a while. I'll be back later and then you can tend her for me." To Nathan he said, "I'll be billeting men here and in every other inn in the town, the Growers' and Vintners' Hall, and any other place I can find. So expect a fair amount of shoeing and tack repair between now and when you leave. You're the only man in Ravensburg besides our company smith who can repair weapons and armor." He looked regretful as he said, "Don't expect much sleep for a few days."

Nathan shook his head and said, "Come with me, Robert, and I'll join you in a glass. I think I'm going to need it."

Kitty kissed Erik. "Hurry back."

Freida kissed him as well and whispered, "She seems a fine girl, Erik, if a little odd at times."

Erik grinned. "You don't know the half of it. I'll be back for supper."

As his mother turned away, he said, "Any word of Roo?"

She stopped. "Two of his wagons got here a couple of days ago. I think they're over at Gaston's. But we haven't heard anything of him. Why?"

"He was on the road, and . . . it's been difficult."

Freida, who never had any use for Rupert, but knew how close her son was to him, nodded and said, "I'll say a prayer."

Erik smiled. "Thank you, Mother." He remounted and headed back out into the town of Ravensburg, to oversee the deployment of the men and get ready for the destruction of the town in which he had lived most of his life.

Roo said, "How are you doing?"

Luis said, "Better." He was riding beside Roo and indeed looking better.

From ahead, Jadow turned and said to Roo, "Man, considering that you almost killed him with that poultice, he looks positively reborn."

"Well, I thought that was the moss Nakor had showed us."

The elves had removed Roo's concoction, found the correct ingredients for a healing poultice, and re-dressed Luis's wound.

Jadow's soldiers had secured enough mounts from the raiders they had killed so Roo, Luis, and the women could ride. The elves were all on foot, so two of them led the horses with the children, while Karli and Helen kept a close eye on their offspring.

They had moved from the scene of combat and made camp. Jadow dispensed with the full entrenchment, since the elves made excellent outer sentries, and Jadow decided the extra two hours a day of movement was more necessary than defensive security.

Twice since leaving that camp in the morning, they had reports of other companies moving south: Kingdom forces to the east, and invaders to the west. It was clear that they were heading straight toward the next battle. Roo knew enough about the surrounding countryside to understand that after Ravensburg the only town of size was Wolverton and the countryside around that hamlet was not conducive to a stout defense. They would hold for a while at Ravensburg, then fall back to Darkmoor.

"How far to Ravensburg?" Jadow asked Roo.

Roo said, "We'll be there in less than an hour."

"Good," said Luis. "I could use a taste of that wine you and Erik used to brag on so often."

"You'll not be disappointed," said Roo. Then he thought of a large portion of the Kingdom army already being in Ravensburg, and said, "Assuming there's any left when we get there."

Ten minutes later they approached the first Kingdom camp, located behind a very defensible rise in the road. They hailed the guards and were passed without question.

As they rode along, they saw more and more elements of the Kingdom army digging in. Roo said, "Looks like they're fighting along ten miles or so of front."

Jadow pointed over his shoulder, to the north. "We've been turning them this way for weeks. We left behind enough men to ensure they don't try to feint this way, turn back, and break through north of us."

Roo knew the local terrain as well as anyone. "Even if they get past you that way," he said, "they're still going to have to turn south when they try to climb Nightmare Ridge."

"That's the plan," said Jadow.

The closer they came to the town of Ravensburg, the more frantic the activity. The road they traveled ran parallel to a low ridge line, a series of interconnecting hills, that had been planted with grapevines for years.

Soldiers were cutting the large vines, some as big as small trees, piling them, along with anything else they could find, to form breastworks along the top of the ridge. While no winemaker, Roo had spent enough time growing up among them to know what a loss those vines would be. Some were three hundred years old, rootstock that would be impossible to replace. He noticed that workers were madly cutting vines, saving them for grafts, in the hope they could someday return to these vineyards and start over. Roo silently wished them luck.

They reached Ravensburg in midafternoon. Roo saw Erik supervising the establishment of a barricade across the main road. He waved and Erik rode over.

"Roo! Luis! Jadow!" said Erik, relief obvious on his face.

Galain waited until greetings were exchanged, and said, "Captain von Darkmoor?"

"Yes," said Erik. "What can I do for you?"

Galain produced a scroll and handed it to him. Erik read it and said, "Good." He pointed toward an inn across the square. "If you'd like to eat, go there and tell them I sent you."

"Thank you," said Galain.

Erik looked at Karli, Helen, and the children and said, "If you'd be so kind as to continue leading those horses, I'd appreciate it." To Karli he said, "Tell my mother I sent you and don't let her give the children too many sweets."

Karli smiled and a tear of relief ran down her cheek, despite her attempts to restrain it. "Thank you," she said.

As the two women and four children were led away, Erik said to Luis, "What happened to your shoulder?"

Luis said, "Long story. I'll tell you tonight."

Erik nodded. To Roo he said, "Why don't you go with your family and we'll visit later. I still have a lot to do."

"Apparently," said Roo. "Until later."

They rode off and Erik accepted Jadow's mocking salute. "Report, Sergeant."

"Yes, sir, Captain sir!" said Jadow with a grin.

"All right, that's enough."

"Anything you say, Captain sir!"

Erik leaned over and said, "Would you like to be a corporal again, Sergeant?"

"Don't tease me with promises you won't keep, you evil man."

Erik grinned. "What have you seen?"

"There's a tough bastard up to the north leading the enemy, named Duko, General Duko. He's staying put, pounding at that little pass between Eggly and Tannerus. The Earl of Pemberton and the Duke of Yabon both have heavy infantry dug in there, with some Cortesian archers holding the higher ridges, keeping the enemy down in the pass. They're tough little bastards and can pick your teeth with their arrows. So most of Duko's men are just hitting the barricades across the trail, over and over. It's a bloody mess, a regular grinder up there, but other than that, most of the enemy's forces are heading this way."

"Any word on Fadawah?"

"None. Seems the Lord High Bad Man is staying close to the Emerald Bitch." Jadow scratched his chin. "This is a pretty messed-up invasion, my friend, if you see what I mean."

"I see exactly what you mean." Erik said, "Go get some food, and when your men are in billets, take a night of rest. I want you and your company to pull back and see what you can do in the next town, Wolverton. The enemy should come right through it, so see if you can come up with some nasty surprises for them so they might slow down a little."

Jadow grinned. "Nasty surprises are my specialty, Captain."

"When you're done, get back here. I need you to supervise the flying company on the northern flank." Erik saluted, and Jadow and his sixty men rode off.

Erik returned his attention to the matter at hand, but part of his mind was preoccupied with his family, particularly with his young wife, who was only a ten-minute ride away.

The inn was crowded, so Milo, the innkeer, put Roo, Karli, Helen Jacoby, Erik and Kitty in the kitchen, all of them packed in around the table used to prepare meals. The children had already been fed and sent off to bed. Even without them, things were so tight Kitty sat upon Erik's knee, a condition neither seemed to mind much.

Erik ate hungrily, his first hot meal in days, and his mother's cooking to boot. Milo had opened several bottles of his better wine and was pouring rounds.

Robert d' Lyes was bunking in with Gunther, Nathan's apprentice, and Milo was at a loss over where he was going to put everyone. Freida said, "The children can have our room for the night."

Nathan said, "Milo's got them upstairs."

"Not Roo's children, I mean Erik and his wife."

Erik blushed and Nathan laughed. "He's hardly what I'd call a child, dear."

Freida said, "He's my boy, and that's little more than a slip of a girl. Anyway, they need some privacy."

"Well," said Nathan, "I'm going to be at the forge all night, anyway, so you're the one who's going to have to find another place to sleep."

"I'll just throw a quilt under this table and sleep here. I'll have to be up early, too, for we've got hungry mouths to feed again."

Erik knew that Nathan and his mother lived in a small building just outside the smithy, and while it had once been little better than a dirty shed when Tyndal, Erik's first master, had lived there, Nathan and his mother had turned it into a tidy little bedroom.

Milo said, "Erik, do we have to leave?"

Erik nodded. "First light, day after tomorrow. A couple of days after that, we'll be fighting a battle here. We have to hold them outside of town while the northern and southern flanks withdraw. Then they hold while we pull back, and if all goes according to plan, we break them at Darkmoor."

Milo sighed. "This inn is all I have."

Erik nodded. "I have some money. When this war is over, I'll help you rebuild."

Milo didn't seem convinced, but he accepted that at face.

Erik said, "How are Rosalyn and the baby?"

"Fine," said Milo, a pleased expression on his face. "She and Randolph had another, a boy they named after me!"

"Congratulations," said Erik.

"I sent word to them you were back, though how they could not know with all these soldiers running around calling your name would be a mystery. I'm a bit surprised they're not here yet."

Erik said, "Well, Randolph and his family have the bakery to dismantle and move."

"That's true. Still, I expect they'll want to see you before they evacuate."

Erik said, "I need to talk to them."

Kitty kissed his cheek. "Talk to them tomorrow."

Erik grinned and blushed again. "Very well," he said softly. Then, looking around the table, he said, "Well, I've got to be up early tomorrow."

Everyone laughed. Erik's blush deepened, and he took Kitty's hand and they left the kitchen.

After they were gone, Nathan said, "Roo, you've done well."

Roo blew out his cheeks in an exaggerated sigh of relief and said, "Now that I know I'm still alive, yes, I'd say I have."

The others laughed, and they began catching up with one another, letting the familiar surroundings lull them into a momentary illusion that trouble was far away.

At dawn the next day, Roo sat on the wagon box, his wife at his side. In the bed of the wagon, Luis rode with Helen and the children. Roo smiled as he asked, "See you soon?"

Erik nodded, astride his horse. "But not for a while, if you're smart. By the time I'm in Darkmoor, you should be halfway to Malac's Cross. Besides, don't you have some estates or something in the East to keep you busy?"

Roo shrugged. "I have enough to keep me afloat if we get through all this. But in a funny way, I hate to miss what's coming."

Erik grinned. "No you don't."

Roo grinned back. "You're right. I'm taking the children to someplace they can play and eat and get fat."

Erik laughed. "Then get out of here!"

Roo had found that two of his wagons had made it to Ravensburg. He did as he had promised and paid the two drivers a year's wages. He then let them go and turned one of the wagons over to Milo and Nathan, keeping the other one for himself.

Erik rode to the second wagon. Milo and Nathan sat on the driver's seat, while Kitty, Freida, Rosalyn, her husband, Randolph, and their sons, Gerd and Milo, huddled in the back. Erik smiled at the older boy, who now clearly resembled his true father, Stefan von Darkmoor. The boy sat in his stepfather's arms, asking excited questions in his own two-year-old's dialect of the King's Tongue, while his mother held the baby in her arms. Erik said to Nathan, "When you get to Darkmoor, find Owen Greylock. He'll find you a safe place to stay."

Kitty stood up and Erik moved his mount close enough to the wagon so that he could embrace her. They held each other without speaking, then Erik let her go.

Nathan flicked the reins and the horses moved away, and Erik sat watching his life move from him. His mother; her husband, who was a rare and wonderful man; Milo, who had been the only thing remotely like a father in his boyhood; Rosalyn, as much a sister to him as if his mother had given birth to her; and Gerd, his nephew, though only a few knew that fact. And, most amazingly, Kitty, a slender young girl who meant more to him than he would have imagined possible before he met her.

Erik watched until the wagon disappeared into the frantic town. Other townspeople piled their belongings into wagons, onto carts, or into bundles they would carry on their backs, in preparation for abandoning their homes. Anything important to a family's livelihood was being carried away: tools, seeds, cuttings from the most productive vines, books and scrolls, inventory. Randolph's family had managed to dismantle their bakery, salvaging every item of hardware—the iron doors to the stone ovens, the flat iron oven bottoms and cooking racks—and every other valuable item, leaving only the empty stone ovens and some wooden cooling racks behind.

Some families had every belonging in their possession piled high atop whatever cart or wagon they owned, while others grabbed only valuables, abandoning years of accumulation, furniture, clothing, and other household goods, sacrificed in the name of speed. Some townspeople had already left, driving small herds of sheep, goats, or cattle, or carrying away chickens, ducks, and geese in wooden crates.

Soldiers hurried by, moving to positions determined months before Erik arrived here. Erik put aside the feeling of personal loss that gripped him, and turned his attention to the defense of his hometown.

He considered everything Greylock had ordered him to do, and thanked the gods that the General and Captain Calis had been so thorough. He knew that soon the most desperate fighting since the fall of Krondor was about to resume.

Everything Erik had read in Knight-Marshal William's library had reinforced one thing overall: war was fluid, unpredictable, and those who were best prepared for any eventuality, able to seize opportunity, were the most likely to survive.

And that was exactly how Erik thought of it these days: survival. Not victory, but simply enduring longer than the enemy. Let them die first, was all he prayed for. And he knew that if any detail of preparation eluded him, it wouldn't be for a lack of effort on his part.

Erik turned his horse and rode off to oversee the first line of defense.

Men dug furiously, building up the breastwork across the pass west of Ravensburg. Axes rang out in the afternoon as trees were felled. Erik wiped his brow and glanced at the hot sun. Thoughts of snow were difficult on a day like this. Yet he knew that in the mountains of his home province, winter could arrive as soon as a month from now. But his homegrown instincts told him this would probably be a late and light winter. The look of the plantlife and the behavior of the wild animals communicated to him silently that eight weeks or more would pass before anything like a serious snowfall would occur, and three months was possible.

Erik remembered the one year—he had been no more than six—when no snow to speak of fell through the entire winter; only a slushy sleet, and that passed quickly.

Erik decided to stop worrying about the weather and concentrate his attention on things over which he had some control. Two riders were heading his way, one from the south, the other from the west.

The rider from the west reached him first, and saluted. He wore the garb of the Krondorian garrison, bloodstained and filthy. He said, "Captain. We got jumped by a company of Saaur. The green bastards cut us up before we could get organized." He glanced over his shoulder, as if expecting to see the enemy come riding into view any minute. "They seem to resent what the lancers did to them, so they go looking for light cavalry and mounted infantry to punish. Anyway, I got loose. I figure they're going to regroup with the advance units and be here by sundown tomorrow or dawn the day after."

Erik said, "Good. Go into town and get some food and rest." He glanced around. "I don't think we're going to need any trailing scouts in the future, so report in the morning to my first sergeant, a loud bully named Harper." Erik smiled. "He'll find you some work."

As the first rider left, the second reined in opposite Erik, and saluted. He wore the uniform of the Pathfinders. "We're getting a bit more pressure than anticipated, Captain. I don't know how much longer we can maintain an orderly withdrawal."

Erik reviewed the troop disposition to the south. "You should be facing moderate pressure. What's happening?"

"I don't know, sir, but the Earl of Landreth is in charge."

"What happened to Duke Gregory?" The Duke of the Southern Marches, a court governor of the Vale of Dreams, had been put in charge of the southern elements of the retreat, coordinating his efforts with Greylock's defense of the center. He had ample resources, given that the garrisons withdrawn from Shamata and Landreth were under his command.

"Dead, sir. We thought you knew. Messengers were dispatched last week."

Erik swore. "They never reached General Greylock or myself." They had assumed the invaders would keep a significant portion of their army turned toward Kesh, in case the Empire sought to take advantage of the confusion to enlarge their domain, but from what this soldier had just said, the southern wing of the defense was collapsing too quickly. Erik said, "Ride into town, get a fresh horse, and grab something to eat. I'm sending two companies of archers to give you some help in the withdrawal." Erik reviewed the maps he had memorized and said, "Suggest to the Earl he let the front to his south collapse, pulling the soldiers on that flank around him, to his left as he withdraws. Then have them dig in at the town of Pottersville. But there he has to hold for another three days; four is better. By then we'll be fighting here and we can't have them flanking us. If he can keep them stationary for that long, he can start sliding northward along the line, using the road to the town of Breonton. Once there, he can turn tail and run to Darkmoor, but not before."

The Pathfinder nodded. With a tired smile, he said, "I assume you won't mind if these *suggestions* originate with General Greylock?"

Erik smiled and nodded. "Of course. I wouldn't presume to order the Earl to do anything." Then he lost his smile. "But we don't have time for you to run to Darkmoor, have Owen tell you exactly the same thing I just did, then run back down to the Earl. So if the Earl asks, tell him those are the General's orders and I'll deal with any problems that might arise from that deception down the road."

The Pathfinder nodded. "You know, Captain, when we all get to Darkmoor, we're going to have a very mixed command; a lot of the nobles aren't going to enjoy being told what to do."

Erik smiled. "Well, that's why Prince Patrick plans on being there."

"The Prince is in Darkmoor?"

"That's the word. Now, get something to eat, then get back down to the Earl of Landreth."

The Pathfinder saluted and rode off. Erik looked at the trees being dragged over to fortify the barrier across the King's Highway. Two large ridges overlooked the position, and while Erik watched, crews of muleskinners were hauling catapults up goat trails to emplacements that had been hand-carved out of the rocks. Any congestion along the highway on the enemy's part would result in high casualties.

Erik nodded in approval. He was going to get more draft animals out in the next hour to drag away the stumps and would turn the men to that task as soon as the last tree was felled. The enemy weren't going to have any cover as they approached Ravensburg if Erik von Darkmoor had any say in the matter.

Twice skirmishers had neared the defenses outside Ravensburg, and at the last minute, darted away, returning to the west. Erik waited on the second crest of the highway, high enough to command a panorama of the center of the battlefield, and close enough to send messages quickly to the front.

Word had reached them an hour before that heavy fighting was under way at both the south and north ends of his ten-mile defense. Those were the two most difficult trouble spots, for everything depended upon them holding, forcing the enemy to slide along conveniently provided routes, down into the center, where Erik could let them spend lives trying to punch through.

When he finally gave the order to withdraw, those northern and southern units were to cut off any engagements, if possible, and hurry to Darkmoor. Erik would try to give them one additional full day, then it would become a full retreat, without any pretense of a delaying action. Owen and Erik had considered Calis's original plan and modified it; Calis had wanted another delaying action, while Erik had argued, and convinced Owen, that the enemy were so conditioned to have the center delay that they would be cautious when the defenders abandoned Ravensburg, giving Erik the time he needed to get as many men away as possible. Erik was positive that each man not lost in a delaying action was going to be twice as valuable to the Kingdom in the defense of Darkmoor.

Now they waited. Swords, spears, and arrows were sharpened, traps were readied, horses were rested. Men sat quietly, some inspecting their armor and weapons again and again, against the possibility of having missed some flaw that might prove fatal. Others waited motionlessly, a few slept, and others said prayers to Tith-Onanka to keep them courageous, while still others made peace with the Death Goddess, against the time of their meeting her.

Erik watched, reviewing every preparation over and over, looking for mistakes, miscalculations, and potential problems. Signal men stood beside him, flags ready, to relay commands to units on the ridges to the north and south.

The chosen field of battle was a small, flat expanse of ground, nestled between a narrowing in the hills, a funnel along the King's Highway, and the first line of defense was a low-running ridge with a notch through which the road passed. That was the point where Erik had erected the first barricade. A log rampart had been thrown across the road, giving Erik an almost level battlement from the ridge lines on the right and left. The enemy might attempt to scale the rocks on either side, but Erik counted on the placement of his bowmen to repulse them.

The battlement had been created to look haphazard and quickly erected, but it wasn't. Erik was counting on the enemy's underestimating the defenders' ability to hold against an all-out rush.

The day passed slowly. Then the sound of enemy riders came from the other side of the clearing. A dozen horsemen emerged at the highest point of the King's Highway, the last rise on the west before reaching the cleared battleground. They reigned in and sat silently, observing the defenders. One man, the leader, spoke, and two of the riders turned back the way they had come and rode off. Then the leader signaled toward the defenders' barricade, and two of his men cantered their horses forward.

Erik said, "Pass the word; if they come within twenty yards of the barricade, they die. If they stay beyond that distance, they can ride their horses into the ground for all I care." A long, narrow trench had been dug before the barricade and carefully concealed. Erik did not want it inspected by the enemy's scouts, but he had no objection to their returning and telling their leaders the way was clear.

The runner saluted and raced off toward the barricade, reaching it and passing the orders. At the farthest reach of the defenders' bow fire, both riders swerved off the road, turning in a quick loop, waiting for the defenders to fire on them. When not one arrow sped in their direction, they came to a stop on the road. Both men turned and looked at their leader. The man signaled, and one signaled in return.

The two riders left the highway, moving to the verge of the road, one on each side. They walked their horses along, slowly.

"The lads are looking for traps," came the familiar voice of Sergeant Harper. "Clever of them."

Erik hadn't noticed Harper's appearance, so focused was he on the two riders. "Everything ready?"

Harper said, "As it has been for hours. What are we going to do about those two?"

"Nothing. Let them think we're saving our arrows for the first assault."

"What if they get too close to the trench?"

"Then they're dead. I've already passed the word."

Harper nodded his approval. "It'll be good to hold here a bit and bloody the bastards. All this running backward tires a body."

"There's going to be nothing good about any of what's about to happen, Sergeant."

"That's what I meant, Captain; I'm just putting it in a different way."

Erik shook his head and smiled. "Well, if you're so ready to be cutting heads, maybe I should move you to the front."

"Well, let's not be doing anything so rash," Harper said quickly. "I expect there'll be enough fighting to go around, this day."

"I expect," agreed Erik.

The advance riders moved along the road, and finally, when they were only a few yards shy of the point where Erik had ordered them killed, they turned and rode quickly back to their leader. The riders then sat motionless, waiting for the column of men who were coming down that road.

After most of the day had passed, the sound of marching feet began to reverberate from the west. At first faint, the sound began to increase, until at last Harper said, "Sounds like they're bringing the whole lot this time, Captain."

"That it does," said Erik.

At the other end of the road, where the riders waited, the woods were thick on both sides of the King's Highway. The sound of the approaching army grew louder, but no soldiers could be seen.

Then, suddenly, men emerged from the woods, an unbroken line of men with shields, wielding battle-axes, swords, spears, and bows. They marched to a point half the distance between the line of trees and the defenders, then halted.

"What have we here?" asked Harper softly.

"Looks like they've learned a few things since they've landed," said Erik. "If they send the infantry first, we're going to lose some advantages."

Since the time when Calis's company had served with the Emerald Queen's forces, the usual tactic had been for them to simply unleash their cavalry at any defensive position when able. Infantry was saved for sieges and for flooding gaps in the defenders' lines.

Erik cursed. "I thought we could steal a day having their cavalry getting themselves butchered."

Harper said, "Don't give up hope yet, Captain. They may do something rash still."

A column of riders crested the distant hill, moving down the road to halt slightly beyond the infantry. Then they waited. Officers rode into view, each moving to a location along the line, stationed before their men. Still they held position.

"If the riders come down the road, while the infantry cross the clearing, it could get interesting," observed Harper.

Erik said nothing.

More riders appeared at the crest, then a trumpet sounded, three short blasts. With a roar, the assembled footmen started running across the clearing. "Signal to catapults," Erik said. He raised his hand, a motion duplicated by the signalman holding a red flag.

Erik watched as the attackers raced toward his defenses. He had studied this terrain so well he could gauge the distances without markers. When the leading edge of the attackers reached the outer range of the catapults, he paused, then dropped his hand. The flag went down an instant later, and then the well-disguised war engines atop the second ridge let fly.

A shower of stones, ranging from ones the size of a man's fist to some the size of a large melon, rained down on the attackers. Men screamed and fell, dead or wounded, with broken bones. Those behind could not halt, and some of the wounded were trampled to death by their own comrades.

As if the rocks had been a signal, the cavalry charged down the King's Highway. "They mean to be here before the catapults reload," observed Harper.

"Black signal!" shouted Erik, holding up his hand again. A second flag went up, and when the charging horsemen reached the appropriate range, Erik's hand came down. The black flag dropped, and another round of missiles rained down. Horses screamed and men were thrown as the second company of catapults unleashed its rain of death upon the invaders.

"Green flag!" shouted Erik, and the third flag went up. When it came down, two special catapults called mangonels, large counterbalanced beams of wood with huge baskets on the long end, flung a rain of caltrops: metal stars with six sharpened points. Those that didn't strike an attacker landed on the ground, with one point always up. Men and horses both stepped on the terrible spikes, which lamed horses and felled men.

By the time the attackers worked through the mass of wounded in the front ranks, the first company of war engines had been reloaded and were launching their missiles. And by the time the third green flag had been raised and fell, the entire attacking front was broken and in retreat.

Hundreds of men and horses lay in the late afternoon sun, and not one Kingdom soldier had been wounded. Erik turned to a grinning Harper and said, "Get the perimeter companies out and start looking for their infiltrators. They'll want those catapults out of action by tomorrow, so expect a lot of unwelcome visitors in the hills tonight."

Harper said, "Sir!" and turned to carry out his orders.

Erik watched the withdrawal and thought they had gotten off as lightly as possible for the first day. He also knew that, starting tomorrow, things would get considerably more difficult.

Dying men groaned in pain, begged for water, or cried. Some called to their gods, or their mothers, or wives, while others could not speak. Erik watched the carnage as the sun sank behind the western hills.

He had been correct in his prediction that the invaders would avoid another confrontation before attempting to neutralize the defenders' catapults. Bands of infiltrators probed through the night, being met at every possible weak point by alert defensive resistance, with Jadow's men acting as a flying company, to reinforce any breach on the north, and another company under a corporal named Wallis did the same on the south.

At dawn it was clear the attackers had tired of trying to find a weak spot, and had decided to simply throw men at the defenders. Erik watched as four times during the day thousands of invaders ran across the battlefield, the Funnel, as Erik thought of it, to die under the devastating fire of the defenders.

Harper said, "Sir, will they ask for truce to give comfort to their wounded?"

Erik said, "No. It's not their way. Their wounded only slow them down."

"It's a bitter thing, then. So we'll have no truce to retrieve our lads on some future occasion?"

"No," said Erik. "My advice if you are wounded is to act dead and hope they don't spare any time to ensure you are. Then crawl off somewhere after they've passed."

"I'll remember that, sir."

Erik watched as three companies of defenders had actually reached the barricades on the last assault, and while none of his men died, several had taken wounds as they killed those who tried to climb over the barricade.

The attackers had found all of Erik's traps the hard way. Pits with stakes and the cleverly disguised trench just below the defensive breastwork had claimed scores of attackers, but now the route was clearly marked. Erik judged the light and thought they might try one more attack before sundown. He prayed they didn't. He had planned to fall back under cover of darkness to the secondary defensive position, a well-placed second barricade that would put the attackers in the clear line of Erik's bowmen as they climbed over the first barricade, and turned the fifty yards of open space between the two lines into a killing ground. If he could hold here another night, then keep them away for one more day after that, he felt sure those fleeing toward Darkmoor would be safely away.

Patrols were riding along the eastern slopes of the hills, ensuring no small companies of invaders had somehow slipped through to trouble the defenders from behind. Erik knew that, yet he feared some unnamed surprise would come to put an end to all his clever planning.

Trumpets sounded and Erik said, "Damn! I was hoping they'd give it a rest."

"Not likely, sir," said Harper, pulling his sword, a large hand-and-a-half affair, which he preferred to the broadsword and shield used by most of the men.

From out of the trees across the field men ran, shouting and exhorting their fellows to get close to the defense and breach it. Erik started giving signals, and the catapults and mangonels dispensed death to the attackers, and then the archers let their bows sing. But this time the attack rolled forward.

When the first few men struck the barricade, and died trying to climb, Erik could see more men emerging from the woods, entering the Funnel, and he knew that whoever commanded on the opposite side was throwing everything at him. Erik pulled his own sword and said, "Sergeant, order the support companies to the ready. I want them right behind our men on the barricade."

"Sir!" said Harper, and started shouting orders.

Three squads each, the support companies numbered one hundred and eighty men, under the direction of a sergeant whose job was to recognize a breach and fill it as quickly as possible. The value of the zone between the two defensive barricades would be lost if defenders were mixed in with the attackers; the archers on the rocks above and on the second barricade would not be able to safely fire into the killing ground.

Erik saw a plumed helmet, a captain in the Emerald Queen's army, who was trying to force himself past a determined attacker who was keeping the defender before him busy. Erik was about to order the archers to pick off the officer, but someone on the ridge above had seen him and sent an arrow flying before Erik could speak.

The battle raged along the barricade, and Erik felt frustrated standing on the second ridge, sword in hand, knowing that if he fought, the advantage was lost. Remembering he was now an officer, in command of the area, he put away his sword and watched.

As the sun sank out of sight, the fight at the barricade remained in balance, attackers swarming across the Funnel to replace men who had fallen. Messages arrived from both flanks, indicating the fighting was uniformly fierce at both ends of the line, but that all sections were holding.

When the western sky began to darken, Erik waited for the recall trumpet to sound, but it didn't come. As darkness approached, torches appeared in the west and soldiers ran toward them carrying illumination to continue the fight into the darkness.

"Damn," said Harper, "they're not about to go away, are they?"

"Apparently not," said Erik. He calculated he had to make a choice now; either beginning the withdrawal, losing the ability to cover the retreat across the killing ground, but getting most of his men to the second barricade, which was almost certain to hold through the night, or continuing to fight and trying to hold them until they withdrew. If they were victorious, it would be a major victory, one that would hold the enemy here in Ravesnburg for at least a week more. But if they collapsed and the invaders overran the second barrier before the Kingdom troops could fall back, the results could be disastrous for the Kingdom.

Erik hesitated. For the first time since he had returned to Ravensburg, he cursed Calis for being absent. He or Greylock should have to make this decision, not a young soldier who had only read about these sorts of problems in books.

Harper had his sword ready. "What are we to do, sir?"

Erik's mind raced. He needed an inspiration and a way to get his men back to the second barricade by sunrise, without letting the enemy follow.

Harper said, "Maybe a few of those lads will trip over something and set fire to themselves."

Erik's eyes widened. "Harper, you're a genius!"

"I know, sir, but that still doesn't tell us what we're to do."

"Charge," said Erik. "Bring up every man we have to the barricades and hold them until sunrise."

"Very well, sir." Harper turned and began shouting orders, and men held in reserve were suddenly tumbling over the second barricade and hurrying to reinforce the first.

Erik said, "Now things get easy."

"If you say so, sir," said Harper. "Do we stand here or join the fight?"

Erik pulled his sword. "We fight." The two men ran forward.

Twenty-three

Retreat

Erik shouted.

It was a mindless howl of agony and fatigue, serving only to focus the rage he needed to continue the struggle. It was an animal sound, without meaning. It was a sound repeated throughout the night by thousands of men.

For the first time since the fall of Krondor, the main elements of the invaders' army were locked in battle with the Kingdom. Throughout the night the wave of attackers had continued unabated.

As dawn hinted in the east, where the sky had softened from its funereal black to a dull grey, men had struggled to control a dozen yards of ground. The dead were piled high on both sides of the barricade, where Erik and Harper stood like anchors in storm.

Three times in the night there had been lulls, when water buckets had come to them, and when young boys from the baggage company could haul away the wounded, dying, and dead. But most of the night had been filled with grueling butchery, with little skill, a simple raising and lowering of the blade, much as when Erik had hammered steel. Yet even steel yielded eventually to the smith's hammer. But this sea of flesh, this never-ending supply of bodies willing to be cleaved and sundered, would not stop.

In a moment of lucidity, after striking down another man attempting to climb the barricade, Erik glanced to the rear. Dawn was less than two hours away. To Harper he gasped, "Hold them here for a few more minutes."

Harper only grunted in reply as Erik stepped away from the fighting. He stumbled a few feet farther, and his legs went out from under him. He scrambled upright and saw he had slipped on a man's leg. Where the rest of the man was, Erik couldn't see.

He was thankful for the darkness. He knew that when the sun rose, the carnage would be unspeakable. The worst slaughterhouse in the Kingdom would appear a clean white room for milady's sewing compared to what the two armies had done that night.

A messenger boy waited nearby with a bucket of water. Erik fell to his knees and picked up the bucket, pouring it over his face, his mouth hanging open. The water ran down his parched throat, reviving him. When he had finished, he told the boy, "Run to the rear and find Lieutenant Hammond. Do you know him?"

The boy nodded.

"He's with the reserve company. Tell him I need him now. And tell him to bring torches. And oil if there's any."

Erik rose on legs so heavy he could barely lift them, yet when he returned to Harper's side, he found instinct and training driving him onward, filling him with a fire to fight, to kill the enemy, and to survive.

Time was suspended, just another series of savage sword blows, repeated over and over. Sometime during the night Erik had lost his shield, and now he grasped his sword with both hands, in imitation of Harper's mighty slices. Those who tried to duck inside the long sword's reach were greeted with a kick to the face, or a downward slash, breaking spines and lopping off heads.

Suddenly a voice at Erik's rear shouted, "Hammond, sir. What are the orders?"

Erik glanced over his shoulder and almost died for the effort. Only a glint in his peripheral vision caused him to dodge the sword point aimed for his side. He slashed backward with his sword and felt it strike, hearing the sound of crushing bone at the same instant. A man screamed. Erik moved back from the fighting and said to Hammond, "Did you bring oil?"

"We have a dozen casks, no more."

"Light the barricade!" he ordered, and then he said to Sergeant Harper, "As soon as the flames take, I want a full withdrawal."

"Sir," said Harper as he cut a man deep enough along the chest that Erik could see the whiteness of ribs.

Erik could smell the fumes as behind them men poured oil around the base of the barricade. "Ready?" came the voice of Lieutenant Hammond.

"Yes!" shouted Erik as he killed another man.

Harper's bellow carried above the sound of battle as he cried out, "Withdraw!"

Trumpeters blew the retreat, and as Erik and the others stepped away from the barricades, dozens of torches were stuck into the wood. Those invaders coming over the barricade were either burned as the flames quickly spread or were trapped on the wrong side of the fire and quickly killed by the soldiers of the King.

Half staggering, half running, the exhausted defenders made their way to the second barricade. Water and food waited there. Those men who could, drank and ate, while those too tired to move just dropped down where they were. A few fainted from the effort, while others closed their eyes, grasping at the chance to sleep, if only for a few minutes.

Other men moved along the barricade, guarding against the possibility of the enemy somehow following closely, but as the fire rose along the first barricade, it was clear no one was crossing over that burning mass for at least the next hour. Harper said, " 'Tis right daft you are, Captain, sir, but it was a hell of a notion."

Erik sat upright, his back against the barricade. He finished drinking his third ladle of water and accepted a wet cloth, which he used to wipe the dirt, sweat, and blood from his face and hands. "Thank you, Sergeant. It gains us an hour's respite, and gives us an open killing ground." He glanced at the east, where the sun would soon be visible above the mountains, and said, "If we can hold here for this day and tonight, we should be able to get safely to Darkmoor with most of the men." Erik stood and shouted for a runner.

"Find another of your company," Erik ordered the youth. "I want orders sent to the north and the south that the time to fall back will come soon. Tell both flank commanders that once they see the enemy moving toward the center, I want a show of offense—make it look like a counterattack—then as soon as the enemy is moving away from those positions, they're to move with all speed to Ravensburg."

The runner sped off.

Erik sank back down behind the barricade and said, "I need some sleep."

"You should have an hour, sir," said Harper, watching the distant fire. When there was no answer, he turned to see Erik's eyes already closed.

"That's a capital idea, sir," said the exhausted Sergeant, who hailed a reserve soldier and said, "I'm grabbing a bit of sleep, so be a good lad and keep a eye on things for the Captain and me, all right?" Without waiting for an answer, Harper slumped down next to Erik and was asleep before his chin touched his chest. Elsewhere along the line, men who had fought all night also tried to rest, while the reserves kept vigil across the burning barricade.

Pug groaned. Miranda said, "Hold still!"

He lay on a table covered with a fresh white cloth while she massaged his back. "Stop acting like a baby," she scolded.

Pug said, "It hurts."

"Of course it hurts," she responded. "You get burned to a crisp by a demon, then as soon as you can, you go find another demon to battle."

"Seven of them, actually," Pug said.

She straddled his back, massaging him as they rested after their ordeal. "Well, you've got one left to deal with, and you're not even going to think about it until you're fit."

"We don't have that much time," Pug said.

"Tomas should be in Sethanon soon, and unless there are more surprises, I think he should be able to deal with this Jakan."

Pug said, "I don't know. What little I witnessed when your father fought Maarg, and what I remember when Jakan attacked me, leads me to believe we should all be at Sethanon when the demon finally reaches there."

Miranda got off his back, and Pug admired her long legs, shown to advantage by a short Quegan-style skirt. He sat up and stretched. "That felt great."

"Good," she replied. "Let's eat. I'm starved."

They left the room in Villa Beata, Pug's home on Sorcerer's Isle, and retired to the dining room. A servant, a Ji-kora reality master, appeared. The creature looked like a large upright walking toad. A year earlier he had appeared unbidden and begged entrance into Pug's school, and Pug had agreed. Like the other students on Sorcerer's Isle, he gave service in exchange for his studies. "You eat?" he asked.

"Please," said Pug, and the ugly creature stalked off toward the kitchen.

The midday meal was pleasant, as it had been each day since they had returned from the Pantathian mines. Though it had been only a week, it felt like ages since they had awakened in darkness, disoriented and exhausted. It had taken all of Miranda's energy for her to create a mystic light by which they could see.

The bisected demon had started to rot, so they assumed they had been in a stupor for at least two or three days. Pug used his last reserves of energy to transport them to Sorcerer's Isle, where Gathis had immediately seen to their needs.

They had been carried to their room and put to bed, where they slept for another day. Upon rising they had eaten, returned to bed, and slept the day through again. It had now been over a week since their return, and Pug felt as if he was getting close to his old strength back.

Gathis approached as they finished their meal and said, "May I have a word with you?"

Miranda rose. "I'll leave you alone."

"No, please," said the goblinlike creature. "This concerns you as well, Mistress."

She sat down. Gathis said, "As I once told you, I shared a bond with the Black One"—looking at Miranda, he said to her—"your father, Mistress."

She nodded.

To Pug, Gathis said, "When Macros last left Midkemia, at the end of the Riftwar, I told you I would know if he should die."

Pug said, "You think he is dead?"

Gathis said, "I know he is dead."

Pug glanced at Miranda whose face was an unreadable mask. Pug said to Gathis, "Of all of us, you knew him best. The loss must be difficult for you. I am sorry."

"Your commiserations are appreciated, Master Pug, but I think you misread me." He motioned for them to follow. "There is something I need to show the two of you."

They rose and followed him down a long hall. He led them outside, across the meadow that rolled away from the rear of the large house, and up a gentle rise to a plain hillside. When they were halfway up the rise, Gathis moved his hand and a cave was revealed.

Pug said, "What is this place?"

"You shall see, Master Pug," said Gathis, leading them into the cave.

Inside the cave they saw a small altar, upon which rested an icon. The image was of a man sitting atop a throne, a man familiar to both Pug and Miranda.

"Father," whispered Miranda.

"No," said Pug, "Sarig."

Gathis nodded. "It is indeed the lost God of Magic."

"What is this place?" asked Miranda.

"A shrine," Gathis said. "When the Black One found me, I was the last of a race that had once held a position of some importance in our world."

"You said you were related to goblins in the way the elves are akin to the moredhel," said Pug.

"That's an oversimplification. Elves and Dark Brothers are the same race, taken to different paths. My people, while distant kin to the goblins, were far more than that. We were a race of scholars and teachers, artists and musicians."

"What happened?" asked Miranda.

"The Chaos Wars lasted for centuries. To the minds of the gods they were nearly instantaneous, but to lesser beings they lasted for generations.

"Humans, goblins, and dwarves were among those who came to Midkemia at the end of the Chaos Wars. My people remained in our birth world. While other races thrived, mine did not. Macros found me, the last of my race, and brought me here."

Miranda said, "I am sorry."

Gathis shrugged. "It is the way of the universe. Nothing lasts forever, perhaps not even the universe itself.

"But one thing my people were as well as those other things I mentioned was a priesthood."

Pug's eyes widened. "You were a priesthood of magic!"

Gathis said, "Exactly. We were worshippers of Sarig, though by a different name."

Pug looked around and found a rock ledge upon which to sit. "Go on, please."

"As the last of my race I was desperate to find someone to carry on the worship of the God of Magic. Before I died I wished to see the continuation of what we believed was a most important cause, the return of magic to Midkemia."

Miranda said, "There's always been magic in Midkemia."

"I think he means the Greater Magic," said Pug.

"More," said Gathis. "The return of magic in the order intended."

"Intended by whom?" asked Miranda.

"By the nature of magic itself."

"There is no magic," said Pug, laughing.

"Exactly," said Gathis. "Nakor believes there is a primary reality in the universe that *anyone* may manipulate, take advantage of, and use beneficially, if he but tries. He is partially right. What is known as the Lesser Magic to humans is an intuitive magic, a magic of poetry and song, of feelings and senses. It is why the Lesser Magicians chose totems and elements with which to identify.

"The priests of the other orders believe that all magic is prayer answered. They are correct, though not in the way they think. It is not their gods answering their prayers, but rather magic itself responding in accordance to the nature of their particular clerical calling. This is also why the high priests and other highly advanced members of each order can effect magic that resembles one another's, while lesser practitioners would find such displays anathema.

"All is of a piece."

"So you're saying that magicians are in actuality worshipping Sarig?" asked Miranda.

"In a manner of speaking, but not exactly that. Each time a spell of the Greater Magic is incanted, the opportunity exists for prayer, for a tiny bit of that worship to feed Sarig, bringing him that much closer to returning to us."

"Well then," said Miranda, "why aren't you down at Stardock gathering converts?"

Pug laughed. "Politics."

"Exactly," said Gathis. "Can you imagine what should occur if one such as I appeared and claimed all that I have told you."

Miranda nodded. "I see your point. I've experienced enough to know you're probably right, and I still find it difficult to believe."

"That's because you're a product of your training, as was I," said Pug. "We must rise above that."

"What does this have to do with us? I mean, why are you telling us this now?"

"Macros the Black was the single most powerful master of magic upon Midkemia until the advent of Master Pug's return from Kelewan," said Gathis. "It is my mission to remain as close to whoever that person may be as long as I live.

"As long as the Black One existed, no matter how far removed, I was bound to him. Now he no longer exists, and I must continue in my mission of working on behalf of Sarig."

"So you want to create a similar bond with me?" asked Pug.

"In a manner of speaking, but you must understand exactly what this entails.

"You know what the bond was between Macros and Sarig. Sarig claimed Macros as his own, his agent on Midkemia, and provided him with his powers. You were the one who severed the bond between them."

Pug said, "But at the last Macros used Sarig's powers to defeat Maarg."

"Perhaps," said Gathis. "I was not a witness to that, but if it is as you described it to me when you first returned, then that was Sarig's last gift to Macros, the power to destroy himself and the demon, rather than fall prey to whatever it was stood behind the demon."

"Whatever it was stood behind the demon?" asked Miranda, and suddenly she was aware again of the knowledge that had been blocked from her memory. "I think I understand."

Gathis nodded. "I think you do, as well. Master Pug, you, on the other hand, are not connected to Sarig. You were not even given your powers on this world. Your ties to the Tsurani heritage and their practices, your native ties to Midkemia conspire to make you something of a neutral agent in this.

"Which is why you now have a choice."

"And that is?"

"You now understand that an ages-old conflict is under way, between powers so vast and ancient our mortal minds can barely comprehend them; we can only serve our tiny part in the great conflict. Your choice is this: you may continue to act as an independent agent for those causes you consider worthy, or you may dedicate yourself to Sarig, taking the place of Macros. If you do so, you gain greater power than you already have, for you will not only have the full measure of the gods' powers and knowledge native to Midkemia, you will also have your knowledge from Kelewan."

"So you're saying I was chosen and trained to be Macros's successor?"

Gathis regarded Pug for a silent moment. "I have come to know this much about the gods: often we act for reasons about which we are uncertain. Who is to say if anything Macros ever did was without Sarig's influences? Macros found you as a baby and unlocked something rare and powerful within you; I do not know if he understood where you would be today. I can't say he chose you to be his successor, but I can say you now stand in the place where you can choose to be such. It is up to you."

"What do I give up?" asked Pug.

"Freedom," said Gathis. "You will find you need to do things without understanding exactly why. Macros claimed he could see the future, and that was partially true, but part of that claim was theatrics, the showmanship of a vain man attempting to make everyone think he was far more than he really was. It's ironic, for he was more powerful than any man I've met, until I met you, Master Pug. But even the most powerful among your race has flaws, I have discovered over the centuries.

"In any event, you will find your life is no longer your own."

Pug said, "You offer a great deal, but you demand a great deal, as well."

"Not I, Master Pug; he does." Gathis pointed to the statue of the god.

Miranda said, "How long does he have to think this over?"

"As long as he needs," said Gathis. "The gods move along a stately course, in their own time, and the lives of mortals are but fleeting heartbeats to them."

Pug said, "You've given me a great deal to think about. What happens if I say no?"

"Then we will wait until another appears, one whose nature and powers are such that the god chooses him to assume the mantle of Sarig's agent."

Pug looked at Miranda and said, "Something else for us to discuss."

She nodded.

Gathis said, "I will leave you alone. Perhaps the god himself will guide your thoughts. If you need anything, I will be back at the villa."

The green-faced steward of the villa departed and Pug said, "What should I do?"

"Be a god? Seems like a hard one to reject."

Pug reached out and pulled her to him. As he held her close, he said, "It also seems like a hard one to accept."

"Well, we have time," said Miranda, hugging him back.

"Do we?" asked Pug as his mind turned to the question of the war.

Erik shouted orders as the battle reached a critical stage. For two days they had fought along the second barricade, suffering one breach, which had taken every reserve at Erik's disposal to close. He had successfully evaluated the demands for defending this position and had set up a schedule for rotating his soldiers in and out of the line, so that those who had fought longest could get some rest.

The wounded were being evacuated along with the support baggage to Darkmoor. Erik knew that it was only a matter of minutes before he would give the order to withdraw and he had to set the torch to his boyhood home.

He'd had moments of regret in anticipation of that act for months, since reviewing Calis's original plan of battle, but at this point he was so exhausted he felt nothing. Perhaps that would change when he actually saw the Inn of the Pintail, the Growers' and Vintners' Hall, and all the other familiar landmarks of Ravensburg in flames, but right now all he was concerned with was an orderly withdrawal.

The enemy seemed limitless. By Erik's rough calculation, they had lost six thousand men at the two barricades, while he had lost fewer than fifteen hundred. But he knew that losses of four to one were acceptable to the

Emerald Queen, while such a ratio was disastrous to the Kingdom. He needed to do better than six to one for the Kingdom to withstand the enemy.

Erik blocked a blow from a particularly muscular man with a war ax, then skewered him with a sword thrust. He stepped back, from the battle, letting a soldier take his place. Glancing around, he judged it time to withdraw. By the time they reached Darkmoor, night would be falling. He moved far enough from the fighting so he need not worry about anything except possibly a stray arrow and signaled for runners. Four of them came to stand before him and saluted. He said, "Pass the word up and down the line. General withdrawal on my signal."

The soldiers hurried off, and Erik saw the magician Robert d' Lyes rushing toward him. "Is there anything I can do to help?" the magician asked.

"Thanks, but unless you have a way to get those bastards on the other side to withdraw for a few minutes, so we can get out of here safely, I think not."

The magician said, "How many minutes?"

"Ten, fifteen. More than that would be good, but in that time I can get the last of the wounded to the wagons and the rest of the mounted infantry in the saddle. The horse archers can hold the enemy at bay while the foot soldiers move out; if we can do that, we might all survive to fight in Darkmoor."

Robert said, "I have an idea. I don't know if it will work, but it might."

"We're pulling out, so give it a try," said Erik.

"How long before you give the order?"

"Five more minutes," said Erik as he signaled for his horse.

As a soldier ran up leading Erik's mount, d' Lyes said, "That should be enough."

The magician hurried to a position a short distance behind the fighting, risking an errant arrow for his troubles. He closed his eyes and started a chant, then put his hand in his shirt and pulled out a small leather pouch. Opening it, he reached inside and took out something—Erik couldn't see what—and made several passes with his hands.

Suddenly a cloud of greenish black smoke appeared at the crest of the barricade. Instantly the invaders inside began to cough and retch. The smoke expanded, following the ridge line, and men on both sides fell back.

Then d' Lyes shouted, "Poison!"

Erik blinked in astonishment; then he shouted in the dialect of the invaders, "Poison! Poison! Withdraw! Withdraw!"

The cry was echoed up and down the line as men from both sides fell back. Erik wasted no time. He signaled up and down the line, crying, "Retreat! Retreat!"

The command echoed up and down the line, and the Kingdom Army withdrew from the barricade. Robert d' Lyes hurried to where Erik sat and said, "They won't be fooled for long. When those men who are vomiting recover, they'll be back."

"What was that you did?"

"It's a useful little spell designed to kill mice, rats, and other vermin in barns. If you breathe the smoke, you get very sick to your stomach for about an hour, but after that you're fine."

Erik was impressed. "Thank you for thinking of it."

"You're welcome. It might be more useful if I could figure a way to make it more toxic, so the enemy would really be poisoned."

"Only if you can also figure out how to keep it on the correct side of the battlefield."

"Yes," said the magician, "I see the problem. Now what do we do?"

"Run like hell," said Erik.

"Very well," said d' Lyes, and he started running as fast as he could to where his horse was tied.

Erik gave the order and watched with relief as the men too wounded to walk were carried to the last of the baggage wagons. Others hurried to mount waiting horses. The archers in the rocks climbed down as fast as they could, and mounted also or joined the general withdrawal, depending on which units they served.

Erik saw the enemy fleeing to the west, many of them rolling on the ground, clutching their stomachs, in what they thought were death throes. A few of his own men, also incapacitated by the smoke, were also helped to safety by their comrades.

Erik counted the minutes, and after ten had come and gone, he said, "Fall back!"

The light cavalry, spears at the ready, were scheduled to be the last units to withdraw before the horse archers. Erik passed them and saw tired, bloody men, but men with a look in their eyes that made his chest swell with pride. He saluted them, then cantered his horse toward town.

As he rode away, he saw firelight on the ridges, as the engineers torched their catapults and mangonels. The machines, too big and difficult to move without dismantling, were destroyed to deny them to the enemy.

Reaching Ravensburg, he saw men with torches at the ready. He glanced around his boyhood home as the baggage wagons rolled through the center of town, taking the wounded and the supplies to the next defensive position. Erik dismounted and loosened his horse's girth, giving the animal a bit of rest. He led the horse to a trough and let him drink a little. Erik watched, waiting for the signal from his rearmost scout that the chase was on, when he would have to burn his boyhood town.

But time passed and no enemy approached. Erik considered they might be leery of approaching the place where d' Lyes had "poisoned" them until they realized it was a ruse. That extra hour would gain them a precious advantage. When he judged they would safely be through, he shouted, "Order the archers and lancers to retire!"

A messenger rode off to the west, carrying word to the last of the Kingdom's scouts to withdraw, and Erik rode toward the Inn of the Pintail. He reached it as a soldier stood ready to ignite hay piled against the fence and outer wall. Erik said, "Give that to me," indicating the torch.

The soldier did as ordered, and Erik threw the torch into the hay. "No one's going to burn my home but me," he said. Then he turned and shouted, "Burn it!"

Everywhere soldiers rode or ran through the town, tossing hundreds of torches. Erik couldn't bring himself to watch the fire destroy the inn, so he put heels to his horse's barrel and rode back to the center of town. Flames were rising quickly on all sides as the first elements of the light cavalry rode through. He knew the horse archers would be the last out, and was determined to ride with them.

The horse archers came fast, in a maneuver created by Calis, one he said originated with riders in Novindus, the Jeshandi. Half the squad would ride, while the other half would cover and fire, then the squad that had ridden would stop and offer cover fire to the group that had just been firing. It required precision and practice, but Calis had drilled these horse archers to perfection, so their withdrawal was nearly flawless. A few enemy arrows sped after them, as the fires announced to the invaders that the Kingdom was withdrawing, but most were fired blindly, arched high from behind the cover of boulders, and fell harmlessly to the ground.

As enemy fire increased, Erik felt it was time to go, so he shouted, "That's enough! Retreat!"

The horse archers turned as one, set heels to their horses, and galloped to the east. They rode furiously until they were sure no enemy followed close on their heels, then they slowed to a relatively relaxed canter, saving the horses as much as they could.

The usual travel time to Wolverton was three hours on a walking horse. Erik reached the town in less than one. The entire way he saw the baggage wagons lumbering down the road, and as he reached Wolverton, he saw them slowing, moving around a building on the edge of town. Jadow and another man from his company stood waving, and Erik rode up. "What is it?"

"Most of your cavalry and infantry went by about ten, fifteen minutes ago. We almost had a disaster when they tried to run over the wagons."

"Are you overseeing traffic?"

Jadow grinned. "More. Got a few of those traps you asked for, enough so that after a couple of them go off, the enemy should slow down a bit." They waited as the wagons rolled on. Again Erik rested his horse. He and Jadow were too concerned with the possibility of the enemy's overtaking the last of the baggage train to engage in small talk. For another two hours the wagons rolled, until suddenly a company of riders could be seen, Erik's rear guard. Jadow motioned toward the company of riders. "They the last?"

Erik nodded. "If you hang around, my advice is, the next rider you see coming down the road, kill him."

Jadow motioned to where he had two horses tied to a broken-down fence and said, "Think I'd rather ride with you." Jadow and his soldier got the two horses, mounted, and returned to Erik's side. "Ride where I tell you, boys, and everything will be fine."

Erik motioned for Jadow to lead and followed him into the small town of Wolverton. "What have you done?"

"Well," said Jadow, "you asked for some nasty surprises, so we obliged. A couple of pits here, a few casks of oil there, some torches we just set burning in that building, some other little things. Nothing will be too damaging, but it should slow them as they start inspecting every building."

Erik nodded his approval. "Very good."

They rode through Wolverton. The town lay across the King's Highway, but it was surrounded on the north and south by flat meadows and groves, providing an impossible defensive position. If Jadow's surprises slowed the enemy a little, making them circle around the town instead of marching straight through, the extra minutes would save lives. Erik and Jadow came up behind the last wagon, slowly working its way along the King's Highway. Erik turned to Jadow. "You and the horse archers guard this and the other stragglers. I have to ride ahead."

"Yes, sir," said Jadow with his customary smile and half-mocking salute.

Erik pushed his tired horse forward, passing the last of the baggage wagons and a few walking wounded who could find no room in the wagons. Twice he found men resting on the side of the road, and he ordered them to keep going, lest they fall too far behind and be killed by the enemy.

As sundown neared, he was forced to rest his horse. Here the road rose steeply, heading to the summit. He looked down the trail and was astonished to see the long line of men and wagons trudging along the highway. He had ridden past every wagon behind him, yet until this moment he had no concept of how many men were still on the road. Torches were lit here and there, and soon a long, flaming line seemed to be creeping along the King's Highway, coming his way, a stately procession.

Erik felt a quickening urgency that precluded his standing idle, so he dismounted and led his horse along. He passed a wagon at the side of the road, where men worked frantically to repair a broken spoke, and when he turned a bend in the road, he saw it: Darkmoor.

Athwart the highway rested the walled city of Darkmoor, and along the eastern side of the mountains ran Nightmare Ridge. There, Erik knew, the fate of the Kingdom and the world of Midkemia would be decided. The city was now ablaze with lanterns and torches along the wall, so from this distance it looked as if a celebration was in progress. Erik knew it was an illusion, for those lights meant the full weight of the Western Realm's defenses would soon be in place.

The region of Darkmoor was actually to the south and east of the city that bore its name. The original Castle Darkmoor had been built as the Kingdom's westernmost defense long before the founding of Krondor. Over the years the town, then the city, of Darkmoor arose, until it, too, had been enclosed by a wall. After Wolverton, Erik had ridden through a relatively empty landscape, as most of the terrain close to the city was rocky and nonarable. Small trees and tough mountain grasses, low brush, and some flowers hugged the roadside. Farther back, trees grew deep in the valleys and gullies running down the west face. Most of the area around the city itself had been forested clear ages ago. Food and other perishables were hauled into Darkmoor from lower-lying farming hamlets.

On the highest peak to the north of the King's Highway, rising like a guardian, was the original Darkmoor Keep. It was now a citadel, for it had originally been been built as a walled fort and the wall and moat around the castle had never been removed. Now the city sprawled out across the pass, and the King's Highway ran through a massive oak gate, bound with iron and flanked by high turrets, each with crenellated, overhanging parapets. Erik judged that no one attempting to reach the gate would be able to do so without being exposed to bow fire, catapults, or hot water or oil from above.

The setting sun threw a red highlight on the castle, and Erik turned to the west. In the distance he saw the sun disapear in a haze of smoke, from the fires in Ravensburg and Wolverton.

Erik reached the gate of the city to discover that the street was packed with refugees from the west. He led his horse past frustrated soldiers trying to deal with the throng of humanity attempting to squeeze into the city.

Erik shouted, "Which way to the keep?"

A soldier looked over his shoulder and, seeing the crimson eagle on Erik's tunic, and the badge of rank, said, "To the center of town, and then left on High Street, Captain!"

Erik led his horse through the throng, occasionally having to shove someone aside to get past knots of confused citizens and fatigued, short-tempered soldiers. The journey took him nearly an hour.

Eventually he reached the ancient drawbridge that crossed the moat separating the citadel from the rest of city. A squad of soldiers had blocked off the street for a hundred yards in all directions, so that those needing quick access to and from the Prince's headquarters would not be impeded.

Erik approached the guard and pointed to the west. "Tell me, is that a clear passage to the western gate?"

The guard said, "It is. Runs along the wall and turns at that corner down there."

Erik sighed. "I wish someone at the gate had mentioned that." He started past the guard, who dropped a spear before Erik's chest.

"Here, now. Where do you think you're going?"

"To see the Prince and General Greylock," said a very tired Erik.

"And suppose you show me some orders, then?"

Erik said, "Orders? From whom?"

"Your officer, assuming you're not another deserter looking to tell the General some cock-and-bull story about being separated from your unit."

Erik slowly reached up, took a grip on the spear shaft, and without apparent effort moved it back upright, despite the soldier's attempts to keep it where he had it. As the man's jaw tightened and his eyes widened, Erik said, "I am an officer. I know I look worse for wear, but I need to see the Prince."

Other soldiers were approaching as they noticed the confrontation. Another shouted, "Hey, Sergeant!"

A sergeant in the uniform of Darkmoor, a black shield with a red raven on a branch on a tan tabard, ran over. "What's this, then?"

The soldier said, "This fellow wants to see the Prince."

The sergeant, a tough old boot used to instant obedience by his men, snapped, "And just who the hell might you be that the Prince would want to see you?"

Erik pushed aside the spear and stepped forward, locking eyes with the sergeant. "Erik von Darkmoor, Captain of the Prince's Special Command!"

At the mention of his name, several of the soldiers stepped aside, while the others glanced at the sergeant. The old veteran grinned and said, "Looks like you've seen a bit of trouble, then, Captain."

"You could say that. Now, step aside!"

The sergeant didn't hesitate, moving briskly to one side. As Erik passed, he handed the reins to the sergeant, saying, "Get him some water and feed him. He's all done in. Then send word where you've stabled him. He's a good horse and I don't want to lose him."

The sergeant took the reins. As Erik walked away, he said without looking back, "Oh, and when my sergeant arrives, send him straight to me. You'll have no trouble recognizing him. He's a tall, Keshian-looking fellow, dark skin, and he'll snatch your head right off your shoulders if you give him one half the trouble you just gave me."

Erik crossed the drawbridge. He looked up at the lights shining in the many windows of the ancient castle. Founded by one of his ancestors, Castle Darkmoor was an alien place to Erik. As a boy he had dreamed of someday being summoned here by his father, to be recognized and given a place in the household. When those dreams died, they were replaced by curiosity. Then they faded altogether. Now the castle had the ominous look of a bad place to die, and as he walked through the gatehouse, entering the ancient castle bailey, Erik realized that the feeling came from the fact that not only was there an army on its way here that wanted him dead, inside was a woman who had vowed to see him dead: Mathilda von Darkmoor, his father's widow and mother of the half brother he had killed.

With a deep sigh, Erik turned to a captain of the Guard and said, "Take me to Greylock. I'm Captain von Darkmoor."

Without a word the captain saluted, turned smartly, and led Erik into his ancestral home.

Twenty-four

Darkmoor

CALIS STUDIED THE GEM.

He was so engrossed in it he almost failed to notice the appearance of four figures in the great hall of the oracle. He glanced at the oracle's attendants, and as they displayed no distress, he assumed there was no danger.

He looked at the new arrivals and saw his father, resplendent in his white-and-gold armor, standing beside Nakor, Sho Pi, and a man dressed in the raiment of a monk of Ishap. Calis forced himself away from studying the gem and rose to greet them.

"Father," he said, hugging Tomas. Then he shook hands with Nakor.

Nakor said, "This is Dominic. He is the Abbot at Sarth. I thought he would prove useful to have with us."

Calis nodded.

Tomas asked, "You were engrossed in the gem when we arrived."

Calis said, "I am seeing things in it, Father."

Tomas said, "We need to talk." He glanced at the others and said, "But first I must pay my respects."

He crossed to the great, recumbent dragon, paused next to the gigantic head, and gently touched it. "Well met, old friend," he said softly.

Then he turned to the senior of her companions and said, "Is she well?"

The old man bowed slightly and said, "She dreams, and in her dreams she relives a thousand lives, sharing them with the soul who will occupy that great body after her." He motioned to a young boy, who came to stand before Tomas. "As I do with my replacement."

Tomas nodded. "Most ancient of races, we have transported you from one doom to another."

"There is risk," said the old man, "but there is purpose. We know that much."

Tomas nodded again and returned to Calis and the others.

Dominic looked past Tomas with wide eyes. "I never would have believed."

Nakor laughed. "No matter what I see, I never imagine I've seen it all. The universe offers endless surprises."

Calis said, "How is it you all managed to arrive together?"

"Long story," said Nakor. He produced a Tsurani transportation globe and said, "Not many of these left. Should get some more."

Calis smiled. "Unfortunately, the rift to Kelewan is on Stardock, and last I looked it's now firmly in the hands of Kesh."

"Not so firmly," said Nakor with a grin.

"What do you mean?" asked Calis.

Nakor shrugged. "Pug asked me to think of something, so I did."

"What?" asked Tomas.

"I'll tell you when we survive this coming ordeal and the fate of Stardock has some meaning."

Tomas said, "Calis, what did you mean about seeing things in the gem?"

Calis looked at his father in surprise, and asked, "Can't you see them?"

Tomas turned his attention to the Lifestone, an artifact he knew in some ways more intimately than any living being on Midkemia. He let his mind relax and watched the cool green surface, and after a moment saw a pulsing light, faint and hard to apprehend if one tried too hard. After a moment he said, "I see no images."

"Odd," said Calis. "They were apparent to me the first few moments I looked at it."

"What do you see?" asked Nakor.

Calis said, "I don't know if I have words. But I think I'm seeing the true history of this world."

Nakor sat on the floor. "Oh, this is most interesting. Please, tell me what you think you see."

Calis sat, as if to compose his thoughts.

Suddenly Pug and Miranda appeared.

Tomas welcomed his old friend and Miranda, motioning for them to sit.

"What is it?" asked Pug.

Tomas said, "Calis is about to tell us what he sees in the Lifestone."

Calis glanced to Miranda and to Pug, and for a moment he held the magician's gaze. Then he smiled. "I'm pleased to see you both again."

Miranda returned his smile. "As we are to see you."

Calis said, "I must speak of the Lifestone."

Nakor turned to Sho Pi and said, "Memorize every word if you want to continue bearing the mantle of disciple."

"Yes, Master."

Calis said, "The Lifestone is Midkemia, in the purest form, a reflection of all life that has gone before, is now, or will be, from the dawn until the end of time."

All fell silent as Calis considered his words.

"At the beginning, there was nothing and then came the universe. Pug and my father bore witness to that creation, as I have heard the story." He smiled at his father. "Several times."

"When the universe was born, it was aware, but in a fashion so far beyond what we comprehend that we have no adequate concepts to understand that awareness."

Nakor grinned. "It is like ants carrying food to their hive, while overhead a dragon sits atop a mountain. The ants have no concept of the dragon."

Calis said, "More, but that is not an entirely faulty comparison.

"This awareness is more than any of us—all of us together—could comprehend. It is so vast and so timeless. . . ." He paused. "I don't think I can say more about it.

"When Midkemia was formed, it was home to powers, basic forces of nature. Mindless, they were forces that built up and tore down."

"Rathar and Mythar," said Tomas. "The Two Blind Gods of Creation."

"As good a name for those forces as any," agreed Nakor.

Calis said, "Then came a reordering of things. Consciousness arose, and the beings that were mindless became purposeful. It is we who define the gods, in a fashion that makes sense to us, but they are so much more than this.

"The order of the universe is like a gem with many facets, and we see only one, that which reflects the existence of our own world."

Pug said, "It is shared with other worlds?"

"Oh yes," said Calis softly. "With all worlds. This is one of the key reasons why what we do here has a profound bearing upon every other world in the cosmos. It is the primal struggle between that which we label good and that which we call evil, and it exists in every corner of creation."

He turned to look at the others in the great cave and said, "I could speak for hours, so let me distill what I think I have discovered."

Calis composed his thoughts, then continued. "The Valheru were more than just the first race to live on Midkemia. They were a bridge between immortal and mortal. They were the first experiment, if you will, of the gods."

"Experiment?" said Pug. "What kind of an experiment?"

"I don't know," said Calis. "I can't even be certain what I'm saying is true, only that it feels true."

Nakor said, "It's true."

All eyes turned toward the little Isalani. He grinned. "It makes sense."

Pug said, "What makes sense?"

Nakor said, "Has anyone besides me wondered why we think?"

As the question came seemingly from out of the blue, everyone exchanged astonished glances. Pug laughed. "Not recently, no."

"We think because the gods have given us the power of apprehension," said Dominic.

Nakor shook his finger at the Abbot. "You know that's dogma, and you know the gods are as much the creation of mankind as mankind is the creation of the gods."

Pug asked, "So, then, what is your point?"

"Oh, just wondering," said Nakor. "I was thinking of that story you told me, about when you and Tomas went to find Macros, and you saw the creation of the universe."

"And?" asked Tomas.

"Well," began Nakor, "it seems to me you have to begin at the beginning."

Pug stared at the little man and burst out laughing. Within seconds everyone was laughing.

"See," said Nakor, "humor is a property of intelligence."

"All right, Nakor," said Miranda, "what are you talking about?"

Nakor said, "Something started it all."

"Yes," said Dominic. "There was a primal urge, a creator, something."

"Suppose," said Nakor, "it was a self-creation?"

"The universe just decided to awaken one day?" asked Miranda.

Nakor pondered the question a moment. "There is something I think we should always keep in mind: everything we talk about is limited by our own perceptions, our own ability to understand, in short by our very nature."

"True," agreed Pug.

"So to say the universe woke up one day is perhaps at one and the same time the most apt and the most incomplete way of putting it," said Nakor.

Dominic said, "This sort of debate is common in the courts of the church. The exercises in logic and faith can often be frustrating."

"But I think we have something here few of your brothers have, Abbot," said Nakor. "Eyewitnesses to creation."

"If that is what they saw," said Dominic.

"Ah," said Nakor and he could barely contain his glee. "We cannot be sure about anything, can we?"

" 'What is reality?' is a common question in those moot courts I spoke of," said the Abbot.

"Reality is what you bump into in the dark," said Miranda dryly.

Nakor laughed, then he said, "You've talked about this big ball thing blowing up to make the universe, right?"

Pug nodded.

"So, what if *everything* was inside that ball?"

"We assume it was," said Pug.

"Well, what was outside the ball?"

"We were," said Pug quickly, "and the Garden and the City Forever."

"But you come from within that big ball," said Nakor, and as the others watched, he stood and began to pace, animated by being on the brink of understanding. "I mean, you were born ages into the future from the creation, but from stuff inside the ball, if you see."

"What about the City Forever?" asked Miranda.

"Maybe it was created far in the future; what do you think?"

"By whom?" asked Pug.

Nakor shrugged. "I don't know, and for the moment I don't care. Maybe when you're a thousand years old you're the one who makes the City Forever and sends it back to the dawn of time so you and Macros have someplace to sit to watch the universe being born."

"Baby universes and thousand-year-old magicians," said Dominic, obviously trying to be patient and losing the attempt.

Nakor held up his hand. "Why not? We know traveling through time is possible. Which brings up, what is time?"

They all glanced at one another and each began to answer, but soon all fell silent. "Time is time," said Dominic. "It marks the passage of events."

"No," said Nakor. "Humans mark the passage of events. Time doesn't care; time just is. But what is it?" He wore a delighted grin as he answered his own question: "Time is what keeps everything from happening at once."

Pug's eyebrows rose. "So in the ball everything was happening at once?"

"And then the universe changed!" said Nakor with glee.

"Why?" asked Miranda.

Nakor shrugged. "Who knows? It just did. Pug, you told me when you found Macros this last time, he had begun to merge with Sarig. Was he Macros or was he Sarig?"

"Both for a short while, but he was still mostly Macros."

"I wish I could ask him, 'As you were merging, did you lose your sense of being Macros?' " For a moment Nakor looked genuinely regretful, but then his grin returned as he said, "I think it safe to say that the more you become one with a god, the less you stay you."

"Then I understand," said Dominic.

"What?" asked Miranda.

"What this madman is driving at." The old Abbot put his finger to his head. "Mind. The spirit of the gods, the 'everything' he talks about as 'stuff.' If everything was occurring at once, before this creation, then everything was everything. No differentiation."

"Yes!" said Nakor, delighted at the Abbot's observations.

"So, for reasons we will never know, the totality of creation acted to differentiate itself. This 'birth' of the universe was a means for the universe . . ." The Abbot's eyes widened. "It was the universe attempting to become conscious!"

Tomas's eyes narrowed. "I don't follow. Humans are conscious, as are other intelligent races, and the gods are conscious, but the universe is . . . it is, that's all."

"No," said Nakor. "Why humans? Why other thinking creatures?"

"I don't know," said Pug.

Nakor's expression turned serious. "Because becoming mortal is the means by which the universe, this 'stuff' I talk about, becomes self-conscious, self-aware. Each life is the universe's experiment, and each of us brings back knowledge to the universe when we die. Macros attempted to become one with a god, and learned that the further you get from mortality, the further you stray from that self-consciousness. Lesser Gods are more detached from 'self' than mortals; Greater Gods even more so, I wager."

Dominic nodded. "The Tear of the Gods allows the Order to communicate with the Greater Gods. It is a very difficult task. We rarely attempt it and when we do, often the communications are incomprehensible." The old Abbot sighed. "The Tear is a valuable gift, for it lets us work the magic that proves to those who serve us that Ishap is still living, so we can worship and work toward his return, but the nature of the gods, even that one we worship, is far beyond our ability to know."

Nakor laughed. "Very well, now if this universe was born the day Macros, Pug, and Tomas were watching, what does that say about the universe?"

"I don't know," admitted Pug.

"It's a baby," said Nakor.

Pug laughed. He couldn't help himself. "The universe is several billion years old, by my calculations."

Nakor shrugged. "That may be a two-year-old universe for all we know. What if it is?"

"What's the point?" said Miranda.

Tomas said, "Yes. While all this is fascinating, we still have some problems to solve."

Nakor said, "True, but the more we know about what it is we're involved with, the more we have a chance of solving those problems."

"Agreed, but where to begin?"

"I asked earlier, why do we think? I may have some idea." Nakor paused, then continued, "Suppose for a moment the universe, everything in it, and everything that ever was or will be is linked."

"We share something in common?" asked Dominic.

"No, more than that; we are all the same." Looking at Pug and Miranda, Nakor said, "You call it magic. I call it tricks." To Dominic he said, "You call it prayer. But it's all the same thing, and what it is . . ."

"Yes?" prompted Pug.

"That's where I run into a problem. I don't know what it is. I call it 'stuff.' " He sighed. "It's some sort of basic thing, something that everything is made up of."

"You might have called it spirit," suggested Dominic.

"You might have called it laundry," said Miranda dryly.

Nakor laughed. "Whatever it is, we're all part of it, and it's part of us."

Pug was silent for a moment. "This is maddening. I feel as if I'm almost at the edge of understanding something, but it's just outside my grasp.

"And what does this have to do with putting things right?"

"Everything. Nothing. I don't know," said Nakor agreeably. "It's just something I was thinking of."

Tomas said, "Much of what you say echoes things I knew once, when I was one with Ashen-Shugar."

Nakor said, "I think so. The universe is alive, a being of impossible complexity and vastness. It is, for want of a better term, a god. Maybe The God. I don't know."

"Macros called it the Ultimate," said Tomas.

"That's good!" said Nakor. "The Ultimate God, the One above All, as the Ishapians call Ishap."

"But you're not talking of Ishap," said Dominic.

"No, he's an important god, but he's not the Ultimate. I don't think this Ultimate even has a name. He just Is." Nakor sighed. "Can you imagine a being with stars in its head, billions of them? We have blood and bile, it has worlds and comets and intelligent races . . . everything!"

Nakor was obviously excited by the image, and Pug glanced at Miranda, seeing her smile reflecting his own amusement at the strange little man's pleasure.

"The Ultimate, if you will, knows everything, is everything, but He's a baby. How do babies learn?"

Pug, who had raised his children, said, "They watch, they are corrected by their parents, they mimic—"

"But," interrupted Nakor, "if you're God, and there's no Mama God or Papa God, how do you learn?"

Miranda was caught up in the discourse and began to laugh. "I have no idea."

"You experiment," said Dominic.

"Yes," said Nakor, and his grin became even wider. "You try things. You create things, like people, and you turn them loose to see what happens."

Miranda said, "So we're some sort of cosmic puppet theater?"

"No," said Nakor. "God isn't watching us on a celestial stage, because God is also the puppets."

"I'm completely lost," admitted Pug.

"We're back to why we think," explained Nakor. "If God is everything, mind, spirit, thought, action, dirt, wind"—he glanced at Miranda—"laundry, everything that is and can be, then each thing He is must be accounted for as having a purpose.

"What is life for?" he asked rhetorically. "It's a way to evolve thought. And what is thought for? It's a way to be aware, a stage between the physical and the spiritual. And time? It's a good way to keep things separated. And lastly, why humans, and elves, and dragons, and other thinking creatures?"

Dominic said, "So that spirit can be self-conscious?"

Nakor said, "Right!" He looked to be on the verge of doing a dance. "Each time one of us goes to Lims-Kragma's hall, we're sharing our life experience with God. Then we go back and do it again, over and over."

Miranda didn't looked convinced. "So you're saying we live in a universe where evil is just as much this God's fault as good?"

"Yes," said Nakor. "Because God doesn't see it as good or evil; God's learning about good and evil. To Him, it's just the odd way certain creatures behave."

"Seems He's slow," said Pug dryly.

"No, He's vast!" insisted Nakor. "He's doing this over and over a billion billion times a day, on a billion worlds!"

Tomas said, "At one time Pug and I asked Macros what the point was if we live in a universe this vast, this complex, should one little planet succumb to the Valheru. He told us the nature of the universe changed after the Chaos Wars and that a reemergence of the Valheru into Midkemia would change the order of things."

"I think not," said Nakor. "Oh, I mean it would be a very unhappy situation for everyone on Midkemia, but eventually the universe would right itself. God is learning. Of course, billions of people could die before something happened to set things right again."

Miranda said, "You make it all sound so pointless!"

"If you look at it that way, yes," said Nakor. "But I like to think the point is we're teaching God to do the correct thing—we're correcting a baby—and that good is worth struggling for, that kindness is better than hatred, that creation is better than destruction, and many other things as well."

"Anyway," said Pug, "it's far more of an academic question to the people living in the Kingdom."

Calis said, "Nakor's right."

All eyes returned to Calis. "He has just made it possible for me to understand what it is that is being done and why I'm here."

Miranda asked, "Why?"

Calis smiled. "I need to unlock the Lifestone."

Erik drank deeply. The wine was a chilled white, a variety common to this part of the duchy. "Thank you," he said as he put down the flagon.

Prince Patrick, Owen Greylock, and Manfred von Darkmoor sat at a table with Erik. Around the room stood a half-dozen other nobles, some dressed like court dandies and others as dirty and blood-soaked as Erik.

Patrick said, "You've done well considering the rapidity with which Krondor fell."

"Thank you, Highness," said Erik.

Greylock said, "I just wish we had more time to prepare."

Patrick said, "There is never enough time. We must trust that we have done enough so that we can hold them here, at Darkmoor."

A messenger hurried in, saluted, and handed a message to Greylock. He opened it and said, "Ill news. The southern reserves are overrun."

"Overrun," said Patrick, slamming the table in frustration. "They were supposed to be cleverly hidden away, ready to strike at the enemy and bleed them from behind. What happened?"

Owen handed the scroll to the Prince, but he said for the benefit of the others in the room, "Kesh. She's moved her army just south of Dorgin. The enemy's southern wing was being pinched too tightly, and when they ran into the Keshians on one flank, and the dwarves ahead, they turned north and overran our fortification."

"Kesh has taken a hand?" asked a tired-looking old noble whom Erik didn't recognize.

"It was to be expected," said Patrick. "If we survive this war, we'll worry about Kesh after."

"What of Lord Sutherland?" asked the noble.

"The Duke of the Southern Marches is dead. Gregory as well as the Earl of Landreth died in the fighting. My lords, if this report is accurate, for all intents and purposes the southern reserves no longer exist," said Greylock.

One of the fancily dressed nobles said, "Perhaps we should consider falling back to Malac's Cross, Highness?"

The Prince threw the man a withering look, but refused to dignify the suggestion with a comment. Looking at Erik, he said, "Those of you just in, please follow the squires outside to your quarters. You'll find fresh clothing and a bath waiting. I'll be pleased to dine with you in an hour's time." He rose, and the others followed suit. "We'll continue this discussion at dawn tomorrow. We will have more intelligence by then." He turned and left the room.

After the Prince had departed, Manfred motioned to Erik and Owen to move away from the door. "Well, we have an awkward situation, it seems, gentlemen."

Erik nodded. "I understood what I was in for the moment I crossed the drawbridge."

Owen said, "We are the Prince's men, may I remind your lordship."

Manfred waved away the comment. "Tell that to my mother." Then he gave a rueful smile. "Better yet, don't."

Erik said, "We can't conduct the business of this war while attempting to avoid your mother, Manfred."

"Erik has that right," said Owen.

Manfred sighed. "Very well. Owen, I've instructed our current Swordmaster to turn your old quarters back over to you; I thought you might be more comfortable there, and truth to tell, it's getting a little bit crowded around here."

Owen smiled. "I bet Percy is not happy."

"Your former assistant was never a happy man; he was born with a long face." Turning to Erik, Manfred said, "You'll stay in a room near mine. The closer you are to me, the less likely Mother is to send someone after you."

Erik looked dubious. "Duke James tried to reason with her."

"No one 'reasons' with Mother. I suspect you'll find that out before this night is through. Now, let me show you to your quarters." Turning to Greylock, he said, "Owen, I'll see you at supper."

"My lord," said Owen. The three left the conference hall, and while Owen went one way, Manfred took Erik another.

"This castle is quite large," said Manfred. "It's easy to get lost. If you do, ask any servant where to go."

"I don't know how long I'll stay," said Erik. "Owen and the Prince haven't told me what my next position is to be. I replaced Calis in the fallback, but now that phase is over."

"I suspect something similar," said Erik's half brother. "It appears you've done quite well." He glanced around the ancient halls of Darkmoor Castle. "I hope I acquit myself as well when the time comes."

"You will," said Erik.

They walked around a corner, and Erik almost stumbled. Coming along the corridor was a stately procession, an older woman in regal raiment, followed by two guards and several lady companions. She stopped for a moment when she saw Manfred, but when she recognized Erik, her eyes grew enormous. "You!" she said with a near-hiss of contempt. "It's the *bastard*. The murderous bastard!"

She turned to the nearest guard and said, "Kill him!"

The stunned guard looked from Mathilda, mother of the Baron, to Manfred, who motioned with his hand for the guard to step away. The guard nodded to the Baron and stepped back. Manfred said, "Mother, we've been all over that. Erik has a pardon from the King. Whatever has gone before is over."

"Never!" said the old woman with a hatred that surprised Erik. He had imagined her distaste for him, from the years when his mother demanded Erik's father acknowledge him to the murder of her son, but never had he experienced anything like this firsthand. Of all the men he had faced in battle, none had regarded him with the pure, naked hatred Mathilda von Darkmoor revealed in her eyes.

"Mother!" said Manfred. "That's enough. I'm ordering you to desist!"

The woman turned her gaze upon her son, and Erik saw instantly that her hatred wasn't limited to Erik alone. She stepped forward, and for an instant Erik feared she would strike her son. In a strident whisper she said, "You order me?" She looked her son up and down. "If you were the man your brother was, you'd have killed this murdering bastard before he got away. If you were even half as much a man as your father, you'd have married and had a son by now, and this bastard's claim would mean nothing. Do you want him to kill you? Do you want to lie in the dirt while this killer takes your title? Do—"

"Mother!" Manfred roared. "Enough!" He turned to the guards and said, "*Escort* my mother to her quarters." He told his mother, "If you can compose yourself, dine with us tonight, but if you can't maintain a shred of dignity before Prince Patrick, do us the courtesy of dining in your room! Now go!"

Manfred turned and began walking, and Erik followed, but he glanced over his shoulder. She never took her eyes from him, and each step of the way Erik knew the old woman wished him dead.

Erik was so intent on the woman he almost knocked Manfred down when he turned the corner. Manfred said, "Sorry about that, Erik."

"I never imagined. I mean, I thought I understood . . ."

"Understand Mother? You'd be the first." He waved for Erik to follow and said, "Your room is down here, at the end of the hall."

When he opened the door and Erik entered, Manfred followed. "I picked this one for two reasons," said Manfred. He pointed to the window. "It's a quick exit. And this is one of the few rooms in Darkmoor that doesn't have a secret passage leading to it."

"Secret passage?"

"Quite a lot of them, really," Manfred said. "This castle was enlarged several times since the original Baron built the first tower keep. There had been some quick exits should the castle fall, then some additional rooms added with back passages so the lord could visit his favorite servant in the middle of the night. Some of them serve a useful purpose, so servants can move through the castle without getting underfoot, but for the most part they're deserted old byways, useful for those who wish to spy on their neighbors or for assassins."

Erik sat down on a chair in the corner. "Thank you."

"You're welcome," said Manfred. "If I may suggest, a bath and change of clothing. I'll have the servants fetch you some water straightaway. The clothes in the wardrobe should fit." He grinned. "They were Father's."

Erik said, "Do you delight in upsetting your mother?"

Manfred's face took on an edge of anger. "More than you'll ever know."

Erik sighed. "I thought about some of the things you said about Stefan, when you came to visit me in jail. I guess I never appreciated how hard it must be for you."

Manfred laughed. "You'll never know."

"Do you mind if I ask you something?"

"What?"

"Why does she hate you? I know why she hates me, but she looked at you the same way."

Manfred said, "That, brother, is something I may or may not choose to disclose someday, but for the time being, let us just say that Mother has never appreciated the way I choose to live my life. As the second son, who would not inherit, it was only a source of some slight conflict. Since Stefan's . . . demise, the tension has increased significantly."

"Sorry to have asked."

"That's all right. I can appreciate why you'd be curious." Manfred turned toward the door. "And sometime I may just tell you. Not because you have any right to know, but because it would make Mother supremely unhappy if I did."

With what Erik considered an evil smile, Manfred left the room. Erik sat back, waiting for the servants to bring his bath water. He had dozed off when they knocked. Sleepily he rose and opened the door, and a half dozen servants entered, carrying buckets of steaming water and a large metal tub.

He allowed the two men who had carried the tub inside to remove his boots for him, while the others filled it. Sitting in the hot water made Erik feel as if every ache and pain was going to fade away. He lay back a moment, then suddenly sat bolt upright as one of the servants began to wash him.

"Is anything wrong, m'lord?"

"I'm not a lord. You can call me 'Captain,' and I can bathe myself," said Erik, taking the washing cloth and soap from the man. "That will be all."

"Shall we lay out clothing before we go?"

"Ah yes, that would be fine," said Erik, now fully awake. The other servants left, while the one who had spoken selected clothing from the wardrobe. "Shall I fetch boots, Captain?"

"No, I'll wear my own."

"I'll try to clean them before you leave, sir." He was out the door with them before Erik could object. Erik shrugged and started washing in earnest. He had rarely had the luxury of a hot bath, and as the water cooled, he found himself reviving. He knew that as soon as supper was over, unless the Prince demanded more meetings, he was going to turn in and sleep the sleep of the dead.

Then he reconsidered that image and decided he'd sleep lightly, even with the door barred. Erik had no idea of the time, but decided he didn't want to be late for dinner with the Prince of Krondor. He dried himself off and inspected the clothing chosen for him by the servant. The man had laid out a pair of pale yellow leggings, a light blue tunic, and a stylish cloak of very light grey, almost white. Erik decided to leave aside the cloak, and donned the hose and tunic. Just as he was finishing, the servant opened the door and said, "Your boots, Captain."

Erik was astonished. In a few minutes the man had managed to get all the blood and filth off, and return the leather to a passable shine. "Thank you," said Erik as he took the boots.

The servant said, "Shall I have the bathtub removed while you dine?"

"Yes," said Erik as he donned his boots. The servant departed, and Erik ran his hand over his chin. He wished for a razor and some soap and supposed that had he asked for them, they would have been provided, but he hadn't, so he decided some whiskers were preferable to keeping the Prince of Krondor waiting.

He went out into the hall and went around the corner, to where he had left the council room, and found a pair of guards standing at the door to that chamber. He asked directions to the dining hall and the guard saluted and said, "Follow me, Captain."

He did so and the man led him through a series of passages, to what Erik expected was part of the original keep, or a series of rooms added soon after, for the dining hall was surprisingly intimate. There was a square table, with room for a dozen diners aside, but the walls were only a few feet behind each of them, so if too many people attempted to move at the same time, things could become quite tangled. Erik nodded to several of the nobles he had met at Krondor and was pointedly ignored by several others who were deep in private conversations. Owen was already there and indicated he should come and sit next to him.

Erik moved around the table and saw the three seats on the right next to Greylock were empty. Greylock said, "Take this one," indicating the seat on his left. He patted the seat on his right and said, "This is the Prince's."

Then Erik noticed every noble at the table was watching him and suddenly he felt embarrassed. Dukes and Earls, Barons and Squires, all were seated below him at the table. He knew that where one sat in relationship to the Prince had serious implications in matters of court intrigue, and he suddenly wished he had thought to take the chair opposite the Prince, at the farthest table on the other side of the room.

A few minutes later, the door behind them opened, and Erik turned to see Prince Patrick enter. He rose, as did the other nobles, and they all bowed their heads.

Then came Baron Manfred, their host, followed by his mother.

The Prince took his place at the center of the head table, and Manfred moved to his right hand. Mathilda moved to her chair, but when she saw Erik she said, "I will not sit at the same table as my son's murderer!"

Manfred said, "Then, madam, you shall dine alone." With a nod of his head, he ordered the guards to escort his mother from the hall. She turned and silently left with her escort.

Several of the nobles in attendance spoke softly to one another until the Prince pointedly cleared his throat. "Shall we begin?" he asked.

Manfred bowed his head and the Prince sat. The others followed suit.

The food was splendid and the wine was the best Erik had ever tasted, but fatigue made it hard for him to keep alert. Still, the discussions around him were all-important, for men spoke about the coming fight.

At one point someone observed that the northern flank was holding so well it might prove wise to send for some of their soldiers to reinforce Darkmoor. The Prince overheard the remark and said, "That wouldn't be wise. We can't assume they won't return there in force the next day."

Discussion around the table turned to speculation about the coming fight, and after a while, Prince Patrick said, "Captain von Darkmoor, you more than any man here have fought the enemy. What can we expect?"

Every eye in the room turned toward Erik. He glanced at Greylock, who gave him a slight nod.

Erik cleared his throat and said, "We can expect between a hundred and fifty and a hundred and seventy-five thousand soldiers to arrive outside the city walls and along the entire length of Nightmare Ridge."

"When?" asked one richly dressed court dandy.

"Anytime," answered Erik. "As early as tomorrow."

The man went pale at the news and said, "Perhaps, Highness, we should call up the Army of the East. They are only camped down in the hills to the east."

Patrick said, "The Army of the East will be called when I decide it's time." He glanced at Erik. "What sort of men do we face?"

Erik knew the Prince had read every report sent back by Calis on his three trips to Novindus, during his grandfather Arutha's reign, during his uncle Nicholas's reign, and the last time. He had also spoken to the Prince on this very subject no less than five times, so Erik knew he was asking for the benefit of those nobles in the room who were untested in battle.

Erik glanced at Greylock, who again gave him a faint nod and a slight smile. Erik knew Owen well enough to understand what he was being asked to do.

Erik cleared his throat. "Highness, the enemy is composed of what were originally mercenary companies, men who fought for pay under a hard-and-fast code of conduct. They have since been forged by murder, terror, and dark magic into a force unlike any that has waged war on the Kingdom in history." He looked around the room and said, "Some are soldiers who have been fighting their way across half a world, from the fall of the Westlands in Novindus to the destruction of Krondor. For twenty years they have known nothing but war, plunder, pillage and rape." He caught the dandy's eye. "Some of them are cannibals."

The man went pale and seemed as if he might faint.

Erik continued. "They will come at us because they have no other option. We have destroyed their fleet behind them, and they have no food. They also number some ten to twenty thousand Saaur—we don't know the exact number." Some of the eastern nobles looked blank at the name. "For those who haven't been briefed, the Saaur are lizardmen, something akin to the Pantathians, but nine feet tall. They ride war-horses twenty-five hands at the withers, and the sound of them charging is like thunder across the mountains."

"Oh, dear gods!" said the dandy and he rose up, holding his hand over his mouth. He dashed from the room, and after a moment of silence, several of the lords in the room exploded into laughter.

The Prince laughed as well. Then after the mirth had subsided, he said, "My lords and gentlemen. Despite the levity, every word Captain von Darkmoor has uttered is true. More: if anything, he underestimates the foe."

"What are we to do?" asked another well-dressed lord who looked as if he had never held a sword in his life.

"My lord, we will fight. Here we stand, at Darkmoor and along Nightmare Ridge. And we will not be budged, for if the enemy passes us, the Kingdom is doomed. It will be victory or death. There is no other choice."

The room fell silent.

Twenty-five

Revelations

DRUMS SOUNDED.

Trumpets blew and men ran along the walls of Darkmoor. Erik was dressed and out the door as fast as he could, racing for the council hall.

He was the third man in the room, after Patrick and Greylock, and was only there for a few moments before a half dozen other nobles came running in. Manfred entered, calmly looked around, and said, "They are here."

No one had to ask who "they" were.

Patrick wasted no time. "Owen," he said, "I want you and Earl Montrose to ride to the south, along the eastern ridge. Take a company and see what we have on that flank. If the entire southern reserves are gone, as reported, I need to know what the enemy brings north. Don't engage unless you're attacked, and then try to get back here as fast as possible. If you run into any remnants of the southern reserves, bring them back with you."

At that moment, Arutha, Lord Vencar, and his two sons entered the room. Erik nodded.

"Arutha," said Patrick. "Your arrival is timely. I want you to oversee the administration of the city. We're going to lock down the gates, and we'll need to control the consumption of food and make sure no one compromises our security by leaving or smuggling." He turned to Manfred. "You're in charge of the citadel, as is your right, but I will oversee the conduct of the war from these headquarters."

Manfred nodded. "Highness."

The Prince turned to Erik. "Erik, I want you to ride north, and oversee the northern defenses. If the south is as weak as I fear, we need to ensure we have no breaches in the north." He looked Erik in the eyes, and said, "Unless you're recalled, defend to the last man."

Erik nodded. "I understand." He didn't wait for further orders but hurried out of the room, to the bailey, and asked for his horse, and rode out.

An hour later he was moving on one of the newly constructed roads, cut into the eastern face of the mountains, a dozen yards below the ridge line. Along the peaks above him, he could see defensive emplacements. He could tell the men were ready, as they ran, carrying supplies, shouting commands, and readying weapons. The fighting hadn't started yet, but Erik could tell the enemy was close.

He rode as fast as he could. He studied every foot of the ridge above him as he rode past.

While the front was a hundred miles long, roughly fifty on each side of Darkmoor, the northern command post was located just twenty miles north of the city. Erik reached it by midday.

Jadow Shati stood outside a small command tent, obviously distressed, with a short man wearing the tabard of Loriél. When Erik entered the camp, Jadow said, "Man, I am glad to see you."

Handing the reins of his horse to a soldier, Erik said, "Why?"

Jadow indicated the other man with a nod of his head..

The short man, who had a square head, short-cropped grey hair, and a square jaw, said, "Who the hell are you?"

Erik realized that he had dressed in his blue tunic and yellow leggings, and had left his uniform back in Castle Darkmoor. Quickly sizing up the short man, Erik said, "I'm your commander. Who the hell are you?"

The man blinked. "I'm the Earl of Loriél!" Then he lowered his voice. "And you are?"

"Knight-Captain von Darkmoor, of the Prince's Special Command, and I'm to command the northern flank."

"Well, we'll just see about that," said the man, his face growing florid. "I'm sworn vassal to the Duke of Yabon, and I'll take orders from the Prince of Krondor, but this special army and you jumped-up boy officers are more than I can stomach! I'll be down to Darkmoor to talk to the Prince himself."

"My lord," said Erik in a soft but firm tone.

"What?"

"Have a nice ride."

After the man left, Jadow burst out laughing. "Man, that little fellow is about as pleasant as a boil on the ass. I hope he stays away for a month."

"Well, given the mood our Prince was in when I left, I suspect his lordship will find little sympathy for his protests. Now, what's the situation?"

"As best I can judge, we have about six companies intact north of here, with ample supplies down at the bottom of the ridge. Some of the boys are pretty beat up, lads who were fighting along the northern front for the last month, but there are some fresh reserves, so overall we're in good shape. The bad news is we're facing Duko."

"I've heard of him. What do we know?"

"Not much. Rumors. A few things we've learned from captives. He's smart, has survived where some others, like Gapi, haven't, and he's still able to command a large contingency. Man, I don't know. If I was to guess, I think he's the best they've got after Fadawah."

"Well then," said Erik, "I guess we have our work cut out for us."

Jadow grinned. "The nice part is we're where they want to be, and they're not."

"You have a happy facility to put things in perspective," said Erik.

Jadow asked, "What are the orders?"

"Simple. Kill anyone who comes up that slope."

"I like simple," said the former mercenary from the Vale of Dreams. "I'm tired of this moving backward."

"No more of that," said Erik. "From this point on, if we move backward, we've lost."

"Well," said Jadow, "we must make sure we don't move backward."

Erik said, "I couldn't have put it better myself."

A trumpet sounded and Jadow said, "Seems they're coming."

Erik drew his sword. "Then let's greet them."

As they climbed the slope to the ridge line, Erik said, "Who else is on this flank?"

"Your old friend Alfred. He's got a company to the north of this one, and then Harper, and Jerome, who's anchoring the end of the line. Turner is to our south, Frazer after him, then it's the Prince's command at the city."

Erik smiled. "With sergeants like that, how can we lose?"

Jadow grinned. "How, indeed?"

Erik looked down the western slope, below the ridge line, and said, "A lot of men are about to die over twenty yards of dirt."

Jadow said, "That's the truth. But if what Captain Calis told us, on that beach in Novindus, is true, it's a pretty important twenty yards."

Erik said, "No doubt about it." He turned and looked down the slope at the men climbing toward him. The archers started firing and Erik could feel the tension in his shoulders as he waited for the first man to close, so he could engage the enemy and get this matter over with.

Then, as if men sprang from the ground, a sea of attackers appeared before him. Erik began to fight.

Pug frowned. "Unlock the Lifestone? How do you propose to do that?"

"What does it mean?" asked Tomas, looking at his son. "Does that release the Valheru?"

Calis shook his head. He sighed, as if very tired. "I'm not sure I can answer either question. I don't know how to unlock the forces inside this thing." He pointed at the pulsing green stone, with the golden sword protruding from it. "I just know that once I begin, I should be able to manipulate the energies within."

"How do you know this?" asked Nakor.

Calis smiled at him and said, "As you are so fond of saying, 'I just know.'

But once I've begun, I may not be able to stop, so I want to be certain I'm doing the correct thing." He pointed at the stone. "This is something that never should have been allowed."

Tomas rubbed his chin. "Ashen-Shugar said basically the same thing to Draken-Korin."

"This is what caused the Chaos Wars," said Nakor.

All eyes turned to him. Tomas asked, "How can you be certain?"

"Think about it. You have a Valheru's memory. Why was the Lifestone created?"

Tomas let his mind drift back, recalling memories he had first experienced fifty years before, but memories that originated with a being ages dead. Suddenly the memories washed over him.

A call came. Ashen-Shugar sat alone in his hall, deep below the mountains. His mount, the golden dragon Shuruga, lay curled in sleep below the huge vertical shaft that gave him access to Midkemian skies.

It was a strange call, unlike any he had heard before. It was a summoning, but one without the bloodlust that drew the Dragon Host together to fly across the stars for pillage and plunder. In his hall, Ashen-Shugar had found himself changing, as another presence, a being named Tomas, had come to him, in thought, from a distant place. By his nature, he should have felt outrage, a murderous reaction to the presence in his mind, yet this being, Tomas, seemed to be a part of him, as natural as his left hand.

With a mental command he woke Shuruga, and leaped upon the back of the great beast. The dragon jumped upward and with mighty wings beat for the sky, heading out of the mountain hold that was the domain of the Ruler of the Eagles' Reaches.

Eastward he flew above the range of mountains that would someday be known as the Grey Towers, and over another range that would be called the Calastius Mountains, to a vast plain, upon which the race met. He was the last to arrive.

He circled Shuruga and ordered the great dragon to descend. Each Valheru waited as the mightiest among them touched down. In the center of the circle stood a figure resplendent in black and orange armor, Draken-Korin, who called himself the Lord of Tigers. Two of his creatures, tigers bred by magic to walk upright and speak, stood on either hand, snarling, their powerful arms crossed. They were objects of indifference to the Ruler of the Eagles' Reaches, for despite their fierce appearance, these lesser creatures were of no danger to a Valheru.

By common opinion, Draken-Korin was the strangest of the race. He had ideas of new things. No one knew from where those ideas came, but he was obsessed by them.

* * *

Tomas blinked. "Draken-Korin! He was *different*!"

Nakor asked, "Have you never wondered why?"

Tomas said, "No. I mean, Ashen-Shugar never wondered why."

Nakor said, "The Valheru appear to be a race with a surprising lack of curiosity. Anyway, what do you remember?"

"I remember being summoned."

"For what?" asked Pug.

Tomas said, "Draken-Korin summoned the race, and he proclaimed that the order of the universe was changing. The old gods, Rathar and Mythar, had fled . . ." Tomas's eyes widened. "He said, *'or have been deposed'*!"

"Deposed?" said Miranda.

"By the Controller Gods!" said Dominic.

"Wait!" said Tomas. "Let me remember!" He closed his eyes.

". . . but for whatever cause, Order and Chaos have no more meaning. Mythar let loose the strands of power and from them the new gods arise," said Draken-Korin. Ashen-Shugar studied the one who was his brother-son, and saw something in his eyes, something that he now realized was madness. "Without Rathar to knit the strands of power together, these beings will seize the power and establish an order. It is an order we must oppose. These gods are knowing, are aware, and are challenging us."

"When one appears, kill it," answered Ashen-Shugar, unconcerned by Draken-Korin's words.

Draken-Korin turned to face his brother-father, and said, "They are our match in power. For the moment they struggle among themselves, seeking each dominion over the others as they strive to gain mastery of that power left by the Two Blind Gods of the Beginning. But that struggle will end, and then shall our existence be threatened. They *will* turn their might upon us."

Ashen-Shugar said, "What cause for concern? We fight as we have before. That is the answer."

"No, there needs be more. We must fight them in harmony, not each alone, lest they overwhelm us."

Ashen-Shugar said, "Do what you will. I will have none of it." He mounted Shuruga and flew home.

Tomas said, "I never dreamed."

"What?" asked Pug.

Looking at Miranda, Tomas said, "Your father knew! He wasn't just creating a weapon to balk the Tsurani conquest or even to stem the return of the Dragon Host to Midkemia, he was preparing us for this fight!"

"Explain, please," said Nakor.

"Something changed Draken-Korin," said Tomas. "He was mad by the standards of his own race. He had these strange notions and odd compulsions. He was the driving force behind the creation of the Lifestone. He masterminded the race's vesting its powers in that crystal."

"No," said Calis quietly. "He was a tool. Something else was the mastermind."

"Who?"

"Not who," said Nakor. "What?"

All eyes turned toward the strange little man. "What do you mean?" asked Pug.

Nakor said, "In each of you, something is locked away." He moved his hand in an arc, and a golden nimbus of light sprang up, washing the room. Pug's eyes widened, for while he knew that Nakor had far more power than he ever admitted to, this shell of protection was something beyond Pug's experience. He recognized it for what it was, but had no idea how the little man could so effortlessly create it.

Miranda asked, "Who are you?"

Nakor grinned. "Just a man, as I have said many times."

"But you are more," Dominic said flatly.

Nakor shrugged. "I am also a tool, in a sense." He looked at each of them in turn. "Several of you have heard me speak of my life, before, and all I told you is true. When I was a child, powers came to me and my father threw me out of the village for my pranks. I traveled and learned, and have been much as you see me now for most of my life.

"I met a woman named Jorna, whom I thought I loved—young men often think physical hunger is love—and in my vanity thought she loved me; we also can rationalize anything when it suits our purposes. Look at me!" He smiled. "A young and beautiful woman falling under my charms?" He shrugged. "It doesn't matter. What matters is that I was left a wiser if sadder man." He looked at Miranda. "You know what came next. Your mother came looking for someone who could teach her more than I, for as I have always said, I am but a man who knows a few tricks."

Miranda asked, "Why do I get the feeling you may be the only person on this planet who would use that description?"

"Be that as it may," continued Nakor, "Jorna became Macros's wife, and I became a traveler." He looked around the room. "My life changed one day when I slept in a burned-out shack on the side of the hills in Isalani. I had always had the ability to do tricks, little things, but that night I dreamed, and in my dream I was told to seek out something."

"What?" asked Pug.

Nakor opened his ever-present carryall and reached deep inside. It was not the first time Pug had seen the little man stick his arm inside up to the shoulder, when from the outside the bag appeared to be only two feet deep. Pug knew there was something inside, like a tiny rift, that allowed Nakor to reach through the bag to a location where he had stored an astonishing assortment of items. "Ah!" he said, pulling out one. "I found this."

Dominic's eyes widened, while the others stared in curiosity. Nakor held a cylinder, perhaps eighteen inches long, four inches in diameter. It was a cold, greyish white color. At each end of the cylinder was a knurled knob.

"What is it?" asked Miranda.

"A very useful thing," said Nakor. "You would be astonished at the information this object has." He twisted one end, and the device opened with a click; a half inch section of the cylinder detached from the side, allowing Nakor to pull out a long piece of what appeared to be a pale, translucent white parchment or paper. "If you pull long enough, you can fill up this room." He pulled and pulled, and the device continued to emit the long paper. "This stuff is amazing. You can't cut it or tear it or write on it. Dirt doesn't stick." The paper was covered in fine writing. "But whatever you want to know about, I bet it's in here."

"Amazing," said Pug. He looked at the writing and said, "What language is that?"

"I don't know," said Nakor, "but over the years, I've gained the ability to read some of it." He turned the knurled end and the page slid back into the cylinder, and again it was without apparent line or flaw, a single piece of unbroken metal. "I just wish I could figure out how to make it work the way it was supposed to."

"You would have to study years, most of the surviving lost lore of the God of Knowledge. It's the Codex," said Dominic in a reverent tone.

"And that's . . . ?" asked Miranda.

"The Codex of Wodar-Hospur. It was assumed to be lost."

"Well, I found it," said Nakor. "The problem is, when I open it, it tells me about things, but never the same thing twice. Some of the material is impossible to understand. Some of it is pretty boring. I think there is a way to get it to give you information that you want, but I haven't figured it out yet." He grinned. "But you would be astonished at what you learn if you just sleep with this under your head."

Dominic said, "It is also known as the Thief of Dreams. Those who sleep too close to it are robbed of their dreams and, after enough time, driven mad."

"Well, you wouldn't be the first person to call me a little crazy," said Nakor. "Besides, I stopped sleeping with it in my room over a hundred years ago. It took me a while, but I deduced it was keeping me from dreaming." He shook his head. "Strange things happen when you don't dream at night. I was beginning to hallucinate and, frankly, I was getting a little irritable."

"What is it?" asked Miranda. "These names mean nothing to me."

"It is the most holy artifact from the temple of the God of Knowledge," said Dominic. "It is a text with all the knowledge of the temple of the Lost God of Knowledge contained within it. Wodar-Hospur was a lesser god, but one deemed critical to understanding all the issues we are discussing now," said Dominic. "What this vagabond has been carrying around for who knows how many years is an item that would have provided an amazing amount of insight and knowledge to our order if we had possessed it."

Nakor said, "Perhaps, but then again, you might have sat around for a couple of centuries staring at the thing without ever really understanding what it does." Nakor looked around the room. "Knowledge is power. You all have power. I have knowledge. Together we have the means of defeating the Nameless One."

As Nakor said that phrase, it was as if the room darkened a little and turned slightly colder. "The Nameless One?" asked Miranda, and suddenly she touched her temple. "There's something I know, but . . . don't know."

Nakor nodded. "I won't name him." He looked pointedly at Dominic. "There are advantages to being a little mad and to having tremendous knowledge." He looked around the room and said, "Here is the rest of the story.

"The Nameless One is nameless, because even to imagine his name is to call his attention to you. If you do, you're lost, for no mortal creature has the power to resist his call"—Nakor grinned—"except me."

Dominic said, "How is this possible?"

"As I said, it helps to be a little mad. And there are tricks that can let you think of one thing without knowing you're really thinking of it, so when the Nameless One hears his name and comes looking for you, you're not there for him to find. Even a Greater God can't find you where you're not."

Miranda said, "I am totally confused."

"You are not alone," said Pug.

Calis smiled. "I think I'm following."

Nakor grinned at him. "That's because you're young." He looked at the others. "When the Chaos Wars raged, one of the Controller Gods, this Nameless One, whose nature is what you would call evil, attempted to upset the balance of things.

"It was he who warped Draken-Korin and who set the Valheru on their self-destructive path. What they did not realize was that the gods were no threat to them. I imagine this would have been nearly an impossible concept to them, but the gods would have been just as satisfied with Valheru worshippers as with humans, elves, goblins and the other intelligent races who live here now."

Tomas smiled. "I think it safe to say you're right. 'Impossible concept' sums it up."

"Anyway," continued Nakor, "when the Valheru rose to challenge the gods, the Chaos Wars ensued." He looked at Tomas. "How long did they last?"

Tomas said, "Why . . . I don't know." He closed his eyes as if attempting to remember, but at last opened them and said, "I have no idea."

"They dragged on for centuries," said Nakor. "The gods as we think of them are localized, specific to Midkemia, yet they reflect larger realities, ones which affect millions of worlds."

"I'm lost again," said Miranda. "Local, yet they stretch across a vast number of worlds?"

Nakor said, "It's the same as if we're all sitting around a mountain. Each of us sees it from a different perspective, but it's the same mountain.

"The goddess you and I call Sung the Pure represents certain aspects of reality, a sense of something profoundly basic, unsullied, without flaw, absolutely perfect, and that aspect of reality exists in a lot more places than just around the corner from here." He looked at Miranda. "Which is to say, if you tried to destroy Sung the White, you'd not only create havoc on Midkemia but create problems for a very large portion of reality."

"Everything's connected," said Calis, intertwining his fingers. "You can't disrupt one part of reality without doing harm to another."

"So, this Nameless One," said Nakor, "attempts to disrupt things, to steal an advantage, to create a disharmony in the order of things. He influenced Draken-Korin and the Valheru to do two things: they created the Lifestone and they rose to fight the gods.

"As a result, a lot of the Lesser Gods were destroyed, or at least as destroyed as a god gets, which means they won't be around for a long time; and others were . . . changed. Killian has sovereignty over the Oceans, where Eortis once ruled. It sort of makes sense, as she's a goddess of nature, but it's really not her job." Nakor shook his head. "You know, this Nameless One, he did some serious damage, all things considered, and we're still dealing with it." He pointed in the general direction of Darkmoor, to the west, and said, "A big demon is coming this way, with an army, and he wants that thing." Nakor pointed at the Lifestone. "He probably doesn't even know why he wants to come here, or even that this Lifestone is here. And once he gets here, he won't know what he's going to do with it. But he'll do anything to get it. And once he has it . . ."

Calis said, "He'll end life on this world as we know it." All eyes turned toward Calis. "It's the nature of the Lifestone that everything in this world is connected. If you disrupt it, everything dies."

"That's the trap," said Nakor. "That's what Draken-Korin didn't understand when he thought he'd created the perfect weapon. He thought that if he unleashed the power of the Lifestone, the energy would blast away the gods, or something like that." He glanced at Tomas.

Tomas nodded.

"But it doesn't work like that," said Nakor. "What would have happened is the world would have died, save for the gods. The Lesser Gods would have been weakened, because there would have been no one around to worship them. But the Controller Gods, they would have been just as they always were."

Miranda said, "I'm getting a headache. If nothing changed for the Controller Gods, what good does all this do this Nameless One?"

"Nothing," said Nakor. "That's the irony. I think he imagined—if I may presume to think like a god—that the general disruption would somehow benefit his cause, would put the other Controller Gods at a disadvantage."

"Wouldn't it?" asked Pug.

"No," said Dominic. "Each god is cast in a fixed role, and within that role they can act, but not outside their nature."

Miranda stood up, obviously exasperated. "Then what is going on? Why is this god acting outside his nature?"

"Because he's mad," said Calis.

"The Days of the Mad God's Rage," said Tomas. "That's the other name for the Chaos Wars."

"What drives a god to madness?" asked Sho Pi.

The others looked at the student, heretofore silent. Nakor said, "You're not as stupid as I think, sometimes, boy. That's a wonderful question." He looked around the room. "Anyone have an answer?"

No one spoke.

Nakor said, "Maybe it's in his nature, but the Nameless One did things that defeated his own purpose. He created a situation that resulted in his being cast out, imprisoned far away.

"Seven gods once lived in balance, each according to its nature. Whatever the reason, the balance was upset. The Chaos Wars caused the destruction of two of the Controllers, for they had to act to preserve what was left of this world. The Matrix, Ishap, the most important god of the seven, is gone. The Good Goddess, Arch-Indar, is also gone, and the Nameless One had to be banished, confined by the other four. His counterpart is dead and the god who kept all in balance is dead, so the remaining four, Abrem-Sev, Ev-Dem, Graff, and Helbinor, had to act. They had no choice.

"So in the end, we're left with a world out of control, unbalanced, lacking cohesion. This is why so many strange things occur on Midkemia. It makes it an interesting place to live, but a little dangerous."

Pug said, "Is this speculation or do you know these things?"

Nakor pointed to the artifact. "Dominic?"

"He knows," said the Abbot of Sarth. "That device was carried by the High Priest of Wodar-Hospur, the God of Knowledge. Reputedly, any question that a man can ask is answered in the Codex. But the price to carry it is extreme. It requires the combined effort of dozens of other clerics in the temple to combat the madness that results from the High Priest's inability to dream." He looked at the Isalani. "Nakor, how did you escape the madness?"

Nakor grinned. "Who said I did?"

Pug said, "I have often thought you a little odd, but never have I judged you truly mad."

Nakor said, "Well, the thing about madness is you can only be crazy so long. After that you either kill yourself or you get better. I got better." He grinned. "It also helped when I stopped sleeping in the same room with the damn thing."

Sho Pi said, "How is it that you"—he pointed to Tomas—"who wear the mantle of the Valheru, and you"—he pointed to Pug—"who was the master of two worlds of magic, and you"—he pointed at Nakor—"who possess this item, and Macros, who was Sarig's agent, are all together at this point in history?"

"We are here to help," said Nakor. "The gods may have planned it this way, but for whatever reason, we need to repair the damage done so many centuries ago."

"Can we?" asked Miranda.

Nakor said, "We cannot. Only one being in this world possesses the nature to attempt this." He turned and looked at Calis. "Can you?"

"I don't know," answered Calis. "But I must try." His eyes returned to the Lifestone. "Very soon."

Nakor said, "And our job is to keep him alive long enough to try."

Erik stood behind the lines, watching as his men repulsed another attack, waiting for another assault; Duko was good, and none of his attacks during the day had been wasted effort. It had taken every trick he knew, and calling in the reserves, for Erik to repulse him. Runners carried messages from the other areas of the line, and the news was not good.

The Kingdom was holding, but the entire line was sorely pressed. Patrick feared there was going to be a breakthrough eventually. It was the reason he was withholding the elements of the Army of the East that were camped below the eastern foothills. They stood ready to respond to any incursion. A small army had been sent to impose itself between any forces that might get through and the abandoned city of Sethanon.

It was late afternoon, and when Erik heard the enemy trumpets sound the retreat, he breathed a sigh of relief. A runner had returned from Darkmoor with his uniform, and he welcomed fresh clothing. He was covered in dirt, blood, and smoke, and while he didn't take the time to bathe, a fresh shirt and trousers would improve his mood.

After he had changed, Jadow came into the tent and said, "We've got word some of the enemy have slipped across the ridge line and are holed up in a little canyon a mile north of here."

"Get a squad and go root them out," said Erik. "If you need help, grab whoever's close by, but get those men dug out of there."

Jadow left and Erik sat down in the command tent. He pawed through the pile of reports and dispatches, and found nothing that required his immediate attention. He rose and left the tent and hurried to where food was being served to the men. He refused to move to the front of the line, so he was only a few feet away from getting his rations when a horseman rode up.

It was Dashel Jamison, who waved. Erik looked at the bubbling pot of stew with some regret as he left the line and said, "Hello!"

Dash dismounted. "The Prince sent me to tell you that the Earl of Loriél has been found other duties." Lowering his voice, he said, "If any other noble rides through and troubles you, I'm to . . . facilitate."

Erik said, "Thanks." He found the next question awkward. "Any word on . . . your grandfather?"

Dash's expression turned grim. "No. Nor my grandmother." He looked westward, facing toward Krondor. "We are resigned to the fact they chose to die together." He sighed. "My father is not dealing with this well, but he'll come out of it soon." Dash shrugged. "Truth to tell, I'm not dealing with it particularly well, either." He looked at Erik. "How can I help?"

"I need someone to sort through all the dispatches as they arrive and save me from the ones that don't need my attention. The command structure along the ridge is very disorganized."

Dash said, "We've lost a lot of nobles, and many of their second in commands are garrison soldiers, with no field experience."

Erik said, "I've noticed." He looked at Dash. "A lot of nobles?"

Dash looked disturbed. "The Duke of the Southern Marches is dead. The Duke of Yabon lies injured and may not live. At least a dozen earls and barons are dead. More before this is through, I think." He lowered his voice. "While you were up in the mountains training, Patrick ordered all the lords who were coming here to leave one son home if they could. If we survive, we're going to have a lot of new members of the Congress of Lords next year. We're paying a bloody price in this war."

"That we are." Then the trumpets sounded and alarm was raised as another attack commenced. "And that we will," said Erik as he pulled his sword and hurried to his chosen place of command.

Calis said, "It's time."

Pug moved to stand beside his old friend's son and asked, "Are you certain?"

Calis said, "Yes."

He looked at his father, and something passed between them; something silent but profound, needing no words. Then he looked at Miranda, and she smiled at him.

Calis stood before the Lifestone, the huge green emerald pulsing with energy. He said, "Father, take back your sword."

Tomas didn't hesitate. He leaped atop the dais upon which the stone rested and placed a booted foot on the gem. He seized the hilt of his white and gold sword and pulled. At first the sword resisted his efforts, then suddenly it slid free.

Tomas lifted his sword, feeling complete for the first time since the end of the Riftwar, and a primal shout of victory escaped his lips.

The gem began to pulse and Calis rested his hands upon it. "I am

Valheru! I am human!" He closed his eyes and said, "I am eledhel!"

Nakor said, "Interesting. His nature is unique and he possesses the attributes of three races."

Calis's eyes opened and he stared into the gem. "It's so obvious!" he said, and he lowered his head until his brow touched the gem. "It's so easy!"

Pug looked at Tomas and they both asked the same silent question: What was so obvious and so easy?

In a grand pavilion, surrounded by servants and advisers, the demon Jakan seethed. Something called to him, something compelling and demanding, something that insisted he move toward it. He did not know what this thing was, but it haunted his dreams and sang to him. He knew where it was, a place to the north and east, Sethanon, and he knew that those who opposed him were denying him this thing.

The self-styled Demon King of Midkemia stood, and to those around him, the illusion of the Emerald Queen still held. She seemed to command them to depart, save those attendants she kept close by, the remaining Pantathian serpent priest, one named Tithulta, and the human General, Fadawah. They knew of the deception and were the only survivors of that bloody night when Jakan had devoured the Emerald Queen. It had been so easy. She had been alone with one of her victims, who died held in her arms and legs as she drank his life from him. The demon had used his growing powers to appear as one of her servants. He had slipped into her tent and quickly killed her and her newest lover. The woman's power was significant, but wasted on keeping a youthful appearance. The demon didn't understand this; it was so much easier to build an illusion, as he had.

In that moment of consuming the woman, the demon had encountered something alien, yet familiar. He had been touched by this agency and knew its name, Nalar. But beyond knowing of its presence, the mystic echoing within the Emerald Queen, the demon was otherwise unconcerned.

Maarg had made a pact with someone to have those odd creatures who looked like Pantathians open the rift to the Saaur world and to this world. But that was Maarg's worry. Let him rot on Shila or return to the demon realm and its limited pleasures. Jakan was the only one of his kind on this world, and his power was growing by the day.

He glanced at his left arm and saw the tremendous growth that had occurred. The last human he had devoured he had swallowed whole, and had found a wonderful moment of delight as the creature screamed for almost a full minute inside his gullet. And now he was pleased to see the human's face appearing on his belly. He flexed his shoulders and felt his great wings nearly touch the sides and tops of the pavilion. He would have to have it enlarged. The illusion of the Emerald Queen could move easily through the tent, but Jakan was now close to twenty feet tall, and as long as he fed, he would continue to grow. For a brief instant, he considered limiting his feeding, then dismissed the idea as too alien.

He ducked as he moved under the tent flap held open for the Queen by her guards. Fadawah and Tithulta appeared to be following at a respectable distance; no one without magic sight could see the mystic chains and collars Jakan had fashioned to keep them in tow.

The nearby army saw the Emerald Queen reach the large tent she had erected for the wounded. She entered and found a few soldiers attempting to tend the dying. "Leave," she commanded, and those able to do so obeyed, for most suspected what was about to happen.

Jakan moved to the first man, unconscious but still alive. The demon scooped him up with one hand and bit his head off, swallowing it. The blood and life forces that ran down the demon's throat filled him with an almost painful pleasure. Never had a demon risen so rapidly, become so powerful, and still had so much potential before him. He would be the mightiest Demon King in the history of the race! Nothing would withstand his march, and when he had devoured this planet, he would use the rift knowledge these people possessed to reach other worlds. Eventually, he thought, I will be a god!

He turned toward a man who could barely move for his injuries, but whose eyes were wide with terror as he attempted to crawl away from the horror he had just witnessed. Jakan realized that, in his bloodlust, he had let his illusion drop, and now sick and dying men moaned in terror. Grinning, with blood still running down his chin, Jakan moved to the man and impaled him on a single talon, lifting him before him. Then with a snap, he devoured him, delighting in the feel of the twitching body sliding down his huge gullet. Never has there been one such as I, he thought.

Jakan turned to his puppet, Fadawah, and said, "Order the attack! We overrun the puny humans today!"

The vacant eyes of Fadawah didn't register any reaction. He turned and stuck his head outside the tent and said, "Order all units to attack!"

Soon, thought Jakan, I will feast on thousands and then I will reach this place, Sethanon, and see what it is that calls me there.

Calis smiled. "It's like untying a knot!"

He had two hands upon the Lifestone and the pulsing green light was bathing him, washing over him, infusing him. Though he didn't move a muscle he had never looked more animated, alive, and powerful to those who knew him.

His father came to stand next to him and asked, "What do you see?"

"Father," said Calis, enraptured, "I see everything!"

A six-foot-tall spinning column of green energy sprang up atop the gem like a flame, and undulated, emitting a keening sound. Faces flickered in the flame, and Tomas's golden blade came to the ready.

"The Valheru!" he said in a hoarse whisper, his every sense tuned and ready for battle.

"No," said Calis. "This is but an echo of their former existence. What they sought to become eluded them. What they returned to recover was never theirs." He turned to look at his father. "Stand ready."

"For what?"

"For the change." Calis closed his eyes, and the flame shot upward, into the ceiling of the cavern, and ran along the rocky surface, fanning out in a circle. As it spread out from the point of impact, it thinned, diminishing to nothing more than a faint green overlaying the golden shimmer of Nakor's protective screen.

Tomas dropped to his knees, the sword falling from his hands, as a moan of pain escaped him. He clutched his chest and stomach, as if in agony. Pug rushed to his side, saying, "What is it?"

Tomas's teeth were clenched and he shook. He was unable to answer.

Calis said, "That which was Valheru is returned to the world."

Pug left Tomas and came to Calis's side. "Will he live?"

"He will," answered Calis. "He is more than Valheru. As am I."

Then Pug saw that Calis was also undergoing a painful transformation, as whatever part of his heritage also was Valheru was being torn from within. Perspiration ran down his forehead, and his arms trembled, but his eyes were afire and his gaze was locked within the stone.

"What is happening?" Pug asked softly.

"Something that was taken from this world is being returned to it," said Calis. "I am the instrument of that return."

After a moment, tiny flecks of green light spun away from the glowing nimbus that surrounded Calis and the stone, flying in random directions. Pug dodged the first spray of light and it went past him, then as he turned another struck him in the chest. Instead of its causing injury or pain, he felt nothing but a sense of energy, something warm and healing passing through him.

He looked at Tomas, bent over in agony, but as the tiny green flecks struck, Tomas began to recover. After a moment, he looked up at his boyhood friend, and Pug saw his eyes were clear, free of pain.

Tomas rose and slowly moved over to Pug and Calis. He looked at Pug, and the magician saw wonder in Tomas's eyes, wonder he had not witnessed since Tomas had taken on the mantle of Ashen-Shugar, last of the Valheru. For the first time in fifty years, Tomas looked more like the boy from Crydee than Pug had ever seen him, and in a voice filled with amazement, Tomas said, "My son is healing the world."

Then, a cry of joy, a note so profound Pug couldn't tell if it was a sound or a feeling, rang through the cave, and the gem seemed to erupt, casting an awe-inspiring flame of life throughout the room. Nakor nearly danced in delight, while Dominic made the sign of his god.

Nakor said, "We don't need this," and dropped his spell of protection.

As it vanished, an echo from across the world, as black and evil as the previous note had been alive and good, resonated, and Nakor's eyes widened. "Oops!"

The demon's head came up from its feasting. "No!" it roared as it felt something being taken away from it. *Sethanon!* the voice in his head screamed.

All dreams of power and primacy were forgotten. The mystic leashes to the two slaves were released as the demon strode to the front of the tent.

Two guards turned as Jakan emerged from the tent. They grew pale and fled.

General Fadawah blinked as if coming out of a daze, and he saw the demon rip apart the entrance to the tent, sending tatters in all directions. He only glimpsed the horror before it leaped to the skies, but it was enough.

The General turned to see the confused Pantathian high priest, also coming out of his daze. Rage gripped the General, and he pulled his decorative dagger. He raised it high and plunged it between the neck and shoulder of the Pantathian, driving the serpent priest to his knees. For a moment the creature rocked on his knees, then he toppled over.

Fadawah didn't even attempt to remove his blade from the last dying member of the Pantathian race. He hurried out the rear of the Queen's pavilion and found terrified officers standing in the command tent. He looked to where their eyes were fixed and saw the demon soaring toward the mountains, in the direction of the castle at Darkmoor.

One of the captains of the mercenary companies who had risen to the staff of the Queen's army saw their commander before him, and stammered out, "Orders, sir?"

Fadawah said, "What has happened? I have been in the power of a monster and don't know what has happened. Tell me!"

"You just ordered a full-scale attack. All units. We are engaging the enemy along the entire ridge."

"Damn!" said the general. He had no idea how long he had been in thrall to the demon, but he knew he had to discover quickly what had occurred. The last thing he remembered clearly was being in the Queen's tent outside the City of the Serpent River; then he had lived in a timeless haze, a vague dream of horror and fear; and now he was on the other side of the world in the middle of a war and he had no idea whom they were fighting, where his units were deployed, or if they were winning or losing. And with the Queen dead, he had no idea why they were continuing to fight.

Looking at his staff he said, "Maps! I want to see where we are, where every unit is, and what we know about the enemy." As the staff jumped to obey, a few of them stealing glances at the diminishing figure of the demon as it sped eastward, Fadawah was consumed by one goal: Survival.

Twenty-six

Confrontation

ERIK FOUGHT.

What had begun as a moderate push, a probing engagement to discover potential weaknesses in the defenders' line, without warning had turned into an all-out offensive. Erik kicked the man he had just killed, letting him roll back down the ridge into the trees below.

All along Nightmare Ridge, the Kingdom army struggled with the invader, a slaughter unmatched since the Riftwar. Erik looked around as he found himself in a relative lull. The wounded and dead were being dragged away by their comrades, and others quickly drank from water buckets carried by the boys from the baggage trains.

Jadow came running along, Sergeant Harper behind him. "They've turned our northern flank," said Harper, blood splattered across his face. "Jerome is dead, and his entire company with him. Duko's got men on our side of the ridge and they're pushing us to the south."

"Damn!" said Erik. He turned to a runner and said, "Orders to the Flying Company—"

Jadow interrupted. "There is no Flying Company. I sent them in as soon as Harper reached me. They're up there right now."

Erik rubbed his face, feeling as if fatigue was ground into his skin like grit. His thoughts were chaotic from lack of sleep and constant fighting over the last two days. "All right," he said to the two sergeants. "Take every third man from here, and bolster the north. If you can't hold, pull back, and when you get to the first defensible position on our side of the ridge, facing north, dig in. You hold them there, and if they turn east and go down the mountain, they're the Army of the East's problem." He turned to the messenger and said, "Go to Darkmoor. Tell Prince Patrick we have a turned flank on the north and are trying to dig in. We need reinforcements. Got it?"

The young soldier said, "Yes, sir!," saluted, and ran to his horse.

Erik turned to see Jadow and Harper already pulling every third man off the ridge and leading them northward. He saw Dash standing a short way off, his sword drawn and blood all over his well-cut tunic and trousers, and he said, "I thought I told you to read dispatchs."

Dash smiled. "There's nothing in there that can't wait, and it seemed an extra sword was needed."

Erik nodded. "You have that right."

Suddenly the enemy was pushing over the ridge again, and Erik became embroiled in the struggle.

Tomas said, "Something is coming!"

Pug said, "I can feel it, too." He paused, then said, "I recognize that presense. It's Jakan!"

Nakor said, "Sho Pi, you and the good Abbot must hide."

Sho Pi said, "I will stay with you, Master."

Nakor grabbed the younger man and propelled him toward a hole in the wall. It was the dusty underground remnants of the last battle that took place in the ancient city created by the Valheru, beneath the destroyed city of Sethanon. "My protection trick could hide us from the Nameless One's hearing, but it can't stop an angry demon who wants to come here! In there!" insisted Nakor. "Hide in that hole, for what is coming may destroy us all, but at least the rest of us have some means to protect ourselves!"

The broken masonry was the result of the titanic battle between the dragon Ryath, whose sleeping body was now occupied by the Oracle of Aal, and a Dreadlord, used by Nalar as a distraction as the spirits of the Valheru attempted to reenter Midkemia. "Get down and stay out of sight."

Nakor hurried back to stand next to Miranda, while Pug and Tomas took up stations on either side of Calis. Miranda said, "Can you protect yourself?"

"I'm tougher than I look," said Nakor, but his grin was gone.

Calis was lost within the dismantling of the Lifestone, his face a mix of rapture and calm. His eyes were now fixed upon a spot at the center of the stone, which was growing smaller as more and more shreds of the life energy flew from it.

Miranda said, "Whatever he's doing, it's making me feel good."

"If we weren't facing the coming rage of a Demon King, I think we'd be enjoying this."

Miranda felt a large speck of the green life force pass through her stomach; her eyes widened and she said, "Oh!"

Nakor giggled. "That looked interesting."

"It felt interesting," she said. She ran her hand over her stomach. With a look of mixed apprehension and uncertainty, Miranda said, "Something's going on."

Nakor looked around the hall, which was now almost universally illuminated in green light, and said, "The life structure of this world is being set right. It's a healing, a rejuvenation. Ancient souls trapped in that thing for centuries are being freed to return to the universe, as they were intended to do." He glanced at Miranda. "Some of the side effects might prove very unexpected."

Miranda said, "I don't doubt it."

Tomas's eyes narrowed and he tilted his head, as if listening to something. "It's coming."

"What is?" asked Miranda.

"Jakan," said Pug. "It can be the only thing on this world to disturb the harmony of life to the point where we can sense its approach."

Tomas held his sword. "I think soon. Within the next hour, two at the latest."

Pug glanced at Calis, who was still consumed by his task. "Will he be finished?"

Tomas said, "I do not know."

They waited.

Erik crouched low as another flight of arrows sped overhead. The instant they had passed, his own archers rose and fired back. The attack had picked up intensity all afternoon, and now he feared he was about to lose domination of the ridge.

Suddenly enemy soldiers were atop the ridge and he was again facing hand-to-hand combat. The determination of his men was unmatched, but their endurance was flagging.

No word had reached him from the north since he had sent Jadow and Harper to reinforce the northern flank, and the men he had sent were now critically needed here. Erik worried that he might have compromised both positions in an attempt to protect them.

The press of battle took his mind off worries for a moment, as he felt the line around him sag, as more and more of the enemy appeared and fewer and fewer defenders stood next to him. Erik let his sword swing like a scythe, cutting down attackers like wheat. He heard men scream, grunt, and curse on all sides, and focused upon the moment. The battle was now in that place he knew where no amount of coordination was possible; the battle would be decided by the strength of the men who fought it. If the defenders had more resolve, they would win.

Erik saw two enemies before him, and in that instant he felt in his soul that the battle was lost. He struck down the first man, shattering his shield with a tremendous blow, but barely dodged a thrust by the second.

Then a third man and a fourth came at him, and in that moment, Erik knew he was going to die. He slashed out and took the second man in the face, cutting his cheek to the bone, which shattered as the blade dug in. He pulled back his sword and tossed the man as a cat tosses a mouse, sending him into the two men who came after.

Erik knew it was just a matter of moments, and he was determined to take as many of the enemy with him as possible before he was overwhelmed.

He struck out against one man, and took a sliding blow to the ribs that caused him to turn suddenly, opening himself up to another sword thrust. A blade struck his left arm, glancing off the leather of his gauntlet to leave a long angry red cut on his forearm.

Erik took a glancing blow to the side of the head, and his knees weakened. He couldn't stand upright, and as he tried to step back, his heel slipped, saving his life. Erik fell back, struck rock and dirt, and rolled head over heels a dozen yards. He came to rest on his back, staring up over his boots at five enemy soldiers rushing down the hill to end his existence.

As the first man reached Erik, his sword held high overhead to deliver a killing blow, a goosefeather shaft appeared in the man's neck. He seemed to take a step, go to one knee, then fall facedown at Erik's feet.

Erik scrambled back as the other four men turned, looking to their left, Erik's right, and another arrow lifted an attacker off his feet, propelling him backward. Only a longbow could unleash that much power. Erik looked and saw a half-dozen men in leather standing a dozen paces down the trail, firing at the attackers while children ran forward.

Erik blinked. They weren't children but dwarves, dressed in armor and carrying war hammers and axes. Shouting their war cries, they were charging into the invaders, cutting them down.

Strong hands reached under Erik's shoulders and hauled him to his feet. "How are you, man?" asked a familiar voice, and Erik turned to see the smiling face of Jadow Shati.

"Better," said Erik. "Much better."

Sergeant Harper said, "We were being handed our heads, sir, when suddenly the lads who were trying to kill us got very concerned about their own rears." He grinned, ignoring the dried blood that spattered his face. "The dwarves and elves were coming down the ridge, doing a grand job of slaughter as they went."

As if a wind blew away a cloud of smoke, the dwarves and elves cleared the ridge before Erik's eyes. A dwarf wearing a large gold torque, and carrying a hammer of obvious power, approached and asked, "You the officer here?"

Erik nodded. "Sir?"

The dwarf smiled. He set down his hammer, drew himself up to his full height, slightly under five feet, and slapped his chest with his balled fist. "I hight Dolgan, King of the Dwarves of the West, chief of village Caldara, and Warleader of the Grey Towers dwarven people!" Then he smiled and said, "It looks as if you could use some help."

Erik grinned. "With thanks."

An elf approached and said, "I'm Galain. Tomas asked us to come through the ridge line from above Hawk's Hollow, making sure that uninvited guests weren't hanging about."

Erik smiled. "Your arrival was most timely."

"Well," said Dolgan. "Better late than never, and it's still a bonny fight. My lads will be pleased to thump a few heads." Lowering his voice, he said, "Tomas has been forthright with what is at stake, and I pledge we will keep these murderers on the west side of the ridge."

Erik said, "Thank you."

Jadow said, "You've got a few wounds here."

Erik sat on a rock and Jadow began field dressings.

More of his men came down the ridge from the north, and Harper reported, "We're rolling them south, sir."

"Good," said Erik. "Keep the pressure on. If we can collapse them down around Darkmoor, we can win this fight."

Erik waited until his bandages were finished, then stood and returned to his observation point, a large rock that gave him a good view of the immediate battlefield.

Below the ridge line, the enemy was dug in behind some sheltering rocks. The elven bowmen had turned the twenty yards of open space above them into a killing ground, and none ventured from behind the rocks.

Erik looked around, saw a boy holding his horse, and signaled for him to be brought over. He told Jadow, "Send a patrol up the line and make sure they're not trying to climb back up there. I'm riding to Darkmoor to inform Patrick of the dwarves' and elves' arrival."

As he mounted his horse, he said, "King Dolgan—"

"Just Dolgan will do," interrupted Dolgan. "No need for titles."

"Dolgan, how many men are with you?"

"Three hundred dwarves and two hundred elves. Enough for a right grand fight."

Erik smiled. "Fine." To Harper, Erik said, "Hold here until I return."

Harper said, "Right, sir!"

Erik rode south, and as he did he saw that the assault on the enemy's northern flank by the elves and dwarves had sent ripples down the line, stalling the assault. A stable line was established, and while the exchange of arrows was constant, the fighting was now sporadic.

He reached Darkmoor in an hour's time, and only a reinforced barricade from the northern gate to the foothills north of the city kept the route open. The enemy had burned every building in the foulburg to the west, and the buildings to the north were abandoned.

Erik rode with an escort he had picked up at the outer limit of the city's defense, men wearing the tabard of Darkmoor. The big northern gate was barred, while the small sally port cut within the gate was left open. Erik rode through, and on to the castle.

He went straight to the Prince's conference chamber, and reported.

After he told Patrick of the arrival of the dwarves and elves, the Prince said, "Now it makes sense. We've been facing steady pressure all day." He pointed to a map. "While you've freed up the northern flank, we've had reports from the south that the same withdrawal along the ride is taking place—"

Erik said, "The dwarves from Dorgin."

"We can assume that much," said the Prince, ignoring the breach of protocol. "That's putting inordinate pressure on the center." He stuck a finger on the city of Darkmoor. "We have mounting attacks here, and we are close to losing the outer wall."

Erik looked around the room. He was the only other officer present, the rest of the room being staffed by runners and scribes. Erik volunteered, "The Army of the East?"

Patrick said, "I sent word to bring up the bulk of the army, but they won't be here until tomorrow morning." He pointed to another map, one of the city. "Here we have three potential weaknesses." He outlined the overall defense of the city and the areas of concern. Erik calculated. "Let me bring down a squad from the northern flank, and plug this breach here." He pointed to the center of the three potential breaches. "If we plug that, we can move to either flank as needed."

"Can you get a squad down here in time?"

Erik motioned to a runner. "With Your Highness's permission?"

Prince Patrick nodded.

Erik said to the runner, "Head north, on the fastest horse you can find, and tell Sergeant Jadow Shati to come here with as many mother-murderers as Harper can spare. He'll know what I mean."

The runner glanced at the Prince, who nodded, and the messenger ran from the room. Patrick said, "Your wounds?"

Erik looked at his bandaged lower left arm and ribs and said, "I got sloppy. I'm fine."

Patrick smiled. "You don't look fine, Captain, but I'll take your word for it."

Just then Greylock entered the room, dirty, sweating, and bloody. He said, "I need the reserves, now, Highness."

Patrick shrugged. "Take them. We have nothing left to lose."

Erik glanced at the Prince and said, "I'll go with the General. I think we need every sword at the wall."

Patrick drew his sword and said, "Very well."

Greylock turned and grabbed the Prince of Krondor's tunic. To lay hands on royalty was a hanging offense, but at that moment he wasn't a General offering insult to his liege lord, he was the old Swordmaster of Darkmoor training an impulsive young soldier. "Highness, your position is here. And if you go get yourself killed, and we win this war, then I have some very difficult explaining to the King and I would rather be spared that conversation with your father. Be a good lad and do your job, and we'll do ours." He released Patrick's tunic, then brushed aside an imaginary speck of dirt, saying, "I think that's it." Turning toward the door, he said, "Erik, shall we go?"

Erik followed, leaving a chastened ruler, who swore as he realized his commander was correct.

The demon bellowed as he swooped down toward the abandoned city of Sethanon. He challenged any who might interfere with his goal, and none answered.

Jakan landed before a destroyed gate, leading into a burned-out keep. He looked around and saw no one.

Something called to him and he felt frustrated he could not locate the origin of the call. He turned, bellowing a challenge toward every compass point. No one answered.

Screaming his rage to the sky, he set out searching, looking for something to fight, someone to kill, the source of the calling that sang to him, pulling him toward a goal he didn't understand, but one which filled him with a hunger that surpassed anything he had known before. Then a thought came to the demon. The demon didn't recognize that the thought was not his own, that a vast and evil being an unimaginable distance away was reaching out to plant in the demon's mind knowledge: how to reach the Lifestone.

Nakor looked upward. No one heard the demon roar, but they sensed it. "He's near."

Tomas nodded, holding the golden blade in his hand. He glanced at Pug and said, "I didn't realize how much I missed this."

Pug said, "I really wish you didn't have to use it."

Miranda said, "I feel the same way."

All waited as the demon above stalked the city, searching for the source of his hunger. "Maybe he won't find us," Nakor said.

"Want to bet on that?" asked Miranda.

Nakor grinned. "No."

Pug said, "If he doesn't figure out how to shift his place in time slightly, he could look for us for years and not find us."

Nakor said, "If he's stupid, maybe, but I think the Nameless One might turn him in the right direction."

"Right," said Miranda, glancing upward. "You would think of that."

Again they felt the demon's rage, reverberating through the ground into the chamber.

Miranda looked at Calis, who stood with eyes closed and hands on the Lifestone. The gem was now half the size it had been when they had found it, and the specks of green energy were flying through them constantly. Miranda said, "Nakor, you look younger."

Nakor grinned. "Am I handsome yet?"

Miranda laughed. "Hardly, but you do look younger."

"It's the Lifestone," said Pug. "It's rejuvenating us."

Miranda's forehead furrowed. "That explains it," she said as she put her hand on her stomach.

"What?" asked Nakor.

"Cramps. I haven't had them for a hundred and fifty years."

Nakor laughed.

Suddenly the room erupted in a howl of rage, echoing through the rocks from above.

"I think," said Nakor, "he's very close."

Erik stood on the wall overlooking the main gate. A huge ram was being rolled toward the outer wall and Manfred shouted, "Fire!"

Catapults unleashed a veritable rain of rocks, and many of the attackers were struck down, but the ram rolled toward them. It had a wooden roof, protecting the men below, and Manfred said, "If they breach this gate, they're into the inner city. We can't fight house to house. We'll have to fall back to the citadel."

Erik said, "Reinforcements are on the way."

"Well, they better get here in the next hour," said Manfred. "Otherwise we're going to be overrun." He turned and shouted, "Oil!"

Cauldrons of hot oil were poured over the wall, showering scalding death over those below. Men screamed and some retreated, but another wave rushed the wall, carrying scaling ladders.

"Down!" shouted Greylock, and Erik and his half brother both acted instinctively, ducking behind the wall over the main gate to the city as a hundred arrows flew overhead.

Men who had been slow to react screamed, many falling from the wall into the city streets.

Manfred crouched next to Erik, both with their backs against the cold stone of the city walls. Manfred looked around at the injured and dying. "If your reinforcements don't get here in the next ten minutes, I'm giving the order to withdraw."

Erik, hunkering down, said, "They can't get here in ten minutes."

"Well, then we'd better begin an orderly withdrawal." He turned to a man in the tabard of Darkmoor, with a sergeant's chevrons embroidered above his heart. "Tell the men to withdraw by sections. Start at the south wall, and get them to High Street. We'll fight our way back from there. Destroy the catapults. We can't allow them to be turned on us."

A thunder of hooves and Erik risked a glance between two merlons. Saaur riders were massing at the far end of the gate. Erik said, "Manfred, as soon as that gate is open, you're going to have a company of Saaur riders coming through!"

Manfred turned to glance over the wall. "Always wondered what they look like—" His eyes widened. "Mother of gods!"

"We need to leave now," suggested Erik.

Manfred agreed. To the sergeant he said, "Burn the catapults, then general withdrawal. Every man for the citadel!"

Word was passed and archers fired down into the streets below, while men with poles pushed over scaling ladders. But as soon as the withdrawal began, ladders were again put up and invaders began climbing.

Manfred and Erik ran down the stone steps to the street. Already chaos was let loose. A few civilians who had been too stubborn or too stupid to evacuate were now in the streets with sacks over their shoulders, running for the citadel. Wounded soldiers were being carried by healthy ones, and a few bowmen kept their heads and fired at the enemy as they came over the wall, but generally the retreat was turning into a rout.

"Have you seen Greylock?" demanded Manfred.

"Not since he went to look over the southern wall."

"I hope he makes it," said Manfred. An arrow struck the ground inches from his boot and he jumped.

Erik grabbed him by the sleeve and pulled him hard to the left, almost yanking him off balance, as three more arrows flew through the spot he had just occupied.

"Thanks," Manfred panted as they hurried around a corner.

"Archers usually work in groups," said Erik.

They ran down a cross street and turned to their right, then left again, and Erik could see the lights from the citadel's highest tower above the rooftops. The streets sloped upward, toward the old castle, and by the time they reached High Street the thoroughfare was clogged with terrified refugees, out-of-breath soldiers, and men carrying their wounded comrades.

"Make way!" shouted a voice and Erik saw Manfred had been recognized by one of Darkmoor's soldiers. "The Baron's here! Make way!"

Erik stayed close to his half brother. They bullied their way through the press and made it to the edge of the drawbridge. Soldiers lined the sides of the bridge, frantically waving though those moving across it.

Erik and Manfred both slumped to the cobbles in the bailey as soldiers ran to their aid. "Water," gasped the Baron.

Erik gasped, "I forgot how tired you can get running at this altitude."

"I forgot how tired you can get just running," said Manfred.

A bucket of water appeared and Manfred drank from it, then passed it to Erik, who gulped from it as it poured over his chest and arms.

Manfred shouted, "Sergeant!"

His sergeant appeared, and said, "M'lord?"

"Word to the lookout above. The moment he sees the enemy at the other end of High Street, close the drawbridge."

Erik said, "Manfred, you can't wait that long. You've got to start clearing it now or you'll never get it closed in time." He pointed to the flood of humanity, the civilians with slow-moving carts, the old men and women on foot, who were trying to squeeze through the gatehouse, and who were only succeeding in getting in one another's way. "Look!"

Manfred studied the situation, then said to the sergeant, "Clear the drawbridge. Tell those on the other side to hurry to the eastern gate. We can keep that one open a little longer. The others will have to make do as best they can."

Both men knew that being trapped outside the citadel was a death sentence.

Manfred stood and motioned for Erik to follow. "We'd better report to the Prince."

Erik rose and moved after his half brother. They trudged through the central entrance to the keep and from behind could hear the angry shouts and tearful pleading of those being forced away from entrance in anticipation of the gate's being closed.

Manfred led Erik up the stairs to the office occupied by the Prince.

Patrick looked up and said, "Full retreat?"

Manfred said, "Everyone is moving back here."

Patrick looked at Erik. "Greylock?"

Erik motioned toward the city. "Out there somewhere."

Patrick said, "Damn!" He glanced out the window and saw fires beginning in the outer districts of the city. "Is there anything good in all of this?"

Erik said, "The one good thing is they're now fighting on three fronts. We've got men along the ridges with the dwarves and elves who will be harrying their flanks, and if we can hold out until morning, the bulk of the Army of the East will be here."

The Prince motioned for them to sit and both men did. Manfred said, "Unfortunately, the Army of the East will be on the wrong side of the city walls, and unless someone slips out and opens the gates for them, we may have a serious problem."

Erik said, "Manfred, you have any secret passageway to the eastern gates?"

Manfred shook his head. "Nothing that clever, sorry to admit. The palace is lousy with bolt-holes and passages, but the old city walls are just solid stone with a few storage houses built in. We'll have to wait, and when morning comes, if we must, we might be able to sally forth and seize the eastern gate closest to the citadel, letting our army in."

Erik said, "We have a long afternoon and a longer night ahead, Manfred."

Manfred said, "Highness?"

Patrick remained calm in the face of all the ill news. "I need a situation report as quickly as you can get one to me. You and Erik find out how many of our men made it back, how many we think might still be out in the city fighting, and what we need to do to defend this citadel. Food and water are not problems, as this matter will be decided within one day."

Erik and Manfred both rose, bowed to the Prince, and departed. Outside, Manfred said, "I know the disposition of the units assigned to the castle, so I'll start there. You head down to the courtyard and see who got here, and get them organized."

Erik smiled. "M'lord."

Manfred looked at Erik. "Mother always feared you'd attempt to usurp the office of Baron. Right now I'll give it to you."

Erik smiled. "No thanks. Then I'd be the one to have to climb all those stairs to the towers."

"As I suspected, a practical man." Manfred turned to quickly climb the steps to the next level of the keep, while Erik headed down toward the courtyard.

Suddenly it went quiet.

Pug held up his hand and tilted his head as if listening.

Then the demon stood in the room.

Nakor whispered, "I didn't know demons could transport themselves."

"Or time-shift," added Miranda.

Then the demon realized he wasn't alone in the cavern. A roar that rattled the rock walls, causing dust to fall from cracks in the ceiling, shook everyone to their bones.

Pug unleashed his first spell, while Tomas interposed himself between his son and the monster.

Crackling blue energies sprang up around Jakan, who howled. But he wasn't screaming from pain but rather in outrage at what he saw before him: Calis manipulating the Lifestone, freeing the trapped energies within.

"No!" the beast bellowed in the tongue of Novindus. "It is mine!"

To Pug, Jakan resembled Maarg, but a leaner, more muscular-looking version. There were no accumulated rolls of fat, nor was he covered in as many tortured skins of his victims. Pug noticed that his tail was pointed, lacking the serpent's head Maarg had possessed.

Jakan struck out at Tomas, but Tomas had reflexively put up his white shield, causing the mighty blow to skid along the surface, leaving no mark on the golden dragon embossed upon it. Then Tomas's blade slashed out, and Jakan howled as he drew back, a venomous red-black poison dripping from his wound. It hissed and smoked where it hit the stones.

Miranda sent a stream of energies toward the creature, and struck him hard enough to move him a little to his left. Tomas seized the moment to strike while Jakan turned to see from where the new attack came. Tomas's blade bit deep in the creature's right thigh, and Jakan lashed out with his right hand, claws the size of daggers swiping at Tomas.

Tomas turned the attack and thrust, again drawing poisonous blood.

"Press the attack!" cried Nakor.

Pug loosed a bolt of energy, a blue spear of light that passed through the demon's wing, ripping a hole the size of a man's fist. The demon stepped back, his wings brushing against the stone wall of the cavern, and lashed out again at Tomas.

Tomas stepped back, preferring to dodge the blow rather than attempt to block it.

The creature hung back, obviously confused by the sudden opposition. Then Nakor shouted, "It's healing!"

Pug watched and saw that the first wound Tomas had caused was closing rapidly.

Nakor said, "The Lifestone! It's healing the wounds."

Pug calculated. Calis had reduced the stone to less than a third its original size, and it appeared that the diminution was accelerating, giving him hope they would be done with this trial in less than an hour, but that meant keeping the creature at bay until Calis was finished. Pug turned to Miranda and said, "Rest. Tomas and I will try to keep this creature away from Calis until we're done. If one of us falters, you must take over."

He turned and hurried to stand as close as he dared to the monster, and he crossed his wrists. A stunning bolt of red light shot out, striking Jakan hard enough in the face to slam him back into the wall.

Tomas didn't hesitate. He hurried forward and delivered a murderous backhand slash with his sword, cutting deep into the creature's leg and sending a gout of poisonous blood spurting across the stones. The blood smoked upon contact and a stench of rotting things filled the air.

Jakan howled in a murderous rage and leaped at Tomas. Tomas tried to move back and succeeded in getting far enough distant that the demon didn't land atop him, but it put Jakan close enough that he could attempt to seize Calis.

A clawed hand the size of a man shot out toward Calis, and Tomas reacted by slashing down as hard as he could with his golden sword. He hacked through a wrist four feet thick, and the creature screamed in pain and pulled away, his hand severed from his body.

A stream of the foul black blood shot through the air and drenched Calis, who screamed in pain and fell back from the Lifestone.

"Calis!" shouted Miranda, and she and Nakor ran to him. Immediately Pug and Tomas threw themselves into the battle. Energy lashed out, and Tomas struck with his sword, forcing the wounded demon back. Jakan clutched the bleeding stump of his arm to his chest, letting them force him to the wall.

Nakor hurried to Calis, grabbing one of his hands, while Miranda took the other, and they dragged him out of the pool of black blood. Instantly the Lifestone ceased being active.

Calis lay on the floor twitching as his skin burned, peeling as if he had been bathed in acid. He clenched his teeth and kept his eyes closed, and made low animal noises of agony. Miranda and Nakor both felt their hands stinging and quickly wiped their hands on their clothing. Holes appeared in the fabric, but at least their hands stopped burning.

Miranda looked around and saw the servants of the Oracle huddling in the farthest corner of the great hall, sheltered behind the recumbent form of the dragon. She ran to them and said, "We need help!"

The oldest member of the band, the one who had spoken to her before, said, "There is nothing we can do."

Miranda grabbed the old man by the arm, hauling him to his feet. "Think of something!"

She dragged the old man closer to the scene of battle and pointed to Calis, who lay moaning. She pointed at him and said, "Help him!"

The old man motioned for two others to come, and they managed to get Calis completely out of the pool of demon blood. The leader motioned for them to carry Calis around to the other side of the Lifestone and then he said to Nakor, "If he can be made to work his will on the stone again, it may save him."

Nakor's eyebrows shot up and his eyes widened. "Of course, the healing energy!" He looked at Miranda. "It's like reiki! It serves him first."

Nakor turned to the two servants of the Oracle and said, "Hold him close to the stone."

They did so, though every movement caused Calis to moan in agony. Nakor took Calis's hands, burned and blistered as they were, and placed them on the surface of the stone. Nakor said, "I hope this works." He made several passes in the air over the hands, and muttered a few phrases, then he placed his hands over Calis's.

Nakor felt warmth under his hands, and looked down. A faint green light bathed Calis's hands and his own. "The energy flows," he said. He waited for a minute while the battle between Pug, Tomas, and the demon continued, neither side able to gain the upper hand.

Nakor said to the two servants of the Oracle, "Hold him here. Keep him in contact with the stone." Then he ran to Miranda's side.

Miranda said, "This isn't working."

"I know."

Pug let loose with a blast of mystic energy, invisible to the eye but causing the air to sizzle as it struck the demon. Tomas showed no sign of tiring, for his Valheru-created armor protected him from any incidental harm. The demon would have to get claws on Tomas to cause him serious injury.

Pug fell back. "The best we can hope for is to keep him at bay. How's Calis?" he asked Miranda.

She pointed and Pug looked. Calis sat upright, held in place by the two servants, and a green glow was now suffusing the air around him, shrouding him in an emerald-colored nimbus. Pug watched for a moment, and said, "He's getting stronger."

Nakor said, "Yes, as he continues to hold the gem it heals him, and as it heals him he becomes strong enough to continue his work on it. Look!" Nakor pointed.

Calis's eyes were now open, and while his expression showed he was still in a great deal of pain, Tomas's son was once again unlocking the Lifestone.

Again the room was filled with tiny motes of green energy, life being returned to its rightful place. Pug pointed to the demon's severed hand, which was fading from view, and to the bleeding stump that was now in the process of growing a new one. Pug said, "This is healing the demon, too." Then Pug's eyes widened. He said to Miranda, "Do you know a powerful spell of binding?"

Miranda said, "Powerful enough for that thing?"

"You only need confine it for two minutes."

She looked dubious, but said, "I'll try."

"Tomas!" shouted Pug. "Keep it back for another minute!"

Pug closed his eyes and began chanting while Miranda did the same. Suddenly crimson bands of energy surrounded the creature, seizing him and crushing his mighty wings across his back. Then they constricted, and Jakan howled in pain.

"Tomas!" Pug shouted. "A killing blow!"

Tomas drew back his golden blade, then plunged it deep between two of the crimson bands, almost to the hilt, piercing whatever served as Jakan's heart. The demon's black eyes widened, and blood began to flow from his mouth and nose. Tomas yanked loose his sword.

Pug dropped one hand and suddenly the room was still as the demon vanished.

They all stood in silence a moment, then Miranda said, "Where is it?"

"Gone," said Pug. "We couldn't kill it, but I knew some place it couldn't survive."

Nakor said, "Where?"

"I transported it to the bottom of the ocean, between here and Novindus. It's a trench more than three miles straight down." Pug suddenly felt tired and sat down on the stone floor. "I found it doing some random searches of the planet years ago, and remembered what your father said at the end." He looked at Miranda.

"He said, 'They are creatures of fire.' " She laughed in nervous exhaustion. "Now I remember. I wondered what he meant."

Nakor sat down next to Pug and said, "That's wonderful. I hadn't thought of that." He shook his head. "It's obvious."

"What's obvious?" said Tomas, putting away his sword and coming to join them.

Nakor said, "Even the biggest demon is little more than a fire elemental at heart."

Pug said, "Once I fought some air elementals near Stardock and, by forcing them into contact with the water, destroyed them." He pointed to the space the demon had occupied and said, "A dunking won't kill Jakan, but trying to swim upward through three miles of seawater, with Miranda's bands around him and Tomas's wound to his heart, will."

Nakor said, "That's wonderful. Now it's over."

"No," said Pug. He pointed to Calis.

Calis now sat unaided, and again had his eyes focused upon the heart of the Lifestone, which was now less than a fifth its original size. Already the wounds on his face and hands were fading as if they had not existed.

"He will be done soon, I think," said Nakor. "We can wait."

Tomas said, "Men are losing their lives while we wait."

Nakor said, "It is a sad thing. But this is more important."

Dominic and Sho Pi came from their hiding place, and Dominic said, "He's right. This may be the most important thing ever done by a mortal on this world. Now the strangled life of this world is set right, and the order of things will begin to return."

"Begin?" asked Miranda.

Dominic nodded. "You don't correct damage on this scale quickly. It's been centuries, millennia, in the making. But now the healing will begin. The way is open for the return of the gods, now, where before the Nameless One blocked their return."

"How long do we have to wait?" asked Miranda.

Nakor laughed. "Several thousand years, but"—he stood up—"each day things will be a little better than the day before, and eventually the old gods will return, and then this planet will become as it was supposed to be."

Pug said, "Do you think we'll ever find out what drove the Nameless One mad?"

Dominic said, "Some mysteries never are solved. And even if we found the answer, we might never understand it."

Nakor reached deep into his bag and pulled out the Codex. He handed it to Dominic. "You take this. I think now you can do some good with it."

"What about you?" asked Pug. "As long as I've known you, I've judged you the most curious individual on the planet. Don't you want to continue to decipher that thing?"

Nakor shrugged. "I've been playing with it for more than two hundred years. I'm bored. Besides, Sho Pi and I have work to do."

"What sort of work?" asked Miranda.

Nakor grinned. "We have to found a religion."

Pug laughed. "A new scam?"

"No, I'm serious," said Nakor, attempting to look injured, and failing.

He grinned. "I'm the new patriarch of the Order of Arch-Indar, and this is my first disciple."

Dominic looked aghast, and Tomas laughed. Pug said, "Why?"

Nakor said, "If these old men can bring back the Matrix, someone still has to bring back the Good Goddess, to offset the Nameless One. Else Ishap will have nothing to balance the Nameless One with."

Dominic said, "A . . . worthy ambition, but . . ."

Miranda finished for him, "Ambitious?"

Dominic could only nod slightly. "Very ambitious."

Pug slapped Nakor on the shoulder. "Well, if anyone can do it, it's our friend here."

Calis said, "It's over."

They turned to look at him, and as he spoke, he put his hands under the tiny remnant of the Lifestone and with a gentle motion tossed it into the air.

Like a thousand emerald butterflies, the last of the life energy trapped for centuries flew, and then the room was again dark. The servants of the Oracle relit torches that had been allowed to go out during the battle, returning a gentle yellow glow to the huge chamber. The jeweled dragon slept, undisturbed.

Calis rose, steadily. His clothing was still damaged from the demon's blood, but he appeared unharmed. He crossed to his father and the two embraced.

Tomas said, "You were incredible. You—"

Calis interrupted. "I merely did what I was born to do. It was my fate."

Pug said, "But it took courage."

Calis smiled. "No one in this room today can be accused of lacking courage."

Nakor said, "I can. I don't have much. I just couldn't think of a good way to get out of here."

Miranda said, "Liar," and pushed him playfully.

Calis looked at his father and said, "Mother will be surprised."

"Surprised at what?" asked Tomas.

Pug said, "You look different."

"Different? How?"

Nakor reached into his bag and felt around a moment, then produced a hand mirror, silver-backed glass. "Here, take a look."

Tomas took the mirror and his eyes widened as he saw what his son had meant. Gone was the alien edge to his appearance, what he judged the Valheru legacy. Now he looked mortal, a human male with elvish ears. He looked at Calis and said, "You've changed as well."

Dominic said, "We've all changed." He pulled back his hood and Pug said, "Your hair!"

Dominic said, "Black again, right?"

"You look as you did when we traveled to Kelewan, so many years ago!"

Miranda said, "Give me that mirror," and snatched it out of Tomas's hand. She inspected herself and said, "Gods! I look as if I'm twenty-five again!"

Then she turned the mirror toward Pug and his eyes widened. Looking back at him was a face he hadn't seen since he had returned from Kelewan, a youthful man without a hint of grey in his hair or beard. "I'll be . . ." he said softly. Then he flexed his hand and said, "I don't believe it."

"What?" asked Miranda.

"Years ago, I cut my right hand, damaging it enough I've never since enjoyed full strength in it." He stared at it a moment, flexing his fingers again. "I think it's completely healed."

Nakor said, "How old do I look?" He took the mirror from Miranda and inspected himself. "Hmmm. I look about forty."

"You seem disappointed," said Miranda.

"I was hoping I'd be handsome." Then he grinned. "But forty's not bad."

Calis said, "I now understand what that key was the Pantathians were forging with the captured life, and what the alien presence was."

Tomas said, "The Nameless One?"

Calis shook his head. "No, some other presence. Perhaps those creatures who created the rifts for the Pantathians. But one thing was clear, that alien key would have permitted Maarg or Jakan to use the Lifestone."

"As a weapon?" asked Dominic.

"No," said Calis. "As distilled life energy. That's food to demons. Can you imagine Jakan ten times the size and with a hundred times the power he had moments ago? That would have been the result of a demon using that key to tap the Lifestone."

Miranda shook her head in amazement. "And we still don't know how all these different players, the demons, the Pantathians, those"—she looked at Pug—"what did you call them?"

"Shangri," answered Pug.

"Shangri, got together," finished Miranda.

Pug said, "There are still mysteries, but we have to put them aside for a while."

Calis nodded. "There is but one thing we need to do now."

"What's that?" said Miranda.

Calis's expression turned somber. "We must stop a war."

Twenty-seven

Truth

A BATTLE RAGED.

It was a scene from hell, as men seethed in the city streets under torchlight. The castle had held until nightfall, but the enemy hadn't withdrawn under cover of darkness. It was obvious to Erik that a change in command had taken place, for though he was facing the same motley mercenaries he had faced since the war began, now they were acting in coordination, using their numbers to good effect, and grinding down the defenders.

Erik directed his men along the southern wall of the keep, as the invaders attempted to fill the moat with anything that would give them a means of reaching the wall. Furniture, broken wagons, dirt, anything they could find was being thrown into the water.

The defenders were shooting as many arrows as humanly possible, but the attack was unrelenting.

Manfred peered over the wall at the sea of humanity, thousands of soldiers pressing toward the ancient keep. "This hardly looks good," he said.

"You have a knack for understatement," said Erik. He put his hand on Manfred's shoulders, pushing down slightly.

Manfred ducked as some rocks thrown by slingers on the roofs of the buildings on the other side of the moat whizzed by.

"How do you do that?" asked Manfred.

"Do what?"

"Know when to duck?"

Erik smiled. "I saw the slingers crawling on the roof at sundown. I've been keeping an eye on them. It gets to be a habit."

"If you live long enough."

Erik said, "What sort of shape are we in?"

"I just told the Prince that if we can keep them from getting ladders to the wall, we should hold until morning without much difficulty. The tricky part is going to be getting to the eastern gate to admit the Armies of the East."

Erik said, "I told Patrick I'd lead a sally at dawn."

Manfred laughed. "So did I."

"You can't," said Erik.

"Why not?"

"Because you're the Baron and I'm just a . . ."

"Bastard?"

"Yes."

Manfred said, "But you have a wife and I don't."

Erik said, "That means nothing," and he knew the words sounded just as hollow to Manfred's ears as they did to his own.

"You'll have to come up with a better argument than that," said Manfred.

"How about you're a noble and I'm not? You have people depending on you?"

"And you don't?" said Manfred. "Besides, doesn't a Knight-Captain in the Prince's Army carry the office of Court Baron with it?"

"That's different. I don't have estates and tenants who depend on my protection. I don't have to administer justice or sort out legal wrangles the courts can't solve. I don't have cities and towns, villages and . . . It's not the same!"

Manfred smiled. "Are you *sure* you wouldn't rather be Baron?"

Erik said, "You have Father's title!"

"There is that." Manfred glanced over the wall again and said, "Is there no end to them?"

Erik said, "Not that you'd notice."

For a moment, they rested, crouching behind the wall. Erik said, "How is it you never married? I thought the Duke of Ran had someone in mind for you."

Manfred laughed. "The lady came to visit and I think I failed to impress her."

Erik said, "I find that hard to believe."

Manfred looked at his half brother. "I thought you might deduce it, but obviously not." He glanced around, making sure no one was climbing over the wall. "When you have a mother like mine, it tends to distort your opinion of women. Stefan liked to hurt them. I prefer to avoid them."

Erik said, "Oh."

Manfred laughed. "If we survive, I'll tell you what. You can do me a service. I'll marry some prize the Prince picks for me, and you can father the next heir to the Barony of Darkmoor. It'll be our secret, and I suspect the lady in question will thank me for sending you to her bedchamber."

Erik laughed as a flight of arrows sped overhead. "I don't think my wife would approve." Then he said, "There's something you should know."

"What?" asked Manfred.

"You have a nephew."

"What?"

"The girl Stefan raped, Rosalyn: she bore his baby."

"My gods!" said Manfred. "Is it certain?"

Erik said, "Just one look. He's a von Darkmoor."

Manfred said, "Well, that changes things."

"How?" asked Erik.

"For certain one of us must survive, else the lad will be left to Mother's tender mercies."

Erik laughed. "Only if you tell her."

"Oh, she'll find out, eventually. Mother may be crazy, but she's well connected and enjoys her intrigues." He lowered his voice, as if someone might overhear. "There are moments I think Father's seizures were Mother's doing."

"You think she poisoned him?"

Manfred said, "Sometime get me to tell you Mother's family history. Poison played a large role in her great-grandfather's rise to his title."

A huge boulder slammed into the citadel then, rocking the outer keep wall. "Well," said Manfred as he brushed off the dust, "seems our guests have found a catapult."

Erik glanced over and saw the war engine had been dragged out into the middle of High Street. He motioned for a soldier and said, "Get word to Sergeant Jadow to have that catapult taken care of." Another boulder came slamming into the wall, and the soldiers in the street beyond the moat let out a cheer. "Fast!"

The soldier ran into the keep. Manfred said, "It's pretty straightforward, isn't it?"

"What?"

"They knock a hole in the wall, fill up the moat with whatever they can throw in, and come swarming over."

Erik said, "Basically."

"Well, let's make it interesting," said Manfred. He signaled to another of his soldiers, and said, "Tell Sergeant Macafee to release the oil."

The soldier ran off. Erik said, "Going to fire the moat?"

"Why not?" said Manfred.

Erik sat back. "How long can you keep the oil burning on the moat?"

"Three, four hours."

Another boulder slammed into the wall, and Erik said, "Jadow!"

As if hearing Erik's voice, a catapult atop the central keep fired, releasing half a dozen barrels of oil. They came crashing down around the catapult in the street, drenching the machine and its crew.

The enemy catapult crew began to run. The oil spreading in the street quickly reached one of the many fires nearby, and suddenly the war engine was ablaze. Erik's men on the walls of the citadel let out a cheer.

Erik said, "Well, that's that."

Manfred said, "When the oil in the moat is burned out, they'll start filling it in again."

"That will keep them out until sunrise, though."

"Yes," said Manfred. "But it still doesn't solve one problem."

The half brothers looked at each other and at the same moment they both said, "The eastern gate."

Pug said, "Rejuvenation is all fine and wonderful, but I'm tired."

Tomas said, "I feel I need to sleep."

Calis said, "Men are dying."

Tomas looked at his son and said, "I know. Even though the Lifestone is no more, there's a very large army attempting to sack Darkmoor."

Calis said, "Even if he's free now of the demon's control, by reputation Fadawah is not one to just quit and quietly withdraw." He sighed. "Only we in this room and a few others know of the real stakes, but now we have a cunning, dangerous leader who still has most of his army intact, and he controls most of the Western Realm."

Pug said, "This won't end quickly."

Miranda said, "At least we can get the Saaur out of the war."

Pug said, "If I can convince them what Hanam told me was true."

Tomas said, "We can only try."

"How do we get there?" asked Nakor.

"We don't," said Pug. "Tomas and I will go to Darkmoor. Unless we end this battle, there's no reason to take the rest of you into harm's way."

Calis said, "Remember, I'm the Prince's man."

Miranda said, "And you're not leaving me here."

Nakor motioned to Sho Pi, and Dominic, then grinned and shrugged. "Us too."

Pug's eyes widened, and he let out a slightly exasperated breath. "Very well. Gather around."

Miranda turned to the leader of the Oracle's servants and said, "Thank you for your help."

The old man bowed and said, "No, we thank you for saving us."

Miranda hurried to Pug's side, and the magician said, "Hold on."

They all held hands and suddenly they were standing in the courtyard of Villa Beata at Sorcerer's Island. "This isn't Darkmoor," said Miranda.

"No," said Pug. "I've never been to Darkmoor. So unless you want to materialize in the middle of the battle or inside a stone wall, you'll give me an hour."

Gathis hurried out of the house and welcomed them. "Hot food will be ready shortly," he said, ushering them inside.

Tomas took aside Pug and said, "Is this where you live?"

"Most of the time," said Pug.

Looking around the lovely estate, with the soft summer breeze from the ocean blowing across the meadows, he said, "I should have visited you a long time ago."

Pug said, "We've changed. Until this morning, you could not bring yourself to leave Elvandar."

Tomas said, "We've both lost a great deal. Even though my parents were fortunate and lived long lives, everyone else we knew as boys in Crydee has long since passed. But you, to have lost your children . . ."

Pug nodded. "I sensed over the last dozen years or so that I would outlive both of them, as Gamina and William aged and I didn't." Pug looked down at the ground, and was silent for a moment, lost in thought. Then he said, "Even though I expected it, the pain is still very real. I'll never see my children again."

Tomas said, "I think I understand."

The two old friends stood quietly for a time, and Pug remained motionless. Then Pug looked up at the stars. "It's such a vast universe. Sometimes I feel so insignificant."

"If what Nakor suspects about the nature of that universe is correct, we are, all of us, at once insignificant and important."

Pug laughed. "Only Nakor could come up with that."

Tomas said, "You've known him awhile. What do you make of him?"

Pug put his hand on his friend's arm and led him to the house. "I'll tell you while I work on getting us to Darkmoor. He's either the biggest confidence man in history or the most brilliant and original mind I've ever encountered."

Tomas said, "Or both?"

Pug laughed. "Or both," he agreed as they entered the house.

Pug moved his hands in a circle and a huge sphere of bluish light, shimmering with golden highlights, appeared. Taller than a man, it was as wide as a six-passenger coach,. "What is it?" asked Miranda.

"It's what is going to take us to Darkmoor." Pug said, "I don't know enough about Darkmoor to get us anywhere safely within sight of the city. If I don't have a pattern to fix on, a location I know well enough, well, let's just say it's too dangerous."

"I know the procedure," said Miranda. "I thought we were coming here to get one of those Tsurani devices."

"No good," said Nakor, taking his out of his bag, "unless you've got it set for a place known to you." He shook it. "If it still works."

He laid the device aside.

Nakor grinned. "I'll fly with you in your bubble."

"How do we get in?" asked Miranda.

"Just step inside," said Pug, and did so.

They followed him. "I had to dig up the spell to make this thing, but once I remembered how to do it"—he waved his hands, and the sphere lifted off the ground—"it's easy."

Gathis waved good-bye as the four friends flew high above the roof of the estate, and the sphere turned on a long, curving flight toward Krondor. "It's easier if I follow landmarks I know, like the King's Highway."

"How long to get to Darkmoor?" asked Calis.

"We'll arrive a little after dawn," said Pug.

They sped across the sea, a hundred feet above the tops of the whitecaps. As the last of Midkemia's three moons sank into the west, the predawn sky to the east lightened. A breeze blew, but they were comfortable inside the sphere. They stood in a circle, each with just enough room to move slightly.

Miranda said, "It would be nice if we could sit."

Pug said, "After this is done, I'll happily loan you the volume from which I got this spell, and if you can modify it to put seats in it, feel free."

Nakor laughed.

"How fast are we going?" asked Tomas.

"As fast as the fastest bird," said Pug. "We should be over Krondor in an hour."

The time passed, and they watched the sky turn from jet black to dark grey. As morning approached, they could see the spindrift on the tops of the waves below, grey upon grey as the sea churned beneath them. "Are you sure that demon is dead?" asked Nakor.

Pug said, "He's dead. Water is anathema to his kind. He was powerful enough to withstand it for a while, but not from that depth with the wounds Tomas gave him."

"Look," said Miranda. "Krondor."

Pug had them coming in a direct line from Sorcerer's Isle, so they approached the Prince's city from almost directly west.

"Oh, gods!" said Miranda.

Across the horizon, where once a large city had teemed with life, only a lifeless black spot on the horizon loomed. Even at this hour of the morning, the city should have been alive with lights, as workers made their way along the streets in the predawn gloom. Boats should have been leaving from the fishing village outside the northern wall, and ships departing for distant ports should have been setting sail.

"There's nothing left," said Nakor.

Calis said, "Something's moving." He pointed up the coast, and in the murky light they could see a large company of horsemen moving north along the sea road.

"It looks like some of the Queen's army has deserted," said Sho Pi.

"Now that they're free of the demon's control, that should become more commonplace," said Pug.

As they sped over the outer breakwater of Krondor harbor, the masts of burned ships stuck up above the bay, like a forest of blackened bones reaching for the sky. Beyond the water, everything was burned beyond recognition. The docks were gone, as were most of the buildings. Here and there a portion of a wall stuck up, but mostly it was rubble. The Prince's palace was recognizable from its position atop the southern point of the harbor, high atop the hill that originally gave the first Prince of Krondor command of the harbor.

"It'll be a long time before anyone uses that harbor again," said Calis.

Tomas put his hand on his son's shoulder. He knew the destruction of the city he had sworn to protect burned deeply. He also knew that Calis, better than anyone, understood what had been achieved by the destruction of the Lifestone, yet he recognized the pain Calis felt over the dear price paid by so many.

Pug willed the sphere along the King's Highway. For mile after mile they witnessed wholesale destruction. Every farm and house was burned, and so many bodies lined the way the buzzards and crows couldn't fly for their gorging. Dominic said, "We must get as many clerics as we can to come here, for plague will certainly follow such carnage."

Nakor said, "All of the Order of Arch-Indar will help."

Miranda said, "All two of you?"

Even in the midst of such destruction, Pug found it almost impossible not to laugh.

Tomas said, "Many of the priests will have perished during the destruction of the city."

Calis said, "Not really. We passed word to the various temples months ago, and slowly they've been getting their clerics to safety. Duke James knew we would need much help after, if we survived."

Miranda said, "And it helps to stay on the good side of the temples."

Pug said, "In all my concern over the threat from the Emerald Queen and the demon, and our fears over the Lifestone, I lost sight of the simple fact that the Kingdom has been invaded by a very large army."

Calis said, "I didn't." He pointed ahead. "Look."

They were entering the foothills of the mountains, and Pug saw a sea of campfires, small shelters, and an occasional command tent. Then they were suddenly speeding over a huge command pavilion, the size of a large house. The closer they got to Darkmoor, the more mobilization they saw. "My gods," said Tomas. "I've never seen such an army. Even during the Riftwar the Tsurani never threw more than thirty thousand men into the field, and never all in one place."

Calis said, "They brought almost a quarter million men across the sea." Dispassionately he said, "This below is the half we haven't killed yet."

"So many deaths," said Nakor. He sighed with a heavy note of sadness. "And for no good reason."

Tomas said, "Pug has heard me ask more than once if there was ever a good reason for war."

"Freedom," said Calis. "Preserving what is ours."

Pug said, "Those are good reasons to resist. Even those aren't good enough reasons to start a war."

As the terrain rose, Pug kept the sphere at an even height. But as they found more and more men below pointing at them, and some starting to shoot arrows, Pug elevated the sphere.

At cloud level, they had a panorama of the battlefield below. "Incredible," said Dominic.

An army of eighty or ninety thousand men lay sprawled out below them, like ants climbing up a hill. At the top of the hill was the city of Darkmoor. The foulburg and most of the city seemed to be in the enemy's hands, and the fighting throughout the remainder of the city was fierce.

"Can we stop it?" asked Miranda.

Calis said, "I doubt it. The invaders are stuck on the wrong side of the ocean with no food." He glanced at Pug and said, "Unless you have some magic means of removing them back to Novindus."

Pug said, "A few at a time, perhaps, but . . . nothing like this."

Tomas said, "Then we shall have to stop the fighting and sort it all out after men are no longer killing one another."

"Do you see the Saaur?" asked Pug.

Tomas pointed to a corner of the city, near the southwest, where a small market was packed with the huge green riders. Pug stopped the sphere and said, "Let's see if we can get their attention."

He lowered the sphere, slowly, and as soon as the first Saaur saw it, they loosed their arrows at the humans.

But the arrows struck the walls of the sphere and bounced off, and Pug continued to lower the sphere slowly, and after it was clear no immediate threat was offered by the device, the arrows stopped.

Pug landed the sphere before a group of riders, the centermost of whom wore a particularly splendid horsehair-plumed helmet, and who carried an ornate shield and an ancient-looking sword. Pug said, "Get ready in case this doesn't work."

When the sphere vanished, Pug spoke in the language of Yabon, closely related to the Novindus dialect. "I seek Jatuk, Sha-shahan of all the Saaur!"

"I am Jatuk," said the impressive rider. "Who are you, wizard?"

"I am called Pug. I have come to you to seek peace."

The Saaur's expression was alien, but Pug sensed he was being regarded with suspicion. "Understand we are bound by oath to the Emerald Queen and cannot make a separate peace."

Pug said, "I bring word from Hanam."

The reptilian face then proved quite expressive, as shock was clearly revealed in his features. "Hanam is dead! He died upon the world of my birth!"

"No," said Pug. "Your father's Loremaster used his arts to seize the mind and body of a demon, and in that body he came to this land. He sought me out and we spoke. He is now dead, but his soul is back on Shila, riding with the Sky Host."

Jatuk urged his mount forward, and when he was right before Pug, he looked down, a towering presence. "Say what you will."

Pug began, speaking of the ancient war between good and evil, the insanity of the Priests of Ahsart, and the betrayal of the Saaur by the Pantathians. At first the Saaur warriors appeared dubious, but as Pug spoke he told them what Hanam had told him to say. He concluded, "Hanam said to tell you that you must know, as will Shadu, your Loremaster, Chiga, your Cupbearer, and Monis, your Shieldbearer, that all I have said is true. The honor of your race demands you accept the truth, and the betrayal of your people is more than just lies. The Pantathians and the Emerald Queen and the demons—all have robbed you of your home world. *They* were the ones who destroyed Shila, and took from you, forever, your birthright."

The Saaur rumbled in consternation. "Lies!" said one. "Clever falsehoods fashioned by a master of evil arts!" said another.

Jatuk held out his hand. "No. There is a ring of truth. If you are what you claim, if you have words from Hanam, then he must have told you one thing to let me know this is no clever lie."

Pug nodded. "He said to remind you of the day you came to serve your father. You were the last of your father's sons to serve. All your brothers were dead. You trembled in anticipation of meeting your father, and there was one who took you aside, and spoke softly into your ear to tell you all would be well."

Jatuk said, "This is true. But name the one who comforted me."

"Kaba, your father's Shieldbearer, who told you what to say to your father. He said you were to say, 'Father, I am here to serve the race, to avenge my brothers, and to do thy bidding.'"

Jatuk leaned back, turned his face to the sky, and screamed. It was an animal sound of pure rage and anguish. "We have been betrayed!" he roared.

Without saying another word to Pug he turned to his companions. "Let it be known! Our bond is severed. We serve no one but the Saaur! Let death be the reward for those who have wronged us! Death to the Pantathians. Let no snake survive! Death to the Emerald Queen and her servants!"

Suddenly Saaur riders were heading back toward the city gate, and Jatuk said, "Human, when this is done, we will seek you out and make our peace, but there is a terrible debt of blood that must be paid!"

Tomas said, "Sha-shahan. Your warriors have known years of fighting. Put down your weapons. Withdraw from this fight. An army marches to this city to drive out the invaders. Step aside and let your wives and children know their fathers are returning to them alive."

Holding his sword like a live thing, Jatuk's eyes blazed. "This is *Tualmasok*, Blood Drinker in the ancient tongue. More than any other thing, it is the mark of my office and the badge of my people's honor. It will not be put aside until this wrong is righted."

Pug said, "Then know the Emerald Queen is dead. She was destroyed by a demon."

Jatuk looked as if he could barely contain himself. "Demon! Demons destroyed our world!"

"I know," said Pug, "and the demon is also dead."

"Then who is there to pay the price?" demanded the Sha-shahan.

Tomas put away his sword. "No one. They are all dead. If there are any Pantathians alive they are hiding under the rocks of a distant land. The only ones left living are the victims, the tools, the dupes."

The Saaur leader screamed in frustration to the skies. "I will have my revenge!"

Pug shook his head. "Spare your people, Jatuk!"

"I will have blood for blood!"

Tomas said, "Then go, but leave this city in peace."

Jatuk pointed his sword at Tomas. "My soldiers will depart, and no more will we trouble this place. But we are a nation without a home, and our honor is stained. Only by blood can we cleanse that stain." He turned his horse in the direction of the city gate and with a hard kick sent the giant mount heading for the city gate.

The rest of his company followed after, and while the war in the city raged on, the southwest corner of Darkmoor was suddenly quiet. From behind the barricade a voice said, "Are they gone?"

Pug motioned and Owen Greylock climbed over a pile of furniture, grain sacks, and part of a wagon bed.

"Magician!" said Owen. "I think we owe you thanks."

Pug said, "No thanks needed. There's still fighting."

"If you got rid of the Saaur, we thank you." Owen shook his head. "Damn, but they are a handful."

"Well, they're the invaders' handful," said Tomas. "They've been told of their betrayal and they are not happy."

Owen smiled. "That I can imagine. I've only seen a few Saaur up close, and they don't strike me as having much of a sense of humor." He turned to the men behind him and said, "Spread out and see if you can find any more of our lads. The citadel is under attack, and I mean to hit the enemy from behind."

Tomas pulled his sword. "I may be of some help."

"Glad to have you," said Owen. He glanced up and down Tomas's impressive six inches over six feet and said, "How do you keep all that white clean?"

Tomas laughed. "It's a long story."

"Tell me after the battle," said Owen, motioning for his small band of soldiers to follow him to the fighting around the citadel.

Pug said, "We'll see you later."

Tomas asked, "Where are you going?"

"Inside the keep, to see if I can end this madness."

Tomas nodded, turned, and ran alongside Owen Greylock. Pug motioned for the others to hold hands. He fixed his vision upon the distant citadel, and then they all vanished.

Manfred and Erik both looked up as a shout came from above. "What now?" asked Erik, pulling his sword.

Men on the roof shouted, but the tone was surprise rather than alarm. Manfred pulled his own sword and stepped between Prince Patrick and the door, in case the citadel had been breached.

Reaching a hall at the base of the keep's old central stairwell, Erik saw Calis hurrying down the stone steps, with Nakor, Miranda, and the others behind.

Erik grinned. "Captain!"

Calis returned his smile and said, "Captain."

Erik said, "I am so pleased to see you. How did you get here?"

Calis pointed to Pug.

Erik said, "Magician!" He looked relieved. "Is there anything you can do?"

Pug said, "Yes, I could kill every man outside the wall, but that includes any number of Kingdom soldiers fighting house to house. I would rather think of a way to stop the killing. The demon who led the Emerald Queen's army is dead. The Lifestone is no more. There is no more reason for fighting."

Erik said, "Tell that to those murderers out there."

Pug said, "That's the problem. Even if I did, would they listen?"

Calis said, "No. As I said, they're hungry, and they know what's behind them. They have only one way to go, ahead."

Erik said, "If this demon you talked about is dead, what about the Emerald Queen?"

"She's been dead for months," said Pug. "We'll explain later."

"What about Fadawah? Maybe we can negotiate a truce with him? He's a murderous bastard, but he'd know the old truce terms of Novindus," said Erik.

Calis said, "Right now Fadawah's got a very angry Saaur army looking for someone to vent that anger on. He's their most likely candidate. If he's half as smart as I think he is, he's already looking for a place to hole up in for the winter."

Nakor said, "Winter!"

Pug said, "Yes?"

Nakor pushed past Calis and said to Erik, "Your original plan was to hold this army here until winter, right?"

"Yes. We knew that once the snows came, they'd be forced to withdraw."

Nakor turned to Pug. "If we go to Stardock, can you bring us back here?"

"Yes," said Pug. "Why?"

"No time to explain. Just do it!"

Pug looked at Miranda, Calis, and the others, and shrugged. He put his hand on Nakor's shoulders and they vanished.

"What was that about?" asked Patrick, as he and Manfred entered the hall.

Calis said, "Highness, Baron," and nodded in greeting.

"Captain," said Patrick. "I hope you bring us some good news."

"Well, for one thing, the major threat to all of us is now over."

Patrick said, "The Lifestone is safe?"

Calis said, "It is no more. It is safely undone and can no longer be used to harm anyone."

Patrick said, "Thank the gods!" Every member of the royal family knew exactly what the stakes were since the Lifestone had been discovered under Sethanon fifty years before. "I feel ordering a celebration." The thunder of a catapult above firing on the attackers added a counterpoint to his next remark. "That just may be a bit premature. We are waiting for the Armies of the East."

Manfred put his hand on Erik's shoulder. "My brother and I were having an argument about who was going to go open the Eastern Gate and let the Armies of the East in to save us. Do you have a better plan?"

Calis said, "No, but I hope Nakor does."

Miranda said, "I'm going to the roof to see if the Armies of the East are outside the eastern gate." She looked at Manfred and Erik like a couple of slow children and said, "It wouldn't do to go get yourselves killed opening the gate if the Armies of the East weren't on the other side, would it?"

Erik and Manfred exchanged startled looks, but Miranda was already mounting the stairs to the top of the keep. Calis said, "I'll be back, my lord, Captain," and hurried after her.

They reached the top of the old keep, a relatively small area of the large citadel. Two lookout positions were manned, directing fire from two large catapults located on a roof segment a dozen feet below. Miranda looked to the east and began a soft, almost inaudible, chant. Then she opened her eyes wide and Calis was surprised to see they had changed. Deep amber with vertical slits, they now resembled a bird of prey's. She surveyed the horizon and after a moment, she closed her eyes and rubbed them, and when she opened them they were normal again. She said, "The Armies of the East are moving in stately fashion towards the city. I would wager they might get here by sundown. More likely, tomorrow at dawn."

Calis swore. "If we survive all this, remind me to have some sharp words with the King about the sense of alacrity of some of his Eastern nobles." He leaned over the edge of the wall and looked down as the fighting continued unabated. Men died as they attempted to fill the moat, others as they attempted to prevent them.

"This is all so pointless!"

Miranda put her arms around his waist and said, "You can't save them all."

Calis turned to take her in his arms. "I've missed you so very much."

Miranda said, "You know that I'm going with Pug."

"Yes, I know."

"He's my other half. I've hidden much of my life from you, and someday, when there's time, I'll tell you the truth of who I am and why I've lied to protect my secrets, but what I say to you now is the truth: I love you, Calis. You are one of the best men I have known in a very long life."

Calis looked at her, studying her features as if trying to memorize them. "But you love Pug more."

She nodded. "I don't know if 'more' is the way I'd say it. He's what I need. I am what he needs, though he hasn't discovered that yet; he's still got too much pain locked away."

Calis nodded and held her so her face was against his chest. "William," he said softly.

"And Gamina. She and James stayed in Krondor."

Calis closed his eyes. "I didn't know." He sighed.

"It will take a while, but he'll heal," she said. Then she stepped back and said, "And so will you."

Calis smiled. "I'm fine."

"No you're not." She poked him in the chest with a finger and said, "You must make me a promise."

"What?"

"When we get done with this war, you must go home to see your mother."

Calis laughed. "Why?"

"Just do it. Promise."

He shrugged. "Very well. I'll go home with my father and I'll visit my mother. Anything else?"

"Yes," she said, "but I'll tell you later. We need to tell the Prince that help isn't just outside the eastern wall."

They returned to the conference room and found everyone huddled around a table. The sound of fighting outside was a constant, if low rumble.

Miranda told Patrick what she had seen, and the Prince said, "Well, we must wait, then, for Pug to solve this mess."

An hour later, Pug, Nakor, and a half dozen men in robes appeared in the hall outside the room. Nakor ran in and said, "You've got to watch this!"

Prince Patrick and the others hurried to where Pug and the other men in robes stood, and one of them said, "I protest!"

"Protest all you want, Chalmes," said Nakor. "You're the best weather witch on Midkemia, even if you are a pain in the backside. Now do it!"

Chalmes pointed his finger at Nakor. "You will stick by our bargain?"

"Yes," said Nakor, "of course. But we must stop this war first."

"Very well." The most senior magician from Stardock turned to the other five who had accompanied him and said, "Once this has begun, I will grow faint. If I falter, you will have to continue for me until I recover." He turned to Nakor and said, "I need a table."

"This way," said Nakor.

Chalmes took in his surroundings as he followed the others back into the conference room. As he passed through the door he said, "Excuse me?"

The Prince of Krondor said, "Yes?"

"Could you fetch me a burning taper?"

Patrick's eyebrows rose, and Manfred said, "I'll see to it."

Chalmes opened a bag he was holding. He took out a candle and some other items, and said, "May I have the taper." A servant produced it and Chalmes lit the candle. He drew around it with a waxy stick, then set it down. Closing his eyes, he began to chant.

After a moment, a cool breeze blew through the window. Nakor grinned. "It's working."

Miranda went to stand next to Pug and put her arm around his waist. "Why couldn't you do this?"

Pug said, "I could have done a hurricane, but that's pretty indiscriminate. I never studied much weather magic. You?"

Miranda shrugged. "Me either." She laid her head on his shoulder and watched.

Chalmes concentrated, and those in the room with magic training could feel the energies growing as the very air became electric.

And colder.

By the minute the air cooled, and from outside the sounds of battle were punctuated by shouts of alarm. The room grew colder and colder. Finally Manfred ordered cloaks brought for those with him.

Then the snow began to fall.

Shouts of confusion issued on both sides of the moat. Erik said, "Pass the word to our own men that we're doing this, Highness."

Prince Patrick nodded, ordering a servant to pass the word that the unusual weather was part of the defense of the castle. Manfred hurried to the window and said, "Look!"

They stood on the large balcony, overlooking the outer bailey and the wall over the moat. A few of the enemy ran across slippery rooftops opposite the keep. Erik saw one man turn, draw his bow, and fire. As Erik started to shout, "Down!" the arrow struck.

Erik's eyes widened in shock as he saw Manfred struck in the neck. Pug unleashed a bolt of energy, and the bowman fell from the roof. Others urged the Prince away from the balcony until the area outside was cleared of other archers.

Erik caught Manfred as he slid down the inside of the balcony wall. Erik didn't have to examine his half brother to know he was dead. Holding Manfred, Erik quietly said, "Damn."

Within an hour it was clear that the attacking army was withdrawing in confusion. The defenders on the walls of the citadel, having heard the weather was the Prince's plan, cheered.

Chalmes began to go weak at the knees, and Pug helped him to a chair, while another magician took over the continued manipulation of the weather. Prince Patrick turned to Pug as a servant rushed forward with some spiced wine for the weakened Chalmes, and asked, "How big an area does this storm cover?"

"About five miles in every direction, but we can enlarge it if you'd like."

Patrick shook his head in wonder. "How long can you make it last?"

Pug smiled. "That depends on how many magicians I need to drag up here from Stardock."

Patrick ran a hand over his face. Fatigue had left dark circles under his eyes. "Cousin Pug," he said, "pardon the observation, but . . . are you younger than I remember?"

Pug smiled. "It's a long story. I'll tell you tonight."

For another hour snow fell in continuing flurries, until it was knee-deep in drifts along the walls of the city. The sky was completely grey and birds sat in confusion on the walls of the citadel, undecided if they should be heading south.

Then a band of men came trudging down the boulevard, and Erik looked out to see they were led by Owen Greylock, with Tomas at his side. Owen shouted up, "Will you lower the drawbridge! It's damned cold out here!"

Erik laughed in relief, leaned over the balcony, and shouted, "Lower the drawbridge!"

Twenty-eight

Rebirth

ERIK SHIVERED.

Darkmoor lay under a blanket of snow, though it was beginning to melt as summer reasserted itself. Erik turned his back to the wall, watching the city begin to come back to life, as the soldiers of the Armies of the East cleared the streets of any stragglers from the invading host who had tried to hole up in the burned-out buildings.

The eastern gates had been opened at dawn by Erik and a patrol, who had easily reached them. The few elements of the invaders' army that were still in the city gave them wide berth. They were too tired, cold, hungry, and dispirited to offer much opposition after the sudden snowfall.

Erik turned to watch as new units of the King's army marched slowly into the city. His own men were checking in, slowly, as Patrick dispatched newly arrived soldiers up and down Nightmare Ridge, and Erik expected Jadow, Harper, and the other surviving sergeants to be in Darkmoor soon. Word had arrived that the dwarves and elves were also returning home.

A familiar voice said, "Von Darkmoor!"

Erik saw Jadow Shati standing below, waving. "How did we do?"

"Well enough, until this damnable snow arrived. I nearly froze my backside off!"

Erik hurried down the flight of steps next to the gatehouse and gripped his old friend's hand. Wanting to get the bad news over first, he said, "How many?"

"Too many," said Jadow. "I won't have exact numbers for a few days, but too damn many." He turned and watched as cavalry from Salador entered, banners flapping in the morning air. "We lost Harper two nights ago."

"Damn," said Erik.

Jadow said, "We're running short of sergeants, Erik."

"Well, we'll just have to make sure you stay alive."

"What are we to do next?"

"The Prince will tell us."

Jadow said, "Will we rest?"

"I think Patrick intends to let the Eastern Army drive the invaders down the hill a bit. So, until you hear otherwise, find a billet near the palace and get the men some food and blankets."

"Yes, sir," said Jadow. "They'll like that."

Erik said, "Send word to the citadel where you are when you're situated. I've got some things to do."

"Sir!" said Jadow, and he turned and hurried off.

Erik returned his attention to the eastern gate, and after a few minutes of watching the procession of brightly colored uniforms, clean horses, and unbloodied weapons, he turned and started walking back toward the citadel.

Slowly the city began to revive. Three days after the last of the invaders were reported to be safely on the far side of Ravensburg, Erik heard a familiar sweet voice from the courtyard.

"Erik!"

He spun, and in the wagon pulling into the castle, Kitty sat behind Roo and his wife, next to their children and the Jacoby family.

Erik almost knocked over a squire as he raced down the steps to the courtyard, and was almost knocked over in turn as his wife flew into his arms. He kissed her and held her. Then he pushed her back to arm's length and said, "What are you doing here?"

He looked at Roo. "You were supposed to have everyone safely down at Malac's Cross."

"Well, we almost got there," said Roo. He jumped down and said, "Then we ran into this army and, given the situation, I judged it pretty safe tagging along behind them."

"Where's Luis? Nathan, my mother?"

"They're on their way," said Roo. "I sent them down to Malac's Cross with a list while I stayed close to the army. They should get here tomorrow."

"A list of what?"

"Things to bring to Darkmoor," said Roo. He motioned for Karli and the others to get out. He tapped Erik on the chest as Kitty kissed his cheek. "You and I have suffered a great deal of financial loss, my friend."

Erik laughed and kissed Kitty again. Then he said, "That money I lent you—I never expected to see it again."

"Well, be that as it may," said Roo, "you're a partner." He threw his arm around Karli's waist, and Helen Jacoby came to stand next to them. "We're all partners."

"In what?" asked Erik.

"Avery, Jacoby, and von Darkmoor! Milo and Nathan are loading up in

Malac's Cross with things that will be needed here, and I expect that shortly we'll have a brisk trade set up."

Erik laughed. "Roo, you'll never change."

Karli said, "He's changed." She blushed. "We're going to have another baby."

Erik laughed. "Well, go inside and I'll see what I can do about getting us something to eat."

They headed for the keep, and Erik looked at Kitty. "You have no idea how wonderful you look."

She said, "No, but I know how wonderful you look."

Erik said, "Let's eat, then I'll show you where I'm staying." He put his arm around her and they slowly walked to the keep, just enjoying the nearness of each other.

Erik entered the room and Patrick said, "Captain! Is your family settled in?" Everyone in the room laughed. Erik saw Owen, Calis, Arutha, and the other surviving nobles of the Western Realm in the conference room, and saw Pug and Miranda standing in an anteroom beyond.

Erik blushed. "Yes, sir." He had introduced Kitty to the Prince the night before. It had taken a messenger pounding on Erik's door with a summons from the Prince to get Erik out of Kitty's arms this morning. Nathan, Milo, Rosalyn, and the others had arrived, and had found their way to the keep. Roo was off bartering and making deals, so the Prince had sent for Erik to find quarters for his family.

Patrick said, "I've got enough governance and military matters before me to confound two Kings and a dozen Dukes, Erik, but I wanted to take care of one issue before things dragged out much longer."

The door opened and Erik tensed as he saw a soldier escorting Mathilda into the chamber. The old Dowager Baroness bowed before the Prince, but when her eyes met Erik's, they burned with hatred.

"Milady," said Patrick. "I wanted you here so I could put a certain matter to rest."

"Highness?" asked Mathilda.

"It's fairly common knowledge you harbor Erik von Darkmoor some ill will—"

Mathilda interrupted, "Don't use that name! He doesn't deserve to be called von Darkmoor!"

"Madam!" said Patrick, slamming his hand on the table. "You forget yourself! I forgive much because of your pain, but speak cautiously!"

The old woman almost bit her tongue to keep from speaking, but she bowed her head slightly. Patrick's tone was ice. "Your late husband pointedly refused to deny Erik that name! More, he has earned it! You will put aside any ill will you have against Captain von Darkmoor. He is my man and serves me. If any harm comes to him that I can trace back to your offices, madam, your rank or family connections will do nothing to spare you my wrath. Is that clear?"

"Yes," she said in tones as cold as the Prince's. Then she looked at Erik and with barely controlled rage she said, "Well, bastard, there is nothing to stop you now, is there? With Manfred dead and you the only one of Otto's bastards to wear his name, your friend here can name you Baron now."

"Madam! How dare you!" Patrick motioned for a guard to take Mathilda away.

"Your Highness," said Erik. "Please forgive me, but let her stay. There's something I need to say to her."

Patrick didn't look pleased, but he said, "What?"

Erik looked at Mathilda. "Madam, you have hated me without knowing me for my entire life. I can only blame my father's weakness for other women as the cause, though knowing you as briefly as I have, I can now understand it." She bristled at this. "Perhaps if you had been loving, kind, and gentle, he might still have strayed and there is no fault in you.

"It doesn't matter. My father is dead and so are your sons. But I will not be the next Baron of Darkmoor." Erik looked directly at the old woman and locked gazes with her. "You have a grandson."

Mathilda said, "What? What nonsense is this?"

Erik said, "No nonsense. He's Stefan's son."

Mathilda's hand came to her mouth and moisture gathered in her eyes as she asked, "Where is he?"

"Here, in the castle."

"Who is his mother? I want to see him!"

Erik motioned for a guard and said, "Go to the inn across the bridge and find Milo, the innkeeper from Ravensburg, and his daughter, Rosalyn. Bring them and the baby here."

Patrick said, "Somewhere else, Captain, if you don't mind."

Erik said, "Bring them to the great hall."

Patrick said, "Madam, please wait for them there. I'll send Erik along in a minute."

After Mathilda had departed, Patrick, Prince of Krondor, said, "Captain?"

Erik said, "Highness?"

"Out there," said Patrick, "just a few miles beyond the walls this city, is the new western boundary of the Kingdom of the Isles. I'm the Prince of Krondor, and Krondor no longer exists!

"While all of us here are aware of the terrible destruction we avoided, this war is far from over. I have a commission for you, should you be willing to accept."

"Sir?"

"Retake the Western Realm. Get me back my Principality!"

Erik looked at Calis, who shook his head. "I'm going home," he said softly. He glanced across the room, through the door, to where Pug and Miranda stood watching from the balcony. "I made a promise."

Owen said, "You are the new Eagle of Krondor, Erik."

As Erik stood still in amazement, Patrick said, "That is, as soon as you recapture my city." Bitterly he said, "Or what's left of it, so we can begin rebuilding.

"That's the first order. We winter here, rest and refit, and then we move to Krondor in the spring. We drive out what's left of this invading army, and rebuild. After that, we take it a day at a time."

Erik knew the task before him was tremendous. Owen said, "But you and your wife can have a quiet winter together before we start."

Erik stood silently for a moment, then said, "Highness."

Whatever momentary satisfaction at the acknowledgment that Erik was now in charge of Calis's Special Command was quickly lost as the Prince continued. "Arutha," he said, and Lord Vencar stepped forward from the corner where he had been standing. "I need a new Duke of Krondor, and you're it. Father will ratify the choice as soon as I send word. You and those sons of yours are going to be very important to me. Oh, by the way, James and Dashel are now Barons of the Court."

Arutha bowed. "Highness." It was obvious that holding the office held by his father was a source of honor to Arutha. Erik noticed the strain in Arutha's features and realized the pain he felt because of his parents' and uncle's death. Then he grinned and Erik caught a fleeting glimpse of Arutha's father as he said, "I think the boys will find their new titles amusing."

Patrick smiled at Arutha. "No doubt." He turned his attention back to the list before him. "Greylock, you're the new Knight-Marshal of Krondor, until I find someone better."

"Won't be hard, Highness, so please don't dawdle too long," said Owen.

Patrick leaned forward and softly said, "Well, you better hope it is, because if I do, you and I are going to have words over your yanking me about the way you did. I don't take kindly to being manhandled, even if you were right."

"Understood, Highness," said Owen gravely.

Patrick said, "We've got to find out if we have any navy left, before spring. Erik, I want you to send some of your black shirts to Sarth and have them snoop around. See if any of our ships surived."

Calis said, "If we do find any of them, Highness, where do we tell them to go? Ylith?"

Patrick looked at a map. "No, I'm going to want to open trade with the Far Coast and the Sunsets as quickly as possible. Tell them to make for that harbor Lord Vykor created down in Shandon Bay. It was supposed to be a temporary anchorage, but we'll have to turn it into a permanent one." Patrick had been told that Krondor's harbor was now impassable and would remain so for at least a year. "In fact, that's what we'll name it. Port Vykor."

The appointment and redistribution of the newly reemerging Western Realm continued.

* * *

Outside the chamber, Miranda and Pug watched. Calis left the conference and came over to them. He said, "Father and I leave tonight." Calis looked at Miranda. "You said I must do you one more favor."

Miranda said, "Yes." She slipped her arm from around Pug's waist and took Calis aside. "There's a woman in Elvandar. Her name is Ellia."

"I don't know that name," said Calis.

"She is from across the sea. Her husband died and she is alone in a strange place with her sons."

Calis's eyes narrowed slightly and he said, "Twin boys?"

"Yes."

"I've seen them, teaching the other children to play football," said Calis. "They are beautiful children."

Miranda said, "I do not know the ways of your people, more than you have told me, but I sense something in her. She and you have much in common. Seek her out, that's all I ask."

Calis said, "We are both within our home, yet we are outsiders."

Miranda touched his cheek. "Not for much longer, I think."

Tomas came down the stairs and said, "Son, it is time."

"Yes, Father," said Calis.

Pug came up to his boyhood friend and said, "Let it not be years before we see each other again."

"Agreed," said Tomas. They embraced. "And you? Do you return to Sorcerer's Isle?"

"No. There are things that Miranda and I can do here to help, for a while at least."

"When you have time, come visit."

"We will."

Tomas and Calis left and Miranda came to stand beside Pug. After a moment of silence, she said, "Well?"

Pug said, "What?"

"Don't you have something to say?"

Pug laughed. "Such as?"

She punched him in the chest. "Younger men! Why are you all so thick-headed?"

Pug grabbed her and pulled her to him. "What would you have me say? You are my life, Miranda. You fill up a place I thought would never again know happiness. Stay with me. Marry me."

Miranda said, "One thing."

"What?" he asked, half playfully, half concerned.

"I want a baby."

Pug's mouth fell open as he stepped back. "A baby?" He blinked. "How? You're two hundred years old!"

She grimaced. "The Lifestone. I'm young again, and I'm ready to be a mother." She grabbed the front of his robe and pulled him toward her. Kissing him, she said, "Unless you'd rather I find someone else?"

"No!" he said. "It's just . . ."

"I know," she said softly. "But I regret not having children the first time around, and now I have another chance." Her voice dropped and she said, "Beloved, I know you are suffering over the death of your children, and you've spoken about the pain of outliving them, but this time it will be different, I promise you."

Looking in her eyes, he said, "I have no doubt."

"Good," she said, leading him down the stairs to the quarters Manfred had set aside for them. "Let's go make a baby."

Pug laughed.

Roo, Nathan, and the others had accompanied Erik to the keep when Rosalyn, Milo, and Gerd had been summoned. They entered, Roo with his usual bravado, the others more timidly. None but Roo had ever been inside a great lord's audience hall before, even one somewhat worse for the wear of recent battle.

Mathilda moved slowly to stand before Rosalyn, who held the little boy on her hip. Gerd's attention was drawn by a necklace the Baroness wore, and he reached for it. Rosalyn gently held his hand and Mathilda said, "No, let him play with it."

"He's teething," the young woman said softly. Randolph, her husband, put a reassuring hand on Rosalyn's shoulder.

Mathilda's eyes began to brim with tears and she said, "He looks so much like his father."

Rosalyn blushed and said, "He's a good baby."

Mathilda turned to Erik. "What do you suggest?" Her manner was again controlled and commanding.

Erik said, "I suggest nothing. Stefan was Baron when he fathered Gerd." He saw Rosalyn lower her eyes at the reminder of the rape, and Randolph's hand tightened ever so slightly, in reassurance. "It's clear to me, Gerd is Baron of Darkmoor." Then Erik's tone became steel. "And Patrick will name *me* Baronial Regent." The woman's eyes widened, as Erik could almost read her thoughts: it was a ploy for Erik to seize control of the barony. But before she could speak, Erik said, "But I have duties in the West. So I must delegate someone else to conduct the business of the duchy." He crossed to stand before his nemesis. "You govern here, milady. Let Rosalyn and her husband live here or in the city as they choose, and see the boy daily. But you make him the next Baron of Darkmoor." Then he lowered his voice even more. "But do a better job than you did with Stefan, or I will be back." The woman's face was a mask. "Manfred was a good enough man. Despite your disagreements with him, he could have been a good teacher for the boy. Treat Gerd as you should have treated your sons, and you and I will have no issue. But should any harm come to him, I will be back. Is that clear?"

Mathilda looked past Erik and saw the baby smile. She stepped toward him, saying, "Let me hold him."

Rosalyn handed Gerd to the old woman. Then she said, "Gerd, this is your grandmother."

Erik left the hall and Roo followed after. Outside, Roo said, "Is this going to work?"

Erik said, "It better." Then he turned to his friend and said, "For the next year or so you're going to be around here like flies on dung, so if anything happens that I should know about, get word to me."

Roo grinned. "And where are you going to be?"

Erik smiled and shook his head. "Recapturing a Kingdom, it seems."

The herald blew a trumpet and Patrick said, "Well, let's go talk."

Word had arrived that morning that a large force of heavy cavalry was moving up from the south, slogging along the roads from the west of Dorgin, as a heavy rain had struck the day before.

Scouts reported that the banner of Kesh flew over the force that made its way toward Darkmoor. Now they stood outside the gate, as the evening sun set, and Patrick was riding with Erik, Owen, Pug, and Arutha to see what a Keshian army was doing this far north.

"Maybe they came to help," suggested Nakor as he walked alongside Pug's horse.

"Somehow I doubt that," said Pug.

They reached the Keshians, and one of Darkmoor's men, acting as herald, said, "Who comes before Krondor's Prince?"

The Keshian herald said, "Highness, my lords, I have the honor to present his most esteemed lord General Beshan Solan."

"General," said Prince Patrick. "May we inquire as to your presence in our Kingdom? Are you perhaps lost?"

"Highness," said the General. "Let us be brief. It is wet, and I would like to return to my camp. We have closely watched this invasion, as you have provided us with remarkably candid intelligence regarding the enemy, their disposition, and intent.

"We did, however, incur losses as they attempted to expand into territory occupied by our forces," the leather-faced old soldier said. "So my master, His Most Imperial Majesty, has decided that the former boundaries between Great Kesh and your Kingdom are no longer agreeable to us."

Patrick looked ready to explode. "You dare ride into my own Principality and inform me the Empire is trying to annex territories beyond those agreed to?"

"In a word: yes."

"Well, General, look around. It may come to your attention that the bulk of the Armies of the East are currently here in Darkmoor. Come spring, I can order them southward just as easily as westward. I am certain I can convince my father that we can wait a year to reclaim the Western Realm while we sort out some Keshian adventurers."

The General seemed unimpressed. "Highness, with all due respect, your Western Armies are scattered and decimated, your Eastern Armies cannot stay here long, else you'll face difficulties on your eastern borders. You have no significant navy left of which to speak. In short, while you could most certainly create some difficulties for Great Kesh for a short while, in the long run, to what advantage?" He took out a rolled-up parchment, and said, "Here are the terms of a treaty my Imperial Master sends to your father."

Patrick nodded and a soldier took the scroll from the Keshian General. Patrick nodded to Arutha, who took it, opened it, and read it. "Damn!" he said after a moment.

"My Lord?" said Patrick.

"They want it all. We keep everything from where we sit to the East. Kesh claims all lands between the Great Star Lake and the Teeth of the World west of the Calastius Mountains."

"Kesh's historical boundaries, as you know," said the General, "before the unfortunate war with the rebellious Confederacy to the south forced us to abandon our hereditary lands."

"Hereditary lands!" said Patrick. "Not in the worst fever dream of your most deluded monarch, General."

Arutha said, "What of Queg and the Free Cities of Natal?"

The General said, "Kesh will deal with her recalcitrant children in time."

Patrick said, "If you will be so kind as to wait, my lord, I will pen a reply to your Imperial Master. And you can tell Digaai for me that the formal declaration of war from my father will arrive shortly."

Nakor said, "Highness?"

"What!" snapped Patrick, obviously close to a rage.

"I think I can help."

Pug said, "What do you have in mind?"

"Watch!" He took out the Tsurani transport sphere and vanished.

"What is that odd little man up to?" asked the Prince.

Pug said, "I don't know, but he usually manages to come up with unexpected results. I think we can afford to wait a little while."

Patrick said, "Very well."

A few minutes later, Nakor was back. "Look to the south," he said.

The entire company of officers from both sides did as Nakor bade, and to the south a vast column of ruby light pierced the sky.

"What is that?" asked the Keshian General.

"That is Stardock," said Pug.

"Stardock!" said the General. "That's impossible! Stardock is hundreds of miles from here."

"Nevertheless," said Pug, "that light is coming from Stardock."

Nakor said, "It's a demonstration of power. It's to let you know there are seven hundred very angry magicians down there who don't like the way you honor treaties."

"Seven hundred?" said Pug. "I thought there were four hundred."

Nakor grinned. "We invited some of your old Tsurani friends to come visit."

Pug rolled his eyes and said, "Three hundred Black Robes?"

"Well, maybe a few less."

The General said, "Seven hundred magicians?"

"Angry magicians," said Erik.

"And one very angry Prince, with the Armies of the East camped ten miles from here!" added Patrick. "Come spring, you can expect a two-front war, General. And from the look of that little demonstration, you don't even want to consider what that means for the Empire."

The Keshian General looked around and at last said, "What do you propose, Highness?"

Patrick said, "We'll make it simple. You return to the *old* border, and come spring my father's diplomats and your Emperor's can start renegotiating the boundary between our two realms all over again."

"The old boundary!"

"Yes," said Patrick. "We take back Shamata!" His yell caused his horse to turn completely around. "You think on this as you ride south, and you'd better be moving that way at dawn, else I'll turn my army south and start marching that way myself, rain or no rain! Do you understand?"

The General glanced over his shoulder and saw the red light in the sky. "I understand, Highness."

"Good!"

Patrick turned his horse and rode off, Erik and Greylock at his side.

Pug waited as the Keshians returned the way they had come, and Patrick rode off. When only the two of them remained in the street, Pug on his horse and Nakor at his side, Pug asked, "Nakor, what did you promise Chalmes and the others to get them to pull that stunt?"

Nakor smiled. "I gave them Stardock."

"You what?" asked Pug.

Nakor said, "Well, you told me to think of something."

Pug asked softly, "You gave away my duchy?"

"I had to. Independence from both the Kingdom and Kesh was the only thing I could think of that they'd fight for. And the Tsurani like having a neutral way into Midkemia, too. Which is why they helped.

"Either way, though, you lose Stardock, to the magicians or to the Empire. This way is better, I think."

"But you gave away a duchy! What am I going to tell the King?"

Nakor shrugged. "You'll think of something." He grinned.

Epilogue

Consequences

FADAWAH FROWNED.

He looked at the maps his aides had provided and said, "What is the situation here, Kahil?"

"It is the city called Ylith," said the captain who had been charged with gathering intelligence. "It is a major seaport and the only sea entrance into the province of Yabon. It is relatively untouched, and most of its garrison was already sent south to defend Darkmoor. There is only a small force there as well as a few ships. There is another garrison in Zūn, as well as in Loriél and Yabon." He indicated the different locations on the map. "However, if we can seize and hold Ylith until spring, those garrisons should be easy to destroy."

Outside, his regrouped army was settling in around the town of Questor's View. They had overrun the town in under a day's fighting, as it had been defended by less than one company of regular soldiers and a half company of militia.

Fadawah nodded. "Good. We will take Ylith."

Twenty thousand men had made their way up the coast, after Fadawah had judged the situation hopeless at Darkmoor. As soon as he had seen the disposition of the men when he had come out from under the demon's trance he knew that even if they took Darkmoor, they would possess a useless mountain of stone and dead bodies.

The reports that had followed him along his retreat, about the sudden snows and the arrival of another army from the east, only made him all the more certain they had been on a fool's errand, attempting to drive across the mountains, to seize a city reported to be abandoned. He had briefly wondered at the sanity of the demon, but given what had happened since, he said a prayer each night to Kalkin, thanking the god of gamblers for blessing him. How he had survived when so many others had been destroyed by the Emerald Queen or the demon was beyond him.

But now he had more immediate needs. His army was a long way from home and hungry. The good news was that as he traveled north the lands were more abundant, and his men were starting to eat well again. He said to Kahil, "Word is to be sent south that any of those who managed to get away from Darkmoor could come to Ylith, to winter there."

"Very well, General," said the intelligence officer, who saluted and left the tent.

Fadawah also knew the Saaur were out there somewhere, and he was concerned. If he could speak to Jatuk he might convince the leader of the lizard people that he was also a dupe, a tool used and almost discarded, but if he failed that, the angry lizard would seek someone upon whom to vent his rage. As the highest remaining officer of the Emerald Queen's army, Fadawah was a logical choice.

Fadawah sat back on the small stool in his tent. He had been cast upon a distant shore by a capricious fate, but it was his nature to turn an advantage wherever he might. That was why he had become the most successful general in Novindus, rising from mercenary captain in the Eastlands, to Military Overlord of the Emerald Queen.

His senior captain, Nordan, said, "What will we do once we've taken this Ylith, General?"

Fadawah said, "We've paid in blood for other people's greed and ambition, my old friend." He leaned forward, putting his elbows on his knees. "Now we serve our own." He smiled at his old companion. His thin face looked especially sinister in the faint light from the small lantern that hung from the tent pole. "How would you like to be General of our armies?"

Nordan said, "But if I become General, what about you?"

Fadawah said, "I become King."

His finger outlined the coast between Krondor and Ylith. "The Kingdom's Western Capital is in ruins, and no law exists between it and Ylith." He considered his options. "Yes, King of the Bitter Sea. How does that sound?"

Nordan bowed. "It sounds . . . appropriate. Your Majesty."

Fadawah laughed as the cool fall wind blew outside the tent.